Praise for DARK FIRE

'One of the author's greatest gifts is the immediacy of his descriptions, for he writes about the past as if it were the living present'
Colin Dexter

'Sansom's magnificent books set in the reign of Henry VIII bring to life the sounds and smells of Tudor England . . . *Dark Fire* is a creation of real brilliance, one of those rare pieces of crime fiction that deserves to be hailed as a novel in its own right'
Sunday Times

'I've discovered a new crime writer who's going to be a star. He's C. J. Sansom, whose just-published second novel, *Dark Fire*, is wonderful stuff, featuring a sort of Tudor Rebus who moves through the religious and political chaos of the 1540s with sinister élan'
James Naughtie, *Herald*

'Sansom gives us a broad view of politics – Tudor housing to rival Rachman, Dickensian prisons, a sewage-glutted Thames, beggars in gutters, conspiracies at court and a political system predicated on birth not merit, intrigue not intelligence . . . a strong and intelligent novel'
Guardian

'Spellbinding . . . Sansom's vivid portrayal of squalid, stinking, bustling London; the city's wealth and poverty; the brutality and righteousness of religious persecution; and the complexities of English law make this a suspenseful, colourful and compelling tale'
Publishers Weekly

Praise for DISSOLUTION

'Terrific . . . a remarkable, imaginative feat. A first-rate murder mystery and one of the most atmospheric historical novels I've read in years'   *Mail on Sunday*

'Extraordinarily impressive. The best crime novel I have read this year'   Colin Dexter

'Remarkable . . . The sights, the voices, the very smell of this turbulent age seem to rise from the page'   P. D. James

'As good a new thriller as I have come across for years. The London of the 1530s smells real, the politics and the religious machinations are delicious and Sansom's voice rings true. His troubled hero Shardlake is a kind of Tudor Morse and a character to treasure'   *Sunday Times*

'Matthew Shardlake combines engrossing historical detail with a first-rate murder mystery'   *Independent on Sunday*

'As clever and enthralling as *The Name of the Rose* . . . Matthew Shardlake deserves a place in the pantheon of detective fiction'   *Tablet*

'*Dissolution* is not just a fascinating detective story, but a convincing portrait of a turbulent period'   *Sunday Telegraph*

'Sansom paints a vivid picture of the corruption that plagued England during the reign of Henry VIII, and the wry, rueful Shardlake is a memorable protagonist . . . cunningly plotted and darkly atmospheric'   *Publishers Weekly*

'Terrific. Historical fiction at its finest'   Peter Robinson

Lamentation

C. J. SANSOM was educated at Birmingham University, where he took a BA and then a PhD in history. After working in a variety of jobs, he retrained as a solicitor and practised in Sussex, until becoming a full-time writer. Sansom is the bestselling author of the critically acclaimed Shardlake series, as well as *Winter in Madrid* and *Dominion*. He lives in Sussex.

Discover more at www.cjsansom.com
and facebook.com/CJSansomAuthor

Also by C. J. Sansom

WINTER IN MADRID

DOMINION

The Shardlake series

DISSOLUTION

DARK FIRE

SOVEREIGN

REVELATION

HEARTSTONE

C. J. SANSOM

Lamentation

§

PAN BOOKS

First published 2014 by Mantle

This paperback edition published 2015 by Pan Books
an imprint of Pan Macmillan, a division of Macmillan Publishers Limited
Pan Macmillan, 20 New Wharf Road, London N1 9RR
Basingstoke and Oxford
Associated companies throughout the world
www.panmacmillan.com

ISBN 978-1-4472-8918-0

1 3 5 7 9 8 6 4 2

A CIP catalogue record for this book is available from
the British Library.

Map artwork by Neil Gower
Typeset by Ellipsis Digital Limited, Glasgow
Printed and bound by CPI Group (UK) Ltd, Croydon, CR0 4YY

To Roz Brody, Mike Holmes, Jan King
and William Shaw, the stalwart writers' group,
for all their comments and suggestions for
Lamentation as for the last seven books.

Author's Note

The details of religious differences in sixteenth-century England may seem unimportant today, but in the 1540s they were, literally, matters of life and death. Henry VIII had rejected the Pope's supremacy over the English Church in 1532–33, but for the rest of his reign he oscillated between keeping traditional Catholic practices and moving towards Protestant ones. Those who wanted to keep traditional ways – some of whom would have liked to return to Roman allegiance – were variously called conservatives, traditionalists, and even papists. Those who wanted to move to a Lutheran, and later Calvinist practice, were called radicals or Protestants. The terms conservative and radical did not then have their later connotations of social reform. There were many who shifted from one side to the other during the years 1532–58, either from genuine non-alignment or opportunism. Some, though not all, religious radicals thought the state should do more to alleviate poverty; but radicals and conservatives alike were horrified by the ideas of the Anabaptists. Very few in number but a bogey to the political elite, the Anabaptists believed that true Christianity meant sharing all goods in common.

The touchstone of acceptable belief in 1546 was adherence to the traditional Catholic doctrine of 'transubstantiation' – the belief that when the priest consecrated the bread and wine during Mass, they were transformed into the physical body and blood of Christ. That was a traditionalist belief from which Henry never deviated; under his 'Act of Six Articles' of 1539, to deny this was treason, punishable by burning at the stake. His other core belief was in the Royal Supremacy; that God intended monarchs to be the supreme arbiters of doctrine in their territories, rather than the Pope.

The political events in England in the summer of 1546 were dramatic and extraordinary. Anne Askew really was convicted of heresy, tortured, and burned at the stake, and she did leave an account of her sufferings. The celebrations to welcome Admiral d'Annebault to London did take place, and on the scale described. The story of Bertano is true. There was a plot by traditionalists to unseat Catherine Parr; and she did write *Lamentation of a Sinner*. It was not, though, so far as we know, stolen.

Whitehall Palace, taken by Henry from Cardinal Wolsey and greatly expanded by him, occupied an area bounded roughly today by Scotland Yard, Downing Street, the Thames and the modern thoroughfare of Whitehall, with recreational buildings on the western side of the road. The whole palace was burned to the ground in two disastrous accidental fires in the 1690s; the only building to survive was the Banqueting House, which had not yet been built in Tudor times.

Some words in Tudor English had a different meaning from today. The term 'Dutch' was used to refer to the inhabitants of modern Holland and Belgium. The term 'Scotch' was used to refer to Scots.

The name 'Catherine' was spelt in several different ways – Catherine, Katharine, Katryn and Kateryn – it was the last spelling which the Queen used to sign her name. However, I have used the more common, modern Catherine.

PRINCIPAL DRAMATIS PERSONAE

and their places on the political–religious spectrum

In this novel there is an unusually large number of characters who actually lived, although, of course, the portrayal of their personalities is mine.

The royal family

King Henry VIII

Prince Edward, age 8, heir to the throne

The Lady Mary, age 30, strongly traditionalist

The Lady Elizabeth, age 12–13

Queen Catherine Parr

Family of Catherine Parr, all reformers
(see Family Tree, pp. xxii–xxiii)

Lord William Parr, her uncle

Sir William Parr, her brother

Lady Anne Herbert, her sister

Sir William Herbert, her brother-in-law

Principal Dramatis Personae

Members of the King's Privy Council

John Dudley, Lord Lisle, reformer

Edward Seymour, Earl of Hertford, reformer

Thomas Cranmer, Archbishop of Canterbury, reformer

Thomas, Lord Wriothesley, Lord Chancellor, no firm
alignment

Sir Richard Rich, no firm alignment

Sir William Paget, Chief Secretary, no firm alignment

Stephen Gardiner, Bishop of Winchester, traditionalist

Thomas Howard, Duke of Norfolk, traditionalist

Others

William Somers, the King's fool

Jane, fool to Queen Catherine and the Lady Mary

Mary Odell, the Queen's maid-in-waiting

William Cecil, later Chief Minister to Queen Elizabeth I

Sir Edmund Walsingham

John Bale

Anne Askew (Kyme)

Lamentation

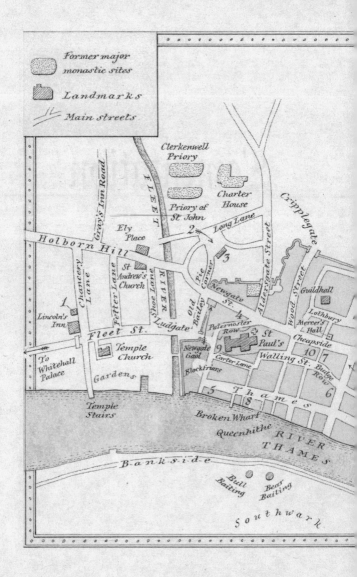

Former major monastic sites

Landmarks

Main streets

Clerkenwell Priory

Charter House

Priory of St. John

Cripplegate

Gray's Inn Road

FLEET

Ely Place

2

Long Lane

Holborn Hill

Aldersgate Street

RIVER

3

Pie Corner

Wood Street

Guildhall

Chancery Lane

St Andrew's Church

Newgate St.

Lothbury

1

Fleet Street

Shoe Lane

Old Bailey

4

Mercer's Hall

Lincoln's Inn

Fetter Lane

Ludgate

Paternoster Row

St Paul's

Cheapside

Fleet St.

9

10

7

To Whitehall Palace

Temple Church

Newgate Gaol

Carter Lane

Walling St.

Bridge Row

Blackfriars

Gardens

5

Thames

6

8

Temple Stairs

Broken Wharf

Queenhithe

RIVER THAMES

B a n k s i d e

Bull Baiting

Bear Baiting

S o u t h w a r k

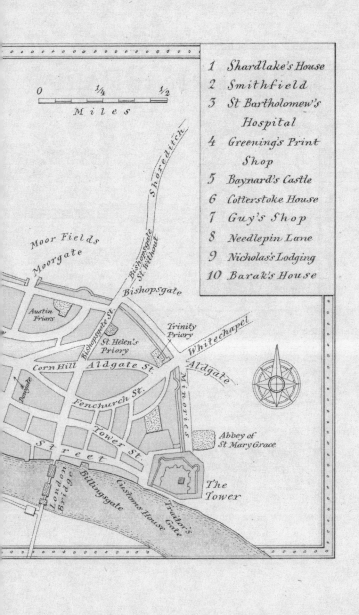

1   Shardlake's House
2   Smithfield
3   St Bartholomew's Hospital
4   Greening's Print Shop
5   Baynard's Castle
6   Cotterstoke House
7   Guy's Shop
8   Needlepin Lane
9   Nicholas's Lodging
10 Barak's House

0   1/4   1/2
Miles

Moor Fields
Moorgate
Shoreditch
Bishopsgate St Without
Bishopsgate
Austin Friars
Bishopsgate St.
St Helen's Priory
Trinity Priory
Whitechapel
Corn Hill
Aldgate St.
Aldgate
Minories
Fenchurch St.
Poultry
Tower St.
Abbey of St Mary Grace
Street
London Bridge
Billingsgate
Customs House
Traitor's Gate
The Tower

CATHERINE PARR

Sir William
Parr

Maud
Green
(1492 - 1531) = Sir Thomas
Parr
(1478 - 1517)

m.
1509

(1) CATHERINE
PARR
b. 1512 = (i) Edward
Borough
d. 1533 = (ii) John Neville
Lord
Latimer
d. 1543 = (iii) HENRY
VIII

m.
1529

m.
1534

m.
1543

ABBREVIATED FAMILY TREE

Elizabeth
Fitzhugh

Others

William, Lord
Parr of Horton
b. c. 1480

Maud
Lady Lane
b. c. 1515

② William
Earl of Essex
b. 1513
=
Lady
Anne
Bourchier

③ ANNE
b.c. 1515
=
SIR WILLIAM
HERBERT
b. c. 1501

Issue

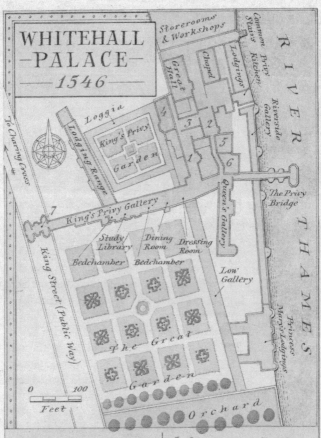

WHITEHALL PALACE 1546

To Charing Cross

Loggia

Lodging Range

King's Privy Garden

Storerooms & Workshops

Great Hall

Chapel

Common Privy Stairs

Kitchen

Lodgings

Riverside Gallery

R I V E R

4

3 2

5

1

6

King's Privy Gallery

7

Queen's Gallery

The Privy Bridge

King Street (Public Way)

Study Library

Dining Room

Dressing Room

Bedchamber

Bedchamber

Low Gallery

Princess Mary's Lodgings

0   100

Feet

The Great Garden

T H A M E S

Orchard

1 King's Privy Chamber	5 Queen's Privy Chamber
2 Queen's Presence Chamber	6 Queen's Bedchamber
3 King's Presence Chamber	7 Holbein Gate
4 King's Guard Chamber	a.k.a. Great Gate
(Great Chamber above)	(King's Secret Study above)

Chapter One

I DID NOT WANT to attend the burning. I have never liked even such things as the bearbaiting, and this was to be the burning alive at the stake of four living people, one a woman, for denying that the body and blood of Christ were present in the Host at Mass. Such was the pitch we had come to in England during the great heresy hunt of 1546.

I had been called from my chambers at Lincoln's Inn to see the Treasurer, Master Rowland. Despite my status as a serjeant, the most senior of barristers, Master Rowland disliked me. I think his pride had never recovered from the time three years before when I had been — justly — disrespectful to him. I crossed the Inn Square, the red brickwork mellow in the summer sunshine, exchanging greetings with other black-gowned lawyers going to and fro. I looked up at Stephen Bealknap's rooms; he was my old foe both in and out of court. The shutters at his windows were closed. He had been ill since early in the year and had not been seen outside for many weeks. Some said he was near death.

I went to the Treasurer's offices and knocked at his door. A sharp voice bade me enter. Rowland sat behind his desk in his spacious room, the walls lined with shelves of heavy legal books, a display of his status. He was old, past sixty, rail-thin but hard as oak, with a narrow, seamed, frowning face. He sported a white beard, grown long and forked in the current fashion, carefully combed and reaching halfway down his silken doublet. As I came in he looked up from cutting a new nib for his goose-feather quill. His fingers, like mine, were stained black from years of working with ink.

'God give you good morrow, Serjeant Shardlake,' he said in his sharp voice. He put down the knife.

I bowed. 'And you, Master Treasurer.'

He waved me to a stool and looked at me sternly.

'Your business goes well?' he asked. 'Many cases listed for the Michaelmas term?'

'A good enough number, sir.'

'I hear you no longer get work from the Queen's solicitor.' He spoke casually. 'Not for this year past.'

'I have plenty of other cases, sir. And my work at Common Pleas keeps me busy.'

He inclined his head. 'I hear some of Queen Catherine's officials have been questioned by the Privy Council. For heretical opinions.'

'So rumour says. But so many have been interrogated these last few months.'

'I have seen you more frequently at Mass at the Inn church recently.' Rowland smiled sardonically. 'Showing good conformity? A wise policy in these whirling days. Attend church, avoid the babble of controversy, follow the King's wishes.'

'Indeed, sir.'

He took his sharpened quill and spat to soften it, then rubbed it on a cloth. He looked up at me with a new keenness. 'You have heard that Mistress Anne Askew is sentenced to burn with three others a week on Friday? The sixteenth of July?'

'It is the talk of London. Some say she was tortured in the Tower after her sentence. A strange thing.'

Rowland shrugged. 'Street gossip. But the woman made a sensation at the wrong time. Abandoning her husband and coming to London to preach opinions clear contrary to the Act of Six Articles. Refusing to recant, arguing in public with her judges.' He shook his head, then leaned forward. 'The burning is to be a great spectacle. There has been nothing like it for years. The King wants it to be seen where heresy leads. Half the Privy Council will be there.'

'Not the King?' There had been rumours he might attend.

'No.'

I remembered Henry had been seriously ill in the spring; he had hardly been seen since.

'His majesty wants representatives from all the London guilds.' Rowland paused. 'And the Inns of Court. I have decided you should go to represent Lincoln's Inn.'

I stared at him. 'Me, sir?'

'You take on fewer social and ceremonial duties than you should, given your rank, Serjeant Shardlake. No one seems willing to volunteer for this, so I have had to decide. I think it time you took your turn.'

I sighed. 'I know I have been lax in such duties. I will do more, if you wish.' I took a deep breath. 'But not this, I would ask you. It will be a horrible thing. I have never seen a burning, and do not wish to.'

Rowland waved a hand dismissively. 'You are too squeamish. Strange in a farmer's son. You have seen executions, I know that. Lord Cromwell had you attend Anne Boleyn's beheading when you worked for him.'

'That was bad. This will be worse.'

He tapped a paper on his desk. 'This is the request for me to send someone to attend. Signed by the King's secretary, Paget himself. I must despatch the name to him tonight. I am sorry, Serjeant, but I have decided you will go.' He rose, indicating the interview was over. I stood and bowed again.

'Thank you for offering to become more involved with the Inn's duties,' Rowland said, his voice smooth once more. 'I will see what other – ' he hesitated – 'activities may be coming up.'

✝

ON THE DAY of the burning I woke early. It was set for midday but I felt in too heavy and mopish a frame of mind to go into chambers. Punctual as ever, my new steward Martin Brocket brought linen cloths and a ewer of hot water to my bedroom at seven, and after bidding me good morning laid out my shirt, doublet and summer robe. As ever, his manner was serious, quiet, deferential. Since he and his wife Agnes had come to me in the winter my household had been run like clockwork. Through the half-open door I could hear Agnes asking the boy Timothy to be sure and fetch some fresh water later, and the girl Josephine to hurry with her breakfast that my table might be made ready. Her tone was light, friendly.

'Another fine day, sir,' Martin ventured. He was in his forties, with thinning fair hair and bland, unremarkable features.

I had told none of my household about my attendance at the burning. 'It is, Martin,' I replied. 'I think I shall work in my study this morning, go in this afternoon.'

'Very good, sir. Your breakfast will be ready shortly.' He bowed and went out.

I got up, wincing at a spasm in my back. Fortunately I had fewer of those now, as I followed my doctor friend Guy's exercises faithfully. I wished I could feel comfortable with Martin, yet although I liked his wife there was something in his cool, stiff formality that I had never felt easy with. As I washed my face and donned a clean linen shirt scented with rosemary, I chid myself for my unreasonableness: as the master it was for me to initiate a less formal relationship.

I examined my face in the steel mirror. More lines, I thought. I had turned forty-four that spring. A lined face, greying hair and a hunched back. As there was such a fashion for beards now – my assistant Barak had recently grown a neat brown one – I had tried a short beard myself a couple of months before, but like my hair it had come out streaked with grey, which I thought unbecoming.

I looked out from the mullioned window onto my garden, where I had allowed Agnes to install some beehives and cultivate a herb garden. They improved its look, and the herbs were sweet-smelling as well as useful. The birds were singing and the bees buzzed round the flowers, everything bright and colourful. What a day for a young woman and three men to die horribly.

My eye turned to a letter on my bedside table. It was from Antwerp, in the Spanish Netherlands, where my nineteen-year-old ward, Hugh Curteys, lived, working for the English merchants there. Hugh was happy now. Originally planning to study in Germany, he had instead stayed in Antwerp and found an unexpected interest in the clothing trade, especially the finding and assessing of rare silks and new fabrics, such as the cotton that was coming in from the New World. Hugh's letters were full of pleasure in work, and in the intellectual and social freedom of the great city; the fairs, debates and readings at the Chambers of Rhetoric. Although Antwerp was part of the Holy Roman Empire, the Catholic Emperor Charles V did not interfere with the many Protestants who lived there – he did not dare imperil the Flanders banking trade, which financed his wars.

Hugh never spoke of the dark secret which we shared from the time of our meeting the year before; all his letters were cheerful in tone. In this one, though, was news of the arrival in Antwerp of a number of English refugees. '*They are in a piteous state, appealing to the merchants for succour. They are reformers and radicals, afraid they will be caught up in the net of persecution they say Bishop Gardiner has cast over England.*'

I sighed, donned my robe and went down to breakfast. I could delay no more; I must start this dreadful day.

†

THE HUNT FOR heretics had begun in the spring. During the winter the tide of the King's fickle religious policy had seemed to turn towards the reformers; he had persuaded Parliament to grant him power to dissolve the chantries, where priests were paid under the wills of deceased donors to say Masses for their souls. But, like many, I suspected his motive had been not religious but financial – the need to cover the gigantic costs of the French war; the English still remained besieged in Boulogne. His debasement of the coinage continued, prices rising as they never had at any time before in man's memory. The newest 'silver' shillings were but a film of silver over copper; already wearing off at the highest point. The King had a new nickname: 'Old Coppernose'. The discount which traders demanded on these coins made them worth less than sixpence now, though wages were still paid at the coins' face value.

And then in March, Bishop Stephen Gardiner – the King's most conservative adviser where religion was concerned – returned from negotiating a new treaty with the Holy Roman Emperor. From April onwards there was word of people high and low being taken in for questioning about their views on the Mass, and the possession of forbidden books. The questioning had reached into both the King's household and the Queen's; among the many rumours circu-

6

lating the streets was that Anne Askew, the best known of those sentenced to death for heresy, had connections within the Queen's court, and had preached and propagandized among her ladies. I had not seen Queen Catherine since involving her in a potentially dangerous matter the year before, and knew, much to my grief, that I was unlikely to see that sweet and noble lady again. But I had thought of her often and feared for her as the hunt for radicals intensified; last week a proclamation had been issued detailing a long list of books which it was forbidden to possess, and that very week the courtier George Blagge, a friend of the King's, had been sentenced to burn for heresy.

I no longer had sympathies with either side in the religious quarrel, and sometimes doubted God's very existence, but I had a history of association with reformers, and like most people this year I had kept my head down and my mouth shut.

I set out at eleven from my house, just up Chancery Lane from Lincoln's Inn. Timothy had brought my good horse Genesis round to the front door and set out the mounting block. Timothy was thirteen now, growing taller, thin and gawky. I had sent my former servant boy, Simon, to be an apprentice in the spring, to give him a chance in life, and planned to do the same for Timothy when he reached fourteen.

'Good morning, sir.' He smiled his shy, gap-toothed grin, pushing a tangle of black hair from his forehead.

'Good morning, lad. How goes it with you?'

'Well, sir.'

'You must be missing Simon.'

'Yes, sir.' He looked down, stirring a pebble with his foot. 'But I manage.'

'You manage well,' I answered encouragingly. 'But perhaps we should begin to think of an apprenticeship for you. Have you thought what you might wish to do in life?'

7

He stared at me, sudden alarm in his brown eyes. 'No, sir – I – I thought I would stay here.' He looked around, out at the roadway. He had always been a quiet boy, with none of Simon's confidence, and I realized the thought of going out into the world scared him.

'Well,' I said soothingly, 'there is no hurry.' He looked relieved. 'And now I must away – ' I sighed – 'to business.'

☦

I RODE UNDER Temple Bar then turned up Gifford Street, which led to the open space of Smithfield. Many people were travelling in the same direction along the dusty way, some on horseback, most on foot, rich and poor, men, women and even a few children. Some, especially those in the dark clothes favoured by religious radicals, looked ser-ious, others' faces were blank, while some even wore the eager expression of people looking forward to a good enter-tainment. I had put on my white serjeant's coif under my black cap, and began to sweat in the heat. I remembered with irritation that in the afternoon I had an appointment with my most difficult client, Isabel Slanning, whose case – a dispute with her brother over their mother's Will – was among the silliest and costliest I had ever encountered.

I passed two young apprentices in their blue doublets and caps. 'Why must they have it at midday?' I overheard one grumble. 'There won't be any shade.'

'Don't know. Some rule, I suppose. The hotter for good Mistress Askew. She'll have a warm arse before the day's done, eh?'

☦

SMITHFIELD WAS crowded already. The open space where the twice-weekly cattle market was held was full of people, all facing a railed-off central area guarded by soldiers wearing metal helmets and white coats bearing the cross of St George. They carried halberds, their expressions stern. If there were any protests these would be dealt with sharply. I looked at the men sadly; whenever I saw soldiers now I thought of my friends who had died, as I nearly had myself, when the great ship *Mary Rose* foundered during the repelling of the attempted French invasion. A year, I thought, almost to the day. Last month news had come that the war was almost over, a settlement negotiated but for a few details, with France and Scotland, too. I remembered the soldiers' fresh young faces, the bodies crashing into the water, and closed my eyes. Peace had come too late for them.

Mounted on my horse I had a better view than most, better than I would have wished for, and close by the railings, for the crowd pressed those on horseback forward. In the centre of the railed-off area three oaken poles, seven feet tall, had been secured in the dusty earth. Each had metal hoops in the side through which London constables were sliding iron chains. They inserted padlocks in the links and checked the keys worked. Their air was calm and businesslike. A little way off more constables stood around an enormous pile of faggots – thick bunches of small branches. I was glad the weather had been dry; I had heard that if the wood was wet it took longer to burn, and the victims' suffering was horribly prolonged. Facing the stakes was a tall wooden lectern, painted white. Here, before the burning, there would be a preaching, a last appeal to the heretics to repent. The preacher was to be Nicholas Shaxton, the former Bishop of Salisbury, a radical reformer who had been sentenced to burn with the others but who had recanted to save his own life.

On the eastern side of the square I saw, behind a row of fine, brightly painted new houses, the high old tower of St

Bartholomew's Church. When the monastery was dissolved seven years before, its lands had passed to the Privy Councillor, Sir Richard Rich, who had built these new houses. Their windows were crowded with people. A high wooden stage covered with a canopy in the royal colours of green and white had been erected in front of the old monastic gatehouse. A long bench was scattered with thick, brightly coloured cushions. This would be where the Lord Mayor and Privy Councillors would watch the burning. Among those on horseback in the crowd I recognized many city officials; I nodded to those I knew. A little way off a small group of middle-aged men stood together, looking solemn and disturbed. I heard a few words in a foreign tongue, identifying them as Flemish merchants.

There was a babble of voices all round me, as well as the sharp stink of a London crowd in summer.

'They say she was racked till the strings of her arms and legs perished – '

'They couldn't torture her legally after she was convicted – '

'And John Lassells is to be burned too. He was the one who told the King of Catherine Howard's dalliances – '

'They say Catherine Parr's in trouble as well. He could have a seventh wife before this is done – '

'Will they let them off if they recant?'

'Too late for that – '

There was a stir by the canopy, and heads turned as a group of men in silk robes and caps, many wearing thick gold chains around their necks, appeared from the gatehouse accompanied by soldiers. They slowly mounted the steps to the stage, the soldiers taking places in front of them, and sat in a long row, adjusting their caps and chains, staring over the crowd with set, stern expressions. I recognized many of them: Mayor Bowes of London in his red robes; the Duke of Norfolk, older and thinner than when I had encountered him six years before, an expression of contemptuous arrogance on his haughty, severe face. To Norfolk's side sat a cleric in a white silk cassock with a black alb over it, whom I did not recognize but I guessed must be Bishop Gardiner. He was around sixty, stocky and swarthy, with a proud beak of a nose and large, dark eyes that swivelled over the crowd. He leaned across and murmured to Norfolk, who nodded and smiled sardonically. These two, many said, would have England back under Rome if they could.

Next to them three men sat together. Each had risen under Thomas Cromwell but shifted towards the conservative faction on the Privy Council when Cromwell fell, bending and twisting before the wind, ever with two faces under one hood. First I saw William Paget, the King's Secretary, who had sent the letter to Rowland. He had a wide, hard slab of a face above a bushy brown beard, his thin-lipped mouth turned down sharply at one corner, making a narrow slash. It was said Paget was closer to the King than anyone now; his nickname was 'The Master of Practices'.

Beside Paget sat Lord Chancellor Thomas Wriothesley, head of the legal profession, tall and thin with a jutting little russet beard. Finally Sir Richard Rich completed the trio, still a senior Privy Councillor despite accusations of corruption two years before, his name associated with all the nastiest pieces of business these last fifteen years, a murderer to my certain knowledge, and my old enemy. I was safe from him only because of the things I knew about him, and because I still had the Queen's protection – whatever, I wondered uneasily, that might be worth now. I looked at Rich. Despite the heat, he was wearing a green robe with a fur collar. To my surprise I read anxiety on his thin, neat features. The long hair under his jewelled cap was quite grey now. He fiddled with his gold chain. Then, looking over the crowd, he met my gaze. His face flushed and his lips set. He stared back at me a moment, then turned away as Wriothesley bent to speak to him. I shuddered. My anxiety communicated itself to Genesis, who stirred uneasily. I steadied him with a pat.

Near to me a soldier passed, carefully carrying a basket. 'Make way, make way! 'Tis the gunpowder!'

I was glad to hear the words. At least there would be some mercy. The sentence for heresy was burning to death, but sometimes the authorities allowed a packet of gunpowder to be placed around each victim's neck so that when the flames reached it, the packet would explode, bringing instantaneous death.

'Should let them burn to the end,' someone protested.

'Ay,' another agreed. 'The kiss of fire, so light and agonizing.' A horrible giggle.

I looked round as another horseman, dressed like me in a lawyer's silken summer robe and dark cap, made his way through the crowd and came to a halt beside me. He was a few years my junior, with a handsome though slightly stern face, a short dark beard and blue eyes that were penetratingly honest and direct.

'Good day, Serjeant Shardlake.'

'And to you, Brother Coleswyn.'

Philip Coleswyn was a barrister of Gray's Inn, and my opponent in the wretched case of the Slanning Will. He represented my client's brother, who was as cantankerous and difficult as his sister, but though, as their lawyers, we had had to cross swords I had found Coleswyn himself civil and honest, not one of those lawyers who will enthusiastically argue the worst of cases for enough silver. I guessed he found his client as irritating as I did mine. I had heard he was a reformer – gossip these days was usually about people's religion – though for myself I did not care a fig.

'Are you here to represent Lincoln's Inn?' Coleswyn asked.

'Ay. Have you been chosen for Gray's Inn?'

'I have. Not willingly.'

'Nor I.'

'It is a cruel business.' He looked at me directly.

'It is. Cruel and horrible.'

'Soon they will make it illegal to worship God.' He spoke with a slight tremor in his voice.

I replied, my words noncommittal but my tone sardonic, 'It is our duty to worship as King Henry decrees.'

'And here is his decree,' Coleswyn answered quietly. He shook his head, then said, 'I am sorry, Brother, I should watch my words.'

'Yes. In these days we must.'

The soldier had laid the basket of gunpowder down carefully in a corner of the railed-off area. He stepped over the rail and now stood with the other soldiers facing outwards at the crowd, quite close to us. Then I saw Wriothesley lean forwards and beckon the man with a finger. He ran across to the canopied stage and I saw Wriothesley gesture at the gunpowder basket. The soldier answered him and Wriothesley sat back, apparently satisfied. The man returned to his position.

'What was that about?' I heard the soldier next to him say.

'He asked how much gunpowder there was. He was frightened that when it blew up it might send burning faggots flying towards the stage. I told him it'll be round their necks, well above the faggots.'

His fellow laughed. 'The radicals would love it if Gardiner and half the Privy Council ended up burning, too. John Bale could write one of his plays about it.'

I felt eyes on me. I saw, a little to my left, a black-robed lawyer standing with two young gentlemen in doublets bright with expensive dye, pearls in their caps. The lawyer was young, in his twenties, a short thin fellow with a narrow, clever face, protuberant eyes and a wispy beard. He had been staring at me hard. He met my gaze then looked away.

I turned to Coleswyn. 'Do you know that lawyer, standing with the two young popinjays?'

He shook his head. 'I think I've seen him round the courts once or twice, but I don't know him.'

'No matter.'

There was a fresh ripple of excitement through the crowd as a procession approached from Little Britain Street. More soldiers, surrounding three men dressed in long white shifts, one young and two middle-aged. All had set faces but wild, fearful eyes. And behind them, carried on a chair by two soldiers, an attractive, fair-haired young woman in her twenties. As the chair swayed slightly she gripped the sides, her face twitching with pain. So this was Anne Askew, who had left her husband in Lincolnshire to come and preach in London, and said the consecrated wafer was no more than a piece of bread, which would go mouldy like any other if left in a box.

'I had not known she was so young,' Coleswyn whispered.

Some of the constables ran to the faggots and piled several bundles round the stakes, a foot high. We watched as the three men were led there. The branches crunched under the constables' feet as they chained two of the men — back-to-back — to one stake, the third to another. There was a rattle

as the chains were secured round their ankles, waists and
necks. Then Anne Askew was carried in her chair to the
third stake. The soldiers set her down and the constables
chained her to the post by the neck and waist.

'So it's true,' Coleswyn said. 'She was racked in the
Tower. See, she can no longer stand.'

'But why do that to the poor creature after she was convicted?'

'Jesu only knows.'

A soldier brought four brown bags, each the size of a
large fist, from the basket and carefully tied one round the
neck of each victim. They flinched instinctively. A constable
came out of the old gatehouse carrying a lit torch and stood
beside the railing, impassive. Everyone's eyes turned to the
torch's flame. The crowd fell silent.

A man in clerical robes was mounting the steps to the
lectern. He was elderly, white-haired and red-faced, trying to
compose features distorted with fear. Nicholas Shaxton. But
for his recantation he would have been tied to a stake as well.
There were hostile murmurs from some in the crowd, then a
shout of, 'Shame on you that would burn Christ's members!'
There was a brief commotion and someone hit the man who
had spoken; two soldiers hurried across to separate them.

Shaxton began to preach, a long disquisition justifying
the ancient doctrine of the Mass. The three condemned men
listened in silence, one trembling uncontrollably. Sweat
formed on their faces and on their white shifts. Anne Askew,
though, periodically interrupted Shaxton with cries of, 'He
misses the point, and speaks without the Book!' Her face
looked cheerful and composed now, almost as though she
were enjoying the spectacle. I wondered if the poor woman
was mad. Someone in the crowd called out, 'Get on with it!
Light the fire!'

At length Shaxton finished. He slowly descended and was led back to the gatehouse. He started to go in but the soldiers seized his arms, forcing him to turn and stand in the doorway. He was to be made to watch.

More kindling was laid round the prisoners; it reached now to their thighs. Then the constable with the torch came over and, one by one, lit the faggots. There was a crackling, then a gasping that soon turned to screaming as the flames licked the victims' legs. One of the men yelled out, 'Christ receive me! Christ receive me!' over and over again. I heard a moaning wail from Anne Askew and closed my eyes. All around the crowd was silent, watching.

The screaming, and the crackling of the faggots, seemed to go on forever. Genesis stirred uneasily again and for a moment I experienced that awful feeling I had known frequently in the months since the *Mary Rose* sank, of everything swaying and tilting beneath me, and I had to open my eyes. Coleswyn was staring grimly, fixedly ahead, and I could not help but follow his gaze. The flames were rising fast, light and transparent in the bright July day. The three men were still yelling and writhing; the flames had reached their arms and lower bodies and burned the skin away; blood trickled down into the inferno. Two of the men were leaning forward in a frantic attempt to ignite the gunpowder, but the flames were not yet high enough. Anne Askew sat slumped in her chair; she seemed to have lost consciousness. I felt sick. I looked across at the row of faces under the canopy; all were set in stern, frowning expressions. Then I saw the thin young lawyer looking at me again from the crowd. I thought uneasily, Who is he? What does he want?

Coleswyn groaned suddenly and slumped in his saddle. I reached out a hand to steady him. He took a deep breath and sat upright. 'Courage, Brother,' I said gently.

He looked at me, his face pale and beaded with sweat. 'You realize any of us may come to this now?' he whispered.

I saw that some of the crowd had turned away; one or two children were crying, overcome by the horrific scene. I noticed that one of the Dutch merchants had pulled out a tiny prayer book and was holding it open in his hands, reciting quietly. But other people were laughing and joking. There was a smell of smoke round Smithfield now as well as the stink of the crowd, and something else, familiar from the kitchen: the smell of roasting meat. Against my will I looked again at the stakes. The flames had reached higher; the victims' lower bodies were blackened, white bone showing through here and there, their upper parts red with blood as the flames licked at them. I saw with horror that Anne Askew had regained consciousness; making piteous groans as her shift burned away.

She began to shout something but then the flames reached the gunpowder bag and her head exploded, blood and bone and brains flying and falling, hissing, into the fire.

Chapter Two

A S SOON AS IT WAS OVER, I rode away with Coleswyn. The three men at the stakes had taken longer than Anne Askew to die. They had been chained standing rather than sitting and it was another half-hour before the flames reached the bag of gunpowder round the last man's neck. I had shut my eyes for much of the time; if only I could have shut my ears.

We said little as we rode along Chick Lane, heading for the Inns of Court. Eventually Coleswyn broke the uneasy silence. 'I spoke too freely of my private thoughts, Brother Shardlake. I know one must be careful.'

'No matter,' I answered. 'Hard to keep one's counsel when watching such a thing.' I remembered his comment that any of us could come to this, and wondered whether he had links with the radicals. I changed the subject. 'I am seeing my client Mistress Slanning this afternoon. There will be much for both of us to do before the case comes on in September.'

Coleswyn gave an ironic bark of laughter. 'That there will.' He gave me a look which showed his view of the case to be the same as mine.

We had reached Saffron Hill, where our ways divided if he were to go to Gray's Inn and I to Lincoln's Inn. I did not feel ready to go back to work yet. I said, 'Will you come for a mug of beer, Brother?'

Coleswyn shook his head. 'Thank you, but I could not. I will return to the Inn, try to lose myself in some work. God give you good morrow.'

'And you, Brother.'

I watched him ride away, slumped a little over his horse. I rode down to Holborn, pulling off my cap and coif as I went.

✝

I FOUND A QUIET INN by St Andrew's Church; it would probably fill up when the crowds left Smithfield, but for now only a few old men sat at the tables. I bought a mug of beer and found a secluded corner. The ale was poor, cloudy stuff, a husk floating on the surface.

My mind turned, as it often did, to the Queen. I remembered when I had first met her, when she was still Lady Latimer. My feelings for her had not diminished. I told myself it was ridiculous, foolish, fantasy; I should find myself a woman of my own status before I grew too old. I hoped she possessed none of the books on the new forbidden list. The list was long – Luther, Tyndale, Coverdale, and of course John Bale, whose scurrilous new book about the old monks and nuns, *Acts of the English Votaries*, was circulating widely among the London apprentices. I had old copies of Tyndale and Coverdale myself; an amnesty for surrendering them expired in three weeks. Safer to burn them quietly in the garden, I thought.

A little group of men came in. 'Glad to be out of that smell,' one said.

''Tis better than the stink of Lutheranism,' another growled.

'Luther's dead and buried, and Askew and the rest gone now too.'

'There's plenty more lurking in the shadows.'

'Come on, have a drink. Have they any pies?'

I decided it was time to leave. I drained my mug and went outside. I had missed lunch, but the thought of food revolted me.

✝

I RODE BACK under the Great Gatehouse of Lincoln's Inn, once again in my robe, coif and cap. I left Genesis at the stables and crossed to my chambers. To my surprise, there was a flurry of activity in the outer office. All three of my employees – my assistant Jack Barak, my clerk John Skelly, and my new pupil, Nicholas Overton – were searching frantically among the papers on the desks and shelves.

'God's pestilence!' Barak was shouting at Nicholas as he untied the ribbon from a brief and began riffling through the papers. 'Can't you even remember when you last saw it?'

Nicholas turned from searching through another pile of papers, the freckled face beneath his unruly light-red hair downcast. 'It was two days ago, maybe three. I've been given so many conveyances to look at.'

Skelly studied Nicholas through his glasses. It was a mild look but his voice was strained as he said, 'If you could just remember, Master Overton, it would narrow the search a bit.'

'What is going on?' I asked from the doorway. They had been so busy with their frantic search they had not seen me come in. Barak turned to me, his face an angry red above his new beard.

'Master Nicholas has lost the Carlingford conveyance! All the evidence that Carlingford owns his land, which needs to be presented in court on the first day of the term! Dozy beanpole,' he muttered. 'Bungling idiot!'

Nicholas's face reddened as he looked at me. 'I did not mean to.'

20

I sighed. I had taken Nicholas on two months before, at the request of a barrister friend to whom I owed a favour, and half-regretted it. Nicholas was the son of a gentry family in Lincolnshire, who at twenty-one had, apparently, failed to settle to anything, and agreed to spend a year or two at Lincoln's Inn, learning the ways of the law to help him run his father's estate. My friend had hinted that there had been some disagreement between Nicholas and his family, but insisted he was a good lad. Indeed he was good-natured, but irresponsible. Like most other such young gentlemen he spent much of his time exploring the fleshpots of London; already he had been in trouble for getting into a sword fight with another student over a prostitute. The King had closed the Southwark brothels that spring, with the result that more prostitutes had crossed over the river to the city. Most gentry lads learned sword fighting, and their status allowed them to wear swords in the city, but the taverns were not the place to show off such skills. And a sharp sword was the deadliest of weapons, especially in a careless hand.

I looked at his tall, rangy form, noticing that under his short student's robe he wore a green doublet slashed so the lining of fine yellow damask showed through, contrary to the Inn regulations that students must wear modest dress.

'Keep looking, but calm down, Nicholas,' I said. 'You did not take the conveyance out of this office?' I asked sharply.

'No, Master Shardlake. I know that is not permitted.' He had a cultivated voice with an undertone of a Lincolnshire burr. His face, long-nosed and round-chinned, was distressed.

'Nor is wearing a slashed silken doublet. Do you want to get into trouble with the Treasurer? When you have found the conveyance, go home and change it.'

'Yes, sir,' he answered humbly.

'And when Mistress Slanning comes this afternoon, I want you to sit in on the interview, and take notes.'

'Yes, sir.'

'And if that conveyance still isn't found, stay late to find it.'

'Is the burning over?' Skelly ventured hesitantly.

'Yes. But I do not want to talk about it.'

Barak looked up. 'I have a couple of pieces of news for you. Good news, but private.'

'I could do with some.'

'Thought you might,' he answered sympathetically.

'Come into the office.'

He followed me through to my private quarters, with its mullioned window overlooking Gatehouse Court. I threw off my robe and cap and sat behind my desk, Barak taking the chair opposite. I noticed there were odd flecks of grey in his dark-brown beard, though none yet in his hair. Barak was thirty-four now, a decade younger than me, his once lean features filling out.

He said, 'That arsehole young Overton will be the death of me. It's like trying to supervise a monkey.'

I smiled. 'Fie, he's not stupid. He did a good summary of the Bennett case papers for me last week. He just needs to get himself organized.'

Barak grunted. 'Glad you told him off about his clothes. Wish I could afford silk doublets these days.'

'He's young, a bit irresponsible.' I smiled wryly. 'As you were when first we met. At least Nicholas does not swear like a soldier.'

Barak grunted, then looked at me seriously. 'What was it like? The burning?'

'Horrible beyond description. But everyone played their part,' I added bitterly. 'The crowd, the city officials and Privy Councillors sitting on their stage. There was a little fight at one point, but the soldiers quelled it quickly. Those poor people died horribly, but well.'

Barak shook his head. 'Why couldn't they recant?'

'I suppose they thought recantation would damn them.' I sighed. 'Well, what are these pieces of good news?'

'Here's the first. It was delivered this morning.' Barak's hand went to the purse at his waist. He pulled out three bright, buttery gold sovereigns and laid them on the table, together with a folded piece of paper.

I looked at them. 'An overdue fee?'

'You could say that. Look at the note.'

I took the paper and opened it. Within was a scrawled message in a very shaky hand: '*Here is the money I owe you for my keep from the time I stayed at Mistress Elliard's. I am sore ill and would welcome a visit from you. Your brother in the law, Stephen Bealknap.*'

Barak smiled. 'Your mouth's fallen open. Not surprised, mine did too.'

I picked up the sovereigns and looked at them closely, lest this was some sort of jest. But they were good golden coins, from before the debasement, showing the young King on one side and the Tudor Rose on the other. It was almost beyond belief. Stephen Bealknap was famous not only as a man without scruples, personal or professional, but also as a miser who was said to have a fortune hidden in a chest in his chambers which he sat looking through at night. He had amassed his wealth through all manner of dirty dealings over the years, some against me, and also by making it a point of pride never to pay a debt if he could avoid it. It was three years since, in a fit of misplaced generosity, I had paid a friend to look after him when he was ill, and he had never reimbursed me.

'It's almost beyond belief.' I considered. 'And yet –

remember, late last autumn and into the winter, before he became ill, he had behaved in an unexpectedly friendly manner for a while. He would come up to me in the court-yard and ask how I did, how my business was, as though he were a friend, or would become one.' I remembered him approaching me across the quadrangle one mellow autumn day, his black gown flapping round his thin form, a sickly ingratiating smile on his pinched face. His wiry fair hair stuck out, as usual, at angles from his cap. 'Master Shard-lake, how do you fare?'

'I was always short with him,' I told Barak. 'I did not trust him an inch, of course, I was sure there was something behind his concern. I think he was looking for work; I remembered him saying he was not getting as much from an old client. And he never mentioned the money he owed. He got the message after a while, and went back to ignoring me.' I frowned. 'Even back then he looked tired, not well. Perhaps that was why he was losing business; his sharpness was going.'

'Maybe he's truly repenting his sins, if he is as ill as they say.'

'A growth in his guts, isn't it? He's been ill a couple months now, hasn't he? I haven't seen him outside. Who delivered the note?'

'An old woman. She said she's nursing him.'

'By Mary,' I said. 'Bealknap, paying a debt and asking for a visit?'

'Will you go and see him?'

'In charity, I suppose I must.' I shook my head in won-derment. 'What is your other piece of news? After this, were you to tell me frogs were flying over London I do not think it would surprise me.'

He smiled again, a happy smile that softened his features.

'Nay, this is a surprise but not a wonder. Tamasin is expecting again.'

I leaned over and grasped his hand. 'That is good news. I know you wanted another.'

'Yes. A little brother or sister for Georgie. January, we're told.'

'Wonderful, Jack; my congratulations. We must celebrate.'

'We're not telling the world just yet. But you're coming to the little gathering we're having for Georgie's first birthday, on the twenty-seventh? We'll announce it then. Will you ask the Old Moor to come? He looked after Tamasin well when she was expecting Georgie.'

'Guy is coming to dinner tonight. I shall ask him then.'

'Good.' Barak leaned back in his chair and folded his hands over his stomach, contentment on his face. His and Tamasin's first child had died, and I had feared the misery would tear them apart forever, but last year she had borne a healthy son. And expecting another child so soon. I thought how settled Barak was now, how different from the madding fellow, who carried out questionable missions for Thomas Cromwell, I had first met six years before. 'I feel cheered,' I said quietly. 'I think perhaps some good things may come in this world after all.'

'Are you to report back to Treasurer Rowland about the burnings?'

'Yes. I will reassure him my presence as representative of the Inn was noted.' I raised my eyebrows. 'By Richard Rich, among others.'

Barak also raised his eyebrows. 'That rogue was there?'

'Yes. I haven't seen him in a year. But he remembered me, of course. He gave me a nasty glance.'

'He can do no more. You have too much on him.'

'He had a worried look about him. I wonder why. I thought he was riding high these days, aligning himself with Gardiner and the conservatives.' I looked at Barak. 'Do you still keep in touch with your friends, from the days when you worked for Cromwell? Heard any gossip?'

'I go to the old taverns occasionally, when Tamasin lets me. But I hear little. And before you ask, nothing about the Queen.'

'Those rumours that Anne Askew was tortured in the Tower were true,' I said. 'She had to be carried to the stake on a chair.'

'Poor creature.' Barak stroked his beard thoughtfully. 'I wonder how that information got out. A radical sympathizer working in the Tower, it has to be. But all I hear from my old friends is that Bishop Gardiner has the King's ear now, and that's common knowledge. I don't suppose Archbishop Cranmer was at the burning?'

'No. He's keeping safely out of the way at Canterbury, I'd guess.' I shook my head. 'I wonder he has survived so long. By the by, there was a young lawyer at the burning, with some gentlemen, who kept staring at me. Small and thin, brown hair and a little beard. I wondered who he might be.'

'Probably someone who will be your opponent in a case next term, sizing up the opposition.'

'Maybe.' I fingered the coins on the desk.

'Don't keep thinking everyone's after you,' Barak said quietly.

'Ay, 'tis a fault. But is it any wonder, after these last few years?' I sighed. 'By the way, I met Brother Coleswyn at the burning, he was made to go and represent Gray's Inn. He's a decent fellow.'

'Unlike his client then, or yours. Serve that long lad

Nicholas right to have to sit in with that old Slanning beldame this afternoon.'

I smiled. 'Yes, that was my thought, too. Well, go and see if he's found the conveyance yet.'

Barak rose. 'I'll kick his arse if he hasn't, gentleman or no . . .'

He left me fingering the coins. I looked at the note. I could not help but think, What is Bealknap up to now?

✞

MISTRESS ISABEL SLANNING arrived punctually at three. Nicholas, now in a more sober doublet of light black wool, sat beside me with a quill and paper. He had, fortunately for him, found the missing conveyance whilst I had been talking to Barak.

Skelly showed Mistress Slanning in, a little apprehensively. She was a tall, thin widow in her fifties, though with her lined face, thin pursed mouth and habitual frown she looked older. I had seen her brother, Edward Cotterstoke, at hearings in court last term, and it had amazed me how much he resembled her in form and face, apart from a little grey beard. Mistress Slanning wore a violet dress of fine wool with a fashionable turned-up collar enclosing her thin neck, and a box hood lined with little pearls. She was a wealthy woman; her late husband had been a successful haberdasher, and like many rich merchants' widows she adopted an air of authority that would have been thought unbefitting in a woman of lower rank. She greeted me coldly, ignoring Nicholas.

She was, as ever, straight to the point. 'Well, Master Shardlake, what news? I expect that wretch Edward is trying to delay the case again?' Her large brown eyes were accusing.

'No, madam, the matter is listed for King's Bench in

September.' I bade her sit, wondering again why she and her brother hated each other so. They were themselves the children of a merchant, a prosperous corn chandler. He had died quite young and their mother had remarried, their stepfather taking over the business, although he himself died suddenly a year later, upon which old Mrs Deborah Cotterstoke had sold the chandlery and lived out the rest of her long life on the considerable proceeds. She had never remarried, and had died the previous year, aged eighty, after a paralytic seizure. A priest had made her Will for her on her deathbed. Most of it was straightforward: her money was split equally between her two children; the large house she lived in near Chandler's Hall was to be sold and the proceeds, again, divided equally. Edward, like Isabel, was moderately wealthy – he was a senior clerk at the Guildhall – and for both of them, their mother's estate would make them richer. The problem had arisen when the Will came to specify the disposition of the house's contents. All the furniture was to go to Edward. However, all wall hangings, tapestries and paintings, '*of all description within the house, of whatever nature and wheresoever they may be and however fixed*', were left to Isabel. It was an unusual wording, but I had taken a deposition from the priest who made the Will, and the two servants of the old lady who witnessed it, and they had been definite that Mrs Cotterstoke, who though near death was still of sound mind, had insisted on those exact words.

They had led us to where we were now. Old Mrs Cotterstoke's first husband, the children's father, had had an interest in paintings and artworks, and the house was full of fine tapestries, several portraits and, best of all, a large wall painting in the dining room, painted directly onto the plaster. I had visited the house, empty now save for an old servant kept on as a watchman, and seen it. I appreciated painting – I had drawn and painted myself in my younger days – and this example was especially fine. Made nearly fifty years before, in the old King's reign, it depicted a family scene: a young Mrs Cotterstoke with her husband, who wore the robes of his trade and the high hat of the time, seated with Edward and Isabel, young children, in that very room. The faces of the sitters, like the summer flowers on the table, and the window with its view of the London street beyond, were exquisitely drawn; old Mrs Cotterstoke had kept it regularly maintained and the colours were as bright as ever. It would be an asset when the house was sold. As it was painted directly onto the wall, at law the painting was a fixture, but the peculiar wording of the old lady's Will had meant Isabel had argued that it was rightfully hers, and should be professionally removed, taking down the wall if need be – which, though it was not a supporting wall, would be almost impossible to do without damaging the painting. Edward had refused, insisting the picture was a fixture and must remain with the house. Disputes over bequests concerning land – and the house counted as land – were dealt with by the Court of King's Bench, but those concerning chattels – and Isabel argued the painting was a chattel – remained under the old ecclesiastical jurisdiction and were heard by the Bishop's Court. Thus poor Coleswyn and I were in the middle of arguments about which court should have jurisdiction before we could even come to the issue of the Will. In the last few months the Bishop's Court had ruled that the painting was a chattel. Isabel had promptly instructed me to apply to King's Bench which, ever eager to assert its authority over the ecclesiastical courts, had ruled that the matter came within its jurisdiction and set a separate hearing for the autumn. Thus the case was batted to and fro like a tennis ball, with all the estate's assets tied up.

'That brother of mine will try to have the case delayed again, you wait and see,' Isabel said, in her customary self-righteous tone. 'He's trying to wear me down, but he won't. With that lawyer of his. He's a tricky, deceitful one.' Her voice rose indignantly, as it usually did after a couple of sentences.

'Master Coleswyn has behaved quite straightforwardly on this matter,' I answered sharply. 'Yes, he has tried to have the matter postponed, but defendants' lawyers ever will. He must act on his client's instructions, as I must on yours.' Next to me Nicholas scribbled away, his long slim fingers moving fast over the page. At least he had had a good education and wrote in a decent secretary hand.

Isabel bridled. 'That Coleswyn's a Protestant heretic, like my brother. They both go to St Jude's, where all images are down and the priest serves them at a bare table.' It was yet another bone of contention between the siblings that Isabel remained a proud traditionalist while her brother was a reformer. 'That priest should be burned,' she continued, 'like the Askew woman and her confederates.'

'Were you at the burning this morning, Mistress Slanning?' I asked quietly. I had not seen her.

She wrinkled her nose. 'I would not go to such a spectacle. But they deserved it.'

I saw Nicholas's lips set hard. He never spoke of religion; in that regard at least he was a sensible lad. Changing the subject, I said, 'Mistress Slanning, when we go to court the outcome of the case is by no means certain. This is a very unusual matter.'

She said firmly, 'Justice will prevail. And I know your skills, Master Shardlake. That is why I employed a serjeant at law to represent me. I have always loved that picture.' A touch of emotion entered her voice. 'It is the only memento I have of my dear father.'

'I would not be honest if I put your chances higher than fifty–fifty. Much will depend on the testimony of the expert witnesses.' At the last hearing it had been agreed that each side would instruct an expert, taken from a list of members of the Carpenters' Guild, who would report to the court on whether and how the painting could be removed. 'Have you looked at the list I gave you?'

She waved a dismissive hand. 'I know none of those people. You must recommend a man who will report the painting can easily be taken down. There must be someone who would do that for a high enough fee. Whatever it is, I will pay it.'

'A sword for hire,' I replied flatly. There were, of course, expert witnesses who would swear black was white for a high enough fee.

'Exactly.'

'The problem with such people, Mistress Slanning, is that the courts know the experts and would give little credibility to such a man. We would be much better off instructing someone whom the courts know as honest.'

'And what if he reports back to you against us?'

'Then, Mistress Slanning, we shall have to think again.'

Isabel frowned, her eyes turning to narrow little slits. 'If that happens, then we will instruct one of these "swords for hire", as that strange expression puts it.' She looked at me haughtily, as though it were I, not her, who had suggested deceiving the court.

I took my copy of the list from the desk. 'I would suggest instructing Master Jackaby. I have dealt with him before, he is well respected.'

'No,' she said. 'I have been consulting the list. There is a Master Adam here, he was Chairman of his Guild; if there

31

is a way to get that painting off – which I am sure there is – he will find it.'

'I think Master Jackaby would be better. He has experience of litigation.'

'No,' she repeated decisively. 'I say Master Adam. I have prayed on the matter and believe he is the right man to get justice for me.'

I looked at her. *Prayed on it?* Did she think God concerned himself with malicious legal cases? But her haughty expression and the firm set of her mouth told me she would not be moved. 'Very well,' I said. She nodded imperiously. 'But remember, Mistress Slanning, he is your choice. I know nothing of him. I will arrange a date when the two experts can meet together at the house. As soon as possible.'

'Could they not visit separately?'

'The court would not like that.'

She frowned. 'The court, the court – it is my case that matters.' She took a deep breath. 'Well, if I lose in King's Bench I shall appeal to Chancery.'

'So, probably, will your brother if he loses.' I wondered again at the bitterness between them. It went back a long way, I knew that; they had not spoken in years. Isabel would refer contemptuously to how her brother could have been an alderman by now if he had made the effort. And I wondered again, why had the mother insisted on using that wording in her Will. It was almost as though she had wished to set her children against each other.

'You have seen my last bill of costs, Mistress Slanning?' I asked.

'And paid it at once, Serjeant Shardlake.' She tilted her chin proudly. It was true; she always settled immediately, without question. She was no Bealknap.

'I know, madam, and I am grateful. But if this matter

goes on into next year, into Chancery, the costs will grow and grow.'

'Then you must make Edward pay them all.'

'Normally in probate matters costs are taken out of the estate. And remember, with the value of money falling, the house and your mother's money are going down in value too. Would it not be more sensible, more practical, to try and find some settlement now?'

She bridled. 'Sir, you are my lawyer. You should be advising me on how I can win, surely, not encouraging me to end the matter without a clear victory.' Her voice had risen again; I kept mine deliberately low.

'Many people settle when the outcome is uncertain and costly. As it is here. I have been thinking. Have you ever considered buying Edward's half-share of the house from him and selling your own residence? Then you could live in your mother's house and leave the wall painting intact, where it is.'

She gave a braying little laugh. 'Mother's house is far too big for me. I am a childless widow. I know she lived there alone but for her servants, but she was foolish; it is far too large for a woman by herself. Those great big rooms. No, I will have the painting down and in my hands. Removed by the best craftsmen in London. Whatever it costs. I shall make Edward pay in the end.'

I looked at her. I had had difficult, unreasonable clients in my time but Isabel Slanning's obstinacy and loathing of her brother were extraordinary. Yet she was an intelligent woman, no fool except to herself.

I had done my best. 'Very well,' I said. 'I think the next thing is to go over your most recent deposition. There are some things you say which I think would be better amended. We must show ourselves reasonable to the court. Calling your brother a pestilent knave will not help.'

33

'The court should know what he is like.'

'It will not help you.'

She shrugged, then nodded, adjusting her hood on her grey head. As I took out the deposition, Nicholas leaned forward and said, 'With your leave, sir, may I ask the good lady a question?'

I hesitated, but it was my duty to train him up. 'If you wish.'

He looked at Isabel. 'You said, madam, that your house is much smaller than your mother's.'

She nodded. 'It is. But it suffices for my needs.'

'With smaller rooms?'

'Yes, young man,' she answered tetchily. 'Smaller houses have smaller rooms. That is generally known.'

'But I understand the wall painting is in the largest room of your mother's house. So if you were able to remove the painting, where would you put it?'

Isabel's face reddened and she bridled. 'That is my business, boy,' she snapped. 'Yours is to take notes for your master.'

Nicholas blushed in turn and bent his head to his papers. But it had been a very good question.

☦

WE SPENT AN HOUR going over the documents, and I managed to persuade Isabel to take various abusive comments about her brother out of her deposition. By the time it was over, my head was swimming with tiredness. Nicholas gathered up his notes and left the room, bowing to Isabel. She rose, quite energetic still, but frowning; she had looked angry ever since Nicholas's question. I got up to escort her outside, where a serving-man waited to take her home. She stood facing me – she was a tall woman and those determined, staring eyes looked straight into mine. 'I confess, Master Shardlake, sometimes I wonder if your heart is in this case as it should be. And that insolent boy . . .' She shook her head angrily.

'Madam,' I replied. 'You can rest assured I will argue your case with all the vigour I can muster. But it is my duty to explore alternatives with you, and warn you of the expense. Of course, if you are dissatisfied with me, and wish to transfer the case to another barrister—'

She shook her head grimly. 'No, sir, I shall stay with you, fear not.'

I had made the suggestion to her more than once before; but it was an odd fact that the most difficult and hostile clients were often the most reluctant to leave, as though they wanted to stay and plague you out of spite.

'Though . . .' She hesitated.

'Yes.'

'I think you do not truly understand my brother.' An expression I had not seen before crossed her face. Fear – there was no doubt about it, fear that twisted her face into new, different lines. For a second, Isabel was a frightened old woman.

'If you knew, sir,' she continued quietly. 'If you knew the terrible things my brother has done.'

'What do you mean?' I asked. 'Done to you?'

'And others.' A vicious hiss; the anger had returned.

'What things, madam?' I pressed.

But Isabel shook her head vigorously, as though trying to shake unpleasant thoughts out of it. She took a deep breath. 'It does not matter. They have no bearing on this case.' Then she turned and walked rapidly from the room, the linen tappets of her hood swishing angrily behind her.

Chapter Three

It WAS PAST SIX when I returned home. My friend Guy was due for dinner at seven – a late meal, but like me he worked a long day. As usual, Martin had heard me enter and was waiting in the hall to take my robe and cap. I decided to go into the garden to enjoy a little of the evening air. I had recently had a small pavilion and some chairs set at the end of the garden, where I could sit and look over the flower beds.

The shadows were long, a few bees still buzzing round the hive. Wood pigeons cooed in the trees. I sat back. I realized that during my interview with Isabel Slanning I had not thought at all about the burning; such was the power of her personality. Young Nicholas had asked a clever question about where she would put the picture. Her answer had been further proof that, for Isabel, winning the quarrel mattered more than the picture, however genuine her attachment to it. I thought again of her strange remark at the end, about some terrible things her brother had done. During our interviews she usually liked nothing better than to abuse and belittle Edward, but that sudden spasm of fear had been different.

I pondered whether it might be worthwhile having a quiet word with Philip Coleswyn about our respective clients. But that would be unprofessional. My duty, like his, was to represent my client as strongly as I could.

My mind went back to the horror I had watched that

morning. The great stage would have been taken down now, together with the charred stakes. I thought of Coleswyn's remark that any of us could come to the fate of those four; I wondered whether he himself had dangerous connections among the reformers. And I must get rid of my books before the amnesty expired. I looked towards the house; through the window of my dining room I saw that Martin had lit the beeswax candles in their sconces, and was setting the linen tablecloth with my best silver, meticulously, everything lined up.

I returned to the house and went into the kitchen. There, all was bustle. Timothy was turning a large chicken on the range. Josephine stood at one end of the table, arranging salads on plates in a pleasing design. At the other end, Agnes Brocket was putting the finishing touches to a fine marchpane of almonds and marzipan. They curtsied as I entered. Agnes was a plump woman in her forties, with nut-brown hair under her clean white coif, and a pleasant face. There was sadness there too, though. I knew that the Brockets had a grown son who for some reason they never saw; Martin had mentioned it at his interview, but nothing more.

'That looks like a dish fit for a feast,' I said, looking at the marchpane. 'It must have cost you much labour.'

Agnes smiled. 'I take pleasure in producing a fine dish, sir, as a sculptor may in perfecting a statue.'

'The fruits of his labours last longer. But perhaps yours bring more pleasure.'

'Thank you, sir,' she replied. Agnes appreciated compliments. 'Josephine helped, didn't you, dear?' Josephine nodded, giving me her nervous smile. I looked at her. Her cruel rogue of a father had been my previous steward, and when I had – literally – booted him out of the house a year before, Josephine had stayed with me. Her father had terrified and intimidated her for years, but with him gone she had gradually become less shy and frightened. She had begun to take care of her appearance, too; her unbound blonde hair had a clear lustre, and her face had rounded out, making her a pretty young woman. Following my look, Agnes smiled again.

'Josephine is looking forward to Sunday,' she said archly.

'Oh? And why is that?'

'A little bird tells me that after church she will be walking out again with young Master Brown, that works in one of the Lincoln's Inn households.'

I looked at Josephine. 'Which one?'

'That of Master Henning,' Josephine said, reddening. 'He lives in chambers.'

'Good, good. I know Master Henning, he is a fine lawyer.' I turned back to Agnes. 'I must go and wash before my guest comes.' Though goodhearted, Agnes could be a little tactless, and I did not want Josephine embarrassed further. But I was pleased; it was more than time Josephine had a young man.

As I left the kitchen, Martin returned. He bowed. 'The table is set, sir.'

'Good. Thank you.' Just for a second I caught Josephine glance at him with a look of dislike. I had noticed it once or twice before, and been puzzled by it, for Martin had always seemed a good master to the lower servants.

✠

GUY ARRIVED shortly after seven. My old friend was a physician, a Benedictine monk before the Dissolution of the Monasteries. He was of Moorish stock; past sixty now, his dark features lined and his curly hair white. As he entered I noticed he was developing the stoop that tall men sometimes

her hatred of her brother, but after what she said this after-noon I think there may be more to it.'

Guy looked sad. 'It sounds as though this quarrel goes back a very long way.'

'I think so. I have thought of talking quietly about it with my opponent – he is a reasonable man – see if we can work out some way to get them to settle. But that would be unpro-fessional.'

'And may do no good. Some quarrels go so deep they cannot be mended.' The sadness in Guy's face intensified. Martin and Agnes brought in the next course, platters of chicken and bacon and a variety of vegetables in bowls.

'You are not usually so pessimistic,' I said to Guy when we were alone again. 'Besides, only recently I was offered an olive branch by the last person I would expect to do such a thing.' I told him the story of Bealknap's note, and the money.

He looked at me sharply. 'Do you trust him? Think of all he has done in the past.'

'It seems he is dying. But – ' I shrugged my shoulders – 'no, I cannot bring myself to trust Bealknap, even now.'

'Even a dying animal may strike.'

'You are in a dark humour tonight.'

'Yes,' he said slowly. 'I am. I think of what happened at Smithfield this morning.'

I put down my knife. I had avoided discussing religion with Guy during these recent months of persecution, for I knew he had remained a Catholic. But after a moment's hesitation I said, 'I was there. They made a vast spectacle of it, Bishop Gardiner and half the Privy Council watching from a great covered stage. Treasurer Rowland made me go; Secretary Paget wanted a representative from each of the Inns. So I sat and watched four people burn in agony because they would not believe as King Henry said they should. At least they hung gunpowder round their necks; their heads were eventually blown off. And yes, when I was there, I felt the ground shift beneath me again, like the deck of that foundering ship.' I put a hand up to my brow, and found it was shaking slightly.

'May God have mercy on their souls,' Guy said quietly.

I looked up sharply. 'What does that mean, Guy? Do you think they need mercy, just for saying what they believed? That priests cannot make a piece of bread turn into the body of Christ?'

'Yes,' he said quietly. 'I believe they are wrong. They deny the Mystery of the Mass – the truth that God and the church has taught us for centuries. And that is dangerous to all our souls. And they are everywhere in London, hiding in their dog-holes: sacramentarians and, worse, Anabaptists, who not only deny the Mass but believe all society should be over-thrown and men hold all goods in common.'

'There have only ever been a few Anabaptists in England, just some renegade Dutchmen. They have been raised up into a bogey.' I heard the impatience in my voice.

Guy answered sharply, 'Well, the Askew woman boasted herself that she was a sacramentarian. Askew was not even her name; her married name was Kyme and she left her hus-band and two little children to come and harangue the people of London. Is that a right thing for a woman to do?'

I stared at my old friend, whose greatest quality had always been his gentleness. He raised a hand. 'Matthew, that does not mean I think they should have been killed in that horrible way. I don't, I don't. But they were heretics, and they should have been – silenced. And if you want to talk of cruelty, think of what the radical side has done. Think what Cromwell did to those who refused to accept the Royal

Supremacy ten years ago, the monks eviscerated alive at Tyburn.' His face was full of emotion now.

'Two wrongs do not make a right.'

'Indeed they do not. I hate the cruelties both sides have carried out as much as you. I wish I could see an end to it. But I cannot. That is what I meant when I said some quarrels go so deep they are impossible to mend.' He looked me in the eye. 'But I do not regret that the King has taken us halfway back to Rome and upholds the Mass. I wish he would take us all the way.' He continued, eagerly now. 'And the old abuses of the Catholic Church are being resolved; this Council of Trent which Pope Paul III has called will reform many things. There are those in the Vatican who would reach out to the Protestants, bring them back into the fold.' He sighed. 'And everyone says the King grows sick. Prince Edward is not yet nine. I believe it wrong that a monarch should make himself head of a Christian church and declare that he instead of the Pope is the voice of God in making church policy. But how can a little boy exercise that headship? Better that England take the opportunity to return to the Holy Church.'

'To the Church that burns people, in France, in Spain under the Inquisition? Many more than here. And besides, the Holy Roman Emperor Charles is making fresh war on his Protestant subjects.'

Guy said, 'You have turned radical again?'

'No!' My own voice rose. 'Once I hoped a new faith based on the Bible would clearly show God's Word to the people. I hate the babble of divisions that has followed; radicals using passages from the Bible like black-headed nails, as insistent they alone are right as any papist. But when I see a young woman taken to the stake, carried in a chair because she has been tortured, then burned alive in front of the great

43

men of the realm, believe me I look with no longing for the old ways either. I remember Thomas More, that indomitable papist, the people he burned for heresy.'

'If only we could all find the essence of true godliness, which is piety, charity, unity,' Guy said sadly.

'As well wish for the moon,' I answered. 'Well, then, on one thing we agree: such divisions have been made in this country that I cannot see ever mending until one side bludgeons the other into defeat. And it made me sick this afternoon seeing men whom Thomas Cromwell raised up, believing they would further reform, now twisting back to further their ambition instead: Paget, Wriothesley, Richard Rich. Bishop Gardiner was there as well; he has a mighty thunderous look.' I laughed bitterly. 'I hear the radicals call him the Puffed-up Porkling of the Pope.'

'Perhaps we should not discuss these matters any more,' Guy said quietly.

'Perhaps. After all, it is not safe these days to speak freely, any more than to read freely.'

There was a quiet knock at the door. Martin would be bringing the marchpane. I had no appetite for it now. I hoped he had not heard our argument. 'Come in,' I said.

It was Martin, but he was not carrying a dish. His face, always so expressionless, looked a little perturbed. 'Master Shardlake, there is a visitor for you. A lawyer. He said he must speak with you urgently. I told him you were at dinner, but he insisted.'

'What is his name?'

'I am sorry, sir, he would not give it. He said he must speak with you alone. I left him in your study.'

I looked at Guy. He still seemed unhappy at our argument, picking at his plate, but he smiled and said, 'You should see this gentleman, Matthew. I can wait.'

'Very well. Thank you.' I rose from the table and went out. At least the interruption would allow my temper to cool.

It was full dark now. Who could be calling at such an hour? Through the hall window I could see two link-boys, young fellows carrying torches to illuminate the way, who must have accompanied my visitor. There was another with them, a servant in dark clothes with a sword at his waist. Someone of status, then.

I opened the door to my study. To my astonishment I saw, standing within, the young man who had been watching me at the burning, still dressed soberly in his long robe. Though he was not handsome – his cheeks disfigured with moles – his face had a strength about it, despite his youth, and the protuberant grey eyes were keen and probing. He bowed to me. 'Serjeant Shardlake. God give you good evening. I apologize for disturbing you at dinner, but I fear the matter is most urgent.'

'What is it? One of my cases?'

'No, sir.' He coughed, a sudden sign of nervousness. 'I come from Whitehall Palace, from her majesty the Queen. She begs you to see her.'

'Begs?' I answered in surprise. Queens do not beg.

'Yes, sir. Her message is that she is in sore trouble, and pleads your help. She asked me to come; she did not wish to put her request in writing. I serve in a junior way on her majesty's Learned Council. My name is William Cecil. She needs you, sir.'

Chapter Four

I HAD TO SIT DOWN. I went to the chair behind my desk, motioning Cecil to a seat in front. I had brought in a candle, and I set it on the table between us. It illuminated the young man's face, the shadows emphasizing the line of three little moles on his right cheek.

I took a deep breath. 'I see you are a barrister.'

'Yes, of Gray's Inn.'

'Do you work with Warner, the Queen's solicitor?'

'Sometimes. But Master Warner was one of those questioned about heretical talk. He is – shall we say – keeping his head low. I am trusted by the Queen; she herself asked me to be her emissary.'

I spread my hands. 'I am nothing more than a lawyer practising in the courts. How can the Queen be in urgent need of my help?'

Cecil smiled, a little sadly I thought. 'I think we both know, Serjeant Shardlake, that your skills run further than that. But I am sorry; I may give you no more particulars tonight. If you consent to come, the Queen will see you at Whitehall Palace tomorrow at nine; there she can tell you more.'

I thought again, Queens do not beg or ask a subject to visit them; they order. Before her marriage to the King, Catherine Parr had promised that while she would pass legal cases my way she would never involve me in matters of

politics. This, clearly, was something big, something dangerous, and in wording her message thus she was offering me a
way out. I could, if I wished, say no to young Cecil.

'You can tell me nothing now?' I pressed.

'No, sir. I only ask, whether you choose to come or no,
that you keep my visit entirely to yourself.'

Almost everything in me wanted to refuse. I remembered
what I had witnessed that morning, the flames, the screams,
the blood. And then I thought of Queen Catherine, her
courage, her nobility, her gentleness and humour. The finest
and most noble lady I had ever met, who had done me nothing but good. I took a deep, deep breath. 'I will come,' I
said. I told myself, like a fool, that I could see the Queen and
then, if I chose, still decline her request.

Cecil nodded. I got the sense he was not greatly impressed
with me. Probably he saw a middle-aged hunchback lawyer
deeply troubled by the possibility of being thrown into
danger. If so, he was right.

He said, 'Come by road to the main gate of the palace at
nine. I will be waiting there. I will take you inside, and then
you will be conducted to the Queen's chambers. Wear your
lawyer's robe but not your serjeant's coif. Better you attract as
little notice as possible at this stage.' He stroked his wispy
beard as he regarded me, thinking perhaps that, as a hunchback, I might attract some anyway.

I stood. 'Till nine tomorrow, then, Brother Cecil.'

He bowed. 'Till nine, Serjeant Shardlake. I must return
now to the Queen. I know she will be glad to have your
reply.'

✝

I SHOWED HIM OUT. Martin appeared from the dining
room bearing another candle, opened the door for Cecil and

bowed, always there to perform every last detail of a steward's duty. Cecil stepped onto the gravel drive, where his servant waited beside the link-boys with their torches to light him home, wherever that was. Martin closed the door.

'I took the liberty of serving the marchpane to Dr Malton,' he said.

'Thank you. Tell him I will be with him in a moment. But first send Timothy to my study.'

I went back into my room. My little refuge, my haven, where I kept my own small collection of law books, diaries and years of notes. I wondered, what would Barak think if he knew of this? He would say bluntly that I should cast aside my sentimental fantasy for the Queen and invent an urgent appointment tomorrow in Northumberland.

Timothy arrived and I scribbled a note for him to take round and leave at chambers, asking Barak to prepare a summary of one of my more important cases which I had intended to do tomorrow. 'No, pest on it! Barak has to chase up those papers at the Six Clerks' office . . .' I amended the note to ask Nicholas to do the job. Even if the boy came up with a jumble, it would be a starting point.

Timothy looked at me, his dark eyes serious. 'Are you all right, Master?' he asked.

'Yes, yes,' I replied irritably. 'Just harried by business. There is no peace under the sun.' Regretting my snappishness, I gave him a half-groat on his way out, before returning to the dining chamber, where Guy was picking at Agnes's fine marchpane.

'I am sorry, Guy, some urgent business.'

He smiled. 'I, too, have had my meals interrupted when a crisis overtakes some poor patient.'

'And I am sorry if I spoke roughly before. But what I saw this morning unmanned me.'

'I understand. But if you think all those who oppose reform – or those of us who, yes, would have England back in the bosom of the Roman family – support such things you do us great injustice.'

'All I know is that I hear thunder rolling all around the throne,' I said, paraphrasing Wyatt's poem. I then remembered again Philip Coleswyn's words at the burning and shuddered. Any of us may come to this now.

✝

EARLY NEXT MORNING Timothy saddled Genesis and I rode down to Chancery Lane. My horse was getting older; round in body, his head growing bony. It was another pleasant July day; hot but with a gentle cooling breeze stirring the green branches. I passed the Lincoln's Inn gatehouse and rode on to Fleet Street, moving to the side of the road as a flock of sheep was driven into London for slaughter at the Shambles.

Already the city was busy, the shops open and the owners' apprentices standing in doorways calling their wares. Peddlers with their trays thronged the dusty way, a rat-catcher in a wadmol smock walked nearby, stooped under the weight of two cages hung from a pole carried across his shoulders, each one full of sleek black rats. A woman with a basket on her head called out, 'Hot pudding pies!' I saw a sheet of paper pasted to a wall printed with the long list of books forbidden under the King's recent proclamation, which must be surrendered by the 9th of August. Someone had scrawled 'The word of God is the glory of Christ' across it.

As I reached the Strand the road became quieter. The way bent south towards Westminster, following the curve of the river. To the left stood the grand three- and four-storeyed houses of the wealthy; the facades brightly painted and

decorated, liveried guards at the doorways. I passed the great
stone Charing Cross, then turned down into the broad
street of Whitehall. Already I could see the tall buildings of
the palace ahead, turreted and battlemented, every pinnacle
topped with lions and unicorns and the royal arms, gilded so
they flashed in the sun like hundreds of mirrors, the brightness making me blink.

Whitehall Palace had originally been Cardinal Wolsey's
London residence, York Place, and when he fell the King
had taken it into his possession. He had steadily expanded it
over the last fifteen years; it was said he wished it to be the
most lavish and impressive palace in Europe. To the left of
the broad Whitehall Road stood the main buildings, while
to the right were the pleasure buildings, the tennis courts
where the King had once disported, the great circular cock-
pit and the hunting ground of St James's Park. Spanning
the street, beyond which became King Street, and connecting the two parts of the palace was the Great Gate designed
by Holbein, an immense towered gatehouse four storeys
high. Like the walls of the palace itself, it was tiled with
black-and-white chequer-work, and decorated with great
terracotta roundels depicting Roman emperors. The gateway
at the bottom was dwarfed by the size of this edifice, yet wide
enough to enable the biggest carts to pass two abreast.

A little before the Great Gate, the line of the palace walls
was broken by a gatehouse, smaller, though still magnificent,
which led to the palace buildings. Guards in green-and-
white livery stood on duty there. I joined a short queue
waiting to go in: behind me, a long cart pulled by four horses
drew up. It was piled with scaffolding poles, no doubt for the
new lodgings being constructed for the King's elder daughter, Lady Mary, by the riverside. Another cart, just being
checked in, was laden with geese for the kitchens, while in

front of me three young men sat on horses with richly decorated saddles, accompanied by a small group of servants. The young gentlemen wore doublets puffed and slashed at the shoulders to show a violet silk lining, caps with peacock feathers, and short cloaks slung across one shoulder in the new Spanish fashion. I heard one say, 'I'm not sure Wriothesley's even here today, let alone that he's read Marmaduke's petition.'

'But Marmaduke's man has got us on the list; that'll get us as far as the Presence Chamber. We can have a game of primero and who knows who might pass by once we're in.'

I realized these young men were aspiring courtiers, gentry most likely, with some peripheral connection to one of Sir Thomas Wriothesley's staff, some of the endless hangers-on who haunted the court in the hope of being granted some position, some sinecure. They had probably spent half a year's income on those clothes, hoping to catch the eye or ear of some great man – or even his manservant. I remembered the collective noun used for those who came here: a threat of courtiers.

My turn came. The guard had a list in his hand and a little stylus to prick off the names. I was about to give mine when, from an alcove within the gatehouse, young Cecil appeared. He spoke briefly to the guard, who marked his paper and waved me forward. As I rode under the gatehouse arch I heard the young men arguing with the guard. Apparently they were not on the list after all.

I dismounted beyond the gatehouse near some stables; Cecil spoke to an ostler, who took Genesis's reins. His voice businesslike, he said, 'I will escort you into the Guard Chamber. Someone is waiting there who will take you to see the Queen.' Cecil wore another lawyer's robe today, a badge sewn onto the chest showing the head and shoulders of a young woman crowned: the Queen's personal badge of St Catherine.

I nodded assent, looking round the cobbled outer court-yard. I had been there briefly before, in Lord Cromwell's time. To the right was the wall of the loggia surrounding the King's Privy Garden. The buildings on the other three sides were magnificent, the walls either chequered in black and white, or painted with fantastic beasts and plants in black relief to stand out more against white walls. Beyond the Privy Garden, to the south, I could see a long range of three-storey buildings reaching along to the Great Gate, which I remembered were the King's private apartments. Ahead of us was a building fronted with ornately decorated pillars. More guards stood at the door, which was ornamented with the royal arms. Behind soared the high roof of the chapel.

The courtyard was crowded, mostly with young men. Some were as richly dressed as the three at the gate, wearing slashed and brightly decorated doublets and hose in all col-ours, and huge exaggerated codpieces. Others wore the dark robes of senior officials, gold chains of office round their necks, attended by clerks carrying papers. Servants in the King's livery of green and white, HR embroidered on their doublets, mingled with the throng, while servants in work-aday clothes from the kitchens or stables darted between them. A young woman accompanied by a group of female servants passed by. She wore a fashionable farthingale dress; the con-ical skirt, stitched with designs of flowers, was wide at the bottom but narrowed to an almost impossibly small waist. One or two of the would-be courtiers doffed their hats to her, seeking notice, but she ignored them. She looked pre-occupied.

'That is Lady Maud Lane,' Cecil said. 'The Queen's cousin and chief gentlewoman.'

'She does not seem happy.'

'She has had much to preoccupy her of late,' he said sadly. Cecil looked at the courtiers. 'Place-hunters,' he said. 'Office-seekers, opportunists, even confidence tricksters.' He smiled wryly. 'But when I first qualified I, too, sought out high contacts. My father was a Yeoman of the Robes, so I started with connections, as one needs to.'

'You also seek to rise?' I asked him.

'Only on certain terms, certain principles.' His eyes locked with mine. 'Certain loyalties.' He was silent a moment, then said, 'Look. Master Secretary Paget.' I saw the man with heavy, slab-like features, brown beard and slit of a downturned mouth, who had been at the burning, traverse the courtyard. He was attended by several black-robed servants, one of whom read a paper to him as they walked, bending close to his ear.

'Mark him, Serjeant Shardlake,' Cecil said. 'He is closer to the King than anyone now.'

'I thought that was Bishop Gardiner.'

He smiled thinly. 'Gardiner whispers in his ear. But William Paget makes sure the administration works, discusses policy with the King, controls patronage.'

I looked at him. 'You make him sound like Cromwell.'

Cecil shook his head. 'Oh, no. Paget discusses policy with the King, but goes only so far as the King wishes, no further. He never tries to rule him. That was Cromwell's mistake, and Anne Boleyn's. It killed them both. The great ones of the realm have learned better now.' He sighed heavily. 'Or should have.'

He led me across the cobbles. Two burly men in the King's livery, each with a ragged boy in his grasp, passed us, went to the gate, and threw them outside with blows about the head. Cecil said disapprovingly, 'Such ragamuffins are always getting in, claiming to be the servant of a servant of some junior courtier. There aren't enough porters to throw them all out.'

'There's no security?' I asked in surprise.

'In the outer court, very little. But inside – that, you will see, is a different matter.'

He led me across to the door bearing the King's arms. Two Yeomen of the Guard carrying long sharp halberds stood there in their distinctive red doublets decorated with golden Tudor roses. Cecil approached one and said, 'Master Cecil and lawyer for Lord Parr.' The yeoman marked his list, and we passed inside.

☫

WE ENTERED a large hall. Several men stood there on guard. Their clothes were even more magnificent than those of the yeomen; black silk gowns, and caps with large black feathers, their brims embroidered with gold. Round their necks each wore a large golden badge on a chain. All were tall, and powerfully built. They carried sharp poleaxes. This must be the King's personal guard, the Gentlemen Pensioners.

The walls were decorated with bright tapestries, painted wooden chests standing by the walls. And then I saw, covering the whole of one wall, a picture I had heard of, painted last year by one of the late Master Holbein's disciples: The King and His Family. It showed an inner room of the palace; in the centre, the King, solid, red-bearded and stern, sat on a throne under a richly patterned cloth of estate, wearing a broad-shouldered doublet in gold and black. He rested one hand on the shoulder of a little boy, Prince Edward, his only son. On his other side Edward's mother, Henry's long-dead third wife Jane Seymour, sat with hands folded demurely in her lap. Standing one on each side of the royal couple were a young lady and an adolescent girl: Lady Mary, Catherine of Aragon's daughter, and Lady Elizabeth, daughter of Anne Boleyn, both restored to the succession two years before. Behind each of the young women was an open doorway giving onto a garden. In the doorway behind Mary, a little woman with a vacant expression on her face was visible, while behind Elizabeth stood a short man with a hunched back, a monkey in doublet and cap on his shoulder. I stood for a second, enraptured by the magnificence of the painting, then Cecil touched my arm and I turned to follow him.

The next chamber, too, contained a fair number of richly dressed young men, standing around or sitting on chests. There seemed no end of them. One was arguing with a guard who stood before the only inner door. 'There will be trouble, sir,' he said hotly, 'if I do not get to see Lord Lisle's steward today. He wishes to see me.'

The guard looked back impassively. 'If he does, we'll be told. Till then, you can stop cluttering up the King's Guard Chamber.'

We approached. The guard turned to us with relief. Cecil spoke quietly: 'Lord Parr awaits us within.'

'I've been told.' The guard studied me briefly. 'No weapons?' he asked. 'No dagger?'

'Certainly not,' I replied. I often carried a dagger, but I knew weapons were forbidden within the royal palaces. Without another word, the big man opened the door just wide enough for us to pass through.

✝

AHEAD OF US was a broad flight of stairs, covered with thick rush matting that deadened the sound of our footsteps as we ascended. I marvelled at the decorations on the walls; everything a riot of colour and intricate detail. There were brightly painted shields displaying the Tudor arms and heraldic beasts, intertwined leaves of plants painted on the walls between, and areas of linenfold panelling – wood intricately carved to resemble folded cloth – painted in various colours. More Gentlemen Pensioners stood guard at intervals on the stairs, staring impassively ahead. I knew we were approaching the Royal Apartments on the first floor. We had passed out of the ordinary world.

At the top of the stairs a man stood waiting for us, alone. He was elderly, broad-shouldered, and carried a staff. He wore a black robe bearing the Queen's badge and there was a gold chain of unusual magnificence round his neck. The hair beneath his jewelled cap was white, as was his little beard. His face was pale and lined. Cecil bowed deeply and I followed. Cecil introduced us. 'Serjeant Shardlake: the Queen's Lord Chancellor, her uncle Lord Parr of Horton.'

Lord Parr nodded to Cecil. 'Thank you, William.' Despite his age, his voice was deep and clear. Cecil bowed again and walked back down the stairs, a trim little figure amidst all the magnificence. A servant passed us, hurrying silently down the steps after him.

Lord Parr looked at me with sharp blue eyes. I knew that when the Queen's father died young, this man, his brother, had been a mainstay of support to his bereaved wife and children; he had been an associate of the King in his young days and had helped advance the Parr family at court. He must be near seventy now.

'Well,' he said at length. 'So you are the lawyer my niece praises so highly.'

'Her majesty is kind.'

'I know the great service you did her before she became

Queen.' He looked at me seriously. 'Now she asks another,' he added. 'Has she your complete and unquestioning loyalty?'

'Total and entire,' I said.

'I warn you now, this is a dirty, secret and dangerous matter.' Lord Parr took a deep breath. 'You will learn things it is potentially fatal to know. The Queen has told me you prefer life as a private man, so let us have that out in the open now.' He looked at me for a long moment. 'Knowing that, will you still help her?'

My answer came immediately, without thought or hesitation. 'I will.'

'Why?' he asked. 'I know you are no man of religion, though you were once.' His voice became stern. 'You are, like so many in these days, a Laodicean, one who dissembles on matters of faith to keep quiet and safe.'

I took a deep breath. 'I will aid the Queen because she is the most good and honourable lady I have ever met, and has done naught but good to all.'

'Has she?' Lord Parr, unexpectedly, gave a sardonic smile. He looked at me for a long moment, then nodded decisively. 'Then let us go on, to the Queen's apartments.'

He led me down a narrow corridor, past a magnificent Venetian vase on a table covered with a red turkey-cloth. 'We must pass through the King's Presence Chamber, then the Queen's. There will be more young courtiers waiting to see the great ones of the realm,' he added wearily. Then, suddenly, he paused and raised a hand. We were by a small, narrow mullioned window, open against the heat of the day. Lord Parr looked quickly round to see if anyone was in the offing, then laid a hand on my arm and spoke, quietly and urgently. 'Now, quick, while we have the chance. You should see this, if you are to understand all that has happened. Look through the window from the side, he does not care to be seen thus. Quick now!'

I looked out and saw a little courtyard covered with flagstones. Two of the sturdy, black-robed Gentlemen Pensioners were helping an immense figure, clad in a billowing yellow silk caftan with a collar of light fur, to walk along, supporting him under the arms. I saw with a shock that it was the King. I had seen him close to twice before – during his Great Progress to York in 1541, when he had been a magnificent-looking figure; and again on his entry to Portsmouth last year. I had been shocked then at his deterioration; he had become hugely fat, and had looked worn with pain. But the man I saw now was the very wreck of a human being. His huge legs, made larger still by swathes of bandages, were splayed out like a gigantic child's as he took each slow and painful step. Every movement sent his immense body wobbling and juddering beneath the caftan. His face was a great mass of fat, the little mouth and tiny eyes almost hidden in its folds, the once beaky nose full and fleshy. He was bare-headed and, I saw, almost bald; his remaining hair, like his sparse beard, was quite grey. His face, though, was brick-red and sweating from the effort of walking round the little courtyard. As I watched, the King suddenly thrust up his arms in an impatient gesture, making me jump back instinctively. Lord Parr frowned and put a finger to his lips. I glanced out again as the King spoke, in that strangely squeaky voice I remembered from York: 'Let me go! I can make my own way to the door, God rot you!' The guards stepped aside and the King took a few clumsy steps. Then he stopped, exclaiming, 'My leg! My ulcer! Hold me, you clods!' His face had gone ashen with pain. He gasped with relief as the men once again took him under the arms, supporting him.

Lord Parr stepped aside, gesturing me to follow. Quietly, in a strangely toneless voice, he said, 'There he is. The great Henry. I never thought the day would come when I would pity him.'

'Cannot he walk unaided at all?' I whispered.

'A mere few paces. A little more on a good day. His legs are a mass of ulcers and swollen veins. He rots as he goes. He has to be carried round the palace in a wheeled chair sometimes.'

'What do his doctors say?' I spoke nervously, remembering it was treason to foretell the death of the King.

'He was very ill in March, the doctors thought he would die, and yet, somehow, he survived. But they say another fever, or the closing of his large ulcer – ' Lord Parr looked round. 'The King is dying. His doctors know it. So does everyone at court. And so does he. Though of course he will not admit it.'

'Dear God.'

'He is in near-constant pain, his eyes are bad, and he will not moderate his appetite; he says he is always hungry. Eating is the only pleasure he has left.' He gave me a direct look. 'The only pleasure,' he repeated. 'It has been for some time. Apart from a little riding, and that grows more difficult.' Still speaking softly, and watching lest someone come, he said, 'And Prince Edward is not yet nine. The council think of only one thing – who will have the rule when the time comes? The kites are circling, Serjeant Shardlake. That you should know. Now come, before someone sees us by this window.'

He led me on, round a little bend to another guarded door. A low hubbub of voices could be heard from within. From behind, through that open window, I heard a little cry of pain.

Chapter Five

THE GUARD ON DUTY recognized Lord Parr and opened the door for him. I knew that the Royal Apartments were organized on the same principle in each palace: a series of chambers, with access to each more and more restricted as one approached the King's and Queen's personal rooms at the heart. The King's Presence Chamber was the most colourfully extravagant room yet in its decoration; one wall was covered with a tapestry of the Annunciation of the Virgin, in which all the figures were dressed in Roman costume, the colours so bright they almost hurt my eyes.

The room was full of young courtiers, as Parr had predicted. They stood talking in groups, leaning against the walls; some even sat at a trestle table playing cards. Having got this far through bribery or connections, they would probably stay all day. They looked up at us, their satin sleeves shimmering in the bright light from the windows. A little man dressed in a green hooded gown entered behind me and crossed the room. Small, sad-faced, and hunchbacked like me, I recognized the King's fool, Will Somers, from the painting in the Guard Chamber. His little monkey sat on his shoulder, picking nits from its master's brown hair. The courtiers watched as he walked confidently across to one of two inner doors and was allowed through.

'Sent for to cheer the King with his jests when he returns from that painful walk, no doubt,' Lord Parr said sadly. 'We go through the other door, to the Queen's Presence Chamber.'

One of the young men detached himself from the wall and approached us, removing his cap and bowing deeply. 'My Lord Parr, I am related to the Queen's cousins, the Throckmortons. I wondered if there may be a place for my sister as a maid of honour—'

'Not now.' Lord Parr waved him away brusquely, as we approached the door to the Queen's Presence Chamber. Again the guard allowed us through with a bow.

We were in another, slightly smaller version of the Presence Chamber, a group of tapestries representing the birth of Christ decorating the walls. There were only a few young would-be courtiers here, and several Yeomen of the Guard, all wearing the Queen's badge. The supplicants turned eagerly when Lord Parr came in, but he frowned and shook his head.

He led me to a group of half a dozen richly dressed ladies playing cards at a table in a large window-bay, and we bowed to them. All were expensively made-up, their faces white with ceruse, red spots on their cheeks. All wore silken farthingales, the fronts open to show the brightly embroidered foreparts and huge detachable sleeves, richly embroidered in contrasting colours. Each gown would have cost hundreds of pounds in labour and material, and I considered how uncomfortable such attire must be on a hot summer's day. A spaniel wandered around, hoping for scraps from the dishes of sweetmeats on tables beside them as they conversed. I sensed tension in the air.

'Sir Thomas Seymour was at Whitehall the other day,' one of the ladies said. 'He looks more handsome than ever.'

'Did you hear how he routed those pirates in the Channel in May?' another asked.

A small, pretty woman in her thirties tapped the table to gain the dog's attention. 'Heel, Gardiner,' she called. It trotted over, panting at her expectantly. She looked at the other women and smiled roguishly. 'Now, little Gardiner, nothing for you today. Lie down and be quiet.' The dog was named for Bishop Gardiner, I realized; an act of mockery. The other women did not laugh, but rather looked anxious. One, older than the others, shook her head. 'Duchess Frances, is it meet to mock a man of the cloth so?'

'If he deserves it, Lady Carew.' I looked at the older woman. This must be the wife of Admiral Carew, who had died with so many others on the *Mary Rose*. She had seen the ship go down while standing on shore with the King.

'But is it safe?' I saw the speaker was the Queen's cousin, Lady Lane, whom Cecil had pointed out to me in the courtyard.

'Well asked, daughter,' Lord Parr said brusquely.

One of the other ladies gave me a haughty look. She turned to Lord Parr. 'Is the Queen to have her own hunchback fool now, like his majesty? I thought she was content with Jane. Is this why we ladies have been sent out of the Privy Chamber?'

'Now, my Lady Hertford,' Lord Parr chided. He bowed to the ladies and led me towards the door the servant had passed through. 'Malaperts,' he muttered. 'Were it not for the loose tongues of the Queen's ladies we might not be in this trouble.' The guard stood to attention. Parr spoke to him in a low voice. 'No one else in the Queen's Privy Chamber till we finish our business.' The man bowed, opened the door and Lord Parr ushered me in.

Another magnificent room. A series of tapestries on the theme of the miracle of the loaves and fishes hung on the walls; there was more linenfold panelling, as well as vases of roses on several finely carved tables, an ornate chess set on another. There were only two people within. The Queen sat on a raised chair under a cloth of estate. She was dressed even more magnificently than her ladies, in a farthingale of crimson under a French gown in royal purple. The farthingale was covered with geometric designs; and as it caught the light I saw the intricacy of the needlework: hundreds of tiny circles and triangles and squares shot through with gold leaf. The bodice tapered to a narrow waist from which a gold pomander hung, and I caught the sharp-sweet smell of oranges. The bodice was low-cut; round the Queen's white powdered neck jewels hung on gold chains, among them a magnificent teardrop-shaped pearl. A French hood was set far back on her auburn hair. Yet beneath the magnificence, and the white ceruse covering her fine, intelligent features, I could see strain in Catherine Parr's face. She was thirty-four now, and for the first time since I had known her she looked her age. As I bowed deeply, I wondered what had happened to her, even as I asked myself what the other man, standing beside her, was doing here: Archbishop Thomas Cranmer, the man I had heard was keeping out of trouble down in Canterbury.

I raised myself. The Queen's eyes were downcast; she did not meet my gaze. Cranmer, however, had no such hesitation. He wore a silken cassock over a black doublet, a simple black cap over his grey hair. His large, expressive blue eyes were troubled.

'Serjeant Shardlake,' Cranmer said in his quiet voice. 'Why, it must be three years since we met.'

'And more, my Lord Archbishop.'

The Queen looked up, cast her sorrowful eyes over my face, and smiled tightly. 'Since the time you saved my life,

Matthew.' She sighed, then blinked and turned to Lord Parr. 'Is Elizabeth gone to sit for her portrait?'

'Not without some swearing. She thinks it unseemly to be painted in her bedroom.'

'So long as she went. This portrait is important.' The Queen looked at me again, then said quietly, 'How have you fared this last year, Matthew?'

'Well enough, your majesty.' I smiled. 'I labour away at the law, as usual.'

'And young Hugh Curteys?'

'Well, too. Working for the clothiers in Antwerp.'

'Excellent. I am glad some good came out of that bad business.' She bit her lip, as though reluctant to continue.

There was a moment's silence, then Cranmer spoke. 'As the Queen remarked, once you saved her life.'

'It was my privilege.'

'Would you save it again?'

I looked at the Queen. Her eyes were cast down once more. This subdued figure was not the Catherine Parr I knew. I asked quietly, 'Has it come to that?'

'I fear it may,' Cranmer answered.

The Queen pressed her hands together. 'It is all my fault. My vanity, my forwardness—'

Lord Parr interrupted, his voice authoritative. 'I think it best we start at the beginning and tell Serjeant Shardlake all that has happened since the spring.'

The Queen nodded. 'Fetch chairs, all of you.' She sighed. 'It is no simple tale.'

We obeyed, sitting in a semi-circle before the throne. She turned to her uncle. 'Tell it all, tell it straight. Begin with what the King said in March.'

Lord Parr looked at me hard. 'You will be only the fifth person to know this story.'

I sat still, trying to keep my hands unclenched on my knees. I realized that I had truly launched myself into a deep well this time. The Queen was looking at me with a sort of desperation, toying with the pearl at her neck.

'The King was very ill in the spring,' Lord Parr began. 'He did not leave his rooms for many weeks. He would call the Queen to him for company; her presence much comforted him. The talk turned often to matters of religion, as it does with the King. At that time, though, Bishop Gardiner had just returned from abroad, in high feather from his success in negotiating his new treaty with the Holy Roman Emperor Charles.'

'And then I made my great mistake,' the Queen said, quietly and sadly. 'I have ridden high for three years, always careful in everything I have said. But I was overcome by the sin of vanity, and forgot I am a mere woman.' She looked down again, lifting the pearl on the end of its golden chain and staring at it. 'I argued with the King too forcefully, trying to persuade him to lift the ban on those of low rank reading the Bible. I told him that all need access to Christ's Word if they are to be saved . . .'

'Sadly,' Lord Parr said, 'her majesty went too far, and annoyed the King – '

The Queen calmed herself, letting the pearl drop. 'My greatest foolishness was to talk in such manner to the King once in the presence of Bishop Gardiner. After I left, the King told Gardiner – ' she hesitated – '"So women are become clerks, and I am to be lectured by my wife in my old days."' I saw tears prick the corners of her eyes.

Cranmer explained. 'We know this from one of the King's body-servants who was present. And we know that Gardiner, like the ravening wolf he is, told the King that the Queen and her ladies were heretics; they had had men to preach in the Queen's chambers during Lent who denied the bread and wine became the body and blood of Christ in the Mass, and who discussed forbidden books with them. Gardiner said such people were no better than Anabaptists, who would destroy royal rule.'

The Queen bowed her head. Lord Parr glanced at her, then continued. 'But the King was suspicious of Gardiner. Ever since Cromwell fell, he has been wary of those who would whisper in his ear about heretic plots. And despite his anger that night, he loves the Queen; the last thing he would want is to lose her. Hold fast to that, niece, hold fast.'

'But I have done dangerous things,' she said. I frowned. I had always known she was a radical in religion, and wondered with a chill whether she had indeed become a sacramentarian. For a second I smelled the smoke at Smithfield again.

'Your uncle is right,' Cranmer said reassuringly. 'The King loves you, for your goodness and the comfort you have brought him. Remember that, Kate, always.' I thought, Kate? I had not known the Queen and the Archbishop were so close.

Lord Parr continued. 'The King allowed Gardiner to search for evidence. And at the same time to order a general investigation into heresy throughout the country. He was worried already over the discontent caused by the price rises and the war – though, thanks be, God has led his majesty to see the sense of making peace.' He looked again at his niece. 'The Queen has loyal friends, and she was warned that searches were afoot. Any books that she or her ladies possessed, which Gardiner might twist as evidence to mean a supporter of heresy, were removed by me. And those who were questioned about discussions in the Queen's chamber stayed loyal and said nothing incriminating.' I wondered what those books had been. But any book with even a mildly Lutheran flavour could be used by Gardiner and his people.

The Queen spoke again. It was as though she had divined my thoughts. 'There were no books of a heretical nature, and nothing forbidden was said in the King's chambers. Though Gardiner set his dogs loose on my friends, my ladies, he came away empty-handed.' So that was why they had seemed brittle, and why Lady Carew had been anxious about Duchess Frances's mocking of Gardiner. 'Even though the place-seekers on the Privy Council became his willing tools. Lord Chancellor Wriothesley, and a man you know well, who would be glad to see me burn: Richard Rich.'

I shifted uncomfortably on my chair. 'It was through your protection of me last year that Rich became your enemy,' I said quietly.

Cranmer shook his head. 'No, Master Shardlake, Rich and Wriothesley saw the chance to rise in Bishop Gardiner's wake, and that of the Duke of Norfolk, who is hand in glove with Gardiner, and they both took it. As the senior peer of the realm, the Duke would like to be Regent for Prince Edward, should anything happen to the King. Though I pray daily for Our Lord to preserve him many years.' I remembered what I had seen from the window and saw from his face that Cranmer, man of faith as he was, had little hope those prayers would be answered.

Lord Parr took up the story again. 'You see, if Gardiner and his people could bring down the Queen and those of her ladies associated with radicalism, that would mean the end for their husbands, too: Lord Lisle, Sir Anthony Denny, the Earl of Hertford – whose wife made that unpleasant remark about you outside—'

The Queen looked up angrily. 'What has Anne Stanhope said now?'

I murmured, 'It was nothing, your majesty.'

Lord Parr said, 'She was discontented you sent the ladies out.'

'She may talk like a good Christian, but she has no charity. I will not have it!' For a moment the Queen sounded regal again, and I could not help but feel a little glow that it was mistreatment of me that had stirred her anger.

Lord Parr went on, 'So you see, Gardiner and his people sought to attack the reformers on the council through their wives. But when the investigations in the Queen's household found nothing, the King became angry; he divined that this was a deceitful plot to get him to change policy. And the rumours that Anne Askew had been tortured seemed to anger him, too.'

'No rumours,' I said. 'I was at the burning. She could not stand, she was put to death sitting in a chair.'

'We fear the torture was used to try and extract damaging information about the Queen. Though her majesty had never met the woman, Lady Hertford and Lady Denny had sent her money while she was in prison—'

'Lest she starve!' the Queen burst out. 'It was charity, charity. Mistress Askew—'

'Mistress Kyme,' Cranmer corrected gently.

'Mistress Kyme, then! That I may have been the cause of her torture . . .' Tears had appeared at the corners of the Queen's eyes again — she who had always been so self-controlled. I thought, what must it have been like for her these last months, knowing she was under investigation, but unable to say anything; all the time trying to behave normally with the King. I saw she was at the end of her tether, in no condition even to tell her story without help.

'We do not know that was the reason.' Lord Parr placed a gnarled hand on his niece's. 'But in any event, it seems the

King has now had enough. He was angry, too, that his friend George Blagge was sentenced to burn; he has pardoned him.'

Cranmer nodded agreement. 'Gardiner's plot has failed. The King decided it was time to cry, "Enough!" So that, I thought, explained Rich's worried look at Smithfield. Perhaps it explained, too, why Cranmer felt it safe to come back to court now. With a wry smile he added, 'And so he decided to teach the heresy hunters a lesson they would not forget.' He looked at the Queen. She closed her eyes.

The Archbishop took a deep breath. 'Three years ago, when Gardiner was after my head, hunting for heretics in my diocese, the King called me to see him. He said he had agreed that I should be examined by the Privy Council.' The Archbishop paused, and his face worked: a memory of fear. He took a deep breath. 'But his majesty told me the investigation into my diocese would be headed by me, and gave me his ring to present to the Privy Council to show I had his favour. Though not before he had frightened me by telling me he knew, now, who was the greatest heretic in Kent. Frightened me, warned me, but at the same time showed me I had his confidence.' He paused. 'And last week he used the same strategy with her majesty.' Cranmer looked pointedly at the Queen.

She lifted her head. 'I was called to the King's private chamber. Near two weeks ago, on the third. What he said astounded me. He said quite directly that Gardiner and his friends had tried to make him believe wicked lies about me, but now he knew better. He was unaware that I knew what had passed. Or perhaps he did know, but said nothing; he can be so – ' She broke off, fingering the pearl again, before resuming in strangely wooden tones. 'He said his love for me was undiminished, and asked for my help in teaching Gardiner and Wriothesley a lesson. He said he would have articles drawn up for my arrest, and tell Wriothesley to take me into custody. But we would pretend a copy of the articles had fallen into my hands by accident. I would be heard crying out in despair, and he would come to comfort me.' Her voice broke for a second and she swallowed hard. 'So that is what we did.' My heart beat hard with rage that the King should manipulate her so.

'Then the next evening I was to call on him in his chamber, and, in front of his gentlemen, apologize for going too far in discussing religion.' She closed her eyes. 'I was to say I knew a woman's duty is to be instructed by her husband, and that I was only seeking to distract him from the pain in his legs. I did as he asked, playing my part in the performance.' I discerned a note of bitterness, quickly suppressed, in her voice.

'The next day, I was to walk in the garden with him and my ladies. By prearrangement with the King, Wriothesley was to come and arrest me with fifty of the guard. Wriothesley thought he had won, but when he arrived the King tore the warrant from his hand, called him a beast and a knave in front of the men of the guard and my ladies, and ordered him from his presence.' She smiled sadly. 'Since then his majesty has been loving and attentive to me in front of all. I am to have new jewels; he knows I love bright jewels. I have ever had good measure of the sin of covetousness, as well as vanity.' She lowered her head.

'Then – then the crisis is over?' I said. 'That dreadful burning and the new proclamation on forbidden books – that was the last act? Wriothesley and the conservatives have been humiliated?'

'Would that it were the last act!' the Queen cried out. 'I have one book missing, the most dangerous of all, and it is my fault!'

Lord Parr put his hand over hers again. 'Calm, Kate, stay calm. You are doing well.'

Cranmer stood, walking to a window which looked out over a garden to the river, blue in the summer sunshine, dotted with the white sails of wherries and tilt-boats. Another world. There was a distant hammering from where the Lady Mary's new chambers were being built. The Archbishop said, 'I spoke of Bishop Gardiner negotiating a new treaty with the Empire. And Paget has succeeded in making peace with the French. Lord Lisle and the Earl of Hertford played their parts, too; both are abroad just now, but they will return next month, with feathers in their own caps, and the balance on the Privy Council will change in favour of the reformers. That, and the King's annoyance with Gardiner's faction, will help us. But something else is going on, Master Shardlake.' Cranmer turned and I felt the full force of those penetrating eyes. 'We do not know what it is, but we see the senior councillors in the conservative faction – Norfolk, Gardiner, and others like Paget – still smiling and talking in corners, when after their setback they should be cringing like whipped dogs. The other day, after the council, I heard Paget muttering to Norfolk about a visitor from abroad; they fell silent as I approached. Something else, something secret, is going on. They have another card still to play.'

'And I have given them a second,' the Queen said bleakly. 'Placed myself and all those I care for in jeopardy.'

This time neither her uncle nor the Archbishop sought to reassure her. The Queen smiled, not the gently humorous smile that in happier times was ever ready to appear on her face, but a sad, angry grimace. She said, 'It is time for you to know what I have done.'

Chapter Six

W E ALL LOOKED AT HER. She spoke quietly. 'Last winter, it seemed the King was moving in the direction of reform. He had made Parliament pass the bill that gave him control of the chantries; another bastion of popish ceremony had fallen. I had published my *Prayers and Meditations* that summer, and felt the time was safe for me to write another book, a declaration to the world of my beliefs, as Marguerite of Navarre has done. And so I wrote my little volume. I knew it might be – controversial – so I composed it in secret, in my bedroom. A confession – of my life; my sins, my salvation, my beliefs.' She looked at me intently; the light of conviction shone in her eyes now. 'It is called the *Lamentation of a Sinner*. I speak in it of how, when I was young, I was mired in superstition, full of vanity for the things of this world; of how God spoke to me but I denied His voice, until eventually I accepted His saving grace.' Her voice had risen with passion; she looked at Lord Parr and the Archbishop, but they had cast their eyes down. She continued, more quietly. 'It was God who brought me to realize it was my destiny to marry the King.' She cast her own head down, and I wondered if she was thinking of her old love for Thomas Seymour. 'In my *Lamentation* I speak in the most plain terms of my belief that salvation comes through faith and study of the Bible, not vain ceremonies.' I closed my eyes. I knew of books like this, confessions by radical

Protestants of their sinfulness and salvation. Some had been seized by the authorities. The Queen had been foolish to write such a thing in these faction-ridden times, even in secret. She must have known it; but for once her emotions had overridden her political sense. And her hope that the times were shifting in favour of reform had again proved disastrously wrong.

'Who has seen the book, your majesty?' I asked quietly.

'Only my Lord Archbishop. I finished it in February, but then in March the trouble with Gardiner began. And so I hid it in my private coffer, telling nobody.' She added bitterly, 'You see, Matthew, I can still be sensible sometimes.' I saw that she was torn between conflicting emotions: her desire to spread her beliefs amongst the people, her acute awareness of the political dangers of doing so, and her fear for her own life. 'The book stayed locked in my coffer until last month, when I resolved to ask the Archbishop for his opinion. He came to me, here, and read it one evening with me.' She looked at Cranmer, smiling wistfully. 'We have spoken much on matters of faith, these last three years. Few know how much.'

The Archbishop looked uneasy for a moment, then said, his voice composed, 'That was on the ninth of June. A little over a month ago. And I advised her majesty that on no account should the book be circulated. It said nothing about the Mass, but the condemnation of dumb Roman ceremonies, the argument that prayer and the Bible are the only ways to salvation – those could be read, by our enemies, as Lutheran.'

'Where is the manuscript now?' I asked.

'That is our problem,' Lord Parr said heavily. 'It has been stolen.'

The Queen looked me in the eye. 'And if it finds its way to the King's hands, then likely I am dead and others, too.'

'But if it does not deny the Mass—'

'It is too radical for the King,' the Queen said. 'And that I should be its author, and have kept it secret from him . . .' Her voice faltered.

Cranmer spoke quietly. 'He would see that as disloyalty. And that is the most dangerous thing of all.'

'I can understand that,' the Queen said sadly. 'He would feel – wounded.'

My head reeled. I clasped my hands together in my lap to force my mind to focus, realizing the others were waiting for me to respond. 'How many copies are there?' I asked.

The Queen answered, 'Only one, in my own hand. I wrote it in my bedchamber, secretly, with my door locked.'

'How long is it?'

'Fifty pages of small writing. I kept it secure, in the strong chest in my bedchamber. I alone have the key and I keep it round my neck. Even when I sleep.' She put her hand to her bodice and lifted out a small key. Like the teardrop pearl, it was on the end of a fine chain.

Cranmer said bluntly, 'I advised her majesty to destroy the book. Its very existence was a danger.'

'And that was on the ninth of June?' I asked.

The Queen answered, 'Yes. I could not, of course, meet with the Archbishop in my bedchamber, so I brought it to this room. It was the only time it has left my bedchamber. I asked all the ladies and servants to leave so our discussion could be private.'

'And you told nobody about your meeting?'

'I did not.'

They were all looking at me now. I had slipped into the question-and-answer mode of the investigating lawyer. There was no pulling back from this. But I thought, if this goes wrong, it could be the fire for me as well as for them.

The Queen continued. 'My Lord Archbishop told me the book must be destroyed. And yet – I believed, and still believe, that such a work, written by a Queen of England, could bring people to right faith.' She looked at me pleadingly, as though to say: see, this is my soul, this is the truth I have learned, and you must listen. I was moved, but lowered my gaze. The Queen clasped her hands together, then looked between the three of us, her voice quietly sombre now. 'Very well. I know. I was wrong.' She added wearily, 'Such faith in my own powers is itself a token of vanity.'

I asked, 'Did you return the manuscript directly to your chest?'

'Yes. Almost every day I would look at it. For a full month. Many times I nearly called you, Uncle.'

'Would that you had,' Lord Parr said feelingly.

'Had it not been summer, had there been fires lit in the grate, once, twice, I would have burned it. But I hesitated, and days lengthened into weeks. And then, eleven days ago, the day after that scene with Wriothesley, I opened the chest and the book was gone. It was gone.' She shook her head. I realized what a shock that moment must have been to her.

'When had you last seen it?' I asked gently.

'That afternoon I looked over the manuscript again, wondering whether there were changes I might make that would render it safe to publish. Then, in the early evening, the King called me to his private chamber, and I was with him, talking and playing cards, till near ten. His legs were paining him; he needed distraction. Then, when I came to bed, I went to take it out, to look at it, to guide my prayers, and it was gone.'

'Was there any sign the lock had been tampered with?'

'No,' she answered. 'None at all.'

'What else was in the chest, your majesty?'

'Some of my jewels. Legacies from my second husband, and his daughter, dear Margaret Neville, who died this spring.' A spasm of sadness crossed her face.

Lord Parr said, 'All those jewels were of considerable value. But nothing apart from the manuscript was removed.'

I considered. 'And this was the day following the incident with Wriothesley?'

'Yes. The sixth of July. I have cause to remember recent days very well.'

Lord Parr said, 'My niece contacted me at once. I was horrified to learn of the existence of the book, and what had happened to it.'

I looked at the old man. 'I imagine the nature of the theft would make enquiries within the household – difficult.'

He shook his head. 'We dare tell nobody. But I checked with the guards who had been in and out of the Queen's bedchamber during those crucial hours. Nothing unusual: two pages to clean, a maid-in-waiting to prepare the Queen's bed. And Jane her fool, wandering in to see if the Queen was about. Jane Fool is allowed to go everywhere,' he added crossly. 'But she has not the wit to steal an apple.'

'Finding out who was seen to enter the chamber during those hours is important,' I said. 'But someone could have found out about the book earlier, and chosen the hours when her majesty was with the King to make the theft.'

'How could anyone have known,' the Queen asked, 'when I wrote it in secret, told no one, and kept it locked away?'

Lord Parr nodded agreement. 'We cannot see how this has been done – we have not known what to do. We have felt – paralysed.'

The Queen closed her eyes, clutching the pearl round her

neck hard. We all watched her with concern. Finally she unclenched her hand. 'I am all right.'

'Are you sure?' Lord Parr asked.

'Yes. Yes. But you continue the story, Uncle.'

Lord Parr looked at me. 'It was then,' he said, 'that we heard of the murder by St Paul's.'

'Murder?' I asked sharply.

'Yes, there is murder in this, too. The book was stolen from the coffer sometime on the evening of the sixth of July. At dusk last Saturday, the tenth, a printer in a small way of business in Bowyer Road, hard by St Paul's, was murdered in his shop. You know how these little places have multiplied· round the cathedral these last few years. Printers, booksellers, often just tiny businesses in ramshackle sheds.'

'I do, my Lord.' I knew, too, that many printers and booksellers were radicals, and that several had had their premises raided in recent months.

'The printer was a man called Armistead Greening,' Lord Parr continued. 'His shop was one of those little sheds, with only a single printing press. He had been in trouble before for publishing radical literature; he was investigated in the spring but nothing was found against him. Recently he had been printing schoolbooks. Last Saturday evening he was working in his shop. Several of the local printers were at work nearby; they toil away until the last of the light, to make the most use of their presses. Greening had an apprentice, who left at nine.'

'How do you know these details?'

'From the apprentice, but mainly from his neighbour, who owns a larger print~shop next door. Geoffrey Okedene. At around nine, Master Okedene was closing down his shop when he heard a great commotion, shouts and cries for help, from Greening's shed. He was a friend of Greening's and went to investigate. The door was locked, but it was a flimsy thing; he put his shoulder to it and broke it open. He caught a glimpse of two men running through the other door, at the side – these print-shops get so hot, and full of vile smells from the ink and other concoctions they use, that even small ones have two doors. Master Okedene did not pursue them, for an attempt had been made to set Greening's print-shop on fire. His stock of paper had been strewn around and set light to. Okedene was able to stamp it out – you may imagine that if such a place caught it would burn like a torch.'

'Yes.' I had seen these poorly erected wooden sheds that were built against the cathedral walls or in vacant plots nearby, and heard the loud rhythmic thumping that constantly resounded from them.

'Only when he had put out the fire did Okedene see poor Greening lying on the earthen floor, his head beaten in. And, clutched in Greening's hand, this . . .' Lord Parr reached into a pocket in his robe and carefully extracted a small strip of expensive paper covered in neat writing and dotted with the brown stains of dried blood. He passed it to me. I read:

The Lamentation of a Sinner, Made by Queen Catherine, Bewailing the Ignorance of her Blind Life.

Most gentle and Christian reader, if matters should be rather confirmed by their reporters than the reports warranted by the matters, I must justly bewail our time, wherein evil deeds be well worded, and good acts evil turned. But since truth is, that things be not good for their praises, but praised for their goodness, I do not . . .

There the page ended, torn off. I looked at the Queen. 'This is your writing?'

She nodded. 'That is the opening of my book. *Lamentation of a Sinner.*'

Lord Parr said, 'Okedene read it and of course grasped its import from the heading. By God's mercy he is a good reformer. He brought it personally to the palace and arranged for it to be delivered into my hands. I interviewed him at once. Only then did he call the coroner. He has told him all he saw, except, at my instruction, about this piece of paper. Fortunately, the coroner is a sympathizer with reform, and has promised that if anything comes to light he will inform me. And he has been very well paid,' he added bluntly. 'With the promise of more to come.'

The Queen spoke then, an edge of desperation in her voice, 'But he has discovered nothing, nothing. And so I suggested we come to you, Matthew. You are the only one whom I know outside the court who could carry out such an investigation. But only if you will. I know the terrible dangers—'

'He has promised,' Lord Parr said.

I nodded. 'I have.'

'Then I thank you, Matthew, from the bottom of my heart.'

I looked at the torn paper. 'The obvious conclusion is that Greening was trying to keep the manuscript from the intruders, and whoever killed him snatched it out of his hands, but part of the top page tore away.'

'Yes,' said Lord Parr. 'And whoever killed him heard Master Okedene breaking down the door and fled. So desperate were they to avoid identification that they did not even pause to prise the piece of paper from the dead man's hands.'

'Or did not notice it at the time, more likely,' I said.

Lord Parr nodded. 'You should know that this was not the first attempt on Greening's life. He lived as well as worked in that hovel, in the most wretched poverty.' He wrinkled his nose in aristocratic distaste. 'As I mentioned, he has a young apprentice. Five days before, this boy arrived for work early in the morning and found two men trying to break into the shed. He called the alarm and they fled. From the apprentice's account they were different men from those who attacked and killed Greening shortly after.'

Cranmer said, 'Our first thought was that Greening had the manuscript given to him for printing. But that makes no sense. A Catholic might print it, so the book could be distributed around the streets, to the Queen's ruin, but no reformer.'

'Yes.' I considered. 'Surely if it fell into Greening's hands and his views were as you say, he would do exactly what Okedene did, return it. Could Greening have been a secret Catholic?'

Cranmer shook his head. 'I have had discreet enquiries made. Greening was a radical, a known man, all his life. And his parents before him.' He gave me a meaningful look.

A 'known man'. That meant Greening's family belonged to the old English sect of Lollardy. Over a hundred years before Luther, the Lollards had come to similar conclusions about the centrality of the Bible in the cause of salvation, and were known for their radical views about the Mass. Many of them had gravitated to the most extreme edges of Protestantism; with their long history of persecution, they had experience of being an underground community. They were as unlikely as any radicals to wish the Queen harm.

I asked, 'Is there anything else in the document that could identify it as the Queen's work?'

'It is all in the Queen's hand.'

'But the work as a whole would not be instantly identifiable, like that opening passage?'

'Even a superficial reading would identify the author.' Lord Parr looked at the Queen. 'It is, after all, a *personal* confession of sinfulness and salvation. It is obviously the Queen's work.' He shook his head. 'But we have no idea who has it now, or how it came into Greening's possession. The inquest was held two days ago; it returned a verdict of murder by persons unknown.'

The Queen looked at me. 'We have been waiting like rabbits caught in a snare for something to happen, for the book to appear on the streets, but there has been nothing for eleven days save silence. We three have fretted day and night over what to do and decided the matter must be investigated, and not by someone closely associated with the court.' She held my gaze, her eyes full of appeal. 'And so Matthew, forgive me, my mind turned to you. But even now, I say again, I only *ask* if you will help me. I do not command; I will not. I have enough blood on my hands through my writing of that book; but for me, poor Greening would still be alive.' She added sadly, 'I meant only to do good, but truly the Bible says, "Vanity of vanities, all is vanity."' She sat back, exhausted.

I said – could only say, 'How would you have me proceed?'

Cranmer and Lord Parr exchanged a glance. Relief? Hope? Doubt as to the wisdom of placing this thing in my hands? Lord Parr stood abruptly and began pacing the room. 'We have a plan, though you must tell us if you see flaws in it. The matter is urgent and I think must be approached from both ends. So far as Greening's murder is concerned, agents of the Archbishop have spoken with his parents through their vicar. They know nothing of the book, of course, but want the murderer found. They live in the Chilterns, so cannot easily come to London.'

'The Chilterns, yes.' I knew the district had long been known for Lollardy.

'They have willingly given you a power of attorney on their behalf. So far as they are concerned, wealthy friends of their son wish to discover his murderer, nothing more. Now the inquest is over, investigations have been left in the hands of the local constable, a man called Fletcher, a plodder. You will know, Serjeant, that if a murderer is not found within forty-eight hours the constables lose interest, as the chances of finding the perpetrator are slim. I should think Fletcher will be glad if you take over the work from him. Speak to Greening's apprentice, his neighbours, his associates; look round the workshop. But say nothing about the book. Except to Okedene, who, thank God, is a man who knows how to keep his mouth shut. He is utterly loyal to reform and understands the importance of this.' Lord Parr looked at me with steely intensity.

'I will, my Lord.'

'The other aspect of the mission is to discover who stole the manuscript from here. It has to be someone with access to the Queen's chamber. You will have to be sworn in as an assistant on the Queen's Learned Council, as of this afternoon. You will be given a new robe with the Queen's badge sewn into it; wear the robe when you are making enquiries within the palace. Wear your ordinary robe when you are looking into the Greening murder – there you should not be visibly connected to the Queen.'

'Very well.'

Lord Parr nodded approvingly. Cranmer glanced at me, then quickly away; a look of pity, I thought, or perhaps doubt.

Lord Parr continued, 'So far as investigations at the palace are concerned, you are known to have worked for the Queen on legal cases before. The story we will put around is that a valuable jewel, a ring bequeathed to her by her stepdaughter, has been stolen from the Queen's coffer. Just to be sure, I have taken the ring and have it in safekeeping. It is worth a great deal. The Queen's closeness to Margaret Neville, too, is well known; everyone will understand her eagerness that it be found. You will have authority to question servants in the Queen's household about who might have gained access to that coffer. As it happens, some time ago a pageboy stole a jewel from one of the Queen's ladies and after an investigation was caught. At the Queen's insistence he was pardoned, because of his youth. People will remember that.' He looked at me. 'I would conduct the investigation myself, but for someone of my seniority to be seen taking this on personally would cause surprise. And in this place an outsider can often see things more clearly.' He sighed. 'The world of the court is an incestuous one. I am happier on my estates, I confess, but my duty lies here now.'

'I am known as an enemy to certain on the King's Council.' I spoke hesitantly. 'The Duke of Norfolk; above all, Richard Rich. And I once angered the King himself.'

Cranmer said, 'Those are old matters, Matthew. And your investigations will be confined to the Queen's household. If you uncover anything that seems to go wider, tell us and we will deal with it. I will not be returning to Canterbury until this is settled.'

'Forgive me, my Lord Archbishop,' I said, 'but word may still get to Norfolk or Rich. You spoke of spies reporting what Gardiner said to you from the King's Privy Chamber . . .'

'Sympathizers,' Cranmer replied reprovingly, 'not spies.'

'But may there not be those within the Queen's household

who sympathize with the opponents of reform? The very fact the manuscript was stolen suggests as much.'

'That is the strange thing. We guard secrets very carefully in the Queen's household.' Cranmer looked at the Queen. 'Her majesty inspires great loyalty, which was tested during the heresy hunt. We can identify no one who could, or would, have done this.'

There was a moment's silence, then Lord Parr said, 'Begin now, Serjeant Shardlake; try to unravel the threads. Go to the printer's this afternoon. Come back this evening and I will swear you in, give you your robe and brief you further.'

I hesitated again. 'I am to work entirely on my own?'

'Young William Cecil may be useful, he has contacts among the radicals and is trusted by them. But he does not know of the *Lamentation*, and we will keep him out of it for now, I think.' He continued, in a lighter tone, 'Would you believe Cecil is already twice married, though only twenty-five? His first wife died in childbirth, and now he has a second. A woman with good connections. I think he will soon be a rising man.'

The Archbishop added, 'And where the printer's murder is concerned, you may employ your man Barak to help you. I understand he has been useful in the past.'

'But — ' Lord Parr raised a warning finger — 'he must know only that you are acting for the dead man's parents; make no mention of the Queen or the *Lamentation*.'

I hesitated. 'Barak is married now, with a child and another on the way. I would not put him in the way of even the possibility of danger. I have a student, Nicholas, but—'

Lord Parr interrupted. 'I will leave that to your discretion. Perhaps he can be employed in routine matters. So long as you tell him nothing of the *Lamentation*.' He looked at me intently again.

I nodded agreement, then turned to the Queen. She leaned forward and picked up the pearl on its chain round her neck. 'Do you know to whom this once belonged?' she asked quietly.

'No, your majesty. It is very fine.'

'Catherine Howard, who was Queen before me and who died on the block. A quicker death than burning.' She gave a long, desperate sigh. 'She, too, was foolish, though in a different way. All these rich things I wear, the cloth of gold and silken tissue and bright jewels, so many of them have been passed down from Queen to Queen. Always, you see, they are returned to the Department of the Queen's Wardrobe, to be preserved or altered. They are worth so much that they cannot be discarded, any more than the great tapestries.' She held up her richly embroidered sleeve. 'This was once worn with a dress of Anne Boleyn's. I have constant reminders of past events. I live in fear now, Matthew, great fear.'

'I will do all I can, put all other work aside. I swear.'

She smiled. 'Thank you. I knew you would succour me.'

Lord Parr inclined his head, indicating I should rise. I bowed to the Queen, who essayed another sad smile, and to Cranmer, who nodded. Lord Parr led me out, back to the window from which we had watched the King in the courtyard. The yard was empty now. I realized the window was in an angle of the corridor from which we could not be seen from either direction; ideal for private conversation. He said, 'Thank you, sir. Believe me, we do not underestimate the difficulties, or the dangers. Come with me now and I will give you more particulars of Greening, and the power of attorney from his parents.' He looked out over the courtyard, hesitated, then leaned closer. 'You saw the physical state of the King. But as you will have realized from what we told you, his mind is still, mostly, sharp and clear. And it has always been full of anger and suspicion.'

Chapter Seven

I T WAS WITH a sense of relief that I rode out under the gate of the palace again. I made my way slowly towards Charing Cross. Genesis sneezed and shook his head at the dust from the Scotland Yard brickworks, which endlessly laboured to produce materials to embellish and improve Whitehall. The day was hot and the street stank. I decided I would take Nicholas with me to the printers' quarter. It would do no harm to have someone young and sizeable beside me.

At the steps of the great Charing Cross, dozens of beggars sat as usual. More and more of them these last two years, with the polling and nipping of poor men's wages caused by the collapsing value of the coinage. There were those who said that beggars were leeches, licking the sweat from hardworking labourers' brows, but most of the beggars had once been working men themselves. I glanced at them, men and women and children, wearing ancient dirty rags, faces red and harsh from constant exposure to the sun, some displaying their sores and weeping scabs to invoke pity from the passers-by. One man who sat with the stump of one leg exposed wore the tatters of a soldier's uniform; no doubt he had left his leg in Scotland or France during the last two years of war. But I averted my eyes, for it was well known that to catch the eye of one could bring a whole horde descending on you; and I had much to think on.

I was involved in a matter potentially more deadly than

anything in my prior experience. It reached right into the heart of the royal court, at a time when the manoeuvring of various factions had never been more vicious. Recalling that spectacle of the King in the courtyard, I realized now that everything which had happened since the beginning of the year was part of a struggle to decide who would control the realm when Henry died and his throne passed to a child. In whose hands would the King leave the realm? Norfolk? Edward Seymour? Paget? The Queen?

I had let myself in for long days of fear and anxiety, as a harbourer of dangerous secrets which I did not want to possess. But a wise man knows he is a fool, and I was aware, of course, of my true motives. It was because I had long cast a fantasy of love around the Queen. It was an ageing man's hopeless foolishness, but that morning I realized how deeply I still felt.

And yet I knew I must see Queen Catherine clearly: her religious radicalism had led that most careful and diplomatic of women to risk all. She had called it her vanity but it was more like a loss of judgement. I wondered uneasily if she were verging towards fanaticism, like so many in these days. No, I thought, she had tried to draw back by submitting to the King and by asking for Cranmer's approval of the *Lamentation*; and yet her refusal to dispose of the book had led to potentially disastrous consequences.

The thought came to me, why not let the factions fight it out to the death? Why was the radical side any better than the conservative? But then I thought, the Queen would harm no man willingly. Nor, I believed, would Cranmer. I wondered, though, about Lord Parr. He was old and looked ill; but I had seen his devotion to his niece and sensed a ruthlessness about him, too — I was useful to him, but probably dispensable as well.

Lord Parr had handed me the power of attorney from Greening's parents. I would go to the streets around St Paul's to talk to the constable, then to Greening's neighbour Okedene, and finally the dead man's apprentice, who had witnessed the earlier break-in. And I should try and find out who Greening's friends were.

Lord Parr wanted me back at the palace by seven. I was likely to be heavily involved with this for many days. Fortunately it was out of law term and the courts were not in session. I would have to ask Barak to do some extra preparation work on cases I had in hand, and supervise Nicholas and Skelly. Uncomfortably I realized that I would have to lie to Barak and Nicholas; I could tell them I was involved in investigating the printer's murder, but only on behalf of his family, and I must say nothing about the hunt for the Queen's missing book. I hated the thought of lying to Barak especially, but there was no obvious alternative I could see.

On impulse, I turned north, heading for the street of little houses where Barak lived with his wife, Tamasin. He would be at work but she would likely be at home this time of day. Like Barak, Tamasin was an old friend; the three of us had been through much together, and I had an urge to talk with someone ordinary, commonsensical, with no taste for intrigue; and to see my little godson. I wanted a moment of normality, perhaps the last I would be allowed for some time.

I tied Genesis to the post outside their house and knocked on the door. It was answered by their servant, Goodwife Marris, a formidable widow of middle age. She curtsied. 'Master Shardlake, we were not expecting you.'

'I was nearby, I came on impulse. Is Mistress Barak in?'

'Ay, and the master, too. He came home for lunch. I was about to clear the plates away.' I realized I had had nothing to eat. Goodwife Marris showed me into the little parlour overlooking Tamasin's small, immaculately kept garden. The shutters were open and the room was filled with the scent of summer flowers. Barak was sitting at the table with Tamasin, empty plates and mugs of beer before them. Jane began clearing the plates away. Tamasin looked well, her pretty face contented and happy. 'This is a welcome surprise, sir,' she said. 'But you have missed lunch.'

'I forgot about it.'

She clicked her tongue. 'That is not good for you.'

Barak looked at me. 'I came home to eat. I thought Skelly could keep an eye on young Nick for that long.'

'That is all right.' I smiled as a little figure in a white robe and a woollen cap tied in a bow came crawling out from under the table to see what was happening. He looked at me with Barak's brown eyes, smiled and said, 'Man!'

''Tis his new word,' Tamasin said proudly. 'See, he begins to speak.'

'He is well out of his swaddling clouts now,' I said, admiring George's progress as he crawled over to his father and then, furrowing his little brow with concentration, man-aged to stand for a moment before clutching at his father's hose. Smiling at his achievement, he lifted a foot and kicked at his father's ankle.

Barak lifted him up. 'Do you kick, sirrah?' he said with mock seriousness. 'In the presence of your godfather, too? Shameless imp.' George chuckled happily. I reached down and patted his head. A few curls, blond like Tamasin's and fine as silk, escaped from under his cap.

'He grows by the day,' I said wonderingly. 'Though I still cannot see whom he most resembles.'

'Impossible to say with that fat chubby face,' Barak said, tapping his son on his button nose.

'I hear you are to be congratulated, Tamasin.'

She blushed. 'Thank you, sir. Yes, George will have a little brother or sister next January, God willing. We both hope for a girl this time.'

'You feel well?'

'Apart from a little sickness in the mornings, yes. Now, let me fetch that bread and cheese. Jack, you have a pea in your beard. Please take it out. It looks disgusting.' Barak pulled the pea from where it had lodged, squashed it between his fingers, and gave it to a delighted George. 'I think I might grow one of those long forkbeards people have now. I could drop so much food in it I would have a nice snack always to hand.'

'You'd have to find a new house to eat it in,' Tamasin called from the kitchen.

I looked at Barak, sprawled comfortably in his chair, the little child playing at his feet. I was right to keep him out of this. 'Jack,' I said, 'I have a new piece of business which is likely to keep me out of the office a good deal for the next few days at least. Could I ask you to take charge, to supervise Nicholas and Skelly – though I may use Nicholas a little. I will see the more important clients if I can.'

'Like Mistress Slanning?' I knew Barak could not abide her.

'Yes, I will deal with her.'

He looked at me keenly. 'What is the business?'

'A printer murdered down by St Paul's. It is a week now, and no sign of catching the culprit. The coroner's office is lazy as usual. I have a power of attorney to investigate, from the printer's parents. They live in the Chilterns.'

'They gave you the case?'

I hesitated. 'It came through a third party.'

'You don't do jobs like that any more. Could be dangerous.'

'I felt a duty to take this on.'

'You look worried,' he said in his direct way.

'Please, Jack,' I answered, somewhat pettishly. 'There are some aspects to this I must keep confidential.'

Barak frowned. I had never left him out of such a matter before. 'Up to you,' he said with a touch of grumpiness.

George, meanwhile, left his father and toddled a couple of steps over to me. I picked him up, only to realize as he laid pudgy hands on my shirt that he had smeared the squashed pea all over it. I set him down again.

'That's a mess,' Barak said. 'Sorry. But you have to be careful picking him up.'

Tamasin came back with a plate of bread and cheese and a couple of wrinkled apples. 'Last year's,' she said, 'but they've been well stored.' She saw my shirt and took George. 'You muttonhead, Jack,' she scolded. 'You didn't give him that pea, did you? He could choke on it.'

'He hasn't eaten it, as you can see. Anyway, he tried to eat a slug from the garden last week, and it did the little squib no harm.'

'Fie, give him here.' Tamasin reached down and picked up her son, who gave her a puzzled look. 'You encourage him to trouble.'

'Sorry. Yes, it's best to keep out of trouble.' Barak looked at me meaningfully.

'If you can,' I answered. 'If you can.'

✝

I RODE HOME TO CHANGE my shirt before going down the street to Lincoln's Inn. I went into the kitchen. Josephine was standing there wearing a dress I had not seen before; of good wool, violet-coloured with a long white collar. Agnes knelt beside her, working at the skirt with pins. Agnes stood hurriedly and both women curtsied as I came in.

'What do you think of Josephine's new dress, sir?' Agnes asked. 'She got it for her walking out tomorrow. I helped choose it.'

Josephine, as ever, blushed. The dress became her. I could not, though, but reflect how the dye looked pale, washed out, in comparison with the extraordinary bright colours that I had seen everywhere at Whitehall. But such clothes were all most people could afford.

'You look fine, Josephine,' I said. 'Master Brown cannot fail to be impressed.'

'Thank you, sir. Look, I have new shoes as well.' She lifted the dress a little to reveal square white shoes of good leather.

'A picture,' I said, smiling.

'And the dress is finest Kendal wool,' Agnes said. 'It will last you many a summer.'

'Where will you go walking?' I asked.

'Lincoln's Inn Fields. I hope it will be another fine afternoon.'

'The skies are clear. But now, I must hurry. Agnes, I need a new shirt.' I opened my robe to reveal a green smudge. 'My godson,' I said ruefully.

'What a mess! I will call Martin.'

'I can fetch one from the press,' I said, but Agnes had already called her husband's name. He appeared from the dining room, clad in an apron. He must have been cleaning the silver for his clothes smelled of vinegar.

'Could you get a new shirt for Master Shardlake, please, Martin?' As always when she spoke to her husband, Agnes's tone was deferential. 'His little godson has spoiled the one he has.' She smiled, but Martin only nodded. He seldom laughed or smiled; he seemed one of those men born without a sense of humour.

I went up to my room, and a couple of minutes later Martin appeared with my new shirt. He laid it on the bed and stood waiting. 'Thank you, Martin,' I said, 'but I can put on a shirt myself. I will leave the stained one on the bed.' Always he wanted to do everything. He looked a little put out, but bowed and left the room.

I changed the shirt and left my bedroom. At the foot of the stairs, I saw Josephine carrying a jug of hot water, held out carefully in front of her so as not to touch her new dress. She took it through the open door of the parlour to where Martin was still cleaning the silver.

'Put it on the table,' he said. 'On the cloth there.'

'Yes, Master Brocket.' She turned away, and I saw her give Martin's back a look of dislike, mingled with contempt, similar to the one she had given him yesterday. It puzzled me. Surely Martin's cold manner alone was not sufficient to evoke a look like that from someone as good-natured as Josephine.

☦

I LEFT GENESIS AT HOME and walked the short distance to Lincoln's Inn. Barak had not yet returned, but both Skelly and Nicholas were occupied at their desks. Skelly stood up and brought me a note, eyes shining with curiosity behind his wooden spectacles. 'This was just delivered for you, sir, by the woman who attends Master Bealknap.'

I took the note and broke the seal. Inside was another note, painfully scrawled. '*I am told I must soon prepare to meet my maker. Could you, as a kindness, visit me after church tomorrow? Stephen Bealknap.*'

I sighed. I had forgotten all about him. But I could not ignore this. I scribbled a reply, saying I would be with him after church, and asked Skelly to run across with it. When he had gone I turned to Nicholas. He was dressed soberly today, in a short black robe, in accordance with the regulations. He handed me a sheaf of papers. 'My summary of the main points in that conveyance case, sir.'

I glanced through them quickly. The notes were scrawled, but seemed thought through and logically set out. Perhaps the boy was settling down after all. I looked up at him – he was six feet tall, I had no choice but to look up. His green eyes were clear and direct. 'I have a new case,' I said. 'It is a confidential matter, requiring discretion, and unfortunately for the next few days at least I will be much out of chambers and you will need to put in more hours. Are you willing to do that?'

'Yes, sir,' he answered, but I heard the unwillingness in his tone. It would mean fewer hours spent in the taverns with the other young gentlemen.

'Hopefully it will not be for long. I would also welcome your assistance with some aspects of this new case. I would like you to come with me now to interview some witnesses.' I hesitated, then said, 'It is a matter of murder, and at the request of the victim's parents I am helping the investigation. I am going to interview the constable, and then some witnesses.'

Nicholas immediately brightened up. 'To catch a villain, that is a worthy task.'

I answered seriously, 'If I take you with me on these enquiries, you must keep everything you hear entirely confidential. This is not a matter for discussion in the taverns. That could lead me, and you, into trouble.'

'I know that cases must be kept confidential, sir,' he answered a little stiffly. 'Any gentleman must respect that.'

'None more than this one. I have your promise?'

'Of course, sir,' he said in an injured tone.

'Very well. Then walk with me now to St Paul's. The

murdered man was a printer. When I am asking people questions, listen hard, and if any questions occur to you, and you think them sensible, you may ask them. As you did with Mistress Slanning yesterday,' I added. 'You did well there.'

Nicholas brightened. 'I wondered if I had gone too far. Whether she might leave you.'

'That would be a tragedy,' I answered sardonically. 'And now, let us go.' A thought occurred to me. 'Did you bring your sword with you today?'

'Yes, sir.' Nicholas reddened. He liked to wear his sword when walking abroad, it was all part of his swagger.

I smiled. 'Since your father's being a landowner decrees you are a gentleman and gentlemen wear swords in public, we may as well turn the sumptuary laws to our advantage. It might impress the people we will be talking to.'

'Thank you.' Nicholas retrieved his sword, in its fine leather scabbard, tooled with a design of vine leaves. He buckled it on. 'I am ready,' he said.

Chapter Eight

WE WALKED ALONG the Strand, under Temple Bar and down Fleet Street. It was afternoon now, and I was glad of the bread and cheese Tamasin had given me earlier. Nicholas's natural walk was a fast lope, and I told him to slow down a little, reminding him that lawyers are men of dignity and should walk gravely. We crossed the Fleet Bridge, and I held my breath at the stink of the river. A rooting pig had fallen in and was thrashing about in the mud. Its owner stood knee-deep in the green, scummy water, trying to get it out.

We passed the Fleet Prison where, as always, the dirty hands of prisoners stretched through the bars seeking alms, for if no one brought them food, they starved. I thought of Anne Askew in Newgate, being brought money by the Queen's ladies. From there she had gone to the Tower to be tortured, and then to the stake. I shuddered.

We went under the city wall at Ludgate, the great edifice of St Paul's Cathedral ahead, its soaring wooden spire reaching five hundred feet into the blue sky. Nicholas looked at it with wonder. 'No building so fine in Lincolnshire, eh?' I said.

'Lincoln Cathedral is beautiful, but I have only seen it twice. My father's estate is down in the southwest of the county, near the Trent.' I caught a bite of anger in the boy's voice when he mentioned his father.

Beyond Ludgate, Bowyer Row was busy with trade. A butcher had set up a stall on which lay some stiff-looking, greenish meat. Prices were so high these days that stallholders could get away with selling rancid meat. To attract customers, he had set a live turkey in a cage at the end of his stall. People paused to stare at this extraordinary bird from the New World, like a gigantic chicken, with enormous brightly coloured wattles.

An elderly peddler approached us, his tray full of pamphlets newly purchased from the printers. He leered at us. 'Buy my new-printed ballads, sirs. Full of naughty rhymes. *The Milkmaid and the Stallion Boy*, *The Cardinal's Maidservants*.' Nicholas laughed and I waved the man aside. Another peddler stood in a doorway, an old arrowbag full of canes over his shoulder. 'Buy my fine jemmies!' he called. 'Buy my London tartars! Well soaked in brine! Teach wives and sons obedience!'

A group of seven or eight little children, ragged shoeless urchins, ran towards us. I had glimpsed the sharp knife one boy was carrying. 'Cutpurses,' I murmured to Nicholas. 'Watch your money!'

'I saw them.' He had already clapped a hand to his purse, grasping his sword hilt with the other. We looked directly at the children and, realizing we had guessed their intent, they ran off to one side instead of crowding round us. One shouted, 'Crookback devil!', another, 'Carrot-head clerk!' At that Nicholas turned and took a step towards them. I put a hand on his arm. He shook his head and said sadly, 'People were right to warn me; London is a wild sea, full of dangerous rocks.'

'That it is. In more ways than one. When I first came to London I, too, had to learn things for myself. I am not sure I have ever got used to the city; I sometimes dream of retiring to the country, but distractions will keep coming.' I looked at him. 'One thing I should tell you. The murdered man and his friends were religious radicals. I take it dealing with such people will not be a problem for you.'

'I worship only as the King requires,' Nicholas said, repeating the formula of those who would be safe. He looked at me. 'In such matters I wish only to be left in peace.'

'Good,' I said. 'Now, turn up here, we are going to visit the constable first, in Ave Maria Lane.'

✝

AVE MARIA LANE was a long narrow street of three-storey buildings, a muddle of shops, houses and tenements, all with overhanging eaves. I noticed a couple of booksellers' shops, their publications laid out on a table in front, watched over by blue-coated apprentices with wooden clubs to deter thieves. Most of the books were aimed at the upper end of the market – Latin classics and French works – but among them there was also a copy of Becon's new *Christian State of Matrimony*, which urged women to quiet and obedience. Had it not been so expensive I might have bought a copy for Barak as a jest; Tamasin would throw it at his head. I wished I had not had to dissemble with him earlier.

'The constable is called Edward Fletcher,' I told Nicholas. 'He lives at the sign of the Red Dragon. Look, there it is. If he is not at home we shall have to try and find him about his business.'

The door was answered by a servant, who told us Master Fletcher was in and ushered us into a little parlour, with a desk and chairs all heaped with papers. Behind the desk sat a thin man of about fifty in the red doublet and cap of a city constable. He looked tired, on edge. I recognized him; he had been one of the constables who carried the faggots to the fires the day before.

'God give you good morrow, Master Fletcher,' I said.

'And you, sir.' He spoke deferentially, impressed no doubt by my robe. He stood and bowed. 'How may I help you?'

'I am here about the murder last week of Armistead Greening, God pardon his soul. I understand the coroner has put you in charge of the investigation.'

Fletcher sighed. 'He has.'

'I am Serjeant Matthew Shardlake, of Lincoln's Inn. My pupil, Master Overton. Master Greening's parents are sore grieved at his loss, and have asked me to assist in the investigations, with your permission. I have a power of attorney.' I passed the document to him.

'Please sit, sirs.' Fletcher removed papers from a couple of stools and laid them on the floor. When we were seated he regarded me seriously. 'You will know, sir, that if a murderer is not caught within the first two days, and his identity is unknown, the chances of finding him are small.'

'I know it well. I have been involved in such investigations before, and understand how difficult they are.' I glanced at the papers piled around. 'And I know how heavy the duties are for the city constables in these days.' I smiled sympathetically. 'Investigating a brutal murder must be yet one more burden.'

Fletcher nodded sadly. 'It is indeed.' He hesitated, then said, 'If you would take on the investigation I should be grateful.'

I nodded. I had read the man aright; many London constables were lazy and venal but Fletcher was conscientious and hopelessly overburdened. And affected, perhaps, by what he had had to do yesterday. The burning.

'I would keep you informed of any developments, of

course,' I said. 'And you would be the one to report any dis,
coveries to the coroner.' And take the credit, I implied.

He nodded.

'Perhaps I could begin by asking you what you know of
the circumstances of the murder. My pupil will take notes,
if you will permit.' Nicholas took quill and paper from his
satchel. Fletcher gestured to him to help himself from his ink,
well, then folded his arms and sat back.

'I was visited somewhat after nine on the evening of the
tenth, just as the light was fading, by one of my watchmen.
He told me that a printer of Paternoster Row, Armistead
Greening, had been murdered, and also reported the hue and
cry raised by his neighbour, Master Okedene, who discov,
ered the body. I sent a message to the coroner and went across
to Paternoster Row. Okedene was there, looking in a bad
state. He said he had been working late in his print,shop
with his assistant, using the last of the light, when he heard a
loud cry for help from Greening's works next door, then
bangs and shouts. Master Okedene is a man of some sub,
stance, but Greening was in a small way of business, his
workshop little more than a wooden hut.'

'Not a very secure place, then?'

'No indeed. Master Okedene told me that when he ran to
investigate the door was locked, but he forced it open, just in
time to see two men, big ragged,looking fellows, run out of
the side door. Master Okedene's assistant, an old man, had
stayed in the doorway of Okedene's shop, but saw the two
men run out and climb over the wall behind the shed, into a
garden. He gave a good description. Master Okedene would
have pursued them, but he saw the print,shop had been set
alight, a lamp dropped on a pile of paper.'

'They wanted to burn the place down?' Nicholas asked.

I said, 'If it burned down and a charred body were found

in the ruins, Greening's death might have been attributed to his accidentally setting the place on fire.'

Fletcher nodded. 'That was my surmise. In any event, Master Okedene saw the fire and hurried to put it out before it reached more papers and the inks and other materials printers use. They are very flammable, a fire could have spread to his place.'

I nodded agreement. Fire in summer was one of the terrors of London, and probably a greater terror still among printers.

'Then he saw Master Greening lying in a pool of blood by his press, his head staved in.' The constable frowned. 'I was a little annoyed with Master Okedene, because after giving me his statement he went off and disappeared for several hours. At the inquest he said he had been so shocked by what had happened that he had had to get away and have a drink, and had wandered down to one of the taverns by the river that stay open after curfew.' The constable shrugged. 'Still, he told me all he knew before he left, and he is known as an honest man.' I reminded myself: during those hours, Okedene was actually at Whitehall Palace.

Fletcher hesitated, then continued, 'I should tell you, I was already under orders to keep a watch on Master Greening. He was known for having extreme views in religion, and radical friends. Three years ago he was closely questioned by Bishop Bonner about some books of John Bale, which were smuggled in from Flanders; there were reports that Greening was one of the distributors. But nothing was proved. It is a strange thing, though, that while his shop is small, with only one press and one apprentice, he has been able to keep the business going for some years, though you will know how risky the printing trade is.'

'Indeed. You need money to invest in the equipment.

And once you have printed a book you must sell many copies to recoup any profit.'

Fletcher nodded agreement. 'And he was a young man, only thirty, and his parents I believe are not rich.'

'Small yeoman farmers only, I understand.'

The constable gave me a look of sudden suspicion. 'And yet they can afford to hire a serjeant at law.'

'They have connections to someone I owe a favour to.'

Fletcher studied me closely, then continued. 'Greening's known acquaintances were questioned, including some other radicals the Bishop has ordered us to keep an eye on. All had alibis, and no motive for killing him. He kept no money at the shop. He lived there, slept on a little truckle bed in a corner. There were several shillings in his purse, untouched. He was unmarried, and seems to have had no woman.'

I asked, 'What sort of radical was he?'

Fletcher shrugged his shoulders. 'He and his friends were thought to be sacramentarians, maybe other things. I have heard it said Greening's parents were Lollards from generations back. And old Lollards might be Anabaptists today. But no proof was ever found.' Fletcher gave me another suspicious look, perhaps wondering if I were a radical myself.

I said lightly, 'My pupil was just saying on the way here, it should suffice simply to worship as the King commands.'

'Yes,' Fletcher agreed. 'Safer that way, too.'

'What about his apprentice?'

'A hulking, insolent fellow, I wouldn't be surprised if he were another radical. But he was at home with his mother and sisters on the night of the murder, and all agree he got on well with his master. Master Okedene has taken on the boy now.'

'And the two men Master Okedene's assistant saw?'

'Vanished into thin air. From the descriptions they're not local men. I'd have taken it for a random attack by some beggars, hoping perhaps to steal some paper, which of course has some value – but for one thing . . .'

'What is that?'

The constable frowned. 'It was not the first attack on Greening.' I looked surprised, as though hearing the news for the first time. 'The apprentice, young Elias, told me that, some days before, he came to work early to find two men trying to break in, smash the lock. He shouted to waken Master Greening, who was asleep within, and called out, "Clubs!", which as you will know brings any apprentice within reach to aid one of his fellows. The two men fled at once. And according to young Elias's description, they were not the same men who killed Greening. He sticks to that.' Fletcher spread his arms. 'And that is all. The inquest returned its verdict of murder yesterday. I was asked to continue the investigation, but I have no further leads – nothing to investigate.'

'Do you have the names of the suspected radicals Greening associated with?'

'Yes. There were three.' Fletcher rummaged among his papers and wrote down the names and addresses of three men. We leaned over the desk as he pointed at each in turn. 'James McKendrick is Scotch; he works at the docks, used to be a soldier but turned into one of those radical preachers the Scotch have thrown out of their kingdom. Andres Vandersteyn is a cloth merchant from Antwerp; he trades between there and London – they say in forbidden books as well as cloth. The third, William Curdy, is a candlemaker, moderately prosperous. They all attend church regularly on Sunday and are careful what they say in public, but they were all friendly with Greening and sometimes used to meet

together at his shop. And they were friends with other radicals of various sorts.'

'How do you know?' Nicholas asked.

'Informers, of course. Mine and the Bishop's. And I am
told that these three have not been at their homes lately.' He
raised his eyebrows. 'They may be keeping out of the way of
officialdom.'

Nicholas said, 'A strange group to meet together. A
Dutch merchant trading with the Low Countries would be
of gentleman status, a candlemaker would be the middling
sort, but a poor printer and a dockworker are from quite a
different class.'

'Some radicals believe social divisions between men are
wrong,' I replied. 'But meeting together is not an offence.'

'Nor being Dutch, nor a Scotch exile,' Fletcher said.
'More's the pity, for both groups are often radicals.' He
sighed, shook his head at the restrictions that bound his
work, then added, 'Nonetheless, the Bishop's men raided
Greening's place back in April –'

'I did not know that,' I said, leaning forward.

'They raided several print-shops in search of some pamphlets by John Bale that had appeared in London. Printed
somewhere in the city. Nothing was found anywhere.'

Yet somehow the most dangerous book in the kingdom
had found its way into that shop. 'What do you think happened, Master Fletcher?' I asked.

'Greening obviously had enemies who were out to kill
him. But no one seems to know of any. Perhaps there was a
falling-out with another radical group; these people will turn
from love of each other to hatred over the tiniest point of
doctrine. The descriptions of the two sets of people who
tried to break in tally with nobody known locally, and this

is a close-knit district. You can see why the investigation is at a standstill.'

I nodded sympathetically. 'If you would not object, I would like to question Master Okedene and his assistant. And the apprentice. Perhaps these friends of Greening's. And I would like to look at Master Greening's shop, too. Is there a key?'

Fletcher produced a small key from his desk. 'I put a new padlock on. You may as well keep this for now. The shop is at the sign of the White Lion. I wish you well.' He waved his hands at the papers littered around. 'As you see, I am burdened with duties. This year I have had to hunt for heretics as well as criminals, though the hunt for the former seems to have died down now.' He looked me in the eye. 'I saw you at the burning yesterday, on your horse; your friend looked set to faint.'

'I saw you, too.'

'I have to carry out the duties the mayor gives me,' he said defensively, though for a moment his eyes looked haunted.

'I understand.'

He gave me a hard look. 'You will report anything you find in this case back to me, remember. I have jurisdiction under the coroner.'

'All and anything I discover,' I lied. 'By the way, what happened to the body?'

'It couldn't be kept lying around till his parents were able to get here from the Chilterns; not in summer. He was buried in the common pit.'

✝

WE WALKED UP Ave Maria Lane into Paternoster Row; a longer, wider street, which was the centre of England's small but growing printing trade. There were several more booksellers, some with printer's shops above, and a few smaller print-shops; as Fletcher had said, some were mere sheds fixed to the side of buildings, or erected on small plots of land leased from the owner. I thought of Greening's possible involvement with the printing of forbidden books by John Bale. Once a favourite of Lord Cromwell's, but now the most detested of radicals, Bale was hidden in exile somewhere in Flanders.

'What did you think of Fletcher?' I asked Nicholas.

'He was at the burning?'

'Yes. Doing his duty,' I added heavily.

'I would rather die than carry out such a duty.'

It was an easy thing for a young man of means to say. 'I do not think he liked it,' I observed.

'Perhaps. I noticed his fingernails were bitten to the quick.'

'Well spotted. I did not see that. Noticing things, that is the key in this business. We will make a lawyer of you yet. And what did you make of the murder?'

Nicholas shook his head. 'Two attacks, as Fletcher said; that sounds like Greening had enemies. Or perhaps he had something precious in his shop – something more than paper and ink.' I looked at the boy sharply; he had come a little too close to the mark for my comfort with that observation. 'Gold, perhaps,' Nicholas went on, 'that the thieves managed to take before they were interrupted.'

'If people have gold they spend it, or deposit it somewhere safe; only misers hoard it at home.'

'Like your friend Bealknap? I have heard he is such a one.'

'He is not my friend,' I answered shortly. Nicholas reddened, and I continued more civilly, 'Greening does not sound like such a man.'

'No, indeed.' Nicholas added, 'The constable looked over-worked.'

'Yes. In some ways London is a well-policed city. The constables and watchmen look out for violence, and violations of the curfew. If a few taverns open after hours they wink at it, so long as the inn keepers do not let customers get violent.' I looked at Nicholas and raised my eyebrows. His own tavern sword fight had become an item of gossip round Lincoln's Inn, to my discomfort. He reddened further.

I went on, 'The constables check that people obey the sumptuary laws regarding the clothes that may be worn by men of each station, though again they wink at minor infringements. And they run informers to report on crime and religious misdemeanours. But when it comes to investigating a murder requiring a long-term, detailed investigation, they have not the resources, as Fletcher said.'

'I confess I do not fully understand about the different types of radical,' Nicholas said. 'Sacramentarians and Lollards and Anabaptists, what are the differences?'

'That is something it is as well to know in London. But lower your voice,' I said quietly. 'Open discussion of these matters is dangerous. Sacramentarians believe the bread and wine are not transformed into the body and blood of Christ during the Mass, which properly should be regarded only as a remembrance of Christ's sacrifice. By law, to express that belief is heresy. In most of Europe such opinion is new, but in England a man called John Wycliffe propounded similar doctrines more than a century ago. Those who followed him, the Lollards, were persecuted, but Lollardy has lived on here and there, in small secret groups. The Lollards were delighted, of course, by the King's break with Rome.'

'And the Anabaptists?'

They were one of the religious sects that sprang up in

Germany twenty years ago. They believe in going back to the practices of the earliest Christians; they are sacramentarians, but they also believe that the baptism of children is invalid, that only adults who have come to knowledge of Christ can be baptized. Hence "Anabaptists". But also, and most dangerously, they share the belief of the earliest Christians that social distinctions between men should be abolished and all goods held in common.'

Nicholas looked astonished. 'Surely the early Christians did not believe that?'

I inclined my head. 'Looking at the Scriptures, there is a good argument they did.'

He frowned. 'I heard the Anabaptists took over a city in Germany and ran it according to their beliefs, and by the end blood was running in the streets.' He shook his head. 'Man cannot do without authority, which is why God has ordained princes to rule over him.'

'In fact, the Anabaptists were besieged in Münster, the Protestant Prince allying with Catholic forces to take the city. That was the real cause of the bloodshed. Though I have heard that yes, the Anabaptists' rule inside the city had become violent. But afterwards most of them renounced violence. They were run out of Germany and Flanders, too; a few from Flanders came here across the North Sea. The King burned those he could find.'

'But there could still be others?'

'So it is said. If they exist they have been forced underground as the Lollards were. Anyone with a Dutch name is looked at askance these days.'

'Like that friend of Greening's the constable mentioned? Vandersteyn?'

'Yes.'

Nicholas's brow furrowed. 'So the Anabaptists have

renounced violence, but not the belief that rulers must be put down?'

'So it is said.'

'Then they remain a great danger,' he said seriously.

'They are a useful bogey.' I looked at Nicholas. 'Well, now you have seen what a murder enquiry begins to look like. It is seldom an easy thing to investigate, nor safe.'

He smiled. 'I am not afraid.'

I grunted. 'Fear keeps you on your toes. Remember that.'

✝

ALL THE SHOPS and printworks in Paternoster Row had little signs outside: an angel, a golden ball, a red cockerel. The sign of the White Lion, crudely painted on a board, hung outside a one-storey wooden building which was made to seem all the poorer by the fine-looking house which stood next to it. That must be the neighbour, Okedene's. I used the key to open the padlock the constable had fixed to the splintered door, and pushed it open. It was dim within. There was a second door at the side of the shed, with a key in the lock, and I got Nicholas to open it. It gave onto a weed-strewn patch of ground. I looked round the shed. The single room was dominated by a large printing press in the centre, the press itself raised on its screw, the tray of paper empty. Nailed to the walls, cheap shelves held paper, ink and solutions in bottles, and blocks of type in boxes. A harsh smell permeated the place.

In one corner was a pile of printed pages, and others had been hung on lines to dry. I looked at the top page: *A Goodly French Primer.* I glanced at the pages hanging to dry: *Je suis un gentilhomme de l'Angleterre. J'habite à Londres . . .* I remembered such stuff from my schooldays. Greening had been printing a schoolbook for children. There was a straw bed in a corner, a blanket and pillow. Beside the bed was a knife and plate with some stale bread and mouldy cheese. Greening's last meal.

'Nicholas,' I said, 'would you look under the printing press and see if there is any type in the upper tray? I am not sure I could manage it.' If there was, I would have to get the boy to detach the tray somehow, so that I could see if it was the same type used in printing the French book, or something else; had Greening been planning to print the *Lamentation*?

Nicholas twisted his long body under the press and looked up with an easy suppleness I envied. 'No print in the tray, sir. It looks empty.'

'Good,' I said, relieved.

He rose and stood looking around. 'What a poor place. To have to live as well as work here, amidst this smell.'

'Many live in far worse conditions.' Yet Nicholas was right, a man who was able to keep a printer's business going should have been able to afford a home. Unless his business was failing; perhaps he had not been sharp enough for this competitive trade. Lord Parr had said Greening's parents were poor, so where had he got the capital to buy the press and other equipment to start the business? I saw, by the bed, a dark stain on the floor. Blood, from the injuries Greening had received. Poor fellow, not yet thirty, now rotting in the common graveyard.

There was a plain wooden coffer beside the bed. It was unlocked, and contained only a couple of stained leather aprons, some shirts and doublets of cheap linen, and a well-thumbed New Testament. No forbidden books; he had been careful.

Nicholas was bending over a little pile of half-burned papers on the floor. 'Here's where they tried to start the fire,' he said.

I joined him. 'Under the shelf of inks. If Okedene

hadn't come the place would have gone up.' I picked out one of the half-burned pieces of paper '... *le chat est un animal méchant ...*' 'Pages from the book he was printing,' I said.

Nicholas looked around the room. 'What will happen to all this?'

'It belongs to his parents now. The power of attorney gives me the right to take out probate on their behalf. Perhaps you and Barak could deal with that. The author will have paid Greening to print his book, that money will have to be repaid. Otherwise the materials will be sold and the proceeds given to his parents. The printing press will be worth something.'

I looked at the paper on the shelf. Not a large stock, but with nearly all paper in England imported, it had a market value, and as Fletcher had suggested, it would be worth stealing, as would the working type. But it hardly explained two attempted burglaries by separate parties.

I went to the side door and stepped outside, pleased to be away from the harsh fumes, and looked out. The little patch of weedy ground ended at a brick wall, seven feet high. I had a thought. I needed to speak to Okedene on his own, without Nicholas. Besides myself, Okedene was the only other person outside the palace walls who knew of the *Lamentation*.

'Nicholas,' I said, 'go and look over that wall.'

He did so, pulling himself up easily. 'A garden,' he said. 'In little better state than the ground this side.'

'Will you climb over, see where those men might have gone after they killed Greening, whether they left any traces? Then join me at Okedene's house.'

He looked worried. 'What if the owners see me poking about in their garden?'

'Make some excuse.' I smiled. 'A good lawyer should always be able to think on his feet.'

Chapter Nine

MASTER OKEDENE'S establishment was a three-storey house. The bottom floor was a bookshop, volumes displayed on a table outside. They were varied; from Eliot's *Castle of Health* to little books on astrology and herbs, and Latin classics. There were a couple of prayer books, approved ones, small volumes no larger than a man's hand, which one could carry as one walked. From the upper floors came a thumping, clacking sound: newly inked pages would be put under the press, it would be rapidly screwed down, the page taken out and a new one inserted. An old man stood in the doorway, guarding the bookshop; he was stringy and arthritic-looking, his hands knotted. He studied me warily; he would have seen Nicholas and me enter Greening's shed.

I smiled. 'God give you good morrow, goodman. I am a lawyer, representing the parents of the late Master Greening.'

He took off his cap, revealing a bald pate beneath. 'God pardon his soul.' He gave a wheezing cough.

'I have authority from Constable Fletcher to investigate the matter. Would you be Master Okedene's assistant, that saw the two men run from the building?'

'I am, sir,' he answered more cheerfully. 'John Huffkyn, at your service.'

'I am Master Shardlake. Would you tell me what happened?'

He nodded, clearly pleased to tell his story again. 'It was evening, I was helping Master Okedene run the press. He is printing a book on the voyages to the New World, with woodcuts showing the wondrous creatures there. A big contract. We were working till the light was done.' He sighed. 'Now that Master Okedene has taken on that lump Elias as apprentice, I am put to mind the shop during the day.' He paused. 'But thirty years in this business have worn my joints to shreds. And my chest—'

'That night . . .' I said, bringing him back to the point.

'Work had just finished, we were pinning up pages to dry overnight. The windows were open and we heard a commotion next door. Cries, then a loud shout for help. Master Okedene and I looked at each other. Master Greening could occasionally be heard in loud discussions with his friends, but these were sounds of violence. We ran downstairs. The master ran next door, but I stayed in the doorway. With my poor bent limbs and bad chest I could be of little assistance . . .' He looked ashamed.

'I understand,' I offered solicitously.

'From here I saw it all. Master Okedene battered the door in, and a second later I saw two men run out of there.' He pointed to Greening's side door. 'As I told them at the inquest, they were both in their twenties, dressed in dirty wadmol smocks. Vagrants, they seemed to me, masterless men.' He made a grimace. 'Both carried nasty-looking clubs. They were strongly built; one was tall and, young as he was, near bald. The other was fair-haired and had a big wart on his forehead; it was visible even in the poor light. Both had raggedy beards.'

'You observed well.'

'My eyes at least are still sound. I would be glad to identify them, help see them hang. Master Greening was a good neighbour. I know he was a radical, but he was quiet, he wasn't one of those who buttonholes people and starts preaching at them, putting them in danger of the law. He did no man harm – that I know of,' he added, looking at me sharply.

'I have heard no ill spoken of him.'

Huffkyn continued, 'When the two men had gone I went across to the shed, for I could smell burning. Master Okedene was putting out a fire, a heap of papers set alight on the floor, and poor Greening was lying there. A dreadful sight, the top of his head bashed in, blood and brains spilling out.' He shook his head.

'Thank you, Goodman Huffkyn.' I took out my purse and gave him a groat. 'And now, if I may, I would speak to your master. Can I go in?'

'Of course. He is at work with Elias, on the first floor.'

☩

I WALKED THROUGH the shop and went upstairs. The rhythmic thumping was louder now. The whole first floor had been knocked into one room, a larger equivalent of poor Greening's. Again there were shelves of paper and chemicals, printed pages in piles, more hung up on ropes stretched across the room, like linen on drying day. Although the shutters were open, the chamber was hot and smelled of heavy leaden dust; I felt sweat on my brow.

Two men were working at the press. Both wore stained leather aprons. A tall, clean-shaven, grey-haired man in his fifties was smoothing out a fresh piece of paper on the bottom tray. Holding the handle of the great screw above the upper tray, where the inked letters were set, was a large, strongly muscled boy of about eighteen, with a dumpish, heavy countenance. They looked round as I entered.

'I am Master Shardlake,' I said quietly. 'I have been sent to investigate poor Master Greening's murder.'

The older man nodded. 'Geoffrey Okedene,' he said. 'I had a message to expect you. Let us go to the book-binding room. Elias, we will be down in a while.'

The boy looked at me directly for the first time. His brown eyes were afire with anger. 'It was a wicked, godless thing,' he said. 'Good Christian people are no longer safe in these days.'

'Keep your place, boy.' Okedene frowned at him, then led me up to the top floor, where a middle-aged woman sat at a table, carefully sewing pages into a binding of thick paper. Okedene said, 'Could you go down to the kitchen for a few minutes, my dear? I need a private word with this gentleman of the law. It concerns the contract for the new book. Perhaps you could take Elias a jug of ale.'

'I heard you chide Elias just now. That boy needs a whipping for his insolent tongue.'

'He is strong and works hard, that is what matters, sweetheart. And the loss of his old master hit him hard.'

Mrs Okedene rose, curtsying to me before stepping out. The printer closed the door behind her. 'My wife knows nothing of this matter,' he said quietly. 'You have come from Lord Parr? He said he would send someone.'

'Yes. You acted well that night, Master Okedene.'

He sat at the table, looking at his work-roughened hands. He had a pleasant, honest face, but it held lines of worry. 'I had a note from Whitehall that a lawyer would be coming. They asked me to burn it, which I did.' He took a deep breath. 'When I saw the words on that page poor Greening held – I am no sacramentarian, but I have ever been a supporter of reform. I had work from Lord Cromwell in his time. When I saw the title page of that book, I knew it was a personal confession of sinfulness and coming to faith, such as radicals make these days, and could be dangerous to her majesty, whom all reformers revere for her faith and goodness.'

'How did you gain access to Whitehall Palace?'

'There is a young apprentice printer living on the street who is known as a fiery young radical. As is often the case with such young men, he has contact with other radicals among the servants at court. I went to him, told him I had hold of something the Queen's councillors should know about. He told me of a servant I should approach at Whitehall, and thus I was led to Lord Parr himself.' He shook his head wonderingly.

'Is this boy friendly with Elias?'

'No. Elias tended to mix only with Master Greening and his circle.' Oakdene passed a hand across his brow. 'It is hard to find oneself suddenly inside Whitehall.'

I smiled sympathetically. 'It is.'

'It was – frightening.' He looked at me. 'But I must do what I can, for conscience's sake.'

'Yes. Lord Parr is grateful to you. He has asked me to take up the investigation into the murder, which the coroner has all but abandoned. I have told the constable and everyone else – including my own pupil, whom I have set to search the gardens behind Greening's shed – that I am acting on behalf of Greening's parents. I took the liberty of questioning Goodman Huffkyn, and I would like to speak to Elias as well. I understand he thwarted an earlier attempt to break in.'

'So he says, and Elias is truthful, if unruly.'

'You must not speak of that book to him or anybody else.'

He nodded emphatically. 'By our Lord, sir, I know how

much discretion this matter demands. Sometimes good Christians must speak with the wisdom of the serpent as well as the innocence of the dove, is it not so?'

'In this matter, certainly. Now, would you tell me in your own words what happened that night?'

Okedene repeated what Huffkyn had told me about hearing a noise and rushing outside. 'As I ran up to the shed, I heard Master Greening call out to someone to leave him alone. I think he was fighting them. I tried the door and found it locked so I put my shoulder to it. It gave way at once.'

'It was locked from inside?'

'Yes, Master Greening lived there, as you know, and would lock the door at night. I can only guess the people who attacked him knocked at the door, pushed their way in when he answered, then locked the door behind them.'

'Huffkyn gave me a description of them.'

'Yes, I only caught the merest glimpse.'

'He seems a clever old man.'

'Poor fellow, he has a bad chest, as many of us in the trade do. I am afraid I took the chance, when poor Greening died, to take on Elias and put John Huffkyn to lighter work.'

'Probably a good arrangement for everyone.'

'I hope so.'

'When you entered, apart from that glimpse of the attackers, what did you see?'

'My eyes were drawn at once to the fire. I had to put it out.' He looked at me seriously. 'With all the paper and printing materials in this street, fire is a constant worry. Fortunately the pile of paper had only just started to burn, and I was able to stamp it out. Then I saw poor Greening – ' he took a long breath – 'on the floor. I hope never to see such a thing again. And then I saw the torn sheet of paper in his hand – the best quality paper on the market. I read it, and knew this was more than a matter of murder. I heard Huffkyn coming and stuffed the page into my pocket.'

'Do you think they killed him before they heard you trying to enter?'

He shook his head. 'When I first put my shoulder to the door Greening was still shouting. But then the noise stopped, save for a horrible crash – I think one of them clubbed him then, and he went down.'

'And they grabbed the book from his hands,' I mused, 'but left behind part of the title page. Probably failed to notice it in their hurry to get out; they set the fire and ran.'

'I think that might be how it was.' Okedene shook his head sadly. 'I wonder whether, had I not broken in just then, they might not have panicked and killed him.'

'I think they would have killed him in any case, in order to wrest that book from him.' He nodded sadly. 'How well did you know Armistead Greening?' I asked.

'He came to Paternoster Row five years ago. He said he had come from the Chilterns – he spoke with the accent of those parts – and wanted to set up as a printer. He had been married, he told me, but his wife died in childbirth and the baby, too, so he came to London to seek his fortune. Poor young man, he often had a sad cast of face. He leased that piece of land his shed stands on from the Court of Augmentations – it belonged to a little monastic house whose remains stand on the land behind the shed.' He smiled sardonically. 'Ironic, given his religious views. He built the shed himself with a couple of friends. I remember thinking I was glad he had found some friends in London. I did not know him well, he kept to himself, but – I heard and saw things, especially recently.' He hesitated.

'Nothing you tell me about him can harm him now. Goodman Huffkyn dropped some hints.'

'It might harm Elias. If it reached the ears of Gardiner and his wolves.'

'I report to no one but Lord Parr and the Queen.'

His eyes widened. 'The Queen herself?'

'Yes. I knew her when she was Lady Latimer,' I added, a note of pride in my voice.

'I think Greening was very radical.' Okedene looked at me seriously. 'A known man.'

I drew a sharp breath. The code for the old Lollards and, now, the Anabaptists. Okedene continued, 'Can you guarantee that nothing I tell you about Elias will get him into trouble?' He spoke quietly, intently, reminding me again how dangerous it was to discuss radical religion.

I hesitated. I knew Lord Parr, at least, would be quite ruthless if he thought it necessary to protect the Queen. And any mention of Anabaptism would be to shake a stick in a wasps' nest. 'Anything that might harm the apprentice I will speak of only to the Queen,' I answered. 'Her mercy and loyalty are well known.'

Okedene stood. He looked from the window at Greening's shed. 'The walls of that rickety place are thin. Armistead Greening had friends and visitors with whom he would have loud religious discussions. This summer especially, with everyone's windows open in the hot weather, I would sometimes hear them talking – arguing, rather – sometimes a little too loudly for safety. Mostly it was just a hubbub of voices I heard, the occasional phrase, though the phrases were enough to set my ears pricking. They were an odd mixture of people. Six or seven sometimes, but there were three constant regulars – a Scotsman, a Dutchman and an Englishman, all known as local radicals.'

'McKendrick, Vandersteyn and Curdy.'

Okedene nodded. 'I think Master Curdy is quite a

wealthy man. Master Greening told me he sent one of his assistants to help build that shed. The Scotsman helped as well; I remember seeing him. A big, strong fellow.'

'So Greening knew them almost from the time he came to London? Were you acquainted with them?'

'Only to nod to in the street. They kept themselves to themselves. I only really knew Armistead Greening as a neighbour and fellow printer. Sometimes we would discuss the state of business; once or twice we lent each other paper if we had a job in, and our stocks were running low.'

'What did you hear Master Greening and his friends arguing over?' I asked. 'The sacrament?'

He hesitated again. 'That, and whether we are predestined to heaven or hell. It is just as well, Master Shardlake, that I am no Catholic and John Huffkyn takes care to mind his own business.'

'They were careless.'

'They seemed much agitated this summer.' He set his lips. 'One evening I heard them arguing over whether people should only be baptized when they were adults, and whether all baptized Christians had the right to equality, to take the goods of the rich and hold them in common.'

'So Armistead Greening might have been an Anabaptist?'

Okedene shook his head, began walking to and fro. 'From the way he and his friends argued I think they had differing views. You know how the radicals disagree among themselves as much as with their opponents.'

'I do.' The last decade had been a time of shifting faiths, men moving from Catholicism to Lutheranism to radicalism and back again. But it was obvious that Greening and his friends were at least exploring the radical fringes. I wondered where those other three men were now: McKendrick, Vandersteyn and Curdy. Had they gone to ground?

Okedene said, 'I often used to wonder how Armistead made ends meet. I know some of the books he printed did not sell well, and sometimes he seemed to have no work at all. At other times he was busy. I wondered if he was involved in the trade in illegal books and pamphlets. I know a few years ago a large pile of books was delivered to him.'

'Books already printed?'

'Yes. Brought in from the Continent, illegally perhaps, for distribution. I saw them in his shed, in boxes, when I visited him to ask if he wanted to buy some surplus type I had. One box was open and he closed it quickly.'

'I wonder what those books were.'

'Who knows; works by Luther, perhaps, or this Calvin, who they say is making a new stir in Europe; or John Bale.' He bit his lip. 'He asked me not to tell anyone about these books, and I swore I would not. But he is dead now, it cannot hurt him.'

I said quietly, 'Thank you for trusting me, Master Okedene.'

He looked at me seriously. 'If I had reported what I heard to the wrong people, Armistead Greening and his friends could have ended up burning with Anne Askew yesterday.' His mouth twisted with sudden revulsion. 'That was a wicked, disgusting thing.'

'It was. I was made to go and watch, to represent my Inn. It was a horrible, evil act.'

'It is hard for me, Master Shardlake. My sympathies are with the reformers. I am no sacramentarian, still less an Anabaptist, but I would not throw my neighbours into Gardiner's fires.'

'Was Elias part of this radical group?' I asked quietly.

'Yes, I think he was. I heard his voice from Master Greening's shed this summer, more than once.'

'I must question him, but I will be careful.'

'Loutish as he is, he was devoted to his master. He wants the killers caught.'

'And he has one important piece of information for us. I understand he interrupted an earlier attack on the shop a few days before.'

'Yes. He is the only one who saw it, but he certainly raised the alarm and brought other apprentices running.' He paused. 'One strange thing I will tell you, for I doubt Elias will. A few days before the first attack, Master Greening and his friends – Elias, too – were holding one of their evening meetings. They were having a particularly loud argument. His windows were open and so were mine, a passing watchman could have heard them from the street – though even the watchmen are reformers round here.'

I knew that in many of London's parishes the people were increasingly grouping together into reformist and traditionalist districts. 'Is everyone in this street of a reformist cast of mind? I know most printers are.'

'Yes. But the sort of talk I heard that evening would be dangerous in any district. I was angry with them, for if they found themselves arrested I would be questioned too, and I have a wife and three children to think about.' His voice trembled a little, and I realized how much the thoughtless talk of his neighbours, to say nothing of finding himself at Whitehall facing Lord Parr, had frightened him. 'I went outside, intending to knock at the door and tell them they should have regard for their safety and mine. But as I reached the door I heard the Dutchman – he has a distinctive accent – saying a man was coming to England who was an agent of the Antichrist himself, who could bring down and destroy the realm, turn true religion to ashes. They mentioned a name, a foreign name. I'm not sure I heard it aright.'

'What was it?'

'It sounded like "Jurony Bertano".'

'That sounds Spanish, or Italian.'

'That was all I heard. I banged on the door, called to them to speak more quietly and shut their windows, lest they find themselves in the Tower. They did not answer, but thank God they pulled the window shut and lowered their voices.' He gave me a searching look. 'I tell you this only because of the danger to the Queen.'

'I am truly grateful.'

'But there is one thing that has puzzled me all along,' Okedene said. 'Why would radicals have stolen Queen Catherine's book and put her in danger?'

'That is something I wonder about, too.'

'Certainly I never overheard any mention of the Queen's name. But as I say, apart from that particular night when I heard that name Jurony Bertano, it was mostly just the occasional phrase I heard.' He sighed. 'But nowhere is safe in these days.'

Footsteps sounded outside. Someone had come up the stairs, quietly, and we had not heard. Okedene and I looked at each other in alarm. The door opened. Nicholas came in, looking pleased with himself. 'Could you not knock?' I said angrily. 'Master Okedene, this is my pupil, Nicholas Overton. I apologize for his manners.'

Nicholas looked hurt. He bowed to Okedene, then turned quickly back to me. 'I am sorry, sir, but I found something in the garden.'

I wished he had not blurted that out in front of Okedene. It was best for his safety that he knew as little as possible. But Nicholas went on. 'I climbed over the wall. The garden on the other side is very overgrown, with high grass and brambles. There was only a family of beggars there, taking shelter in the ruins of what looks like an abandoned monastic building.'

Okedene said, 'It was, boy, a little Franciscan friary. After the Dissolution, many of the stones were taken for building, and no one has bought the site yet. There is still a glut of land in London.'

Nicholas rattled on. 'I looked to see if there was still a trail through the long grass. There has been no rain, and I am a good tracker. I learned well when hunting at home. And there was a trail of flattened grass, as though people had run through it. And on a bramble bush, I found this.' He pulled a piece of cloth from his pocket, fine white silk embroidered with tiny loops and whorls of blackwork. I saw it was from a shirt cuff such as only a gentleman could have afforded. It looked quite new. Nicholas said proudly, 'My guess is that when the killers ran away one caught his shirt on the bramble thorns.'

Okedene looked at the scrap of cuff. 'A fine piece of work, best silk by the look of it. But you have it wrong, boy, my assistant saw the assailants clearly and they wore rough wadmol smocks. Someone else must have passed through the garden and torn his shirt.'

I turned the fabric over in my hand. 'But who would go wandering about an abandoned garden full of brambles wearing such finery?'

Nicholas said, 'Perhaps men who were not poor at all, but put rough clothes over their shirts so that people in the street would not notice them.'

'By Mary, Nicholas,' I said, 'you could have the right of it.' And whoever stole the *Lamentation* had access to the highest reaches of the court. 'Nicholas, did you speak to this beggar family?'

'Yes, sir. A cottager and his wife from Norfolk. Their

piece of land was enclosed for sheep and they came to London. They are camping out in the one room that still has a roof. They were frightened of me; they thought someone had bought the land and sent a lawyer to throw them out.' He spoke of them scornfully; Okedene frowned disapprovingly. 'I asked if they had seen anything on the night of the murder. They said they were woken by the sound of men running through the garden. They saw two men with clubs, big young fellows; one was almost bald, they said. They escaped by climbing over the far wall.'

'So John Huffkyn saw aright.' Okedene looked at the piece of silk cuff. 'This worries me, sir. The killing could have been carried out by men of status.'

'Yes, it could. You have done well, Nicholas. Please, Master Okedene, keep this secret.'

He laughed bitterly. 'I can swear that, right readily.'

I put the scrap of lace in my pocket and took a deep breath. 'And now I must question young Elias.'

✝

THE APPRENTICE looked up from inking a tray of type. 'Master,' he said to Okedene as we entered, 'we will be falling behind –'

'We have a large order on hand,' Okedene explained. 'But Elias, these gentlemen are investigating Master Greening's killing, for his parents. We must help them.'

I put out a hand. 'I am Matthew Shardlake, of Lincoln's Inn.'

'Elias Rooke.' The boy's eyes narrowed. 'Master Greening told me his parents were poor folk. How can they can afford a lawyer?'

It was a brave question for a mere apprentice. 'Elias . . .' Okedene said warningly.

'I only want to find the truth of what happened, Elias, and bring Master Greening's killers to justice. I would like to ask you some questions.' The boy still looked at me suspiciously. I spoke encouragingly. 'I understand you were at home on the night of the murder.'

'With my mother and sisters. And a neighbour called in. I told them so at the inquest.'

'Yes. I understand you thwarted an earlier attack on Master Greening's premises.'

'I told them about that, too. I came to work early one morning – there was much to do – and two men were standing outside the shed, trying to pick the lock. They were very quiet, I think they knew Master Greening was within.'

'Not the same two who attacked him later?'

'No. Old Huffkyn described the men who killed my poor master as big and tall. These two were quite different. One was short and fat. The other was slim, with fair hair, and had half an ear missing. Looked like a slash from a sword, not the great hole you get from having your ear nailed to the pillory.'

'Were they carrying weapons?'

'They had daggers at their waists, but so do most men.'

'What were they wearing?'

'Old wadmol smocks.'

'Cheap garments, then?'

'Ay.' Elias relaxed a little, realizing I was just going over old ground. 'But those are all most folk can afford these days, with the rich land-grabbers and idle rout of nobles taking everything.'

Nicholas said, 'Do not be insolent to my master, churl.'

I raised a hand. I could put up with boyish insolence if it would get me information. And it seemed this boy held radical social views. 'When was this first attack?' I asked. 'I was told it was some days before the murder.'

'Just over a week. Monday, the fifth.'

I frowned, realizing that was the day before the *Lamentation* was stolen from the Queen. That made no sense. 'Are you sure of the date?'

Elias looked back at me directly. ''Tis my mother's birthday.'

'What did you do when you saw the men?'

'What any good apprentice would do. Shouted "Clubs!" to let the other lads in the street know there was trouble. A few came out, though they weren't quick – it was early, they were probably hardly awake. They will confirm the date if you doubt me. The two men were already gone, they went over the garden wall behind Master Greening's shed, the same way as the other two. Some fellows went in pursuit, but they lost them.' So these men, too, had probably surveyed Greening's place before attacking it, to find the best escape route. 'I stayed to knock up my master.'

'How did Master Greening react when you told him?'

'He was alarmed, what do you think?' Elias replied curtly. Nicholas gave him a warning look, but he ignored it.

'Did your master have any idea who the men could have been?'

'Casual thieves, he thought. But they must be connected to the men who came later, and killed him. Mustn't they?'

I caught a slight tremor in his voice; under his bravado Elias was seriously afraid. I thought, if Greening had his premises attacked a week before his murder, why did he let the two killers in when they knocked? Had he perhaps been reassured by a request to enter from two men with cultivated accents; one with a silk shirt under his jerkin? I looked at Elias again. I thought, did he know about the book? If he did, he was in danger. Yet he had not gone to ground, as it seemed Greening's three friends had, and he had taken a job at the works next door. I asked, 'What do you know of your master's friends? I have the names McKendrick, Vandersteyn and Curdy.'

'I have met them.' The apprentice's eyes narrowed. 'Good, honest men.'

'They were all able to give account of their movements on that night,' I said with a reassuring smile. 'Though they have not been seen for some days.'

'I haven't seen them since the murder.'

'McKendrick is a Scotch name,' Nicholas said bluntly. 'Until just recently we were at war with them.'

Elias glared at him. 'The papists threw Master McKendrick out of Scotland for calling the soul of the Pope a stinking menstruous rag. As it is.'

Okedene snapped, 'Elias, I will not have such language in my shop!'

I raised a pacifying hand. 'Was there any woman Master Greening was close to? Your master was still a young man.'

'No. Since his poor wife died he devoted himself to his work and the service of God.'

I was considering how to broach the question of Elias's involvement in the religious discussions between his master and his friends, when Nicholas asked him suddenly, 'What about this Jurony Bertano that I heard my master mention as I came upstairs? Did your master know him?'

An expression of utter fear came over Elias's face, his ill-mannered surliness vanishing. He took a step back.

'How do you know that name?' he asked. He looked at Okedene. 'Master, these men are agents of Bishop Gardiner!' Before Okedene could reply, Elias shouted at me, his face red with fear and anger, 'You crawling crouchback papist!' And with that he punched me hard in the face, making me stagger. He threw himself on me, and with his size could have done me damage had not Nicholas put an arm around his throat and dragged him off. The boy twisted, grasped Nicholas, and the two fell grappling to the floor. Nicholas reached for his sword, but Elias threw him off and ran through the open door of the print-shop, his footsteps crashing down the stairs. I heard Okedene's wife call out, 'Elias!' The front door slammed.

Nicholas was on his feet in a second, running downstairs after him. Okedene and I looked from the window to see my pupil standing in the crowded street, looking up and down, but Elias had already disappeared. The boy would know these streets and alleys like the back of his hand.

Okedene stared at me in amazed horror. 'Why did that name cause him such terror? I never saw Elias react like that before.'

'I don't know,' I said quietly as I wiped blood from my cheek.

Nicholas came back upstairs. 'He's gone,' he said. 'Are you hurt, master?'

'No.'

Okedene's face darkened with anger. 'Elias was terrified. I doubt he will return.' He glared at Nicholas. 'Now I will have to find a new apprentice in the middle of a print run. All because you blurted out that name. Master Shardlake, I have done enough. I wish to have no more to do with this matter. I have a business, and am responsible for my wife and children.'

'Master Okedene, I am sorry.'

'So am I. Sorry, and sore afraid.' He looked out of the window again, breathing hard. 'And now, please go. And I beg you, involve me no more in this.'

'I will try to ensure you are not troubled again. But if Elias returns, can you send word to me at Lincoln's Inn?'

Okedene did not look round, but nodded wearily.

'Thank you,' I said again. 'I am sorry.' I turned to Nicholas. 'Come, you,' I snapped.

✝

I BEGAN WALKING fast down Paternoster Row. My cheek stung where Elias had struck it. I would have a nice bruise soon. 'We should go to the constable,' Nicholas said. 'For an apprentice to run away from his master is an offence.'

'We don't know that he's run away yet,' I answered. I was not going to involve the authorities in this without first consulting Lord Parr. I stopped and turned to Nicholas, 'What did you think you were doing, mentioning that name?'

'I heard you and Master Okedene discussing it as I came to the door. It seemed important. I thought it might be a good thing to scare that insolent boy into answering.'

'Could not you see that beneath his surliness was fear?'

'I saw only that he spoke to you as a lumpish apprentice should not to one of your rank.'

'Yes, Nicholas, you are full of your rank and class, and Elias annoyed you, so you thought to put him in his place. I was trying to soothe him, in order to gain his confidence. Do you not know the saying, never prick the stirring horse more than he needs? You have just lost us our most important witness.'

He looked crestfallen. 'You said I could ask questions.'

'Only after careful consideration. You didn't consider, you just reacted. The worst thing a lawyer can do.' I jabbed a finger on his doublet. 'Do not ever play the lusty-gallant gentleman again in my service.'

'I am sorry,' he said stiffly.

'So am I. So is poor Master Okedene.'

'It seems this murder touches the most delicate matters of religion,' he said quietly.

'All the more reason to be delicate ourselves,' I snapped back. 'Now, return to Lincoln's Inn and ask Barak what needs doing there. And do not say one word about where we have been. I think even you will realize the importance of confidentiality here. And now I will leave you. I have business elsewhere.'

I turned my back on him and walked away, down to the river, to get a boat to Whitehall.

Chapter Ten

WHEN I REACHED the Thames Street stairs there were plenty of boatmen waiting along the riverside, calling, 'Eastward Ho!' or 'Westward Ho!' to indicate whether they were going up- or downriver. I called to a man who was going upriver, and he pulled into the steps.

We rowed past Whitehall Palace; I had asked the boatman to take me to Westminster Stairs, just beyond. At the Whitehall Common Stairs servants were unloading great armfuls of firewood from a boat, presumably destined for the palace kitchens. I thought again of yesterday's burning, and shuddered. The boatman gave me an odd look. I lowered my eyes, watching him pull the oars in and out. He was a young man but his hands were already hard and knotted; I knew that older boatmen often got painful arthritis, the joints in their hands frozen into grasping claws. And all to take rich folk like me where they wanted to go.

We passed the King's Stairs: a wide covered gallery painted in green and white, jutting out fifty feet into the water, and ending in a broad, covered landing stage where the King's barge would pull up. Beyond, the long line of the palace facade was beautiful, the red brickwork mellow in the late afternoon sun, interspersed with projecting, richly glazed bastions, with tall glass windows, and at the south end the Lady Mary's new lodgings, covered in scaffolding. I paid the boatman and walked back up the Whitehall Road, beside the west wall of the palace, to the Gatehouse. I was hot in my robe, dusty, tired and troubled.

This time there was no one to meet me, but my name was on the list and the guard at the gate allowed me in. I walked underneath the Gatehouse, across the courtyard, then up the stairs and into the King's Guard Chamber; my name checked at every door.

I went up to the King's Presence Chamber. A brown-robed servant carrying a silver ewer of water hurried past as I entered, almost colliding with me. I looked around. It was strange; already the effect of all the fantastic magnificence had worn off a little, though I was conscious of the Gentlemen Pensioners around the wall; their dress magnificently decorative. But they were big men, and carrying heavy pole-axes. Here I saw fewer young men come to fish for a name of fame standing around. My eye was drawn again to the picture of the royal family, the square solid frame of the King a total contrast to the grotesque, sad figure I had seen earlier that day.

Two of the would-be courtiers sat gambling with silver dice. One suddenly stood and shouted, 'You cheat! That is the third time you have thrown a five!'

The other stood up, moving his short Spanish cloak aside to free his arm. 'Dirt in your teeth! You insult me –'

Two of the Gentlemen Pensioners instantly moved forward, each grasping one of the popinjays by an arm. 'You forget where you are, churls!' one of them shouted. 'Do you dare think you can make a bray in this place, as though it were a common tavern? Get out! The King's Chamberlain will hear of this!' The two gamblers were marched to the door, now watched by everyone in the room.

I drew in my breath sharply at the sight of two men in black robes and gold chains, who had entered from the stairs and stood staring at the brawlers. I had seen both of them at the burning. One was Chief Secretary William Paget, his square face frowning above the bushy brown beard that framed his odd, downturned slash of a mouth. The other, his spare frame contrasting with Paget's solid build, and with a sardonic smile on his thin face, was Sir Richard Rich. They had not seen me; I moved quickly to the door leading to the Queen's Presence Chamber and whispered my name to the guard. He opened the door and I slipped through. On the other side another guard in the Queen's livery looked at me interrogatively. 'Serjeant Shardlake,' I said breathlessly. 'Here to see Lord Parr.'

The Queen's uncle was already waiting for me in the chamber; someone below must have told him I had arrived. Among all the magnificent decoration, and the sumptuous clothes of a pair of courtiers, Lord Parr made a sober figure in his black robe, the only colour the Queen's badge on his chest and the heavy gold chain around his neck. I bowed low. He said, 'Come to my private office, Master Shardlake.'

I followed him through another door. He led me on down a corridor, our footsteps making no sound on the thick rush matting that covered the floors from wall to wall. Through an open door I glimpsed the Queen's Presence Chamber, and caught sight of the Queen herself sitting sewing at a window, dressed in red, with some of the ladies who had also been present earlier. Gardiner, the Duchess of Suffolk's spaniel, sat on the floor, playing with a bone.

'We are passing on to the Queen's privy lodgings,' Lord Parr said. 'My office is there. The Queen likes me close to her since I was recalled from the country in the spring.' He opened the door to a small, dark office, with a window giving onto another courtyard, the papers on chests and the little desk in neatly ordered piles. 'Here,' he said, taking a lawyer's robe in fine silk from a chair and handing it to me. 'Change into this.' The Queen's brightly coloured badge of St Catherine, I saw, was sewn onto the breast. Before taking his place behind the desk he went over and closed the window. Then he bade me sit.

'I prefer it open these summer days,' he said ruefully. 'But in this place one never knows who may be listening from the next window.' Lord Parr sighed. 'As you have probably realized, the court is a place full of fear and hate; there is no real amity anywhere. Even among families; the Seymours quarrel and scratch like cats. Only the Parr family is united; we are loyal to each other.' He spoke with pride. 'It is our strength.'

'You have been here only since the spring, my Lord?' I ventured.

'Yes. For much of the last few years I have delegated my duties and stayed on my estates. I am old now, not always well. No longer the man I was, when I served the King.' He smiled in reminiscence. 'As did my brother, the Queen's father; and the Queen's mother was lady-in-waiting to Catherine of Aragon. The Parrs have been a part of the court for a long time. The Queen's mother died just before the full storm of the King's Great Divorce broke. Well, she was spared that.' He looked up, eyes sharp again under the white brows. 'I have stood *in loco parentis* for my niece since then. I will do anything to protect her. When she asked me to come back to court, I did so at once.'

'I understand.'

'I should swear you in.' He took a Testament from a drawer, and I solemnly swore to serve the Queen loyally and honestly. Lord Parr nodded brusquely, returned the Testament to the drawer, and said, 'Well, what news?'

I took a deep breath. 'Not good, my Lord.' I told him that the first of the attacks on Greening had taken place before the *Lamentation* was stolen, that the authorities had given up on the case, that Greening's friends seemed to have gone to ground and might even be Anabaptists. Finally I explained how Elias had fled. I had promised to tell only the Queen of anything that might endanger the boy, but Lord Parr had to know of his plight. None of it made good hearing, and I had to mention Nicholas's careless use of the name Bertano, which had caused such distress to Elias, though I praised his discovery of the scrap of silk. I had brought it with me, and now laid it on the table. Lord Parr examined it.

'A fine piece of work, expensive,' he said. 'The black-work decoration is distinctive.' He turned it over. 'The Queen's embroiderer, Hal Gullym, has worked all his life at the Queen's Wardrobe in Baynard's Castle; he knows all the fine shirt-makers in London. He might be able to find out who made this.'

'From a mere piece of sleeve?'

'Of this quality, possibly.' He frowned. 'The apprentice was certain that the first attack on Greening happened before the *Lamentation* vanished?'

'Certain. I am sorry he ran away. When that name Bertano was mentioned he became terrified.'

'I have never heard it before. And Okedene, he overheard them talking of this Bertano as one who would bring down the country, an agent of the Antichrist?'

'He is quite sure. And I believe Okedene is an honest man.' I added hesitantly, 'He asks that we leave him alone now; he fears for his family.'

'As I fear for mine,' Lord Parr answered bluntly. 'And yet – eleven days now since the book was stolen and not a word, nothing. Who could have taken it?'

'Not a religious radical, surely.'

'And yet if it was a papist, surely the book would be public knowledge by now, and God knows what would have happened to my niece. The King has a hard view of anything that smacks of disloyalty.' He bit his lip.

'We should find that apprentice,' I said.

He looked at me sternly. 'You should not have lost him.'

'I know, my Lord.'

'And those three associates of Greening's. Gone to ground?'

'It looks like it. Though they may just be keeping quiet for a while. The constable knows where they live. He has been keeping an eye on them this year, as suspected sacramentarians.'

Lord Parr frowned angrily, spots of colour forming on his pale cheeks. 'God's death, these extreme radicals with their mad ideas. They are a danger to those of us who know that reform must be sought through quieter means. They have no idea of the reality of politics. This Bertano, he may not even exist, may be some phantasm of their fevered minds!' He took a long breath, calming himself, then said, 'You must seek out these three friends of Greening's, talk to them, find what they know. Likely that apprentice has taken refuge with them.' He frowned again. 'And if you take your pupil this time, make sure he knows when to keep his mouth shut.'

'Rest assured, my Lord, I will.'

I thought, this meant even more work, and among people who could be dangerous to those they thought their enemies. I thought also of the work in chambers that I could not leave to my staff – the inspection of the wall painting in the Slanning case was coming up – and I had a moment's panic, felt the chair shifting under me. I grasped the arms hard.

'What is the matter?' Lord Parr asked sharply.

'I am sorry, my Lord, I – it has been a long day, and I was

at the burning yesterday. Sometimes when I am tired I feel strange, the world seems to rock – '

I expected him to snap at me for being a mumping weakling, but to my surprise he spoke quietly. 'The Queen told me you were on the *Mary Rose* when she went down last year. That was a great tragedy. Though it is not permitted to speak of it at court, the King felt much humiliated by the foundering of his favourite ship.'

'I lost good friends, and nearly died myself. At times of strain – forgive me, my Lord.'

He grunted. 'I, too, am sometimes unwell. I have long suffered from fevers, and they grow more frequent. Sometimes I am so tired – ' He shrugged, then gave a tight smile. 'But we must go on. You know the Queen's motto?'

'To be useful in all I do.'

'And so must we be. I know this is a hard load, Serjeant Shardlake.'

'Thank you, my Lord, but is it really the best course for me to try to find and question these men? The radicals are suspicious of everybody. They will surely see me, as the apprentice did, as an inquisitive lawyer who may serve some master who would hurt them.'

Lord Parr smiled wryly. 'Yes, people are suspicious of your trade, they think all lawyers will serve any master for a fee.'

'Perhaps if someone else could approach these men initially, someone known as a sympathizer, who could reassure them that the lawyer who will be coming is not an enemy. No more than that need be said.'

The old man nodded. 'You are right. You met young William Cecil last night?'

'Yes.'

'He is known to have certain – contacts, shall we say. He

is a very junior employee of the Queen's Learned Council, but I have already marked his cleverness, and his commitment to reform. As well as his ambition for himself, which is considerable.' He gave his sardonic smile again. 'Very well, I will send him to try and find these people, and reassure them that you merely wish to question them about the murder of Greening, but that you mean them no harm. That is all Master Cecil needs to be told. He does not know about the *Lamentation*, of course.'

'That may help our quest.'

Lord Parr stroked his beard. 'You say Greening was only printing some French primer when he was killed?'

'Yes. I checked the print-shop thoroughly.'

'The Queen, you may imagine, has no connection with such small-scale printers. Her *Prayers and Meditations* went to the King's Printer, John Berthelet.' He shook his head, then grasped the arms of his chair resolutely. 'And now,' he said, 'I would like you to question some servants of the household.'

'Yes, my Lord.'

'But first, look at this.'

He reached into his robe, and held up a little key on a gold chain. 'I have persuaded my niece to entrust this to me. It is the one she kept around her neck, that opens her private chest.'

I examined it, and saw it had several teeth of different sizes. 'It does not look like a key that would be easy to copy.'

'No. The chest itself I have removed to a place of safety, where it can be inspected.' Lord Parr replaced the key in the folds of his robe. 'Now, are you ready to question these servants?' He gave me a hard look.

'Yes, my Lord. Forgive me, I had but a weak moment.'

'Good.' He consulted a paper on his desk. 'I have

checked the records and discovered who was on duty that evening. The Queen was in her chamber all that afternoon; she went to her bedchamber after lunch, looked at the book and thought again about disposing of it, then spent some time studying Spanish – she is working to increase her knowledge of languages, that she may be of most use in diplomatic functions.'

'She is often on her own during the afternoons?'

'No. But when an afternoon is free she does like to take the chance to be alone for a little – it is not always easy in this place,' he added feelingly. 'Then at six she was called to the King, as you know, and returned at ten of the evening. It was during those four hours that the *Lamentation* was stolen. According to the guards, the only people who came into the Queen's privy lodgings during that time were the two page boys whose duties are to clean the rooms and the Queen's Gallery, and feed Rig, the Queen's spaniel, and her birds. Also you will interview two women who have more or less free access – Mary Odell, a maid-in-waiting who has served the Queen for years, who makes sure her bed is ready and often sleeps with her in her chamber; and Jane, the fool she shares with the Lady Mary. Jane is much wanting in wit. Apparently she came into the Privy Chamber that evening, where some of the Queen's ladies were sitting, demanding to see my niece, saying she had something that would entertain her. She did not believe the ladies when they told her the Queen was with the King, and Jane can make a great fuss if she does not get her way – the Queen and the Lady Mary both overindulge her – so the guard let her into the Queen's privy lodgings to see for herself. She came out after a few minutes. And that is all.'

'How many rooms make up the Queen's privy lodgings?'

'Six. The bathroom, bedchamber, the closet for prayer, a

study, and dining room. And beyond those the Queen's Privy Gallery, where she often walks. I have searched every inch of each chamber myself, by the way, in case the book was somehow secreted there. And found nothing.'

'Are two pages needed to clean each day?'

Lord Parr laughed scoffingly. 'Of course not. But this is the royal household, and a multitude of servants is a sign of the Queen's great status. There is another pair who come to clean in the morning. Only the King has more.'

'And the staff on duty vary?'

'Yes. There is a rota. I see what you are thinking. Another servant could somehow have discovered the book's existence earlier? But they could not have arranged in advance for the book to be taken on that day, as nobody knew the King would call the Queen to him that evening.'

'But he must do so fairly often?'

'Not every evening. And in recent days he has often had meetings in the evening with the councillors and ambassadors.'

'So, it seems the book must have been taken by one of these four servants, unless someone had secreted themselves in the Queen's Gallery.'

'Impossible. Nobody could. The guards at the doors to the Privy Chamber entrances check everyone who goes in and out. They are an absolute bar.'

I thought a moment. 'What about the guards themselves? Can they be trusted?'

'All selected by the Queen. On a rota, again, but if any guard left his post by one of the doors, it would be noticed instantly. Not least by would-be courtiers, who are ever eager to gain closer access to places they shouldn't. No, the only people who had entry when the Queen was absent were the two page boys, Mary Odell, and Jane Fool.'

'Four people only.'

'I have had both boys called in, and the two women. Using the pretext of the stolen ring, I want you to check the movements of each of them on that day. Present the jewel's loss as a matter of great sorrow to the Queen. She has given authority for you to see Mary Odell alone, but you will have to question Jane in her presence; Jane is so foolish she would be afraid if you were to question her alone, perhaps even defiant.' He frowned; he obviously thought her an unmitigated nuisance.

'Very well, my Lord.'

'Mary Odell is one of four chamberers. It is a junior post, but Mary is especially close to the Queen. She is her cousin once removed. There are many distant Parr relatives in the Queen's household now, just as once there were Boleyns and Seymours. As well as being her dependants, they all owe their posts to the Queen, so their loyalty can be counted on. But Mary Odell, particularly, is the Queen's close friend as well as her servant. Handle her gently. As for Jane Fool – ' he inclined his head – 'there are two types of fool: those skilled at gentle clowning, like the King's man, Will Somers, and natural fools like Jane. She has great licence. But she has a sharp wit as well.' Lord Parr looked at me closely. 'One never knows if fools are always so foolish as they seem,' he concluded darkly.

'And Jane serves as fool to the Lady Mary as well. So she has joint loyalties,' I ventured.

'I have considered that. It is ten years since the Lady Mary ended her defiance and agreed to the Royal Supremacy. She is conservative in religion, but has followed the King's wishes all this time. The Queen has tried to bring all three royal children together, but although Mary is fond of little Edward, she does not like the Lady Elizabeth.' He shrugged. 'Understandable, as Elizabeth's mother displaced hers. The

Queen has done everything to befriend Mary. They are of an age, and often together.'

'But Mary is no reformer.'

'She has avoided all taint of plotting. She is safe. And now I will leave you.' Lord Parr stood. 'The pages will be sent in. It will attract less notice, as I told you, if the questioning is conducted by one of the Queen's Learned Council rather than myself. I will return later. The missing ring is plain gold with a large square ruby in the centre, and the initials of the Queen's late stepdaughter, MN, for Margaret Neville, on the inside of the band.' He stepped to the door. 'Watch the page Adrian Russell, he can be an insolent pup. Later I will show you the chest. By the way, I heard today the King is moving to Hampton Court next month. The rat-catchers have already been sent in. Everything and everybody in the Royal Apartments will be moved there by barge. So it is important that you see everything here as it was at the time of the theft, while you still can.'

✝

A GUARD SHOWED in the first page, a skinny fair-haired lad of about sixteen, with a haughty manner. He wore the Queen's red livery, her badge on his chest, and a black cap which he removed. I looked at him sternly, as though he were a hostile witness in court.

'You are Adrian Russell?'

'Yes, sir, of Kendal. My father is a distant relation of the Queen, and owns much property in Cumberland.' He spoke proudly.

'I am Serjeant Shardlake, of the Queen's Learned Council, set to investigate the matter of the ruby ring stolen from the coffer in the Queen's bedchamber. You have heard of the theft?'

'Yes, sir.'

'It was stolen while the Queen was with his majesty on the sixth of July, between six and ten in the evening. You were one of those on duty that night?'

Russell looked at me boldly. 'Yes, sir. Garet Lynley and I came in at six, to bring fresh candles, clean the rooms, and scent them with new herbs. I left at eight. Garet stayed. To attend to the bedchamber,' he added.

'Did you enter the Queen's bedchamber at all?' I asked sharply.

'No sir, only Garet Lynley. Only one page is allowed in there each evening, and it was not my turn that day.'

'Two pages carry out this work every day for two hours?'

'That is our assignment on the rota. We have to attend to the Queen's gallery, too, feed the birds there. And her dog.'

I did not like this lad's arrogant tone. I spoke coldly. 'Mayhap it does not always take two hours? Perhaps you sometimes sit down, rest?'

'All servants do, sir.'

'And boys are prone to meddle. A page stole something from the Queen before, you may remember. And he was sentenced to hang until the Queen pardoned him.'

Russell's eyes widened. He began to bluster. 'Sir, I would do nothing like that, I would steal nothing, I swear. I am of good family—'

'So you say. Did you see anyone else while you were there? Or anything unusual at all?'

'No, sir.'

'Think. Think hard. Perhaps the thief left something out of place, moved something?'

'No, sir. I swear, I would tell you if I had noticed any-thing out of place.' Young Russell was kneading his hands together with anxiety now, his childish arrogance gone. I could not see this callow lad being involved in the book's theft. In gentler tones, I got him to go over his exact movements, then told him he could go. He scurried from the room with relief.

The second page, Garet Lynley, was afraid from the outset; I could see that at once. He was the same age as Russell, tall and thin, his neatly combed brown hair worn long. I bade him sit and asked him about his duties in the Queen's bedchamber.

'I go in there, put new candles in the holders, lay out fresh linen on the coffer, then change the flowers and place fresh herbs and petals about the room. I feed the Queen's dog, Rig, if he is there, but he was not that night. I do not touch her majesty's bed or clothes, of course, that is for her chamberers. Mary Odell, I think it was, that day.'

I nodded. 'You put the linen on the chest. You know valuables are kept within?'

'I swear, sir, I did not touch it. I never do. I believe it is locked.'

'Have you ever tried the lock to find out?'

'Never,' he answered. 'I am loyal to her majesty – ' His voice rose in fear.

I made my tone friendlier. 'Did you notice anything unusual in the room that evening? About the chest, perhaps?'

'No, sir. It was dusk by then. I carried a lamp.' He frowned. 'But if anything had been amiss with the chest I think I would have seen. I placed the linen there every night that week.'

'Have you ever seen the stolen ring?'

'No. I am told the Queen wears it on her finger sometimes, but I always have to bow low each time she passes, so I have never seen it.'

'Very well.' I believed him, but Garet Lynley, I was sure,

was frightened of something more than just my interrogation. 'Where are you from, boy?' I asked lightly. 'You have a
northern cast of tongue.'

The question seemed to disturb him greatly; his eyes swivelled as he answered me. 'Lancashire, sir. My mother was
once a maid-in-waiting in Catherine of Aragon's household. It was through her that my family were granted their
lands. She knew the present Queen's mother, old Lady Parr.'

'And that was how you got this post? Through your family's connection with the Queen's mother?'

'Yes, sir. She wrote to Lord Parr as to whether there
might be a place for me.' His breath was coming noticeably
fast now.

'Are both your parents still alive?'

'Not my father, sir.' The boy hesitated. 'He was imprisoned in the Tower after the Northern Rebellion ten years
ago, and died there.'

I considered carefully. A boy whose mother had served
Catherine of Aragon and whose father had taken part in the
Northern Rebellion. 'Your family history, then, might make
people wonder about your religious sympathies,' I said
slowly.

Garet's collapse was sudden, and total. Almost falling off
his chair, he knelt on the floor, wringing his hands. 'It is not
true! I swear I am no papist, I loyally follow the King's dis-
pensations. I keep telling people, if only they would leave me
alone – '

'Get up,' I said gently. I felt sorry to have unmanned him
so. 'Take your chair again. Now, listen, I am not here to
harm you. What people?'

He shook his head desperately. Tears were coursing down
his cheeks now.

'Come, Garet. If you have done nothing wrong you will

suffer no harm. If you have – and if you confess – the Queen will be merciful.'

The boy took a long, shuddering breath.

'I have done nothing, sir. But it is as you say, because of my family's past, people think I might be one who would spy against the reformers. Though Lord Parr and the Queen know my family wish only to live quietly and serve loyally. But since coming to the palace – ' He hesitated.

'Yes?'

'A man has approached me, twice, and asked if I would observe what I could about the Queen and report to those who would serve what he called true religion. I refused, I swear – ' He stared at me miserably, his face puffy with tears, and I realized suddenly what it must be like for an innocent boy to step into this gilded sewer-pit.

'Did you report this to your superiors? Lord Parr?'

'No, sir, I didn't dare. The man, he – frightened me.'

'When did this happen?'

'When I first came, last autumn. Then again in April, when the hunt for heretics began.'

'The same man approached you both times?'

'Yes. I did not know him. I told one of the other pages and he said it sometimes happens when you first come to court, an approach from one side or the other, and if you would keep your skin whole you should always say no. The approach is always by someone unknown at court, a servant of one of the great men, but from outside the palace.'

'What was his name?'

'He would not tell it. He approached me the first time in the street. The second occasion he was waiting for me outside an inn I frequent. There was something in his face that frightened me.' The boy looked down, ashamed of his weakness.

'Can you describe him?'

The boy looked up at me again. He realized it was all or nothing now. 'He was in his twenties, thin but wiry and strong. He wore cheap clothes but spoke like a gentleman. I remember he had half of one ear missing, like it had been cut off in a fight.' Garet shuddered.

Half an ear gone, like one of the men Elias had disturbed trying to break into the print-shop that first time. I tried not to let my excitement show. Garet continued, 'Both times he said that if I agreed to spy on the Queen I would earn the gratitude of a very great personage of the realm, who would reward me and advance my career at court.'

'Surely an enticing prospect,' I observed.

'No.' Garet shook his head fiercely. 'Now I only want to leave here as soon as possible.'

'You did the right thing in telling me,' I said soothingly. 'You have nothing to fear. Now, after you turned this man down for the second time, did you see him again?'

'Never. It is like that, I'm told, if they cannot turn you they give up. I wish I could go home to my family, sir,' he added in a small voice. 'Without disgrace.'

'I think that may be arranged.'

Garet wiped a satin sleeve across his face. I could not but sympathize with his weakness. If I had found myself in the same danger at his age my reaction would probably have been the same. I let him leave, and sat alone in Lord Parr's office. At last, I thought, a clue.

Chapter Eleven

MARY ODELL was a tall, plump woman in her early thirties, dressed in black silk livery, the Queen's badge fixed to the cap atop her fair hair. She had soft features, and something of a motherly air, although she wore no wedding ring. Her green eyes were keen and alert. I stood and bowed, inviting her to sit. She did so, folding her hands in her lap, looking at me with curiosity and, I thought, a touch of speculative amusement.

'I am Serjeant Matthew Shardlake.'

'I know, sir. The Queen has spoken of you. She believes you an honest and most clever man.'

I felt myself blush. 'I apologize for troubling you, Mistress Odell, but I must speak with everyone who was in the Queen's privy lodgings the night her ring was stolen.'

'Certainly. Her majesty asked me to do all I could to help you.'

'Lord Parr says you have been chamberer and friend to the Queen for some time.'

'We are related. I knew her majesty before she was Queen.' Mary Odell smiled slightly, with that hint of secret amusement the Queen herself had so often shown in happier days. 'Poor relations do well when a person reaches such exalted status.' She paused, and then continued, her voice serious now. 'But my loyalty to her majesty goes far deeper than gratitude for my post. She has favoured me with her trust and good friendship, and I tell you frankly I would die for her.' Mistress Odell took a deep breath. 'She has told me much of what has happened these last months. Her — troubles.'

'I see.' But not about the *Lamentation*. That would be too dangerous.

Mistress Odell looked at me quizzically. 'The Queen seems extraordinarily upset over the loss of her ring. She loved the good Margaret Neville, but even so seems somehow stricken very hard by the theft.' I could see this intelligent woman had guessed that more was involved here than a stolen jewel. But of course I could not comment.

'I understand you were on duty as chamberer that night. And that you — pray, excuse me — share the Queen's bed on occasion.'

'I do sometimes. For company, when my mistress is feeling lonely, or troubled.'

'Could you tell me everything that happened when you came to prepare the Queen's bedchamber the night the ring was stolen? Anything even slightly unusual that you saw or heard might help.'

She nodded, seeming to approve that I was getting down to business. 'I have two rooms in the lodgings by the gatehouse. That evening I left them perhaps ten minutes early, a little before nine; I was tired and wanted to get my duty done and out of the way. I crossed the courtyard to the Royal Apartments. The routine is that the pages clean the rooms, and then I go in to prepare the bed, make sure all is in order in the bedchamber, and lay out the Queen's nightgown and hairbrushes.'

'One of the pages always cleans the bedchamber first?'

'Yes.'

'Are the pages obedient? Boys are prone to mischief.'

'Once or twice I have caught them playing cards in the Queen's Gallery and reported them to the gentleman usher, but they would not dare to make any real trouble in the Queen's quarters. The boys on duty that evening had done a good enough job. One of the guards told me her majesty was with the King that evening. Sometimes when she returns she likes to talk with me, so as I went back to my lodgings I told the guard I would be there if she wanted me. I have to say, Serjeant Shardlake, it seemed a very ordinary evening. Nothing unusual, nothing out of place. Only – ' She wrinkled her nose. 'There was a slightly unpleasant smell in the bedchamber. So slight you could barely catch it.'

'What sort of smell?'

'Begging your pardon, of ordure. I thought perhaps it had come from the river, and closed the window. I looked round the room closely with my lamp as well, but could see nothing amiss. As I said, the smell was very faint.'

'And did you notice anything about the Queen's private chest? Where the ring was kept?'

'The page had laid the linen on top of it as usual. There was nothing untoward.' She paused. 'I wish I could help you more with this, sir, given the Queen's distress.' She spoke now with feeling. 'But there was nothing.'

'You will have seen inside the chest?'

'A few times. The Queen has sometimes taken out her jewels, or a half-finished letter in front of me; she always kept the key round her neck.' Her voice grew sad. 'But not these last few months. Recently her majesty has seemed reluctant to let me see inside it.'

I had to deflect her from this path, even if it meant lying. 'Sometimes when a person has been under strain for a while, as I know the Queen has, some final event, such as the loss of a ring from a loved one, can unbalance their humours.'

She nodded. 'True.' But she looked at me keenly.

'You are quite sure, then, there was nothing unusual that night.'

She thought hard, then something seemed to occur to her. 'Apart from the smell, which soon vanished, there was only one thing, something so small I hesitate to mention it.'

'What?' I leaned forward over Lord Parr's desk. 'Anything might help.'

'I told you I came over from my lodgings. You will have discovered how many guarded doors one must pass through in this place – at the entrance to the King's Guard Chamber, the Presence Chambers, the Privy Chamber, the privy lodgings . . . When I am on duty I am always on the list of people to be admitted. Sometimes a guard new to his duties will ask who I am, check that I am on the list and make a prick against my name with his pin. I do not complain, it is their duty. But in the Queen's apartments nearly all the guards know me; they just mark my name as I pass. That night the guard on the door to the privy lodgings was a man who has often been on duty there, named Zachary Gawger. To my surprise he stopped me and made a fuss about being unable to find my name on his list. I told him not to be foolish, but he insisted on checking the list twice before he finally found it and let me through. And he spoke in a loud, bullying tone, not fit for addressing a lady of my station.' She bridled slightly. 'I wondered if he might be drunk, but the guard captain always checks the guards are sober, and their equipment in order, before he allows them on duty.'

'It certainly sounds strange,' I agreed. 'I shall discuss it with Lord Parr.' I stood and bowed. 'I thank you for your time.'

Mistress Odell got up. 'I am asked to take you to the Queen's private prayer closet now. The Queen will meet you there. I understand you are to speak to Jane Fool.'

''Tis so.'

That touch of a humorous smile again, like Queen Catherine's. 'I wish you good luck with her, sir.'

She opened the door, and I followed her out.

✝

WE WALKED DOWN the hallway. A rich perfume of roses and lavender filled the air, the scent coming from petals laid alongside the wainscotting. Through an open door at the end of the hall I had a glimpse of an immensely long, brightly painted gallery with tall windows, and of caged songbirds within that made a pretty trilling. The Queen's Gallery, I surmised.

Mary Odell knocked on a side door and, receiving no reply, bade me enter. I found myself in a private closet, a room for prayer. The design was impeccably orthodox; richly painted like everywhere in the palace, with an altar covered with embroidered white linen and candles burning in niches. The Queen would make sure her private chapel presented no visible sign of reformism for her enemies to use against her.

Mary Odell turned in the doorway. 'The Queen and Jane should be here soon.'

'Thank you, Mistress Odell.'

She gave me a sudden winning smile. 'I know you will do all you can to help the Queen. God speed your efforts, Serjeant Shardlake.'

'You are kind.'

She went out with a rustle of silken skirts, leaving me alone. In the distance I could hear faint voices: the daily hubbub of the palace. At last, I thought, I gain a little ground. The man with half an ear who had been at the first attack on Greening was linked to someone at the top; Mary

Odell's strange episode with the guard should be investigated, too. Even that odd smell should be considered further. And now I was about to see the Queen again. I looked at one of the red candles burning in the chapel, and for a moment felt an odd sense of contentment.

So thick was the rush matting that I did not hear approaching footsteps, and started as the door opened. Four women entered, but Queen Catherine was not among them. Two were young, dressed sumptuously in long-sleeved dresses. The two others, I realized with a shock, were familiar to me from the great portrait of the King and his family. One was the little round-faced woman who had been standing behind the Lady Mary in the doorway; the other was the Lady Mary herself. The little woman, who I realized must be Jane Fool, had with her, of all creatures, a fat white duck, which waddled beside her, a leathern collar and leash round its neck.

Jane was conspicuous in the comparative plainness of her dress, though her grey high-collared gown and white coif were of the best material. Her blue eyes darted around the chapel then fixed on me with a blank, frightened look. Beside her, scarcely taller, but magnificently dressed and with a bearing of regal authority, the Lady Mary studied me. I bowed almost to the floor, my heart thumping hard.

'Rise, master lawyer.' The voice was rich, surprisingly deep.

I looked at the King's eldest child. I knew Catherine of Aragon's daughter was much older than the Lady Elizabeth and Prince Edward; well into her twenties and, with her thin, narrow features, looking older still. She had auburn hair under a round French hood studded with diamonds, and a green gown decorated with pomegranates; a popular design but also the emblem of her long-dead, rejected mother.

Small, shapely hands played with a golden pomander which she wore at her waist.

'Forgive me, my Lady,' I said. 'I did not know – '

She nodded and smiled pleasantly, though her dark eyes were coldly watchful. She struck me as someone who had been watchful all her life, despite her poised manner. She waved a hand. 'You were expecting the Queen, I know. But my father called on her to sit with him a little. Jane was with me when Mary Odell came to fetch her, and I said I would accompany her instead.' She looked at me quizzically. 'I believe you have been asked to investigate the Queen's stolen ring.'

'That is correct, my lady. By Lord Parr.'

Mary made a movement of her thin shoulders, a hint of a shrug. 'I had heard vaguely of it. But I have been much engaged these last few days observing the building of my new lodgings.' A touch of pride entered her voice. 'I have brought two of my ladies along, as you see, for propriety's sake.' She did not introduce them, but continued to address me. 'I am surprised poor Jane is to be questioned.'

She looked fondly at the little woman, who stared back at her appealingly and spoke, in a high voice. 'I haven't done aught amiss, my lady.'

I wondered, was Jane genuinely slow-witted and anxious, or was she acting? I could not tell; there was something oddly inscrutable about her moon face, either because her mind worked strangely or because she was a skilled actress. Perhaps it was both.

I said, 'The Queen wished it, because Jane – ' it seemed the custom to refer to her by her Christian name – 'was one of only four people who entered her majesty's bedchamber on the evening the ring was stolen.' I turned to Jane. 'You are not suspected of anything. It is rather a matter of whether you might have seen or noticed anything amiss—'

The Lady Mary's voice, suddenly sharp, interrupted me. 'I require that you address any questions to Jane through me, sir, as I am sure the Queen herself would wish, were she able to attend. I will not have her frightened.' She gave a slight frown, which the two ladies-in-waiting instantly copied. The duck pulled at its leash, keen to investigate a scattering of herbs lying in a corner of the prayer closet.

'Then may I request, my Lady, that you ask Jane where she went, and what she might have seen, from the time she entered the privy lodgings on the sixth of July?'

'Well, Jane?' the Lady Mary asked encouragingly. 'Do you remember anything?'

Jane Fool gave me a quick look before addressing her mistress. 'I wanted to show the Queen a new trick I have taught Ducky, to seek out herbs which I have hidden. But the ladies would not let me past the Privy Chamber, they said she was not in.' To my surprise Jane then stamped her foot like a child, and raised her voice. 'Often they try to keep me from the Queen, though I alone can divert her when she is sad. She has often been sad of late—'

Mary raised a hand, and Jane was instantly silent. 'Yes,' Mary said dryly. 'She has. And now such a fuss over a missing ring.' However hard the Queen might have tried to bring the King's children into amity with her and each other, it seemed that with Mary at least her success had been limited.

'It was of great sentimental value,' I murmured. 'My Lady, if Jane could say where she went – '

Mary turned back to Jane. She spoke patiently. 'When you went past the ladies into the privy lodgings, where did you go? Did you see anything strange?'

'I looked in all the rooms for the Queen,' Jane replied.

'And when I saw she was truly not there, I came out again into the Privy Chamber. Nobody was in her quarters, the pages had gone and Mary Odell not yet come.'

'Then all is well.' Mary spoke in a tone of finality and Jane Fool shot me a quick, triumphant look.

I persisted. 'Did she notice anything unusual in the Queen's bedchamber? About her private chest, perhaps, where she kept the ring and other valuables?'

'No. Nothing,' Jane said – too quickly, I thought. 'The Queen never lets me near it. My Lady, this crookback frightens me.' I thought, you are lying. From the change in the Lady Mary's expression I realized she saw it too.

'Any information would be received most gratefully by the Queen,' I dared to venture.

The Lady Mary looked at Jane. 'Be calm, my dear. You know I can tell when you are playing games. Tell the gentleman anything you know, and I give you my word you will come to no harm.'

Jane Fool was red-faced now. Like a child, she pouted and stuck a finger in her mouth.

'Jane – ' A stern note had crept into the Lady Mary's voice.

'It's rude, it's naughty,' Jane blurted out.

'What is, Jane?'

There was a long moment of silence. Then she said, 'When I went into the bedchamber to see whether the Queen was there – '

I leaned forward. The Lady Mary said encouragingly, 'Yes – ?'

'I had Ducky with me, and – '

'Yes – ?'

'He shat on the floor.'

Whatever I had expected, it was not that. So that

explained the smell. 'A little trail of shit on the matting,' Jane continued. 'I was afraid the gentleman ushers might have Ducky sent away. I took a cloth and cleaned it up, using water from the Queen's rosewater bowl. The scent of herbs in the room was so strong, I thought the smell might not be noticed. I went away at once, and told no one.' Suddenly she yanked the duck's leash, pulling it towards her with almost enough force to break its neck, then bent down and hugged it to her. It looked startled, as well it might. 'Don't let the hunchback tell, my Lady, I beg you. I love Ducky.'

'No one will tell, Jane,' the Lady Mary said. She looked at me then, her mouth twitching slightly, and I discerned she had a quality I had not guessed at before: a sense of humour.

'Does that satisfy you, master lawyer?' she asked.

'Of course, my Lady.'

'I will allow you to report the duck's misdemeanour to Lord Parr,' she said gravely. 'But only on condition Jane is not parted from it. I think the Queen would agree.'

'Of course, my Lady.'

'Then we will leave you to your business.'

One of the ladies-in-waiting helped Jane to her feet; the other opened the door for the Lady Mary. I bowed low again. They went out, the duck waddling after the group on its webbed yellow feet. As I rose, the Lady Mary turned, looked at me, and gave a sardonic little smile. The door closed. I stood there, shaken by the unexpected and ridiculous turn of events. Ridiculous? I could not help but wonder whether I had just been made the victim of an elaborate charade, and whether Jane Fool knew more than she had said. But if so, she was an accomplished actress. And I had no evidence, none at all. I thought of her childlike demeanour. Perhaps that was what had attracted the Queen and the Lady Mary to her, two mature women who were childless and likely to remain so.

Perhaps she was a substitute child for them and nothing more. But there was something about Mary Tudor that made me afraid to think of the *Lamentation* ending in her hands.

✝

I STAYED IN the prayer closet, with the candles and incense. Half an hour passed, the light outside beginning to fade, before the door opened again and Lord Parr entered. He was frowning. 'I am told the Lady Mary accompanied Jane Fool to see you. You gave her no hint about the book?' He looked at me anxiously.

'None, my Lord.' I told him the absurd story about the duck, what I had gleaned from Garet Lynley about the man with half an ear missing, and Mary Odell's story of the guard.

He nodded. 'I will make discreet enquiries. A man with half an ear serving a great man of the realm . . .'

'The page said one of the great *personages* of the realm.'

He studied me closely. 'You mean the Lady Mary? That she might have sent Jane Fool to steal the book that evening after all?'

'We must make absolutely sure the Queen dropped no hint about the book to Jane.'

Lord Parr shook his head. 'Jane has always appeared a natural idiot.'

'Perhaps. Yet her speech, even though childish, is fluent. And sometimes one can be – indiscreet – before fools.'

He nodded, taking the point, but said, 'The Queen would not be. Not on this. And as I said before, the Lady Mary has stayed strictly orthodox for a decade. Nonetheless, I will speak to the Queen about Jane. Though even that theory begs the question of how someone managed to get the coffer open yet leave no signs of forced entry.' He sighed. 'Thank you, Master Shardlake, we may be starting to make progress. Now, the Queen is still with the King. A good time for us to take a look at the coffer. Come.'

✞

THE QUEEN'S bedchamber overlooked the river. It was a large, feminine room, richly scented, with flowers in vases and large embroidered cushions scattered on the floor where one might lie and read. A huge four-poster bed dominated the room. There was a desk, bare save for an ornate inkwell: here, at this desk, the Queen had written *Lamentation of a Sinner*. Next to the desk stood a solid wooden chest, two and a half feet high, a red-and-gold turkey carpet fixed to the top. On the front two carved nymphs flanked a Tudor rose. There was no bed linen on the chest; tonight's page had not arrived yet.

Lord Parr knelt down, with surprising suppleness for a man of his age, and I followed more slowly. He banged the side of the coffer, bringing forth a hollow echo.

'Firm, solid oak,' he said. 'All the Queen's valuables have been removed and placed elsewhere.'

I studied the lock. It was small but very solid, set firmly into the wood. I ran my fingers over it. 'No sign of scratches on the metal, nor the wood surrounding it. It was either opened with a key, or by a very skilled locksmith.'

'I have had the Queen's valuables taken elsewhere,' Lord Parr said, opening the chest carefully.

I looked at the empty interior, then bent carefully to study the lock from within. My back was hurting after this long day. No sign of scratches there, either. 'I have seen many chests and coffers for securing valuables,' I said. 'Mostly documents in my case. Often they have two or three locks, and complicated mechanisms inside.'

He nodded agreement. 'Yes. But this coffer was given to the Queen by her mother. She is very attached to it.'

I looked up at him. 'But the lock is surely new.'

'Yes indeed. When the hunt for heretics and the questioning of those within the royal household started this spring, the Queen had the locks on all her cupboards and coffers replaced. I asked if she wanted a more complex lock for this one, too, but she said it might damage the coffer. I remember her telling me, "If I have the only key and the new lock is strong, surely it is safe."' 'Of course,' he added, with a note of bitterness in his voice, 'I did not know then what lay within.'

'Who made the new lock?' I asked. 'They could have made another key.'

Lord Parr shook his head. 'You are right, it is an obvious point. But the Queen's own coffer-maker constructed this lock, as well as all the other new locks. He is well trusted. He has been the locksmith to successive Queens for twelve years, and you do not keep a man in such a post if he is not trustworthy.'

'Have you questioned him?'

'Not yet. Again, I thought it best to leave that to you. But I do not consider him a likely suspect.'

'Nonetheless, he is an obvious one.'

'He works down at Baynard's Castle. I thought perhaps on Monday you might go down there and question him. And talk to the embroiderer about that sleeve. Of course, they will not be there tomorrow, it being Sunday. That is a nuisance, but it will allow you a day of rest, and reflection.'

'Thank you.' I was grateful for the old man's consideration. But then he continued, 'What we really need is an expert on locks. Someone from outside the palace.' He raised his eyebrows. 'Your assistant Jack Barak is known to have experience in such matters. From the days when he was employed by Lord Cromwell.'

I drew a deep breath. So Lord Parr had been making enquiries about Barak. My assistant's experience in such matters had indeed come in useful over the years, and yet — 'I would rather not involve him,' I said quietly.

'It would help the Queen,' Lord Parr pressed. 'Barak need not know what this is about — in fact must not know. We will keep to the story of the jewel. But now the chest is empty I can send it down to Baynard's Castle, and he can look at it when you are there on Monday.'

'He would not claim to be a great expert — '

Lord Parr looked at me hard. 'He knows locks. And has experience of how the royal household works, the underside of it at least.'

I took a deep breath. 'I will speak to him tomorrow, see what he says — '

'Good.' Lord Parr spoke brusquely. 'Be at Baynard's Castle at nine on Monday. You can inspect the lock, speak to the cofferer and the embroiderer. I will arrange for William Cecil to be there, too; he can tell you what news he has of these religious makebates.' He rubbed his hands. 'We make a little progress.'

'And yet,' I said. 'Whoever has the book could still make it public at any moment.'

'I know that,' he answered testily. 'I have feared every day that someone will hand it to the King. Or that some papist printer is setting it into type in order to print it and distribute it in the streets. And it is not a long book, by now many copies could have been printed.' He shook his head. 'Yet day after day passes, and nothing happens. Someone is keeping it hidden. Why?' He looked suddenly old and tired. He stood up, his knees creaking. 'Tonight's page will be arriving soon, we should go. Take a good day of rest tomorrow, Master Shardlake. We still have much to do.'

Chapter Twelve

THE LAWYERS AND THEIR wives progressed out of Lincoln's Inn chapel, slowly and soberly as always after service; the men in black robes and caps, the women in their best summer silks. I stepped into the July sunshine, fresher that morning for a thunderstorm that had broken in the night, waking me from an uneasy sleep. Some rain would help the crops. And now I had to keep my promise to visit Stephen Bealknap. As I walked down the side of the chapel, Treasurer Rowland came over to me, a hard smile on his narrow face.

'Good morrow, Serjeant Shardlake,' he said cheerfully. 'A fine service.'

'Yes, Master Treasurer. Yes, indeed.'

In fact I had scarcely heard any of it, even though tomorrow would be the anniversary of the sinking of the *Mary Rose*. I should have been praying for the souls of my friends and the hundreds of others who had died, although I was no longer sure there existed a God who would listen. But even on that of all Sundays, I could not get my mind away from thinking of the *Lamentation*.

Rowland inclined his head to one side like an inquisitive crow. 'I thought you looked a little strained during service. I hope it was not the effect of attending the burnings.'

'I have many matters on just now,' I answered brusquely.

'Well, the Inn notes with gratitude your representing us

on Friday. And you may be called upon to represent us again next month, at a further public occasion.'

'Indeed,' I answered slowly, apprehensively.

'A celebration, though, not an execution.' Rowland smiled thinly. 'It is confidential still. But this will be a marvellous thing to see.' He nodded, bowed briefly, and was gone. I looked after him. Next month. Just now I could think no further ahead than tomorrow. I put his words from my mind.

✝

I WALKED SLOWLY on across the courtyard, ruminating. For all that I had found some leads yesterday, they were but threads in a great tangled skein. Why had the man with the damaged ear tried to break into poor Greening's premises *before* the Queen's book was stolen? How had someone managed to get into the coffer without leaving any marks, when the only key was around the Queen's neck? Could the locksmith have made a second key? And I wondered who this Jurony Bertano was, of whom Elias the apprentice was so terrified. The name sounded Spanish or Italian; I wondered if I dared ask Guy.

I almost tripped over a cobble which had become detached from its setting, and kicked it angrily away. I asked myself if I had done right to involve myself in a matter which could easily turn deadly. Images chased each other through my head: the weeping page, Garet Lynley, talking of the man with the slashed ear who would recruit him for a spy; Jane Fool, yanking at her duck's leash; Mary Tudor's severe face. I knew that if the *Lamentation* appeared in public I myself could be in danger, as would the Queen and Lord Parr. And that danger would extend to those who worked with me, like Nicholas: I had seen him standing on the far side of the chapel with the other clerks, a head taller than most of them, looking a little the worse for wear as he often did on Sundays.

The best protection I could give those who worked for me was to make sure they knew as little as possible of the true facts. But an order from Lord Parr was not to be denied. And so, before church that morning, I had gone round to Jack and Tamasin's house.

When I arrived at their house Jane Marris let me in, then went up to wake Barak and Tamasin from a late morning in bed. I had to sit uncomfortably in the parlour, listening as they clumped about getting dressed overhead, murmuring irritably. Jane brought George down. He was grizzling, and gave me a sad, tear-stained look. She took him to the kitchen, where I heard her starting to prepare breakfast.

Eventually Barak and Tamasin came down. I stood. 'I am sorry to disturb you so early.'

Tamasin smiled. 'It was time we were up. Will you have breakfast with us?'

'Thank you, I have eaten. How do you fare, Tamasin?'

'The sickness seems to have ended, praise be.'

'Good. I will not stay, I must get back to Lincoln's Inn, to church.'

'We don't bother any more than we have to,' Barak said. I knew both of them had had enough of religion for a lifetime.

'It's soon noticed if I stay away from the chapel too long,' I said. 'Besides, I have promised to see Bealknap.'

'You should leave him to rot, after all the harm he's done you,' Barak said. 'You're too soft.'

Tamasin nodded agreement. 'He is the worst of men.'

'Well, I confess I am curious to see what he has to say.'

'Curiosity killed the cat, sir,' Tamasin pressed.

I smiled sadly. 'Cats have nine lives, and perhaps mine are not all used yet. Jack, I wonder if I might have a quick word with you. It concerns – a work matter.'

Barak and Tamasin looked at each other knowingly. Perhaps they, like Rowland, could see the strain on my face. Tamasin said, 'I must see to Georgie. He is teething. He shall have a chicken bone to suck.'

Barak looked at me shrewdly as she left us. 'Young Nicholas was very subdued yesterday afternoon. He wouldn't say where you'd been, said you'd instructed him not to. I got the impression you'd told him off. Not that he doesn't need it sometimes.'

'I am sorry to have to leave so much to you.'

'We'll be all right for a few days. I've got Nicholas working hard. As I said, he seems quiet. Not his usual boisterous self.' Barak raised an eyebrow. He had guessed something serious was afoot.

I took a deep breath. 'Jack, I am afraid I have got myself involved in a piece of – delicate business. For Lord Parr, the Queen's Chamberlain.'

He frowned, then spoke with angry puzzlement. 'What is it that keeps drawing you back there? With all the rumours there have been about the Queen these last months, surely you should stay clear.'

'Too late now. The matter concerns a stolen jewel.' There, the lie was told.

Barak was silent a moment, then spoke quietly. 'You want my help? In times gone by, yes; but – ', he nodded at the doorway. Yes, I thought. Tamasin, George, the new baby.

I bit my lip. 'There is one small aspect where your expertise might be of help. I did not suggest it, the idea came from Lord Parr. I am sorry.'

'I still have a reputation in certain quarters?' His voice sounded surprised, but I detected some pleasure in it, too.

'So it seems. There is a chest at Whitehall Palace from which a valuable ring was stolen. Yet there is only one key, which the owner wore round her neck constantly, and there is no sign of forced entry.'

'You've seen this chest?'

'Yes. I spent much of yesterday at Whitehall Palace.'

'Whose is it?' he asked bluntly. 'The Queen's?'

'I must not say. It is being taken to the Queen's Wardrobe at Baynard's Castle for us to examine at nine tomorrow. Could you be there to look at it for me, see what you think?'

He gave me a long, hard stare. 'And that's all that is wanted of me?'

'Yes.'

'For myself, I wouldn't mind. But if Tamasin thought for a second that I was putting myself in peril again, she – ' he shook his head – 'she'd be furious. And she'd be right.' He sighed. 'But if it's an order from the Queen's Chamberlain – '

'It is. And I promise, I will keep you from further involvement.'

'I sensed trouble from your face when I came downstairs. So did Tamasin. You spoke of a cat having nine lives. Well, you must be on number nine by now. So must I, come to that.'

'I am bounden to the Queen.'

'All over a stolen jewel?' He gave me a sidelong look. 'If you say so. Anyway, I'll come. I won't tell Tamasin, though I don't like misleading her.'

'No, this must be kept confidential.'

He nodded, then looked at me hard again. 'But remember. Only nine lives.'

✝

LIES, LIES, I thought, as I approached Bealknap's chambers, which stood more or less opposite to mine. Then I heard a voice behind me, calling my name. I turned round irritably; what now? To my surprise, I saw Philip Coleswyn, the lawyer acting for Isabel Slanning's brother, whom I had seen at the burning. I doffed my cap. 'Brother Coleswyn, God give you good morrow. You have not been at the Gray's Inn service?'

'I attend my local church,' he said a little stiffly. I thought, a church with a radically inclined vicar, no doubt. 'I came here after service, because I wished to speak with you.'

'Very well. Shall we go to my chambers? They are just at hand. Though I have another appointment . . .' I glanced up at Bealknap's shuttered window. 'I cannot tarry long.'

'It will take but little time.'

We walked to my chambers. I unlocked the door and led Coleswyn into my room, threw off my robe and invited him to sit. He was silent a moment, looking at me with his clear blue eyes. Then he said hesitantly, 'Occasionally, Serjeant Shardlake, a case comes up where it can be – useful – to talk to the other side's representative, in confidence.' He hesitated. 'If I think that, like me, the representative would wish to avoid an unnecessary degree of conflict.'

'The Cotterstoke Will case?'

'Yes. When we met two days ago, Serjeant Shardlake, at that dreadful event at Smithfield – ' he blinked a couple of times – 'I thought, here is a man of probity.'

'I thank you, Brother. But strictly, probity means we must each represent our clients' interests, however troublesome they are. Their wishes must come first.'

'I know. But is it not a Christian thing to try to resolve conflicts where one can?'

'If it is possible.' I remembered Guy's assertion that some conflicts could never be resolved. I remembered, too, what Isabel had said: *If you knew the terrible things my brother has done.*

'I will hear what you have to say.' I added, 'And I promise it will go no further.'

'Thank you. We have the inspection of the wall painting on Wednesday. Your expert, of course, will be briefed to look for any ways in which the painting may be removed without damaging it.'

'While yours is likely to say it cannot be brought down.'

'My expert is an honest man,' Coleswyn said.

'So is mine.'

'I do not doubt it.'

I smiled. 'Yet both men are working to a brief, for a fee. I fear stalemate is the most likely outcome.'

'Yes,' Coleswyn agreed. 'It is in the nature of the system.' He sighed. 'And so the experts' charges will be added to the bills, and both the debt and the paperwork will grow.'

I replied wryly, 'What is the saying? "Long writing and small matter."'

'Yes.' And then Coleswyn laughed. I do not think he meant to; it was a release of tension. It made his hitherto serious face look quite boyish. I found myself laughing, too. We both stopped at the same moment, looking guiltily at each other.

'We cannot prevent them from fighting,' I said. 'Though I would happily be rid of this. Tell me, in confidence, does Master Cotterstoke hate Mistress Slanning as much as she does him?'

He nodded sadly. 'Edward Cotterstoke is never happier than when telling me what a wicked, vicious and evil-minded woman his sister is. Oh, and he also says she is a traitor, a popish Catholic who observes the old ceremonies in secret. He was introduced to me through my church congregation; I have just come from him.' He raised his

eyebrows. 'My appeals to his Christian charity go unheard.'
I nodded sympathetically.

'And Mrs Slanning tells me her brother is a heretic whom
she would happily see burned.' I paused, then added, 'And,
I fear, you also.'

He frowned. 'They should both be careful with their
tongues in these times.' He took a deep breath, then looked
at me. 'Edward Cotterstoke will listen to no reason. I know
his wife and children have tried to dissuade him from this
battle with his sister. Without success.'

'Isabel is a childless widow, but even if she had family, I
doubt they could move her either. Tell me, Master Coleswyn,
have you any idea why they hate each other so?'

He stroked his short beard. 'No. Edward will only say
that his sister has been a bad creature since they were children. And yet, though he enjoys abusing her – and we have
both seen them standing in court glaring mightily at each
other – I have a sense Edward is afraid of her in some way.'
He paused. 'You look surprised, Brother.'

'Only because Mistress Slanning said some words that
made me think *she* was afraid of *him*. How strange.' Though
it was strictly a breach of confidence, I was sure of Coleswyn's honesty now, and I decided to tell him what Isabel
had said about her brother – *the things he has done*.

When I had finished he shook his head. 'I cannot think
what that might mean. Master Cotterstoke is very much the
respectable citizen.'

'As is Mistress Slanning. Has it struck you how the wording of the old woman's Will was very odd? The specific
reference to wall paintings.'

'Yes. It is almost as though old Mistress Cotterstoke
wished to provoke a quarrel between her children, laugh at
them from beyond the grave.' He shivered.

'She must have known they loathed each other. Perhaps there were not two members of this family hating each other because of Heaven knows what old grievance, but three. The mother, too,' I finished sadly.

'Possibly. But I know nothing of their early days. Only that their father, a Master Johnson, who can be seen in the picture, died not long after it was painted. And that their mother soon remarried, to Cotterstoke, who took over her late husband's business. But he, too, soon died, leaving everything to his widow. There were no other children, and Edward and Isabel took their stepfather's name.'

'That tallies with what I know,' I answered. 'It does not sound as though there was an evil stepfather in the picture.'

'No.' Coleswyn stroked his beard again. 'If we could find what has brought them to this – '

'But how? Have you noticed that, though the two of them constantly abuse each other, it is always in general terms; nothing is ever specified.'

'Yes.' Coleswyn nodded slowly.

I heard the Inn clock strike twelve. 'Brother, I must go to my appointment. But I am glad you came. Let us each consider what we may do.' I stood and offered a hand. 'Thank you for speaking to me. So many lawyers would happily drive this witless matter on to Chancery, for the profits.' Bealknap would have, I thought, except that he would never have had the patience to deal with Isabel's carping and sniping. He had ever preferred some crooked land deal where everything was done in the dark.

Coleswyn smiled shyly. 'And to seal our little agreement, perhaps you would do me the honour of dining with my wife and me. Perhaps on Wednesday, after the inspection.'

The rules prevented barristers on opposing sides from discussing their clients behind their backs, but dining together was not prohibited. Otherwise, what would have become of our social lives?' I would be glad to. Though I have a separate matter that is taking much time just now. May I take the liberty of agreeing subject to the possibility I may have to cancel at the last moment?'

'Certainly.'

I sighed. 'This other matter makes the Cotterstoke case look – trivial.'

'It *is* trivial.'

I smiled sadly. 'Yes. Though not to our clients, unfortunately.'

I showed him out, and through the window watched his trim stocky figure as he walked away to the gate. Then my eyes turned to Bealknap's shuttered chambers, and I took a deep breath.

Chapter Thirteen

I WENT ACROSS the courtyard to the building that housed Bealknap's chambers, remembering his odd behaviour at the end of last year, those unexpected overtures of friendship, which I had rejected because he was not to be trusted. I knocked at the door and a porter answered. 'I have called to see Brother Bealknap.'

He looked at me gloomily. 'According to his nurse this may be the last day anyone will visit him. I will take you up.'

We climbed a long wooden staircase, passing other chambers, empty on the Sabbath. Very few barristers, save Bealknap, lived in chambers. I had not been inside his rooms for years; I remembered them only as untidy and dusty. He was rumoured to keep his great chest of gold there, running his fingers through the coins at night.

The porter knocked and the door was opened by an elderly woman in a clean apron, a short coif over her grey hair.

'I am Serjeant Matthew Shardlake.'

She curtsied. 'I am Mistress Warren. Master Bealknap has employed me to nurse him. He received your note.' She continued in the same cool, disinterested tone, 'He has a great growth in his stomach, the doctor says he has little time left now. The end will come in the next day or two.'

'Has he no family who might be summoned?'

'None he wished to contact. I think there was some falling

out, many years ago. When I asked him, he said he had not seen his family since the old King's time.'

I thought, that was near forty years past. Bealknap must have been only in his teens at the time. Another old family quarrel perhaps, such as the one I had just been discussing.

The old woman looked at me curiously. 'You are the only one he has asked to see. Other than the doctor and the builder, no one has been to visit.' *Builder?* I thought. 'Apart from the priest,' she added. 'Master Bealknap received the last rites this morning.' His death, then, was truly close. 'I will take you in,' Mistress Warren said, leading me along a dusty hallway. She lowered her voice. 'He refuses to have his shutters open, I do not know why. I warn you, his room smells bad.'

She spoke true. As she opened the door to a half-dark chamber a fusty smell of unwashed skin and diseased, rotten breath hit me like a blow. I followed her in. The room was poorly furnished, with a chest for clothes, a couple of wooden chairs, a bed and a crowded table filled with bottles and potions. The bed, at least, was large and comfortable-looking.

Bealknap had always been thin, but the figure under the covers was skeletal, the skin stretched tight over his skull, his ears and big nose prominent, the hands that lay on the sheet like white claws.

'I think he is asleep,' Mistress Warren said quietly. She bent over the dying man. 'Yes, asleep. Each time I think to find him gone, but he still breathes.' For the first time I heard a note of human sympathy in her voice. She shook Bealknap's shoulder gently. His eyes opened, those forget-me-not-blue eyes that had always roved around, never quite meeting yours. But today he stared right up at me, then smiled effortfully, showing his yellow teeth.

'Brother Shardlake.' His voice was scarce above a whisper. 'Ah, I knew if I sent you the gold, you would come.'

I brought one of the chairs over to the bed. Bealknap looked at the nurse. 'Go, Mary,' he said curtly. She curtsied and left.

'Is there anything I can get you?' I asked.

He shook his head wearily. 'No. I just wanted to see you one last time.'

'I am sorry to find you in this condition.'

'No,' he said softly. 'Let us speak the truth. You have always hated me, and I you.'

I did not reply. Bealknap's breath rasped painfully in his chest. Then he whispered, his breath in my face stinking, rotten, 'What is going to happen now?'

'None of us can know that for certain, Brother Bealknap,' I said uncomfortably. 'We must all hope for God's mercy on our souls – '

His eyes stayed fixed on mine. 'You and I know better than that. I think it is the one thing we agree on. We both know men have no souls, any more than cats or dogs. There is nothing afterwards, nothing. Only darkness and silence.'

I shook my head. 'I am not so sure as you. There is no way to know for certain. I do not know what or who God is, but – perhaps he exists.'

'No.' Bealknap sighed. 'I have had the rites, but only because that was necessary if my legacy is to be fulfilled.' He smiled again, and a dreamy quality came into his eyes. 'All my money, all my gold, is to go to the building of a great marble tomb in the Inn church, gilded and painted, with a stone image of me in my robes atop the tomb edged with gold so that all future generations of Lincoln's Inn lawyers will remember Brother Stephen Bealknap. I have been arranging the details with the man who will build it.' He laughed weakly. 'Treasurer Rowland took much persuading, but gold won the argument, as it wins them all.'

For a moment I could not think what to say. Bealknap must know how he was disliked. Was the commissioning of this memorial a last act of defiance? I thought sorrowfully, a lifetime's earnings put into such a thing. But something puzzled me. 'You said you are certain there is no afterlife, yet just now you asked what will happen now.'

He gave a throaty, painful laugh. 'I did not mean what will happen to *me*, Matthew Shardlake. I meant, what is going to happen to *you*?'

'I do not understand you.'

'I wanted to live to see what would happen to you.' He took a breath, winced with pain. 'Together with your good friend the Queen.'

My eyes widened. All the Inn knew that I had not worked for the Queen for a year. What could he know? 'What are you talking about?' I asked sharply, leaning over him. Bealknap gave me a look of satisfaction, then closed his eyes. I was angry now, realizing that he was playing games to the end. I shook him, but he had gone back to sleep and did not stir. I looked at him for a long moment. Then I could stand the terrible fug no longer; I was starting to feel sick. I went to the window and threw the shutters wide. The figure on the bed, now caught in full sunlight, lay white and wasted.

The door opened and the nurse came in. She went over to Bealknap, checked his breathing, then crossed to me, looking angry. 'Master, what are you doing? He wants the shutters closed. If he finds you have opened them he will complain fiercely when he wakes. Please.'

I let Mistress Warren close the shutters again. She looked at Bealknap. 'You must leave now, sir. Every effort tires him.'

'There is something I need to ask him.'

'Then return a little later. After lunch. Come now, please.' She took my arm, and I let her lead me to the door. From the bed I heard a grunt, then another. Bealknap was dreaming, and from those sounds, not of anything pleasant.

✝

I SAT IN MY ROOM in chambers, nursing a mug of small beer. I had been there for over an hour, trying to make sense of what Bealknap had said. Him, involved in all this? But how? He knew I once worked for the Queen, and must have heard the gossip that she was in trouble. But it was well known by everyone that I had stopped working for her a year ago. No, I thought, it is just that Bealknap knew that I had worked for Catherine Parr, knew she was in trouble as so many did, and hoped I might fall with her. I looked across the sunlit courtyard at the chamber where Bealknap lay. I would have to go over there again later, try to get more information from him. I shook my head. Vicious to the end. I thought of that great memorial Bealknap had planned; it would become a joke, a jest round Lincoln's Inn. But he would not foresee that. He had always been blind in so many ways.

I heard the outer door of my chambers open, then close again. I had locked it when I came back; it must be Barak come in for something. I got up and opened the door. To my surprise I saw Nicholas taking papers from a table to his desk. His freckled face still looked tired, and there was a beer-stain on his robe. He stared at me.

'Nicholas? Here on a Sunday?'

He looked a little shamefaced. 'Some notes of cases came in yesterday from the Court of Requests, matters for the Michaelmas term. With your being busy, Barak asked me to summarize them. I was at the Inn for the service, and thought I might as well come in here and do some work.' To my amusement he looked embarrassed at being caught out coming in to work extra hours. It did not fit with the image he liked to convey.

'Nicholas,' I said. 'I was too sharp with you yesterday. You asked the apprentice Elias that question at the wrong time, and you must learn to judge more carefully. But – I should have made allowance for your youth, your inexperience. I apologize.'

He looked at me in surprise. 'Thank you, sir.'

'Are you getting a taste for the law?'

'I confess at first I found it – well – boring, but now – it seems less so. There are some matters I find interesting.'

'Most of all if a hunt for a murderer is involved, eh?'

He smiled. 'Does that not add some spice?'

'That is one way of putting it. The law is seldom so exciting, as you know. But it is necessary to see all aspects of it if you are to return to Lincolnshire and help manage your father's lands.'

The boy's face fell, the first time I had seen him look sad. 'I doubt I will go back, sir.'

I realized how little I knew of Nicholas; he had volunteered almost nothing about himself. 'How so?' I asked.

He looked at me with his dark green eyes. 'I was sent to law because my father disapproved of something I did.' He hesitated. 'Involving a proposed marriage.'

I nodded sympathetically. 'You wished to marry someone below your station?' I knew such cases were not uncommon.

Nicholas shook his head vigorously. 'No, sir. I am of age, I may marry where I like.' His eyes flashed with sudden anger, his chin jutting forward.

'Of course,' I soothed.

He hesitated. 'As my father's only son, the marriage I make is important. Our estates have suffered from the fall in money like so many, the value of our rents has fallen and the tenants can afford no more. A marriage to the wealthy daughter of a neighbouring estate would have brought a valuable dowry.'

'Yes. I know such arrangements can be – difficult. What is it they say of gentlefolk? Marry first and learn to love later.'

Nicholas's face brightened a little. 'You understand, sir. Well, a marriage was planned for me, with the daughter of a large estate near our manor at Codsall.'

'And you did not like her? Or she you?' I smiled sadly. 'Neither position is easy.'

His face set hard. 'We liked each other very much. But we did not love each other. I am no great catch, and nor in truth was she, so they thought we would go well together.' He spoke bitterly. 'So my father and mother put it to me. But Anys and I both desire, in God's good time, to marry for love. We have seen enough marriages of convenience that have ended in discord. So she and I made a pact, during one of the walks we were encouraged to take in my father's garden, as they watched us from the windows. We agreed to tell our parents we would not marry. My father was sore angry; he was already discontented with me for spending too much time hunting and hawking rather than helping on the estate, so he sent me here. As a sort of punishment, I think, though I was glad enough to leave the country and see London,' he added. 'Anys and I still write to each other, as friends.' He smiled ruefully. 'Well, sir, now you know me for a truly disobedient fellow.'

'It sounds as though you and Anys might have rubbed along together quite happily.'

'That is not enough.'

'No,' I said. 'Many would disagree, but I think like you, it is not.'

'The poor have it easier,' he said bitterly. 'They may marry for love.'

'Only when they can afford to, and that is often later than they would wish these days. As for the effects of the war, the taxation and the ruin of the coinage – well, your father still has his manor house, but his poor tenants will find it hard to pay the rent and eat.'

Nicholas shook his head firmly. 'Now the war is over, prosperity will surely return. And the security of everyone depends on people staying within the ranks to which they were born. Otherwise we would have the anarchy of the Anabaptists.'

That bogey again. I said, 'I confess that the more I see of mankind, the more I think we are all of one common clay.'

He considered for a moment, then said, 'My family have been gentlefolk by birth for centuries. Since before the Conquest, my father says; since the Norsemen settled Lincolnshire. It is our heritage to rule.'

'They became gentlefolk by conquest alone. The Norsemen took plenty from the English, as did the Normans. That is how most of our families become wealthy; I know, I am a property lawyer, I spend much time dabbling in ancient deeds.'

'Land may be taken honourably in warfare, sir.'

'As the Normans doubtless did from your Norse ancestors. You may have had more land once.'

'Too late to fight for it now, I suppose. A pity, perhaps.' He smiled.

I was starting to like Nicholas; he was showing signs of wit, and for all his upholding of gentlemanly conformity, he had himself defied convention. I said, 'Well, we shall have the chance to talk more of land and who owns it as the new law term approaches. But now I must go home for lunch.'

'Has there been any further progress on the murder of the printer?' Nicholas asked.

'No.' I raised a finger. 'And remember, do not speak of it.'

'You have my promise as a gentleman.'

'Good.' My eye was drawn to Bealknap's window. After lunch, I would lie down for an hour or two; I needed to rest. Then I would return.

✝

I WENT HOME. AS I walked up the path, Josephine appeared in the doorway in her new dress, a young man in a sober doublet at her side. Agnes Brocket held the door open, smiling at them, while Timothy stood at the corner of the house, looking on nosily. Josephine's companion was in his early twenties, slim, dark-haired and moderately handsome; this must be the young man she was walking out with. She blushed as I approached, and the boy doffed his cap and bowed.

'I am Edward Brown, sir. Servant to your brother-in-the-law, Master Peter Henning.'

'Ah, yes. A good man. I was sorry to hear his wife died – some months ago, was it not?'

'In December, sir. My master was much affected. He is thinking of retiring, going home to Norfolk.'

'I hope he will not,' Josephine ventured.

'I thank you for permitting me to take Josephine out walking,' Goodman Brown said.

I smiled at Josephine. 'I am glad to see her getting out and about. You are going to Lincoln's Inn Fields, I believe. It should be pleasant there today.'

'Watch you take good care of her,' Agnes said from the doorway.

'I will.'

I turned to Timothy. 'Did you need to speak to me, lad?'

'I – I just wanted to tell you Genesis will need some more hay.'

'Then get some tomorrow,' Agnes said. 'And for now, be off.'

Timothy scurried away. Josephine and young Brown looked at each other and smiled. Timothy had permission from me to buy new hay whenever it was needed; it was obvious he had come to have a look at Goodman Brown. That the young fellow seemed amused rather than annoyed was another mark in his favour.

I stood with Agnes and watched the two walk down the gravel path. Then I heard a sound, from up the road at Lincoln's Inn. The slow tolling of a bell. I felt a shiver down my spine. It was the dead-bell, sounded when an Inn member died: that must surely mean Bealknap. I would not now get the chance to question him again; even in death, he had cheated me.

'It is good to see Josephine so happy,' Agnes said.

I smiled at her. 'It is.'

She hesitated, then added, 'She has told me a little of her past. She owes you much.'

Martin appeared behind her from inside the house, moving quietly as usual. He looked down the path, where Josephine and Goodman Brown were just turning onto the roadway. A disapproving look. So the dislike between Martin and Josephine was mutual, I thought. I wondered what was behind it. Martin spoke sharply to his wife, 'Never mind them. Have you told Master Shardlake of his visitor?'

Agnes put a hand to her mouth. 'Oh, I am sorry—'

Her husband cut across her. 'The young lawyer gentle‑man who called two nights ago is come again. He still will not give his name.' Martin frowned at the breach of eti‑quette. 'I told him you would be back shortly for lunch. He is waiting in your study.'

'Thank you.' I went quickly inside. In the study, the slight figure of William Cecil sat in a chair, his thin face thoughtful and worried. He rose and bowed as I entered.

'I am sorry to disturb you on the Lord's Day, sir,' he said quickly, 'but there has been a serious development.'

'You visited Greening's friends? Lord Parr said you would.'

'I did. But all are fled from their lodgings. They have disappeared, all three. Nobody knows where.' He sighed heavily. 'But it is the apprentice, Elias, that we need to talk about.'

'Have you found him?'

Cecil took a deep breath, fixed his protuberant eyes on me. 'What is left of him. His mother found him last night, in the alley next to their house, beaten about the head and weltering in his own blood.' A spasm crossed his face.

'Jesu.'

'There was something he managed to say to her, a woman's name, just before he died.'

'What was it?' I dreaded to hear the Queen's name. But instead Cecil said, 'Anne Askew. He managed to say, "Killed for Anne Askew".'

Chapter Fourteen

ELIAS'S MOTHER LIVED IN one of the narrow lanes between Paternoster Row and St Paul's Cathedral, whose great shadow and giant steeple loomed over the poor tenements below. Cecil and I walked there from my house.

On the way, talking quietly, he told me what had happened. 'Lord Parr asked me to speak to Greening's three friends. He told me about Greening's murder, that there was no suspect yet, but there were delicate political ramifications and he wanted you to talk to them. I understand he has told you more.' He looked at me, and I saw a quick flash of curiosity in his large eyes.

'A little more. This must have been a busy day for you,' I concluded, sympathetically.

'It has. My wife was unhappy at me working on the Sabbath, but I told her needs must.'

'Did you know any of Greening's friends yourself?' I asked.

'No,' he answered, a little curtly. 'But a friend in my congregation knows Curdy, the candlemaker. It appears Curdy may be a sacramentarian, his family are certainly old Lollards, like Greening. He may even be an Anabaptist, though that is probably rumour.' He gave me a hard, unblinking look. 'Though be clear, Master Shardlake, I have never spoken for sacramentarianism, and I have nothing but loathing for these Anabaptists, who would overthrow all, interpreting the

Bible after their own wild fantasies. The fact they may have played with such ideas does not mean Greening and his friends held them, of course.' For all his youth, Cecil spoke like an older, more experienced man.

'That is true.'

'All Greening's friends lived around Paternoster Row and the cathedral. I went out very early this morning; I thought it the best time to catch them, before church service. The exiled Scots preacher, McKendrick, lived in a cheap room he rented from Curdy, who was a widower. Curdy apparently was a friendly, jovial man, a journeyman, who worked with other candlemakers. McKendrick, on the other hand, had a reputation for surliness. And he is a big man, and an ex-soldier, so people tended not to get into quarrels with him.'

'These two friends of Greening's are very different people.'

'Which implies common religious affinities. In any event, when I arrived at Curdy's house both were gone. According to Curdy's housekeeper, they vanished overnight nearly a week ago, taking hardly anything with them.'

'Fled somewhere, then.'

'Unquestionably. The other friend of Greening's, the Dutchman Vandersteyn, is in the cloth trade, an intermediary for the Flanders wool buyers. He had a neat little house of his own, but when I got there his steward told me the same story; his master gone suddenly, taking only a few possessions.'

'Could they have been afraid of sharing Greening's fate?'

'Perhaps. Or if they were sacramentarians they might have feared the attentions of Bishop Gardiner's men. If that is the case, the Lord alone knows where they are.'

I remembered young Hugh's letter, the story of the refugees arriving in the Low Countries, fearing persecution. And Vandersteyn hailed from Flanders.

Cecil continued, 'Then I decided to call on the apprentice Elias's mother, to see what news she had, or whether perhaps he had come home. I found her outside, on her knees, frantically washing blood off the wall of the alleyway.'

'Dear God.'

'She has two little daughters. Her husband died of quinsy last year.'

'Perhaps that was why Elias took another job rather than leaving the district as the others seem to have done.'

'Mayhap.' Cecil took a deep breath. 'Elias's mother told me that in the small hours of last night, she heard her son shouting for help outside. She rushed out, like a good mother.' He sighed again and shook his head. 'She saw him killed. Let her tell you the story herself. She has taken the body into the house. Jesu, the sight of it turned my stomach.'

'Has she told the authorities?'

'No. Because of what Elias said to her before he died.'

'The name Anne Askew?'

'Yes.' He lowered his voice. 'Quiet now, look there.'

We were passing along Paternoster Row. All the shops were shut for the Sabbath. However, a man in a black doublet was walking slowly along the sunlit street, peering into the shop windows. Cecil smiled sardonically. 'I know him. One of Bishop Gardiner's spies, trying to spot forbidden titles no doubt, or dubious-looking visitors to the printers.'

We walked past him. Looking back at him from a safe distance, I asked Cecil, 'Have you worked for the Queen's Learned Council for long?'

'Two years only. Lord Parr has been good enough to favour me.'

For Cecil's abilities, I thought; there was no doubting those. And for his reformist sympathies too, most likely.

'Where are you from?' I asked. 'I thought I caught a trace of Lincolnshire. My pupil is from there.'

'Well divined. My first wife came from there, too, like me, but sadly God took her to Him in childbirth, though He left me our son.'

I looked at him. His was an unremarkable face, but for those powerful, protuberant eyes which I had noticed seldom blinked, and that line of three moles running down one cheek. Yet he had been married, widowed and remarried, and become a confidant of the highest in the land, all by his mid-twenties. For all his ordinary looks and reserved manner, William Cecil was a man out of the common run. 'We turn down here,' he said abruptly.

We walked into a narrow alley, made darker by the shadow of the cathedral, onto which it backed. Chickens pecked in the dust. Cecil stopped in front of a door with flaking paint. Beside it, almost blocking the dusty alleyway, stood a cart, a tarpaulin slung over it. Cecil knocked gently at the door: two short raps then a long pause till the next, obviously a prearranged signal.

✝

THE DOOR WAS OPENED by a woman in her forties, as short and spare as Elias had been large and burly. She wore a shapeless grey dress and had not even put on a coif, her dark hair hastily knotted behind her head. Her eyes were wide with horror and fear. On her cuffs I saw flecks of red. She stared at me, then Cecil. 'Who's this?' she asked him fearfully.

'Master Shardlake. A lawyer. And, like me, one who would not have people persecuted for their opinions. May we come in, Goodwife Rooke?'

Her shoulders slumped helplessly, and she nodded. She

led us into a poorly furnished parlour where two thin little girls of about eight and nine sat at table. The younger had her mother's small, birdlike features, the elder Elias's heaviness of face and body. Both stared at us in fear. I noticed a bucket and scrubbing brush on the floor, a discarded apron, stained red, rolled into a ball beside it.

'Girls,' Goodwife Rooke said gently. 'Go and wait upstairs in our bedroom. But do not go in your brother's room. Do you swear?'

'I swear,' the elder girl said. She took her sister's hand and they sidled past us. Their footsteps sounded on a wooden staircase. Goodwife Rooke sat down.

'It is no thing for his sisters to see,' she said. 'Nor a mother either,' she added, her voice breaking.

'Do the girls know?' Cecil asked gently.

'Only that Elias has been hurt, not that he is dead. I had a mighty job keeping them in our room last night, while I was heaving his body up the staircase. The noise made the girls call out to ask what was happening.' She rested her brow on a trembling hand for a moment, then looked at us desperately. 'I don't know what to *do*, sirs.'

Cecil said, 'We shall try to help you. Now, can you tell this gentleman what happened?'

'If it is not too much,' I added reassuringly.

'After seeing it, telling is little,' she answered starkly, and took a deep breath. 'My husband died last year. Elias, thankfully, had his job with Master Greening. But he spent too much of his spare time there, talking with Master Greening and his friends. Some of the things he said they discussed – ' her eyes flickered between us – 'they were dangerous.'

Cecil prompted, 'About faith and the Bible being the only keys to Grace, you told me, and questioning whether the social order was ordained by God.'

She nodded. 'I was angry with Elias for speaking of such things in front of his sisters. His father would have beaten him. Yet – ' her voice softened – 'my son was young, angry over the injustice in the world, full of newfound ideas. He was a good boy, he did not drink or roister, and his wages kept all of us.' She ran her hands through her hair. 'I do not know what will happen to us now. The girls – '

'I shall see what can be done,' Cecil said gently.

'What happened last night?' I asked after a moment.

She looked at me. 'It was around ten, the girls were in bed, thank God, and I was about to go up myself. I was worried, for Elias had not come home the night before. He had been surly, distracted, since poor Master Greening's murder. Then I heard his voice outside, shouting, "Help! Mother!"' She shook her head desperately. 'Almost the last words he ever said, and they were too late. I think he had been hanging around the house, checking to see whether it was safe to come home.' She swallowed. 'I threw open the door at once. Two men were running from the alleyway. One carried a cudgel. They ran past me, past that cart outside, and disappeared. I looked into the alley. There was my son. His head – ' she squeezed her eyes shut. 'There was blood, blood everywhere. Yet he was still just alive; he grasped my hand. He said, "Tell them, tell my friends, I was killed for Anne Askew." And then,' she added starkly, 'he died. I don't know how I found the strength but I dragged him indoors and upstairs and laid him in his room. I should have gone to the constable, I know, but after what he said – that name – ' Her voice fell to a whisper. 'Anne Askew. The one who was burned on Friday.' She looked at us. 'Elias wanted to go to the burning, shout cries of encouragement to the poor souls there. I think his friends persuaded him he would only end in the fire himself.' Her eyes grew angry. 'He would not be the first young apprentice to be burned these last few years.'

'No,' Cecil said. 'But they, and Elias, are safe now from the evils of this world, in Jesus' arms.' The words could have sounded trite, but he spoke them with quiet sincerity.

Goodwife Rooke pleaded again, desperately, 'What should I *do*, sirs?'

Cecil took a deep breath. 'Say nothing to the coroner, not yet. If people ask, say Elias never came back.'

'Lie to the officials?'

'Yes. For now. We have powerful friends, we can protect you from any trouble. Do not ask us more just now, but rest assured we shall hunt down Elias and Master Greening's murderers.'

I glanced at Cecil. 'They may be the same people. Could you describe them, Goodwife Rooke?'

She spoke in a dead tone. 'I could not see them clearly, it was dark. They were dressed roughly, like vagrants. Both young and strong. One, though, was near-bald. He looked at me for a second. A strange, wild look. It sore frightened me. He carried a club.' The poor woman put her face in her hands and shook violently. Then she seemed to collect herself; she glanced upstairs towards her daughters. 'Please,' she whispered, 'keep them safe.'

Cecil nodded.

I asked, 'That cart outside. Have you any idea who it belongs to?'

She shook her head. 'I never saw it before last night.'

I exchanged a glance with Cecil. Greening's killers – and it was obvious from Goodwife Rooke's description that it was they who had also killed Elias – might have learned that Elias had vanished, and been waiting around the alley lest he came home, a cart ready to remove the body. Had the boy not managed to shout out, he would never have been seen again.

Cecil said, 'I will arrange to have Elias's body taken away.'

For the first time, Goodwife Rooke looked hostile. 'Is my son to have no proper funeral?'

'It is safest, believe me. For you and your daughters.'

'And as we have told you,' I added, 'Elias's death will not go unpunished.'

She bowed her head.

'And now, might Master Shardlake look at Elias's body?' Cecil took her hand. 'We will say a prayer.'

She looked at me angrily. 'See what was done to my poor son.' She addressed Cecil. 'Was he killed for his beliefs? Was Master Greening?'

'As yet we do not know. But it may be.'

Goodwife Rooke was silent. She knew she was at our mercy. 'Come, Master Shardlake,' Cecil said quietly.

'Do not let my daughters see,' Goodwife Rooke called after us with sudden passion. 'If you hear them outside Elias's room, send them downstairs. They must not see that.'

✞

ELIAS LAY FACE UP on a straw bed in a tiny bedroom, the afternoon sun full on his bloodied face. He had been struck on the right cheekbone, hard enough to shatter it, for splintered shards of white bone showed through the dark mess of his face. He had also been struck on the top of the head, his hair a mess of gore. The shutters were open and blowflies had entered and settled on his head. In sudden anger I waved them away.

'Head wounds make much blood,' Cecil observed –

calmly enough, though he stayed a couple of feet from the bed.

'He was killed the same way as Greening,' I said. 'Struck on the head. And that cart and tarpaulin were almost certainly arranged to take him away. They didn't want a great hue and cry.' I looked at the body again. I thought of Bealknap, lying in his bed. But he had been rotten with sickness, ready to die, whereas Elias had been but eighteen, full of young life. I turned to Cecil. 'Did you believe what you said, about Elias being safe in the arms of Jesus?'

The young lawyer looked stung. 'Of course. Do you wish to say a prayer with me now, as I told his mother we would?' he asked stiffly.

'No,' I answered, and asked bluntly, 'What do you plan to do with the corpse?'

'Lord Parr has some contacts. I should think he will arrange to have it buried out on the Lambeth marshes.'

I looked at him. 'Lord Cromwell used to do that, with inconvenient bodies. I remember.'

Cecil looked at me hard with those protuberant eyes. 'In high politics, Serjeant Shardlake, there are always people who work in the dark. You should know that. Do you want a commotion about the murder of two radical Protestant printworkers? Men with possible links to the Queen? There must be a link, mustn't there, or Lord Parr would not be involved?'

I nodded reluctantly, turning away from the sight of Elias's shattered head. 'What of Greening's three friends, Master Cecil? What if they are dead too?'

He shook his head. 'The evidence suggests they all fled their homes. They may have learned that the two men who killed Greening were about.'

I nodded agreement. That sounded right. 'I want something done for that poor woman.'

'As I said, I will ask Lord Parr.'

'It is what the Queen would wish. Send someone soon,' I added.

✣

WE LEFT GOODWIFE ROOKE sitting wearily at her table and went back outside. We examined the cart; it was just a cheap wooden one, the tarpaulin old. But it was not valueless; it was unlikely someone would have just left it in these streets.

We walked slowly back to Paternoster Row. 'Why did Elias not flee with those others?' Cecil asked.

'Because he had a mother and two sisters to support, and could not just abandon them.'

He nodded agreement. 'I will report back to Lord Parr now. He will probably want to talk to you when you go to the Queen's Wardrobe tomorrow morning. With your assistant, the one who used to work with Lord Cromwell,' he added, looking at me curiously.

'Cromwell was a hard and ruthless man. But he had beliefs. If he could see how those he promoted turned out — Paget, Rich, Wriothesley, helping Gardiner fight against everything he believed in.' I shook my head.

'The balance on the Privy Council is about to change. Lord Hertford and Lord Lisle return from France soon. With the peace treaty well ensured. That will be a feather in their caps with the King.'

'Will the peace hold?'

'Oh, I think so. The coinage is so debased now that any English money is distrusted in Europe. The German bankers who lent the King so much to finance the war will allow him no more.' He smiled sadly. 'England is bankrupt, you see.'

'Bankrupt indeed,' I said ruefully.

'But if we can solve this matter without trouble to the Queen the reformists may begin to turn things round.' His manner was neutral, detached, but I realized William Cecil knew a very great deal. He fixed me again with those staring eyes, then raised his cap and bowed. 'God give you good evening, Master Shardlake.' He turned away, heading for the river and a wherry to Whitehall.

Chapter Fifteen

I WALKED HOME THROUGH the quiet streets, thinking hard. Two men were dead now, three had fled, and I was no nearer to a solution to the problem of who had stolen the Queen's book, or why. I felt very alone. I had been unable to say too much to Cecil; he did not know about the missing book. The only ones I could talk to honestly were Lord Parr and the Queen.

When I reached Chancery Lane I turned into Lincoln's Inn; I had to confirm whether that tolling bell had been for Bealknap. The porter was sunning himself in the gatehouse doorway. He bowed. 'God give you good morrow, Serjeant Shardlake.'

'And you. I heard the chapel bell tolling earlier.'

He spoke in a pious voice. 'Master Stephen Bealknap has died, God's mercy on his soul. The woman who was nursing him has ordered the coffin already.' He inclined his head towards the courtyard. 'It's just been brought in. They'll take him to the coroner's till the funeral, as there's no family.'

'Yes.'

His eyes narrowed. 'I daresay you won't miss him that much.' The porter knew all the doings at the Inn, including my long enmity with Bealknap.

'We are all equal in death,' I replied. I thought, when news of Bealknap's planned monument got out, the porter would have a rich feast of gossip. I walked on to Bealknap's chambers. The shutters in his room were open now. There was a noise in the doorway as two men manhandled a cheap coffin outside.

'Light, ain't he?' one said.

'Just as well, on a hot day like this.'

They carried the coffin out of the gate. The sunlit quad, rangle was quite empty. It was the custom that when a member of the Inn died his friends would stand outside as the coffin was taken out. But no one had come to mourn Bealknap.

I walked away, up to my house. I was hungry; I had missed lunch again. As I opened the door I heard Martin Brocket's voice, shouting from the kitchen. 'You obey *me*, young Josephine, not my wife. And you account to *me* for where you've been.'

I stood in the kitchen doorway. Martin was glaring at Josephine, his normally expressionless face red. I remem, bered how her father used to bully the girl, reduce her to trembling confusion, and was pleased to see Josephine was not intimidated; she stared back at Martin, making him redden further. Agnes stood by, wringing her hands, while Timothy was by the window, pretending to be invisible.

'No, Martin,' I said, sharply. 'Josephine answers to me. She is my servant, as you are.'

Martin looked at me. It was almost comical to watch him compose his face into its usual deferential expression. 'What makes you nip the girl so sharply?' I asked.

'My wife – ' he waved an arm at Agnes – 'gave the girl permission to walk out with that young man this afternoon without asking me. And she is late back. She told Agnes she would be back at three and it is nearly four.'

I shrugged. 'It is Josephine's day of rest. She can come back when she likes.'

C. J. Sansom

'If she is seeing a young man, I should be informed.'

'You were. By your wife. And I saw you watch Josephine leave.'

'But for decorum's sake, she should be back when she said.' Martin was blustering now.

'She is an adult, she can return when she wishes. Mark this, Josephine. If you are seeing Goodman Brown on your free day, so long as you inform Martin, or Agnes, or me in advance, you may come back any time before curfew.'

Josephine curtsied. 'Thank you, sir.' Then she gave Martin a little triumphant look.

'And no more shouting,' I added. 'I will not have a brabble in my house. Josephine, perhaps you could get me some bread and cheese. I missed my lunch.'

I walked out. It was not done to support a junior servant against a steward in his presence, but Martin had annoyed me. I wished I understood what was the matter between him and Josephine. From the window, I saw Timothy leave the kitchen and cross the yard to the stables. On impulse, I followed him out.

✝

THE LAD WAS SITTING in his accustomed place, atop an upturned bucket beside Genesis. He was talking softly to my horse, as he often did. I could not hear the words. As my shadow fell across the doorway he looked up, flicking his black hair from his face.

I spoke casually. 'Master Brocket seemed much angered with Josephine just now.'

'Yes, sir,' he instantly agreed.

'Has he ever shouted at her like that before?'

'He – he likes to keep us in order.' His look was puzzled, as though to say that is the way of things.

198

'Do you know, is there some cause of enmity between them? Come, I know you are fond of Josephine. If there is a problem I would help her.'

He shook his head. 'They do seem to dislike each other, sir, but I do not know why. It was not bad at first, but these last few months she is always giving him unpleasant looks, and he never misses a chance to chide her.'

'Strange.' I frowned. 'Have you thought any further about what I said, about your maybe going for an apprenticeship?'

Timothy spoke with sudden vehemence. 'I would rather stay working here, sir. With Genesis. The streets outside – ' He shook his head.

I remembered how, until I found him, he had spent most of his early years as a penniless urchin. My home was the only place of safety he had ever known. But it was not right, a young boy knowing nobody his own age. 'It would not be like before you came here,' I said gently. 'I would ensure you had a good master, and you would learn a trade.' He stared back at me with large, frightened brown eyes, and I went on, a little testily, 'It does a lad your age no good to be alone so much.'

'I am only alone because Simon was sent away.' He spoke defensively.

'That was to ensure his future, as I would ensure yours. Not many lads get such a chance.'

'No, sir.' He bowed his head.

I sighed. 'We shall talk about it again.'

He did not answer.

✝

I WENT TO MY ROOM, where Josephine had left bread, cheese and bacon, and a mug of beer. I sat down to eat. Outside, the garden was green and sunny; at the far end my little summer pavilion was pleasantly shaded. A good place to go and set my tumbling thoughts in order.

I saw there was a new letter from Hugh Curteys on the table. I broke open the seal. Hugh had been promoted, I read, to a permanent position with one of the English trading houses, and was now thinking of a merchant's career. The letter went on to give the latest news of Antwerp:

In a tavern two days ago I met an Englishman, glad to find someone who spoke his language. He had been tutor to a Wiltshire family, well-connected folk, for some years. He is a radical in religion, and the family, though they had no complaint of him, feared that association with him might do them harm in these days. They gave him some money and arranged for a passage here. I marvel, sir, at what is happening in England. I never remember such times. I hope you are safe.

I wondered if Greening's three friends would also make for the Continent. Lord Parr should arrange for a watch to be kept at the docks, though I reflected gloomily that it might already be too late. I read the rest of Hugh's letter:

I was in the counting-house by the wharves yesterday, and a man was pointed out to me, standing with some others looking at the ships. He had a long grey beard and dark robe and a clever, watchful face, set in a scornful expression. I was told it was John Bale himself, the writer of plays against the Pope and much else; if King Henry got hold of him he would go to the fire. The Inquisition dare not interfere too much in Antwerp because of the trade, for all the Netherlands are under Spanish dominion, but I am told Bale does not parade himself publicly too often. Perhaps he was arranging the export of more forbidden books to England. I was glad to see him turn and leave.

I put the letter down. I thought, John Bale, Bilious Bale. Indeed he was a great thorn in the side of Gardiner and his people. As well for him that he was safe abroad.

I went into the garden, with pen, ink and paper and a flagon of wine, and sat in the shade of the pavilion. The shadows were lengthening but the air was still warm, and it would have been a pleasure to close my eyes. But I must get my thoughts in order.

I began by writing a chronology of recent events, beginning with the Queen's writing of the *Lamentation* during the winter. It had been in June, she said, that she had shown the completed manuscript to Archbishop Cranmer in her Privy Chamber, and argued with him when he said she should destroy it.

Then, on the 5th of July, came the first attack on Greening's premises, witnessed by Elias. By two roughly dressed men, one with half an ear sliced off. Then, on the 6th, the Queen discovered the manuscript was missing, stolen while she was with the King, at some time between six and ten that evening. Nobody would have known in advance that the King would call for her, which implied that someone had been waiting for their chance, with a duplicate key ready. I shuddered at the thought of someone in the Queen's household watching and waiting for an opportunity to betray her.

I turned my mind back to the key. The Queen had kept it round her neck at all times, so surely there *had* to be a duplicate. And that must have been made either by her locksmith, or somebody who had got hold of the original key before it was given to the Queen. Tomorrow's visit to Baynard's Castle would be important.

I leaned back, thinking of those I had questioned at Whitehall. I could not see either of the pages or Mary Odell taking the book. But I was not so sure of Jane Fool. I had a feeling she was less stupid than she pretended, though that in itself was not proof of guilt. And she served the Lady Mary as well as the Queen. I remembered Mary Odell's account of the strange behaviour of the guard on duty the night the manuscript was stolen. I must see what Lord Parr turned up there.

I looked up at the green branches of the large old elm beside the pavilion. The leaves moved in the faint breeze from the river, making a kaleidoscope of pretty patterns on the pavilion floor. I looked over at the house, shaking my head. For the most important question remained unanswered: how could anyone have learned that the *Lamentation* existed at all?

I wrote down the next important date. The 10th of July. The murder of Armistead Greening; the stolen manuscript of the *Lamentation* grabbed from his hand by two men who had come to kill him and hide the deed by setting his shed on fire. Different men from the earlier attack, on the 5th, though again young and roughly dressed. One of the earlier attackers seemed to have worn an embroidered sleeve, the mark of a gentleman. I remembered what Okedene's old servant had said about the man from the first group, who was missing half an ear. *It looked like a slash from a sword, not the great hole you get from having your ear nailed to the pillory.* So he had probably been in a sword fight; and the only people who were allowed to carry swords were those of gentlemen status, like Nicholas. I thought, what if *both* attacks were carried out by people of high status, dressed like commoners to escape notice? What if all four attackers were working for the same person? Yet that left unresolved the central problem that, at the time of the first attack, the *Lamentation* had not yet been stolen. Could both sets of attackers have been after something else and found the *Lamentation* by chance?

After Greening's murder, his associates had, except for Elias, fled. They had first been questioned by the constable, and all had alibis. Had they left because they were frightened of religious persecution, I wondered, or for some other reason? Only poor Elias had stayed because his mother and sisters needed him, and he had been killed by the same people who killed Greening.

And then there was that new mystery: Elias's dying words to his mother. *Killed for Anne Askew.* I wondered, had Greening's group had some association with her before her capture?

I thought more about Greening's group of friends. According to Okedene, apart from Greening himself and Elias, there had been one or two people who came from time to time, but the core of the little fellowship remained the three men who had vanished. I wrote down '*McKendrick, the Scottish soldier. Curdy, the candlemaker. Vandersteyn, the Dutch trader.*' Religious radicals, meeting for potentially dangerous discussions. Possibly sacramentarians, or even Anabaptists. And somehow, the *Lamentation* had come into Greening's hands.

The radical groups were well known to be disputatious, often falling out among themselves. Okedene had overheard them arguing loudly. I thought, what if *they* had somehow stolen the manuscript and planned to print it as proof that the Queen sympathized with religious radicalism? They might even have thought it would stir up the populace in support of their stance, so popular was the Queen. Of course, the notion was mad – the only result would be the Queen's death. But the religious radicals were often ignorant and naive when it came to actual political realities.

I stood up, pacing to and fro. This, I told myself, was pure speculation. And the person Okedene had heard them arguing over just before Greening's murder was not the

Queen, but this mysterious Jurony Bertano, that they called the 'agent of the Antichrist', who was soon to arrive, but about whom nobody at court appeared to know anything. I wrote the name down phonetically, as I was unsure of the spelling, and decided I would ask Guy about the possible nationality of its owner.

Then I wrote another, final name: *Bealknap*. What he said was a complete mystery, and a worrying one. He had seemed certain that both the Queen and I had an ill fate in store. But I crossed out his name; his deathbed words had, surely, referred to the heresy hunt and his hope to live to see me and the Queen caught up in it.

I put down my pen, and stared over the garden, almost completely in shadow now. I thought of the Queen. That evangelism of hers, that desire to share her faith, had caused her to forget her habitual caution and common sense. She regretted it now, was full of guilt. The *Lamentation* itself might not be strictly heretical, but she had shown disloyalty to Henry by writing it in secret. That would not be easily forgiven. The King had not allowed her to be prosecuted without evidence, when Gardiner was after her, but if that manuscript were to be given to him – or, worse still, printed in public . . . I shook my head at the thought of what her fate might be then.

Chapter Sixteen

THE NEXT MORNING, Monday, Barak called at the house early. Like Genesis, his black mare, Sukey, was getting older, I noticed, as we rode out along Fleet Street, under the city wall. The sky had taken on that white milky colour that can portend summer rain.

'Bealknap died yesterday,' I said.

'There's one gone straight down to hell.'

'He told me he did not believe in an afterlife. And he was unpleasant to the last.'

'Told you so.'

'Yes, you did.'

'And this business. This chest. What's behind it?'

I saw Barak's curiosity had got the better of him. I hesitated, but realized I would have to give him something to satisfy that curiosity. 'A ring was stolen from it. Best you do not know more.'

We had just passed under Fleet Bridge, and the horses shied at a rattle of pots and pans. A middle-aged woman, dressed only in a shift, was seated backwards on a horse, facing the animal's tail and wearing a pointed cap with the letter S on it. Her head was bowed and she was crying. A man, his expression stern, led the horse along, while a little band of children ran alongside, banging sticks on pots and pans; several adults too.

'A scold being led to the stocks,' Barak said.

'Ay, Bishop Bonner's courts do not like women overstepping themselves.'

'No,' said Barak. 'And those folk will be her neighbours. How little excuse people need to turn on each other.'

✝

WE RODE DOWN to Thames Street, where Baynard's Castle stood by the river. It was an old building, renovated and expanded, like all the royal properties, by Henry. I had seen it from the river many times; its tall four-storey turrets rose straight from the Thames. Since Catherine of Aragon's time it had been the Queen's official residence, doubling as the Wardrobe, where her clothes and those of all her household were looked after and repaired. Catherine Parr's sister, Anne, resided there now with her husband, Sir William Herbert, a senior officer in the King's household. All the Parrs had found advancement in these last years; the Queen's brother, named William like his uncle, was on the Privy Council.

Baynard's Castle was reached from the street by a large gate, well guarded by men in the Queen's livery, for there was much of value inside. We dismounted, our names were checked off on the usual list, and our horses taken to the stables. The courtyard of Baynard's Castle seemed even more a place of business than Whitehall; two merchants were arguing loudly over a bolt of cloth they held between them, while several men unloaded heavy chests from a cart.

Those in the yard fell silent as a group on horseback clattered under the gate; two richly dressed men and a woman, accompanied by half a dozen mounted retainers. They rode towards an archway leading to an inner courtyard. I saw that the woman bore a strong resemblance to the Queen, and I realized it was Anne Herbert. The man riding beside her, in his forties, black-bearded with a military air, must be Sir William. The other man accompanying them was tall and slim, with a thin, hollow-cheeked face and a short auburn beard. His own resemblance to the Queen allowed me to recognize him as William Parr, Earl of Essex. They looked down at the people in the courtyard with haughty expressions – we had all doffed our caps as they passed. Yet all three were known as radicals, who would certainly fall if the Queen did.

A door in the main courtyard opened and Lord Parr stepped out. He wore his dark silk robe and cap, and his thick gold chain of office. Anne Herbert waved and hailed him from her horse. The little retinue halted as Lord Parr walked slowly over to them. He was leaning on a stick today. His nephew and niece greeted him and they exchanged a few words; I took the opportunity to open my satchel and take out my robe bearing the Queen's badge. Barak whistled quietly. 'So you're sworn to her household now?'

'Only while this investigation lasts.'

Lord Parr left his relatives, who rode on to the inner courtyard, and approached us.

'He doesn't look too well,' Barak whispered.

'No. He's near seventy and feeling the strain of the job, I think.'

'All over this stolen whatever-it-is,' Barak replied sceptically. I did not answer. We bowed deeply to Lord Parr.

'Serjeant Shardlake. You are on time,' he said approvingly. 'And this must be Goodman Barak, who knows about keys and locks.'

'I will assist in any way I can, my Lord.' Barak knew when to be deferential.

'Good. The chest is inside. I had it brought across, saying

it needed repair. But first, Master Shardlake, a word in confidence.' He put his arm around my shoulder and led me a little away, leaving Barak looking put out.

'I heard from William Cecil what happened to the apprentice boy.' Lord Parr stroked his white beard, looking grave.

'I thought Cecil might be here today.'

Lord Parr shook his head. 'The fewer people seen to be making enquiries the better. Officially I am here to dine with my niece and nephew. So, what do you make of the apprentice's death?'

I told him about my reflections in the garden. 'Greening, Elias and the other three all had reason to fear danger. But I do not know whether any of them, other than Greening, had any connection with the *Lamentation*. I wonder, my Lord, whether Mistress Askew might have had any contact with the Queen, could have had knowledge of her book; whether she might not in fact have been tortured to try and find those things out.'

He shook his head. 'The Queen and Anne Askew never met. Mistress Askew had contacts on the fringes of the court, yes, and would have loved to preach at the Queen, but my niece and I were too careful to permit that. I made sure Anne Askew never came near her household.'

'Yet she must have been tortured for some reason. By the way, the news of that must have been leaked by someone inside the Tower. Is there any chance of finding out who that could have been?'

Lord Parr considered. 'When it became obvious at the burning that the street gossip about Askew's torture was true, I thought there would be a hue and cry in the Tower to find who set those rumours. Someone there, as you say, must have talked. But I have heard nothing.' He furrowed his brow. 'The Constable of the Tower, Sir Edmund Walsing-ham, was my predecessor as Queen's Chancellor and is a friend. I shall make enquiries. In the meantime I want you to come to the palace tomorrow to question the guard who was on duty the night the manuscript was stolen and who Mary Odell said behaved oddly. He comes back on duty in the morning.'

'Thank you, my Lord. And those three runaways: Curdy, McKendrick and the Dutchman. It is essential to interview them. I wonder whether they may even have taken the Queen's book in connection with some hare-brained scheme of their own. Perhaps even fallen out over it, so that one killed Green-ing and made off with the book.'

Lord Parr's face set hard. 'Then we are dealing with wild fools rather than an enemy at court.' He shook his head. 'But how could such people get hold of the book in the first place?'

'I do not know.'

'But nevertheless they should be found.'

'Yes.' I added, 'I was thinking about Okedene the printer, whether they might come after him now.'

'He has already told us what he knows.'

'Even so, his safety – '

Lord Parr looked irritable. 'I do not have a limitless supply of people I can employ on this matter; and none I would completely trust, apart from Cecil. I have no network of spies like your old Master Cromwell, or Secretary Paget,' he added caustically. 'I have asked Cecil to keep his ears and eyes open, which he will do. And I can arrange for him to bribe someone at the customs house. Cecil suggested that, to see whether anyone resembling these three men books passage on a ship. Perhaps he can bribe one of the dockers to keep a watch.'

I remembered Hugh's letter. 'Many radicals are going abroad these days,' I said.

Lord Parr grunted. 'And provided they are just little fish, the authorities wink at it. Glad to be rid of them.'

'Then they may already be gone. But if they are seen, would it be possible to detain them? Perhaps on suspicion of involvement in the theft of a missing jewel?'

'Yes, that may be a good idea. I will talk to Cecil.' Lord Parr raised a monitory finger. 'But remember, Master Shardlake, my powers are limited. And the Queen still has to watch every step.' He sighed deeply. 'For myself, I wish I were back in the country.' He shook his head. 'Nearly a fortnight since the *Lamentation* disappeared, and not a whisper of it.'

'And two men murdered.'

'I am hardly likely to forget. And I have still heard nothing about this man with half an ear sliced off, in the employ of someone at court.' All at once, beneath his finery, I saw a puzzled, frightened old man. 'We are in the midst of a deadly business. Surely the two attacks on Greening's premises must be connected. Yet the *Lamentation* had not yet been stolen when the first attack took place. Pox on it!' He spoke querulously, banging his stick on the cobbles. Then he collected himself, turned and looked at Barak. 'Will he be acting as your right-hand man in this?'

'No, my Lord. I'm sorry, but I fear his family commitments—'

Lord Parr grunted impatiently. 'Too much softness is not a good thing with those who work for you. It gets in the way of business. However, I am arranging for some money to be sent to the apprentice's mother when his body is taken away. Together with advice to leave London.'

'Thank you, my Lord.'

Another grunt. 'I would be in trouble with her majesty if

I did not help the woman. And she is safer off the scene. Have you brought the piece of embroidery your boy found?'

'In my satchel.'

'Good. You will be taken to the embroiderer after seeing Master Barwic, the carpenter and locksmith. You can also tell the embroiderer the story of the stolen jewel. His name is Hal Gullym.'

'Has he been with the Queen long?'

'He is not an old retainer like Barwic, the cofferer. He was employed at court three years ago, when the Queen's household was set up. Like everyone at Baynard's Castle he is part of the *domus providenciae*, a servant, a craftsman. And he has a strong motive for loyalty and obedience. Working for the court takes you to the top of your profession. Every guildsman in London longs to work here.' He spoke patronizingly, I thought, an aristocrat talking dismissively of men who worked with their hands. 'So Hal Gullym will be happy to assist. Now –' From his robes Lord Parr produced the Queen's key, still on its gold chain, and gave it to me. 'Handle that with great care.'

'I will.'

'The guard with a fair beard you see over at that door has been told you are coming to investigate a jewel theft; he will guide you, and wait while you examine the chest. Give the key to him afterwards to return to me; he can be trusted. Then he will take you to Barwic and then Gullym. If you find anything important, send word to Whitehall. Otherwise, attend me there at ten tomorrow morning.' Lord Parr turned and called to Barak. 'Over here, sirrah, your master has instructions.' Then he hobbled away to the inner courtyard to join the members of his family.

✝

THE INTERIOR OF the building into which the guard led us was nothing like Whitehall, for all the fine tapestries adorning the walls. This part of Baynard's Castle was a clothing enterprise; embroiderers and dressmakers working at tables in the well-lit hall. The shimmer of silk was everywhere, the air rich with delightful perfumes from the garments. I thought of what the Queen had said, how the richest of these clothes had passed from Queen to Queen.

Barak shook his head at it all. 'All these people are working on the clothes of the Queen's household?'

'It has a staff of hundreds. Clothes, bedlinen, decorations, all have to be of the finest quality and kept in good repair.' I nodded to the guard, and with a bow he led us over to one of the many side doors. We were taken down a corridor to a large room where several clothes presses stood, bodices and skirts kept flat beneath them. The Queen's chest stood on a table; I recognized the distinctive red-and-gold fabric covering its top. It was oak, with strong iron brackets at each corner. Barak walked round it, felt the wood, looked at the lock, then lifted the lid and peered inside. It was a bare wooden box, empty except for the tills in the side where small valuables were kept.

'Good strong piece. You'd need an axe to break in. The chest is old, but the lock's new.' He leaned in and thumped the sides and bottom. 'No hidden compartments.'

'It is an old family heirloom.'

He looked at me sharply. 'Of the Queen's?'

'Yes. She had a new lock fitted in the spring, the other one was – old.'

He bent and peered closely at the lock, inside and out. Then he said, 'I'd better see the key. I saw Lord Parr give it to you.'

'Don't miss much, do you?'

'Wouldn't still be here if I did.'

I handed him the key. I wished he had not asked about the Queen. But if I limited his involvement to the chest, surely he would be safe. He studied the key's complicated teeth closely, then inserted it in the lock, opening and shutting the chest twice, very carefully. Finally he took a thin metal instrument from his purse and inserted it in the lock, twisting it to and fro, bending close to listen to the sounds it made. Finally he stood up.

'I'm not the greatest expert in England,' Barak said, 'but I would swear this lock has only ever been opened with a key. If someone had tried to break in using an instrument like mine, I doubt they'd have succeeded – the lock's stronger than it looks – and I'd expect marks, scratches.'

'The Queen says she kept this key always round her neck. So no one would have had the chance to make an impression in wax to construct another. I think there must be another key.'

'And the only person who could have made that is the locksmith, isn't it?' Barak said, raising his eyebrows.

'So it seems.'

He rubbed his hands, his old enthusiasm for the chase clearly visible. 'Well, let's go and see him.' He smiled at the guard, who looked back at us impassively.

✝

THE CARPENTER'S workshop was at the rear of the hall, a large, well-equipped room smelling of resin and sawdust. A short, powerfully built man with regular features only half-visible through a luxurious growth of reddish hair and beard was sawing a plank, while his young apprentice – like his master, wearing a white apron emblazoned with the Queen's badge – was planing another piece of wood at an adjacent table. They stopped working and bowed as we entered. At the back of the workshop I noticed a set of lock-smith's tools on a bench.

'Master Barwic?' I asked.

'I am.' He looked a little apprehensive, I thought, at the sight of my lawyer's robe with its own Queen's badge. But then he would know of the theft, and that he might be under suspicion.

'I am Matthew Shardlake, Serjeant at Law. I am enquir-ing for Lord Parr into the loss of a jewel belonging to the Queen, which she values greatly.' I turned to the apprentice, who was small and thin, a complete contrast to poor Elias. 'Does this boy help you with lock-making?'

'No, sir.' He gave the boy an unfavourable look. 'I have enough trouble training him up on the carpentry side.'

I looked at the lad. 'You may leave us.' Barwic stood, hands on the table, frowning a little as the boy scurried from the room. 'I heard of the jewel's loss, sir. I think someone must have stolen the key.'

I shook my head. 'Impossible. The Queen wore the key round her neck at all times.' I saw his eyes widen; he had not known that. 'Come,' I said. 'I would like you to see the chest.'

'It is here?'

'In one of the rooms nearby.'

We led Barwic to the chamber, where he examined the chest carefully. 'Yes, I made this lock, and fitted it to the chest, back in the spring.' I gave him the key and he studied it. 'Yes, this is it.'

'And you made no copies?' Barak asked.

Barwic frowned, obviously annoyed at being questioned by someone junior. 'On the Queen's instructions,' he answered. 'It was unusual, but those were her majesty's orders. The chest was brought to my workshop. The lock was as old as the chest, though serviceable enough. I made the new lock and key, tested them, then took the key and chest back to Whitehall myself, as instructed. I gave the key directly into the hands of Lord Parr.'

'Normally, though, you would make a spare key, in case the original was lost?'

'Yes, and send both keys to the Chamberlain.' His calmness deserted him and his voice rose. 'I did as I was ordered, sir, simply that.'

'I have to question everyone connected with this chest,' I answered mildly.

'I am a senior craftsman.' Barwic rallied a little. 'I was Chairman of the Carpenters' Guild last year, responsible for its part in all the ceremonies and processions, and raising troops for the war.'

I nodded slowly. 'An honourable duty. Did you know what was kept in the chest?'

'They told me jewels and personal possessions. Sir, if you are accusing me—'

'I accuse you of nothing, good Master Barwic.'

'Ay, well, I am not used to being questioned like this.' He spread his hands. 'Perhaps someone was able to make an impression of the Queen's key. If so, they could open the lock, if the duplicate were made carefully enough. Someone in that great warren, the Queen's household. Surely she did not wear it all the time. I am a man of honest reputation, sir,' he added. 'Ask all who know me. A simple carpenter in his workshop.'

'Like Our Lord himself,' Barak said, straight-faced.

✝

BARAK ACCOMPANIED ME back out into the courtyard, the guard assigned us walking a little behind. 'Jesu,' Barak said. 'All that just to clothe a few women.'

'More than a few, I think. The ladies are granted the cloth, but pay for the work themselves.'

He stood rocking on his heels. 'That cofferer, he looked worried.'

'Yes. And he was Chairman of his guild last year. That's an expensive business, as he said.'

'He'll be well paid in this job.'

'It would be an expense, even so. And with the value of money falling, and all the taxes to pay for the war that are due this year, everyone has to be careful. He may have need of money.' I slowed. 'Could he have made a second copy for someone else? He did not know the Queen wore the only key constantly round her neck.' I considered. 'I think we'll let him sweat a little.'

'It would be a dangerous matter, stealing from the Queen. He'd hang if he was caught.'

'We both know the things people are capable of risking for the sake of money. Especially those who have gained status and wish to keep it.'

Barak looked at me askance. 'You said *we'll* let him sweat a little.'

'A slip of the tongue, I'm sorry. I told you, I just wanted your help with the chest and lock.'

He looked around the courtyard. Another cart was unloading. 'Jesu,' he said again, 'all this to keep fine clothes on the backs of great ladies. Just as well we didn't bring Tamasin. We'd never have got her out.'

'Remember she doesn't know you're here. And would be displeased if she did.'

'I won't forget. What do you want to see the embroiderer for?'

I sighed. He was interested now; he would not easily let it go. 'I'm only trying to trace a piece of fine silk sleeve Nicholas found, that may be connected to the case,' I answered. 'The embroiderer may be able to help me, perhaps suggest who might have made it.'

'If he gives you a name you may need someone to pay him a visit.'

'I think that might be a job for Nicholas. He found the sleeve, after all.'

Barak looked disappointed, then nodded. 'You're right, it's a job for a junior.'

'And now I have an appointment with the embroiderer.'

He fingered his beard, reluctant to leave, but I raised my eyebrows. 'All right,' he said, shrugging his shoulders, and quickly walked away to the gate.

✝

I NODDED TO the guard and he took me back into the hall, knocking at another side door before entering. Within, a man was working at a desk set close by the window to get the best light. He was embroidering flowers on a piece of fabric, flowers so tiny he needed to look through a large magnifying glass on a stand. To my surprise, he was a big, black-bearded fellow, though I saw his fingers were long and delicate. He stood up at my entrance, wincing a little. For a man of his height, a life spent constantly hunched over was a recipe for a bad back.

'Master Gullym,' I asked, 'the Queen's head embroiderer?'

'I am.' His voice had a Welsh lilt.

'Matthew Shardlake. I am investigating the theft of a jewel from the Queen.'

'I'd heard something about a ring gone missing.' Gullym sounded curious, but unlike Barwic, unconcerned. But of course he was not under any suspicion. I took the piece of torn silk and laid it on the desk. 'We think this may belong to the thief. Is there any way of identifying who made it?'

Gullym picked up the scrap of silk, wrinkling his features in distaste, for it was a little dirty now. 'Looks like an English design,' he said. 'Very fine, expensive. Someone in the embroiderers' guild made it, I'd warrant.' Carefully he slid the delicate silk he was working on from under the magnifying glass and replaced it with the piece of cuff. 'Yes, very well made indeed.'

'If the maker of this piece could tell me who commissioned it, it might help us. They would gain the favour of the Queen,' I added.

Gullym nodded. 'I can write you a list of names. Perhaps a dozen embroiderers in London could have made this. It was done recently, I would say, that design of little vines has only been popular this year.'

'Thank you.'

With slow, deliberate steps, Gullym crossed to a desk, wincing again as he moved. He took quill and paper and wrote out a list of names and addresses, then handed it to me. 'I think these are all the people who might help you.' He smiled complacently. 'I have been in the guild since I came to London thirty years ago, I know everyone.'

I looked at the list. Someone would have to visit all these London shops.

'Thank you, Master Gullym,' I said. 'By the way, I could not help but notice you have some problems with your back.'

'Goes with the job, sir.'

'I do, too, as perhaps you may imagine.'

Gullym nodded tactfully.

'There is a physician who has helped me much. He practises down at Bucklersbury, Dr Guy Malton.'

'I have been thinking I should see someone. It gets bad in the afternoons.'

'I can recommend Dr Malton. Tell him I sent you.'

Chapter Seventeen

THAT EVENING, AFTER DINNER, I rode down to Bucklersbury to visit Guy. We had not parted on the best of terms three nights before, and I wanted to try and mend fences. I also hoped he might tell me about that name, Bertano.

The cloud had disappeared during the afternoon and the sun was out again, setting now, casting long shadows on the row of apothecaries' shops. Although Guy had come originally from Spain and qualified as a physician in the great French university of Louvain, his status as a foreigner — a Moor — and a former monk, had meant a long struggle for acceptance as a member of the College of Physicians. Before qualifying, he had practised as an apothecary and, although he now had a large practice and the status of an English denizen and could have moved to a good-sized house, he preferred to stay here; partly because of his old monkish vow of poverty, and because he was getting old and preferred the familiar.

As I dismounted and tied Genesis to the rail outside his house, I reflected that, apart from Guy, all my friends and contacts now were either reformers or people who preferred to keep out of the religious struggles. But I knew there were plenty in London, and many more in the countryside, who would welcome a return to the Catholic church.

Francis Sybrant, the plump, grey-haired man of sixty

who served as Guy's general assistant these days, answered my knock. I liked Francis; he had worked for a neighbouring apothecary and when the man's business failed last year had come to work for Guy. He was grateful to have found a new berth at his age. A cheerful fellow, he was a good counter to Guy's habitual melancholy.

'Master Shardlake.' He bowed.

'God give you good evening, Francis. Is Master Guy at home?'

'In his study. Working with his books as usual of an evening.' He led me down the narrow hall, knocking gently on the door of Guy's study. Guy was sitting at his desk, reading his copy of Vesalius, with its gruesome anatomical diagrams, using the light of a candle to compare what was on the page with a human thigh bone he held up. He put it down carefully and stood. 'Matthew. This is a surprise.'

'I hope I am not interrupting you.'

'No. My eyes are getting tired.' He pinched the bridge of his nose. 'Francis says I should get spectacles, but I cannot face the thought somehow.'

'I am sorry I had to leave you so suddenly on Friday. After we – ' I hesitated – 'disagreed.'

He smiled sadly. 'That argument resounds all over England, does it not?'

'I was not myself that day.'

'I understand. You still look tired. A glass of hippocras?'

'That would be welcome. I have been working hard.'

Guy called to Francis, who fetched two mugs of warm spiced wine. I sat looking into mine then said, 'My old foe Stephen Bealknap is dead. A growth in his guts.'

Guy crossed himself. 'God pardon him.'

I smiled sadly. 'He did not want God's pardon. I was with him near the end, he said he had no faith. He has left all his money to build a great memorial to himself in Lincoln's Inn chapel.'

'Had he no family?'

'Nor friends. Nor God.'

'That is sad.'

'Yes.' I looked into my wine again, then pulled myself together. 'Guy, there is a piece of information I seek. About a foreign name. I have only my Latin and poor French, and with your experience of languages I hope you may be able to help me.'

'If I can.'

'In strict confidence.'

'Of course.'

'It has come up in the context of something I am working on. Reported second-hand. The name sounds foreign, and may be mispronounced, but I wondered if you could guess its origin.'

'What is the name?'

'Jurony Bertano. Could it be Spanish?'

He smiled. 'No. That is an Italian name. The first name is Gurone, spelt G-U-R-O-N-E.'

'Close enough then.'

'One of the Italian merchant community in London, perhaps?'

'Possibly.' I gave him a serious look. 'But I cannot discuss the matter.'

'I understand. The rules of confidentiality.'

I nodded unhappily. We were silent for a moment. Then I said, 'You know, on the way here I was thinking how few Catholic or traditionalist friends I have now. These last years most people have withdrawn into one circle or the other, have they not? Often without even thinking about it?'

'For safety, yes, sadly they have. I have few patients among the radicals or reformers. My practice began with people from – dare I say – my side, and they refer their friends to me, and so it goes on. It is probably much the same with you.'

'It is. Though, by the way, I have recommended you to someone else with back troubles. An embroiderer from the Queen's court.'

He smiled. 'A reformist sympathizer, then.'

'I have no idea.' I looked up at him. 'Do you ever doubt, Guy, that your view of God is the right one?'

'I have been prey to doubt all my life,' he said seriously. 'For a time, as once I told you, I doubted God's very existence. But I believe that if faith and doubt battle together within a human soul, that soul becomes the stronger and more honest for it.'

'Perhaps. Though I have far more doubt than faith these days.' I hesitated. 'You know, I have always considered that people who were unshakeable in their faith, on either side, to be the most dangerous sort of men. But just recently I wonder whether that is wrong, and rather it is those, like some of the highest at court – Wriothesley, or Rich – who shift from one side to the other to further their ambitions, who are truly the worst men.'

'What are you involved in now, Matthew?' Guy asked quietly.

I answered with sudden passion, 'Something I must protect my friends from knowing about.'

He sat silent for a moment before saying, 'If I can help, at any time –'

'You are a true friend.' Yet one whose conscience placed him on the other side of the divide from Catherine Parr, I thought. To change the subject, I said, 'Tell me what you are trying to learn from that old bone. Something far more useful to humanity than anything lawyers or Privy Councillors do, I'll warrant.'

✝

NEXT MORNING, I left home early to visit chambers before going on to Whitehall Palace. Everyone — Barak, Nicholas and Skelly — was already there and working. I felt grateful to them. John Skelly had always been a hard and loyal worker, and Nicholas, given a little trust, was responding well, while Barak was relishing being in charge. As I came in he was giving Nicholas a heap of case papers to be filed on the shelves. 'And don't lose any conveyances this time,' he said cheerfully.

I thanked them all for being in early. 'Nicholas,' I said, 'there is a particular job I would have you do for me.' I gave him the list the embroiderer Gullym had prepared the day before, together with the piece of silk, carefully wrapped in paper. I added some shillings from my purse, the copper already shining through the silver on the King's nose. 'I want you to visit the embroiderers on this list and see whether any of them can identify this work. It was likely made by one of them. Say that I have consulted with Master Gullym, who is one of the most important members of the Embroiderers' Guild. Do not reveal what it is about. Can you do that? Use your gentlemanly charm?'

Barak gave a snort of laughter. 'Charm? From that long lad?'

Nicholas ignored him. 'Certainly, Master Shardlake.'

'This morning, if you would.'

'At once.' Nicholas took the pile of work from his desk and dumped it back on Barak's. 'Afraid I'll have to leave you with these,' he said with a cheery smile.

✝

THIS TIME, I caught a wherry upriver to the Whitehall Palace Common Stairs, donning my robe with the Queen's badge as we approached. At the Common Stairs, watermen unloading goods for the palace mingled with servants and visitors. A guard checked my name as usual and directed me to the King's Guard Chamber. I walked along a corri-dor adjoining the Great Kitchens. Through open doors I glimpsed cooks and scullions preparing meals for the sev-eral hundred people entitled to dine in the Great Hall and lodgings. They wore no badges of office, only cheap linen clothes, and in the July heat some worked stripped to the waist. I passed on, through the Great Hall with its magnifi-cent hammer-beam roof, and out into the courtyard.

It was dole day, and officials from the almonry stood at the main gate handing packets of food to a crowd of beggars, who were being closely watched by the guards. The remains of each palace meal, which consisted of far more than any one man could eat, were usually distributed daily to hospitals and charitable organizations, but twice a week the 'broken meats' were given out at the gate, a sign of the King's gener-osity.

Though most in the courtyard ignored the scene, going about their business as usual, I saw that two men were watching. I recognized both from the burning four days ago. One, in silken cassock and brown fur stole, was Bishop Stephen Gardiner. Close to, his dour countenance was truly formidable: heavy, frowning brows, bulbous nose and wide, broad-lipped mouth. Standing with him was the King's Secretary, William Paget. As usual, he wore a brown robe and cap; the robe had a long collar of miniver, thick snow-white fur with black spots. He ran the fingers of one square hand over it softly, as though stroking a pet.

I heard Gardiner say, 'Look at that woman, shamelessly

pushing her way past the men, thrusting out her claws at the food. Did this city not have sufficient demonstration at Smithfield that women must keep their place?'

Paget said, 'We can show them again if need be.' They made no attempt to lower their voices, quite happy to be overheard. Gardiner continued frowning at the beggar crowd; that glowering disposition seemed to be how this man of God turned his face to the world. Paget, though, seemed only half-interested in the scene. As I passed them I heard him say, 'Thomas Seymour is back from the wars.'

'That man of proud conceit,' Gardiner replied contemptuously.

Paget smiled, a thin line of white teeth in his thick beard. 'He will get himself in trouble before he's done.'

I walked on. I remembered the ladies talking about Thomas Seymour in the Queen's Privy Chamber. Brother of the leading reformist councillor, Edward Seymour, now Lord Hertford, Catherine Parr would have married him after her second husband died, had not the King intervened. I knew the Queen and Seymour had been carefully kept apart since, with Seymour often sent on naval or diplomatic missions. I had had dealings with him before, not pleasant ones. Paget was right, he was a foolish and dangerous man, a drag on his ambitious brother. I wondered what the Queen would be feeling about his return.

Again I passed into the King's Guard Chamber, up the stairs, and through to the Presence Chamber. The magnificence everywhere still astounded me whenever I paused to let it. The intricacy, colour and variety of the decoration struck me afresh; the eye would rest for a moment on some design on a pillar, drawn to the intricate detail of the vine leaves painted on it, only to be at once distracted by a tapestry of a classical scene hung on a nearby wall, a riot of colour. My gaze was drawn again to the portrait of the King and his family; there was Mary, and behind her Jane Fool. I passed through, attracting no notice; a hunchback lawyer from the Queen's Learned Council, come no doubt to discuss a matter connected with her lands.

The guard checked me through into the Queen's Privy Chamber. Again a group of ladies sat sewing in the window. Once more Edward Seymour's wife, Lady Hertford, gave me a haughty look. The Duchess of Suffolk's spaniel saw me and gave a little bark. The Duchess scolded it. 'Quiet, foolish Gardiner! 'Tis only the strange-looking lawyer come again.'

The inner door opened, and Lord Parr beckoned me in.

✝

LORD PARR WENT to stand beside the Queen. She sat in her chair cushioned with crimson velvet, under her cloth of estate. Today she wore a dress in royal purple, with a low-cut bodice, the forepart decorated with hundreds of tiny Tudor roses. She was laughing at the antics of the third person in the room: dressed all in white, Jane Fool was executing a clumsy dance in front of her, waving a white wand. I exchanged a quick glance with Lord Parr. Jane ignored us, continuing with her steps, kicking up her legs. It amazed me that intelligent adults, let alone the highest in the land, could laugh at such a scene, but then it struck me that amid the formality of the court, with the endless careful watching of words and gestures, the antics of a fool could provide a welcome relief.

The Queen glanced at us and nodded to Jane. 'Enough for now, my dear. I have business with my uncle and this gentleman.'

'This gentleman,' Jane mimicked, giving me an exaggerated bow. 'This hunchback gentleman frightened me, he would have had Ducky taken away.'

I said nothing; I knew licence to insult and mock was part of a fool's role. Nonetheless the Queen frowned. 'That is enough, Jane.'

'May I not finish my dance?' The little woman pouted. 'One minute more, I beg your majesty.'

'Very well, but just a minute,' the Queen replied impatiently. Jane Fool continued the dance and then, with a skilled athleticism I would not have expected, bent over and performed a handstand, her dress falling down to reveal a linen undergarment and fat little legs. I frowned. Surely this was going too far.

I became conscious that someone else had entered the room through an inner door. I turned and found myself looking at the magnificently dressed figure of the Lady Elizabeth, the King's second daughter. Lord Parr bowed deeply to her and I followed suit. I had met Elizabeth the year before, in the company of the Queen, to whom she was close. She had grown since then; almost thirteen, she was tall and the outline of budding breasts could be seen under the bodice of her dress. It was a splendid concoction; crimson, decorated with flowers, the forepart and under-sleeves gold and white. A jewelled French hood was set on her light auburn hair.

Elizabeth's long, clever face had matured, too; despite her pale colouring I saw in her features a resemblance to her disgraced, long-dead mother, Anne Boleyn. She had acquired, too, an adult's poise, no longer displaying the gawkishness of a girl. She stood looking at Jane's antics with haughty disapproval.

The Queen seemed surprised to see her. 'My dear. I thought you were still with Master Scrots.'

Elizabeth turned to her stepmother. 'I have been standing still for hours on end,' she answered petulantly. 'I insisted upon a rest. Will the painting of this picture never end? Kat Ashley that is attending me fell asleep!'

'It is important you have your own portrait, child,' the Queen said gently. 'It helps establish your position, as we have discussed.'

Jane Fool sat down on the floor, pouting, clearly annoyed at the Lady Elizabeth for taking the attention of her audience. Elizabeth glanced at her, then turned to the Queen. 'Can you ask Jane Fool to go? She is unseemly, waving her great bottom in the air like that.'

Jane, quick as a flash, appealed to the Queen in a tone of injured innocence. 'Your majesty, will you let the Lady speak to me so, I that seek only to entertain you?'

Elizabeth's face darkened. 'God's death,' she snapped in sudden temper, 'you do not entertain me! Get out!'

'Leave now, Jane.' The Queen spoke hastily. Jane looked alarmed for a moment, then picked up her wand and left without another word.

The anger left the Lady Elizabeth's face, and she smiled at Lord Parr. 'My good Lord, it is a pleasure to see you.' She looked at me. I bowed deeply. When I rose, her dark eyes were puzzled for a moment but then her face cleared. 'This gentleman, too, I know. Yes, Master Shardlake, you and I once had an agreeable discussion about the law. I thought long on it.'

'I am greatly pleased it interested you, my Lady, though I am surprised you remember.'

'God has blessed me with a good memory.' Elizabeth smiled complacently. If she was half a woman in body now, she was more than half in mind and demeanour. Yet her remarkably long fingers fiddled nervously with the rope of pearls at her waist.

She said, 'You told me that lawyers acting even for wicked clients have a duty to find what justice there is in their case and bring it to court.'

'I did.'

'And that it is a virtuous undertaking.'

'Yes, my Lady.' I thought suddenly of the Slanning case. The inspection of the wall painting was due to take place tomorrow. Was fighting that case virtuous?

'But it seems to me,' Lady Elizabeth continued, 'for that to be so, there must be at least *some* virtue in the case.'

'Yes, my Lady, you are right.' And in the Slanning case, I realized there was no virtue on either side, only hatred. Young though she was, Elizabeth had nailed a central point.

'Elizabeth,' the Queen said gently, 'will you not go back to Master Scrots? You know the portrait is almost done. And there is business I must conduct here. Come back in an hour, perhaps.'

Elizabeth nodded and gave her stepmother an affectionate smile. 'Very well. And I am sorry for shouting at Jane Fool, but I fear that, unlike you and my sister, I do not find her amusing.' She gave me a brief nod. 'Master Shardlake. My Lord Parr.'

We bowed again as she left by the inner door. The Queen closed her eyes for a second. 'I am sorry for that scene. It appears I cannot even control the people in my own privy quarters.' I noticed the strain and tension writ large on her face.

Lord Parr addressed her. 'I told you what Master Shard-lake said about Jane Fool. About her having been in your chambers that night, about her closeness to the Lady Mary.'

The Queen shook her head firmly. 'No. Jane Fool knew

nothing of my book, and would not have had the wit to steal it.'

'Perhaps the Lady Mary would.'

'Never. Mary is my friend.' She frowned sadly, then said, 'Or at least not my enemy. The trouble over her mother, Catherine of Aragon, is long over.'

'Well, we may have some answers soon.' Lord Parr smiled at me, rubbing his thin hands together. 'The Captain of the Guard spoke to the man who was on duty guarding the Queen's lodgings on the night the book was stolen. And mark this, it was not Zachary Gawger, whose odd behaviour Mary Odell reported. It was another man entirely, called Michael Leeman. It seems there was a substitution. The captain has had Gawger placed in custody, though on my instructions has asked no questions of him yet. And Leeman was to be taken when he came on duty this morning. That was at six; he will have him under guard now. I ordered both to be held for you to question, Master Shardlake.' He smiled triumphantly at the Queen. 'I think we are about to find the answer.'

'I hope so.' But she spoke doubtfully. Lord Parr gave a quick frown of impatience. The Queen turned to me.

'First, Master Shardlake, may we go over the other developments? My uncle has told me, but I would like to hear first-hand from you.'

'Quickly,' her uncle murmured.

Rapidly, I summarized everything that had happened since we last met: Elias's murder, the disappearance of Greening's three friends, Bealknap's strange last words, my suspicion that all was not quite right with Barwic the carpenter. I added that the mysterious name Bertano was Italian in origin, and suggested that perhaps we could find out whether the name was known among the Italian merchants in the city.

'I will arrange that,' Lord Parr said. 'Discreetly. First, though, let us see what these guards have to say. And if after that there remains any question of the carpenter's involvement, I will come with you to Baynard's Castle and speak to the man myself.'

'But Lord Parr, I thought you wanted to keep your involvement in the enquiries to a minimum.'

'I do. But those at Baynard's Castle are household staff, responsible to me, and therefore frightened of me.' He smiled tightly. 'As for the docks, Cecil has persuaded one of the customs house officials to inform us if any of Greening's three friends are spotted and try to flee on a ship. All goods and persons entering or leaving the country have to go through there. And Cecil has also got one of the dockers to keep an eye on everything that happens on the waterfront. With a promise of a goodly sum in gold if these jewel thieves are captured.' He smiled wryly.

'That poor apprentice boy,' the Queen said. 'I cannot understand why he should say he was killed for Anne Askew. I made sure she and I never met.' She looked sadly at her uncle. 'At least there I was properly careful.'

Lord Parr nodded. 'I have spoken to my old friend Sir Edmund Walsingham,' he said. 'I am going to the Tower tomorrow. I have invented a piece of household business to justify the visit.' He turned to me. 'You will come too. We shall see what we can dig out about the news of Mistress Askew's torture being leaked. But now – the guard.'

The Queen, however, seemed reluctant to let me go. 'This man Bealknap?' she asked. 'Which side did he follow in religion?'

'Neither. But he was associated with Richard Rich.'

'Those words of his. Did they sound like a warning, or a threat?'

'Neither, your majesty. Merely a last gloating, a hope to see me charged with heresy, and you.'

Lord Parr said firmly, 'That's surely what it was.'

'Bealknap could not have been involved with the theft,' I said. 'He has been ill in his room for many weeks.'

'Then forget him,' Lord Parr said resolutely. He turned to the Queen. She swallowed, gripping the arms of her chair. Her uncle put his hand on hers. 'And now,' he said, looking at me, 'the Captain of the Guard, Master Mitchell, is waiting for you. With his prisoners. Question them. Alone, of course.'

Chapter Eighteen

THE GUARDROOM, I WAS TOLD, was on the other side of the Presence Chamber. As I crossed the chamber, a plump middle-aged man, sweating in a furred robe, stepped into my path, doffed a feathered cap and gave me an exaggerated bow. 'Good master lawyer,' he said in honeyed tones, 'I saw you come from the Queen's Privy Chamber. I regret interrupting you, but I am an old friend of the late Lord Latimer, visiting London. My son, a goodly lad, wishes to serve at court—'

'Such things are not my business,' I answered curtly. I left him clutching his cap disconsolately and made my way quickly towards the door to which I had been directed. 'Sent to Master Mitchell from Lord Parr,' I said to the yeoman standing with his halberd outside. He opened the door and led me into a small anteroom, where two black-robed guards sat playing dice. He crossed the room to another door and knocked. A deep voice called, 'Come in.' The guard bowed and I entered a cramped office.

A strongly built, fair-haired man in a black robe sat behind a desk, the Queen's badge set on his cap. My heart fell when he looked up; I could tell from his sombre expression that he had no good news.

'Serjeant Shardlake?' He waved a hand to a chair. 'Please sit. I am David Mitchell, Head of the Queen's Guard.'

'God give you good morrow. I believe Lord Parr has

explained that I wish to question Michael Leeman, who was on duty the night the Queen's b—, I mean, ring – was stolen.' I cursed myself. I had nearly said 'book'. That one word, uttered to the wrong person, could bring everything crashing down.

Mitchell, for all that he was a big man, looked uncomfortable, somehow shrunken inside his uniform. He spoke quietly. 'I have Zachary Gawger in custody here. But I am afraid we do not have Michael Leeman.'

I sat bolt upright. 'What?'

Mitchell coughed awkwardly. 'I checked the rotas yesterday afternoon, when Lord Parr asked me to. Gawger and Leeman were both on the evening shift on the sixth of July, and it was Leeman that was assigned to stand guard at the door of the Queen's Privy Chamber. Yet according to Mary Odell it had actually been Gawger. Gawger was on duty last night and I had him immediately placed in custody. Leeman was supposed to be on duty at six, but he never arrived and when I sent for him, his chamber in the guards' lodgings was empty. His possessions had gone too.'

I closed my eyes. 'How did this happen?'

It was strange to see the Guard Captain, a military man of considerable authority, squirm in his chair. 'Apparently one of the other soldiers had seen Gawger taken into custody. He went to spread the news, and apparently Leeman was in the wardroom, heard the gossip. I was not quick enough. The sergeant I sent to arrest him must have arrived minutes after he left.' He looked at me. 'Lord Parr shall have my resignation this morning.'

'Is there any indication where Leeman may have gone?'

'He was checked out of the palace at eight last night. He said he was going into the city for the evening; he often did, it was not remarked upon, though the guard on duty noted he was carrying a large bag. Containing the Queen's lost ring, no doubt,' he added bitterly.

I stared up at the ceiling. A fourth man disappeared now. I turned back to Mitchell. There was no point in being angry with him. I little doubted Lord Parr would accept his resignation.

I said, 'I think the best thing will be for Gawger to tell me all he knows.'

'Yes.' He nodded at a door to the side of the office. 'He is in there. Christ's mother!' he spat in sudden anger. 'It will be his last morning at Whitehall; tonight he will be in the Fleet Prison, the rogue.'

I looked at him. 'That is for Lord Parr to decide.'

Mitchell got up slowly, opened the door, and dragged a young man into the office. He was dressed only in undershirt and hose, his brown hair and short beard were bedraggled and there was a bruise on his cheek. He was tall and well-built, like all the guards, but he made a sorry figure now. Mitchell thrust him against the wall. Gawger sagged, looking at me fearfully.

'Tell the Queen's investigator all you told me,' Mitchell said. 'I shall be waiting outside.' He looked at the young man with angry disgust, then turned to me. 'I should tell you, Master Shardlake, that during the twelvemonth Gawger has worked here I have had cause to discipline him for drunkenness and gambling. He is one of those young fools from the country whose head has been turned by the court. I was already thinking of dismissing him. Would that I had.' He glared at Gawger. 'Spit out the whole story, churl!'

With that, Mitchell turned and left his office. The young man remained cowering against the wall. He took a deep breath, then gulped nervously.

'Well?' I asked. 'Best you tell the whole truth. If I have to tell Captain Mitchell I have doubts, he may be rough with you again.' It was no more than the truth.

Gawger took another deep breath. 'About three weeks ago, sir – it was at the start of the month – one of my fellow guards approached me in lodgings. Michael Leeman. I did not know him well – he had not made himself popular, he was one of the radicals, always telling us to amend our souls.'

'Really?' I leaned forward with interest.

'He said the palace soldiery were mired in sin and that when his term was done he would go to new friends he had, godly friends.'

'Do you know who they were?'

Gawger shook his head. 'I'm not sure. But they lived somewhere around St Paul's, I think. He was always off there during his free time. But I steer clear of talk about religion. It's dangerous.' He stopped, breathing rapidly now, perhaps realizing that he was in deep danger. The rules governing the Queen's Guard were strict, and I had little doubt that what Gawger was about to confess to constituted treason. I took a deep breath.

He continued, a whining, desperate note in his voice now. 'I – I have had money troubles, sir. I have been playing cards with some of my fellows. I lost money. I thought I could win it back, but lost more. I appealed to my father; he has helped me before, but he said he had no more to spare. If I did not find the money soon I knew there would be a scandal, I would lose this post, have to return home in disgrace – ' Suddenly he laughed wildly. 'But that was nothing to what will happen now, is it sir? I gambled everything on this throw, and lost.'

'And exactly what was this throw Leeman wanted you to make?'

'He was in the middle of a fortnight's evening duty. He

told me he had had a dalliance with one of the chamber servant women and had left a pair of monogrammed gloves, that could be traced to him, in the Queen's Long Gallery. He had taken this girl in there when no one else was around. If the gloves were discovered both of them would be dismissed.'

I raised my eyebrows. 'And him such a man of God?'

'I was surprised, sir, but men who lust fiercely after religion can often turn out to have strong lusts of the flesh as well, can they not?' He gulped again, then added, 'Leeman showed me a bag with ten sovereigns, old ones of pure gold.' The man's eyes lit up for a moment at the memory. 'He said it was mine if I would take his place as guard outside the door to the privy lodgings, just for a few minutes, while he fetched his gloves. We would both be on duty in the Presence Chamber for several days, and could change places when the Queen and her servants were absent. He said it needed to be done as soon as possible. But it was many days before we were able to do it.'

'So the switch happened on the sixth?'

'Yes, sir.'

I leaned back in my chair. It all fitted. Somehow Leeman had found out about the *Lamentation*, and had decided – why, I had no idea – to steal it. He had looked for an accomplice, found the wretched Gawger, and taken his opportunity when it came on the 6th of July. He was a religious radical. He had friends by St Paul's. Was he a member of Greening's group? I looked at Gawger. Such a young man as this could easily be won over with the promise of gold. And Leeman's story was plausible; even in July, carrying silk gloves of fine design was common round the court as yet another symbol of status. But how had Leeman learned of the book? Why had he stolen it? And how had he got a key to that chest?

I asked Gawger, 'How would Leeman know for sure when the Queen's lodgings were unoccupied?'

'Everything runs according to routine in this place, sir. In the evenings, the servants arrive and depart at fixed hours. If the Queen is called to the King, as she frequently is in the evenings, her personal attendants go with her and for a short time nobody is present in her apartments. I was on duty, but in reserve rather than at post. My arrangement with Leeman was that I would remain in the guardroom – the room you came through just now – and if the Queen was called away he would run across to tell me. Then I would take his place while he went inside for a few minutes. That would not be noted; there is always someone in reserve in case a guard is taken ill or has to relieve himself and cannot wait. And at that time of night, if the Queen was with the King, there was normally nobody in the Presence Chamber either. There wasn't that night.'

'Go on.'

Gawger took a deep breath. 'Just before nine, Leeman came into the Guard Chamber. I was the only one there. I remember how set his face was. He nodded to me, that was our signal. Then the two of us went back to the Presence Chamber and I took his position by the door while he slipped inside. I waited at the door – in a sweat, I may say.'

'Had you had a drink?' I asked.

'Just a little, sir, to give me courage. But I had only been there a minute when Mistress Odell arrived. I tried to delay her – '

'I know,' I said. 'You pretended her name was not on the list, and when she insisted on going in, as you opened the door you said loudly that everything must be done properly, no doubt to alert Leeman. She told me. It was that which first aroused my suspicions.'

Gawger lowered his head. 'Leeman must have hidden

somewhere till Mary Odell had passed by him. Then he came out again.'

'Was he carrying anything?'

'Not that I could see.'

I thought, the manuscript was small, he could have concealed it under his voluminous cloak. Suddenly I felt angry. 'What if Leeman had been unbalanced? What if he had planned to murder the Queen, who you are sworn to protect? What then, master gambler?'

Gawger bowed his head again. 'I have no answer, sir,' he said miserably.

I went across to the door. Mitchell was waiting outside. I let him in and told him all that Gawger had told me; both, of course, thought that at issue was a stolen ring. 'It seems you have your answer, Serjeant Shardlake,' Mitchell said bleakly.

'I would rather have Leeman as well,' I answered curtly. 'Now I will report back to Lord Parr. Do not have this man publicly accused yet. Is there somewhere you can keep him?'

'Surely now he should be imprisoned and tried for conspiracy in this theft, and for endangering the Queen's person.'

'Lord Parr must say,' I answered firmly.

Mitchell stood up, grabbed the wretched guard, and thrust him back into the antechamber. He returned and sat behind his desk again, looking haggard. I said, 'I want this kept quiet till you receive further orders.'

'I place myself in the hands of the Queen. It is my responsibility Leeman is gone.' Mitchell shook his head. 'But it is hard sometimes, having to take on these young country gentlemen because their fathers have influence. And these last months have been terrible. All the rumours – I have served the Queen loyally these three years, but since the spring I have never known when I may be ordered to arrest her.'

I did not answer. I could feel no sympathy for him. However well organized, however disciplined a system of security might be, it only took one slip from a man in a crucial position for the line to be broken. 'Tell me more about Leeman,' I said eventually.

'His father is a landowner in Kent. He has some distant connection to the Parrs through their Throckmorton cousins, one of whom petitioned for a post for him. I interviewed young Leeman last year. I thought him suitable; as a gentleman, he was well trained in the arts of combat and he is a big, handsome young fellow, well set up. Though even then he struck me as a little serious. And godly; he said his main interest was the study of religion. Well, being a reformer was no hindrance then.' He sighed. 'And he was a good and loyal guard for two years. Never a hint of trouble, except that twice he had to be warned against evangelizing among his fellow guards. It annoyed them. I warned him early this year such talk was becoming dangerous.' Mitchell leaned forward. 'He is the last one I would have expected to have concocted a plot to steal one of the Queen's jewels. And Leeman is not rich, his family are poor and distant cousins of the Queen, delighted to have a son in such a post. How could he have come by such a huge sum as ten sovereigns to offer Gawger?'

'I do not know.'

Mitchell swallowed. 'I expect there will be a search for Leeman now.'

'It rests with the Queen and Lord Parr,' I said quietly, standing up. 'For now, keep Gawger close confined – and tell nobody.' I bowed and left him.

✝

I RETURNED TO the Queen's Privy Chamber. Lord Parr was pacing up and down, the Queen still sitting beneath her cloth of estate, playing with the pearl that once belonged to Catherine Howard. Her spaniel, Rig, lay at her feet.

I told them what had happened with Mitchell and Gawger.

'So,' Lord Parr said heavily. 'Thanks to you, we now know *who*, but not *how* or *why*. And thanks to that fool Mitchell, Leeman is gone.'

'As for the how, I think another word with the carpenter is called for. Especially now we know Leeman had money to wave before people. As to the why – I begin to wonder whether a whole group of radical Protestants may be involved in this, reaching from Leeman to the printer Greening. But that brings us back to the question of why. Why would they steal the book?'

'And how did they come to know of its existence in the first place?' Lord Parr asked.

Suddenly the Queen leaned forward, her silks rustling, and burst into tears: loud, racking sobs. Her uncle went and put a hand on her arm. 'Kate, Kate,' he said soothingly. 'We must be calm.'

She lifted her face. It was full of fear, tears smudging the white ceruse on her cheeks. The sight of her in such a state squeezed at my heart.

'Be calm!' she cried. 'How? When the theft has already caused two deaths! And whoever these people are who stole my book, it looks as though someone else was after them and has it now! All because of my sin of pride in not taking Archbishop Cranmer's advice and destroying the manuscript! *Lamentation*! Lamentation indeed!' She took a long, shuddering breath, then turned a face of misery upon us. 'Do you know what the worst thing is, for me who wrote a book urging people to forget the temptations of the world and seek salvation? That even now, with those poor men dead, it is not of them that I think, nor my family and friends in danger, but of myself, being put in the fire, like Anne Askew! I imagine myself chained to the stake, I hear the crackle as the faggots are lit, I smell the smoke and feel the flames.' Her voice rose, frantic now. 'I have feared it since the spring. After the King humiliated Wriothesley I thought it was over, but now – ' She pounded her dress with a fist. 'I am so selfish, selfish! I, who thought the Lord had favoured me with grace – ' She was shouting now. The spaniel at her feet whined anxiously.

Lord Parr took her firmly by the shoulders, looking into her swollen face. 'Hold fast, Kate! You have managed it these last months, do not crumble now. And do not shout.' He inclined his head to the door. 'The guard may hear.'

The Queen nodded, and took a number of long, whooping breaths. Gradually, she brought herself under control, forcing her shaking body to be still. She looked at me, ventured a watery smile. 'I imagine you did not think to see your Queen like this, Matthew?' She patted her uncle's hand. 'There, good my lord. It is over. I am myself again. I must wash my face and get one of the maids to make it up again before I venture outside.'

'It sore grieves me to see you in such distress, your majesty,' I said quietly. But a thought had come to me. 'Lord Parr. You told her majesty that if she shouted the guard might hear?'

The Queen's eyes widened in alarm. Lord Parr patted her hand. 'I exaggerated, to calm her. These doors are thick, deliberately so that the Queen may have some privacy. The guard might make out a raised voice, but not each individual word.'

'What if it was a man who shouted?' I said. 'A man with a loud, deep voice, the voice of a preacher, trained to carry far?'

He frowned. 'No man would dare come here and shout at the Queen.'

But the Queen leaned forward, eyes wide, balling a

handkerchief in her palm. 'Archbishop Cranmer,' she said. 'That evening when we argued over the *Lamentation*, and I resisted his arguments, I shouted and – yes – he shouted, too.' She gulped. 'We are good friends, we have discussed matters of faith together many times, and he was very afraid of what could happen if I let the *Lamentation* become public. How many times must he have feared the fire himself these last dozen years? And he was right, as I realize now.' She looked at me again. 'Yes, if the guard outside could have distinguished the words of anyone shouting in here, it would have been the Archbishop's. Telling me that if I tried to publish the *Lamentation* now, the King's anger might know no bounds.'

Lord Parr frowned. 'He had no right – '

I said, 'That was in early June, you told me?'

The Queen nodded. 'Yes.' She frowned. 'The ninth, I think.'

I turned to Lord Parr. 'My lord, do you know the evening duty hours?'

'Four till midnight.'

'It would be interesting to find out who was on duty outside on the night of the argument. Captain Mitchell will have the records.'

The Queen said, aghast, 'Then Leeman might have been outside when the Archbishop and I argued?'

I spoke with quiet intensity. 'And could have heard of the existence of the book, and made his plans to steal it. So long as he was able to get a copy of the key. It all rests on that. My Lord, let us find out who was on duty then. And afterwards, I think we should question the carpenter again.'

✝

IT WAS LEEMAN on duty that night; Mitchell confirmed it. That made it almost certain: he had overheard Cranmer and learned of the existence of the *Lamentation*. Then he had planned, and waited, and bribed. But with what money, I wondered. I felt sure he was not acting alone.

Lord Parr and I left the distraught captain, and took the smaller of the Queen's two barges to Baynard's Castle, the rowmen in her livery sculling fast down the Thames, a herald with a trumpet signalling other craft to get out of the way. Mary Odell had been called to the Queen and would be with her in her private apartments now, making her fit to face the public again.

Lord Parr and I sat opposite each other under the canopy. In the sunlight he looked his age, with pale seamed skin and tired eyes. I ventured, 'My Lord, has her majesty often been – like that?'

He looked me in the eye for a moment, then leaned forward and spoke quietly. 'A few times, these last months. You have little idea of the control and composure she must have. It has always been one of my niece's greatest qualities, that control. But underneath she is a woman of powerful feeling, more so as her faith has grown stronger. And since the spring – the questioning of those close to her, the persecutions, the knowledge that the King might turn on her – yes, she has broken down before. In front of me, and Mary Odell, and her sister. She is lucky to have those she can trust.' He paused and looked at me hard.

'She can trust me, too, my Lord,' I said quietly.

He grimaced. 'For a commoner to see the Queen as you did – well, let us say you are the first. And I pray the last.' He sat up straight, looking over my shoulder. 'Here, the Baynard's Castle steps are close ahead.'

✝

THE TWO OF US had agreed our approach, the words we would use to bring a confession if Barwic was guilty. We had no time to waste. Lord Parr strode through the courtyard and then the central hall, looking stern, all the guards saluting the Queen's Chancellor in turn. He came to the carpenter's door and flung it open. Barwic was planing a length of oak – I noticed little pieces of sawdust in his russet beard – while his assistant sanded another. They both looked up at our entrance, the assistant in astonishment and Barwic, I saw, in fear.

Lord Parr slammed the door shut and stood with his arms folded. He inclined his head to the apprentice. 'Go, boy,' he said bluntly, and the lad fled with a quick bow. Barwic faced us.

'Michael Leeman, the thief, is discovered,' I said, bluntly. 'And his confederate, Zachary Gawger.'

Barwic stood there for a second, his face expressionless, his wild red hair and beard, flecked with sawdust, looking almost comical. Then, like a puppet, he sank slowly to his knees, lowering his head and clasping his work-roughened hands together. From this position he looked up at the Queen's Chancellor, the clasped hands trembling.

'Forgive me, my Lord. At first I only made a copy of the key lest the original be lost. It is not a good thing for a chest containing valuables to have only one key.'

'So you made another secretly and kept it?' I asked. 'Where?'

'Safe, my Lord, safe. In a locked chest to which only I have the key.' All the while he did not shift his gaze from Lord Parr's face.

'Have you ever done this before?'

Barwic looked at me, then turned back to Lord Parr. 'Yes, my Lord, forgive me. If ever I am asked to make a lock with only one key, I make a second. I can show you the place

I keep them all, show you the keys. It was for security only; security, I swear.'

'Then how did Leeman get hold of it?' I asked.

'Stand up when you answer, churl!' Lord Parr snapped. 'I will get a crick in my neck looking down at you.'

Barwic stood, still wringing his hands. 'He came to see me, near three weeks ago. I did not know him, but he wore the uniform of the Queen's Guard. He told me the key to the Queen's chest had been lost, said he had heard I might have another. I – I thought he came on behalf of the Queen, you see—'

Lord Parr brought his hand down on the bench with a bang, sending the plank of wood crashing to the floor. 'Don't lie to me, caitiff! You know well enough a member of the Queen's Guard would have no authority to demand a key. Especially when you kept the very existence of copies a secret!'

The wretched man swallowed nervously. 'I let it be known, to certain people, that I made extra copies of keys. Not officially, but you see – if a key was lost, I could provide a replacement for anyone who lost it.'

'At a price?'

Barwic nodded miserably.

'How long have you been doing this?'

'Since I first became the Queen's carpenter and lock-smith twelve years ago. Perhaps half a dozen times I have provided a spare key to a chest or coffer, usually to a lady who has lost hers. But always to someone who is trusted, sir, and nothing has been stolen in all that time as a consequence. Nothing.'

Lord Parr shook his head. 'Dear God, the Queen's household has been lax.'

'Yes,' I agreed, 'and Michael Leeman, I would wager,

ferreted out where the weak points were. How much did he pay you, Barwic?'

'Ten sovereigns, sir. I – I couldn't resist.' I thought, the same bribe as for Gawger. 'He told me the Queen had gone out and left the key with him for safekeeping and he accidentally dropped it through a gap in the floorboards. He did not want to have them taken up.'

'Did you believe him?' Lord Parr's voice was scornful.

'I was uncertain, my Lord. I told him to come back on the morrow. In the meantime I asked friends at Whitehall for information on Leeman – had he been there long, was he honest? I was told he was known as an honest man, godly. I wouldn't just hand out a key to anybody, sir, I swear.'

Lord Parr gave him a look of contempt. 'No. I imagine you would not, for fear of being hanged. But Michael Leeman *was* a thief. And you are deep in the mire.' He looked at me. 'I will have this man held close at my house for the moment. Come with us, Master Barwic. I'll put you in the charge of a guard, as a man suspected of conspiracy to rob the Queen. And you don't say a word about keys. Leeman, and his confederate, are discovered, but Leeman has escaped and you'll keep all this quiet till he is captured.'

Barwic sank to his knees again. His voice shook. 'Will – will I hang, sir? Please, would you ask the Queen to show mercy? I have a wife, children – it was all the expenses of being Guild Chairman, the taxes for the war – '

Lord Parr bent over him. 'You'll hang if I have any say,' he said brutally. 'Now, come.'

☩

BARWIC WAS PUT in the charge of a guard and led away, sobbing, across Baynard's Castle yard. Another man whose life now lay in ruins. Some men lifting bolts of silk from a cart turned to look at the weeping prisoner being taken away under guard.

'Well,' Lord Parr said quietly. 'You have taken us far, Serjeant Shardlake. We have the whole story of the theft, the how and the who. But still not the why. And who has the damned manuscript now? And why are they keeping quiet about it?'

'I do not know, my Lord. My young assistant is trying to trace the maker of that piece of torn sleeve he found near Greening's print-shop, but for now there are no other leads. We need to catch Greening's friends.'

He stirred the dust of the courtyard with his foot. 'I will send Cecil a detailed description of Leeman; I'll get it from Captain Mitchell. He can add it to those who are to be watched out for.'

'They will likely try to leave under false names.'

'Of course they will,' he said impatiently. 'But the customs house has the descriptions, and if any of them try to board a ship they will be arrested and held close till I can question them.' He shook his head. 'Though they may try to go via Bristol, or Ipswich.'

'That leaves our enquiries in the Tower,' I reflected. 'It may be possible we could find that it was another radical who leaked the truth about Anne Askew. Possibly someone linked to the others.'

He nodded slowly. 'I certainly smell some sort of radical conspiracy here. I wish I knew what it was about.'

'Whatever it was, that original group has been attacked and blown apart.' I looked at him. 'By internal dissension, or perhaps it could even be that someone in the group was a spy, maybe for someone in the conservative camp.'

His eyes widened. 'By God, you could be right. Secretary Paget has the main responsibility for employing spies to watch for internal dissension. But others could be doing the same, on their own account. Someone perhaps with a taste for plotting.'

He looked at me. 'Who are you thinking of?' I asked. 'Sir Richard Rich?'

'He has been assiduous in the heresy hunt.'

I paused, then said, 'My Lord, I am worried about Greening's neighbour, the printer Okedene.'

He inclined his head. 'I think we have got all the information we can out of him.'

'I was thinking of his safety. Two men have been killed already. I wondered if Okedene might also be at risk; whether our enemies, whoever they are, might try to stop his mouth for good.'

'He has told us all he knows. He has no further use.'

'All the same, much is owed to him. Could you not arrange some protection, perhaps a man to lodge in his house?'

'Do you not understand?' Lord Parr burst out. 'I've already told you, I do not have the resources! I cannot help him!' I did not answer, did not dare provoke him further, and he continued. 'Now, the Tower is next.'

'Yes, my Lord.'

'Until he retired recently, the Queen's Vice Chamberlain, my immediate junior in the Queen's household, was Sir Edmund Walsingham. He has also been Constable of the Tower of London for twenty-five years.'

'He combined both jobs?' I asked in surprise.

'Both are ceremonial rather than administrative roles. At the Tower the Constable, Sir Edmund, is a very old friend of mine; in fact he is almost as old as me.' He smiled wryly. 'Naturally he knows how everything works there. I have arranged to visit him tomorrow at eleven; I could not obtain an earlier appointment, though I tried.' He looked at me.

'Now, this is what we shall do. On the pretext that some information is needed for a legal case, we will see if you can get sight of the duty rosters that cover the period when Anne Askew was tortured. Between the twenty-eighth of June, when she was taken there, and the second of July when the rumours first began to fly around London. It will not be easy; I imagine the Tower authorities will be very reticent about what happened. My nephew William, Earl of Essex, tells me no investigation has been ordered by the Privy Council, which is strange. In any event, a good meal and good wine can loosen tongues between friends.'

Eleven o'clock. That would at least allow me time to carry out the Cotterstoke inspection early the next morning. I looked at Lord Parr; the old man's face had become quite animated at the prospect of progress. But I did not want to visit the Tower again. Five years before, thanks to a conspiracy between Rich and Bealknap, I had briefly been imprisoned there. I wondered whether Lord Parr knew about that. But, I reflected, he probably knew everything about me. He looked back at me quizzically. 'Is there a problem?'

'My Lord, forgive me, but the number who know that the Queen has suffered some sort of a theft is growing. News could reach the King. I cannot help wondering – well, whether the Queen might serve her interests best by going now and confessing all to him. He will surely be more merciful than if the book is hawked round the streets and he finds out then that she kept it secret from him.'

Lord Parr rounded on me. In the crowded courtyard he kept his voice low, but his tone was fierce as he spoke. 'You are not qualified to advise her majesty on such a matter. And remember, great danger still threatens her; it is common knowledge on the Privy Council that there is still something going on, secret talks are occurring between Paget and

Gardiner and the King. My nephew William, the Queen's brother, like most of the Privy Council is outside the circle, but something is afoot that keeps Gardiner looking confident despite the failure of the persecution, that makes him look on with a secret smile when William passes him.'

'But the book is not heretical,' I said. 'And Sir Edward Seymour is expected soon at court, as, I heard, is Lord Lisle. Both are reformers, and in alliance with the Parrs they will be strong—'

'It is *not* safe for the Queen to tell the King.' The old man's voice shook with anger and I saw the strain on his face. 'You overstep the mark, sir, by God you do! The alliance between the Parr and Seymour families is none of your business. You know nothing of it, nor of the machinations at court.' He lowered his voice. 'But you should have come to realize, after all these years, that the one thing this King will not tolerate is any suspicion of disloyalty.'

'I only thought to help, my Lord.'

'Then keep your nose out of matters far above your station. And remember, Master Shardlake, you answer to me alone. Be at the Middle Tower gate at eleven tomorrow, with your horse, and wearing your robe.' And with that Lord Parr turned and limped away.

I watched him go, the hot sun beating down on my head. Stepping away, I tripped. I righted myself, yet still the ground seemed to rock under my feet, as it had when the *Mary Rose* foundered. I closed my eyes. The picture that came to my mind, though, was not the great ship turning over, nor the men falling into the sea, but Anne Askew on fire, Anne Askew's head exploding.

Chapter Nineteen

NEXT MORNING I SET OUT early again. The last four days had passed in a blur; but if the Queen's book was to be recovered, time was of the essence. The previous evening I had sent a note to Okedene; I was worried about him. I warned him that Greening's killers were still at large and urged him to make arrangements for his security. Lord Parr had not authorized me to write, but I felt it my duty nevertheless.

Downstairs, Josephine served my breakfast. I wondered again about her difficulties with Martin Brocket, but she seemed cheerful enough today.

Outside it was warm and sunny again. I remembered I was due for dinner at Coleswyn's that evening. I would be at the Tower later in the morning and I thought of cancelling the meal, but decided it might be good to have some ordinary human company after that particular visit.

First I called in at chambers. Barak and Skelly were there working already, doing my work as well as their own. Nicholas had left early, Barak said, to continue checking the embroiderers' shops, having had, apparently, no luck the previous day. His tone was slightly aggrieved; Barak really did not like being kept out of things. I said I was going to the painting inspection, and would also be out in the afternoon now.

'Why don't you just tell that Slanning creature to piss off and get another lawyer since you're so busy?'

'I can't, not without good cause,' I answered stubbornly. 'I've taken on the case, I have to see it through.'

'Even when you have this other thing on your mind?'

'Yes.'

I left him, feeling not a little uneasy.

✟

THE COTTERSTOKE HOUSE was at Dowgate, on the other side of the city, so I rode down Cheapside; the shops were just opening, market traders setting up their stalls. I remembered my last conversation with Coleswyn; our pact to try and bring this case to a decent resolution. It had crossed my mind to make discreet enquiries at the Haberdashers' Guild about the Cotterstoke family history, but that would be unprofessional, and besides I had no time.

Ahead of me I saw another black-robed lawyer riding along slowly, head bowed as though in thought, and realized it was Philip Coleswyn. I caught him up.

'God give you good morrow, Brother Coleswyn.'

'And you. Are you ready for the inspection?'

'My client will be there. And yours?'

'Master Cotterstoke. Oh, undoubtedly.' Coleswyn smiled ironically, then added, 'My wife looks forward to meeting you tonight. Around six, if that is not too late?'

'That would be convenient. I have business in the after-noon.'

We rode on. Coleswyn seemed preoccupied today and spoke little. Then we passed the mouth of an alleyway, where a commotion was taking place. A couple of burly men were bringing out furniture from a house in the alley: a truckle bed, a table, a couple of rickety chairs. They loaded them on a cart, while a woman in cheap wadmol clothing, several small children clinging to her skirts, stood by stony-faced. A middle-aged man was arguing loudly with a large fellow who had a club at his waist and was supervising the removal.

'We're only a month behind with the rent! We've been there twelve years! I can't help it trade's so bad!'

'Not my problem, goodman,' the big fellow answered unsympathetically. 'You're in arrears and you've got to go.'

'People don't want building repairs done this year, not with all the taxes there have been for the war! And the rise in prices – ' The man turned to a little crowd that was gathering. There were murmurs of agreement.

'An eviction,' Coleswyn observed quietly.

'There have been many of those this year.'

The builder's wife suddenly lunged forward and grasped a chest which the two men had brought from the alleyway. 'No!' she cried. 'That's my husband's tools!'

'Everything is to be taken to pay the arrears,' the big man said.

The builder joined his wife. His voice was almost frantic. 'I can't work without those! I'm allowed to keep my tools!'

'Leave that chest be!' A man who had joined the crowd shouted threateningly. The fellow with the club – the landlord's agent, presumably – looked round nervously; the number of spectators was growing.

We halted as Coleswyn called out, 'He's right! He can keep the tools of his trade! I'm a lawyer!'

The crowd turned to us; many of their faces were hostile, even though Coleswyn was trying to help. Lawyers are never popular. The man with the club, though, seemed relieved. 'All right!' he shouted. 'Leave that chest, if it's the law!' He could tell his employer later that a lawyer had interfered.

The men lowered the chest to the ground and the woman sat on it, gathering her children round her. 'You can go, pen-scratchers!' someone shouted at us. 'Salved your consciences, have you?'

We rode on. 'Poor men lie under great temptation to doubt God's providence,' Coleswyn said quietly. 'But one day, when we have the godly Commonwealth, there will be justice for men of all ranks.'

I shook my head sadly. 'So I used to believe, once. I thought the proceeds from the monasteries would be used to bring justice to the poor; that the King, as Head of the Church, would have a regard for them the old church did not. Yet all that money went on extending Whitehall and other palaces, or was thrown away on the war. No wonder some folk have gone down more radical paths.'

'Yet those people would bring naught but anarchy.' Coleswyn spoke with a desperate, quiet intensity. 'No, a decent, ordered, godly realm must come.'

✝

WE REACHED THE HOUSE. It was big, timber-framed like most London houses, fronting onto the busy street of Dowgate. An arch led to a stableyard at the back. We tied up the horses and stood in the summer sunshine, looking at the rear of the house. The windows were shuttered, and though the property was well-maintained, it had a sad, deserted air. Dry straw from the days when the Cotterstoke horses had been stabled here blew round the dusty yard on the light breeze.

'This place would fetch a good deal of money, even in these times,' Coleswyn observed.

'I agree. It is silly to leave it standing empty and unsold because of this dispute.' I shook my head. 'You know, the more I think of the strange wording of her Will, the more I believe that old woman intended to cause trouble between her children.'

'But why?'

I shook my head.

We walked round to the front and knocked. There were shuffling footsteps, and a small elderly man opened the door. I remembered him as Patrick Vowell, the servant who had been kept on to look after the place after old Mrs Cotterstoke died. He was fortunate. The other servants, including the witnesses to old Deborah Cotterstoke's Will, had been dismissed, as usually happened when the owner of the household died.

'Serjeant Shardlake with Master Coleswyn,' I said.

He had watery blue eyes, heavy dark pouches beneath, a sad look. 'Mistress Slanning is already here. She is in the parlour.'

He led us across a little hall where a large tapestry of the Last Supper hung, worth a good deal of money in its own right. The parlour, a well-appointed room, did not look to have been touched since my first visit, or indeed since old Mrs Cotterstoke died. The chairs and table were dusty and a piece of half-finished embroidery lay on a chair. The shutters on the window giving onto the street were open; through the glass we could see the bustle of the street. The light fell on Isabel Slanning, standing with her back to us before the beautiful painting that covered the entire far wall. I remembered Nicholas saying it would be hard to fit the painting into a smaller house. Not hard, I thought, impossible.

It was, indeed, extraordinarily lifelike: a dark-haired man in his thirties, wearing black robes and a tall, cylindrical hat, looked out at us with the proud expression of one who is getting on well in life. He sat to one side of the very window that now cast light on the painting, on another sunny day at the very start of the century. I had the strange feeling of look‐ing into a mirror, but backwards in time. Opposite the man sat a young woman with a face of English‐rose prettiness, though there was a sharpness to her expression. Beside her stood a boy and a girl, perhaps nine or ten; both resembled her strongly except for their prominent eyes, which were their father's. In the picture little Isabel and Edward Cotterstoke stood hand‐in‐hand; a contented, carefree pair of children.

Isabel turned her wrinkled face to us, the bottom of her blue silk dress swishing on the reed matting. Her expression was cold and set, and when she saw Coleswyn with me anger leapt into those pale, bulbous eyes. She had been fingering a rosary tied to her belt, something strongly frowned on these last few years. She let it fall with a clack of beads.

'Serjeant Shardlake.' She spoke accusingly. 'Did you travel here with our opponent?'

'We met on the road, Mistress Slanning,' I answered firmly. 'Are either of the experts here yet? Or your brother?'

'No. I saw my brother through the window a few min‐utes ago. He knocked at the door, but I instructed Vowell not to allow him in till you were here. I daresay he will return shortly.' She flashed a glare at Coleswyn. 'This man is our foe, yet you ride with him.'

'Madam,' Coleswyn said quietly, 'lawyers who are opponents in court are expected to observe the civilities of gentlemen outside it.'

This made Isabel even more angry. She turned to me, pointing a skinny finger at Coleswyn. 'This man should not be speaking to me; is it not the rule that he should communi‐cate with me only through you, Master Shardlake?'

In fact she was right, and Coleswyn reddened. 'Gentle‐man, indeed!' She snorted. 'A heretic, I hear, like my brother.'

This was appalling behaviour, even by Isabel's standards. To imply that Coleswyn was not a gentleman was a bad enough insult but to call him a heretic was to accuse him of a capital crime. Coleswyn's lips set hard as he turned to me. 'Strictly your client is correct that I should not have direct converse with her. In any case, I would rather not. I shall wait in the hallway till the others arrive.' He walked out and shut the door. Isabel gave me a look of triumph. Her whole body seemed rigid with sheer malice.

'Heretics,' she snapped triumphantly. 'Well, they are getting their just deserts these days.' Seeing my expression, she scowled, perhaps wondering about my own loyalties, although knowing Isabel she would have been careful to ensure I was – at least – neutral in religious matters before appointing me.

A movement outside caught her eye. She looked through the window and seemed to shrink for a second before setting her face hard again. There was a knock at the door and a minute later Vowell showed Coleswyn back in, together with three other men. Two were middle-aged fellows whom I guessed were the experts; they were discussing the various methods by which small monastic houses could be converted into residences. The third was Isabel's brother, Edward Cotterstoke. I had seen him in court but, close to, the resemblance to his sister was even more striking: the same thin face with its hard lines of discontent and anger; the protuberant, glaring eyes, the tall, skinny body. Like the other men present he was dressed in a robe; in his case it was the dark green of a Guildhall employee, the badge of the City of London on his breast. He and Isabel exchanged a look of hatred, all the more intense somehow because it only lasted a second; then they both looked away.

The two experts, Masters Adam and Wulfsee, introduced

themselves. Adam was a small, solidly plump man, with a ready smile. He grinned cheerfully and grasped my hand. 'Well, sir,' he said, 'this is a strange business.' He gave a little laugh. 'Interesting little set of papers I read yesterday. Let's see if we can find some answers, eh?'

I could tell at once from his manner that Isabel had made the wrong choice. Adam was clearly no sword-for-hire expert, but an ordinary man, unaccustomed to testimony, who probably saw this whole thing as an odd diversion from the daily grind. Wulfsee, however, Edward Cotterstoke's expert, was a tall man with a severe manner and sharp eyes. I knew of him as a man who would argue a technical point to death for his client, though he would never actually lie.

Edward Cotterstoke looked at me, frowning, his back turned to Isabel. 'Well, master lawyer,' he said in a dry, grating voice. 'Shall we get this done? I have left my work at the Guildhall for this – nonsense.' Isabel glared at his back, but did not speak.

The experts went over to the wall painting and looked it over with professional interest. The servant, Vowell, had come in and stood unobtrusively by the door, looking unhappily between Edward and Isabel. It struck me that he probably knew as much of the family history as anyone.

The two men ran their practised hands gently over the painting and the adjoining walls, talking quietly. Once, they nodded in agreement; this caused both Edward and Isabel to look anxious. Then Adam, who had been bending to examine the flooring, got up, brushed down his hose, then said, 'May we look at the room next door?' Coleswyn and I exchanged a glance and nodded. The two men went out. We heard the faint murmur of their voices from the next room. In the parlour there was absolute silence, Isabel and Edward still turned away from each other. Edward was looking at the wall painting now, sadness in his eyes.

A few minutes later Wulfsee and Adam returned. 'We will prepare written reports, but I think Master Adam and I are in agreement,' Wulfsee said, a triumphant glitter in his eye. 'This wall painting could not come down without irreparable damage to it. One can see from the room next door that the plaster in the wall has shrunk, leaving a distinct crack in the middle of the wall. It is barely visible from this side, though you can see it if you look closely. Were an attempt to be made to remove the wooden joists, the plaster would simply collapse. You agree, Master Adam?'

Adam looked at me, hesitated, then spread his hands apologetically. 'I do not see how anyone with knowledge of building work could think otherwise.' I heard a sharp indrawn breath from Isabel, and a nasty smirk appeared on Edward's face.

'See, we will show you,' Wulfsee said.

We all went through to the next room, where a fine crack was clearly visible on the wall. Going back to the parlour, looking very closely, we could see a faint line on this side too, under the paint. Edward smiled. 'There,' he said with satis-faction, 'the matter is settled.'

I looked again at the wall. Wulfsee, so far as I could tell, was right; an expert determined to make a fight of it might have blustered and prevaricated, but Adam was not like that. Coleswyn turned to me and said, 'It does seem so, Serjeant Shardlake. The wall painting was always intended to adorn the structure of the house, and can only exist as such. It must therefore be defined as a fixture.'

'I would like to peruse the experts' reports when they are prepared,' I said, to buy time. But I knew this was decisive. By insisting on an expert of her choice, Isabel had doomed her own case. Everyone, even Edward, looked at her. She stood like stone, gazing at the wall painting – so old and beautiful and fragile, that view across the years of her parents, her brother and herself. She had gone deathly pale with the news, but as I watched the colour rose until her normally papery face became scarlet. She pointed at poor Adam. 'What church do you attend?' she snapped.

He frowned, puzzled. 'I do not think that any of your business, madam.'

'Are you afraid to say?' Her voice was sharp as a file.

Edward intervened, throwing up a thin hand. 'Do not answer her, sir, she is not in her right wits.'

Isabel raised herself to her full height, still glaring at Adam. 'You do not answer, sir, but allow my brother to give you orders, though you are supposed to be acting for me. I have little doubt you are a heretic like my brother and his lawyer! You are all in league!'

Edward suddenly lost control. 'You are mad, Isabel!' he burst out. 'Truly mad! You have been since we were children, since you forced me—'

Vowell stepped quickly into the room, arms waving, so that everyone turned to look at him. 'Master! Mistress! Remember your mother and father – ' He was almost in tears. Edward stared at him, his mouth suddenly tight shut. Isabel, too, fell silent, taking long, deep breaths, but then continued, her tone quieter but still full of anger. 'I will find out, sir, I will discover whether you have associations with the heretics.' She pointed at Coleswyn. 'You and my brother are heretics; I know your priest has been under investigation by the Bishop, it is said he denied the body of Jesus Christ is present in the Mass!'

'Nothing was proven against him.' Coleswyn answered

with dignity, though his voice shook with anger. 'I stand by all he has said.'

Edward gave Coleswyn an anxious glance. Isabel saw it and her eyes narrowed. 'I shall find out what he has said, mark that.'

Both Wulfsee and Adam were looking very uneasy at the turn the discussion had taken. Adam spoke, anxious now. 'I attend St Mary Aldgate, madam, and worship as the King commands. All know that.'

'You are an evil woman,' Edward Cotterstoke spat. 'You know what things I could say of you – '

Isabel looked at her brother fully in the face for the first time. 'And I of you,' she hissed. Brother and sister were glaring at each other now, eye to eye. Then Isabel turned and marched out of the house, slamming the door. I looked at the servant. Vowell stood clasping his hands, still near to tears.

Wulfsee and Adam bowed hastily to Coleswyn and me, then hastily followed Isabel out. I heard Master Adam say from the hallway, 'By Mary, sir, I had no idea what I was getting into, coming here.'

Edward said, 'I shall leave too. Thank you, Master Coleswyn.' He looked troubled by his exchange with Isabel as he gave his lawyer a nod of thanks. He was shown out by Vowell, to whom neither he nor Isabel had spoken a word throughout. Coleswyn and I were left alone.

'I do not think you should have said what you did about your preacher,' I said quietly.

He looked shaken. 'I have never let someone provoke me like that before. Forgive me. It was unprofessional.'

'It was dangerous, sir. Your preacher, did he – ' I broke off as Vowell returned.

'Please, sirs,' the old servant said anxiously. 'I think it better you leave as well, if you would.'

He accompanied us to the door. I said, 'Thank you, Goodman Vowell.'

'And to think that this was once a happy house,' he replied, blinking tears from his eyes, then bowed and closed the door.

Coleswyn and I were left standing in the busy street, under the hot sun. He spoke quietly as we went round to the stables. 'My preacher has said nothing against the Mass.' He paused and added, 'In public.'

I did not ask, *And in private?* Instead I looked down at my feet, where two large black beetles were fighting in the dust, head to head. Philip said, 'How like our clients.'

'Yes,' I agreed. 'They snap at each other, but each is protected by a carapace.'

'But underneath there is softness, vulnerability, is there not? They are not hard right through.'

'Beetles, no. But some humans, I wonder.'

'After this morning, I would understand if you preferred not to come to dine tonight,' he said quietly.

'No, I will come.' To refuse the invitation now struck me as ungentlemanly, cowardly, especially after the insults he had borne from my client. Obstinacy, too, would not allow me to let that poisonous woman determine whom I saw socially. 'You said nothing actionable,' I added reassuringly. 'Only that you agreed with your preacher. Mistress Slanning was merely looking for a stick to beat you with.'

'Yes,' he said.

'I must return to chambers now.'

'And I have to visit a client near the river.'

As I rode away I could not help but wonder whether Coleswyn's preacher had said something dangerous to the wrong person, or whether Isabel was merely repeating gossip.

I reminded myself the man had only been investigated, not prosecuted.

☦

I RODE BACK TO Lincoln's Inn. Genesis trotted along slowly. I thought how with his increasingly bony face and stiff whiskers he was starting to resemble a little old man, though mercifully a good-natured one. I remembered Isabel and Edward shouting about the things they could say about each other. What had they meant? I recalled again what Isabel had said to me in chambers: 'If you knew the terrible things my brother has done.' And Vowell, the servant whom they had otherwise ignored, intervening as though to stop them saying too much. Edward had said his sister was not in her right wits, and neither sibling had seemed entirely sane that morning. I hoped my client could now be made to accept that she could not win her case, but I doubted it.

I half expected her to be at chambers when I arrived, ready for a fight, but all was quiet. Barak was making notes on some new cases to be heard at the Court of Requests when the Michaelmas term began in September.

'What happened at the inspection?' he asked eagerly.

'The experts agreed that any attempt to remove the wall painting will make the plaster collapse.'

'That's it then? We'll never have to see that woman's sour face again?'

'Oh, I think we will. She stormed out in high dudgeon; but somehow I suspect she'll present herself here soon, probably today.'

Barak nodded to where Nicholas sat copying out a conveyance. 'He has some news for you. Won't tell me what it is. Been looking like the cat that got the cream.'

Nicholas stood. There was indeed a self-satisfied expression on the boy's freckled face. 'Come through,' I said. As Nicholas followed me to my office I saw Barak frown and Skelly smile quietly to himself. Barak indeed seemed jealous of my involving my pupil in a mission from which he himself was excluded. I felt a momentary annoyance. I was only protecting him; Tamasin would skin him alive if she suspected I had involved him in court politics again, as well he knew.

I closed the door. 'What is it?' I asked Nicholas. 'News of that sleeve?'

'It is, sir.' He removed the silk carefully from his pocket and laid it on the desk with his long, slim hands. 'The second embroiderer I visited today recognized it instantly. He sewed the shirt for a client. Mention of Master Gullym's name did the trick; the embroiderer knows him. He looked at his records. The shirt was made for a gentleman called Charles Stice. He gave me an address, down by Smithfield.'

'Well done,' I said.

'There's more. I noticed he wrinkled his nose when he spoke of Stice, so I asked what he was like. He said Stice was one of those young men who come into money or position and put on haughty airs.' Nicholas was finding it hard to keep the excitement from his voice. 'But here's the thing, sir. Charles Stice is a tall, brown-haired young man with half an ear missing. Looked like he got the injury from a knife or a sword in a fight, the man said.'

I looked again at the little, ragged piece of silk. Nicholas said, 'So this was left not by the men who killed Greening, but by those who fled into the garden after young Elias discovered them trying to break in earlier. They escaped the same way.'

I thought, and this Charles Stice was the man who had

tried to suborn the Queen's page, young Garet. 'You have done well, Nicholas. Very well.' I looked at him seriously. 'But leave the matter with me now. This man is dangerous.'

Nicholas looked disappointed. 'Will you arrange for him to be found?'

'This afternoon.' I must get the news to Lord Parr.

There was a gentle knock on the door, and Skelly entered. He spoke apologetically. 'A visitor, sir. Will not wait. Must see you immediately.'

I smiled wryly at Nicholas. 'Mistress Slanning?'

'No, sir. It is a man called Okedene. He says he is a printer, that he knows you, and that it is a matter of life and death.'

Chapter Twenty

S KELLY SHOWED OKEDENE IN. He wore a light wool doublet and his face was red and sweating, as though he had been running. As Skelly closed the door behind him I saw Barak looking in at us curiously. I stood. 'Master Okedene, what is it?' I wondered with a thrill of horror whether, as I had feared might happen, he or his family had been attacked.

The printer slowly regained his composure. The constant physical activity of his trade meant he had to be fit, but he was not young any more. 'Master Shardlake,' he said quickly, 'I've come to see you about that note you sent. To tell you I am leaving London. I am selling the business and putting the proceeds into my brother's farm, out in Norfolk. I have feared for my wife and children since the night poor Armistead was murdered.' He frowned at Nicholas, doubtless remembering his part in provoking Elias's flight. He did not know his former apprentice was dead.

'I am sorry,' I said. I saw how the lines of strain and worry on his face had deepened since we last met.

He raised a hand. 'Never mind that now,' he said. 'There is no time.'

'No time for what?' Nicholas asked.

'I stopped on the way here to buy a glass of beer — I was thirsty, it is a warm day. At the sign of Bacchus near St Paul's. It is a big inn —'

'I have been there,' I said.

'Inside, I saw two men sitting at a table by the window. I am sure it was the men who killed Armistead, even though they were wearing gentlemen's clothes today; the Bacchus is a respectable place.' He took another deep breath. 'I have never been able to get my old assistant Huffkyn's description of them out of my mind. Two young men, both big and tall, one fair and with a wart on his brow and the other near bald, young as he is. I have feared to see them ever since. Those murderers,' he added bitterly, 'sitting quietly supping beer in full view of everyone.' He looked from me to Nicholas, then squared his shoulders. 'I ran all the way here. The inn is less than fifteen minutes if we go fast.'

Nicholas said, 'The authorities—'

'There is no time, boy!' Okedene snapped. 'They must be taken before they leave. A citizen's arrest!' I saw he was eager to take the chance to capture Greening's killers himself, and perhaps to lift the cloud of worry from his family. 'Master Shardlake, have you any other people here who could help us?' he asked. 'Perhaps that bearded man in your outer office?'

I sighed. Okedene was right, this might be our only chance. But these were killers, young, fit men, experienced in violence. Nicholas might give a good account of himself but Okedene was no youngster, while I would be of little use in a fight. Nor would Skelly. That left Barak, whom I had sworn to involve no further. But here was a chance to take the killers, present them to Lord Parr myself. Nicholas and Okedene looked on impatiently as I considered. Then I crossed to the door and asked Barak to join us. He rose from his desk, an odd mixture of anticipation and reluctance flashing across his face.

I explained that Master Okedene had been a witness to the murder I was investigating, and he had just seen the killers at the Bacchus Inn. I said, 'These are dangerous fellows. I doubt we could take them without you. I've no right to ask you to come, and if you say no, I'll understand.'

Barak took a long, deep breath. 'Is this connected with the — other matter? With Baynard's Castle?'

I nodded slowly. 'This may be our one chance to settle both matters.'

Barak bit his lip. Through his shirt he fingered his father's old Jewish mezuzah, which he wore round his neck as constantly as the Queen had worn the key round hers. Then he said, 'Have we weapons enough? Young Nick wore his sword into work today, showing off as usual. I have a good knife.'

'And I,' Okedene said.

'Mine is somewhere,' I said.

'Then let's go,' Barak said. 'I've been out of things a while, but I haven't forgotten how to fight.'

✝

AN ILL-ASSORTED quartet, we made our way along Fleet Street under a hot mid-morning sun, and under the city wall at Newgate. Skelly had stared as we left; Barak told him cheerfully that if Mistress Slanning called she was to be requested kindly to go and boil her head in a pot. Nicholas loped along, hand on his sword, eyes agleam, clearly looking forward to the fray. There was a reassurance in the presence of his weapon, which I knew Nicholas took pains to keep well-sharpened. But the men we would face were dangerous. I dreaded the thought of anything happening to Nicholas or to Barak, who was stepping along purposefully, his face set and watchful. Okedene and I had to hurry to keep up with them both.

'What's the layout of this place?' Barak asked Okedene.

'A door from the street, one big room with tables inside, a serving hatch with the kitchen behind. They serve food as well as drink. There's a door to a little garden at the rear, with more tables.'

'There'll be one to the kitchens too,' Barak said. 'Where are they sitting?'

'At a table in an alcove by the window.'

'Good,' Nicholas said. 'Then we can surround them, cut off any escape.'

Barak nodded approvingly. 'Well done, boy.'

'My swordsmanship teacher was a soldier in the French wars in the twenties. He always said, knowing the ground is essential in a fight.'

'He was right.'

Okedene looked at Barak curiously. 'You have much knowledge of such matters for a law clerk.'

Barak glanced at me. 'Wasn't always a law clerk, was I?'

We arrived at the Bacchus. It was one of the respectable London taverns where travellers stayed, and families of the middling sort sometimes went for weekend meals or celebrations. Through the open shutters we could see two men sitting at a big round table in the window, heads together, deep in conversation. As Okedene had said, they answered Huffkyn's description exactly. Both wore good clothes, slashed doublets and shirts, lace collars showing. Like Stice at the first attack on Greening, these two had pretended to be poor men when they went out set on murder.

It was a slack time of day, with only a few other people sitting at tables – tradesmen discussing business, by the look of them.

'Are you sure it's them?' I asked Okedene.

'Huffkyn's description is etched in my mind.'

Barak said, 'Did you notice if they have swords?'

'I didn't see. I didn't like to watch too long. They could have them under the table.'

'They're wearing gentlemen's clothes,' Nicholas said. 'They're entitled to carry swords.'

Barak looked at him seriously. 'Then you may need to use yours, Nicky boy. And these fellows may dress well now, but they won't act like young gentlemen in combat. You ready?'

'Ready and able,' he answered haughtily.

'I doubt the clientele will interfere,' Barak said. 'They'll all be scared shitless.'

I took a deep breath, fingering the knife at my belt. 'Come on, then.'

☩

WE STEPPED OVER the threshold, into a smell of beer and pottage. One or two people glanced at my lawyer's robe, which I had kept on to lend our group an air of authority. We walked straight to the table where the two young men sat in the alcove, still talking intently. My heart pounded. Both, I saw, indeed had swords in their scabbards, lying on the benches beside them. As we approached I thought I heard the bald man mention the name Bertano.

The two broke off their talk and looked sharply up at us; hard, hostile faces. The bald one was in his late twenties, large, well-built and handsome, but with more than a touch of cruelty round the fleshy mouth. The fair one with the wart on his brow had narrow, greyhound-like features, and his expression held the same cold intensity as a hunting dog's.

Loudly enough for the other patrons to hear, I said, 'Gentlemen, we are making a citizen's arrest upon you, for the murder of Armistead Greening on the tenth of this month.'

The fair man tensed, his eyes narrowing to slits, but the

bald fellow looked at us with large, unreadable brown eyes, and then laughed. 'Are you mad?' he asked.

'That we aren't,' Okedene said, raising his knife. 'You were seen running with a bloody club from Armistead Greening's workshop after killing him.'

There was a murmur of voices from the other tables. A couple got up hastily and left.

'You're not the authorities,' the fair man growled.

'We do not need to be,' Nicholas answered, putting his hand to his sword. 'Not for a citizen's arrest.'

The bald man laughed. 'What are you, a law student, by your little robe? Scratchy clerks come to arrest us?'

I said, 'I am Matthew Shardlake, Serjeant at Law, charged by the victim's family with investigating the murder under the coroner.'

The two glanced at each other, and I realized with a shiver that they had recognized my name. They looked over our little group more closely, weighing us up. The fair-haired man quietly slipped the hand furthest from us towards his sword, then jerked back as Nicholas swept his own sword from its scabbard and pointed it at the man's throat, a glint of sunlight on the razor-sharp edge. 'Don't dare move, churl,' he said, 'or I'll slit you. Hands on the table.' I had wondered whether, when it came to it, Nicholas's bravado would be matched by action. Now I knew.

The fair man sat stock-still. He looked at me, eyes boring into mine. 'You'd do best to let us go,' he said very quietly, 'or there'll be big trouble from those above us. You've no idea who you're dealing with, hunchback.'

'I can make a guess,' I said, thinking of Richard Rich. 'In any case, you're under-arrest.'

Both men were looking at me now. With his right hand Barak reached swiftly under the table on the bald man's side, his left holding the knife on the table. 'I'll take your sword, matey,' he said.

Then, so quickly I could not follow with my eyes, the man pulled a knife from his belt and stabbed it straight through the muscle between the first two fingers of Barak's left hand, pinning it to the table. Barak yelled and dropped his knife with a clatter. Nicholas turned instinctively, and the narrow-faced man pushed his sword arm away with one hand, grabbing his own from under the bench with the other and slashing at Nicholas with it.

Both had moved with astonishing speed, and for a terrible second I thought Nicholas was lost, but he had raised his own sword in time to parry. Barak, meanwhile, reached for the knife pinning his hand to the table and, with another yell, managed to pull it out. Blood welled up. At the same moment the bald man reached for his sword, but Okedene, who had brought out his own knife, thrust it to the hilt into his shoulder. Quickly I pulled out my own weapon and held it to his throat. Barak could do no more than clutch at his hand.

For a moment I thought we had won, for Nicholas seemed to have the fair man at a disadvantage trying to fight from behind the table. But then with his free hand he reached down and grasped the table's underside. Despite his slim build he was strong, for he managed to tip the table right over on us, sending pewter tankards flying. Nicholas, staggering back, dropped his sword. The fair man slashed at him, catching him on the chest so that blood gushed out. Okedene, caught by the table, fell over with a yell. The fair-haired man jumped from the alcove. His companion, clutching at his shoulder, reached down with his free hand and took up Nicholas's sword.

Both made for the door, the fair man slashing at a potman

who stood gaping at the scene; he jumped back frantically and a woman screamed. The two men turned in the door-way, menacing us with their swords for a moment, the face of the dark-haired man white with pain, Okedene's knife still in his shoulder. Then they turned and ran. I stood looking after them. There was nothing I could do alone. Barak and Nicholas were both hurt, though thank heaven not severely, and Okedene was only now stumbling to his feet, pale and groaning.

The innkeeper appeared with two assistants, each bearing a cudgel. 'What the hell's going on?' he asked angrily. 'Fight-ing and near murder in my inn. I'll have the constable on you!'

'Didn't you hear us say we were trying to arrest two murderers?' I shouted with sudden violence. I took a deep breath and swallowed, for what had happened must have terrified both staff and patrons. I took out my purse and produced a sovereign – one of those Bealknap had given me. I held it up.

'This should more than cover your trouble.'

The innkeeper looked at it hungrily.

I said, 'It's yours if you answer a couple of questions. Have these men been here before?'

'A few times these last weeks. They always sit talking in that corner after ordering something to eat. And I know their names; I remember because once a man came for them, a messenger from somewhere. He asked if Master Daniels and Master Cardmaker were here. Said it was urgent. Then he saw them sitting in the alcove and went over to them. I didn't like the look of them. An innkeeper knows when people may be trouble. By Mary, I was right there,' he added bitterly, looking at the overturned table, the spilled beer on the floor, the deserted room. A few frightened faces peered in from the garden.

I took a deep breath. Learning their names like this was a great piece of luck, though it did not make up for the fact we had lost them, and that Barak and Nicholas had been hurt. I wondered, who had sent that messenger?

'Thank you,' I said. 'We'll go.' Barak was sitting down, his face white, wrapping his hand tightly with a handkerchief. Nicholas had undone his shirt, revealing a pale but muscular torso. To my relief he had suffered no more than a superficial cut. Colour was returning to Okedene's face.

'I must take you and Nicholas to Guy at once,' I told Barak.

'How the fuck am I going to explain *this* to Tammy?' he said thickly.

I helped him to the door. Outside I turned to Okedene. 'Sir, will you come with us?'

The printer shook his head. 'No, Master Shardlake, and I will have no more of this business. I should never have come to you. I will hasten with the sale of my printworks. Thank you for your care in sending that note, but please let us alone now.' He looked again at my injured companions, then walked slowly away.

Chapter Twenty-one

MERCIFULLY, GUY WAS AT HOME. His assistant, Francis, looked astonished when I appeared on the doorstep with two men who were both bleeding profusely. 'Robbers attacked us,' I lied. Francis hurried us through to Guy's consulting room, where he was mixing herbs. 'By Mary!' he cried. 'What has happened?'

I watched anxiously as he examined Nicholas and Barak. Nicholas's chest wound required only a couple of stitches, which he bore well, biting his tongue as Guy sewed. Then he carefully examined Barak's left hand. 'Thank heaven it was a narrow knife,' he said, 'and went through the fleshy part between the long bones of your fingers. But it will require stitching, and lavender and other oils to stop the wound becoming poisoned.'

Nicholas frowned. 'I thought wine was best to clear wounds.'

'Lavender is better. Though it stings. And a bandage.' Guy looked at Barak seriously. 'You will have to wear it for a week, and have it changed regularly. You are right-handed, aren't you?'

'Yes,' said Barak. 'God's wounds, it hurts.'

'It will. But with luck, there should be no damage save a little stiffness.'

Barak turned to Nicholas and me. 'You'll both be seeing Tamasin at George's birthday celebration in a few days. I'll make something up. We'll discuss the details later, to make sure everyone has them right. I'll tell her it was an accident at work. I don't want her catching you out.'

'Surely your wife will believe you?' Nicholas said, surprised.

'Don't bank on it, lad.'

Guy said, 'This is not the first time your master has brought Jack Barak here to be tidied up after – an incident of violence, shall we say. And Jack has brought your master, too.' Guy's tone was severe, but Nicholas looked at me with new respect.

I said, 'May I leave them with you, Guy? I am sorry, but I have an important appointment and I fear I will be late.' On the way I had seen the hand on a church clock showing near eleven.

He nodded agreement. 'A word, though, Matthew, if you please. I will see you out.' His mouth was set, his dark face troubled and angry.

Outside he spoke quietly. 'So, it was not a robbery.' He shook his head. 'Again you bring Jack to me after a dangerous encounter, married with a child and with Tamasin pregnant again. And this boy as well.'

'I am investigating a murder,' I answered. 'A pair of rogues who bludgeoned two innocent men to death. They were seen in a tavern, by a witness who brought the news to me at Lincoln's Inn. It was a chance, perhaps the only chance, to take them. Jack and Nicholas knew there was danger.'

'Did you take these killers?'

I shook my head angrily. 'No, they were experienced fighters. They got away.'

'Matthew,' Guy said, 'you ever follow danger. But now this boy, and Jack. Jack is no longer so young, and used to a quieter life now.'

I ran a hand across my brow. 'I know, I know. But it was my only chance to bring two murderers to justice.' I stared at my old friend defiantly. 'And perhaps stop them killing again.'

'You indicated when we last met that you were involved in something secret, the details of which it would be dangerous for others to know.'

'Yes.'

He inclined his head to the consulting room door. 'Have you made Jack and that boy aware of those details?'

I shook my head.

'Then you should not have involved them,' Guy said. 'I am sorry, but that is what I think.' He looked at me sharply. 'Is it something to do with the Queen?'

'What makes you ask that?'

'I see from your expression that it is. I know you have ever had an immoderate affection for her. I have seen your troubled looks these last months, worrying about her travails. But you should not let it place you in danger – and still less those who work for you.'

'Why?' I answered sharply. 'Because you think her a heretic?'

'No,' he snapped back. 'Because she is the Queen, and because, as you yourself said, thunder circles around thrones. Certainly this King's throne,' he added bitterly. I did not answer. 'Is this man Bertano you asked me about part of it?' he asked.

I remembered Daniels and Cardmaker mentioning his name back at the inn. I said seriously, 'Keep that name close, Guy, as you value your safety.'

He smiled wryly. 'See, you have even involved me in a small way. Think on my words, Matthew. I do not want to have to treat Barak or Nicholas again, and for something worse. Nor you,' he added in a gentler tone.

✝

I HURRIED TO THE TOWER, my mind full of conflict. Guy was right: it was my own feelings for the Queen that had set me on this path, trailing danger in my wake like the bad humours of an illness. But I could not just step aside now, even if I wanted to. Those two men at the inn had known my name.

Tower Hill rose ahead of me, where Lord Cromwell and so many others had died; and beyond, the Tower of London: the moat, the high white walls and there, the huge square bulk of the White Tower, where the conspiracy between Rich and Bealknap five years before had resulted in my briefly being held prisoner in its terrible dungeons.

I saw Lord Parr was already waiting outside the Middle Tower gate, on horseback. To my surprise young William Cecil sat on another horse beside him, two servants in Queen's livery holding the reins. Cecil was dressed in his lawyer's robe, and Lord Parr wore a light doublet, green and slashed at the shoulder to show the crimson silk lining. He sniffed at a pomander that hung by a gold chain from his neck, to ward off the stink from the moat.

'Matthew!' It was the first time he had greeted me by my Christian name, his tone much more civil than when we had last met. 'I brought Master Cecil with me, so that we might exchange news.'

'My Lord, I am sorry I am late, but I have just had an encounter with the men who killed Greening – '

He leaned forward in his saddle. 'Are they caught?' he asked eagerly.

'No, but Barak and my pupil were injured in the attempt. I had to get them medical attention.'

'Tell me what happened.'

I glanced at Cecil. 'William knows all,' Lord Parr said. 'Including about the *Lamentation*. The Queen and I agree he can be trusted, and he has already organized enquiries among the radicals, and agents at the docks.'

I looked at Cecil. Trusted indeed, I thought. I told them about our encounter with Daniels and Cardmaker, that the two seemed to know my name and had, I was sure, mentioned the name Bertano. I also told them Nicholas had identified the torn sleeve as belonging to one Charles Stice, who, from the description of his damaged ear, had been involved in the first attack on Greening, and the attempt to suborn the young page Garet.

Cecil said, 'I have made less progress, I fear. No sign of Greening's three vanished friends, nor the guard Leeman. And though all four have friends among the religious radicals, none are part of any known group. I think Greening and the rest set up their own little circle.'

'I think that may be right,' I agreed.

Lord Parr grunted. 'God knows there are enough of those springing up, even under Gardiner's nose. Maybe even Anabaptists. We know that one of the men is Dutch, and it is from there and from Germany that those wretched people come.'

'What about Bertano?' I asked Lord Parr.

'The name is not known in the Italian merchant community. They all have to be registered, and this name is not on the list.'

'He could have slipped into the country,' Cecil observed.

'Possibly.' Lord Parr shook his head. 'Or he may not be in England at all.' He looked across at the Tower. 'Well,

Matthew, we must go in. They will take the horses at the gate. We are late enough already.' He turned to Cecil. 'There, William: Shardlake has another three names for you to investigate. Daniels, Cardmaker, Stice.' He inclined his head. 'But quietly.'

The young lawyer nodded gravely, then rode away. Lord Parr stroked his beard. 'There's a clever fellow,' he said quietly. 'And discreet.'

'You have told him everything?'

'Yes, the Queen approved it after meeting him. She took to him very much.' I felt an absurd pang of jealousy. Lord Parr watched Cecil's retreating figure. 'He is ambitious. If we succeed in this, it may be a stepping stone for him. Of course, there is religious principle involved for him as well. If we do not succeed, however,' he added bleakly, 'and the book is published for the King to see, all of us may be in dire straits.'

✝

THE GUARD AT the Tower gate saluted Lord Parr. His horse was taken to the stable, and we walked across Tower Green.

'No word of the *Lamentation*, then?' I asked.

'No. More than two weeks now since it was taken. I tell the Queen that each passing day makes it less likely it will appear on the streets, but she does not believe it.' He gave a quick bark of laughter. 'Nor, in truth, do I. These men you encountered,' he continued. 'One said you did not know who you were dealing with. Implying it was somebody senior. And you said earlier you thought Sir Richard Rich might be involved?'

'Possibly.'

'There are so many possibilities: Norfolk, Gardiner,

Paget, acting alone or in concert; perhaps someone else – '
He shook his head. 'But no, not Paget; he always works
strictly to the King's orders.'

'Are you sure, my Lord? Wolsey and Cromwell did so at
first, but later . . .'

He pursed his lips. 'You are right. We cannot be entirely
sure of anything in these whirling days.'

'It still concerns me, my Lord, that when Jane Fool
arrived to be questioned, the Lady Mary appeared with her.'

'That was just unfortunate.'

'I wondered whether it might be something more. Is Jane
truly a woman of little wit, or could she be acting, concealing her true intelligence?'

Lord Parr shook his head. 'She is a mere idiot, of that I
am sure. I cannot see her deceiving her mistress about that;
you know how shrewd the Queen is. In any event she did
not let Jane anywhere near that manuscript.'

'The Lady Elizabeth seemed not to like Jane Fool.'

He snorted. 'The Lady Elizabeth does not like a lot of
people. Particularly anyone who upstages her with the
Queen.'

✝

WE WERE APPROACHING the White Tower. Lord Parr
had slowed down, and I noticed a faint sheen of perspiration
on his forehead. I remembered his age, his remarks about his
health. He looked at me, then said uncomfortably, 'I am
sorry I was short with you when we last met. This business
is a great strain.'

'I understand, my Lord. Thank you.' I realized it could
not come easily to one of Lord Parr's rank and temperament
to apologize to an underling.

He nodded brusquely, then looked towards the Tower. 'As

I told you, Sir Edmund Walsingham used to be the Queen's Vice-Chancellor, and he is an old friend.' I thought, among the high ones of the realm everyone knows everyone, and they are either a friend or an enemy. 'I am going to tell him you have acted for my wife's family, and have a case coming up involving a witness who claims he was being questioned in the Tower sometime between – let us pick a broad range of dates – June the twentieth and July the fifth. We will say that you do not believe this man was in the Tower at all, that in fact he was up to mischief elsewhere.'

'I understand,' I said, uncomfortable at the thought of lying so blatantly to the Constable of the Tower.

'We will say that you wish to check the names of men imprisoned there between those dates,' Lord Parr continued. 'There have been plenty in and out these last few months and if I vouch for you I think Sir Edmund will let you see the records. Could you do that? Then try to find out who was on guard duty when Anne Askew was tortured. That was around June the thirtieth. The news of her torture was leaked the same day.'

'Very well.' The eviction which Coleswyn and I had witnessed that morning suddenly came back to mind. 'I could say the man concerned is trying to give himself an alibi for being part of a group of men who evicted a tenant without due process.'

'A landlord? Yes, you work at the Court of Requests, don't you?' he added, a little superciliously. 'Very well. But on no account mention Anne Askew. I do not wish to draw his mind to that.'

There was a sudden loud roar from the Tower menagerie, probably a lion. Lord Parr smiled. 'I hear they have a new creature there from Africa, an animal something like a horse but with an absurdly long and thin neck. I may ask Sir Edmund to let me see it.'

✝

WE ENTERED the White Tower. A guard took us through the Great Hall, where as ever soldiers stood or sat talking and playing cards. At the far end, I recognized the door leading down to the dungeons.

We were led upstairs, along a corridor with rush matting that deadened the sound of our footsteps. We entered a spacious room where a man a little younger than Lord Parr, with white hair and a lined face ending in a long pointed beard, rose to receive us. There was another man standing by the desk, slightly younger, with grizzled hair and beard and a soldierly air. I bowed low to them, while Lord Parr shook hands.

'Sir Edmund,' Lord Parr said lightly. 'I have not seen you for months. And Sir Anthony Knevet, Master Lieutenant of the Tower, God give you good morrow.'

'And you, my Lord. If you will excuse me – ' the soldierly man tapped a folder of papers under his arm – 'I am due to present a report to Master Secretary Paget at Whitehall.'

'Then we will not detain you.' There was a note of annoyance in Walsingham's voice. The other man bowed and left.

Walsingham gestured for us to sit. Taking a chair, Lord Parr said, 'There are a couple of small matters from your time in charge of the Queen's household which I need to ask you about; I would have written, but thought to take the opportunity to visit you, now the Court is at Whitehall.'

'I am glad you have. This has been a busy few months at the Tower.' Walsingham raised his eyebrows knowingly.

'Does not Sir Anthony Knevet do most of the day-to-day work?'

'Yes, but the ultimate responsibility remains mine. And Sir Anthony has been sticking his nose into one or two places he should not have – ' Sir Edmund broke off, waved a hand dismissively, then changed the subject. 'How go things in her majesty's household?'

'Easier recently,' Lord Parr answered carefully. 'How is your family? Your clever nephew Francis?'

'He is at Cambridge now. Growing up fast,' Walsingham added sadly. 'Reminds me I grow old. I have felt my age these last months.'

'I too,' Lord Parr said feelingly. 'In time of age the humours alter and slow, do they not?' He continued casually, 'Sir Edmund, I crave a small favour. Serjeant Shardlake here is a barrister to the Court of Requests, who has also acted for my wife; he has a case coming on at Michaelmas where the Tower records may shed light on something.'

Walsingham looked at me. 'Oh?'

Lord Parr recounted the story of the fictional witness. Sir Edmund looked at me, his gaze keen from small tired eyes. 'Between June the twentieth and July the fifth, you say?' He grunted, looking at me. 'You know who was here then?'

I paused a moment, as though trying to remember. 'Anne Askew?'

'Just so. Not so many others, the heat was dying down by then.' He grimaced. 'Though not for her.' He looked at Lord Parr. 'You vouch for him?'

'I do.'

Walsingham turned back to me. 'Who was this witness?'

I spoke the first name that came to me. 'Cotterstoke. Edward Cotterstoke.'

Sir Edmund shook his head. 'I don't remember that name. But you can go down to the cells and look at the records, seeing as Lord Parr vouches for you.' He laughed abruptly. 'Don't look like that, master lawyer. I won't detain you down there.'

Lord Parr laughed too. 'Sir Edmund is doing you a favour, Matthew,' he said chidingly. 'Officially those documents are not for the public to see.'

'I am sorry, Sir Edmund. I am grateful.'

The Constable laughed scoffingly. 'Well, it shows the mere name of the Tower dungeons puts people in fear, which is partly what they're for.' He scribbled a quick note, then rang a bell on his desk. As a guard appeared, Sir Edmund said, 'Take this lawyer to the cells to see the record of prisoners between June the twentieth and July the fifth. See he writes nothing down.' He gave me a look of amused contempt. 'And bring him safely back here afterwards.'

✝

THE GUARD LED ME downstairs again, across the main hall. He was a big fellow in his thirties, with a heavy limp. Like Sir Edmund he seemed to take my apprehensive stare at the door as commonplace. 'Looking for a name, are you, sir?' he asked.

'Yes, a witness in a case who says he was questioned in the Tower. I think he is lying.'

'A strange lie.'

'He probably thought I would be unable to make a check here.'

The guard winced. 'May I stop just a moment, sir? My leg pains me.'

'Of course.'

'A Frenchie soldier ran it through with a half-pike in Boulogne last year.'

'I am sorry. I know it was a fierce campaign.'

'They gave me this job afterwards. I won't be going soldiering again. I'm all right to go on now, sir, thank you.'

The door was opened by a guard and we walked down that dreadful stone staircase, slick with green algae once we passed under the level of the river. The light came now from torches, stinking with smoke. At the bottom was a barred door which I remembered. My escort called out and a hard, unshaven face appeared behind the bars.

'Yes, sir?'

'This gentleman has permission to look at the log.' Sir Edmund's note was passed through the bars. The man on the other side looked at it, then closely at me, before turning back to my escort.

'You're to wait and take him back?'

'Yes.'

There was a clank of keys, and the heavy door opened. I went through, into a stink of damp, and entered a long vestibule with bare ancient stone walls, a row of cells with barred windows along its length. It was cold down here, even in high summer. I observed – strange the things one notices at such times – that the layout of the central vestibule had been changed: the desk which was its only furniture was larger than the one that had stood there five years ago, and had been positioned against the wall to allow more space for people to pass. It was covered in papers and a man sat behind it. I saw a large open ledger.

The guard who had let me in looked me up and down. 'Your purpose, sir?' he asked in a voice which was quiet but not respectful.

'Matthew Shardlake, Serjeant at Law.' I told him the story of the dubious witness. Lying was not easy under his hard, watchful eyes.

'Well, if Sir Edmund agrees,' he said reluctantly. 'But

you're to write nothing down, only look through quickly for the name you seek.'

'I understand.'

'My name is Ardengast. I am in charge here.'

Without further comment he led me to the desk. The man sitting behind it was a big, middle-aged fellow in a leather jacket, with an untidy straggling beard. He sat up straight as we approached. Ardengast said, 'This man is to see the logs from June the twentieth to July the fifth, Howitson. Looking for a witness in a case.'

The man in the leather jacket frowned. 'It's not to do with——?'

'No. Some law matter.' Ardengast waved dismissively. He glanced again at Walsingham's note. 'The name is Edward Cotterstoke. I don't remember him.'

'Nor I.'

'That is the point,' I said. 'I think he was lying about being here.'

Ardengast turned to me. 'I'll leave you with Howitson, I've got business.' He walked away, unlocked a door at the far end of the chamber, and passed through. From somewhere beyond I thought I heard a distant scream. I looked through the dark barred windows on the doors of the cells. They seemed empty, but who knew what pitiful souls and broken bodies lay within? I thought of Anne Askew alone and terrified in this place.

Howitson pulled the big ledger over to him. I saw there were two columns. One gave the times that prisoners arrived and left and their names, while the other, smaller column was for the signatures of the officers on duty. The writing was poor, scrawled, and I could not read it upside down. Howitson turned over several pages, pausing occasionally to lick his black-stained thumb. Then he leaned back in his chair.

'No one here called Cotterstoke, sir. I thought as much.' He looked up with a satisfied smile.

'Good,' I said. 'I suspected the witness was lying. However, I will have to see the book myself. The rules of court require me to testify to what I have seen personally. Simply to repeat what another has told me would be what is called hearsay, and thus inadmissible.'

Howitson frowned. 'I don't know about legal rules. But that book is confidential.'

'I know. And I will only testify that this particular name is *not* there, nothing else.' He still looked doubtful. 'It is the law,' I said. 'Sir Edmund said I could see the book.'

'We have our own laws down here, *sir*.' He smiled a little menacingly, an insolent emphasis on the last word.

'I understand, goodman. If you like I can ask Sir Edmund to be more specific, in writing, to satisfy you.'

Howitson grunted. 'All right, but be quick. No lingering over names. We've had enough rumours getting out of this place.'

'I understand.'

He turned the ledger round, going back a couple of pages. I ran my eyes quickly over the entries for late June; I was not interested in those. I noticed, however, that there were always two officers present to sign a prisoner in; one was usually Howitson, the other presumably whichever guard was on duty. From the 28th of June a signature more legible than the others began appearing during the afternoons. Thomas Myldmore. He was on duty when 'Mistress Anne Kyme', Anne Askew's married name, appeared on the record.

Howitson brought his big heavy hand down on the ledger. 'That's it, sir,' he said officiously.

'Thank you. I have seen all I need.'

I stepped away from the desk. As I did so the door at the end of the passage opened again and two men appeared. One was older, wearing an apron darkly stained with I knew not what. The other was young, small and thin, with dark blond hair and an oval face unsuited to the pointed beard he wore. I noticed his shoulders were slumped. The older man began undoing the buckles on his apron, paying me no heed, but when the younger one saw me standing over the ledger his grey eyes widened a little. He came across. Howitson closed the book with a thump and gave the newcomer a glare.

'I'm going off duty now, Master Howitson,' the young man said in a surprisingly deep voice.

'Thank Sir Anthony Knevet you've still got a duty to be *going* off,' Howitson muttered. The young man looked at my lawyer's coif and robe. 'Is there a problem with the book?' he asked hesitantly.

'Nothing to concern you, Myldmore,' Howitson said. 'Don't recall anyone by the name of Cotterstoke, do you, being here late June or early July?'

'No, sir.'

'There you are then, sir,' Howitson said to me triumphantly.

'Then I thank you, sir,' I said with a little bow. I looked at Myldmore. His eyes were wide, burning yet frightened. 'Good day, fellow,' I said and headed for the door, where the veteran stood leaning against the wall outside, gently massaging his leg.

✝

THE GUARD LED ME back to Sir Edmund's room where he and Lord Parr were talking and laughing, drinking wine. I heard Sir Edmund say, 'The first time I saw a woman in one of these farthingales, I couldn't believe it. Waist braced with corsets so tight it looked like you could span it with your hands, and the wide skirt with those hoops underneath – '

'Ay, like barrels – ' Lord Parr looked round as I entered, instantly alert. 'Find your man, Shardlake?'

'His name was not there, my Lord, as I suspected. I thank you, Sir Edmund.'

Walsingham was in a relaxed mood now. 'Will you stay for some wine?'

'I fear I cannot. I have much to do. But I am most grateful to you.'

'Perhaps I should come with you, Shardlake,' Lord Parr said. He would want to know what I had found out.

Sir Edmund protested. 'No, no, my Lord, you have hardly got here – '

Lord Parr looked between us. Clearly he thought it might look suspicious if he left so soon. He said, 'One more drink, then, Edmund. Forgive me, though, I must go to the jakes. Master Shardlake, can you help me?' He made a show of finding it difficult to stand.

'You cannot take your wine any more, my Lord,' Sir Edmund called after him teasingly.

Once the door closed behind us, Lord Parr was instantly alert. 'Well?' he asked impatiently.

'The man who was most often on duty when Anne Askew was here is called Myldmore. I saw him; he looked anxious and seemed in bad odour with the fellow at the desk.'

Lord Parr smiled and nodded. 'Another name for Cecil to investigate. I wonder if he is connected with the others.' He clapped me on the shoulder. 'You are a good fellow, Master Shardlake, for all your long face and – well, never mind.' He spoke with sudden passion. 'We shall have them, end this game of hoodman blind, and unmask who is at the bottom of it all. I shall be in touch very soon. Good man.'

He went down the corridor, leaving me to walk, as fast as I could, towards the exit and the Tower gates.

Chapter Twenty-two

I WALKED SLOWLY home. It had been a long day, even by the standards of this last week. I was utterly weary. It was still afternoon, but the shadows were beginning to lengthen. Looking down a narrow street leading to the river, I saw a fisherman in a boat, casting a long net that turned the water silver as it splashed into the Thames, sending swans flying to the bank. Normality. I remembered Guy's words. Why did I keep walking into danger, taking others with me? My feelings for the Queen had led to my involvement in this case; yet it had been the same even before I met her. It went back to Thomas Cromwell, my association with him that first brought me into contact with the high ones of the realm who, like Cromwell himself, sought to use my skills and exploit my obstinate refusal to give up anything I had started. I thought, if I get through this, perhaps it is time to move out of London. Plenty did. I could practise in one of the provincial towns: Bristol, perhaps, or Lichfield, where I had been born and still had cousins. But I had not been there for years; it was a small place and not all of its associations were happy for me.

My musings reminded me of young Timothy and his reluctance to move on. I decided to speak to Josephine; she was fond of the boy. And I resolved, as well, to ask her directly what was the matter between her and Martin Brocket. My steward did not seem like a bully, but I did not see all that went on in my home. No master does.

I arrived home towards five. Martin opened the door to me, his expression deferential as always; I asked if there had been any messages and he told me none. I thought, perhaps I should visit Barak, then decided, better for him to establish a story first with Tamasin. Damn all the lies.

✝

JOSEPHINE WAS IN the parlour, dusting with her usual care. She rose and bowed as I entered. I looked longingly through the window to my little resting place in the garden, but as I had caught her alone I should take the chance to speak to her. I began in a friendly tone. 'I have had little chance to talk to you of late, Josephine. How go things with you?'

'Very well, sir,' she said.

'I wanted to speak to you about Timothy. You know I have suggested that when he turns fourteen he should go for an apprenticeship, as Simon did?'

'That would be a good thing, sir, I think.'

'And yet he is reluctant to go.'

Her face clouded. She said, 'He did not have a happy time before he came here.'

'I know. But that was three years since.'

She looked at me with her clear blue eyes. 'I think, sir, he sees this house as a refuge.' She blushed. 'As do I. But it is not good to cower from the world too long, perhaps.'

'I agree.' I paused. 'What do you think I should do, Josephine?'

She looked at me in surprise. 'You are asking me, sir?'

'Yes.'

She hesitated, then said, 'I should go carefully, sir. Slowly.'

'Yes. I think you are right.' I smiled. 'And you, Josephine, will you be seeing Goodman Brown again soon?'

She blushed. 'If you are agreeable, sir, he has asked me to walk with him again on Sunday.'

'If he is agreeable to you, so he is to me.'

'Thank you, sir.'

'If I remember, you met him at the May Day revels. At Lincoln's Inn Fields.'

'Yes. Agnes persuaded me to go with her, and to wear a little garland of flowers she had made. Master Brown was standing next to us, he said it was pretty. He asked where we worked, and when he found it was for a barrister he told us that he did, too.'

'The law was ever good for establishing friendships.' I thought of Philip Coleswyn. Was he a friend? Perhaps, I thought. I said to Josephine, gently, 'I think Master Brown is perhaps the first young man you have walked out with?'

She lowered her head. 'Yes, sir. Father, he did not want me — '

'I know.' There was an awkward silence, then I said, 'Make sure you behave in a ladylike way, Josephine, that is all I would say. I think you will not find that difficult.'

She smiled, showing white teeth. 'He asks nothing more, sir.' She added quickly, 'Your approval is important to me.'

We stood for a moment, both a little embarrassed. Then I said, 'You get on very well with Agnes.'

'Oh, yes,' she answered brightly. 'She advises me about clothes. No woman ever has before, you see.'

'She is a good woman. Martin, I suppose, did not come with you to the revels.'

She wrinkled her nose. 'No, sir. He regards such things as silly.'

'But he treats you well enough?'

'Yes, sir,' she answered hesitantly. 'Well enough.'

I pressed her, gently. 'Josephine, I have sensed an – unease – between you and Martin.'

She put the cloth down on the table. Then she took a deep breath and lifted her head. 'I have been meaning to speak to you, sir, yet I did not know if it was right – and Agnes Brocket has been so good to me – '

'Tell me, Josephine.'

She looked at me directly. 'Two months ago, I went into your study one day to dust, and found Martin Brocket going through the drawers of your desk. Agnes was out, perhaps he thought he was alone in the house. I know you keep your money in a locked drawer there, sir.'

I did, and my most important papers, too. Martin had keys to most places in the house, but not to that drawer, nor the chest in my bedroom where I kept my personal items. 'Go on,' I said.

'He snapped at me to get out, said that he was looking for something for you. But Master Shardlake, he had the look of one uncovered in wrongdoing. I have been battling with my conscience ever since.'

I thought, thank heaven there was nothing in writing about the *Lamentation*; even the notes I had made in the garden I had destroyed. And, besides, two months ago it had not even been taken. But the news sent a chill down my spine, all the same. And how many times had Martin nosed around without Josephine seeing?

I said, 'I have never sent Martin to fetch anything from my desk. Thank you, Josephine, for telling me this. If you see him doing something like that again, come to me.'

I had missed no money. But if not money, what had Brocket been looking for? 'You did right to tell me, Josephine.

For now, let us keep it a secret.' I smiled uneasily. 'But remember, tell me if anything like this occurs again.'

'I did not like him from the start, sir, though Agnes has been such a friend, as I have said. Sometimes he speaks roughly to her.'

'Sadly husbands occasionally do.'

'And he was always asking about you when he first came, last winter. Who your friends were, your habits, your clients.'

'Well, a steward needs to find such things out.' It was true, but I felt uncomfortable nonetheless.

'Yes, sir, and it was only at first. Yet there has always been something about him I did not trust.'

'Perhaps because he speaks roughly to Agnes, whom you like?'

Josephine shook her head. 'No, it is something more, though I am not sure what.'

I nodded. I felt the same.

She said, hesitant again, 'Sir, perhaps I should not ask – '

'Go on – '

'If I might say, this last week you have seemed – preoccupied, worried. Have you some trouble, sir?'

I was touched. 'Merely work worries, Josephine. But thank you for your concern.'

I felt uneasy. I thought of the books I possessed, forbidden by the recent proclamation. They were concealed in my chest, and under the amnesty I had another fortnight to turn them in; I thought, if I do that officially, my name will doubtless go on a list. Better to burn them discreetly in the garden. And I would keep a careful eye now on Master Martin Brocket, too.

✝

THAT EVENING I WAS due to visit Philip Coleswyn.

He lived on Little Britain Street, near Smithfield. I walked there by back lanes to avoid seeing Smithfield itself again. His house was in a pleasant row of old dwellings, with overhanging jettied roofs. Some peddlers and drovers in their smocks were pushing their carts back towards the city from the Smithfield market. They seemed to have many unsold goods; I wondered if the troubles caused by the King's debasement of the coinage would ever end. A small dog, a shaggy little mongrel, wandered up and down the street whining and looking at people. It had a collar – it must have come to Smithfield with one of the traders or customers, and got itself lost. Hopefully its owner would find it.

I knocked at the door of Coleswyn's residence, where, as he had told me, a griffin's head was engraved over the porch. He let me in himself. 'We have no servants at the moment,' he apologized. 'My wife will be doing the cooking tonight. We have a fine capon.'

'That sounds excellent,' I said, concealing my surprise that a man of his status should have no servants. He led me into a pleasant parlour, the early evening sunlight glinting on the fine gold and silver plate displayed on the buffet. An attractive woman in her early thirties was sitting with two children, a girl and boy of about seven and five, teaching them their letters. She looked tired.

'My wife, Ethelreda,' Coleswyn said. 'My children, Samuel and Laura.'

Ethelreda Coleswyn stood and curtsied, and the little boy gave a tiny bow. The girl turned to her mother and said seriously, 'I prefer the name Fear-God, Mamma.'

Her mother gave me a nervous look, then told the child, 'We want you to use your second name now, we have told you. Now go, both of you, up to bed. Adele is waiting.' She clapped her hands and the children went to their father, who bent to kiss them goodnight, then they left obediently.

'My sister has come from Hertfordshire to help with the children,' Coleswyn explained.

'I must see to the food.' Ethelreda got up. She left the room. Coleswyn poured me some wine and we sat at the table.

'That was quite a scene at the Cotterstoke house this morning,' he said.

'My client's behaviour towards you was insufferable. I apologize for her.'

'Her manners are not your responsibility, Brother Shardlake.' He hesitated, then added, 'Have you seen her again today?'

'No, I have not been back to chambers. If she called this afternoon, she was unlucky. No doubt there will be a message tomorrow.'

Coleswyn smiled wryly. 'I keep thinking of those two beetles we saw fighting in the stableyard. Why do Edward and Isabel need their carapaces, and what lies underneath?'

'God alone knows.'

He fingered the stem of his glass. 'Recently I met an old member of the Chandlers' Guild, Master Holtby. Retired now, over seventy. He remembered Isabel and Edward's father, Michael Johnson.'

I smiled. 'Met by chance, or design?'

'Not purely by chance.' He smiled wryly. 'In any event, he said that Michael Johnson was a coming man in his day. Shrewd, prosperous, a hard man in business but devoted to his family.'

'You can see all that in the painting.'

'Yes, indeed. He inherited the business from his own father and built it up. But he died way back in 1507; that was one of the years when the sweating sickness struck London.'

I remembered the sweating sickness. More contagious and deadly even than the plague, it could kill its victims in a day. Mercifully there had not been an outbreak for some years.

Coleswyn went on, 'The family were devastated, according to old Master Holtby. But a year later Mistress Johnson remarried, another chandler, a younger man called Peter Cotterstoke.'

'Common enough for a widow left alone to marry a new husband in the same trade. It is only sensible.'

'The children were about twelve, I think. Master Holtby did not remember any trouble between them and their stepfather. They took his name in place of their father's, and kept it. In any case, poor Cotterstoke also died, a year later.'

'How?'

'Drowned. He had been down at the docks on some business to do with a cargo, and fell in, God save his soul. But then to everyone's surprise, Mrs Cotterstoke sold the business soon afterwards, using the proceeds to live on for the rest of her life. Disinheriting her son, Edward, in effect. He would have started as an apprentice in the business in a year or so. Master Holtby told me there was no love lost between the mother and either of her children.'

'But why?'

'He didn't know. But he said old Mrs Cotterstoke was a strong, determined woman. He was surprised she sold the business; he would have expected her to run it herself, as some widows do. But no, she just lived on in that house, alone. Edward started work at the Guildhall soon after, and Isabel married, while she was still very young, I believe.'

I considered. 'So some quarrel divided all three of them. And old Mrs Cotterstoke — we agreed that the wording of the Will looks as though she wished to set her children against each other, taking revenge from beyond the grave.'

'But for what?'

I shook my head. 'These family disputes can start from something small and last till everyone involved dies.'

'Perhaps this one will end now, after today's inspection?' he said hesitantly.

I raised my eyebrows. Knowing Isabel, I doubted that. Coleswyn nodded agreement.

'Did you notice their servant?' I asked. 'The one left to look after the place.'

'He had a sad look,' Coleswyn said. 'And it was strange how he leapt in when Edward and Isabel began shouting of what each could tell about the other. He could probably tell some stories himself. But of course neither of us could question him without our client's authority.'

'Personally, I just want to be done with it. This is one mystery I do not need to solve.'

Coleswyn played with a piece of bread. 'By the way, I have told my wife nothing of what happened today. Those wild accusations of heresy would upset her. What Isabel Slanning said about our vicar being under investigation earlier this year was quite true.' His face darkened. 'My wife comes from Ipswich. She has a family connection to Roger Clarke.'

'I do not know the name.'

'He was burned in Ipswich a few months ago, for denying the Mass. My wife's brother was an associate of his. He was interrogated there but recanted, said he accepted the presence of Christ's body and blood in the Mass.' He gave a grimace of a smile. 'Turn rather than burn, as they say.' I remembered an old friend of mine from years ago: Godfrey, a barrister who had become a radical Protestant and left the law to go and preach on the streets. I had never heard from him again; if he had been prosecuted for heresy it would have been all round Lincoln's Inn, so he must have died on the road, or gone to Europe. But Godfrey had had no wife or children.

'Since then I know there have been eyes on me at Gray's Inn; Bishop Gardiner has his informers among the lawyers. And Ethelreda thinks this house is sometimes watched. But I am a lawyer. I know how to be careful. I have said nothing against the Mass, and will not.'

I was silent a moment. Then I said, 'The persecutions seem to be over. No one has been taken in recently.'

'It started out of the blue,' he said, the skin round one eye twitching. 'And it may start again. That is why I dismissed our two servants. I was not sure I trusted them. But we must get another. Someone in my congregation has recommended a man. Not having servants is something that is noticed, too, among people of our class. And we thought it politic to make our daughter, who was christened Fear-God, use her second name, Laura.'

I shook my head. If the truth be told I did not know whether or not Christ's body and blood were present in the Mass, and now did not much care. But to bring ordinary people to such a state of fear was evil.

He continued quietly, 'When Parliament passed the act dissolving the chantries at the end of last year, our vicar thought the tide was turning his way and said some – well, I suppose, some careless things.' He looked at me with his clear blue eyes. 'He was questioned, and members of the congregation watched.' He took a deep breath. 'Has anyone asked you about me?'

'Nobody. I have heard nothing, apart from Isabel Slanning's rantings.'

He nodded. 'I am sorry to ask, but my wife is anxious.

Ah — ' His voice became suddenly cheerful. 'Here she is. Now you will learn what a fine cook Ethelreda is.'

✠

I HAD EATEN better meals; the capon was a little over-done, the vegetables mushy, but I made sure to praise the food to Ethelreda. Coleswyn and I tried to keep the conversation light, but his wife was preoccupied, smiling bravely at our jests about life at the Inns of Court, only picking at her food.

Coleswyn said, 'You have been a Serjeant at Law for some time. Perhaps you will be awarded a judgeship soon. It is the next step.'

'I have made too many enemies along the way for that, I think. And I have never been sufficiently conformist — in religion or aught else.'

'Would you like to be a judge? I think you would be a fair one.'

'No. I would either let people off or sentence them too severely. And seriously, I would not welcome having to waste time on all the flummery and ceremonial.'

'Some would give their right hands for a judgeship.'

I smiled. 'What is it the psalm says? "Vanity of vanities, saith the preacher. All is vanity."'

'And so it is,' Ethelreda said quietly.

Outside, the light began to fade. The noises from the street lessened as curfew approached; through the open shutters I heard the lost dog whine as it wandered up and down the street.

'This is the finest summer in some years,' I observed. 'Warm, but not too hot.'

'And just enough rain to keep the crops from drying out,' Coleswyn agreed. 'Remember the hailstorms last year? And all the men taken from work in the fields when we thought the French about to invade?'

'All too well.'

'Do you think this peace will last?'

'They are making much of it.'

'Peace,' Ethelreda said with a sort of flat despair. 'Peace with the French, perhaps. But what of peace at home?' She rubbed her hand across her brow. 'Philip says you are a man to be trusted, Serjeant Shardlake. Look at this realm. Last Christmas the King spoke in Parliament about how people call each other papist and traitor, how the word of God is jangled in alehouses. But from him there has been no constancy on religion these last dozen years. However the King's mind turns, we have to follow him. One year Lord Cromwell is bringing about true reform, the next he is executed. One month the King dissolves the chantries for the empty papist ceremonial they are, the next Bishop Gardiner is set to find sacramentarians in every corner, including, some say, in the Queen's circle. Nowadays it is unsafe to hold any settled conviction. You cannot trust your neighbours, your servants – ' She broke off. 'Forgive me, you are our guest – '

Her husband reached across and put his hand on her arm.

'No, madam,' I said quietly. 'You speak true.'

She made her tone light. 'I have strawberries and sugared cream to come. Let me fetch them. A woman's place is to work, not lecture.'

When she had left, Philip turned to me apologetically. 'I am sorry. When it is unsafe to discuss certain things in general company, and one finds someone trustworthy, one talks of little else. It relieves the strain, perhaps. But we should not impose on you.'

'That is all right. I do not like these dinners where one

fears to discuss aught but trivia.' I hesitated. 'By the way, do you think there are any Anabaptists in London these days?'

He frowned. 'Why do you ask?'

'The question has arisen in connection with a case. Their beliefs are very strange – that only adult baptism is valid, that Christ was not of human flesh – and, of course, that earthly powers should be overthrown and all men live in common.'

Coleswyn's mouth turned down in distaste. 'They are violent madmen. They brought blood and ruin in Germany.'

'I had heard that most of them, while holding to their social beliefs, have now renounced violence as a means of attaining them.' I thought, there are always other means, however misguided, including publishing a radical book by the Queen if they believed, however wrongly, that such an action would serve their political ends.

'Any that have been found have been burned,' Coleswyn replied. 'If there are any left they are keeping underground. Some I believe are old Lollards, and they had plenty of experience of living in hiding.'

'But perhaps Anabaptists, too, when in company, are tempted to talk unwisely,' I said thoughtfully. 'They are, after all, merely men like any other.'

He looked concerned. 'All the same, you do not want to meddle with such people.'

'No,' I answered feelingly. 'You are right.'

Ethelreda returned with the pudding, and we discussed politics no more. Master Coleswyn asked where I was from – he could not place my accent – and I told him about Lichfield: amusing stories of the poor monks' school where I received my early education. It grew dark and candles were lit in the sconces. Towards nine I became tired, suddenly finding it hard to keep my eyes open, and excused myself.

Coleswyn showed me to the door. In the porch he shook my hand. 'Thank you for coming, Master Shardlake. Forgive my wife's anxiety, but the times – '

I smiled. 'I know.'

'Thank you for listening to us. I think in truth you are a godly man.'

'Many would disagree.'

'Study the Bible, pray.' He looked earnestly at me. 'That is the way, the only way, to salvation.'

'Perhaps. In any event, you and your good lady must come to dine at my house soon.' I sensed the Coleswyns had been isolating themselves with their worries. More than was good for them.

'That would be most pleasant.' He clasped my hand. 'God give you good night.'

'And you, Master Coleswyn.'

'Call me Philip.'

'Then you must call me Matthew.'

'I shall.'

He closed the door, leaving me to adjust my eyes to the darkness. The moon was up, but the overhanging eaves of the houses meant the sky was but a narrow strip. I began to walk towards the stables.

Ahead I saw a movement near the ground. I flinched, then realized it was nothing more than the lost dog, still wandering up and down the street in search of its owner. I had startled the poor creature, which ran into a doorway opposite.

There was a thud, a sudden yelp, then the dog flew out the doorway and landed at my feet, lifeless, its head at a horrible angle, its neck broken by a kick.

I jumped back, my hand going to my knife as I peered into the darkness of the doorway. Shadows moved within.

I had been too careless. If this was Daniels and Cardmaker they could have me dead in an instant. But then, to my amazement, Isabel Slanning stepped out into the street. Two men in servants' dress followed her; one I recognized as the man she usually brought with her to consultations at Lincoln's Inn. She stood before me, staring right into my face, the moonlight making strange play with her features, those overlarge eyes glinting.

Her expression was triumphant. 'So, Master Shardlake,' she said, her voice a vicious hiss. 'I was right! You not only ride with Master Coleswyn, you dine with him. He calls you a godly man, you are his confederate – '

'Madam,' I said, aware that my voice was shaking with shock. 'I told you before, lawyers observe the courtesies with each other. They are not consumed with blind hatred as you are!' Behind her back, I caught a flash of white teeth as one of her servants smiled.

Isabel jerked her head back. 'I, Master Shardlake, am concerned with justice! A woman alone, faced with a confederacy of heretics! I am sure, now, that the so-called architect who came this morning to represent me is in league with my brother, too!'

'You picked him!'

'It is part of my brother's plot.' She waved a skinny finger in my face. 'But I have time, and will spare no energy in my search for justice! This is not the first time I have waited outside that man's house in the evening, to see who comes and goes. And tonight I see – you!' The last word was an accusing shout. It occurred to me again that Isabel Slanning was more than a little mad.

She smiled; I had never seen Isabel smile before and I had no wish to see it again – a wide grimace, splitting her face and exposing long yellow teeth. There was something savage in it. 'Well, *Serjeant* Shardlake!' Her voice rose. 'You will represent me no more! I will find a lawyer who will prosecute my case honestly, without heretic conspiracy! And I will write to the Lincoln's Inn authorities, telling them what you have done!'

I could have laughed. There could be no better news than that I was to be rid of Isabel. As for a complaint based on such evidence of wrongdoing as she possessed, it would have even Treasurer Rowland sniggering over his desk. I said, 'If your new lawyer will get in touch with me, mistress, I will happily give him the papers and answer any queries he has. And now I must get home.'

Philip's door opened. The noise had brought him and his terrified-looking wife to find out what was going on. He stared in amazement at Isabel. 'Brother Shardlake, what is happening?'

'No matter,' I said. 'Mistress Slanning has, I am delighted to say, just sacked me. Mistress Coleswyn, your husband said you thought someone was watching the house. It was this mad beldame.'

Isabel pointed at me again, her finger trembling. 'I will have you! I will have you all!' Then she turned and walked away, her servants following.

Ethelreda Coleswyn had started to cry. Philip said, 'All right, all right, my love, it was only that poor madwoman.'

'She will not be back,' I added reassuringly. Nonetheless, my eye was drawn to the poor dead dog. That must have been a vicious kick to break its neck like that, and Isabel had been standing in front of her servants in the doorway. It was she who had done it.

Chapter Twenty-three

THAT NIGHT I SLEPT DEEPLY, but woke early with a mind full of fears and discontents. I recalled Isabel Slanning's savage fury; I was sure she would like to serve me as she had that unfortunate dog.

There was a knock at the door and Martin entered, bearing towels and hot water, his face flatly expressionless as usual. 'God give you good morrow, Master,' he said. 'It is another fine, warm day.'

'Good morrow, Martin. Long may it continue.' I looked at his solid back as he laid the bowl on the table, wondering what went on inside that head of close-cropped fair hair. What had he been looking for in my desk that time? And Josephine said he had been constantly enquiring about my friends and contacts when he first came. Trying to nose into my life. Yet Martin, as I had reminded Josephine, needed to know all about me if he were to perform his duties as steward. His old master, another barrister, had given me a glowing reference; Martin and Agnes had been with the man for ten years, and were only leaving because he was retiring and moving to the country. I did not have a forwarding address, so could not get in touch with him.

Martin turned and gave me his tight little smile. 'Is there anything else, sir?'

'No, Martin. Not this morning.'

✝

AFTER BREAKFAST I walked up to Lincoln's Inn, wondering how Nicholas and Barak were, and whether they had come in. I thought, I should have visited them instead of going to Coleswyn's yesterday.

Barak was at his desk, working through some papers clumsily because of the heavy bandage on his left hand. Skelly looked at him curiously through his glasses. I could see no sign of Nicholas.

'Young Overton not in?' I asked with false jollity.

'Not yet,' Barak answered. 'He's late.'

Skelly looked up. 'Mistress Slanning called first thing this morning. She was in a – troubled state. She says she is going to a new lawyer.'

'Yes. I thought that might happen.'

'Should I send her a final bill?'

'Yes, we had better. If we don't she will take it as an admission of guilt or wrongdoing. With luck we shall not have to see her again.'

'She said she was going to take the case to Master Dyrick, whom you had dealings with last year.' Skelly looked at me curiously.

'Really? Well, if she wants someone to run a hopeless case with the maximum vigour, and charge her for the pleasure of it, she could not do better than Vincent Dyrick.' I turned to Barak. 'Come through, would you, Jack?'

He followed me into my office and I motioned him to sit. 'Dyrick again, eh? Well, they'll suit each other,' Barak said, managing a wry smile.

'I am only glad to be out of it. And I doubt Dyrick will encourage her to make trouble for me; remember, I know things about him.' I took a deep breath. 'Jack, I am more sorry than I can say for what happened yesterday.'

'I knew what I could be getting into.'

'I would have come round last night, but I thought you were best left to tell Tamasin – to tell her – '

'A pack of lies,' he finished heavily. 'Yes, you are right. So far as she is concerned I had an accident at the office. I was making a hole in a pile of papers with a knife, to thread a tag through, when my hand slipped. Tammy was full of sympathy, which makes it worse. Listen, when Nick gets in we need to meet to make sure we have the story straight between the three of us. You'll be seeing Tamasin next week at George's party. Please.'

'Yes, we will do that.' I closed my eyes a moment. 'Once again, I am sorry.'

He gave me his most piercing look. 'I just wish I knew what was going on.'

I shook my head. 'No. Safer not. How is your hand?'

'Sore as hell. But I have to play it down for Tamasin's sake, that's why I came in today. I'll survive,' he added.

'Any word from Nicholas?'

'He got but a flesh wound,' Barak said unsympathetically. 'By the way, there's a message for you, from Treasurer Rowland. He wants you to see him this morning. Before ten; he has a meeting then.'

'I'll go now. He did mention he had another task for me.' I got up. 'Dear God, I hope it's nothing like what he had me do last week.'

✝

ROWLAND WAS SEATED behind his desk again, writing. He raised his head, a cold look on his thin face. He had worn a similar expression when I had reported back to him after Anne Askew's burning, complimenting me on finding a place at Smithfield where my presence would be noted. I had, of course, not told him of Rich's glare at me. Looking at his white hair and long beard, I wished that, like Martin Brocket's old employer, he would retire. But he was the sort who savoured power, and would probably die at his desk.

'Serjeant Shardlake,' he said. 'Sit down.' He tapped the paper on his desk with a bony, inky finger. 'You knew the late Brother Bealknap, I believe. Had more than one passage of arms with him, I think.'

'Indeed I did.'

'I have just been composing a note to send round the Inn about his funeral. I am having to make the arrangements; his executor is not interested and there is no family. It will be in two days' time, the twenty-fourth, in the chapel. I doubt many will come.'

'No.' Certainly I would not, after Bealknap's piece of deathbed spite.

'You will appreciate this,' Rowland said. 'Bealknap left a vast sum of money to build what amounts to a mausoleum in the Inn chapel. With a marble image of himself, decorated and gilded and heaven knows what. He paid the Inn a good deal of money to agree to have it done.'

'So he told me. I saw him the day he died.'

Rowland raised his white eyebrows. 'Did you, by Mary?'

'He asked me to visit him.'

'A deathbed repentance?' Rowland's eyes narrowed with malicious curiosity.

'No.' I sighed. 'Not really.'

'You remember all the rumours that he had a great chest of gold in his chambers? Well, it was my duty to go and look for it. That chest did indeed exist, and contained several hundred sovereigns. But it wasn't at his chambers. Bealknap had had the sense to deposit it with one of the goldsmiths, for security. According to this goldsmith, Bealknap used to go there and sit with it of an evening.'

'He was a strange man.'

'There was certainly enough in the chest to pay for this mausoleum. However, many of the benchers have objected. Bealknap was not, after all, a great credit to the Inn, and this thing is hardly in the chapel style. They are refusing point-blank to sanction it. As I suspected they would, at the time I made the bargain with Bealknap. He can lie under a marble slab in the chapel like a reasonable man.' Rowland gave that cynical smile of his, world-weary but also cruel; proud of his outwitting of a dying man.

I said, 'But if it is in his Will – '

Rowland spread his arms, black silk robe rustling. 'If the benchers will not agree, the legacy becomes impossible of execution.'

'Who is his executor?'

'Sir Richard Rich.' I looked at him sharply. 'It is an old Will. I know for a fact he hasn't worked cases for Rich for over a year. Rich stopped using him when he began to get ill.' I wondered, was that why Bealknap had come cosying up to me at the end of last year, in the hope that I could get him some work? I remember him saying he was not getting as much work from one of his clients. It must have been Rich. Rowland inclined his head. 'I keep an eye on which of the great ones of the realm give work to Lincoln's Inn barristers. As the Queen used to do with you. I have been in touch with Rich's secretary, and he said Sir Richard couldn't care less about the mausoleum.' He shrugged. 'And the Will specifically excludes members of his family from having a say. So, this thing will not be built, and all Bealknap's gold will be *bona vacantia*. So in the absence of anyone else, his fortune will go to – ?' He paused on a questioning note, as though I were a law student.

'The Crown,' I said.

'Exactly!' He gave his creaky laugh. 'Rich will be able to boast that he has garnered another few hundred pounds for the King to spend.' Now I really could not help feeling sorry for Bealknap. 'Talking of the King and spending,' Rowland continued cheerfully, 'you remember you promised to undertake more duties for the Inn? Well, there is another big occasion coming up next month.' My face must have fallen, for he continued hurriedly, 'It is nothing like the burning. On the contrary, it will be the grandest celebration in London for years, some say since Anne Boleyn's coronation.'

'A celebration of what?' I asked, puzzled.

'The peace with France. A great chivalric display. I have had another letter from Secretary Paget. Apparently the very admiral who led the invasion fleet last year will bring a retinue of French ships up the Thames, including some that sailed against us. There will be a whole round of celebrations at the Tower and also at Hampton Court. Thousands will be present, royalty and nobility and representatives of the City Guilds and Inns of Court. They want a serjeant from Lincoln's Inn made available for the celebrations and I thought of you. As a sort of reward for that – less enjoyable occasion last week.'

I looked at him levelly. Rowland knew, of course, that I disliked ceremonial; again he was asserting his power. 'The King and Queen will be at many of the ceremonies,' he added, 'and I believe little Prince Edward is to be involved for the first time.'

I spoke quietly. 'There was a time, Master Treasurer, when the King was displeased with me. Perhaps it would be impolitic for me to attend.'

'Oh, the York business.' Rowland waved a dismissive hand. 'That was years ago. And all you'll be required to do is stand among many others in your best clothes and cheer when you're told to.'

I thought, cheer Admiral d'Annebault, who led the invasion fleet in the very battle during which the *Mary Rose* foundered. Chivalry, I thought, is a strange thing.

'I do not know the exact dates you will be required,' Rowland continued. 'But it will be during the last ten days in August, a month from now. I will keep you informed.'

There was no point in arguing. And I had other things to worry about. 'Very well, Treasurer,' I said quietly.

'The Lord alone knows how much it will all cost.' He laughed. 'Well, the King will have Bealknap's money to put towards it now.'

✝

I STEPPED OUT into the quadrangle. It had turned cloudy, that low, light summer cloud that seems to trap and thicken the heat. As I walked back to chambers I noticed a man loitering hesitantly nearby; young, well dressed in a dark doublet and wide green cap. I looked at him, then stared. It was a face I had seen only the day before, by the torchlight of the Tower dungeons. The gaoler Myldmore, who had appeared to be in trouble with his superior. He saw me and walked hesitantly across. His eyes were wide and frightened, as they had been at the Tower. 'Master Shardlake,' he said, a tremble in his voice, 'I must speak with you, in confidence. About – about a certain manuscript.'

Chapter Twenty-four

I TOOK MYLDMORE INTO my chambers. Barak and Skelly gave him curious looks as I led him into my room. I bade him sit. He did so, looking round uneasily. I spoke mildly, to try and put him at ease. 'Would you like a glass of beer?'

'No, sir, thank you.' He hesitated, pulling at his stringy little beard. He was an unimpressive-looking fellow; but as a Tower gaoler he would have seen – perhaps even done – some dreadful things. He spoke again suddenly. 'I believe you are investigating the murder of the printer Armistead Greening.'

'I am.'

'Officially?' His eyes turned on me with anxious intensity. 'They say it is on behalf of his parents.'

'Who says that?' I asked mildly.

'Friends. They told me a man they trust, called William Cecil, had been to see them and said it was safe to cooperate with you. Cecil is trying to trace three friends of Greening's who disappeared as well. His apprentice has vanished, too.' I looked at Myldmore closely. His eyes shifted, would not meet mine. If he knew all this he must have connections with the religious radicals. Suddenly he looked straight at me. 'Sir, why did you come to the Tower yesterday?'

I considered a moment, then said, 'I will answer you. But first let me reassure you that your friends are correct. I am not acting for any foe of the reformed cause.'

He looked at me narrowly. 'Is it believed there is a link between Greening's death and the – the Tower?'

'Rather that he had some connection with Anne Askew. Her name has come up.' I could not mention Elias's dying message; Myldmore did not even know the apprentice was dead.

A bead of sweat appeared on the young gaoler's brow. He said, as much to himself as to me, 'I must trust you then. I cannot understand why they have not come for me. They would give me no mercy.' He shook his head. 'Not if they found out about the book.'

I gripped the arms of my chair, trying not to betray my feelings. In what I hoped was a casual manner, I asked, 'Did you know Master Greening?'

Myldmore clasped his skinny hands together. 'Yes. I was at some of the meetings at his print-shop. With those other men.' He took a deep breath, then said, his voice shaking, 'What I did in the Tower, for Anne Askew – pity and conscience moved me to it. But it is fear now that moves me to come to you.' He cast his head down.

'I think you have important matters to tell me, Goodman Myldmore, and I would give you time. I see you are troubled. Let me tell my assistant we are not to be disturbed.'

I got up. Myldmore nodded. He actually looked a little relieved now, as people sometimes will do when they have decided to confess an important secret. I went to the outer office. Still no sign of Nicholas. I crossed to Barak's desk and swiftly scribbled a note to Lord Parr, telling him I had Myldmore in my chambers, and asking him to send some men to ensure that he, at least, did not get away. Barak looked puzzled, but I put a finger to my lips. I whispered, 'Can you take an urgent message to Whitehall Palace for me? To the Queen's Chamberlain?'

'Will they let me in?'

'Tell them I am working for the Queen's Learned Council, on urgent business for Lord Parr. Quick as you can.' I sealed the note and handed it to him. He gave me a sidelong look but got up and hurried out, making no noise as he closed the door. I ordered Skelly to tell any visitors I was absent, and went back to Myldmore. I was deceiving him, for my presence at the Tower had clearly made him believe, wrongly, that I was following a trail which had led to him. But as with so many others this past week, I had no alternative. This was, after all, a matter of a double murder.

✟

MYLDMORE WAS slumped in his chair, gazing unseeingly through the window at the passing lawyers. I sat behind my desk. 'Now,' I said, 'we have as much time as we need.' I smiled and he nodded dully. I thought, start with the easy questions. 'What is your first name?'

'Thomas, sir.'

'How long have you worked at the Tower, Thomas?'

'Two years. My father was a gaoler there before me. He got me my position at the Tower. I was a guard outside first, and when Father died last year I was offered his place.' He looked at me directly, his eyes passionate. 'Though I did not like the work, especially as I had found God and was beginning to tread the path to salvation. And this year – the arrests of so many poor lambs of God – it put me in great turmoil.'

So he had started work as a gaoler last year. He had probably not wanted the job, but work was hard to come by and it would have kept him from being conscripted to the war. In the Tower that would have been a quiet time. The great ones of the realm were concentrating on winning the war, and the struggles between contesting factions and religious loyalties

319

had been temporarily set aside. But in the spring, with the war over, it had all started again.

'I was sore troubled in conscience, sir.' Myldmore spoke as though I would understand; he obviously took me for another reformer. It was probably what Cecil had put around. 'It was through my church, our vicar, that I came to see that the only way to salvation is through Christ, and the only way to Him is through the Bible.' He continued, scarce above a whisper, 'I have doubted whether Our Lord's body is truly present in the Mass.' Now he did look at me anxiously, though he had not actually denied the Mass in what he had just said. I merely nodded sympathetically.

'My vicar said I was going too far – to deny the Mass is to go against the orders of the King, who is Head of the Church, appointed by God. But then, not long after, I met Master Curdy.'

'Greening's friend, who has vanished. The candlemaker.'

'Yes, sir. He knew my mother slightly. She died early this year. I spoke with him after the funeral, and he asked me to meet him for a drink. He turned the talk to religion. He is a learned man, self-taught, and a pleasant, engaging fellow; we met again and he told me he attended a discussion group of like-minded folk which I might find interesting.'

I looked at Myldmore's face, drawn and pale. A lonely, serious, conflicted young man, probably unpopular because of his job, just the sort who might be recruited to the radical cause. It struck me, too, that all the known members of the group were single, though Vandersteyn might have a wife back in Flanders. Otherwise, no wives or children to distract attention from the cause. 'And you went?'

'I attended my first group in April. They always met at Master Greening's print-shop. Only those invited could come, and we were asked not to tell anyone else about the meetings.' He broke off suddenly, biting his lip. 'And everyone I met there is gone now, vanished. Master Greening is dead and all the others have disappeared, I do not know whether of their own will. Elias the apprentice, Master Curdy, McKendrick the Scottish preacher, Vandersteyn the Dutchman, Michael Leeman that served the Queen at Whitehall – '

I sat up. 'Leeman was a member of your group?' I had wondered whether there might be a connection, and here was confirmation.

'He was.' Myldmore's eyes widened. 'Did you not know? What has happened to him?'

'I know only that he, too, has disappeared.' I drew a deep breath. So Leeman had taken the *Lamentation* and given it to Greening. That was clear now. And Myldmore had mentioned 'the manuscript', too. But I must tread carefully.

Myldmore was looking at me anxiously again. 'Please understand me, sir,' he said, 'I was never fully part of their group. They treated me with caution, asking me questions about my beliefs, always glancing at each other when I answered. It was as though – as though they were testing me.'

'Yes, I think I understand.' This was beginning to sound less like a group of radicals than a conspiracy.

Myldmore continued. 'They did not seem to like it that I was still uncertain about the Mass. Though they had strong arguments – about the Mass not being in the Bible – ' He broke off suddenly; he still did not quite trust me.

'We need not discuss that at all,' I said reassuringly. 'I promise, what anyone believes about the Mass is quite irrelevant to my enquiry.'

He looked relieved, and went on, 'Other things they said or hinted at I did not understand, or did not agree with.

They were strong on the need for people to be baptized as adults, not as children, just as John the Baptist and the disciples had been. And when I said the King was appointed by God to be Head of the Church, that angered them; they said the forbidding of the Bible to poor folk was akin to plucking God's Word from the people, and thanked the Lord that John Bale and others were having works on the gospel sent from the Continent. Though they said Bale had no understanding of the need for the ruling powers to be thrown down.'

'They said that? Used those very words?'

'Yes, sir. And said the King's royal blood mattered not a jot, we were all descended from Adam our common father.' He shook his head vigorously. 'Such words are treason. I said it was not right.' He took a deep breath. 'Shortly after that, they told me there stood too much between us for me to remain a member of their group. And so I left, having sworn not to reveal their existence to anyone. I confess I was glad. I felt them more and more as a weight on me.'

'They were leading you into dangerous waters.'

'Perhaps. I do not know.' His manner had become evasive again, and he avoided my eye. Myldmore was young and callow but he was not stupid. He must have realized, as I had, that with their belief in adult baptism and their fierce criticism of the social order, he had found himself among a group which at least sympathized with the revolutionary Anabaptists. And if they themselves were Anabaptists, planning some extreme act, for them to gain a recruit in the Tower, having already secured one in the Queen's household, could be very useful.

'I am sure you did right,' I said, weighing my words carefully. I was desperate to get to the matter of the book, but must not push him too hard. And I must give Barak time to deliver the note and for Lord Parr to react. I said, 'It must have been sad, though, to break with these folk just as you were getting to know them.'

Myldmore sighed. 'They were not easy people. Curdy was a decent fellow; he would ask how I fared, alone in the world as I am now. And though I think he had succeeded in his business, and had money, he always dressed soberly. I think he supported the Scotchman with money, and Greening's business, too. From things Master Curdy said I think his people were Lollards from the old days, that used to read bibles secretly written in English. Well, he was generous, he practised what he preached about sharing.' Myldmore looked at me, and asked suddenly, 'Are they dead, sir?'

'I think not. But I need to find them. Not to harm them, but perhaps to prevent them from unwittingly doing something foolish.'

'They were not men of violence,' Myldmore said. 'They renounced it as wrong. Though they often spoke most hotly –' He smiled sadly. 'Elias said that all rich men should be cast down and made to labour in the fields like common folk.'

I remembered Okedene saying that he had heard them arguing loudly with each other in Greening's shed, especially recently. 'Did they disagree much between themselves?'

Myldmore nodded. 'Often, though usually on points I found obscure, like whether someone baptized as a child needs a complete immersion when they are rebaptized as an adult.'

'What about matters concerning the social order? Did anyone disagree with Elias's remarks about throwing down the rich, for example?'

'No. No, they all agreed on that.'

I smiled back. 'People fierce in their righteousness?'

'Ay. Though Greening was a gentle and amiable man until you got him on to religion. The Dutchman was the worst; sometimes his accent was hard to understand, but that did not stop him calling you names like "blind simpleton" and "foolish sinner destined for Hell" if you disagreed with him. He was the one who spoke most often of John Bale.' I wondered, did Vandersteyn know the English exile? As a Dutchman involved in the cross-Channel trade it was not impossible.

Myldmore went on. 'The Scotchman, too, was an angry man, bitter, I think, at being thrown out of his own land. He could be frightening, big glowering man that he was. I think they treated him badly in his own country. I know he had a wife left behind there.'

'And Leeman?'

'The gentleman from Whitehall? I felt a brotherly spirit with him, for he was much worried, as I am, over the question of whether God had elected him for salvation. Like them all, Leeman was always talking about the coming of the End Time, as foretold in the Book of Revelation; how the Antichrist was about to come and we must be ready for judgement. I did not understand it all.'

The coming of the Antichrist prophesied in the Book of Revelation. It was another belief characteristic of the Anabaptists and other radical Protestants. Okedene had mentioned Bertano in that connection, and his name had been on the lips of Greening's killers at the inn yesterday. I asked, as casually as I could, 'Many have identified the Antichrist with a particular individual. Did the group ever mention a name?'

He looked genuinely puzzled. 'No, sir.'

'An Italian one, perhaps?'

'The Pope, you mean? They mentioned the Pope only to curse him.'

I realized that if the group had decided this Bertano was the Antichrist they would not mention his name to someone they did not fully trust. I said quietly, 'And this whole group has disappeared now. Why do you think that may be?'

A muscle in Myldmore's cheek twitched for a moment. Then he said, 'I think perhaps they have fled because of the book.'

I looked at his anguished, worried face. Then I took the plunge. 'You mean the book which Michael Leeman took?'

He stared at me blankly. 'Leeman? No, it was I who smuggled the book from the Tower and gave it to Greening. Anne Askew's account of her examinations.'

For a moment my head span. We stared at each other. As calmly as I was able, I said, 'Tell me about Anne Askew's book, Thomas.'

He frowned. 'Do you not know? I thought that was why you were at the Tower yesterday.' He shifted in his seat, and for a moment I feared he might panic and run.

'You are right,' I lied. 'I am concerned with Anne Askew's book. But I was misinformed about who gave it to Greening.' I continued calmly, 'You have told me much, Thomas. Best tell me the rest now. I swear to you, I am no enemy.'

He looked at me again, then bent his head. 'It seems I have no choice.'

I did not reply.

He took a deep breath, then he recounted the next part of his story in quiet, even tones, without looking up at me; his voice trembling occasionally so that I had to bend to catch his words.

Chapter Twenty-five

'IT WAS ON THE twenty-ninth of June, a Tuesday. Three weeks ago, though it seems a year. Anne Askew and those three men had been condemned to death for heresy at the Guildhall the day before. Everyone was talking of it. We expected she would lie in Newgate prison with the others till she was taken to be burned. That afternoon I was on duty in the Tower, checking on the prisoners in the dungeons and giving food to those allowed it. Afterwards I went to report on how they fared to Master Howitson – you met him yesterday.'

'Yes, I remember.'

'While I was with him at the desk I heard footsteps outside, several people coming down. The outer door opened and Master Ardengast, the senior guard, entered, accompanied by a couple of guards holding a young woman. She wore a blue dress of good quality, but to my astonishment she had a dirty sack over her head, so her face could not be seen. She was breathing hard, poor creature, very frightened. It was dreadful to see a woman treated so. Another couple of men followed, carrying a large trunk. Then Master Ardengast told Howitson and me this woman was to be lodged down here, and none of the other prisoners were to know of her presence. He said as we were on duty we must perform a double shift, for the fact she was here was to be known to as few as possible.'

Myldmore's voice fell to little more than a whisper. 'You would think one would protest at such a thing, but you get used to the worst in that place. And I am a weak, sinful creature. I only answered, "Yes, sir." The woman was led away, to a cell within, a place called the "special cell", better appointed than the others, for prisoners of gentle birth. But it is near the room where the rack and the other instruments of torture are kept.' He looked up at me. 'I have seen them.'

So have I, I thought, but did not say.

'After that, all the men left, leaving Howitson and me staring at each other. I began to ask who the woman was, but Howitson said we should not talk about it. So I went about my duties. Then, a couple of hours later, Master Ardengast returned. With him were the Lieutenant of the Tower, Sir Anthony Knevet, and two other men, in fine silk gowns with gold chains of office and jewelled caps. One I did not know, he was thin with a ruddy face and a little jutting red beard. The other I recognized, for I have seen him on business in the Tower before. The King's councillor, Sir Richard Rich.'

I stared at him hard. Rich, and by his description the other man was Lord Chancellor Wriothesley, who at the burning had been worried lest the gunpowder round the victims' necks send burning faggots flying at the councillors. And Knevet, who was in bad odour with his superior Walsingham. So, Richard Rich was deep in this business, as I had suspected.

Myldmore looked back at me now, his eyes frightened. 'Should I go on now, sir?'

I think he feared that at the mention of those names I might call on him to desist, and decide to get involved no further. But I said, 'No, continue.'

'They said nothing to me or Howitson, though Rich

frowned when he saw that I recognized him. They passed on, through the door to where the woman was kept.'

'You still had no idea who she was?'

'No.' There was anger in his voice suddenly. 'But I knew Mistress Askew had been condemned, and that the law forbids torturing someone after sentence.'

'Yes, it does.'

Myldmore passed a hand over his brow. 'It was three hours before they all came out again. Rich and Wriothesley looked angry, and Rich had a sheen of sweat on his face, as though he had been at some hard labour. Sir Anthony Knevet looked worried. I remember Rich flexed his hands, little white hands they are, and winced as though he were in pain. They paused at the desk and Sir Anthony spoke to us roughly. "You two never saw these gentlemen, you understand? Remember your oath to the King." Then they all went out, back up the stairs. I heard Rich say angrily, "Another hour, Knevet, and I would have broken her yet."'

He paused. Outside in the quadrangle two barristers were talking, probably of some amusing incident in court, for both were laughing. Sunlight illuminated Myldmore's head, which he bent again as he continued. 'That evening it was again my duty to feed the prisoners. Howitson told me to take a bowl of pottage to the woman. So I went through to her cell. I knocked lest she was in a state of undress, and a voice bade me come in.

'The room had a table, chairs and a bed with a fine cover, as well as a chest. I recognized Anne Askew at once, for I had twice seen her preach in the streets, but now she sat awkwardly in a heap on the floor, her back against the wall and her legs spread out on the stone flags. It looked almost indecent.' Myldmore flushed, and I thought how young he was, how oddly innocent to be serving in that den of wolves.

'I noticed her dress was torn. She had cast off her coif and her fair hair hung down in rats-tails, bathed in sweat. Her face – a pretty face – was composed, but her eyes were staring, wide.' He shook his head, as though to try and clear it of that terrible image. 'Despite all this, when she spoke to me it was in pleasant, gentle tones. She asked, "Would you put the tray on the floor, please, goodman gaoler. I cannot rise."

'I know what racking does to people. God forgive me, I have seen it, the prisoner stretched out, arms above his head, fixed to the moving table with ropes tied to his wrists and ankles, and then the ropes wound so that the muscles and joints tear; and it came to me in a rush of horror that those men – Privy Councillors – had just racked this woman. I laid the plate and spoon on the floor beside her. She bent forward to pick the spoon up but gave a little cry of pain and leaned back, breathing hard.' Myldmore looked up at me, swallowing. 'In a man, it would have been bad enough. But to see a woman in that state – ' He shook his head. 'I think my expression must have betrayed me. She asked if I knew who she was. I answered, "Yes, Madam, I have seen you preach." Then I said, "What have they done to you?"'

'She smiled in answer. "His majesty's noble councillors would have the Queen down, and her ladies and their husbands. They asked me what dealings I had had with them, the Countess of Hertford, Lady Denny, the Duchess of Suffolk. They wanted me to say they were all heretics who denied the Mass. But I said, truly, that I have never met any of them. So they racked me to get the answers they wanted. Sir Anthony Knevet refused to do it, so Rich and Wriothesley turned the rack." Her eyes seemed to burn into mine as she said, "I do not care who knows; I want the story spread abroad."'

Myldmore swallowed, looked at me. 'I was frightened, sir, I did not want to know this. But Mistress Askew continued, shifting her position as spasms of pain went through her. She said, "It was great agony, and there will be more when they burn me. But I know that this is all but a prelude to the bliss to come." And then she smiled again.' The young gaoler shook his head in wonder.

'I asked Mistress Askew, "Do you believe, then, that you are saved?" And she answered, "Truly, I believe I have God's grace in my heart." Her eyes were blue, bright as though from an inner light. It moved me to the heart, sir.' Myldmore's face worked a moment before he continued: 'I knelt before her and said, "You have endured, as Christ did. I wish I had your courage and certainty."' His eyes were wet now. 'And then she asked me to say the twenty-third Psalm with her. I did.' Myldmore whispered, softly, '*Yea though I walk through the valley of the shadow of death, I will fear no evil: for thou art with me . . .*' Then, as she could not feed herself, she asked me to spoon the broth into her mouth. She could scarce move without terrible pain.' He paused, then added quietly, 'I heard she was most brave at the end.'

'She was,' I answered. 'I was there.'

'Ah.' He nodded. 'You were one of the godly folk who went to comfort her.'

I did not contradict him. Myldmore took a deep breath. 'I left after feeding her. Howitson told me that the next day she was to be removed from the Tower to a house – I do not know whose – where she would be lodged to recover. He reminded me to keep my mouth shut. They hoped she would recover sufficiently to walk to the fire. I was angry, sir, more than ever before in my life.'

'Was it you who set the news afoot she had been tortured?'

'Yes.' He clenched his jaw with a new stubbornness. 'And they know it was. I was in such a fume of anger at what had been done, I told my landlady that same evening that Anne Askew had been tortured in the Tower. But I did not have the courage to name Wriothesley and Rich. My landlady is a good reformer, and also a great gossip. I wanted her to tell others. For that one evening, I did not think of my own safety. Next day it was the talk of the streets.' He said, sorrowfully, 'I confess when I heard the story jangled about everywhere, I began to be afraid again.'

He sighed, then continued, 'And soon enquiries were indeed made, by Master Ardengast. Only those who saw Anne Askew in the Tower, and those in the house to which she was taken, knew what had been done to her. I was questioned by Sir Anthony Knevet himself. I confessed at once. I was so afraid I wet my hose during the interview. Anne Askew did not wet herself,' he added quietly, in self-disgust.

'She was a rare creature,' I said.

'I was sure I would be arrested, but I was told only to keep my mouth shut. Which I have, until you came yesterday. I do not understand why I have not been arrested. But Sir Anthony was very mild with me, and there have been rumours in the Tower that he was so concerned at what Rich and Wriothesley had done, that he privately told the King. But I do not know.'

I considered. Perhaps nothing had happened to Myldmore because if he were put on trial for revealing Anne Askew's torture, that would involve admitting publicly that it had taken place.

'Did Sir Anthony Knevet enquire about your motives?' I asked. 'Your religious associations?'

'Yes. He asked about my church, my associates. But I did not tell him about Master Greening or his group. That would be the end of me because of – because of the book. And I had said nothing about that.'

'I think it is time to tell *me*, Master Myldmore.'

He looked down at his hands, then raised his head again. 'On the day I spoke with Mistress Askew, I was sent again, late in the evening, to take her supper, and to report on how she fared. When I went into the cell I found she was still on the floor, but had managed to drag herself half across the room. Jesu knows what that cost her. A candle had been brought in and she was sprawled next to her chest, which was open. She had managed to take out a bundle of papers, which lay on her lap, with an inkwell and a quill. She was writing, sweating and wincing with the effort. She looked up at me. There was silence for a moment, and then she said, in a strange tone of determined merriment, "Goodman gaoler! You have found me at my letters."

'I laid the bowl of pottage close beside her, and in so doing saw what she had written: ". . . *then the lieutenant caused me to be loosed from the rack. Incontinently I swooned, and then they recovered me again* . . ."

'I said, "That letter will not be allowed out, madam, it says too much."

'"A shame," she said. "It contains the whole truth."

'I asked her if she would like me to feed her again, and she said she would. She leaned back against the chest, like a helpless child, while I fed her and wiped her chin. She told me I was a good man, and a Christian. I said I wished I could be. She said then, "Will you report what I have been writing to Sir Anthony Knevet?" I did not reply and she stared at me, her eyes full of pain but somehow – unrelenting. Then she said, "This is a record, an account, of my examinations since my first arrest last year. I wrote that last piece this afternoon, though my arms sore pain me. It is strange, they have never searched among my clothes, where this testament has been hidden." She smiled again. "The King's councillors will tear the strings and joints of a gentle-woman's body, yet common gaolers hesitate to search her underclothes."

'"It is rare for a woman to be imprisoned there," I said.

'Then she touched my hand and said, "They will search the chest soon, without doubt, and will find this. You are the first to have seen it, I had not the strength to put it away quickly when your key turned in the door. My fate is in your hands, sir, and if you feel you must take my journal to Sir Anthony Knevet, then you must." Those blue eyes, glinting in the candlelight, were fixed on mine. "But I ask you, as you seek salvation, to take my writings, now, and somehow get them published. That would make a mighty storm here. Do you think you can do that?"

'I thought at once of Greening. But I drew back. I said, "Madam, you ask me to risk my life. If I were caught – "

'"Your life, sir?" She gave a little smile and with an effort laid her hand on mine. "Life is fleeting, and beyond lies God's judgement and eternity." Then she asked my name. "To have the world know what is done in the King's name would be a mark of grace, Thomas, a great step to your salvation."'

I felt a sudden anger with Anne Askew. She had used the promise of salvation as a weapon against Myldmore, I thought, a sort of blackmail.

His eyes looked inward for a moment, then he gave me a fierce look. 'I said I would take the writings, her *"Examinations"*, as she called them. The document was not long. I hid it under my jerkin and took it from the cell that night. After speaking to my landlady I went straight to Master Greening's print-shop. He was alone there. He greeted me cautiously at first, but when I told him about the manuscript, and showed it to him, he was almost overcome with joy. "I can have this sent to Bale," he told me. "And five hundred copies smuggled back into England in a few months." I remember him saying, "This will make a mighty uproar.'"

I did a quick calculation. 'That would have been – what – the twenty-ninth of June?'

He looked at me, surprised. 'Yes. I knew I must do it that night; already I could feel my courage beginning to fail. But I think the Lord gave me strength, he moved me to do it.'

I sat back. So there was not one book, but two. Myldmore had brought Anne Askew's *Examinations* to Greening, and later Leeman had brought the Queen's *Lamentation*. Because they knew Greening could get them smuggled out to Bale. A mighty uproar indeed. Yes, both books would certainly cause that. Perhaps these people thought, in their noddle-headed way, that the Queen's confession of faith, and Anne Askew's exposure of what had been done to her, would anger the populace sufficiently to overthrow their rulers in a great riot. They did not fully understand the strength and ruthlessness of those in power. Anne Askew was beyond harm now, but the publication of the *Lamentation* would place the Queen in great danger, and her fall would only advance the reformers' worst enemies.

'So what do you think has happened to them, sir?' Myldmore asked again. 'Greening's group? Why was he killed? Was it – was it because I brought them the book?'

'I do not know,' I answered honestly. 'But I think there was more to it than that.'

'What more? Sir, I have told you everything, I have trusted you. Yet I sense you know things that I do not.'

'I do, and may not tell you, as yet. But be assured, I mean

you no harm.' I asked, 'What would you do now, go back to the Tower?'

'I am not on duty again until next Monday.' He shook his head. 'I tremble with fear every time I go to work. I feel them looking at me, waiting. I am terrified that sooner or later they will find out about the book – '

I heard several pairs of footsteps outside. Myldmore started up, then glanced at me, his eyes wide. The door opened and Barak came in with young William Cecil, who wore a stern look. There were two sturdy fellows at his side, each with a hand on a sword hilt. I thought Myldmore might try to run but he just got up and stood meekly by his chair, shaking. He turned his eyes back to me and said, in tones of quiet horror, 'You have betrayed me.'

'No,' I said. 'To the contrary. You will be protected now.' I looked at Cecil, but his severe expression did not soften.

Chapter Twenty-six

LATE THAT AFTERNOON I stood again in Lord Parr's office at Whitehall Palace. With us were William Cecil and Archbishop Cranmer, whose white surplice made a contrast to the dark lawyer's robes Cecil and I wore. On the table was a large piece of paper covered with my writing, the fruit of much thinking that afternoon. We looked expectantly at the door, waiting.

We were to meet with Lord Parr at four o'clock, Cecil had informed me, when he and his men took Myldmore away from my chambers. He had told the terrified young gaoler only that he worked for people at court who were friends and would see him kept safe, housed somewhere quiet for now; a message would be sent to the Tower officials that he was ill, to buy some time.

Myldmore had been very frightened, pleading to be let go, but Cecil answered brusquely that Greening's killers were still at large and I had encountered them very recently, which I could only confirm. As he was led out, Myldmore looked at me over his shoulder; a look of sorrow and anger, for he had bared his soul to me, while all the time I had been preparing to have him seized. As I stood in Lord Parr's office I remembered that look. Yet Myldmore was safer hidden away somewhere – unless the Queen fell; in that case, he was just one more who would fall with the rest of us.

✝

FOR TWO HOURS AFTER they left I had remained in my office. I pulled the shutters closed, got out pen and paper, and sat thinking; about dates and individuals, and the disappearance, now, not of one but of two crucially sensitive books. I tried to fit Myldmore's story into the rest of what I knew. It all came back to Greening and his group; who and what they were. I lost track of time; then the Inn clock sounded three, reminding me I should be on my way. I gathered up the paper on which I had written some crucial notes, and headed down to the river to catch a wherry to the Whitehall Stairs. Once again, I changed my robe in the boat; at the palace the guards were already beginning to recognize me; some nodded respectfully as they ticked my name off their lists. I was starting to become familiar with the layout of the palace, too; that tightpacked series of extraordinary buildings, all different, interspersed with little hidden courts that had seemed so hard to navigate at first. Even the brightness and beauty of the interiors was becoming almost commonplace to me now, and I could walk along the corridors without constantly wanting to stop and gaze in wonder at a statue, a painting, a tapestry.

I arrived at Lord Parr's office just before four; he arrived soon afterwards. Also in the room when I arrived was William Cecil and, to my surprise, Archbishop Cranmer, looking withdrawn and worried. I bowed deeply to him. Lord Parr told me the Queen would be attending us shortly. 'I have been trying to work out where this new development with Myldmore leaves us,' I said as we waited.

'And where is that, Matthew?' Cranmer pressed quietly.

'I think we are narrowing down the possible scenarios.'

There was a tap at Lord Parr's door and it opened. Lady Anne Herbert, the Queen's sister, whom I had seen at Baynard's Castle a few days ago, stood on the threshold.

She bowed as the Queen herself entered, wearing a magnificent dress of gold silk, the forepart and sleeves white with a design of tiny golden unicorns. Her expression was calm and composed. Behind her stood Mary Odell. We all bowed low.

The Queen said, 'Mary, Anne, you may return to my chamber.' The ladies nodded to us briefly and left. She looked between the four of us and took a long breath; for a moment her composure slipped and she appeared haggard as she turned to address her uncle. 'Your message said there had been developments? Have you recovered my book?'

'No, Kate, but Master Shardlake has some news.' He nodded in my direction.

'Good?' she asked quickly, intently.

'Not bad, your majesty. Complicated,' he replied.

She sighed, then turned to Cranmer. 'Thank you for attending us, my Lord. I know my uncle has been keeping you informed of developments.'

'I was here for the meeting of the King's Council.'

'Now that Gardiner and his people are no longer on the offensive,' Lord Parr said. There was a touch of contempt in his voice, no doubt aimed at Cranmer's tendency to absent himself from the council when matters looked dangerous.

The Queen gave her uncle a severe look. 'We five,' she said, 'we are the only ones who know the *Lamentation* is gone. But first, my Lord Archbishop, what news from the council?'

'Most of the discussion was about the visit of the French admiral next month. The scale of the ceremonies will be huge. Wriothesley argued that with so many taxes falling due this year it may cause murmuring and grudging among the populace, but the King is determined on great celebrations, nevertheless.' He smiled. 'And you are to be at the forefront, your majesty.'

'I know. The King has told me of the new gowns and jewellery my ladies and I are to have. And all the time I deceive him,' she added, a tremble in her voice. I thought how if the *Lamentation* suddenly appeared in public all the new finery could vanish in an instant. I remembered Myldmore's description of Anne Askew in the Tower and suppressed a shudder.

The Archbishop continued, encouragingly, 'Your brother, as Earl of Essex, is to welcome the ambassador and ride with him through London. He will be at the forefront of the ceremonies, too. Gardiner and Norfolk remained quiet throughout the meeting. Their heretic hunt has ended in failure, madam, that is clearer every day.'

'Unless something brings it alive again.' The Queen turned to me. 'I have heard from my uncle that two of your employees were injured. I am sorry for it.'

'Neither was seriously hurt, your majesty.'

'And this man Myldmore, you have him somewhere safe?' she asked Lord Parr.

'Yes, together with the guard and the carpenter who helped Leeman.'

'Each could be open to a charge of treason,' Cecil observed.

Lord Parr shook his head. 'If this matter is settled we should ensure all three move quietly out of London, to somewhere far out in the provinces.'

I said, 'Myldmore can only pretend sickness for so long; eventually there will be enquiries made.'

'There is no connection to us. They'll think he's run away.'

'So many disappeared,' the Queen said quietly. 'And two dead. And all because of me.'

'Anne Askew played her part,' Lord Parr said gruffly. 'God rot her wild heresy.'

Cranmer bit his lip, looking troubled, then said, 'With your leave, your majesty, Master Shardlake would like to show us something he has worked out.' He gestured to the sheet of paper on his desk.

The Queen looked at me and nodded, and I bowed again.

Cecil produced chairs for the Archbishop and the Queen, then stood beside Lord Parr. In front of them was a list of names and dates:

Armistead Greening – *murdered 10th July*
James McKendrick – *vanished 11/12th July*
William Curdy – *vanished 11/12th July*
Andres Vandersteyn – *vanished 11th/12th July*
Elias Rooke – *fled 17th July, murdered 18th July*
Michael Leeman – *suborned carpenter Barwic and*
    guard Gawger with money, almost certainly took
    Lamentation of a Sinner *to Greening on 6th July.*
    Fled Whitehall 19th July

    ///////////////

Thomas Myldmore – *took Anne Askew's writings to*
    Greening on 29th June

I said, 'These seven people constituted a radical group which met at Armistead Greening's house.'

Cranmer pointed to the paper. 'Why is Myldmore's name separated from the others?'

'Because he was never actually accepted into the group. There might also be others who were considered, but these first six are the core. Vandersteyn may have had links to the Anabaptists, while Curdy had the money and may have supplied the bribes which Leeman used to pay the locksmith

Barwic and the guard Gawger. Greening himself almost certainly had links to John Bale in Antwerp, and likely imported forbidden books from Flanders. Myldmore's evidence makes clear that this was more than a discussion group; it shows the fervour of some sort of Anabaptist sect.' I looked round. 'I think the group was trying to recruit people with connections to positions of trust, in high or secret places – the guard Leeman and the Tower gaoler Myldmore being two examples. Myldmore, however, could not accept their views on social order, nor on the Mass, and they asked him to leave. But later, when he saw what happened to Anne Askew, he felt he must act. Greening was the obvious person for him to take the woman's book to. And he, in turn, planned to take it to John Bale.'

The others remained silent. The Queen nervously touched the pearl at her breast; Cranmer fixed me with a troubled stare. William Cecil nodded slowly. 'Then Greening was murdered,' I continued. 'As for the other five – ' I ran my finger down the list of names – 'three immediately vanished: McKendrick, Curdy and the Dutchman. The guard Leeman remained in his place here at Whitehall. And Elias moved to work for his neighbour Okedene.'

'If the other three fled,' said Cecil, 'rather than being murdered, why did not Elias and Leeman go, too?'

'I have pondered that. It may be that Leeman thought, given he worked at Whitehall Palace, that he was safe. He has quarters there. He stayed till he found he was under investigation, and only then disappeared. As for the apprentice Elias, remember times are hard, and he provided the only income for his widowed mother and his sisters.' I sighed. 'He was obstinate, and probably rejected the advice of the others to join them in fleeing. He seemed, when I met him, to think Greening was the murderers' only target. And given his youth, and perhaps limited experience, it may well be that the others did not trust him with the knowledge that they had possession of the *Lamentation*. Though I believe he knew that Greening had been given Anne Askew's writings.'

Cecil said, 'Because he said "killed for Anne Askew" before he died.'

'Exactly.'

'The poor boy,' the Queen muttered. 'He stayed for the sake of his mother and sisters, and died for it.' She walked abruptly to the window and stood looking out over the little courtyard below, her head bowed.

Lord Parr said, 'So these other four? Are they still alive?'

'I do not know. The fact Elias was murdered, too, makes me think the killers were after the whole group. Whether they found them or not we do not know.'

Lord Parr stroked his white beard. 'And whoever killed Greening and Elias is likely to have both Anne Askew's writings and the Queen's.'

Cecil asked: 'Could someone powerful – Wriothesley or Gardiner, Rich or Paget – have an agent inside the group? One of the missing four? How else could anyone outside have come to know that Greening had the *Lamentation*?'

I said, 'Yes, someone within that group could have been working for an enemy. I think we can rule out Leeman – if he was acting for Gardiner, the last people he would take the *Lamentation* to is Greening's group. That leaves Curdy, Vandersteyn and McKendrick; three of them. But if one of them was a spy working for Gardiner or anyone else, and murdered Greening and took the *Lamentation*, Anne Askew's work too, why has nothing been heard of either book since? Anne Askew's work they might destroy, for it incriminates Wriothesley and Rich, but surely the spy, if there is one, would take the *Lamentation* straight to the King?'

Cranmer nodded. 'Yes. Norfolk and Gardiner knew that Lord Hertford and Lord Lisle are about to return to the Privy Council, and that the heresy hunt had failed. It has only been recently that I have felt it prudent to return to the council myself. The sensible thing for them would have been to act at once, so far as the *Lamentation* was concerned.'

I said, 'Yes, my Lord Archbishop, I agree.'

The Queen turned and looked at me, a spark of hope flashing in her eyes. 'So you think it may not be Gardiner's agents who killed Greening and took the *Lamentation*?'

'Possibly. Though Master Cecil's logic about an informer within the group is persuasive.'

She shook her head, mystified. 'Someone working against a group of the godly from within? Pretending to be one of them? How could anyone bear such a betrayal of their souls?'

Lord Parr spoke with sudden impatience. 'In God's name, niece, when will you realize not all are as pure in mind as you?'

The Queen stared back at him, then laughed bitterly. 'I am not pure. If I were, I would never have needed to write a book called *Lamentation of a Sinner* – nor failed, after my Lord Archbishop's good advice, to destroy it through my sinful pride, and hence caused all of this. And deceived my husband in the process,' she added bitterly.

I glanced at her. In other tones the words might have sounded self-pitying, but the Queen spoke with a sad, honest intensity. There was silence for a moment. Then Cecil turned to me. 'The way Greening and Elias were killed, and your description of the two killers – that speaks to me of the involvement of someone powerful, someone who can afford to hire experienced assassins.'

I looked at him. Cecil was young indeed to be included in a council such as this, but his cleverness was as great as his calm. Lord Parr had chosen well. 'I agree,' I said. 'But that does not get round the problem of why the book is still kept hidden.' I shifted my stance, for I had been standing a long time and my back was hurting. 'Lord Parr, my Lord Arch‑bishop, your majesty: with your leave I would show you what I have written on the reverse of this paper. It is a chronology, and may illustrate matters further.' The Queen nodded, touching Catherine Howard's pearl again. I had never seen her so subdued. But she leaned across the table with the others as I turned the paper over:

9th June	Leeman overhears the Queen and the Archbishop arguing over the *Lamentation*. He has his group plot to steal it.
29th June	Anne Askew brought to the tower and tortured.
29th June	Myldmore takes Anne Askew's writings to Greening.
5th July	Two men, one with half an ear missing (likely the same who earlier tried to recruit the Queen's page Garet) are disturbed by Elias trying to break into Greening's premises.
6th July	Leeman, having suborned the carpenter Barwic and the guard Gawger, steals the *Lamentation*. Logic suggests he took it to Greening.
10th July	Greening murdered by two men, different from those involved in the first attack, and the *Lamentation* (and perhaps Anne Askew's writings) stolen.

11th/12th July	McKendrick, Curdy and Vandersteyn disappear.
16th July	Anne Askew burned.
17th July	I question Elias, who flees at mention of the name Bertano (which according to Okedene was mentioned by the group in connection with the Antichrist).
18th July	Elias murdered.
19th July	Having got wind of my enquiries, the guard Leeman flees.
21st July	I encounter the two men who killed Greening (not the same as the men who tried to break into his house earlier). They know who I am and they mention Bertano.

They studied the chronology. I said, 'This timetable allows that there could be two different sets of people involved. One that was after Anne Askew's writings, and another that wanted the *Lamentation*.'

Cecil shook his head. 'But there can only have been one informer, surely. Is it not more likely the informer told Gardiner – or Norfolk, or Rich, or Wriothesley, or whoever – about Anne Askew's *Examinations* first, after Myldmore took them to Greening on the twenty-ninth of June, and agents were then sent to take it, but were interrupted by Elias? Then, on the sixth or seventh of July the *Lamentation* comes into Greening's hands, and two different men, also under the authority of whoever is behind this, are sent to kill him and seize both books – succeeding, apart from the torn page Greening held on to?'

'Possibly. But surely it would have been more sensible to send the original two men on the second visit?' I mused.

Lord Parr burst out, in sudden anger, 'When will we get *any* certainty?'

'Not yet, my Lord. And there is another possibility.' I took a deep breath before continuing. 'What if, after the first attempted attack, the group held divided opinions about what to do next? Perhaps some wanted to send the books abroad for publication, while others, more sensible, realized publication of the *Lamentation* could only damage the Queen? Remember that in terms of their understanding of politics, these people are very naive. What if the majority of the group decided not to publish the *Lamentation*, and those who attacked Greening that night were working for someone within the group who *did* want it published?'

Cranmer said, 'We know the extreme sects are ever prone to splitting and quarrelling with each other.'

'To the extent of murdering one another too?' Cecil asked.

'If enough were at stake,' Cranmer replied sadly. 'We should at least consider it as a possibility.'

The others were silent. Then the Queen nodded wearily. 'At least I know who the traitor within my own household was: the guard Leeman.' She gave me a sad little smile. 'You were wrong, Matthew, to suspect Jane Fool and the Lady Mary.'

'I know, your majesty. But it was my duty to interview all the possible suspects.'

She nodded again.

'Where do we go now?' Cranmer asked.

I turned to Cecil. 'First, as I said, we cannot discount the possibility that one of the missing three men took the books, as part of a quarrel over strategy. If so, they may try to smuggle them out of the country. What sort of watch have you been able to put at the docks?'

'I have arranged discreetly at the customs house for out-going cargoes to be searched thoroughly. Of course, the customs officials' main effort goes into searching goods coming *into* the country, particularly for forbidden litera-ture. Books hidden in bales of cloth, tied in oilskin inside casks of wine—'

'And if they find them?' I cut in.

'They are to be delivered to me.' Cecil touched one of the moles on his face. 'Lord Parr has graciously allowed me much gold to grease those wheels.'

The Queen said, 'But what if the books go from Bristol, or Ipswich, or even on a small boat launched secretly from a creek?'

'Then there is nothing we can do,' Lord Parr answered flatly. He turned to me. 'I can see a radical group sending Anne Askew's writings abroad for Bale or someone like him to print and smuggle back to England. But the *Lamentation*? Surely it is obvious, with even a little thought, that printing and distributing it would do nothing but harm the Queen.'

'I have dealt with the outer fringes of fanaticism before,' I said. 'These people may have actively sought to recruit people in places where secret information could be had, precisely so it could be publicized. They may even realize that harm could come to her majesty, but not care if they had it in their heads that their actions could stir people to revolt.'

Again there was a silence in the room. I continued quietly, 'We still have two leads which have not been fol-lowed to the end, both crucial. Two people. Who is Stice, the man with the torn ear, and who is he working for? And who in God's name is Gurone Bertano?'

'Bertano's name is quite unknown,' Cranmer replied. 'Though, as you know, there is something, some initiative, going on involving only the religious traditionalists close to the King. Whether this man could be involved I have no idea. But it could be that Greening's group somehow got hold of a third secret, this man's name and purpose. But from whom?'

'The name certainly terrified Elias.'

'We dare not question too openly, my Lord Archbishop,' Lord Parr said. 'If this Bertano is involved in some secret machinations of the conservatives, and I come out with the name, they will demand to know where we heard it.'

Cecil said, 'The other man, the one with the torn ear. We know from the page that he works for someone at court, someone who was seeking information against the Queen, and who was involved in the first attempt on Greening.'

'If only he could be found, he might be the key to the whole conspiracy,' I said.

Lord Parr began pacing up and down, his body tensed with frustration. 'All the great men of the realm have large households, and spies.'

Cecil said, 'I still find it odd that Myldmore was not arrested directly after it was discovered he had spoken of Anne Askew's torture.'

The Queen spoke up, her voice strained. 'From what you told my uncle, Matthew, I understand Sir Anthony Knevet was unhappy about the illegality of that poor woman's torture, and said he would report it to the King?'

'Yes, your majesty.'

She took a deep breath. 'I remember dining with the King one evening, about three weeks ago. We were interrupted by a messenger telling him Sir Anthony begged to see him urgently, on a confidential matter. The King was angry, said he wanted to dine in peace, but the messenger insisted it was important. I left the room and Sir Anthony was shown in – the King was not fit to walk at all that night.' She took another calming breath. 'They were together some time and then he left and his majesty called me back. He said nothing about the meeting but he seemed – disturbed, a little upset.'

Lord Parr said, 'The dates certainly tally. And what else could Knevet have wished to discuss so urgently?'

The Queen continued, 'I can tell you this. If Rich and Wriothesley tortured Anne Askew on their own initiative, or on the orders of someone higher – Gardiner or Norfolk – if they had done such a brutal and illegal thing against a woman, the King's sense of honour would have been out-raged. They would have smarted for it. Indeed, it was shortly after this that the King came up with his plan of false charges against me being brought by Wriothesley, so that he could humiliate him.'

She held herself stiffly, as though struggling to contain remembered fear. I had long known she looked on Henry with a loving, indulgent eye, though to me he was a monster of cruelty. Nonetheless, it was also known the King placed great store by traditional, chivalric values; such a mind could be shocked by a gentlewoman's torture, while seeing nothing amiss in burning her alive. 'That could explain why nothing has been done to Myldmore,' I said thought-fully. 'And I remember Rich had a worried, preoccupied look at the burning.' I smiled wryly. 'Perhaps it was not only Wriothesley who felt the King's wrath.'

Lord Parr nodded agreement. 'Yes, my nephew's reports of Rich and Wriothesley being subdued at council meetings date from then. Though, as I say, they seem brighter now.'

Cecil asked, 'But would either of them then dare go on to murder the printer and steal those books?'

'Perhaps,' I said thoughtfully. 'If they had an informer in an Anabaptist sect and were told about the books. Recovering the *Lamentation* and presenting it to the King would then help enormously in restoring their position.'

They considered this theory. Then we all jumped at a sudden knock. We looked at each other nervously – perhaps it was not wise for us all to be seen together with the Queen. Lord Parr went to the door and opened it. One of the Queen's guards was outside. He bowed low to the Queen, then said, 'Master Secretary Paget is outside, my Lord. He would speak with you and her majesty.'

'Very well,' Lord Parr said. 'Give us a moment, then show him in.'

As the man closed the door Cranmer spoke quietly. 'It may be politic for me to leave. Perhaps go down to the Queen's Gallery.'

'Very well, my Lord Archbishop,' Lord Parr agreed.

The Archbishop opened the door and left swiftly. But immediately we heard a deep voice in the corridor. 'My Lord Archbishop. Visiting her majesty?'

'Indeed, Master Secretary.'

'Perhaps you could stay a moment. I have called to discuss arrangements for the French admiral's reception.'

Cranmer returned to the room, frowning a little. Then Secretary Paget entered, alone. He bowed to the Queen, then looked around at us with the confident stare of a man in charge of his surroundings. I remembered that square, hard face from the burning, the mouth a downturned slit between his long moustache and unruly forked beard. He wore a grey robe and cap today, no ostentation apart from his heavy gold chain of office, and carried a sheaf of papers under his arm. 'Meeting with men of the Queen's Learned Council, eh, my Lord?' he asked Lord Parr cheerfully. 'How would our lands ever be administered without lawyers dipping their quills in the ink, hey? Well, I, too, was a lawyer once. I hope you do not trouble her majesty too much?' he added maliciously, regarding Lord Parr with a flat, unblinking stare.

I glanced at the Queen; she had managed in an instant to compose her features. She now radiated quiet regality: a lift of the chin and shoulders, a slight stiffening of the body. 'My councillors simplify matters for my weak woman's wit,' she said cheerfully.

Paget bowed again. 'I fear I, too, must ask to indulge your well-known patience, but on a more congenial subject, I am sure. The King has given orders for new clothes for your ladies who will accompany you at the festivities for the French admiral. He wishes you to be very well attended.'

'His majesty is gracious as ever.'

'I know the festivities are a month away, but there is a great deal to organize. May we discuss the arrangements? Afterwards, my Lord Archbishop, perhaps we could talk about your role, which will also be important.'

Behind Paget's back, Lord Parr looked at Cecil and me, then curtly inclined his head to the door. Fortunately, we were too lowly to be introduced to Master Secretary. We bowed to the Queen and sidled out. Paget was saying, 'The finest cloth has been ordered, to be made up at Baynard's Castle . . .'

Cecil and I walked away up the corridor, saying nothing until we reached the discreetly positioned window overlooking the courtyard, where I had seen the King that first day. The courtyard was empty this afternoon apart from a couple of young courtiers lounging lazily against a wall. The afternoon shadows were lengthening.

I spoke quietly. 'Secretary Paget. I saw him at the burning.'

'Yes.'

'He is a traditionalist, is he not?'

'He was first brought to court under Bishop Gardiner's patronage, but he is not linked to him any more.'

'No?'

'He is the King's man now and nobody else's. With the King so physically weak, he puts more and more of the work in Paget's hands, but Paget never oversteps himself.'

'Yes, I heard he learned that lesson from Wolsey and Cromwell.'

Cecil nodded. 'Whichever way the wind blows, Paget will follow only the King's wishes. If he has any principles of his own they are well hidden away.'

'Bend with the wind rather than break.'

'Yes, indeed.'

'But — are we sure? If Paget is a traditionalist in religion, and on good terms with Rich and Wriothesley? It seems those two may have taken the initiative to torture Anne Askew without consulting the King; perhaps Paget, too, is capable of using his initiative. With the King so ill. And is the Secretary not responsible for all official spies and informers?'

'Official ones, certainly,' Cecil replied slowly. 'But as Lord Parr said earlier, all the great men run unofficial ones. As for the King's health, his body is breaking down, but, from all I hear, his mind and will are as sharp as ever.'

I looked at young Cecil: clever, always coolly in control, with more than a touch of unscrupulousness, I suspected. But nonetheless he had nailed his flag unhesitatingly to the Queen's mast. He gave a heavy sigh and I realized that he, too, must be feeling the strain of all this. I wondered whether he also felt afraid now when he smelled smoke. 'What happens next?' I asked him gently.

'It is in Lord Parr's hands, and mine, for now, I think. Watching the docks, trying to find this man with half an ear, and solving the mystery of Bertano.'

He touched my arm, an unexpected gesture. 'We are grateful to you, Master Shardlake. That talk clarified much –' He broke off. 'Ah, see. Down there.'

I looked into the courtyard. Two men had entered and were walking across it, talking amiably. The two young layabouts who were already there stopped leaning on the wall and bowed deeply to them. One was the Queen's brother, William Parr, Earl of Essex, tall and thin with his gaunt face and trim auburn beard. The other was the man I had heard the Queen's ladies speaking of as being back in England, a man whom the Queen had once loved and whom I despised: Sir Thomas Seymour. He wore a short green robe, with white silk hose showing off his shapely legs, and a wide flat cap with a swan feather on his coppery head. With one hand he was stroking his dark auburn beard, which was long like Paget's, but combed to silky smoothness.

'The Parr–Seymour alliance in action,' Cecil whispered, with the keen interest of a connoisseur of politics. 'The two main reformist families meet.'

'Is not Sir Thomas too headstrong for a senior position?'

'Yes indeed. But for now his brother Lord Hertford is abroad, and Sir Thomas keeps the flag flying. Lord Hertford returns very soon, though. I have contacts in his household.' Cecil looked at me with a quick, vain little smile, then bowed. 'I will leave you now, sir. You will be summoned when there is further news. Thank you again.'

I watched him walk away down the corridor, with his quick, confident steps. That smile made me think: Cecil, too, would one day make a politician; already he had his foot on the first rung of the ladder. I wondered about the alliance between the Parrs and the Seymours. For now, they were united against the religious conservatives. But when the King died both families would have separate claims to govern the realm in the name of the boy Edward: the Parrs as the family of his stepmother, the Seymours as that of his dead true mother. And how long, then, would the alliance last?

Chapter Twenty-seven

A s I WALKED BACK along the corridor towards the gilded public chambers, I heard a strange sound. A creaking, clanking noise from behind the wall, and what sounded like the rattle of chains. I looked around, and saw a door in the corridor I had not noticed previously. Unlike the others it did not have a magnificently decorated surround but was set flush to the wall, with the same linenfold panelling as the walls on either side. There was a small keyhole, but no handle. Overcome with curiosity, I pushed at it gently and to my surprise it opened easily on oiled hinges.

Within was a wide, square platform, lit with torches bracketed to the walls. The platform surrounded a staircase leading down to the ground floor. To my astonishment, in one corner of the platform, four men in the dark uniform of the King's Gentlemen Pensioners were straining to turn the handles of a large winch, hauling something up the stairwell from the ground floor. I heard a wheezy shout from beneath, 'Careful, you dolts, keep me steady!' Then, as the men pulled harder on the ropes, an immense figure rose into view, seated on a heavy wheeled chair, secured by a leather belt round his immense waist. I glimpsed a near-bald head, an immense, red, round face, folds of thin-bearded flesh wobbling above the collar of a caftan. The King's huge cheeks twitched in pain.

Another guard saw me and rushed over; a big, bearded

fellow. He clapped a hand over my mouth and pushed me through the door, back into the corridor. He shut the door quietly, then grabbed the lapels of my robe. 'Who are you?' he spat with quiet fierceness. 'How did you get in there?'

'I – I heard strange noises behind the door. I pushed it and it opened easily – '

'God's death, it should always be locked from inside – I'll have Hardy's balls for this.' His expression suddenly changed, from anger to contempt. 'Who are you, crook-back?' He glanced at my robe. 'I see you wear the Queen's badge.'

'I am new appointed to her majesty's Learned Council.'

He released me. 'Then learn, and quickly, that in White-hall you go *only – where – you – are – allowed.*' He punctuated the last words with painful jabs to my chest with his finger, then glanced nervously over his shoulder. A heavy clunk from behind the door indicated the chair had been pulled in. He spoke hurriedly, 'Now go, and thank your stars he did not see you. You think his majesty likes to be watched like this, being winched upstairs? Be gone, now!' He turned and went back through the door. I scurried away as fast as possible. I knew the King could scarcely walk, but it had never occurred to me to wonder how he got to the Royal Apartments on the first floor. His immobility alone must be humiliating enough for that once famous athlete, but to be seen like that – I shuddered at my narrow escape. If he had glanced up momentarily and recognized me . . .

✝

AGAIN, THERE WAS A period of silence from White-hall. I heard nothing for a day or so. I returned to work, but found it harder this time to settle or rest.

On Saturday morning, the 24th of July, I arrived at chambers late in the morning to find Nicholas absent.

'Perhaps he has had a late night in the taverns,' Skelly observed disapprovingly.

'He said yesterday his chest was hurting,' Barak observed. 'I'll go to his place at lunchtime if he hasn't come in, check he's all right.'

I nodded.

Skelly added reproachfully, 'That witness in that Common Pleas case called, as arranged, to have you take his deposition, and I had to say you had been called away on urgent business. Since I did not know where you were, sir,' he added pointedly.

'I am sorry,' I said, annoyed at having forgotten; things could not go on like this.

'And these notes were delivered for you.' Skelly handed me some papers.

'Thank you.'

I took them into my room and worked alone for the next few hours. Most were routine matters, but one was an official notification from Treasurer Rowland that a complaint had been made against me by my former client, Isabel Slanning. He asked me to call on him on Monday. I sighed. Well, that was not unexpected. There was nothing to it, but no doubt Rowland would enjoy trying to discomfit me.

I was a little worried about Nicholas. Barak had said he would visit him at lunchtime if he did not arrive at chambers. What if he found him ill, his wound infected perhaps, and needed to take him to Guy? But I knew Barak: if it was anything I should know, he would have sent a message. He might have gone home, as I had told him he could if he wished while Tamasin was expecting. I turned my attention back to the work that was still upon my desk.

Shortly after, there was a knock at the door. I hoped it might be Barak returned, but Skelly came in. 'Master Dyrick has called to see you, sir, regarding the Slanning case.'

'Show him in.' I put down my quill, frowning. He must have come to collect the Slanning papers. They were on the table next to my desk. I would have expected him to send a clerk, though. We had had a passage of arms a year before, and I knew things about Vincent Dyrick that gave him an interest in not pushing me too far. Nonetheless, he was a man who loved a fight. I could imagine Isabel looking for the most aggressive barrister available. Someone who did not mind acting for difficult clients with hopeless cases, so long as they paid well. That fitted Dyrick exactly. I knew from experience that he would be relentless in trying to make something of the case; probably even persuade himself that her cause was just.

Dyrick came in with his confident, athletic step, his green eyes sharp as ever in his thin, handsome face, strands of red hair showing under his coif. He bowed briefly and gave me his sardonic smile.

'God give you good morning, Brother Shardlake.'

'And you, Brother Dyrick. Please sit.'

He did so, folding his hands in his lap.

I continued, civil but unsmiling, 'So, you have taken Mistress Slanning's case? I have the papers ready.'

'Good. It is an interesting matter.'

'Hopeless, I think. But profitable.'

'Indeed, yes.' He smiled again. 'Brother Shardlake, I know that you and I have reason to keep apart, but – well – sometimes by chance we will find ourselves on opposing sides in a case.'

'My involvement in this one is over. Was it you who

358

prompted her to complain to the Inn authorities?' I asked abruptly. 'The complaint is nonsense.'

He met my gaze. 'Actually, since you ask, no. I told her she should concentrate on the case. But she was insistent.'

'Mistress Slanning is certainly that.' I thought, he is telling the truth there. As far as the case was concerned, there was no advantage in making a complaint, and while Dyrick would like to make trouble for me, neither would he push matters too far.

'She is most displeased with your conduct of matters,' he said in a tone of mock reproof.

'I know.' I pushed the bundle of documents over to him. 'Here are the papers, and I wish you joy of them.'

He laid the bundle on his lap. 'A lot of meat on this chicken,' he said appreciatively. He switched his look to one of disapproval. 'Mistress Slanning tells me you conspired against her with her brother's lawyer, Master Coleswyn. You have been a guest at his house. Further, she claims that you guided her to an expert for an opinion on the wall painting at the centre of this case, who was unsympathetic. She says this man, Adam, was also in collusion with you and Coleswyn. It would help me in representing her if you could give me your response to those charges.'

For a brief moment I considered offering the sort of earthy response Barak might have made. Instead I spoke calmly. 'You will find she chose the expert herself, from the list I provided, without asking my advice.'

He inclined his head. 'Mistress Slanning also says that, like Coleswyn and her brother, you are an extreme religious radical. I fear she has insisted, despite my opposition, on raising that in court in September. I thought I should warn you.'

Dyrick fixed me with those cold green eyes. I answered,

an edge in my voice, 'I am no extreme radical, as you well know.'

He shrugged. 'Well, it is nothing to me either way, but it is not the sort of accusation to have made in public these days. I should warn you, she has put that in her complaint to Lincoln's Inn as well.'

'You are right. It is not sensible to bandy around accusations of religious extremism in these days. For anyone.' There was a warning note in my voice. Dyrick possessed a reckless streak, a lack of sensible judgement, and enjoyed making trouble for trouble's sake.

He inclined his head again. 'I thought the heresy hunt was over.'

'One can never be sure.'

'Well, perhaps you know more of that than I. You have contacts at court, I remember.'

'Brother Dyrick,' I began, 'you must know this case is nonsense, the expert opinion clear and decisive. And my opponent Master Coleswyn, in case you are fishing for information about him, is a clever man, and a reasonable one. In my opinion both Isabel Slanning and Edward Cotterstoke have no aim other than to hurt each other. It would be in everyone's interest if the matter were settled quickly.'

He raised an eyebrow. 'I think you know as well as I, Brother Shardlake, that Mistress Slanning will never settle. Never.' He was right. A picture came into my mind of Isabel's face; lined, bitter, implacable.

Dyrick rose, slipping the file under his arm. He patted it smugly. 'As I said, there is a lot of meat on this chicken. I came to tell you, I will fight it hard; but I will not encourage Mistress Slanning in throwing around accusations of heresy. I am well aware how dangerous that is. As for her complaint to the Inn, I will have to leave you to deal with that.'

I nodded. I was glad he had some sense at least.

'I now look forward to doing battle with Brother Coleswyn.' Dyrick bowed and left the room.

✝

I SAT THERE AWHILE, more irritated than angry at having Vincent Dyrick back in my life. The notion of a religious conspiracy in the Slanning case was ludicrous. But it remained a worry to Philip Coleswyn – possibly even a threat – if Isabel continued making wild accusations. I would warn him.

Eventually, with a sigh, I returned to work. It was cooler now, the sun fading, and all was quiet outside in Gatehouse Court. Towards seven there was another knock at the door; I hoped again it might be Barak or Nicholas, but it was only Skelly come to bid me goodnight and hand me a note. 'This just came, sir. Someone slipped it under the door.' It was a folded paper addressed to me in scrawled capitals, sealed with a shapeless blob of wax.

When Skelly left I broke the seal and opened the note. It was unsigned, and like my address it was written in unidentifiable capitals:

MASTER SHARDLAKE,
WE HAVE THE BOY NICHOLAS OVERTON.
IF YOU WISH TO SEE HIM AGAIN CALL
AT THE HOUSE WITH GREEN SHUTTERS
TWO DOORS DOWN FROM THE SIGN OF
THE FLAG IN NEEDLEPIN LANE, ALONE,
AT NINE TONIGHT. TELL NO ONE AT THE
PALACE; WE HAVE A SPY THERE. IF YOU
DO NOT COME, WE WILL SEND YOU HIS
HEAD.

Chapter Twenty-eight

I HALF-WALKED, HALF-RAN the few streets to Barak's house, earning curious stares from passers-by. My overwhelming fear was that he had found a similar note at Nicholas's rooms and had gone off on a hunt of his own. I told myself it was not like Barak to act impulsively, certainly not these days. But I was truly frightened now for both of them, and cursed myself anew for the trouble my involvement with the *Lamentation* had brought to all around me.

I was out of breath when I arrived, sweating and panting heavily as I knocked at the door. I realized I had become unfit these last months, doing little more than sitting at my work all day and eating Agnes Brocket's good food at home.

Jane Marris opened the door. She curtsied, then stared at me. 'Have you run here, Master Shardlake?'

'Half-run. From chambers.'

Unexpectedly, she smiled. 'All is well, sir. The mistress had a scare, but it turned out to be nothing. Dr Malton is with her.'

I frowned, not knowing what she meant, but followed her anxiously down the little hallway, breathing hard. In the neat little parlour Tamasin sat on cushions, looking pale. To my immense relief Barak sat on a chair beside her, his unbandaged hand in hers while Guy, in his long physician's robe, leaned over the table, mixing herbs in a dish. From upstairs I heard little George crying.

'Jane,' Tamasin said, 'will you go up to him? He knows there is something out of sorts.'

'What has happened?' I asked when Jane left the room.

Barak looked up. In the warm summer evening he wore only his shirt and hose, and I again glimpsed his father's ancient mezuzah on its gold chain round his neck. 'Tamasin had a pain in her stomach this morning. When I came home at lunchtime it was worse. She feared something was happening to the baby. I went round to Guy.'

Guy spoke soothingly, 'All is well, it was nothing more than wind.' Tamasin looked away, embarrassed.

'She had me worried,' Barak said. Tamasin lifted a hand and stroked his neat beard. He turned his head to look at me. 'Sorry I didn't come back to work. But it's Saturday. Paperwork day. How did you know I was here?'

'I – I didn't, for certain. But there was something I needed to discuss with you urgently, so I came round.'

'I am sorry I discommoded you,' Tamasin said.

''Tis you that needs the commode,' Barak answered with a wicked grin.

'Fie, Jack.' She reddened.

Guy stood up. 'Mix these herbs with some beer and take them with food,' he instructed. 'Sometimes the mixture can ease – what you have.' He smiled. 'There is nothing else to worry about.'

Tamasin took his hand. 'You are good to us,' she said. 'Only we worry, after – '

'I know,' Guy said. She was remembering their first, still-born child.

'I'll see you out,' Barak said.

'Thank you.' I noticed there was still a reserve in Guy's voice when he addressed me. He gave me a formal little bow, which hurt me more than hard words would have done, and

Barak showed him out. I was left with Tamasin. She leaned back on the cushions.

'I was worried,' she said to me quietly.

'I understand. In your condition any – upset – must make you fear some ill to the child.'

'Yes.' She looked wistful. 'I hope for a daughter this time. A little girl to dress in frocks and make rag dolls for.'

'Maybe it will be so.'

She smiled briefly at the thought, then said, 'Guy looked at Jack's hand. It is healing well. But it was unlike him to be so careless, and that is a nasty cut to get just from a paper knife.' Her eyes had narrowed slightly and I had to stop myself shifting uneasily; I knew how sharp Tamasin was.

'I am glad it is healing well,' I replied neutrally.

Barak returned. From the look of me he had guessed something serious was afoot. 'We'll go and talk up in the bedroom, Tammy,' he said. 'You won't want to hear a lot of legal business.'

'I don't mind.'

'Take Guy's advice, woman,' he said with mock severity, 'and get some rest.' He led me up the little staircase to their bedroom, where he sat on the bed, lowering his voice, for Jane Marris was still with George next door. He spoke quietly. 'What's happened?'

'Did you go round to Nicholas's lodgings today?'

'Yes. I promised I would. At lunchtime, before coming home. The other students he shares that pigsty with said he went out yesterday evening and didn't come back. They thought he'd probably found a whore to bed with.'

'He didn't, though. Read this.' I took out the note and handed it to him. 'It was pushed under the chambers door less than half an hour ago.'

After reading the message, Barak closed his eyes a moment before opening them and glaring at me furiously.

'All right,' he said, his voice still quiet. 'What in Christ's name is going on?'

'I can't tell you everything. I'm sworn to secrecy—'

'Fuck that!' His voice rose angrily. 'Something big's happening, isn't it? You've been using me and Nicholas to help with aspects of it. That stolen jewel of the Queen's down at Baynard's Castle, the murdered printer whose parents you're supposed to be acting for, those men who attacked us in that tavern; that scared-looking young man you questioned in chambers. They're all connected, aren't they? You send me with a note to the palace and then a whole troop of men come and take the poor arsehole away. He was terrified. And that young lawyer who came with them, the one with the warty face, he works for the Queen, doesn't he?'

'Yes.'

'I could tell by the manner, the cut of his robe, that he was a palace lawyer – I worked round people like that long enough. And I've known you six years; I know how jumpy and tetchy you get when something dangerous is on!' He stabbed a finger at me. 'The Queen's got you mixed up in something again, hasn't she? Someone's kidnapped Nick because of it, and you want me to help you get him back! Well, tell me everything first! Everything!'

I raised my hands. 'Lower your voice, or the women will hear.' I hesitated; if I told him all I would be breaking my oath and exposing him to dangerous secrets, but if I were to do anything for Nicholas I needed Barak's assistance now. So I told him the whole story: my first summons to the Queen, the missing *Lamentation*, the two men who had died and the others who had vanished, Myldmore's confession,

Anne Askew's writings. I spoke softly, Barak asking a couple of questions now and again in an equally quiet voice.

At the end of my story he sat thinking, stroking his beard, but still looking angry. 'Can't you get the Queen's men to help you?'

'The note says they have a spy in the palace.'

'That could be bluff.'

'I daren't risk it.'

'Can't you get a personal note to the Queen herself – you who would do anything for her?' There was impatience in his voice.

I shook my head. 'There is no time. Nine tonight, remember. It's well past seven now.'

'If there *is* a spy at Whitehall Palace, they won't let you out of this house of theirs alive to tell of it. Let alone release Nick.'

I spoke quietly, 'I just want you to come to the house with me and hide nearby while I go in. You're good at that.' I took a deep breath. 'Then, if I don't come out in twenty minutes, try to get a message to the lawyer William Cecil. There is no danger to you in that.'

He shook his head, suddenly weary. 'You'd die for the Queen, wouldn't you?'

'Yes,' I answered simply.

He paced the room, then said, 'Shit. I'll come. Though I think Tamasin's already suspicious over my hand.'

'Thank you, Jack.' I spoke humbly. 'Thank you. I am more grateful than I can say.'

'So you fucking should be. Now wait here while I go and say goodbye to my wife, tell her some story about a witness that needs to be seen urgently. I don't want her seeing that drawn face of yours again. I'll call you down.'

'We've an hour and a half,' I said.

'Enough, then, to find a tavern, and think and plan properly.'

☩

WE WALKED INTO THE CITY, then down towards the river. Barak had donned an old leather jerkin over his shirt, and brought another for me, which I had placed over my doublet once we left the house. It would not be wise to stand out in the poorer areas for which we were headed. Greening's killers had known that.

'Have you any gold in your purse?' he asked.

'Yes. And some silver.'

'Gold's much better.'

We said little more as we walked along St Peter's Street and into Thames Street. To the south I could see the cranes on the wharves and the river beyond, white with sails. Over to the west the sun was setting. Barak never broke his stride; he had spent all his life in the city and knew every street and alley. Eventually he stopped. A respectable-looking tavern stood where Thames Street intersected with a lane of narrow, tumbledown houses that led down to the river, some of the buildings slanting at odd angles as they had settled, over the decades, into the Thames clay. A little way down the lane I saw a sign marking another, shabbier-looking tavern, painted with the red-and-white cross of St George. It was the Sign of the Flag mentioned in the note.

'Needlepin Lane,' Barak said. 'Mostly cheap lodging houses. Let's go in here to this tavern; sit by the window.'

The place was busy, mostly with shopkeepers and workers come for a drink at the end of the day. Barak got two mugs of beer and we took seats with a view of the lane; the shutters were wide open this hot evening, letting in the stifling dusty stink of the city. We had scarcely sat when Barak rose again. A solidly built man in a London constable's red uniform, staff over his shoulder and lamp in hand, was walking by. Later he would patrol the streets to enforce the curfew. Barak leaned over. 'Your purse. Quick!'

I handed it over. Barak darted outside and I saw him talking with the constable, their heads bent close. At one point the constable turned and stared at me for a moment, then he walked on down Thames Street. Barak returned to the tavern.

'Right,' he said, taking his stool. 'I've squared him.'

'I didn't see money pass.'

'He's good at passing coins unseen. So am I. I told him we're on official business about some stolen jewellery, and we're meeting an informant at the house two doors down at nine. Asked him to be ready to come to the house with anyone else he can muster, if I shout.'

'Well done.' I knew nobody better at such tasks; Barak's instincts were always extraordinary.

'I asked him if he knew who lived there. He said one or two men go there occasionally, but mostly it's empty. He thinks it might be where some gentleman takes a girl, though if so he hasn't seen her. You're four shillings poorer, but it's worth it.' He paused. 'It could well be a house belonging to some courtier, where people meet for unauthorized business. Lord Cromwell had such places; I expect the Queen's people are keeping that gaoler from the Tower in one.' He fell silent as a young boy set a candle on our table; outside it was getting dark. Barak took a draught of beer, then stood again. 'I'm going to take a quick walk up and down the street. See if there are any lights on in that house.' He left again, returning a few minutes later. 'The shutters are green, like the note said. They're closed but I could see a glimmer of light between the slats on the ground floor.' He raised his eyebrows and smiled.

'Nothing to do now but wait till the church clocks strike curfew.' Then he took a long gulp of beer.

'Thank you,' I said quietly. 'I would not have thought of any of that.'

He nodded. 'I quite enjoyed persuading the constable to back us up, spying out that house. And even that sword fight in the inn, if truth be told, for all it hurt my hand. Old habits die hard.' He frowned suddenly. 'But I've not the speed and energy I once had. I've a good wife, a good job, a child and another on the way.' He stared into space a moment, then said, 'Lord Cromwell pulled me out of the gutter when I was a boy. I enjoyed the work I did for him, too, the need for sharp wits and sometimes a sharp knife. But that's a job for the young, and those with little to lose.'

I quoted a biblical verse that came to my mind: '*When I was a child, I spake as a child, I understood as a child, I thought as a child; but when I became a man, I put away childish things.*'

'Never had much chance for childish things.' Barak took another swig of beer, and looked at me hard. 'The old ways – I still love that excitement of having to move, think, watch, quickly, on your feet. I've realized that again tonight.' He sat thinking, then looked at me and spoke quietly. 'I passed my mother in the street, you know, a few months back.'

I stared at him. I knew that after the death of his father, Barak's mother had quickly married another man, whom he detested; he had been out on the streets alone by the age of twelve. He said, 'She was old, bent, carrying a pile of twigs for the fire. I don't know what happened to *him*, maybe he's dead, with luck.'

'Did you speak to her?'

He shook his head. 'She was coming towards me, I recognized her at once. I stopped, I wasn't sure whether to speak to her or not. I felt sorry for her. But she walked straight past, didn't recognize *me*. So that was that. It's for the best.'

'How could you expect her to recognize you? You hadn't seen her in over twenty years.'

'A decent mother would know her own child,' he answered stubbornly.

'Did you tell Tamasin?'

He shook his head firmly. 'She'd press me to look for her. And I won't.' His jaw set hard.

'I'm sorry.'

'What's done is done.' He changed the subject. 'You realize Nick may not be at that house, if he's even still alive. These people want *you*, to find out what you know, and they won't be gentle. After that, they'll have no use for either of you.'

I met his gaze. 'I know. But if they are going to interrogate me, it will take time. That's why I need you to watch. If I don't come out in twenty minutes, call your new friend the constable. I was going to tell you to go to Whitehall, but this way's better and faster.'

'All right.' He fixed me with his hard brown eyes, and spoke seriously. 'You have to separate yourself from the Queen. Every time you go near that cesspit they call the Royal Court you end up in danger.'

'*She* is in danger.'

'Her own fault, by the sound of it.'

I lowered my voice to a whisper. 'The King is dying.'

'I've heard that rumour.'

'It's more than rumour. I've caught glimpses of him, twice. The state he is in – I don't see how he can last more than a few months.'

'And then?'

'Then, if the reformers are in the ascendant, the Queen

may be one of those who governs for Prince Edward. She may even be made Regent, as she was when the King led his army to France two years ago. But that book in the wrong hands could kill her.'

Barak inclined his head. 'Even if she survives, and the reformers win, the Seymours will want to take over. And they're Prince Edward's blood relatives, after all. If they do, perhaps the Queen may marry again.' He looked at me narrowly. 'Another political marriage, probably, to someone powerful at Court.'

I smiled wryly. 'Jack, I have never had the remotest hopes for myself, if that's what is in your mind. Catherine Parr was far above me in status even before she married the King. I have always known that.'

'Then let this be the last time,' Barak said, with sudden fierceness.

☦

AT NINE THE CHURCH BELL sounding through the deepening dusk signalled curfew, and the tavern emptied. We went outside. I saw the constable on the corner, his lamp lit. A large, younger man stood beside him. 'Just about to start my patrol, sir,' he said meaningfully to Barak, who nodded. We left them and walked down Needlepin Lane as far as the Sign of the Flag, where again patrons were dispersing for the night. They were a younger, rougher crowd, several apprentices among them. Barak nodded at a doorway just beyond. 'I'll wait there,' he said. 'Just out of sight.'

I took a deep breath. 'Twenty minutes.'

'I'll count them off. Good luck.'

'Thank you.' I walked on, my legs trembling slightly. I passed a house where a ragged family could be seen through open shutters, eating a late supper by the light of a cheap candle; the next house was the one with the green shutters. Like Barak, I could see a light through the closed slats. Looking up at the upper storey, I glimpsed a faint light there too; someone was watching the street. But they could not have seen Barak from that angle.

I knocked at the wooden door. Immediately I heard heavy footsteps within. The door opened and a short, heavyset man in a stained shirt stared at me. He had a candle in one hand, the other held over the dagger at his waist. Elias's descriptions of the men who had made the first attempt to break into Greening's shop had been vague, but this could have been one of them. He was in his late twenties and under bushy black hair his face was square, craggy, with an angry expression that spoke of temper.

'I am Master Shardlake,' I said. 'I received the note.'

He nodded curtly and stepped aside. I entered a room with rushes on the floor, the only furniture a trestle table bearing a large sconce of candles, with stools around. A rickety staircase led to the upper floor. On one of the stools sat Nicholas, his hands bound behind him and a gag in his mouth. He had a black eye, crusted blood on the gag and in his matted red hair. Behind him stood another young man; tall, in gentlemanly clothing – a good green doublet, with embroidery at the sleeves and neck of his shirt. He had keen, foxy features and a neatly trimmed fair beard. The outer half of his left ear was missing; at some point it had been sliced clean off, leaving only shiny scar tissue. He held a sword to Nicholas's throat; the boy stared at me with frantic eyes.

The man who had let me in closed the door. 'No sign of anyone else, Gower?' his companion with the damaged ear asked in cultivated tones.

'No, Master Stice. And he's watching above.' He cocked his head towards the staircase.

The other man nodded, his sword still held to Nicholas's throat. I thought, they've let me know both their names; that doesn't bode well for us. Stice looked at me then; his grey eyes were cool, appraising. He took the sword slowly away from Nicholas's throat and smiled.

'So, Master Shardlake, you came. We didn't think you would, but our master disagreed. He says you have courage and loyalty both.'

Gower stepped over, looking at me with his angry eyes. 'Perhaps you like the boy, eh, hunchback? Someone like you won't have much luck with women. Would have thought you could have done better than this beanpole, though.'

'Leave him alone, Gower,' Stice snapped impatiently. 'We've business to conduct, no time for jests.'

I looked at Stice contemptuously. 'What have you done to Nicholas?'

'We had to knock him out to get him here. And he wasn't very cooperative when he woke up. Gower had to give him a lesson in manners.'

'I have come as you asked. Release him.'

Stice nodded. 'You can have him, though Leonard here would have relished preparing his head to send you.' He glanced at Gower. 'Full of funny ideas is Leonard. He thinks you're a sodomite.' I would not have dared to mock the man like that, but he took it from Stice, who reached behind Nicholas and untied the gag, then used his sword to slice through his bonds. Gower went and stood beside Nicholas, hand held meaningfully on his knife, as the boy pulled the gag from his mouth. Eventually he spoke in a dry, hoarse voice. 'I'm so sorry, sir.'

'It is my fault,' I said quietly. 'I led you into danger.'

'I'd been to a tavern last night,' he croaked.' I was walk-

373

ing home when I was knocked out from behind. When I woke up I was here. Where are we?'

'A house near the river.' I turned to Stice. 'Well, are you going to let him go?'

He shook his head. 'Not yet. There's someone wants to talk to you, then if he's happy we'll let you both go. Leonard will take Nicky boy out back in the meantime.' Stice, sword still in hand, leaned against the wall, waiting.

Nicholas still sat. 'For mercy's sake,' he cried. 'May I have some water?' He swallowed uncomfortably and grimaced with pain.

'Poor baby,' Stice replied with a mocking laugh. 'Not much forbearance for a gentleman. Oh, get him some water from the barrel, Leonard.'

As Gower went through a door to the back of the house, Nicholas stood, shakily. I heard a creak from the floorboards above, and remembered there was another man in the house. Well, we had been here for five minutes; fifteen more and Barak and the constable would come with his men. In the meantime I would have to dissimulate well. Nicholas stood, stretching, and feeling his bruises. Stice still leaned against the wall, hand on his sword hilt, watching him with amusement.

Suddenly Nicholas launched himself at Stice, clearing the few feet between them with one leap, a hand closing on Stice's wrist before he could grasp his sword. Caught off guard, Stice let out a yell of anger as Nicholas grasped his other wrist and pinned him to the wall, then kneed him hard in the crotch. He cried out and bent over.

'Stop, Nicholas!' I shouted. A fight now was the last thing I wanted, and it was one we could not win. At that moment Gower came back with a pitcher of water. With a shout he dropped it on the floor and reached for his dagger, raising it high to bury it in Nicholas's back. I threw myself at him and knocked him off balance, but he did not fall, and turned on me with the dagger just as Stice managed to push Nicholas away from the wall and raised his sword. His face was white with anger.

Then rapid footsteps sounded on the stairs and a voice called out, 'Cease this mad brawling!' Not a loud voice, but sharp as a file; one I recognized. It was enough to stop Gower in his tracks, and make Stice pause, too. Confident footsteps walked into the room. I turned and beheld, dressed in sober black robe and cap, his thin face frowning mightily, his majesty's Privy Councillor, Sir Richard Rich.

Chapter Twenty-nine

R ICH STRODE IN, SCOWLING. He was the smallest
man in the room, but instantly commanded it. He
pulled off his black cap and smacked Stice round the face
with it. The young man's eyes flashed for a moment, but
he lowered his sword. Rich snapped: 'I told you they were
not to be harmed. You've already dealt with that boy more
roughly than I wanted – '

'He went for me when he woke up—' Gower ventured.

'Quiet, churl!' Rich then turned to me, his voice quiet
and serious. 'Shardlake, I want no violence. I took the boy
because I knew it would bring you here, and I need to talk
to you. I knew that if I made contact with you any other
way you would go yowling straight to the Queen's people,
and what I have to say needs to be kept secret. It may even
be that this time we can be of use to each other.'

I stared at him. This was the anxious Richard Rich I had
seen at Anne Askew's burning. His long grey hair was
awry, the thin face with its neat little features stern, new lines
around the mouth, and his normally cold, still grey eyes
roamed around the room.

I said nothing, for the moment lost for words. Nicholas
stared in astonishment at the Privy Councillor who had suddenly appeared in our midst. Rich's two men watched us
closely. Then there was a knock at the door, making everyone jump except Rich, whose expression changed to a more

characteristic, sly smile. 'Answer it, Gower,' he said. 'Our party is not yet quite complete.'

Gower opened the door. Outside stood the constable with his assistant. Between them, looking furious, was Barak. I saw the dagger was gone from his belt. They pushed him in. Rich nodded at Barak and addressed Stice and Gower. 'Watch that one, he's trouble. Master Barak, let me tell you that violence will not help you or your master.' Rich then walked over to the constable, who bowed deeply. 'There's no one else?' Rich asked.

'No, sir, only this one.'

'Good. You and your man will be rewarded. And remember, keep your mouths shut.'

'Yes, Sir Richard.'

The constable bowed again, and waved his assistant back outside. Rich shut the door on them and turned back to us. He shook his head, the sardonic smile on his face showing his straight little teeth. 'Barak, I would have expected better from you. Did you not consider that if I used a house I would bribe the local constable first? They can be bought, as you know, and I pay well.'

Barak did not answer. Rich shrugged. 'Sit at the table. You too, boy. I want a word with your master, and if it concludes well I will let you all go. Understood?'

Barak and Nicholas did not reply, but at a nod from me they allowed Stice and Gower to lead them to the table. They all sat. 'Watch Barak carefully,' Rich said. 'He's as full of tricks as a monkey.' He crossed to the staircase, crooking an imperious finger to indicate I should follow. 'Come up, Master Shardlake.'

I had no alternative. Once upstairs, Rich led me to a room which was as sparsely furnished as the rest of the house, containing only a desk with a sconce of lit candles, and a couple of chairs. He motioned me to sit, then regarded me silently, his expression serious again. In the candlelight it seemed to me his thin face had more lines and hollows now. His grey eyes were little points of light. I said nothing, waiting. He had said we might be of use to each other; let him say how. I wondered, did he know of the missing *Lamentation*? At all costs I must not be the first to mention that.

He said, 'You are working for the Queen again.' It was a statement, not a question. But it had been clear from his note that he knew that.

I said, 'Yes. And there will be more trouble for you if I disappear. Remember the things her majesty knows about you.' The '*more* trouble' had been a guess, but Rich's eyes narrowed. 'She will not be pleased, for example, to learn that your man Stice once tried to suborn one of her pages – as I know for a fact.' Rich frowned at that. Then I asked, 'Is it really true, as you said in your note, that you have a spy in her household?'

Rich shrugged. 'No. But I spotted you at Whitehall a few days ago, in the Guard Chamber.'

'I did not think you saw me,' I replied, truly alarmed now.

He leaned forward. 'There is very little that I miss.' His tone was both threatening and vain. 'You would hardly be coming to see the King. I thought then, so he is working for her once more, after all this time; I wonder why. And then right afterwards you began your enquiries into the murder of a certain Armistead Greening, printer.'

'On behalf of his parents only.'

'Do not take me for a fool, Shardlake,' Rich said impatiently. 'You are acting for the Queen on this.' I did not reply. He thought for a moment, then said, 'Let me guess what you have found. Greening was part of a little group of religious fanatics, probably Anabaptists. One of their members, Vandersteyn, is a Dutch merchant, and we know that Ana, baptism still festers over there. And another is Curdy, a merchant from an old Lollard family – and we know how many of them have been seduced by the Anabaptists in the past.' He raised a slim hand and ticked off a series of names on the fingers of the other – 'Vandersteyn, Curdy, Elias Rooke, apprentice, McKendrick, a Scotch soldier turned preacher, and –' he leaned forward – 'Leeman, a member of the Queen's guard, no less. And finally –' he took a deep breath – 'it seems, a gaoler from the Tower, called Myld, more. Six of them, all vanished into thin air.'

I took a deep breath. He knew much, then, but not that Elias had been murdered or that Lord Parr had Myldmore in custody. There were four missing men, not six. I said, 'So you, too, are seeking Greening's murderer?'

He leaned forward, linking his hands. 'No,' he said firmly. 'I am looking for a book. An important book to me, and perhaps to her majesty the Queen.'

A book. One book. But I had learned from Myldmore there were two – the *Lamentation* and the *Examinations of Anne Askew*. And the *Examinations* spoke of Rich's torture of her. What if he did not know about the *Lamentation*? 'A book by Anne Askew,' I ventured. 'About her time in the Tower?'

Rich leaned back. 'Good,' he said. 'We have it out in the open. Yes, the lies and ravings of that wretched woman. So you know about it. How?'

'I spoke to the apprentice Elias before he disappeared, and he told me Greening had it,' I lied. 'Tell me, was it because of that book that your men attempted to break into Green, ing's premises before he was murdered?'

Rich frowned. 'Where did you get that information from? Oh, the boy Elias, I would guess. Yes, those two were trying to break in and retrieve Askew's writings, but they were disturbed. And shortly after someone else killed Greening.'

'How did *you* know Greening had it, Sir Richard?'

'The gaoler Myldmore. Who has disappeared as well now. He knew certain things about Anne Askew's time in the Tower, never mind how, and I had him followed.'

'By Stice?' I asked.

'No, it was Gower. You wouldn't think it to look at him, but following people surreptitiously is something he excels at. And he reported back that Myldmore had called on Greening, with a small satchel on his shoulder that was full when he went in and empty when he came out.'

'I see.'

Rich shifted in his chair. 'I had Anne Askew questioned again — she was out of the Tower then, held in a private house under my watch until the day of her burning. She readily admitted she had written a scurrilous account of her time in the Tower, accusing me and Wriothesley of torturing her, among other things, and had it smuggled out. She would not say how, or to whom it was delivered. But she did not need to; having Myldmore followed had given me the answer to that.' Rich frowned and a muscle in his jaw twitched. 'She laughed in my face, cackled triumphantly that she had got her writings out of the Tower.' His voice rasped angrily. 'Oh, Anne Askew loved nothing more than to be the one to have the last word. I wondered if she might say something awkward at the burning; there was a moment when I thought she might, but then — '

He paused, and I ended his sentence, 'The gunpowder exploded. I remember.'

'Yes, I saw you there.'

'What is it you fear she might have said, and written, Sir Richard?' I asked quietly.

'Things about me. And about another. All lies, but in these days of heretic propaganda – '

'If you knew Greening had those writings, why did you not have him arrested? And Myldmore?'

'It was better dealt with as a private matter,' Rich answered shortly. I thought, that is why he is frightened, the King is already angry with him for torturing Anne Askew to obtain information about the Queen, and he fears that if it becomes public knowledge it would be the end of his career. It was clear he knew nothing of the *Lamentation*, thank goodness.

Confidence returned to his voice again. 'Of course, just as I have concerns about Anne Askew's writings being discovered, so – since she employed you – must the Queen. Perhaps Anne Askew wrote something about her own connections with her majesty or her radical friends.' He waved a dismissive hand. 'But the Queen matters nothing to me now.'

'Sir Richard, I can hardly believe that. When you and Wriothesley have spent the last several months trying to entrap her, no doubt at the bidding of Bishop Gardiner.'

'Gardiner's plan failed,' Rich said bluntly. 'It depended on finding evidence against the Queen and none was discovered, as you no doubt know. The King warned us at the start that we must bring him firm evidence: he was annoyed with her for lecturing him, but he still loves the woman. Now he is angry with all those involved, and the Queen is back in favour. I have no more interest in whether she is a heretic or not.'

'So,' I began. 'It remains important to you to find Anne Askew's writings. You are interested in saving your own position. Perhaps even your skin.'

'Who does not want to do that?' A threatening tone had entered his voice. 'The Queen does, I am sure, and as you are involved, now my guess is that there are things in Askew's writings that could still endanger her.'

I did not answer. Rich sighed, then continued wearily. 'It is only the Askews and Gardiners of this world who would risk their lives over such questions as the nature of the Mass.' He pointed a finger at me. 'Working to preserve himself before all else is what any man endowed with reason does. You are right, Master Shardlake, I want to ensure I am safe, just as the Queen does. I have reached a dead end trying to find these missing people. I think you have, too. I have a spy at the docks, and from what he tells me, others are also there, watching for someone trying to get books out. Those people I suspect are working for the Queen.' Again I did not answer. 'I have limited resources, as do you,' he went on in an irritated tone. 'My suggestion is that the Queen and I work together to recover Askew's book.' He gave a bitter little laugh. 'There have been stranger alliances these last fifteen years.'

'I cannot forget the outcome when last I made a bargain with you,' I said finally. 'You tried to kill me.'

He shrugged. 'Oh, I would like you dead, have no doubt. But larger matters are involved. I offer you limited cooperation for a specific end. And you have the Queen's direct protection, of course.'

I sat back. 'I would need a little time to consider.' My feelings about Rich were violent; a mixture of disgust, loathing, and complete distrust. And yet I confess I also felt a certain pleasure sitting there dealing with him on equal terms for the first time, and pleasure, too, at the fact that I knew more than he did. And, in terms of reason, Rich was right. His proposition made sense. Furthermore, working with him would give me the opportunity to try and prevent the worst from happening – that he might get hold of the *Lamentation* as a by-product of retrieving Anne Askew's writings. For that was truly explosive material. This time, it would be me playing a double game with Rich.

He said, 'You mean, you need time to consult the Queen's people. Yes, I understand that.'

'You realize Anne Askew's book may already have been smuggled out of the country, to be printed abroad.' And the *Lamentation*, I thought, but did not say.

'I think not.' Rich leaned back again, interlacing his fingers. 'You know of John Bale? Currently residing in exile in Antwerp?'

'By reputation.'

'The main publisher of heretical books in English. A likely destination for this trash, you agree?'

'Yes.'

'John Bale has been watched, for some time, by agents of the King. Secretary Paget is in charge of that, but I am among the Privy Councillors who see the reports. We would have liked him arrested by the Emperor Charles's authorities and burned, as William Tyndale was a decade ago. But the Emperor's authority is weak in Antwerp now. We can only watch. And it is known that Bale is expecting a consignment. It is not there yet, or at least it was not two days ago, the date of the last report.'

'I see.' That tied in with what Hugh Curteys had told me, too. 'Where does Lord Chancellor Wriothesley fit into this?'

'He leaves the hard work to me. As people do.'

'Who leads your men? Is it Stice?'

'Yes. He has a distant family connection, one of those innumerable young gentlemen who seek a place at court. I watch for those with brains who do not mind getting their hands dirty, too. Gower is one of his lackeys.'

'Gower seems a little – unstable.'

'Stice assures me he is totally loyal to him, as he seems to be. And one must trust one's subordinates to some extent, or one would go mad, would one not?'

'True.'

'If we find Anne Askew's book, I want it agreed that it be destroyed unread.' He spoke slowly and clearly, as if to prevent any misunderstandings.

I nodded. 'I have no problem with that being agreed.' And there I had the advantage over Rich, knowing that there was nothing in it that implicated the Queen. I did not care what happened to it one way or the other. I had already decided I would recommend the Queen to make this tempor, ary agreement with Rich. But I would watch him like a hawk. I was certain that, had I not kept this appointment, Rich would have killed Nicholas. And I would never have known who had done it.

'I will consider what you have said. With the Queen's people.'

He nodded. 'I thought you would.'

I smiled grimly. 'You have not done well these last few years, have you, Sir Richard? Those allegations of corruption when you were in charge of finance during the war? And now months of working for Gardiner and Wriothesley to help bring down the Queen, only for it to end in your total failure. I thought you did not seem your usual confident self at the burning.'

He had spoken civilly up to now, as one grown man negotiating with another, but now he glared and wagged a lean finger at me. 'The Queen may have ridden this storm, Shardlake, but do not be too confident all will go the reform, ers' way from now on. I offer cooperation on a specific issue, for a limited time. Tell that to your masters, and please remember when you speak to me in future that I am a Privy

Councillor.' He frowned. Rich had lost his composure with me and I could see he regretted it. I thought, when he said the reformers should not be too confident, he can only have been referring to whatever new plot the traditionalists were hatching, the one Lord Parr said was afoot. The one plot in which Bertano – whoever he was – might be involved. But I dared not mention that.

I stood, making an ironic little bow. 'How do I get back in touch with you?'

'A note to this house will reach me. Stice will stay here for now, though he thinks the place beneath him.'

'One last thing, Sir Richard. You know that Stephen Bealknap is dead.'

'Yes. I am his executor.'

'His plans to have a monument erected to himself have been refused by Lincoln's Inn.'

He shrugged. 'I heard.'

'Sir Richard, did you ask Bealknap to try and get into my good graces? Last autumn?'

Rich looked genuinely puzzled. 'Why would I do that? Besides, I had ceased instructing Bealknap by then. His health was starting to become unreliable.'

I looked at him. He had appeared genuinely surprised. Whatever Bealknap had been doing, it did not seem to have involved Rich. Then again, Rich was a consummate liar.

'Reply to me tomorrow, please, Master Shardlake, we do not have much time.' He stood in turn. 'Now, you can go and collect that rogue Barak, and that long streak of piss, and get out.'

✝

STICE AND GOWER stood by as the three of us left the house. I knew that for Nicholas, and probably Barak, to leave thus meekly must feel like a defeat. I must get to Whitehall, I thought.

We walked along Thames Street, the city deserted after curfew. Windows were open this warm night, squares of candlelight flickering in the dark. A berobed city official walked past, his way along the dusty street lit by link-boys carrying torches.

'That constable must have been offered a large bribe,' Barak said angrily. 'One that only someone like Rich could afford. Christ's bowels, if I ever find myself alone with that Stice I'll have his balls. He has a scoffing wit. He told me Lord Rich told him I once worked for Lord Cromwell; he asked was it true Cromwell picked all his men off the streets, instead of using proper gentlemen.'

'And that other churl,' Nicholas said, '*his* wits are awry. Some of the things he said – '

I looked at the boy, his face a mass of bruises. 'I am sorry,' I said quietly. 'I did not know we were dealing with Rich. He will stop at nothing.'

Nicholas looked at me. 'That was truly him? The Privy Councillor?'

'Ay,' Barak said angrily.

'I knew he had a bad reputation.'

'We've crossed swords with him before,' Barak said. 'He should have been hung a dozen times.' He turned to me, and burst out, 'What the fuck did he want you for?'

I laughed bitterly. 'To suggest we work together, believe it or not. Nicholas, I should not say more in front of you. It is not safe.'

'Am I to have my life threatened and simply accept it?' Nicholas answered hotly. 'To have no justice against those rogues?' I thought, he is foolhardy but, by God, he has courage to speak so, after what must have been a terrifying captivity.

'He has a point,' Barak muttered.

'I may not say any more, Nicholas, without breaking a promise and nor will I give you information which could be dangerous to you. I've already told Jack far more than I should.' I hesitated, then added, 'Did they hurt you much?'

'Apart from knocking me over the head? That Gower beat me when I tried to fight them after I awoke. But what manner of man in my position would not fight back? Then they said if I kept quiet and waited I would come to no harm. I had no option.' His voice trembled slightly, and I realized he had been more frightened than he would admit. 'Tell me this at least,' he asked. 'Did they use my life as a bargaining counter? Did they make you give them something in exchange for it?'

'No, please be reassured, Nicholas. Rich merely used you as bait to make me come to him. In fact, I got the best of that encounter.'

'I am glad of that at least.'

'How is the wound on your chest?'

'Healing well. But I should bathe these cuts.'

'Then go back to your lodgings directly.' I took a deep breath. 'Nicholas, when you came to work for me you did not expect to be attacked or to be held prisoner by murderous rogues. It might be better if I were to transfer you to another barrister. With the best of references, I promise.'

To my surprise he laughed. 'This is more interesting than the law!' I shook my head, remembering how some young gentlemen loved adventure, had been brought up to think it noble. Even his recent experiences had not knocked that out of him.

We parted at the head of Thames Street. 'So what happened?' Barak asked, when Nicholas had gone.

I told him. He stroked his beard. 'This is quite some

game of hoodman blind we are playing. What will you do now?' he asked.

'Go to the palace, try to see Lord Parr, late as it is.'

'I would have thought you'd had enough for one day.'

'I must tell them about Rich immediately. What I said to Nicholas applies to you too, Jack,' I added. 'I think perhaps you should both walk away now.'

He shook his head. 'Not after this. My blood's up.'

'Your pride, rather. What about all you said earlier? What about Tamasin?'

He frowned. 'My wife doesn't rule me.'

'Jack – '

'I want to see this through. Besides,' he added more quietly, 'you need someone. You haven't anyone you can trust, none of those people at court cares what happens to you. What happens to my job if you get killed?'

'The Queen – ' I remonstrated.

'Her first loyalties are to her family,' he countered impatiently, 'and to the King, for all that she fears him. You need people you can really trust. I'm sure you can trust Nick, too, you know. And he's useful. Think about it.'

He turned and walked away homewards. There was a spring in his step now. He had been torn between his current life and his old ways, I realized, and the encounter had changed the balance for him. Barak's taste for adventure had won out, as it had so easily for Nicholas. I shook my head, and walked down to the river to find a wherry going upriver to Whitehall.

Chapter Thirty

I SAT IN LORD PARR'S OFFICE AGAIN. It was late, well past midnight. Whitehall Palace was dark and silent, everyone asleep apart from the guards ceaselessly patrolling the corridors. Lit only by dim candlelight, all the gorgeous decoration was in shadow, hidden.

Lord Parr was still working in his office when I arrived; his room brightly lit with fat buttermilk candles, the shutters closed. He had called for William Cecil, who arrived within minutes; he must have been staying at the palace. After I told them the story of my encounter with Rich, Lord Parr sent for the Queen; she had been with the King that evening but had returned to her own bedchamber. 'She must be consulted,' he insisted. 'This comes so near to her person.'

Sitting behind his desk while we waited, Lord Parr looked exhausted. 'Richard Rich, eh?' He shook his head and smiled wearily, the old courtier in him perhaps amused by this turn of the political screw.

'I thought Rich might be behind all of it,' I said. 'The murders and the taking of the book. But it seems not so, not this time.'

'But if he gets hold of the *Lamentation*—' Cecil began.

'Yes,' Lord Parr replied. 'He would use it. The campaign against the Queen could revive.' He looked between us. 'Well, you know the saying: keep your friends close and your enemies closer. Let us work with Rich, and keep him close.'

There was a gentle knock at the door. Mary Odell and the Queen's sister, Lady Herbert, stood in the doorway, bearing candles. They stepped aside to allow the Queen to walk into the room between them. Like the others she was dressed informally, in a gold-and-green caftan; there had been no time for the long labour with pins and corsets necessary for her to be dressed fully. Her auburn hair was tied back under a knitted hood. Under hastily applied whitelead, her face was tense. We bowed to her, my back suddenly stiff after the long day. She dismissed her ladies.

'What news?' she asked without preliminaries. 'Please, tell me my book is found.'

'Not yet, niece,' Lord Parr said gently. 'But there has been another development, a – complication. I am sorry to request your presence at this time of night, but matters are urgent.'

He nodded to me, and again I told my story, though missing out the part about Stice's threat to send me Nicholas's head. 'Rich knows nothing of the *Lamentation*,' I concluded. 'He believes there may be something in Anne Askew's writings which would compromise you as well as him.'

'Rich doesn't know we have Myldmore,' Lord Parr added. 'Shardlake did well in foxing him.'

'The rogue, though.' The Queen walked past me to the shutters, a rustle of silk and a waft of scent as she passed. She made to open them. 'It is so hot—'

'Please, Kate,' Lord Parr said urgently. 'You never know who may be watching.'

The Queen turned back to us, a bitter little smile playing on her lips. 'Yes. For a moment I forgot, here one must guard one's every movement.' She breathed deeply, then took a seat and looked at each of us in turn. 'Must we cooperate with Rich?'

'We must at least pretend to,' Lord Parr answered. 'Work

with his people, but watch them every moment. More pairs of eyes at the docks would be useful.' He turned to me. 'That information about Bale is helpful, as well.'

'But who has the books?' Cecil asked. 'The four who have disappeared – McKendrick, Curdy, Vandersteyn, and that wretched guard, Leeman? Or someone else entirely? We do not even know if the missing four are still alive. Who employed Greening's murderers? We know now it wasn't Rich.'

I said, 'I think the four missing men are radicals who want to get both books out of the country. We know from their actions in Germany what the Anabaptists are capable of, even if some have renounced violence now. Greening's killers could have been henchmen of theirs, employed after an internal falling out. I have said before, if it was the conservatives that took the *Lamentation*, all they would need to do is lay a copy before the King.' The Queen winced momentarily, but it had to be said. 'I think the answer lies with Curdy's people within the radical group.'

Lord Parr shook his head. 'We may know the limits of Rich's involvement, but someone else who bears the Queen ill will at the court could still be hiding the book, and could have employed one of the group as a spy.' He shook his head again. 'If so it would almost certainly be a member of the Privy Council, I am sure. But which one? And where is the book now?'

'We still have no idea,' Cecil said.

Lord Parr took a deep breath. 'All right. Shardlake, you liaise with Rich via this man Stice. You and Cecil can work with his people on trying to find the missing men, and keeping an eye on the docks.' He bent forward and scribbled on a piece of paper. 'These are our men at the customs house there. Give this to Stice, and get the names of their agents in return. Our men know only that we are looking for someone trying to smuggle out some writings.'

Cecil looked uneasy. 'There are murderers involved. There could be trouble. We may have to deal with the missing men if they try to escape, and if Stice calls on us we shall need help. We may have to deal with more of Rich's people, too, if the *Lamentation* is found. How many fit young men do you have?'

'There are four in my household whom I would trust with this,' Parr said. 'Though naturally I will tell them nothing about the *Lamentation*.'

The Queen said, 'I would have no violence.'

'There may be no alternative, niece,' Lord Parr answered sadly. 'Shardlake and Cecil may need to defend themselves, and should have help available.' He looked at me closely. 'How much does your man Barak know?'

'All of it now.' Lord Parr raised his eyebrows. 'I had to tell him,' I explained, 'when I asked him to watch for me at Needlepin Lane.'

He considered, then said, 'Then we can use him. And what of your pupil who was kidnapped?'

'He knows only a little. He has shown himself courageous, but he is very young. And Barak has responsibilities. I would not wish to put either into any further danger.'

'Do they want to help?'

I hesitated. 'Yes. They are good men.'

'Then we need them.'

Cecil asked, 'I know of Barak, but this boy, this –'

'Nicholas –'

'Is he truly fit to be trusted with this? To whom does he owe his loyalties?'

I considered. 'Nobody other than me, I think.'

'Would you vouch for him on that basis?'

'Yes, certainly.'

'What of his background? His religious loyalties?'

'He is of Lincolnshire gentry stock. He has no links to anyone at court. As for religion, he told me once he wishes only to worship as the King requires, and believes others should be allowed liberty of conscience.'

'Even papists?' There was a hint of disapproval in Cecil's voice now.

'He said only that. I do not see it as my place to interrogate my servants as to their religious views.'

Lord Parr fixed me with his eyes, bloodshot and tired now, but still keen. Then he came to a decision. 'Include the boy,' he said. 'Tell him the story. He has shown himself useful. But this is a new responsibility; make him swear that he will keep knowledge of the Queen's book secret. Barak as well.'

'This Nicholas sounds like a boy of little faith,' the Queen said sadly.

I replied with an unaccustomed boldness. 'As I said, your majesty, I have not sought to weigh his soul. I do not have the right. Nor, in fact,' I continued, 'do I have the right to involve him, or Barak, in more danger.'

She coloured slightly. Lord Parr frowned and opened his mouth to reprove me, but the Queen interrupted. 'No. Matthew has the right to speak. But – if he and Cecil are to do this, surely there is safety in numbers.' She looked at me. Slowly and reluctantly, I nodded agreement.

Lord Parr spoke brusquely. 'So. Rich knows the heresy hunt is over but believes the reformers have not yet won. The Queen's brother was at the Privy Council meeting today; he tells me that Gardiner and Wriothesley and Paget were whispering together again in corners. He heard them muttering about someone who was about to arrive in London.'

'This Bertano, whose name ever haunts us?' I asked keenly.

'We've no idea,' Lord Parr answered impatiently. 'But if Paget knows, the King knows. He turned to his niece. 'Did his majesty say anything to you tonight of this?'

The Queen frowned at her uncle. 'He spoke only of the preparation for Admiral d'Annebault's visit. Then we had the players in, and I sang to him. He was in much pain from his leg.' She looked away. The Queen hated reporting on what the King had said. But these last months she had needed allies.

Lord Parr stood. 'Very well, Shardlake. Get a message to Rich. Cecil will talk to our people at the customs house. And now I must go to bed.'

He bowed to the Queen. 'Thank you, Uncle,' she said quietly. 'And you, Master Cecil. Master Shardlake, stay. I would talk with you. We can walk a little in my gallery. Mary Odell can accompany us.' A bitter little smile. 'It is always safest for me to have a chaperone when I talk alone with any man not my relative.' Lord Parr gave me a sharp look; I knew he would rather any confidences went through him. Nonetheless he and Cecil left us, bowing deeply to the Queen. As he opened the door I saw Mary Odell and the Queen's sister still waiting outside. The Queen went out and spoke to them for a moment, leaving me alone in the room. Then she returned and said, 'Come with us.'

I stepped outside. Lady Herbert had gone but Mary Odell remained. The Queen spoke quietly. 'You remember Mary, Matthew. You asked her some questions last week.'

'Indeed. God give you good evening, mistress. Your information was most helpful.'

Mary Odell nodded. Her plump face was serious; those who served the Queen as closely as she would have divined that a new danger was afoot.

The Queen led us down the corridor, past her privy lodgings, through a door to a large vestibule where two or three
guards stood at each of the four doors leading from it. They
saluted the Queen as she walked to the door opposite. The
guards opened it, and we passed through into a beautiful
gallery, perhaps two hundred feet long, dark but for a view
of the river from the long glass windows on one side. One
guard took a torch from a bracket in the vestibule and at a
signal from Mary Odell hurried down the gallery, lighting
the sconces of candles standing at intervals on tables covered
with colourful turkey-cloths. I looked around as the details
of the gallery became dimly visible: the roof beautifully
decorated in blue and gold, paintings of biblical and classical scenes lining the walls, occasional tapestries flashing
with cloth-of-gold thread. At intervals large birdcages stood
on poles, cloth over the cages for the night. The guard bowed
and left. The Queen let out a long breath and visibly relaxed.
She turned to Mary Odell.

'Walk a little behind us, Mary. There is something I
would discuss with Master Shardlake.'

'Yes, your majesty.'

We walked slowly down the gallery. There were alcoves
at intervals, each filled with rare treasures displayed on tables
or stone columns: a box of gold and silver coins of strange
design, stones and minerals in many colours, and several
ornate clocks, their ticking an accompaniment to our progress. The Queen stopped at a desk where there was an open
book and some sheets of paper with notes in her handwriting. I stared at it and she gave me a sad smile. 'Do not worry,
Matthew. I am learning Spanish, it is a diversion, and useful
for diplomatic meetings. These are only my notes.' She
looked round the gallery. 'This is my favourite place in this

palace. Where I can walk undisturbed, and rest my eyes on its treasures.'

'There is much beauty here.'

'The clocks remind me that however frantically courtiers plot and plan beyond these doors, time ticks by regardless.' She looked at me directly with her hazel eyes. 'Taking us to our judgement.'

Nearby a bird stirred and cheeped, woken by the noise. The Queen went over and lifted the cover of its cage; a pretty yellow canary-bird looked out at us between the bars. 'A shame to see it caged,' I dared to say.

The Queen looked at it. 'We are all caged, Matthew, in the prison of this earthly world.'

I did not answer. She said, 'I wish you would seek salvation, Matthew. I feel sure God must call to you.'

'I do not hear Him, your majesty.' I hesitated. 'I have recently become acquainted with another lawyer, a man called Philip. He is what would be called a radical. A good man. Yet in some ways – blinkered.'

'Is it blinkered to seek faith, to have faith?'

'Perhaps I am too cross-grained, too contrary, to know faith as you and he would understand it.' I asked quietly, 'Does that mean, do you think, that I am damned?'

Taken by surprise, she stood still, her face pale in the candlelight. Then she answered me softly. 'Only God can answer such questions in the end. But He holds out the joys of true faith, for those who would take them.'

'Does He?' I asked. 'I cannot help but wonder.'

'Then why are you doing this for me? I ask more and more of you. It puts you and those you care for in great danger. I saw just now how concerned you are for those men who work for you.'

'I am. But Nicholas is young and adventurous, and

Barak — ' I sighed. 'Well, he is no longer young, but he is still adventurous, despite himself.'

She looked at me closely. 'Are you doing all this because it is I who ask?'

'For you, and the loyalty I owe you,' I answered quietly. 'And because I hope that if your side wins people may be allowed some liberty of conscience and belief; that apprentices and young gentlewomen and aged clerics will not be burned alive at the stake for their private beliefs, while men like Rich and Gardiner look on.'

She lowered her gaze. After a moment she whispered, 'You mean when my husband is dead?'

I answered, the words suddenly rushing from me, 'The people are sore afraid, your majesty. Afraid that any belief they hold may be approved one month, but the next may send them to the stake. It drives them to a careful, fearful orthodoxy which, whatever it is, is not faith. All fear the prison and the fire,' I added quietly.

'I fear it, too,' she replied. 'Sometimes these last months I have been so convulsed with terror I have scarce been able to rise from my bed, let alone converse and behave as the Queen must.' She shuddered.

I would have dearly liked to touch her then, to comfort her, but that I dared not do. We stood in silence for a moment, opposite a great ornate fireplace where carved heraldic beasts sported above the empty grate. A few yards off Mary Odell waited, hands held before her demurely.

At length the Queen drew a deep breath. 'My family hope that one day I may be Regent for Prince Edward,' she said quietly. 'If that happens there will be no burnings, no persecutions. The rules governing the church would change, and there would be no capital penalties.' She smiled sardonically. 'But the Seymours, as the King's uncles, believe they have a better claim. Although they too, I am sure, would want to lighten the severity of the law. For the moment we stand together against Gardiner and his people, but the future – it is in God's hands.' She added, passion in her voice now, 'That is my comfort, that it is in His hands. Our duty is to be His handmaidens on this poor sorry earth.' She lowered her head again. 'But it is a duty I failed in when, out of pride, I kept that book despite the Archbishop's advice.'

'And my duty is to recover a piece of property stolen from a most noble lady, and bring a pair of murderers to book. That is all I can promise, your majesty. I cannot promise to undertake a quest for faith.'

'It is more than most would do for me.' The Queen smiled, then raised a hand impulsively, as though to touch my arm, but let it fall. When she spoke again her tone was level, even a little formal. 'The hour is very late, Matthew. Mary can arrange a room for you in the outer lodgings, then you can leave tomorrow morning. I know you have much to do.'

✠

I WAS FOUND A PLACE near the gate, in a large room with rush matting and a comfortable bed. I slept well and woke late; the sun was already high in the sky and I heard people talking in the wide courtyard outside. It was Sunday and church bells sounded both within the palace grounds and beyond the precinct. I remembered that Bealknap's funeral had taken place yesterday; I had forgotten about it. I wondered if any mourners had gone. And as for Bealknap's strange deathbed gloating, perhaps that mystery had died with him, too.

I dressed hurriedly – I had a message to get to Stice, and I also wanted to talk to Nicholas. As I left the lodgings I saw people had gathered round three sides of the courtyard, facing the King's Guard Chamber. Servants, courtiers, officials, all seemed to be congregating there. I saw William Cecil a little way off and shouldered my way through the crowd to greet him.

'Brother Shardlake?' he said. 'You have been here all night?'

'Yes. I was given lodgings as it was so late.'

'I often need to spend the night here, too. But I miss my wife and children.' He smiled sadly, then looked at me speculatively. 'You spoke with the Queen?'

'Yes. Mainly of religion.'

'She would have all see the light which she has seen.'

'Yes, indeed.' I changed the subject. 'It seems, Master Cecil, that we shall be working closely, perhaps even facing danger together.'

He nodded seriously. 'Yes. I did not know things would come so far as this.'

'Nor I.' I looked round curiously. 'Why is everyone gathered here?'

'Do you not know? When the King is in residence at Whitehall he always makes a public procession to the chapel on Sunday mornings.'

'The Queen too?'

'Yes. Observe.'

As I watched, a group of guards exited the ornate door of the King's Guard Chamber and took up places before it. Then another group, Gentlemen Pensioners in their black livery decorated with gold, marched out with their halberds. Then came the King. As he was on the side nearest to me, I could only catch a glimpse of the Queen on the other side of that vast bulk, a quick view of a brightly coloured dress. Those who wore caps took them off and then loud cheers erupted from the crowd.

I looked at Henry. Today he was dressed in formal finery: a long cream satin robe with broad padded shoulders furred with marten. He looked slightly less obese than when I had seen him last, and I wondered if he was corseted, as he was said to be when he went abroad in public. Those huge bandaged legs were covered with black hose. He walked very stiffly, leaning on a thick, gold-headed walking stick, his other arm through that of a Gentleman Pensioner.

The King walked round the courtyard and turned to smile at the crowd, at one point doffing his black cap embossed with little diamonds. I saw, though, how his lips were clenched together and sweat stood out on his red brow and cheeks. I could not help but admire his courage in still presenting himself to his public as a man who could walk. It must cost him great pain. He doffed his cap once more, his little eyes darting round the courtyard, and for a moment I thought they rested on me. He passed on slowly, down the other side of the courtyard and in through the doorway of the Great Hall. Senior officials and councillors followed: I saw the stern bearded face of Paget; thin-faced, red-bearded Wriothesley; the red-robed Duke of Norfolk in the procession.

'I thought he looked at me for a second,' I whispered to Cecil.

'I didn't see. I should think he was concentrating on keeping his feet. They'll put him in his wheeled chair as soon as he's out of sight.' He shook his head sadly.

'How long can he go on?' I asked.

Cecil frowned and leaned in close. 'Do not forget, Master Shardlake, it is treason to foretell the death of the King. In any way.'

✝

I AGREED WITH CECIL that I would contact him again as soon as I had spoken with Stice. Once more I took a wherry to Temple Stairs, envying those citizens who, church over, had taken a boat onto the river to enjoy the sunshine. I walked to the narrow lanes off Amen Corner where I knew Nicholas lodged.

A young man who looked like another student answered my knock. He seemed a little reluctant to take me to Nicholas. 'Are you his pupil-master?' he asked.

'I am.'

He said warily, 'Nick's been in a fight. He won't say what happened, but I'm sure it's not his fault – '

'I know about it. And no, it wasn't his fault.'

The student took me up a flight of stairs and knocked on a door. Nicholas answered. He was in his shirt, the strings untied, showing the line of the bandage across his chest. The bruises on his face had come out yellow and black. He made a sorry sight.

'How are you?' I asked.

'It looks worse than it is, sir. And my chest is healing well.'

I followed him into an untidy room thick with dust, unwashed plates on the table, law books scattered about. It took me back to my own student days a quarter-century before; though I had been tidier than this. Nicholas evidently lodged alone, as I had. But whereas my father had not been wealthy enough to send a servant with me, Nicholas's father had chosen not to; another sign, no doubt, of his disapproval. He invited me to take the only chair, while he sat on the unmade bed. I studied him thoughtfully. He had courage and intelligence, but also the reckless bravado of the young. But of his trustworthiness I felt certain now.

I said, 'Nicholas, you saw last night that the matter I am

involved in concerns the highest in the land. The one I am working for is of even higher status than Rich.'

His eyes widened. 'The King himself?'

'No, not that high. Nicholas, you spoke to me once about the religious quarrels that ravage this country. You said you wish to steer clear of it all, to be left alone and have others left alone. That is my wish, too. But what I am working on now concerns a struggle at court. On the one side are those who would keep the Mass, and in some cases perhaps bring back the Pope. On the other, those who would end what Catholic ceremonies remain. Involvement in that struggle can end in torture, murder and burning. For some, it already has.'

He fell silent. I could see my words had impressed him. 'You still have not told me who you are working for,' he said at length.

'Nor can I, unless you swear an oath of secrecy.'

'Is Jack working with you?'

'Yes. He insists.'

'And you need more help?'

'Yes.'

He smiled sadly. 'Nobody has ever asked for my help before.'

'I say in all honesty, it may be better for you to stay out. Not because I doubt your courage or loyalty, but because of the danger. As I said last night, I can arrange for you to work for another barrister. Nicholas, you should not just think of yourself. Consider your parents, your inheritance, your future as a gentleman.' I smiled, thinking that would get through to him as nothing else could.

His reaction surprised me. He spoke with sudden, bitter anger. 'My parents! My inheritance! I told you, sir, why it was I came to London. My father – and my mother – would have had me marry someone I did not love. You know I refused – '

'Yes, and so were sent to London to learn the law. I am sure when your studies are finished your parents will have got over their anger, perhaps even come to respect you for what you have done.'

'That they never will,' he said bitterly. 'My father told me if I would not marry according to his wishes he would dis, inherit me. He sent me to learn law to get me out of his sight. My mother, too; she is even fiercer on the matter than he. She told me that in refusing to marry whom they chose I was no proper man, and not her son. So I have no inheritance.' He looked at me fiercely.

'That is very hard. But things said in anger —'

He shook his head. 'They meant it. I could see it in their faces when they spoke. I remember well the sinking feeling when I realized they did not love me.' There was a choking sound in his throat for a moment; he coughed. 'They have already hired lawyers to see what can be done about barring the estate to me. They would transfer it to a cousin of mine, a young popinjay who would marry a one-legged dwarf if she would bring enough money. No, Master Shardlake, they mean business.' He looked down, and smoothed the sheet on his unmade bed. 'I am their only child. That is a burden on me, as I am on them.'

'I, too, have no brothers and sisters. Yes, that can bring its burdens, though I never had such a hard one placed on me as you have.'

Nicholas looked around the untidy room at the law books. 'Sometimes I find interest in the law, though at others it all seems like rats fighting in a sack. The Slanning case —'

I smiled. 'Fortunately, cases such as that are rare. What matters do you find interest in?'

'Ones where one can sympathize with the client, where one sees an injustice to be righted.' He smiled. 'Exciting ones.'

'Exciting ones are dangerous ones. And as for the others, one cannot just act for those of whom one approves. However, in the autumn term perhaps you could assist with my cases in the Court of Requests.'

He made a face. 'Commoners suing the gentlemen who are their natural rulers?'

'Should everyone not have an equal right to go to law, just as they should have to their private religious views?'

He shrugged.

'Perhaps you would see matters differently if you were to work on the cases.'

'I do not know. For now, an active life, in pursuit of an honourable cause, that is what I want. Even if it means being kidnapped again.' He smiled then, his large green eyes shining.

'Something with meaning?'

He hesitated, then said, 'Yes. I need some – meaning.'

I realized now that Nicholas wanted a life of adventure partly to escape the memory of what his unworthy parents had done. I remembered the story I had heard of him getting into a sword fight over a prostitute. I thought, if he does not find the excitement he needs with me he may find it somewhere else, and end with a sword in the guts. And perhaps if he is with me I can guide him, check that self-destructive urge I detected in him. 'You think the cause I serve is just?' I asked.

He answered seriously, 'If it will bring an end to such persecution as I have seen since coming to London, then yes.'

'If I tell you for whom I am working, and the details of what this is about, you must first swear, on your oath as a gentleman, to tell nobody, nobody at all.'

'I have no bible here – '

'Your word will do.'

'Then I swear.'

'My employer is that honourable lady, her majesty Queen Catherine.'

His eyes widened. 'Skelly told me you used to do legal work for her.'

'I have known her since before she was Queen. She is a good lady.'

'Many say she has been in trouble.'

'She has. She is now. But she is no persecutor of anyone.'

'Then I will help you.'

'Thank you. And Nicholas, do as I tell you, with care; no heroics.'

He blushed under his bruises. 'I will.'

I took his hand. 'Then thank you.'

Chapter Thirty-one

I WALKED FROM Nicholas's lodgings back to Needlepin Lane. In daylight it looked even more dingy, the plaster-work crumbling on the old houses, the lane a narrow track with a stinking piss-channel in the middle. Though it was Sunday, men were standing outside the Flag Tavern, quaff-ing beer from wooden mugs in the sunshine. Among them I saw a couple of girls in bright make-up and low-cut dresses. The King had ordered the Southwark brothels closed that spring, but although prostitution was already illegal in the city and conviction could bring a whipping, many whores had come north of the river. One girl, well in her cups, caught my glance and shouted out, 'Don't glower at me like that, crookback, I'm a respectable lady!' People stared at me, and some laughed. I ignored them and knocked on the door of the house with the green shutters. Stice opened it immediately.

'You're back soon.'

'I have a message for your master.' I nodded over my shoulder. 'I'd best come in; I've attracted notice from the people outside the tavern.'

'Common churls, they're always shouting at passers-by.' He stood aside, and I walked into the bare room. My hand closed instinctively on my knife as he shut the door and went over to the table. He sat down, smiling insolently. The sword with which he had nearly killed Nicholas the night before lay there; he had been polishing it. The sun glinted on its razor-sharp edge. There was a jug of beer and some pewter mugs on the table, too. 'No hard feelings, eh, Master Shardlake?' Stice said. 'We each serve those to whom we are pledged.' Then, with an edge to his voice, 'You have an answer for my master?'

'Yes. Those I work for agree to our collaborating to try and locate these missing people, and Anne Askew's writings. I will liaise with you. We have another man, a lawyer named William Cecil, who has been keeping an eye on the docks. These are the people he has paid to look for writings being smuggled out.' I handed him a copy of Cecil's list. Stice looked it over and nodded. 'Well, between us,' he said, 'I think we have the docks and the custom house covered.'

'How many men do you have there?'

'In our pay, two officials.' He wrote two names on the bottom of the sheet of paper, tore it off and gave it to me.

'Sir Richard said that Bale is expecting a consignment. Let us hope we are in time.'

'Amen to that.'

'One important condition, Master Stice. If either party has word of the cargo, they warn the other at once.'

'Of course.' Stice smiled and spread his arms. 'By the way, if there's any fighting to be done – say with what's left of Greening's people, if they turn up – how many men can you bring to bear?'

'Two for certain. Probably two or three more.'

'Are the first two Barak and the boy?'

'Yes.'

Stice nodded appreciatively. 'They're both handy.'

'Cecil will likely be able to call on more.'

'And I have three on hand, including Gower, whom you met yesterday. He's down keeping an eye on the docks now.

I'm sure my master will agree those terms.' He laughed. 'Who would have thought, when you came in last night, we'd end by working together? Come, sit, let's share a beer.'

Reluctantly, I dropped into a chair opposite him. The more I could learn about these people the better: I had no doubt that if they got hold of the *Lamentation* Rich would betray us in an instant.

Stice poured me a beer, then lounged back in his chair. He was, I reckoned, about twenty-five. He dressed well — again the silk cuff of his shirt was visible below the sleeve of his doublet, like the one he had torn on his aborted raid on Greening's premises. His face was good-looking in a hard way, though that lopped ear was a disfigurement. I wondered that he did not wear his hair long to hide it.

Stice saw me looking and put his hand to the ear. 'Can't miss it, eh? People's eyes get drawn to it, as I daresay they do to your back. I'm not ashamed of it, I came by it in an honest duel, with a mangehound who impugned my ancestry. And in the sort of business Master Rich sometimes has me on, it shows people I'm not to be treated lightly.'

'How long have you worked for Rich?'

'Two years. I come from Essex, where Sir Richard has many properties. My father's land adjoins his, and he sent me to court to try my luck. Sir Richard was looking for young gentlemen with no ties and a taste for adventure.' He smiled again.

I thought, another young gentleman, like Nicholas, in search of excitement. Yet Stice, I guessed, would stoop to anything, including murder, for the sake of rising in Rich's service. That, no doubt, was why Rich had chosen him.

He laughed. 'By Mary, sir, you have a grim look. Sir Richard said you had the manner of a canting Lutheran, though not the religion.'

I did not answer directly. 'You hope to advance under Rich?' I asked.

'I do. Sir Richard is loyal to those who serve him. It is well known.'

I laughed. 'Loyalty is not the word that comes to my mind.'

Stice waved a dismissive hand. 'You speak of his dealings at the King's court. None of the great men is truly loyal to any other. But Sir Richard is known to stick by those who serve him, and reward them well.' His eyes narrowed over his mug. 'I hope the same can be said of the Queen and her people. Who is it you work for? Sir Richard told me it was probably Lord Parr, her uncle.'

I was not going to be drawn. I put down my mug and stood abruptly. 'I will let you know if I have news of any developments. And you can contact me at my house. It is in Chancery Lane.'

He raised his mug in a mocking gesture. 'I know where it is.'

✠

I HAD DECIDED to warn Philip Coleswyn of the latest turn in the Slanning case, but I thought that was best done after I had discussed Isabel Slanning's complaint with Treasurer Rowland on the morrow. I went home; I had what remained of Sunday to myself, and there were two other things I needed to do.

First I went to my study and wrote a letter to Hugh. I wrote of the general news, and my part in the coming ceremonies to welcome Admiral d'Annebault. Then I advised him that John Bale was a dangerous man, that he was to be avoided, and warned Hugh not to write to me of him again. There, I thought: at least I have not drawn Hugh into this.

I sealed the letter and put it in my satchel to be posted from Lincoln's Inn tomorrow.

I went downstairs. The house was silent. As agreed, Josephine had gone walking with her young man again, so I knew she was not at home. There was nobody in the kitchen; a tallow candle was burning on the table there, in order that there should be fire ready for cooking later. I went out to the stables, where Timothy was energetically mucking out the stable, a pile of old straw and horse dung already by the door.

'God give you good morrow, master,' he said.

'And you, Timothy. Remember to keep the horse-dung for Mistress Brocket's vegetable patch.'

'Ay. She gives me a farthing for a good load.'

'Have you thought any more about going for an apprenticeship? I could speak to the Lincoln's Inn stablemaster about what places may be available among the farriers.'

A shadow crossed his face. 'I would still rather stay here.'

'Well, I would like you to give it some more careful thought.'

'Yes, sir,' he replied, but unenthusiastically, his head cast down.

I sighed. 'Do you know where Master and Mistress Brocket are?'

'They went for a walk. Mistress Brocket asked me to keep an eye on the candle in the kitchen, light another from it if it got too low.'

'Good.' So the house was empty. There was nothing illegal in what I planned to do next, but I did not want to be seen by anyone. 'They had a letter delivered this morning, by messenger,' Timothy added. 'I was in the kitchen with them. I don't know who the letter came from but they both looked upset. They ordered me from the kitchen and a little after they said they were going for a walk. Master Brocket looked grim, and I think poor Mistress Brocket had been crying.'

I frowned, wondering what that was about. I said, 'Timothy, there is a job of work I have to do. Can you make sure I am undisturbed for an hour? If anyone comes to the door, say I am out.'

'Yes, sir.'

'Thank you.'

I went upstairs, and unlocked the chest in my bedroom. My heart was heavy as I looked at the books within; several were on the new forbidden list and must be handed in to the city authorities at the Guildhall by the 9th of August. After that date, possession of any of the books would attract severe penalties. With a heavy heart I lifted out my copies of Tyndale's translation of the New Testament, and some old commentaries on Luther dating from twenty years before. These books had been my friends in my old reformist days; one of them had been given me by Thomas Cromwell himself. But given my current employment with the Queen, to say nothing of the trouble with Isabel Slanning, I had decided it was definitely better to burn them privately than hand them in and risk my name appearing on a list of those who had owned forbidden books.

I took them downstairs, lighting another candle from the one in the kitchen, then went out to Agnes's neatly tended vegetable patch behind the house. There was a large iron brazier there, used for burning weeds and other garden rubbish. It was half-full, the contents brown and dry after all the recent sun. I took a dry twig from the brazier, lit it with the candle and dropped it in. The fire flared up quickly, crackling. I looked around to ensure I was unobserved, then, with a sigh, I took the first of my books and began tearing out pages and dropping them on the fire, watching the black

Gothic script I had once read so carefully curling up. I remembered Anne Askew, her skin shrivelling in the flames, and shuddered.

✝

NEXT MORNING, Monday, I went into chambers early and caught up with some work. When Barak arrived I told him of my talk with Nicholas, and my meeting with Stice. I said there was nothing to do for now but wait for news from him or Cecil.

'How is Tamasin?' I asked.

'Does nothing but talk of tomorrow's party. All our neighbours are coming. You know what women are like.' He looked at me shrewdly. 'I think she's forgotten any suspicions she had about what I might be doing. Let's hope she goes on forgetting, eh?' He raised his hand and I saw the bandage was off and the stitches out. 'I'm ready for action,' he said.

✝

LATER THAT MORNING I crossed the sunlit Gatehouse Court to visit Treasurer Rowland. The old man was as usual seated behind his desk, his office shutters half-closed, and he greeted me with a curt nod.

'I looked for you at Bealknap's funeral on Saturday. I wondered if you would come.'

'Actually, I forgot about it.'

'So did everyone else. There were only me and the preacher there. Well, Brother Bealknap lies in the chapel now, under a flagstone like any other, with his name and dates of birth and death inscribed upon it. He merited no mausoleum.'

'Poor Bealknap,' I said.

'Oh no,' Rowland said. '*Rich* Bealknap. Much good it did him in the end.' I did not reply, and he turned to the pile of papers on his desk. 'Secretary Paget's people have sent me more details about the French admiral's visit next month. It is going to be an even bigger event than I thought. I'll show you the correspondence. But first,' his voice deepened, 'I've got to waste my time on this nonsense.' He pulled a letter from the pile on his desk and threw it across to me: Isabel's complaint, two pages covered in her neat, tiny writing. As expected, it accused me, along with Philip Coleswyn, her brother and the expert Master Adam, of collusion to defeat her case, 'out of wicked spite', as she was of honest religion while we were all heretics.

'It's all nonsense,' I said. 'She chose that architect herself.'

'Is he a radical?'

'No. The accusations of heresy she sent flying around at the inspection scared him out of his wits. As I said, it's all nonsense.'

Rowland gave his laugh, a sound as though rusty hinges were opening and closing in his throat. 'I believe you, Brother Shardlake. It is years since you associated with the radicals; we spoke not long ago of how you have been careful. Though you did not attend Mass yesterday.'

'Urgent business. I will be there next weekend.'

He leaned back in his chair and regarded me closely, stroking his long white beard with fingers stained black from a lifetime's working with ink, as mine were. 'You seem to attract trouble, Serjeant Shardlake, despite yourself. How did you end up working for this madwoman?'

'Ill luck. Every barrister has such clients.'

'True. I am glad I am out of such nonsense. What of this Coleswyn, is he a radical?'

'He has a reputation as a reformer.'

Rowland looked at me sharply. 'Mistress Slanning says you went to dinner at his house.'

'Once. We became friendly because we were both frustrated by our clients' behaviour. Mistress Slanning's brother is as much a vexatious litigant as she is. And Mistress Slanning found out about my visit because she sometimes passes the evening spying on Coleswyn's house. That gives you a flavour of the woman.'

'She says her brother met Coleswyn because they both attend the same radical church.'

'It is a common enough way for lawyers to meet clients.'

He nodded agreement, then made a steeple of his fingers. 'Who represents her now? Do we know?'

'Vincent Dyrick of Gray's Inn. He called to get the papers last week.'

Rowland frowned. 'He has a vicious reputation. He'll make something of this conspiracy theory in court. Probably instigated the complaint.'

'He said he did not, it was all Isabel's idea. Actually, I believe him there. But he won't be able to stop her from making her allegations in court.'

'Do you think she might complain to Gray's Inn about Coleswyn?'

'She'd have no right. He is not acting for her.'

Rowland considered. 'Very well. I will try to make this go away. I will write to Mistress Slanning saying she has no evidence to back her complaints, and to warn her about the laws of defamation. That should frighten her off.' He spoke complacently, though I feared such a letter would only anger Isabel further. 'And you, Master Shardlake,' Rowland continued, his voice full of angry irritation, 'stay out of this case from now on. I don't want you mixed up in any religious quarrels when you are to represent the Inn at the celebrations next month.'

'I will step down from attending the ceremonies if you wish,' I answered mildly.

Rowland gave his unpleasant half-smile and shook his head. 'Oh no, Brother Shardlake, you will do your duty. I have already given in your name. Now, see this.' He passed me another sheaf of papers. 'Details of the peace celebrations.'

I looked them over, remembering what Paget and the Queen had said about the jewels ordered for her, the new clothes for the Queen's ladies. Even so, my eyes widened at the scale of what was planned. The admiral was to sail up the Thames on the 20th of August with a dozen galleys. The King's ships, which had met those galleys in battle exactly a year before, were to be lined up along the Thames from Gravesend to Deptford to welcome him. He would be received by the King at Greenwich, then next day go upriver to the Tower of London, before riding through the streets of the city. During this procession the London aldermen and guildsmen – and others including senior lawyers from the Inns of Court – would line the streets to cheer him, all in their best robes. I closed my eyes for a moment and remembered standing on the deck of the *Mary Rose* a year before, watching as those same French galleys fired at our fleet.

'Quite something, is it not?' Rowland said. Even he sounded a little awed.

'It is, Master Treasurer.'

I read on. The admiral would stay in London two days, riding to Hampton Court on the 23rd. On the way to Hampton Court he would be welcomed by Prince Edward, lords and gentlemen and a thousand horses. Next day he would dine with the King and Queen and there would be enormous festivities at Hampton Court. Again my presence would be required, as one of the hundreds in the background.

I put down the papers. 'It is all about impressing him, I see.'

'Great ceremonial was ever the King's way. All you will be required to do is stand around like scenery, richly garbed. Have you a gold chain for such ceremonies?'

'No.'

'Then get one, before they are all sold out.'

'I will be ready.'

'Good,' Rowland said. 'And I will write to Mistress Slanning.' He made a note, then looked up at me and spoke wearily. 'Try to keep out of trouble, Serjeant Shardlake.'

✝

DESPITE ROWLAND'S warning, that afternoon I fetched Genesis from my house, rode up to Gray's Inn and asked for Philip Coleswyn's chambers. His outer office, which he shared with another barrister, was neatly organized – it made me realize that my own chambers were starting to look a mess. I was shown into Coleswyn's office, which again was immaculate, all the papers filed neatly in pigeonholes. He laid down his quill and stood to greet me.

'Brother Shardlake. This is an unexpected pleasure. So Mistress Slanning has dismissed you. I had a note this morning from her new representative, Brother Vincent Dyrick.'

'Yes.' I raised my eyebrows. 'I know Dyrick.'

'So do I, by repute.' He sighed. 'His letter said Mistress Slanning plans to raise in court the nonsense about us and her brother conspiring with Master Adam, because we are all heretics. He said she has also made a complaint about you to Lincoln's Inn.'

'I had a meeting with the Treasurer this morning about that. I came to reassure you he recognizes the complaint for the foolery it is. But also to warn you about Dyrick: he is persistent, and unscrupulous.'

'I think perhaps Brother Dyrick hopes that by airing these allegations of a heretic conspiracy he will frighten me, and perhaps Master Cotterstoke, into coming to a settlement.' Philip shook his head. 'But we both know nothing on this earth will bring those two to settle.'

'Treasurer Rowland ordered me to steer clear of the business, particularly since I am to play a small part in the ceremonial welcoming the French admiral next month.'

'Then I thank you all the more for coming to see me. I spoke to Edward Cotterstoke about these latest allegations yesterday. He will not shift an inch. In fact he lost his temper when I told him of his sister's latest ploy. He said a strange thing: that if the worst came to the worst, he knew things that could destroy her.'

'What did he mean?'

'Heaven knows. He said it in anger, and refused to elaborate. Insisted it was nothing to do with the case and quickly changed the subject.'

'And Isabel once said her brother had done terrible things. What is it with those two, that they hate each other so?'

'I do not know,' Coleswyn said. He shook his head again.

'You remember the old family servant, Vowell, who became upset by their behaviour at the inspection. Is he still taking care of the house?'

'Yes. But Master Shardlake, you should do as your Treasurer advises, and leave the matter alone now.'

'But I will still be involved, if this conspiracy allegation comes up in court. I am named.'

'You are not a radical reformer. You have nothing to fear.'

'Do you?' I asked bluntly.

He did not answer, and I continued. 'Isabel Slanning will make whatever trouble she can. What if she asks you, through Dyrick, to swear in court that the Mass transforms the bread and wine into the body and blood of Christ?'

'I doubt the court would allow it.'

'But if they do?'

Coleswyn bit his lip. 'I am not sure I could do that.'

'That is what I feared,' I said quietly. 'I beg you to think carefully, Philip. That would be an admission of heresy. Think what could happen not just to you, but to your wife and children. To all those associated with you. Even me.'

His face worked. 'Do you think I have not already considered that, agonized over it? I pray constantly, trying to seek out God's will for me.'

I looked at his honest, troubled face. I realized that Philip Coleswyn was a man who, despite his qualities, might put others at risk to save – as he saw it – his soul. I spoke quietly, 'Think what God's will may be for the rest of us as well.'

✝

I HEARD NOTHING further from Stice that day, nor the one following. Little George's party was early that evening. The weather had changed; it was cooler and clouds were coming slowly in from the west. The farmers could do with the rain as harvest approached, but I knew Tamasin hoped to have the party in her garden.

I arrived shortly after four. It was still dry, but the sky was growing slowly darker. The little house was spotless, the table in the parlour covered in a white linen cloth on which stood flagons of beer and, I saw, some wine. Pewter mugs had been laid out. Outside in the tidy little garden another table was set with sweetmeats. About fifteen men and women, mostly in their thirties, stood there talking, all in their best finery; neighbours and clerks and solicitors from Lincoln's Inn and their wives. Sadly, no family was present, for Tamasin's father had abandoned her as a child and her mother was dead. And I remembered what Barak had told me about meeting his own mother in the street; he had not mentioned it again. I saw Guy, standing a little apart nursing a mug of beer.

Barak and Jane Marris were waiting on the guests, taking flagons to and fro to ensure mugs were kept full, Barak looking a little uneasy in this unfamiliar role. Nicholas was there in his best bright doublet, his fading bruises attracting looks from some of the guests. Tamasin stood with George in her arms, the baby in a white robe and bonnet, holding him out for guests to come and admire. They congratulated her, too, on her pregnancy, which had evidently already been announced. She herself wore her best dress of yellow silk. I filled a mug with beer and went outside. Tamasin smiled at me and held out a welcoming hand.

'Master Shardlake.' She addressed me formally. 'My friends,' she said proudly, 'this is my husband's master, a serjeant of the King's courts.' I reddened as everyone looked at me. Fond as I was of Tamasin, the touch of snobbery in her nature could be embarrassing. Behind her I saw Barak nudge Nicholas and wink. I bent low over George, who stared at me with blank eyes. 'A happy birthday, little fellow.' I touched his plump cheek.

'Thank you for coming,' Tamasin said quietly. 'And for all you have done for us over the years.'

'How are you now?' I asked. 'Feeling better?'

'Yes. In good health and spirits.' She looked round, smiling contentedly. 'Our little party goes well.' My conscience pricked at the thought of how Barak and I were deceiving her. I said, 'I should go and speak to Guy, he is on his own.'

'A good idea.'

I went over to my old friend. 'Well, Matthew.' I noted the neutrality of his tone.

'Tamasin says she is feeling better.'

'Yes, everything is going as it should. And how are things with you?' His look was sharp.

'Well enough.'

'Jack's hand is healed. And the boy's chest wound. As well they did not get infected.'

'I know.'

He asked quietly, 'That business which led to their injuries. Is it settled?' I hesitated. I did not want to lie to him. 'I guessed as much,' he said quietly. 'Something in Jack's manner. I have been observing people carefully for forty years, it is part of my trade. I think Tamasin suspected something when he was hurt, though she appears settled now. But she is expecting a child, Matthew, and lost one before. If anything should happen to Jack—'

'Guy,' I spoke with sudden heat, 'sometimes one takes on duties, swears oaths, and sometimes, to do what one is sworn to, one needs – help.'

'Matthew, I know of only one loyalty you have which would let you place yourself – and others – in danger. I thought the Queen had manoeuvred herself out of the trouble she got herself into earlier, but perhaps I am wrong. Well, hers is not my cause. I agree, one must fulfil a debt of honour. But when others are dragged in, one should think also of them.'

'Guy – '

'I worry for my patient.'

I felt something on my hand, and looked down to see a fat

splash of water. More heavy drops were falling from the grey sky. Barak said, 'Indoors, everybody. Come, wife, get George inside.'

We all went in as the rain turned to a downpour, some of the women helping Jane rescue the sweetmeats before they got soaked. When we were in the parlour I looked around for Guy, but he had gone.

Chapter Thirty-two

I STAYED ONLY A LITTLE LONGER. Outside, the rain pattered down relentlessly, then the thunder came. Guy's departure had been noted. I told Tamasin he had said he was feeling unwell. I left myself a short while later. The thunderstorm had ended, and as I walked home the air smelt damp and oddly fresh, though a nasty brown sludge of sewage and offal squelched under my feet.

When I got home I heard a woman weeping in the kitchen. Josephine's young man, Edward Brown, stood in the hall. He looked embarrassed, twisting his cap in his hands.

'What's going on?' I asked sharply. I had thought him a decent young man. If he had done something to upset her –

'It is Goodwife Brocket, sir,' Brown said hastily. 'I came back with Josephine and we found her distraught in the kitchen. Forgive me waiting in your hallway, sir, but Josephine sent me out.'

'Very well.' I went to join the women. Agnes Brocket sat at the table, her coif removed, her head in her hands. Josephine sat beside her. Agnes looked up as I entered, wisps of nut-brown hair falling over her face.

'What is amiss?' I asked.

Josephine answered. 'Mistress Brocket has had some upsetting family news, sir. I found her crying when Edward and I got back. She will be all right, I will take care of her.'

Agnes looked up. 'Forgive me, I am but a silly woman –'

'Where is Martin?'

'Gone into town, sir.' Agnes made an effort to pull herself together, taking out a handkerchief and dabbing her eyes. 'He's not happy with the bread delivered by Master Dove, he has gone to complain. Please don't tell him you saw me thus, Master Shardlake.'

'I would like to know what is amiss, Agnes.'

She took a deep breath and turned to Josephine, who looked uncertain. Then she answered me quietly, 'We have a son, sir. John. Our only child, and he is in deep trouble. Some business matters went wrong, and he is in the debtors' prison in Leicester.'

'I am sorry to hear that.'

She shook her head. 'He was such a handsome, charming boy. He had such plans to rise in the world.'

I sat down opposite her. 'Nothing so wrong in that.'

For the first time since I had known her, Agnes frowned. 'Martin does not think so. He believes everyone should keep to their appointed place in the social order. He was always severe with John; I think that was why the boy left home early.' She looked up quickly. 'But I do not mean to speak ill of my husband, sir. Despite his severity he has always doted on John.'

'How did your son end in prison, Agnes? Perhaps, as a lawyer, I may be able to assist you.'

She shook her head sadly. 'It is too late for that, sir. John managed to persuade some investors in Leicester to lend him money to buy up some of the land belonging to the old monasteries. He planned to hold on to it until land prices rose.'

'They lent money without security?' I said in surprise.

Agnes smiled sadly. 'John can charm the birds out of the trees when he wants.' Then her face fell. 'But the price of land continued to fall, they sued for debt and for the last year he has sat in Leicester gaol, where he will remain until the debt is paid. Martin and I send him money – if you cannot provide food and clothing for yourself, you are left to starve in that dreadful place. And he tries to pay off his debts, little by little. But it is twenty pounds. Now John has written saying what we send does not cover the interest, and his creditors say the balance is larger than ever.' She shook her head. 'I fear he will die in the prison now. Last winter he had a congestion in his lungs, and another winter in there . . .' Her voice tailed off for a moment. 'Please do not tell Martin I have spoken with you, sir. It is shameful, and he is so proud, and does not like others knowing our trouble – '

I raised a hand. 'If you wish, Agnes. But perhaps I may be able to do something – '

'No, sir, please. We have already consulted a lawyer, he said there was nothing to be done. Do not tell Martin,' she pleaded urgently. 'He will be – distressed.'

'Very well. But consider what I said. I will help if I can.'

'Thank you, sir.' But her tone told me she would say nothing to her husband.

✝

I WENT INTO CHAMBERS early next morning, for there was work to catch up on. The weather was hot and sunny again. Martin Brocket attended me as usual on rising, no sign on his face of anything unusual, and I guessed Agnes had not told him of our conversation.

As I was leaving, Josephine asked to speak to me. I took her into the parlour. 'Agnes Brocket asked me to thank you for your kindness yesterday. She asked me to speak for her as she is – well, ashamed.'

'It is not her shame.'

'She thinks it is. And Martin would be angry if anyone

else knew. It would hurt his pride,' she added, a note of contempt in her voice.

'I have been thinking how seldom the Brockets go out, except for walks.'

'And Agnes never buys clothes.'

'All their money must be going to their son. And, Josephine, that makes me think again about the time you found Martin going through the drawers of my desk. I wonder whether, in a moment of desperation, he considered turning to theft.'

'I wondered the same thing yesterday, sir.'

'It would be an explanation. But I have found nothing missing, and you do not think he has done such a thing again.'

'No, sir, I don't. And I have been watching him.' She gave a slight smile. 'I think he knows that. I think that is why he dislikes me.'

'Well, if it was a moment of madness, then no harm done – but it must not happen again. Go on keeping an eye open, will you? I have other matters on my mind just now, but when I have a little more time I will have to decide what is best to do about him.'

Josephine smiled, pleased at the responsibility. 'You can rely on me, sir.'

†

IN CHAMBERS I found everyone already at work; Barak and Skelly at their desks, Nicholas doing some much-needed filing. Apart from the disapproving looks Skelly cast at Nicholas's puffy face, it was like any normal day, spent working with my staff on preparing cases for the new court term in September.

The quiet did not last long. At noon Barak came in and

closed the door to my office behind him, his expression serious. 'Stice has turned up.'

I laid down my quill. 'Here?'

'Yes. Says he has news. Shall I bring him in?'

'Yes. Fetch Nicholas as well.'

Stice walked confidently into the room. He was well dressed as ever, sword at his hip, every inch the young gentleman. I did not invite him to sit and he surveyed the three of us with a cynical grin.

'All together again, hey?' He looked at Nicholas. 'That's a fine pair of shiners you have.'

'They're fading. At least in a few days my face will look normal, which yours never will.'

Stice laughed, but put a hand to his ear. 'Well, I am keeping my part of the bargain,' he said to me. 'There's news from the customs house. I think some birds may be about to fly into our trap.'

'The missing men?' I could not keep the eagerness from my voice.

'Four of them, at least,' Stice said. I exchanged a look with Barak. There were only four survivors of Greening's group, but Stice did not know that.

He continued, 'A balinger arrived yesterday from Antwerp, with a cargo of silks for the peace celebrations. A Dutch crew. They're loading up a cargo of wool now to take back tomorrow, spending the night moored at Somers Key Wharf. Meanwhile my man at the customs house says four men presented themselves there this morning, claiming they had business in Antwerp, and had passage booked on that ship. One Dutch, one Scotch, and two English. He sent word to me. The four answer the descriptions of Vandersteyn, McKendrick, Curdy and Leeman from the Queen's household.' Stice's thin face lit up with excitement. 'Though they gave false names, of course. No sign of Myldmore or that apprentice. They've been told they can go aboard at ten this evening.' He smiled. 'So, we beat your associate Cecil to the quarry.'

'It's not a competition,' I answered calmly. 'If the coming of these four has been recorded at the customs house I have no doubt the news will get to our people today.'

'Isn't ten at night an unusual hour to go aboard?' Nicholas asked.

Stice looked pleased with himself. 'I'd told my man at the customs house to say it would take till ten to process the papers. It'll be dark then, easier to take them. All we need to do is wait at Somers Key Wharf tonight. It'll be quiet, work will have finished for the day. With luck we'll take them all. And hopefully Askew's confession will be in their luggage, or more likely about the person of one of them.' And the *Lamentation* too, I thought. My heart quickened.

'Why tell us?' Barak asked Stice. 'You could have taken them yourselves.'

'Because Sir Richard keeps his word, fellow.' Stice smiled, then shrugged. 'And as you said, your people will likely get wind of it today, in any case. Besides, if we take them on the wharf there may be trouble. I've told the customs people to keep out of it, that this is private business of Sir Richard, but the crew of that Dutch ship may not like us seizing their passengers, particularly if they're all heretics.'

'The crew will probably be getting drunk in the city,' Barak said.

'There will be a couple of men left on board at least,' Stice replied. 'To keep watch, and help the passengers aboard. And these four may bring their own protection with them, of course.'

I had to agree. 'Yes, there is still the question of those two men who murdered the printer.'

'If there is a fight at the wharf, won't that attract people?' Nicholas asked.

'It could do,' Barak agreed. 'But if swords are being waved around, and a good number of men are involved, people are unlikely to intervene.'

'I agree,' Stice said. 'I can bring another two men tonight besides me and Gower. Can you three come?'

Nicholas and Barak nodded, Nicholas looking Stice in the eye. I said, 'And I will send a note to Cecil, to see if he can provide anybody, too.'

Stice thought a moment. I wondered if he was considering, if Cecil brought some more men, whether his own party would be outnumbered if it came to trouble between us. Then he smiled again. 'Wear dark clothes. We can look forward to an exciting evening.'

'My instructions are to see these people are taken alive,' I said. It had occurred to me that Rich might prefer that anyone with knowledge of Anne Askew's writings be put permanently out of the way.

'Of course. Sir Richard and your friend Cecil will doubtless want to question them all. Unless they decide to act the hero and fight back. They're fanatics, remember.' Stice looked serious now.

'Yes,' I agreed. 'Unless they fight back.'

'Nine o'clock then, at Somers Key Wharf. I've been down there and paid the wharfmaster to ensure a big stack of empty barrels is moved to a place opposite the Dutch ship. We wait behind them; it's an ideal arrangement to take them by surprise. We'll meet first at Needlepin Lane at eight, get to the wharf by nine and hide ourselves. There's no moon tonight, it'll be dark. When they come they won't know what's hit them.'

'You have organized everything very well,' I said grudgingly.

Stice gave an exaggerated bow and looked round at the three of us again. Barak met his gaze stonily, Nicholas angrily. 'Come, sir,' Stice said chidingly to him. 'No ill feelings, as I said to Master Shardlake earlier. You gave a good account of yourself, for all you're a lad just up from the country.'

'In an even fight, Master Stice, one on one, I may do even better.'

'Who knows? But we're on the same side now.'

'For the moment,' Nicholas said quietly.

✝

THAT EVENING Barak and I met Nicholas at his lodgings, and the three of us walked into town. It was a beautiful evening, the sun setting slowly, light white clouds in a sky of darkening blue. A cooling breeze had risen from the west. I looked at my companions. Barak's expression was keen and alert, Nicholas's coldly determined. I spoke quietly to him. 'No bravado tonight. Do not let yourself be roused by Stice, and do not put yourself at risk unnecessarily.'

'I will not let you down, sir.' He paused, then added, 'I know how dangerous this is. And that we must watch our allies as carefully as our enemies.'

'If enemies they are. We are not even sure they have the *Lamentation*. But we must find out.'

'Tonight we will.'

I nodded. I was more glad of his and Barak's company than I could say; I did not fancy my prospects were I to be caught on my own between a group of religious fanatics and a clutch of Rich's men. I had received a reply from Cecil to say he would be joining us at Stice's house, with two strong men from Lord Parr's household. I guessed Cecil would be as little use in a fight as myself, so Stice's party and ours would have four fighting men each.

We turned into Needlepin Lane, past the tavern where once again patrons were gathered outside, and knocked on the door of Stice's house. He let us in. The big man Gower was sitting at the table. Two other men sat with him, large young fellows with swords. They looked, as Barak would have said, useful.

Stice was cheerful and animated. He introduced us to his two new men with a mock bow. 'Here is Serjeant Shardlake, representing the interest of a certain personage who also has an interest in seeing the scribbles of Mistress Askew destroyed. And his men Barak and Master Overton. Overton and Gower had a row a few days ago, as you can see from the state of young Overton's face.'

Nicholas gave him a blank look. 'I get bored with your baiting, sir. This is no time for silly games.'

'Quite right,' I agreed.

Stice shrugged. 'Just a little sport.'

There was another knock at the door. Stice opened it again and William Cecil entered, with two heavyset men, a little older than the two Stice had brought. Like all of us they were dressed in dark clothes. Cecil took a deep breath, looking round the gathering with the sort of cool stare he might have given to an assembly of fellow lawyers. Stice grinned at him. 'Young Master Cecil! I had you pointed out to me a little while ago as a rising man in the service of a certain person.'

Cecil's reply was cold and clear. 'You are Stice, I take it, Sir Richard's man. I was told your appearance was – distinctive.'

Stice scowled but nodded, then Cecil asked, 'We are all to go down to Somers Key Wharf?'

'Yes.' Stice looked out of the window. 'It's pretty dark already. We get there by nine, hide behind the barrels, and wait. When they come, we rush them and bring them, and any baggage they have, back here. It's likely the writing we're looking for will be on their persons rather than in their luggage. I've another man waiting near the wharf with a horse and a big cart with a tarpaulin; we'll bind and gag them to keep them quiet on the way back here, knock them out if we have to.'

'We shall have to act quickly, and all together,' Barak said.

'Agreed. And if any watchmen question us about what we're doing, I have Sir Richard's seal.' Stice looked at Cecil. 'But if they fight back, and someone gets killed, that's not our fault. And if the printer's murderers arrive, too, and they get killed, you agree that's no loss?'

'Agreed,' Cecil answered coldly. He pointed to the empty grate. 'And any writings we find on them, we destroy immediately in that fire. That is also agreed?'

Stice hesitated, but Cecil continued smoothly. 'I think your master would prefer that nobody look at anything we find. In case it incriminates him.' He met Stice's eye. I admired his cool judgement. Rich would not want even his own men to see any record of his and Wriothesley's torture of Anne Askew. No doubt Rich would have liked to find something damaging to the Queen among Anne Askew's writings, and I had let him believe that such incriminating statements might exist; but as he had told me, that was not his priority now. Cecil's hope was doubtless that we would be able to quickly burn all writings we found, including the *Lamentation*, if the survivors of Greening's group turned out to have it. And as Greening had torn off the title page when he was attacked, I was hoping it might not be clear, from the face of the manuscript, who had written it.

'Ready then?' Barak asked.

'Yes,' Stice agreed.

'Then let us go.'

Chapter Thirty-three

W<small>E WALKED DOWN</small> Thames Street; ten of us, all in dark clothes, most carrying swords. It was just past curfew, and the few people on the streets gave our intimidating-looking group a wide berth. A watchman did step out to ask what we were about, a little nervously, but Stice answered peremptorily, 'Business of Sir Richard Rich, Privy Councillor,' and produced a gold seal. The watchman held up his lantern to look at it, then bowed us on our way.

We walked past London Bridge; candles were being lit in the four-storey houses built along its length. The tide was full, just starting to ebb; we could hear the roar of the waters as they rushed under the broad stone piers of the bridge. It was dangerous for boats to 'shoot the bridge' and for that reason the wharves dealing with foreign trade were sited immediately downriver. They ran along the waterfront between the bridge and the Tower of London; a line of masts near a quarter of a mile long when trade was busy, as it was now. Behind the waterfront stood a long row of warehouses. I saw the tall, skeleton-like arms of the cranes at Billingsgate Wharf outlined against the near-dark sky; beyond the wharves, the Tower appeared a strange phantom grey in the last of the light.

We turned down Botolph Lane to the waterfront, walking quietly, stumbling occasionally, for we had no lamps. From several buildings came the sound of revelry, even though it was past curfew – illegal ale-houses and brothels, serving sailors ashore for the night, which the authorities tended to leave alone.

We reached the waterfront and the long line of ships. It was quiet here after the noise of the surrounding streets. For a moment I thought I heard something, like a foot striking a stone, from the mouth of the lane from which we had just emerged. I looked back quickly but saw only the black empty passageway. I exchanged a glance with Barak; he had heard it, too.

Stice led the way onto the cobbled wharf, keeping close to the warehouse buildings. Beyond it the ships bobbed gently on the tide; low, heavy, one- and two-masted trading vessels lined stern to prow, secured by heavy ropes to big stone bollards, sails tightly furled. From a few cabins came the dim flicker of candlelight. With the re-opening of French and Scottish trade, and the import of luxury goods for the admiral's visit, the wharves must be busy indeed during the day. Out on the river itself pinpricks of light, the lanterns of wherries, glinted on the water.

Nearby stood a long pile of barrels, three high, secured with ropes. 'No talking now,' Stice said in a whisper. 'Get in behind them.'

One by one we slipped into the dark space. I crouched next to Cecil and Stice, peering between two of the barrels, which smelled strongly of wine. Opposite us a two-masted crayer was berthed, a squat heavy vessel for North Sea carriage of perhaps thirty tons, *Antwerpen* painted on the side. There was a little deck-house, the windows unshuttered; two men in linen shirts sat inside, playing cards by the light of the lamp. They were middle-aged, but strong-looking.

Next to me Cecil's face was quietly intent. I thought, this is not his usual form of business, and wondered whether underneath his coolness he feared the prospect of violence. I whispered to him, 'I thought I heard something, at the mouth of that lane, just as we came onto the docks. Like someone dislodging a stone.'

He turned to me, his face anxious now. 'You mean we have been followed?'

'I don't know. Barak heard it too. I had a strange feeling.'

Stice, on my other side, turned to Barak who had taken a position beside him. 'Did you?'

He nodded yes.

Stice's eyes glittered in the dark. 'Once or twice I've felt the house in Needlepin Lane is being watched. But I've not been able to catch anybody at it.'

'We've never known for sure that Greening's murderers were connected with these Anabaptists,' Cecil said. 'What if there's a third party involved, someone we don't know about?'

'Then perhaps tonight we'll find out,' Stice answered. 'Now be quiet, stop talking, just watch.'

We crouched there for the best part of an hour. My back and knees hurt; I had to keep shifting position. Once, we tensed at the sound of footsteps and voices, and hands reached for swords and daggers, but it was only a couple of sailors, weaving drunkenly along the dockside. They climbed aboard a ship some way off. Apart from an occasional distant shouting from the taverns, all was quiet save for the sound of water lapping round the ships.

Then I heard more footsteps, quiet and steady this time, and from another narrow lane to our left I saw the bobbing yellow glow of a lantern. A whisper passed along our row of men. 'Four of them,' Stice said into my ear. 'Looks like our people. Right, you and Master Cecil stay at the rear, leave it to us fighting men.' And then, with a patter of feet and the distinctive *whish* of swords being pulled from their scabbards, the others ran out from behind the barrels. Cecil and I followed, our daggers at the ready.

The men were taken totally by surprise. The lantern was raised to show four astonished faces. They matched the descriptions I had committed to memory: the tall, powerfully built square-faced man in his thirties must be the Scotch cleric McKendrick, the plump middle-aged man the merchant Curdy, and the rangy fair-haired fellow the Dutchman Vandersteyn. The fourth man, in his twenties, tall, strongly built and dark-haired, had to be Leeman, the Queen's guard who had deserted. He would be trained as a fighting man, and I also remembered that McKendrick had formerly been a soldier. Apart from Curdy, who had the round flabbiness of a prosperous merchant, each looked as if they could give good account of themselves.

All four rallied in an instant, bringing up swords of their own. They were going to make a fight of it. Apart from Curdy, who had been holding the lamp and now laid it down, only the fair-haired man had been encumbered by luggage, a large bag which he let drop to the cobbles. But Stice and his crew, Cecil's two men, and Barak and Nicholas, made eight against them. They fanned out in a circle, surrounding the smaller group, who cast glances, as did I, at the ship from Antwerp. The two crewmen had now left the cabin and stood at the rail, staring at what was happening. Then another man climbed up from below to join them.

Stice called out, 'Lower your swords. You're outnumbered. You are under arrest for the attempted export of seditious literature!'

The fair-haired man shouted something in Dutch to the men at the ship's rail. One of Stice's men lunged at him with his sword but he parried immediately, just as the three men from the boat jumped nimbly over the ship's rail onto the wharf, each carrying a sword. My heart sank; the number of fighting men was almost even now.

One of Cecil's men turned and raised his weapon, but in doing so he turned his back on the blond Dutchman, who thrust his own sword swiftly through his body. The man cried out, his sword clattering onto the cobbles. Then Vandersteyn turned to face the rest of us and, with his three compatriots, began retreating slowly to the boat. I looked at the fallen man; there was no doubt now that we were not dealing with some amateurish group of fanatics but with serious, dangerous people.

'Cut them off!' Stice yelled. A moment later there was a melee of swordplay, blades flashing in the light of the lamp. I stepped forward, but felt Cecil's hand restraining my arm. 'No! We must stay alive; we have to get hold of the book.'

There was a battle royal now going on beside the ship, blades flashing noisily. Watchmen came out to the rails of nearby ships and stood gawping. Curdy, the weakest of the fugitives, lunged clumsily at Gower, who, ignoring our agreement to take these men alive if possible, sliced at his neck with his sword, nearly severing his head. Curdy thumped down on the cobbles, dead, in a spray of blood.

From what I could see of the melee, the surviving fugitives were effectively parrying blows from our side, backing slowly and deliberately towards the *Antwerpen*. We must not let these people get aboard. I stepped closer, though in the feeble lamplight I could see little more than rapidly moving shapes, white faces and the quick flash of metal. Stice received a glancing blow to his forehead but carried on, blood streaming down his face, felling one of the sailors with a thrust to the stomach. I stepped forward, but again Cecil pulled me back. 'We'd only be in the way!' I looked at him;

his face was still coldly set, but the rigidity of his stance told me he was frightened. He looked at Lord Parr's dead servant, face down on the cobbles, blood pooling around him.

Nicholas and Barak had their hands full with the guard Leeman, who was indeed a fierce fighter. He was trying to edge them away from the centre of the fight, towards the little lane we had come down.

'At least I can get this!' I said, darting over to Vandersteyn's bag, which lay disregarded on the ground. I picked it up, thrusting it into Cecil's arms. 'Here! Look after this!' And with that I pulled out my dagger and ran to where Leeman, wielding his sword with great skill, continued to lead Barak and Nicholas back towards the alley, thrusting mightily and parrying their every blow, years of training making it look easy. His aim was clearly to separate them from the others, to allow McKendrick and Vandersteyn to get on board the ship. Beside the *Antwerpen* the fighting continued, steel ringing on steel.

I raised my dagger to plunge it into Leeman's shoulder from behind. He heard me coming and half-turned; Nicholas brought his sword down on his forearm in a glancing blow as Barak reversed his sword and gave him a heavy blow to the back of the head. He went down like a sack of turnips in the entrance to the lane. Barak and Nicholas ran back to the main fight.

It was now seven against five – Vandersteyn and McKendrick and the three surviving Dutch sailors. I hoped the other members of the crew were all in the taverns getting drunk. But suddenly one of the sailors managed to jump back on board the ship. He held out an arm and Vandersteyn, despite having been wounded in the leg, jumped after him, leaving only one sailor and the Scotchman behind.

On deck, Vandersteyn and the crewman used their

swords to sever the ropes securing the ship to the wharf. The sailor snatched up a long pole and pushed off. The *Antwerpen* moved clumsily away from the wharf, instantly caught in the current. Vandersteyn shouted to the two men left behind, 'I'm sorry, brothers! Trust in God!'

'Stop them!' Stice yelled. But it was too late, the *Antwerpen* was out on the river. The current carried her rapidly downstream, bobbing wildly, the two men on board struggling to control her, almost overturning a wherry which just managed to row out of the way in time. A stream of curses sounded across the water as the boat headed for the middle of the river. I saw a sail unfurl.

The remaining Dutchman and McKendrick had their backs to the river now. Realizing it was hopeless, they lowered their swords. 'Drop them on the ground!' Stice shouted. They obeyed, metal ringing on the cobbles, and Stice waved his men to lower their own weapons. I looked at the four prone bodies on the wharf: the Dutch sailor, Curdy, Cecil's man and, a little distance away, Leeman, lying on his front in the entrance to the alley. 'He's dead,' Barak said loudly.

On neighbouring boats watchmen still stood staring, talking animatedly in foreign tongues, but Barak had been right; they had not wanted to get mixed up in a sword fight involving a dozen men. One man shouted something at us in Spanish, but we ignored him. More men, though, might appear from the taverns. I looked at the Dutchman and McKendrick. Returning my look, the Dutchman spoke in heavily accented English. 'Citizen of Flanders. Not subject to your laws. You must let us go.'

'Pox on that!' Stice shouted. 'Your bodies will go in the river tonight!' His head and shoulders were covered with blood from his wound; in the light of the lamp he looked like some demon from a mystery play.

The Dutch sailor seemed shaken, but McKendrick spoke boldly, in the ringing tones of a preacher, his Scotch accent strong: 'Ye've lost! We know Mynheer Vandersteyn had a book, by Anne Askew. Carried on his person, not in that bag. That's why we got him aboard. Ye've lost!' he repeated triumphantly.

Stice turned wildly to Cecil. 'We have to get that boat intercepted!'

'On what grounds?' Cecil said, his voice sharp and authoritative now. 'Exporting heretical literature? The book would be public knowledge in a day. And intercepting a foreign trading vessel could cause diplomatic trouble; that's the last thing we need just now.'

Stice wiped his face with a bloody sleeve, then looked at the bag which Cecil still held. 'Maybe they're lying! Maybe it's in there!' He grasped it from Cecil's arms and upturned it on the ground, dragging the lantern across to examine the contents. I helped him go through them; nothing but spare clothing, a Dutch bible and a purse of coins. He threw the purse down and stood cursing.

'Search those men!' he shouted, pointing to McKendrick and the Dutchman. Two of Stice's men grabbed them and searched them roughly, watched carefully by Cecil and me, then turned back to their master, holding out a couple of purses. 'Nothing but these!'

'Examine them!'

The two men opened the drawstrings and bent to look inside. Seizing his moment, the Scotchman suddenly jumped forward and grabbed his sword. Gower was next to him. Taking the big man by surprise, McKendrick lunged at him, thrusting his sword deep into his stomach. With a cry, Gower staggered back into the man next to him, unbalancing him, and the Scot, with an astounding turn of speed for such a big man, ran for the lane, jumping over Leeman's prone body. Stice's men ran after him, disappearing into the darkness.

'By God's body sacred!' Cecil shouted out. It was the first outbreak of temper I had seen from him. 'We've lost them all!' He approached the Dutchman and, to my surprise, addressed him in Flemish. A brief exchange followed before Cecil turned away. 'He knows nothing,' he said fiercely. 'They all belonged to some heretic congregation in Antwerp, came over knowing their friend Vandersteyn had an important book to bring back. This one says there are two more crewmen who will be back from the tavern soon. And we *can't* have a diplomatic incident over this.' He spoke desperately, looking at the four bodies and at Gower, who had fallen to his knees and was gasping as he clutched the wound in his stomach, blood trickling down between his fingers.

The two who had run after McKendrick returned empty-handed. 'He got away from us, those lanes are pitch-black. The devil knows where he is now.'

'No!' We all turned to the Dutchman, who spoke in heavily accented English. '*God* knows where he is. He is God's servant, unlike you shavelings of the Pope.' Stice and his men looked at him threateningly; they would have given him a beating, but Cecil called them off sharply. 'Let him go,' he said. He looked at the sailor. 'Run, you, while you can!'

The Dutchman disappeared into the lanes. 'Search Leeman and Curdy's bodies,' Cecil said. 'Quick, there's little time.'

'What for?' Stice asked. He had taken out a handkerchief and was dabbing at his face.

Cecil nodded at the direction in which the Dutchman

had fled. 'In case he's lying and one of them has the book on his person.'

Barak and Nicholas went over and searched Leeman's body, while one of Stice's men searched Curdy's, Cecil and I standing over him in case a manuscript should be found. But there was nothing on either man, save more purses full of coins for the men's new life on the Continent. I sighed. Gower had collapsed to the ground now, coughing; Stice went over and knelt beside him. 'We'll get you seen to,' he said in a surprisingly gentle tone.

I turned to the body of Cecil's man. 'Had he family?' I asked.

Cecil shook his head. 'I don't know. The poor fellow was in Lord Parr's household.' He turned to the other man who had come with him. 'Did you know him?'

'Only slightly, sir. But he had a wife.'

'What do we do with the bodies?' Nicholas asked quietly.

'Put them in the river,' Stice answered, standing up. 'There's nothing to identify them, and with luck they'll be carried far downstream before they surface. When the crew return they'll find the ship gone and they'll learn about the fight from the one we let go, who'll be running to them now. But they'll say nothing, their business was illegal and there's nothing to lead anyone to us. Get them in the water, now.'

'Not my man,' Cecil answered firmly. 'You heard, he had a wife. My other man and I will have him taken back to Whitehall in a wherry. We owe him that. We can say he was robbed.'

Stice took a deep breath. 'We've got to get Gower to a doctor. He'll take some carrying to the cart.'

On the next ship the sailor was calling to us in Spanish again – asking questions, by the tone of his voice. Stice turned and shouted, 'Fuck off!'

'All right, Stice,' Barak said briskly. 'We'll dispose of these other two; you're right, if they're left lying here there'll be questions.'

Stice nodded agreement. He turned to me, braced his shoulders and said, 'We have failed, Master Shardlake. Sir Richard Rich will want an accounting for this.'

'He is not the only one,' Cecil said.

Stice left his two remaining men carrying the wounded Gower between them. Barak shook his head. 'Stomach wound like that, doubt he'll make it.'

'No,' I said. 'Well done, Nicholas, for battling with Leeman. He was a powerful fighter.'

Barak smiled. 'Not was. Is. Come and look. Bring the lamp.'

Puzzled, Cecil and Nicholas and I followed him over to where Leeman lay prone. Nicholas turned him over. The wound on his arm had stopped bleeding. Barak put a hand to the man's nostrils. 'There, he's breathing. I only knocked him out.' He looked between me and Cecil and smiled.

Nicholas said, 'You told me he was dead!'

'There's an art to where you hit a man on the head. I thought it a good idea to pretend he was dead. Now that Stice has gone we can take him in to question him alone.' He allowed himself a smile. 'I was scared he might come to and moan, but he's still out cold.'

Nicholas looked at Barak with a new respect. Cecil bent over Leeman dubiously. 'Are you sure he's all right?'

'Pretty sure. He'll come round soon.'

I looked at the young guard's still face. 'It seems Anne Askew's writings have gone, but as for the *Lamentation*, if anyone knows what's happened to it, it's him.'

Cecil smiled with relief. 'Yes. You did well, Barak.'

'He may not want to talk,' Nicholas muttered.

Cecil looked at the boy, his large eyes set hard now. 'One way or another, he will.' He looked round. People were still watching us from the boats, but nobody had come yet from the taverns. 'All right,' he said. 'Get those bodies in the river. Quick!'

Chapter Thirty-four

I QUICKLY BOUND LEEMAN'S injured arm with my handkerchief. Fortunately the blow Nicholas had struck him, though a long gash, was not deep. Cecil and Lord Parr's surviving man stood watching. Meanwhile Barak and Nicholas rolled the bodies of Curdy and the Dutch sailor into the Thames, watched in horror by the Spaniard on the neighbouring boat. I cringed when I heard the splashes. Beside me, Leeman remained unconscious. I feared Barak had hit him too hard and that the business of the Queen's book would bring yet another death after all. *Lamentation* indeed, I thought bitterly as Barak and Nicholas walked back to us, Barak looking grimly determined and Nicholas slightly shocked. In the water I saw a body rolling over as the current carried it rapidly downriver – Curdy's, I thought, from its round shape.

Barak knelt and examined Leeman. 'We have to get him away somewhere, question him when he comes round.'

'Where?' I asked.

'We cannot take him to Whitehall.' Cecil spoke firmly.

'My lodgings are not far,' Nicholas said. 'And I know my fellow students are out. A friend's birthday celebration. It'll go on till very late, they may not be back at all tonight.'

'You left the party to join us?' Barak said. 'We're honoured.'

'Yes, we are,' I said seriously. 'Your help was important. And that was a grim task.'

Nicholas gave a strange, halting laugh. 'I have never seen anyone killed before.'

When Cecil spoke his voice was cool but his large eyes held a shocked look: 'Take Leeman to the boy's place.'

'We could carry him between us,' Barak said, 'pretend he's a drunk friend that's passed out, if we're asked.'

Cecil looked down at the body of Lord Parr's man. 'And we will take this poor fellow straight on to Whitehall and rouse Lord Parr. What is your address, boy? We will send some men there later, to pick up Leeman. It may take a few hours, though. Keep him safe.'

'We must be careful,' I said. 'I had a sense we were followed here. I'm sure I heard someone accidentally kick a stone in that alley.'

'I thought so, too,' Barak said. 'Watch out for us. Nick boy, keep your hand near your sword.'

Barak and Nicholas heaved Leeman up, putting his limp arms over their shoulders. Cecil looked on, his eyes wide. Barak gave him a grim smile. 'Don't worry, he'll come round in a while.' Cecil shook his head, as though wondering whether all this could actually have happened, then motioned Lord Parr's second man to help him lift the dead man's body.

☦

WE REACHED Nicholas's lodgings without incident, taking the conspirators' discarded lamp to light our way. I kept a keen ear out for anyone following us through the dark streets, but heard nothing. Leeman was still unconscious when we reached Nicholas's lodgings. Barak and Nicholas laid him on the bed, which needed a change of sheets. I coughed at the dust in the room. 'Don't you have someone in to clean?' I asked.

'We had a woman, but Stephen next door tried it on with her once too often. We haven't found anyone else yet.'

I looked at Nicholas's bookshelf, noting that along with some legal tomes and a New Testament which seemed suspiciously pristine, there were a couple of volumes on gentlemanly conduct and the *Book of the Hunt.*

'I'm hungry,' Nicholas said. 'I have some pork dripping and bread. I think the dripping's still all right.' Under the fading bruises his face was pale. Barak, too, looked tired and grim. We were all exhausted. I studied Leeman, lying prone on the bed. He was young, tall and strongly built, with dark hair, a neatly trimmed beard and a handsome face with a proud Roman nose. He wore a jerkin of ordinary fustian, a far cry from the finery of the Queen's court. I felt gently round the back of his head; there was a large swelling there.

Barak and Nicholas had sat down at the table, and were hungrily devouring the bread and dripping which Nicholas had brought from a cupboard. 'Here,' Barak said to me. 'Have some food. We could be here a while.'

I joined them, but continued to check on Leeman. I had some time, at least, to question him before Lord Parr's men arrived. I sensed that, like Myldmore, this man might be willing to speak if we could convince him that we were working for the reformist side. It was worth a try. I remembered what I had said to Nicholas that time Elias had fled. Never prick a stirring horse more than he needs. I was desperate to find out what Leeman knew but a soft touch might work here. I remembered Cecil's remark that he would talk in the end, and had a momentary vision of fists thudding in a darkened room.

After a while, Leeman groaned and began to stir. Barak

took some water from a bucket and squeezed a cloth over his face. Leeman coughed, then sat up, clutching his head. Grimacing with pain, he looked down at his bound arm.

'I did that,' Nicholas said. ''Tis but a flesh wound.'

Leeman's pale face darkened suddenly. 'Where am I?' he asked. He sounded angry but I detected an undertone of fear there, too.

I stood up. 'You are held, Master Leeman, if not by friends then not by the enemies you may think, either.'

Leeman looked round the room, gradually taking in the student messiness. 'This is not a prison,' he stuttered, confusion on his face.

'No,' I replied gently. 'You are not under arrest, not yet. Though others will be coming here for you in a while. I am Matthew Shardlake, a lawyer. It would certainly be better for you to talk to me first. I may be able to do something to help you, if you help us.'

Leeman only glared at me. 'You are the agents of Bertano, emissary of the Antichrist.'

'That name again,' Nicholas said.

I pulled a stool over to the bed and sat face to face with Leeman. 'We have heard that name many times recently, Master Leeman,' I said. 'But I swear to you I do not know who Bertano is. Perhaps you could tell me.' I considered a moment. 'By the Antichrist I take it you mean the Pope.'

'The Beast of Rome,' Leeman confirmed, watching carefully for our reaction.

I smiled. 'Nobody here is a friend of the Pope, I assure you.'

'Then who do you work for?'

I took out the Queen's seal which I had been given on the day of my appointment and held it up for him to see. 'For her majesty. Privately. I am trying to find out what happened to a certain book.'

Leeman frowned, then said, 'Lawyer or courtier, 'tis all the same. You all steal bread from the mouths of the poor.'

'Actually I am an advocate at the Court of Requests, and most of my work is done on behalf of the poor.' His look in response was contemptuous; no doubt he despised the charitable doings of the rich. But I persisted. 'Tonight we were looking for a manuscript which we believe you and your friends were trying to smuggle abroad. I also seek, by the way, the murderers of Armistead Greening.'

'Who is now safe in heaven,' Leeman said, looking at me defiantly.

'There is another manuscript, also missing, by the late Mistress Askew, who was cruelly burned at Smithfield.'

'It is gone.' There was a note of triumph in Leeman's voice now. 'Vandersteyn had it with him.' He paused. His face paled. 'Curdy – your people killed him. Good McKendrick, I saw him run. Did you catch and kill him, too?'

'He escaped. And it was not us who killed Curdy, but some others we have been forced to work with. They are concerned with finding Anne Askew's writings, but we are not.' I spoke slowly and carefully: I saw I had his attention. 'I am interested only in the other manuscript, which they do not know about. The one stolen from the Queen.' I leaned forward. 'A book which, if published, could do great damage to the Reformist cause. Just when her majesty's troubles appeared to be over, and the tide beginning to swing against Bishop Gardiner, you steal it. Why, Master Leeman?'

He did not reply, but looked at me through narrowed eyes, calculating. A slight blush appeared on his pale cheeks and I wondered if he was remembering his oath to the Queen, which he had broken. I continued quietly. 'I traced you through the guard Gawger, whom you bribed, and the carpenter who gave you the substitute key for the Queen's chest.'

'You have learned much.'

'Not enough. Where is the book now?'

'I do not know. Greening had it. Whoever killed him took it.'

'And who was that?' He did not answer, but I sensed he knew more. He looked at me, then surprised me by saying, in a scoffing tone, 'You think the danger to the Queen is ended, if the book I took is recovered?'

'So it has seemed. I have lately been at court, Master Leeman.'

He answered, weariness and scorn mingling in his voice: 'It is not over. How did you learn the name Bertano, if you do not know who he is?'

'Greening's neighbour, Okedene, heard you arguing loudly in Greening's shop, shortly before Greening was killed. He heard the name Bertano mentioned as an emissary of the Antichrist.'

Leeman nodded slowly. 'Yes. The Queen may be a good woman, and perhaps in her heart she recognizes the Mass as a blasphemous ceremony, but because of Bertano she is doomed anyway. The King is about to receive a secret emissary from Rome. That can only mean he is going to return to papal servitude. Many would fall then, Catherine Parr chief among them.' And then I felt a chill as I understood. 'Bertano is the *official* emissary of the Pope,' I breathed.

'Whether that is true or not,' Nicholas said angrily, 'you broke your oath to guard and protect her.'

'In the end she is no more than another of the idle rout of nobles and princes, the refuse of mankind.' Leeman spoke so fiercely, I wondered again whether his conscience pricked him.

Nicholas frowned. 'God's death, he *is* an Anabaptist. That mad company of schismatics. He'd have all gentlemen murdered and their property given to the rabble.'

I turned round and gave him a warning look. 'I am in your hands,' Leeman said fiercely. 'And know that I will soon be killed.' He swallowed hard. His angry tones held the defiance of a martyr, but his voice also trembled slightly. Yes, I thought, he is afraid; like all men he fears the flames.

'Indeed,' he continued. 'I am what your boy calls an Anabaptist. I understand baptism may only be allowed once one has come to true knowledge of God. And that just as the Pope is the Antichrist, seducing men's hearts while living in pomp and magnificence, so earthly princes and their elbowhangers are likewise thieves and must be overthrown if Christians are to live as the Bible commands!' His voice rose. 'With all goods held in common, in true charity, recognizing we are all of the same weak clay, and that our only true allegiance is to Our Lord Jesus Christ.' He leaned back, breathing hard, staring at us defiantly.

'That's some lecture,' Barak said sardonically.

'So,' I began quietly, 'you would overthrow the King, who is said to be, by God's decree, Supreme Head of the Church in England?'

'Yes!' he shouted. 'And I know I have just committed treason with those words, and could be hanged and drawn and quartered at Tyburn. As well as burned for heresy for what I said about the Mass.' He took a deep, shuddering breath. 'Best to get it all out now. I can only die once. It is what I believe, and because of that I will be received in Heaven when you kill me.'

'I told you earlier, Leeman, that we are not necessarily your enemies. If you can help guide us to the Queen's book, I may be able to help you.' I looked at him closely before continuing. 'You come from the gentle classes. You must do, to have been appointed to the position of status and trust you held. So what brought you to your present beliefs?'

'You would have me incriminate others?' Leeman took another breath. 'That I will not do.'

'You have no need to. Master Myldmore has already told us all about your group. We have him safe. We know the names – the three who came with you tonight: Curdy who was killed, Vandersteyn who got away in the boat, and McKendrick who fled. And Master Greening and the apprentice Elias, both of whom were murdered.'

A look of astonishment crossed his face. 'Elias, too, is dead?'

'Yes, and by the description and methods of the killers, by the same hands that murdered Greening.'

'But we thought – ' He checked himself and whispered, 'Then Elias is in heaven, by God's mercy.'

I pressed on. 'We also know, through Myldmore, how Anne Askew's *Examinations* came into the hands of your group. And my enquiries at court led me to you as the man who stole the Queen's book.'

Leeman slumped back on the bed. 'Myldmore,' he said despairingly. 'We knew he could not be trusted. That man had been seduced by Mammon.'

'And had residual doubts about the Royal Supremacy.'

Leeman said, 'Yes. We could not let him into our secrets. Master Greening was firm on that.' He shook his head. 'Greening brought me to the truth, he and the others. God rest him.'

I said, 'We would like to find his killers. Please help us.'

Leeman lay quietly, thinking. I burned to know all, but I was sure that, as with Myldmore, gentle persuasion was the best tactic, though Leeman seemed a much tougher and

more intelligent man. Finally he spoke again, in more subdued tones. 'You know so much, it will do no harm to tell
you the rest. As for me, yes, I was born and raised a gentleman. In Tetbury, in the Cotswolds. It is sheep country, and
my father owned many flocks. He had grown fat on the cloth
trade, and by his connections he was able to get me a position
at court as one of the Queen's guard.' He smiled sadly. 'My
father, landowner though he is, at least embraced the new
faith, as did I as I grew up. Though the King himself has
moved steadily back to the old ways. And would now go
further.'

'Back to Rome, you think?' Barak fingered his beard
thoughtfully.

'Yes. My father warned me that when I came to London
I would see things I would not like, but in order to advance
myself I must hold my tongue and wait for better times.
Concentrate on advancement, always advancement.' He
clenched a hand into a fist. 'Towards riches and power, not
towards God. That is all that fills the hollow hearts at court.
My father could not see that,' he added sadly. 'He saw only
part of what Christ demands of us. As through a glass,
darkly.' He turned to me. 'You have seen Whitehall, Master
Shardlake?'

'I have.'

'It is magnificent, is it not? And still a-building. Getting
grander by the day.'

'Some say the King wishes it to be the greatest palace in
Europe.'

Leeman gave a hollow laugh. 'It is designed to reduce
those who come to a state of awe. Every stone speaks of the
King's power and wealth, every stone cries out: "Look, and
fear and wonder." While within,' he added bitterly, 'the dirty
game is played called kingly craft, wherein no man is safe.'

'I agree with you,' I said. 'Certainly about kingly craft.'

Leeman looked at me hard, surprised by my reaction – I think he had intended to provoke me into defending the King and his court. He went on: 'I hate it. The great palace, every stone built with the sweat of poor men, the stench and poverty and misery just beyond its walls. My vicar in Tetbury was a man who had come to see the emptiness of the Mass, and he put me in touch with friends in London, men of faith.' Leeman paused, his eyes seeming to look inward for a moment. 'It is as well that he did, for royal service offers many temptations – debauchery of the flesh, vanity in dress and manner, fine clothes and jewels – oh, they are tempting, as the Queen herself says in her book.'

'You have read it?'

'Yes, when it was in Master Greening's possession.'

The thought of him reading the stolen manuscript made me suddenly angry, but I forced myself to keep my expression open and amiable as he continued. 'Through friends outside I progressed further towards God, and the right understanding of our wicked society.' He looked me in the eye again. 'One discussion group led me to others as my faith deepened, and last year I was introduced to Master Greening.'

I could see how it had happened: a sensitive young man, with a conscience and radical inclinations, tempted by the magnificence of the court but aware of the evil within. His beliefs had deepened as he moved into more radical circles, eventually coming into Greening's orbit. I ventured, 'So, you were accepted into Greening's little group, unlike Master Myldmore. Who also had access to secrets,' I added meaningfully.

Leeman laughed. 'I guessed you had made that connection. Master Vandersteyn had connections, too; not here, but in the courts of France and Flanders, with men who would tell him things. It was his idea to build a similar group here, of true believers who were in a position to find out secrets that might harm both papists and princes, help stir the population to rebel against both.'

'I see.' So Vandersteyn, now heading out into the North Sea, had been the key.

'He met Master Greening on a business trip to London two years ago, and so our little group was born. McKendrick had already come to see the truth. Then the papists came sniffing at his heels and he had to flee Scotland. He had held a junior position at the Scotch court of the child Mary and knew all the schemings and bitings among the rival lords there.'

'And Master Curdy? He does not seem to have been a man of connections.'

'No. But he was a man of faith, with an instinct for truly sniffing out who might be trusted and who might not.'

'So,' Barak said flatly. 'A little cell of Anabaptist spies, rooting for secrets to disclose.'

Leeman looked at him defiantly. 'And we found them. Even Myldmore, whom we had rejected because he had not reached true faith, came back to us when Anne Askew entrusted him with her writings. We knew that if her story of illegal torture by two councillors of state were published abroad and smuggled back into England it would rouse the populace. English printers are too closely watched for it to be done safely here. And it will be published,' he said defiantly. 'The government has agents in Flanders, but Master Vandersteyn's people are adept at avoiding them.'

'I see.' I took a long breath. 'Well, I told you, I do not care about Anne Askew's book. Others did, and it was necessary for me to work with them for a while.'

'Richard Rich?' Leeman asked. 'There is a villain.'

I inclined my head. 'As for you, you overheard the Queen and Archbishop Cranmer disputing loudly one night when you were on duty, and learned of the existence of the *Lamentation.*'

He groaned, wincing at a spasm of pain. 'By my faith, sir, you are a clever man.'

I took another deep breath. 'And I guess you told your group about the Queen's book, and it was decided you would steal the *Lamentation*, even though publication could seal the Queen's fate. Because you believed her fate was already sealed and publication would at least show that she held radical beliefs before she was toppled. And you knew her fate was sealed because of Bertano?'

'Yes. I argued within the group that it was better to expose Bertano publicly, that knowledge of his coming would truly rouse the populace. But others argued against, saying we would not be believed and it was too late to prevent his coming.'

'Who argued that position?'

'Master Curdy and Captain McKendrick both.'

'And how did you find out about Bertano?'

'I told you, Vandersteyn has informants on the Continent. Including a junior official at the French court. Suffice to say that his responsibilities involved accommodation for foreign visitors, which gave him the opportunity, like me, to overhear conversations. Such as the arrival in France of Gurone Bertano, a papal ambassador who once lived in England and was being sent to seek an agreement between the Pope and King Henry. At the King's invitation.'

Barak shook his head firmly. 'The King would never surrender his authority back to Rome.'

'Yes,' Leeman agreed. 'Master Vandersteyn was mightily

shocked when his emissary from Flanders brought him the news.' He looked at me, his dark eyes hard. 'But his people can always be trusted. Bertano is now at the French court, and he will arrive here within a few days. It has been done secretly, only a few men at court know, and nobody with any sympathy for reform. Certainly not the Queen.'

I glanced at Barak, who sat stroking his beard, frowning hard. It was an outlandish, extraordinary story, yet it fitted what Lord Parr had told me – that despite their failure to destroy the Queen and those around her, the conservative faction were not downcast, were rather comporting themselves as though they had something else up their sleeves. If this was their trump card, the stakes could not be higher.

'When did the news about Bertano come?' I asked.

'Just after I told our group about overhearing the Queen's argument with Cranmer over the *Lamentation*. And we all agreed: if the King decides to go back to Rome, it surely follows that the Queen must be replaced. The Pope would insist on it. But if the *Lamentation* were published, the populace would see the King had executed a good and true woman.'

I got up and walked to the window. I was horrified. If what Leeman said about Bertano was true, the Queen was in deadly danger from another source, too, and was a dispensable pawn in a far bigger game. It was hard to take in. But at least it seemed Greening's group had made a majority decision not to publish the *Lamentation* before the Queen fell, but only to keep it in Greening's shop. Safe, they supposed.

Barak spoke bluntly to Leeman. 'Making public that the King was about to receive a secret emissary from the Pope would surely have roused popular anger, perhaps prevented the visit taking place at all.'

'Ay,' Nicholas nodded agreement. 'The outrage among reformers would be tremendous.'

Leeman replied, 'That is what I said when we discussed Bertano in the group. We argued over it for days.'

I came back to him and sat down again. 'But Curdy and McKendrick opposed it? I ask, Master Leeman, because I think one of your group might have been a spy in the pay of a third party, I know not who. I am fairly certain, by the way, that we were followed to the docks tonight, and that events there were watched.'

He nodded sadly. 'That is what we also came to think, after Master Greening was murdered and the *Lamentation* disappeared. That is why we all fled. Vandersteyn had Anne Askew's writings, ready to take abroad, so at least the killers would not get them. Afterwards, we realized there must have been a spy, for nobody else knew what we were doing.' He shook his head. 'But we thought it was Elias, as he was the only one that refused to leave the country.'

'He had not been told about the *Lamentation*, he was too young for such a secret but he could have . . .'

'He could have overheard. That is what we thought, afterwards. And he needed money, with his family to support.' Leeman shook his head. 'Poor Elias.'

'If there was a spy, it wasn't him.' I thought quickly; that left only Curdy, who was dead, Vandersteyn, who was gone, and McKendrick. And I could not see it being Vandersteyn; he had too long a history as a radical and had been at the very centre of the conspiracy. That left Curdy and McKendrick, who had lived in the same house and had both been against exposing Bertano before his arrival. I asked, 'What was Curdy's and McKendrick's argument against making Bertano's visit known immediately?'

'Curdy said we had no clear evidence, and if we set the

story abroad it would simply be denied, and the negotiations would take place anyway. McKendrick agreed, he said stronger evidence was needed, perhaps more detail of where the negotiations were to take place, and with whom. He said he knew from experience in Scotland how rumours can fly, only to be quickly quelled if there is no evidence. He suggested Vandersteyn try to get more information from the Continent, and then break the news in detail, when Bertano was actually here. We knew only that he was coming around the start of August. In the end we agreed to wait, and Vandersteyn sent letters to his associates abroad, in code, to try to get more information.'

'Was there any reply?'

'No.' He sighed. 'Vandersteyn's agents could discover no more. And then came Master Greening's murder; we fled, hid in secret in the houses of good friends, keeping separate, moving from place to place while Master Vandersteyn arranged for a ship to come over and take us to Flanders. We knew we were being hunted. One of the households which sheltered Master McKendrick was attacked by ruffians just after he left.' He looked at me. 'None of that was arranged by you or your confederates?'

'No.'

'How did you know we would be at the docks tonight?'

'It was not difficult to work out that you would try to get yourselves, and perhaps both books, abroad. Spies were placed at the docks. You were too confident, going through the customs house. You should have smuggled yourselves on board the ship.'

Leeman bit his lip.

'Let's get this clear,' Barak said. 'Your little group were Anabaptists, who want to overthrow not just the whole of established religion, but society itself—'

459

'As we one day will! It is clear in the Bible—'

Barak cut in. 'A group which was put together by the Dutchman Vandersteyn, who is part of a similar circle on the Continent, and whose particular goal was to obtain information that could incite the people to rebellion.'

'Ay. The people are deceived by the lies of popes and princes. But believers such as ourselves are the leaven in the yeast.' Leeman spoke as though chanting a prayer.

'But,' I said, angry now, 'because you did not realize there was a spy in your group, someone – almost certainly working for a leading figure on the conservative side – has the Queen's book in their possession, ready to give to the King at any moment, with the intention of making him angry with the Queen again just as this papal emissary arrives!' Leeman lowered his head. I went on, 'You needed money for bribes and materials in order to steal and publish the Queen's book. Substantial sums. Where did you get them?'

'Master Curdy has money. From his business.' A spark appeared in Leeman's eyes again. 'You see, Master Shardlake, we practise what we preach, the holding of all goods in common.'

I sighed, and turned to Barak and Nicholas. 'Both of you, a word in private. Nicholas, can you bring the candle?' I turned to Leeman. 'Do not even think of running, we will be near. Lie here and think on what you have brought about with your foolishness.'

We went out, leaving him in darkness.

Chapter Thirty-five

WE WALKED DOWNSTAIRS to the dusty little entrance hall. I set the candle in its holder on the wall. Noises from the street came to us faintly. I had lost track of time – it must be far past midnight. I wondered when Lord Parr's people would arrive.

'Well,' I asked Barak, 'what do you think? The Bertano story first.'

Barak stroked his beard. '*If* it's true, and the news got out, then Leeman is right, there would be unrest in the streets. I don't mean a revolution, but trouble certainly. You have to hand it to them, their tactic of placing spies in sensitive places paid off. But – ' he looked intently between us – 'if you're going to have a tightly controlled group, with secret knowledge, you have to be sure everyone in it can be completely trusted. But with some of the wilder radicals – ' he shrugged – 'duping them is easy. Provided the person concerned continually parrots the right phrases, I imagine they're all too ready to believe they're genuine.'

'Yes,' I agreed. 'But you said, *if* it's true about Bertano.'

Barak grunted. 'Remember I've been out of politics for six years. But don't forget that after Anne Boleyn was killed, there was no longer any impediment to the King's going back to Rome. But he didn't.' He gave a cynical laugh. 'He enjoys his power as Head of the Church too much, to say nothing of the money he got from the monasteries. But there's something else.' He furrowed his brows, making shadows on his face in the dim candlelight. 'I know Lord Cromwell thought the key to understanding the King was to remember that he truly believes God has appointed him to be Head of the Church in England. That is why every time he changes his mind on the matter of doctrine, the country has to follow – or else.' He shook his head firmly. 'He wouldn't hand all that power back to the Pope easily – not when he believes God himself has chosen him to exercise it.'

'And when Henry dies?' Nicholas asked quietly.

I thought of the shambling wreck I had seen in Whitehall Palace, the groaning figure winched upstairs. 'The Supreme Headship must pass to his son.'

Barak agreed. 'Nothing would ever shake Henry on his right – his duty, as he would see it – to bequeath the Supreme Headship to Prince Edward.'

Nicholas asked, 'But how can a little boy, below the age of judgement, decide the correct path in religion?'

I answered, 'They'll have a Regent, or a Regency Council, until Edward comes of age. Probably the King will decide in his Will who will rule.' And, I thought, it will not be the Parrs, if the Queen has fallen. 'The council will exercise judgement on matters of religion on Edward's behalf, I suppose, till he reaches his eighteenth year. It's theological nonsense, of course, but that's what they'll do. No, Barak is right, if this Bertano is truly coming over, he won't return with a sworn allegiance from Henry in his pocket.' I considered. 'But I have heard all sorts of things are happening in Europe. It is said the Pope is attempting a dialogue with some of the Protestants through his new Council of Trent. I wonder if Henry thinks some sort of compromise is on the cards.'

'What sort of compromise?' Barak asked impatiently.

'Either the headship of the Church lies with the King or with the Pope. There's no halfway house in between. If there was, someone would have proposed it years ago.'

Nicholas shook his head. 'But perhaps the King thinks there *may* be some way to compromise, short of accepting papal allegiance. Perhaps Bertano has been sent to explore that? After all, the King has been keen this year to try and make peace everywhere . . .'

Yes, I thought, because he knows he is dying. I nodded. 'You could be right, Nicholas. A good point.'

'It'll never happen,' Barak said scoffingly.

'But who was the spy in their group?' I asked. 'And who was he reporting to?'

'It certainly wasn't Leeman,' Barak said. 'He's a true believer if ever there was one. Nor Myldmore; he knew nothing of Bertano or the Queen's book. Greening and Elias were murdered. Vandersteyn — I doubt it, he's crossed the Channel in triumph with Anne Askew's manuscript. That leaves Curdy, who's beyond questioning, and the Scotchman McKendrick, who's still out there somewhere.'

'And McKendrick was Curdy's lodger.' Nicholas knitted his brows. 'It has to be one of them, or perhaps both.'

'If it's McKendrick,' Barak said, 'he'll be running to his master at court by now. Whoever that is.'

'Someone who's working with the conservative faction,' I said. 'But who? Secretary Paget runs the official spy net-work. But each of the courtiers has their own network: the Duke of Norfolk, Rich and Wriothesley who have hitched themselves to Gardiner's wagon.'

Nicholas asked, 'You think Rich could have been involved with the theft of the *Lamentation*?'

I sighed. 'Rich was after Anne Askew's book, and he

didn't seem to know anything about the *Lamentation*. But you can never trust that snake.'

Barak said, 'Whoever is holding it may indeed be ready to reveal it to the King when Bertano comes. For maximum impact. That could explain why it hasn't already been made public.'

I shook my head. 'I am sure these men would have done it already, to bend the King's mind further against the reformers and towards making an arrangement with Bertano when he arrives. Use it to turn the wind against the reformers again as soon as possible.'

'Then where is it?' Barak asked angrily. 'Who has it?'

'God's death, I don't know!' I passed a hand over my brow.

'Could McKendrick have it?' Nicholas said thoughtfully. 'If he was the spy, and was given the book by the thieves, then maybe – if he's been on the run with the others – he hasn't had time to hand it over to whoever he's working for?'

'But it's been nearly a month,' Barak answered.

I said, 'It's unlikely. But anything is possible. I'll have to discuss it all with Lord Parr.'

'Or . . .' Nicholas said.

'What?'

'What if the spy was playing both ends? What if McKendrick – assuming it is him – was indeed working to some master at court, but kept his own beliefs, and made sure the *Lamentation* did not fall into the wrong hands? Perhaps he had it stolen, but kept it himself?'

'It's far-fetched, but it's possible. Thank you, Nicholas.' The boy looked pleased.

'Now, Jack, it is late. Nicholas and I will wait here, but you must get back to Tamasin. Where did you tell her you were going tonight?'

'Only that I was meeting old friends for a drink.'

'But the taverns are long closed. She will be worried. And on your way back,' I added, 'remember those two killers are still out there, and that we were watched tonight. Be careful. Nicholas, will you stay here with me to guard Leeman until Lord Parr's people return?'

'You can trust me.' He shook his head. 'Leeman's nothing but a rogue and a villain.'

I sighed. 'He was doing what he believed was right.'

'And that justifies all he has done?' Nicholas answered hotly. 'The betrayal, the bribery, this – chaos? The threat brought to the Queen by stealing her book?'

Barak turned to him, his tone indulgent. 'He gets soft, Nick, it's his way.' He looked up to the top of the stairs. 'But better have God's true representative bound and gagged in case he starts shouting if the students come back. I'll help you.'

Nicholas said with a sort of appalled admiration, 'That Dutchman, Vandersteyn. He already has informers working on the Continent who found the information about Bertano. Meanwhile he is over here, recruiting fanatics who might be able to spy on those in high places in London.'

Barak said, 'He knew the atmosphere here was seething with plots and religious discontent. Decided to come over and further his revolution in England, no doubt.'

'And found Leeman, then Myldmore. Men with access to two sets of writings that could cause great stir.' He shook his head. 'He must truly think God is working through him.'

Barak snorted. 'He got lucky. Twice. But not *really* lucky: it sounds as if what Anne Askew wrote would be damaging only to Wriothesley and Rich, and they're not the top players. And releasing the *Lamentation* would do the radical cause more harm than good. But some in his group were too bone-headed to see that. If they'd found evidence that Gardiner had been in bed with a choirboy, say, that would've been real luck.'

I said, 'Vandersteyn has probably been running schemes like this on the Continent for years. He was skilful in weeding out those among the radicals who might be of use to him.'

'Not skilful enough to notice he had a spy in his midst,' Barak said.

I nodded agreement. 'No.'

†

LEEMAN WAS sitting on the side of the bed. He blinked in the light. 'Are they here for me yet?' he asked in a quiet voice, with a slight tremor. Being left alone in the darkness had given his fear time to grow.

'No,' I answered.

'What will they do with me?'

'You will be taken somewhere safe for now. I will tell them you have cooperated fully.'

He looked at me keenly. 'Do you know, lawyer, I think perhaps you have it in you to see the light.'

'Do you?' I replied heavily.

'Perhaps. Like me, you were brought up on lies and I think you see that. Read the New Testament, read Revelation. These are the last days before Christ's return. It is foreordained.'

'The Book of Revelation, is it? You and your people have found the key to that text?' Anger spilled out of me. 'You should know, Leeman, I once uncovered a killer who slaughtered several innocent people, who believed himself inspired by Revelation! I wish you could see the trail of blood and torture he left.'

Leeman did not answer. After a moment he asked, 'Will you tell the Queen's officials about Bertano?'

'Yes.'

'Then at least they will be warned.'

I looked at him. 'They will undoubtedly want to question you further.'

He swallowed. 'They will torture me, then kill me. I suppose I must prepare myself.'

'You broke an oath to the Queen. Nonetheless, I shall plead with her for your sorry life. I am not even sure why.'

'We'll keep you with Nick to guard you for now, matey,' Barak added in a matter-of-fact way. 'I'm going to bind your hands together, so stretch them out. No trouble, or we'll do it by force.'

Leeman put out his arms. Barak bound them tight with strips torn from Leeman's own shirt. 'Have to gag you as well, matey, though I know you love to gabble on. Nicholas's fellow lodgers may be back sometime.'

'Can I go to the jakes first?' Leeman's face reddened with embarrassment. 'My guts trouble me.'

Barak looked at me. 'Might as well,' I said. Barak raised his eyebrows. I snapped impatiently, 'We don't want a mess in here. Where's your jakes, Nicholas?'

'Out the back, in the yard. But watch it's not a trick. No noise, or I'll knock you out again.'

'We'll all go, bring him back, then Jack will go home, while you and I – ' I took a deep breath as I looked at Nicholas – 'will wait with him for Lord Parr's people.'

⊹

WE WENT BACK DOWNSTAIRS, Barak and Nicholas holding Leeman between them. He was almost as tall as Nicholas and broader, the build of a royal guard. But he

gave no trouble. As we descended, a church clock somewhere struck one. 'No sign of your friends,' I said to
Nicholas, relieved.

'They probably won't be back at all now; they'll have
fallen drunk in a corner.'

'I remember those student birthday celebrations. A bit
rowdy for me.'

'There's a surprise,' Barak said warmly.

We opened a creaking door to the little backyard, where a
ramshackle wooden shed stood in a corner of an untended
garden, against a stone wall separating the students' garden
from the one next door. By the smell, the cesspit beneath
badly needed emptying. Nicholas opened the wooden door,
and we all stepped back at the stink from within. Barak said
to Leeman, 'Get in, then.'

He hesitated on the threshold, so powerful was the stench.

That hesitation killed him. There was a thunderous noise
from the neighbouring garden, and a brief flash of light. In
the second before Leeman crashed to the ground I saw, by the
light of the lamp, that he had lost half his head. We stood
there, shocked for a few seconds, then Nicholas threw me
to the ground, just as there was a second flash and a bang,
and the smell of smoke. Glancing aside I saw that Barak had
also thrown himself down. He kicked over the lamp he
had been holding and it went out, leaving us in almost total
darkness. I smelled gunpowder in the air.

'Quick!' Barak whispered. 'Back inside. Before he has
time to reload. Nick, you know the way in the dark!'

Nicholas scrambled to his feet and, with his long body
bent over, made for the back of the building, which was visible only as a slightly deeper darkness. Barak followed, and
then I, biting my lip as a muscle in my back went. There
was another bang, another flash, and something hit the wall

ahead of us. Then I heard the door creak open, and Nicholas pushed me unceremoniously inside. Barak followed, kicking the door shut behind him. Outside dogs had begun to bark and someone in a neighbouring house, woken by the noise, shouted, 'Hey! What's going on?'

Nicholas led us to the front of the house and the shelter of the stairs. We stood in the darkness, breathing hard. I said, 'What in hell — ?'

'A gun,' he answered. 'An arquebus. I've seen them used in hunting. They're deadly, but take an age to reload. Leeman — ?'

'Dead,' Barak answered flatly. 'It took his head off. So we were followed here, by someone who brought an arquebus. Clever idea to post the assassin in next door's garden; we were bound to come out to the jakes sooner or later. Great way of killing a person from a distance. There may be more of them out the front.' He walked cautiously to the front door and peered through the keyhole. 'Can't see anyone. I'd guess it was Leeman they were after. To stop him talking to us.'

'At least they failed there,' Nicholas said defiantly.

'Come on, back upstairs. Thank God we kept the window of your room shuttered.'

We returned to Nicholas's room. 'Sir,' he said urgently, 'it would be dangerous for Jack to go out now. There may be more of them waiting in the streets.'

Barak shook his head. 'I should think they've run, now we're safe indoors. But you're right. We should all wait here till Lord Parr's men come from Whitehall.'

'But why didn't they follow us in when we first arrived?' Nicholas asked me.

'Perhaps because they thought the house might be full of students, and they'd have a fight on their hands.'

'Tamasin will be in a state,' Barak said, 'but it can't be

helped – ' He broke off, staring at my neck. I put my hand
to it. My fingers came away covered in sticky red and grey
slime. At first I thought I had been hit, then I realized what
it was: I was looking at Leeman's brains.

Chapter Thirty-six

I WALKED WITH LORD PARR through the Great
Garden of Whitehall Palace. It was the next morning,
the sun high in a cloudless sky. The brightness of the white
gravel on the paths hurt my tired eyes, and I turned to look
over the broad squares of lawn, the flowerbeds at their centre,
each ablaze with its own variety of summer bloom. Garden-
ers in smocks laboured endlessly, weeding and trimming.
Heraldic beasts stood on poles at the corners of each path,
and the water in the great fountain at the centre of the garden
made a relaxing plashing sound. Men, and a few women,
strolled along the paths in their finery. The Great Garden
was where courtiers and senior servants came to walk, but
it was also a sort of enormous outdoor waiting room for
would-be courtiers who were not, or not yet, allowed access
to the King's Privy Gallery. Here they strolled, and waited,
and hoped it did not rain. To the south, work continued on
the new quarters for the Lady Mary, the constant banging
and hammering a strange counter-point to the sound of the
fountain. On the north side the garden was bounded by the
King's Privy Gallery and private lodgings; I glanced up at
them nervously.

'He could be watching us,' I said uneasily.

Lord Parr smiled reassuringly. 'I doubt the King even
knows of your presence on the Queen's Learned Council,
nor your hunt for this elusive jewel. And I have made sure
that within the Queen's Court it is known only as a minor

matter.' He, too, glanced towards the three-storey Privy Gallery, the black-and-white chequerwork facade easily a hundred yards long. It ended at the Holbein Gate, which was twice as high as the gallery itself and spanned the public road, connecting the King's quarters with the recreational wing of the palace on the western side. In earlier years the King would have crossed through the gate to play tennis, or joust, but that was long over now. 'Besides,' Lord Parr added, 'I heard his majesty was working in his study in the Holbein Gate this morning. He likes looking down on his subjects passing along the street as he works.'

'I did not know he did that.' That, too, gave me an uneasy feeling.

'As for the real issues, while we may be seen here, we have the advantage that we cannot be heard.'

He stopped at a corner under a pillar painted in stripes of Tudor green and white. A golden lion on top held an English flag, fluttering in the river breeze that also played with Lord Parr's white beard. He leaned heavily on his stick. In the morning light his thin face was pale, dark bags visible under the eyes. He had been wakened by Cecil, who had arrived at the palace near midnight. Since my own arrival with Leeman's body, at three o'clock, he had been busy. After I had told him all that had happened he arranged a room for me in the lodgings again to snatch a few hours' sleep, though hard thoughts kept me awake. Four more men killed last night, including one of Lord Parr's own servants, and a new threat to the Queen divulged, if the story about Bertano were true. At nine in the morning Lord Parr had sent for me and suggested a walk in the Great Garden.

He closed his eyes, breathing in the scent of the herbs planted alongside the path. 'I could lie down and fall asleep here right now,' he said quietly. 'As could you, from your looks.'

I winced at a spasm in my back. I had pulled a muscle when Nicholas pushed me to the ground last night, but his act had saved my life. Lord Parr continued, 'It is a great pity Leeman was killed.' He raised a hand. 'No, sir, I do not blame you. But I would have liked to question the villain myself.' He clutched the silver handle of his stick hard. 'An Anabaptist, those pestilent scum.'

'They were a small group. In Europe too, I understand, there are but few left.'

'They are like rats, a few in the sewers of the common streets may breed and at a time of hardship or discontent become thousands. They can bring fire and death to us all.' He waved his free hand in a gesture of anger. 'They should be extirpated.'

'Have you told her majesty what Leeman said?' I asked.

'Yes. I wakened the Queen early to tell her the latest news. I thought it best. She wept and trembled, she is much afraid. She is worried that the book remains unfound, and now even more about Bertano. But – ' he paused to look me in the eye – 'she is brave, and well-practised in assuming a composed and regal manner, whatever she feels inside.'

He fell silent as a couple of black-robed officials wearing the King's badge passed. They bowed to us. I had sent for my robe after arriving at Whitehall; Timothy had brought it round and I wore it now. Such things mattered greatly here. The two walked on, stopping briefly to admire a peacock with its huge multicoloured tail as it crossed the lawn. 'I have one servant less,' Lord Parr continued soberly. 'Poor Dunmore, who died last night, was a good and useful man.'

'I never even learned his name.'

'Who *is* it?' Lord Parr banged the white gravel with his

stick. 'Who masterminded the theft of her book, employed those two men – of whom we can find no trace – to kill everyone in that Anabaptist group? I do not believe the theory that whoever took the book from Greening would intend to wait until Bertano was about to arrive before revealing it. Not if they know the King. They would show it to him immediately, let his anger against the Queen and the reformers burst out at once, make him more receptive to whatever proposals this wretched emissary of the Pope brings.'

'Would it be so bad as that?'

He spoke quietly. 'The King still loves the Queen, of that I am sure. But that would only make him even angrier at her disloyalty. And hurt. And when he feels hurt – ' Lord Parr shook his head. 'The existence of the book itself is a lesser matter; Cranmer says it is not heretical, though it sails close to the wind.'

I did not reply. I had never heard Lord Parr talk so openly of the King before. 'His majesty has always been suggestible, vain. He listens to the endless whispers in his ear, especially when they concern the loyalty of someone important to him. And once he has made his mind up he has been betrayed, then – '

'How is his health?' I asked.

'A little worse each week.' He fell silent for a moment, perhaps reflecting that he had said more than was wise, then burst out angrily, 'Why keep it for near a month, Shardlake? I cannot work it out, and nor can Cecil.'

'I cannot either, my Lord. You know far more of the court than I.'

'We have to find that Scotchman, God rot him—'

I placed a hand on the arm of his silk robe to quiet him. He frowned at my presumption, but I had seen what his aged eyes had not: two slim figures with long beards approaching us. Edward Seymour, Lord Hertford, Prince Edward's uncle and a leading figure among the reformers on the Privy Council; and his younger brother, Sir Thomas, who had been the Queen's suitor before her marriage to the King. So, I thought, Lord Hertford is back in England.

The brothers halted before us. They had been arguing with quiet intensity as they approached, but now Sir Thomas's large brown eyes fastened on mine. We had crossed swords in the past.

I had seen them together years before, and reflected anew how alike they were, yet how different. Above his light brown beard Lord Hertford's oval face was pale, and not handsome, with slightly knitted brows that gave him an air of half-suppressed impatient anger. He exuded power, but not authority, or not enough. As a politician he was formidable, but they said he was henpecked and embarrassed by his wife. He wore a long brown robe with a fur collar, and a splendid gold chain round his neck befitting his status as a senior Privy Councillor. Sir Thomas Seymour was more sturdily built, his face another oval, but with regular features and compelling brown eyes above that long coppery beard. While Lord Hertford wore a plain robe, Sir Thomas sported a green doublet of finest silk, slashed at the shoulders and sleeves to show a rich orange lining. He too wore a gold chain, though a smaller one.

The two men removed their jewelled caps and bowed, the links of their chains clinking. We bowed in turn.

'Master Shardlake,' Sir Thomas said, a mocking note in his rich deep voice. 'I hear you are sworn to her majesty's Learned Council now.'

'I am, sir.'

Lord Hertford cut across him, addressing Lord Parr. 'I trust the Queen is in good health, my Lord.'

'Indeed. She is viewing the Lady Elizabeth's new portrait this morning, before it is shown to the King. Master Scrots has painted a good likeness.'

'Excellent. Lady Elizabeth should have a portrait, it is fitting for her high estate.' He inclined his head meaningfully to where Mary's new quarters were being built. 'I am sure the portrait will be a pleasure to his majesty.'

'Indeed. He loves both his daughters, of course, but now Elizabeth is growing, she needs more – exposure.'

I recognized the coded exchange for what it was. Lord Parr and Lord Hertford were both on the reforming side, and Elizabeth, her father's least favourite child, was being brought up a reformer, unlike the traditionalist Mary, who had been raised a Catholic before the break with Rome.

Sir Thomas looked bored. He turned to me again. 'I see, Shardlake, you are on the list of those attending on Admiral d'Annebault.'

'Indeed, Sir Thomas.'

'I have a large role on the committee organizing the ceremonies,' he said self-importantly. 'There is much to be done. The admiral is bringing a thousand men with him.' He smiled. 'It will be a magnificent chivalric celebration of reconciliation after honest combat between soldiers.'

I did not reply. I thought again of my soldier friends who had gone down with the *Mary Rose* and all the others killed in that failed, unnecessary war.

Seymour raised his eyebrows. 'Do you not agree? Well – ' he laughed and squared his broad shoulders – 'some of us are built and fitted for war, while others are not.' He glanced ostentatiously at my back.

It was an appalling insult. But Sir Thomas was in a position to make it, and I did not reply. His brother, though, looked at Sir Thomas fiercely as he now turned to Lord Parr and said mockingly, 'Beware of Master Shardlake, my Lord, he is too clever for his own good. He will be after your job.'

'I hardly think so, Sir Thomas.' Lord Parr glared at him.

Hertford snapped, 'You are ever ready with your nips and quips, Thomas. You will nip yourself into trouble one day.'

Sir Thomas's face darkened. Lord Parr gave him a sardonic smile, then turned to his brother.'

'Is there much foreign business now on the Privy Council, my Lord? My nephew William says the French and Spanish treaties are settled.'

Hertford nodded seriously. 'Indeed, though it has been a mighty labour these last months.' He looked across at the Holbein Gate. 'Well, I am due to attend the King in his study. I must not be late.' He gave me an awkward nod, bowed to us both, and walked on with his brother. Lord Parr watched them go.

'Thomas Seymour is a fool and a bully,' he said. 'But Lord Hertford is our ally. His return, and Lord Lisle's, have shifted the balance of the council towards the reformers. And Cranmer is seen more these days.'

'And Sir Thomas?' I added. 'What role does he play?'

He gave me a considering look. 'I know from my niece that you and he worked together once, and dislike each other. I am not surprised, Thomas Seymour is as full of bluster and empty display as that peacock over there. He did not distinguish himself in the positions he held in the war. Sitting on a committee to organize this ceremonial will test the limits of his ability.' He gave a bitter laugh. 'When he returned in the spring he made great play of how he'd escaped some pirates in the Channel. Made himself a laughing stock by telling the story over endlessly.' He smiled sardonically. 'He wants the power his older brother has on the Privy Council. He feels that, as he is also Jane Seymour's brother and Prince Edward's uncle, he should have equal authority. But he lacks judgement and intelligence, with him all is empty show and bluster. The King knows it. He only ever chooses men of ability for the council. Thomas is a drag on his brother.'

'What is Sir Thomas's position on reform?'

Lord Parr shrugged. 'I do not think he has any religion. Some even say he is an atheist. It is extraordinary that the Queen loved him once, they are such opposites in nature.'

'Extraordinary indeed.'

He shook his head. 'I would never have thought Kate was one to be taken in by such a creature; but we have seen how – emotional – she can be. It is the way of women,' he concluded with a sigh.

I spoke suddenly. 'I suppose there is no motive for anyone on the reformist side of the council to steal the *Lamentation*?'

He shook his head. 'None. The reformist group at court, like every faction, is an alliance of family interests – between the Parrs, the Seymours and the Dudleys, whose foremost fig- ure is John Dudley, Lord Lisle. When, in course of time – ' he stressed those words carefully – 'his majesty is gathered to God, the various family interests may find themselves in conflict. But for the present we are united by our common faith. If Henry does agree to take England back under the authority of the Pope, we shall all be in danger, and must run and fetch our rosaries or face a grim death.' He sighed with unexpected emotion. 'When I think of that, I thank God I am a sick old man.'

We stood in silence for a moment. Then I said thought- fully, 'But if Sir Thomas is one of those who has no religion, and seeks only power, he might see an advantage in taking the *Lamentation* to the King – '

Lord Parr looked at me, frowning. 'Why? From ambition?'

'That, and perhaps because he courted the Queen before her marriage, and was rejected. Proud men harbour thoughts of revenge. And finding the *Lamentation* could give him the status in the King's eyes that he longs for.'

Lord Parr considered for a moment. 'Earlier in the summer, though few know of it, there were attempts to unite the reformist and traditionalist factions through a marriage between the Duke of Norfolk's daughter and Thomas Seymour. The negotiations came to nothing, partly because the Duke's daughter did not want him.'

'That surely proves he will bend any way to gain power.'

Lord Parr shook his head decisively. 'No. Thomas Seymour does not have the intelligence, nor the resources, to send spies into the radical groups. I think your dislike of him, Master Shardlake, justified though it may be, is colouring your judgement.'

'Possibly,' I admitted reluctantly. 'But who in court *would* have motive and money to do that?'

'Paget, of course, as Master Secretary. But if he had a spy in the Anabaptist camp, whether Curdy or McKendrick or both of them, that would have been in an official capacity, and as soon as they had taken Askew's book, or the Queen's, he would have had to arrest everyone in the group and report to the King. And I am sure Paget has no loyalty to either faction. He survives, the Master of Practices, by taking orders only from the King. But the other courtiers – Gardiner and his hirelings Wriothesley and Rich – yes, if they got wind of an Anabaptist group, they have the resources to infiltrate it. It is just the sort of business Rich would be good at. But how would they get wind of it? It seems Rich got lucky only in finding that the gaoler

Myldmore had Askew's book. Unless Rich was lying,' he added slowly, turning to me.

'I still think Rich knows nothing of the *Lamentation*.'

'We must find that Scotchman,' he said again emphatically. 'It is very likely he was the spy.'

I considered. 'My assistant suggested there could have been some sort of double agent, working for a master at court while keeping his Anabaptist beliefs. In that case, it is likely he would seek to keep the *Lamentation* safe.'

'Anything is possible. Only finding McKendrick will solve that mystery.'

'Thinking of Rich, if his only interest was Anne Askew's book, since that is now gone I do not think he would put any more resources into finding McKendrick.'

'No. That would indeed be shutting the stable door after the horse has bolted.'

I looked at him. 'But if he *is* interested in finding the Scotchman, that would indicate he is interested in something more – the *Lamentation*, perhaps.'

Lord Parr considered, then nodded. 'Yes, that makes sense.' He smiled wryly. 'Either way, Rich will be sweating in his shoes, dreading the day Anne Askew's words appear in print in London, smuggled back from Flanders.'

'Yes, he will be.' I could not help but feel satisfaction.

'Go and see Rich now,' Lord Parr said. 'Find out how the land lies. I must go to the Queen, see how she fares.' He bowed and then turned, in his abrupt way, and walked slowly back towards the Queen's chambers, leaning on his stick. I took a deep breath. A little way off I heard laughter and saw a couple of ladies throwing seed to the peacock.

✠

LATER THAT DAY I went again to the house in Needlepin Lane to see Stice. I asked Nicholas to attend me. As we walked down Thames Street I thanked him for saving my life. 'I shall not forget it,' I told him.

He replied with unaccustomed seriousness. 'I am glad to have saved a life, sir, when so many have been lost in this business. Leeman – I felt hot with anger against him last night, with his mad beliefs. I was starting to say too much, wasn't I?'

'Yes. He needed to be gentled along.'

'And I remember I was the cause of Elias fleeing,' he said quietly. 'And then later he, too, was murdered. That has been on my conscience ever since.'

'It need not be. We have all made mistakes in this business.'

He shook his head. 'I knew London was a place of violence and murder, but this – '

'It is not my normal trade, though over the years certain people high in the realm have made it seem so.'

He hesitated, then asked, 'Her majesty?'

I hesitated. 'Yes. And others before her. Cranmer and Cromwell, too.'

He looked impressed. 'You have truly known the great ones of England.'

'That can have its disadvantages.'

'Those names are all on one side of the religious divide,' he said hesitantly.

'I was once myself on that side, and as the realm has divided so my contacts have remained there. But my religious loyalties – ' I shrugged – 'they are gone.'

'Surely it is enough just to believe.'

I looked at him. 'Do you believe, Nicholas?'

He laughed uneasily. 'Just about. I know that at heart I

want to save life, not destroy it. Yours was a life I am glad to have saved,' he added, his face reddening.

'Thank you, Nicholas.' Now I was embarrassed, too. Such words from pupil to barrister could have been syco-phantic, but Nicholas had none of that sort of guile in him. I said gruffly, 'Let's see if these villains are at home.'

✝

STICE OPENED the door. He wore a bandage round his forehead. 'You.' He looked at us with displeasure. 'Come to discuss the mess you made last night?'

'We all failed.'

'My master's here.' He lowered his voice. 'He's not pleased.'

'How is Gower?'

'Like to die.'

'I am sorry.'

'My shitten arse you are.'

He led the way upstairs. Sir Richard Rich was sitting behind his desk. The shutters were drawn, making the room stifling. No doubt he did not want people in the street to see him here. He glowered at us. 'Bowels of Judas! You made a fine butcher's shambles of last night's business!'

'They were good fighters. We could not stop Vandersteyn getting away.'

'We did our best, sir,' Stice added. 'Everyone did.'

'Shut your mouth, mangehound! You were all as much use as a rabble of women! And the physician says I will have to deal with Gower's poxy corpse soon!' He glared at Stice. 'God's death, it would have been better if you had lost your whole head in that duel, rather than half an ear.' He pointed at Stice's disfigurement. 'A fine ornament for a gentleman.' Stice's mouth set hard, but he did not reply.

Rich turned his baleful gaze on me. 'I expect you've been to Whitehall, to tell the Queen's minions that Askew's book is gone. Halfway across the North Sea by now, I imagine.' His little grey eyes bored into mine. 'Well, I can expect the lies Askew told about me to surface in due course.' He spoke with self-pity, though he could hardly imagine I would care.

'The Scotchman remains out there,' I said.

'That canting Anabaptist madman. I hope he gets caught and burned.' Rich gave a long, angry sigh. 'Our alliance is over, Shardlake. How could I have ever thought a hunch-backed scratching clerk could be of use to me?' He waved a slim, beringed hand. 'Begone!'

I looked at him. I had told Lord Parr that if Rich showed no interest in McKendrick it would be an indication that he had been concerned only with Anne Askew's book. Yet there was a blustering, half-theatrical quality to his fury that made me wonder. Then again, perhaps it was just anger and fear that what he had done would soon be exposed. He could still pursue McKendrick on his own, of course. Bluff and counter-bluff, everywhere.

'Will you keep this house on?' I asked.

'Mind your own business!' His face darkened. 'Go, or I'll have Stice give that boy some new bruises, and you a few as well.' He banged his fist on the desk. 'Get out! Never let me see you again!'

Chapter Thirty-seven

LATER THAT DAY I reported back to Lord Parr. Cecil was with him in his study. The young lawyer looked strained, and there were large bags under his eyes. He could not have experienced anything like that battle at the wharf before. I told them what had happened with Rich, and that while I doubted he knew of the *Lamentation*'s existence I could not be sure. Lord Parr told me he was arranging for people from his household to look for McKendrick around the London streets. By now he might be reduced to begging, but equally he could have fled the city entirely. Where the Bertano story was concerned, Lord Parr had learned only that members of the King's own guard had been posted outside a house near the Charing Cross, which was kept for diplomatic visitors. An ominous sign, but there was nothing to do now but wait.

✞

A WEEK PASSED . . . July turned to August, with two days of rain before the hot weather returned, and the first week of the month went by with no further news from Whitehall. I feared every day to hear that some new arrangement with the Pope had been struck, and the Queen and her radical associates arrested. However, I forced myself to give attention to my work. Nicholas's bruises faded; he seemed a little restless but nonetheless set himself to work well enough.

He spoke with pleasurable anticipation of the forthcoming ceremonies to welcome the French admiral; apparently additional cannon were being brought to the Tower for a great welcoming cannonade when d'Annebault arrived. I had told Nicholas I would be involved; he envied me, though I told him I would gladly have avoided the task. Meanwhile Barak's hand had healed completely and he, I sensed, was not sorry to return to a normal life.

At home I kept a continued eye on Brocket, but he did not put a foot wrong and Josephine had nothing further to report to me. Brocket and Agnes seemed more cheerful and I wondered whether there had been better news from their son, though I did not ask. Josephine also seemed happy; she was seeing her young man regularly and had a new confidence about her; sometimes I even heard her singing around the house. I smiled at the sound; it was good to reflect, among my troubles, that I had given Josephine a home and a future. Timothy, though, seemed to avoid conversation with me, perhaps afraid I would raise the subject of his apprenticeship again.

I made sure I had all the appropriate finery ready for the admiral's visit, buying a new black doublet and a shirt with elaborate embroidery at the wrists and collar. I would not, however, go to the expense of a gold chain; my purse had suffered enough from the taxes required to pay for the war.

On the 5th of August, I had a letter from Hugh. For the most part it contained only the usual news of business and entertainment in Antwerp. Hugh did mention, though, that a small cargo ship was recently arrived from England, and a certain Englishman had been at the wharf to welcome the owner, a merchant of Antwerp. I checked the date: the ship, I was sure, was the *Antwerpen*, with Vandersteyn on board; and the Englishman who had met it John Bale. So he would have Anne Askew's writings now, for printing. Well, so much the worse for Rich.

⚜

ON FRIDAY the 6th I had been busy with paperwork all morning — I had almost caught up at last — and after lunching by myself in a refectory almost deserted in the heart of the summer vacation, I decided to take some much-needed air. I had a case coming on in the next law term involving the boundaries of some properties in Gloucestershire: the barrister representing the other side, a member of Gray's Inn, had the coloured map which always accompanied the deeds, delineating the boundaries. In accordance with convention I was allowed to make a copy. Normally that was clerks' work, but while neither Barak nor Nicholas had a good hand for drawing, I did, and took pleasure in it. I decided I would do the job myself, though I could only charge a clerk's rate for it.

Thinking of Gray's Inn reminded me of Philip Coleswyn. I had not seen him since warning him about Isabel's complaint — about which I had heard no more from Treasurer Rowland. I walked the short distance to my house and fetched Genesis, reflecting that he, too, needed some air. Young Timothy was with him in the stable, reading something, which at my entry he shoved hastily up his shirt, turning bright red. I had insisted Timothy go to school to learn to write, so he knew his letters at least. Some pamphlet of lewd rhymes, no doubt; what wonders the printed word had brought to the world, I thought sardonically, as I set the boy to saddling the horse.

It was peaceful riding up the lanes, between the hedges where bees droned, the cattle fat and sleek in the fields. It was one of those hot August days when the countryside can seem almost drugged with heat, cattle and sheep grazing lazily, a faint shimmer rising from the dusty highway. I looked forward to my map-work; earlier, while sorting through the little bottles of coloured ink I would need, I remembered the days when I used to paint. Why had I allowed that gentle pastime to slip from me?

I left Genesis with the Gray's Inn porter and crossed the central square. The trees had a dusty look. I was still thinking about my painting days when, turning a corner, I walked straight into the last two people I wished to see: Vincent Dyrick, in robe and cap, his handsome aquiline face a little red from the sun; and Isabel Slanning, in a dark blue summer dress and gable hood, her thin features gaunt, her expression sour as always. Dyrick was frowning and I wondered whether, experienced though he was with difficult clients, perhaps Isabel was too much even for him.

We all stood still a moment, taken aback. Then I removed my cap and bowed. 'God give you good afternoon, Brother Dyrick. Mistress Slanning.'

Dyrick bowed in return and spoke with unexpected civility. 'And you, Master Shardlake.' I moved to pass them, but Isabel, standing rigidly in front of me, fixed me with her steely gaze.

'Master Shardlake, have you been visiting Master Coleswyn to discuss my complaint, or perhaps to conspire with him against another honest believer who cleaves to the miracle of the Mass?' Her voice was loud and shrill, reminding me of the night she had confronted me outside Coleswyn's house.

To my surprise Dyrick took her by the arm. 'Come, mistress,' he said quietly. 'Let me accompany you to the gate.'

She shook off his arm, still fixing me with that steely look, and pointed a skinny finger at me. 'Remember, Master

Shardlake, I know all about the conspiracy: you, and my brother, and that Coleswyn. You will all pay the highest price. Just wait.' She bared her teeth – good teeth for a woman of her age – in a smile of undiluted malice. 'Master Dyrick would spare you, but I will not,' she ended triumphantly, nodding at Dyrick, who looked uncomfortable.

With that, she turned, allowing Dyrick to lead her round the corner. I stared after them. Isabel's behaviour had been absurd, almost unbalanced. But Dyrick had seemed worried, and I could not help but wonder anxiously what she had meant.

✟

I SPENT AN HOUR making a copy of the map in the chambers of my opponent on the case. I found it hard to concentrate, though, for the bizarre encounter with Isabel still preyed on my mind. I decided to see if Coleswyn was in his chambers.

His clerk said he was, and once more I entered his neat, tidy office. He held out a welcoming hand. He was more at ease than I had ever seen him, relaxed and welcoming. 'Matthew, how go things with you?'

'A busy summer. And you, Philip?'

'My wife and I feel happier now the heresy hunt is over.' He shook his head sadly. 'I took some books in yesterday, under the amnesty, good books written by men of true faith, but now forbidden. I have delayed doing it, for I was much attached to them, but the amnesty expires on Monday.'

'I had some, too. I burned them, as I preferred not to have my name appear on a list.'

'The amnesty is public, and many people have brought in books. Perhaps even some from Whitehall.' He laughed uneasily. 'If they prosecuted those who took advantage of the amnesty, that would be a great breach of faith, and illegal.' He smiled sadly, looking out of the window at the quadrangle. 'My books are a big loss to me, but our vicar says we must wait, for better times may be coming.'

I was glad he did not know about Bertano. I said, 'I am visiting Gray's Inn on other business this afternoon, but I have just had a strange encounter with Isabel Slanning and Brother Dyrick. I thought I should tell you.'

His face became serious. 'What now? Dyrick has been pestering and bothering me about the depositions and other aspects of the case, trying to bully me in his usual manner. But he has not mentioned this nonsense about conspiracy again. I had hoped he was discouraging Isabel from going down that path. I would, if I were him. The courts will not welcome it.'

'I think he may be trying to. When I ran into them just now, Dyrick was civil enough for once, and tried to hustle Isabel away. But she told me again she knew all about you, me and her brother conspiring together, and that we would pay, as she put it, the highest price.'

'Dyrick did not back her up?'

'Far from it, which is unusual for him. I begin to think Isabel is seriously unhinged. But Dyrick looked worried, and I cannot but wonder what she may have planned.'

Philip's cheerful manner was gone. 'Is there further word concerning her complaint about you to Lincoln's Inn?' he asked anxiously.

'None. But Treasurer Rowland was going to write her a sharp letter. I should have expected a copy but I have heard nothing yet. I will call on him.'

Coleswyn considered a moment, then said, 'I have discovered something else.' He took a deep breath. 'A few days ago, I was dining in hall when I saw a friend of mine from another chambers, who knows I have the Cotterstoke case – Dyrick's cases are always a source of gossip round Gray's Inn. He introduced me to a retired barrister, now over seventy, but of good memory. When he was young – this is over forty years ago – he acted for Edward and Isabel's mother.'

I looked up with interest. 'Oh?'

He hesitated. 'Strictly, even though old Deborah Cotterstoke is dead, his duty of confidentiality remains. But you know how old fellows like to gossip. And I cannot help but be interested in anything concerning that family.' He frowned. 'I should not tell you, I suppose.'

I smiled gently. Coleswyn's integrity was one of the things I admired in him. 'I no longer represent Isabel. And I promise it will go no further.' I inclined my head. 'And if a former client threatens a barrister, as Isabel did this afternoon, I think he is entitled to seek out anything which might throw light on the circumstances. I take it the old man's story does that, Philip?'

He grunted acknowledgement. 'Not directly. But you and I have both wondered whence came the mutual hatred, and perhaps fear, in which Edward Cotterstoke and Isabel Slanning hold each other.'

'Yes. It is surely something out of the ordinary.'

'We know from the old merchant I spoke to before that Edward and Isabel's father died young, their mother married again, but her second husband also died. And the merchant said that ever after she and both children seemed at odds with each other.' Coleswyn leaned forward in his chair. 'This old barrister I spoke to was consulted in 1507, back in the old King's time. By Mrs Deborah Johnson, as she then was. At the time she was an attractive widow in her thirties with two children.'

'Edward and Isabel.'

'Yes. Deborah's first husband, Master Johnson, had just died. Of the sweating sickness, you remember, which was raging in the city that summer.'

I remembered the confident-looking young father in the painting, with his tall hat, and the pretty wife and two little children. How easily even a rising man could be suddenly cut down.

'Isabel and Edward's mother had inherited his business. She was quite rich. There had recently been a case in Chancery over whether a woman could inherit and run a business and be a member of a Guild. The old barrister was able to reassure her that she could. He remembered her as a formidable woman.'

'I recall her face in the painting. Pretty, but with a sharpness, a hardness to it. Like her daughter's.'

'Yes. A year later, Mistress Johnson consulted him once more. She was minded to marry again, a man in the same trade as her, Peter Cotterstoke, but she was concerned her rights in the business would pass to her new husband on marriage.'

'As they would. Automatically.'

Philip nodded. 'And so she was advised. She said her son and daughter, who were around eleven and twelve then, were worried they would lose their inheritance. But she was set on marrying Master Cotterstoke. And she did. But Cotterstoke proved an honourable man. Deborah Cotterstoke, as she now was, came back to the lawyer a third time, some months later, together with her new husband, and Master Cotterstoke made a Will stating that if he should die before Deborah, the combined business – his own and the late Master Johnson's – would pass to her. He sealed the matter by formally adopting Edward and Isabel; therefore even if Deborah were to die first they would still inherit their share.

Deborah, apparently, was visibly pregnant at the time, and the couple thought it best to formalize arrangements.'

I scratched my cheek. 'So Cotterstoke was a good step-father to the children. And they kept his name, which they surely would not have done if they disliked him. Did this old fellow know anything of a quarrel within the family?'

'Nothing,' Coleswyn replied. 'Only that shortly after, poor Master Cotterstoke drowned. That we knew, but I decided to look out for the coroner's report.' I sat up. 'Apparently one Sunday, shortly after the children were adopted and the Will made, Master Cotterstoke walked from their home just beyond Aldgate, through the city and down to the docks, where a ship had just come in with some goods he had purchased abroad. He took the two children with him, and he also had two servants in attendance, a normal thing for a gentleman walking out. One was Patrick Vowell, which is the name of the old man who is taking care of the house now.'

'Indeed?' I asked, my interest growing.

'Both servants testified that Master Cotterstoke seemed perfectly happy that day, as did the two children. He was looking forward to the arrival of his new child. The servants left him at the customs house; Master Cotterstoke said he did not know how long he would be and they should wait outside. The children went on to the docks with him.

'It was quiet at the docks, being Sunday. A little time later, a labourer heard shouting and crying from the water. He thought it was gulls at first but it came again and he realized it was a human cry. He ran to the water and saw a man floating there. The tide was full and anyone who fell off the wharfside would plunge into deep water. He called for some of his colleagues to help him get the body ashore but it was too late. It was Master Cotterstoke, and his lungs were found to be full of water; he certainly drowned. And apparently it was a misty day in autumn; someone walking near the edge could easily make a misstep.'

'True.'

'Both children gave evidence at the inquest. They said their stepfather had visited the ship, and then said he wanted to take a walk to see what goods might be available on other ships that had come in, and they should go back to the servants, which they did. Not uncommon for a merchant to do on a Sunday, though apparently the wharves were not busy that day.'

'Was this lawyer you met involved in the inquest?'

'No. But he met Deborah Cotterstoke once more afterwards, when he visited the house to help with formalizing the documentation for probate after the funeral. He said he remembered her as being in a piteous state of grief, which was unsurprising in a woman who had lost two husbands in little over two years, and the children also appeared shocked and stunned.'

'Did she ever come back to see him?'

Coleswyn shook his head. 'He wrote to her asking if she wished to make a new Will, but she did not reply. He heard a little later that she had lost the child she had been carrying at that time, again not surprising, given her sad circumstances.' Philip sighed. 'He remembered seeing her and the children in the streets from time to time. Then she sold the business and her son, my client Edward, decided to seek a different trade.'

'And she never married again?'

'No. Apparently she made a point of wearing sober clothes for the rest of her life.'

I considered. 'Are you saying a third party may have been involved in Master Cotterstoke's death?' I caught my breath.

'Or even one of the children? The coroner would only have their word that their stepfather was alive when they returned to the servants.' I frowned. 'Or that old Mistress Cotterstoke held them both responsible for her husband's death? All the evidence indicates she came to dislike both her children; we have said before that the wording of the Will looks like an attempt to set them against each other.' I looked at Philip. 'These are horrible thoughts.'

'They are. But given the Will their stepfather made, the children and his wife Deborah had no reason to dislike or distrust him.' He looked at me seriously. 'But I have been struggling with my conscience as to whether I should go and speak to the old servant, Goodman Vowell. I have no authority from my client, but . . .'

I smiled sadly. 'You would pluck up the roots of this madness.'

'I wonder if their stepfather's death has something to do with this carapace of hatred between them. And each has said they could do great damage to the other.'

'I remember how old Vowell seemed distraught at Edward and Isabel's quarrel at the inspection,' I said. 'He was obviously upset by their behaviour.'

'But I do not see that I have the right to go and question him.'

'You looked out the coroner's report. And if Isabel's behaviour now involves some possible threat to us both – ' I raised my eyebrows.

'A madwoman's bluster.' He sighed heavily. 'Let me consider this further, Matthew. Let me pray on it.'

I would rather that he had gone to the Cotterstoke house at once and taken me with him. But I was not in a position to insist. I rose from my stool.

'When you decide, let me know. And let us keep each

other informed of anything else concerning this case that may affect us – personally.'

He looked up, fixing me with his clear blue eyes. 'Yes. I promise.'

Chapter Thirty-eight

L ATER THAT DAY I called in at Treasurer Rowland's office, only to be told he was in a meeting. On Monday I called again and this time the clerk said he was out, though passing his window on the way in I was sure I had caught sight of his long, black-robed figure leaning over his desk through the half-open shutters. When I went out again the shutters were closed. I wondered uneasily whether Rowland was avoiding me.

That day in the refectory I dined with another barrister I knew slightly; he planned to hire a wherry on the morrow and take his family on a trip down beyond Greenwich. As Rowland had told me last month, virtually all the King's ships, fifty or so, were coming to the Thames to form a line from Gravesend to Deptford, past which the admiral's ships would sail, and they were starting to arrive. 'They say the *Great Harry* is already moored at Deptford,' my colleague said. 'All those ships that were at Portsmouth last year, and saw off the French.'

'The *Mary Rose* will not be there.'

'Casualty of war, Brother Shardlake,' he said portentously. 'Casualty of war.'

✠

ON TUESDAY, the 10th, at the end of the working day, I invited Barak and Nicholas to take a mug of beer with me in the outer office. Skelly had gone home. Thoughts about the missing *Lamentation* still constantly buzzed in my head, and I thought a talk with them might give me some perspective. Barak asked if I had heard any more from the palace.

'Not for over a week now.'

He shook his head. 'Someone's still holding on to that book. But who, and whyever not reveal it to the King, if they wish to harm the reformers?'

'I wish I knew.'

'And this Bertano,' Nicholas added. 'He must be here, if what Leeman said was true. We are well into August now.' He sighed and his green eyes looked inward for a moment. Lord Parr had had Leeman's body removed by the men he had sent to fetch me to the palace on the night of the shooting; fortunately, the students had not returned until the morning. I was sure that, like me, Nicholas would never forget Leeman's face, suddenly destroyed in front of us.

I said, 'We know now that the Anabaptists had the book. And Leeman was right, one of them was a spy; nobody else knew about the *Lamentation*. It must have been either Curdy, who is dead, or McKendrick who escaped. Or both. And whoever it was, they were working for someone at court, they must have been.'

'One of the big men,' Barak agreed. 'But there's still the question of *who* – and why have they not yet shown their hand?' He looked at me quizzically. 'Do you still rule out Rich?'

'I'd never rule out Rich. But whoever it is, it's dangerous for them to wait. As soon as that book came into anyone's possession it was their duty to take it to the King. And if whoever stole it wants to anger Henry, and thus help the negotiations with Bertano to succeed, the best plan would have been to give it to him as soon as possible.'

'If Bertano exists,' Barak said. 'We're not even certain of that. And if he does, I'm still convinced the King would never surrender the Royal Supremacy.'

'Lord Parr thinks the arrival of someone such as this Bertano fits with the comportment of certain councillors recently. And we know there is a house reserved for diplomats at Charing Cross, which apparently is being guarded by the King's men.'

'In that case,' said Nicholas, 'the best moment to reveal the book has surely passed, as you say. And I hear the Queen is to feature prominently at the ceremonies to welcome the French admiral. That must be a sign she is back in favour.'

Barak grunted. 'Thomas Cromwell was at the height of his power when he fell. He was made Earl of Essex, then a few weeks later suddenly hauled off to the Tower and executed.'

Nicholas shook his head. 'What sort of mind does the King have?' He asked the question in a low voice, despite the safety of my office.

'A good question,' I answered. 'Lord Parr and I have spoken on it. He is impressionable, suspicious, and if he turns against someone, ruthless and relentless. A man who thinks he is always right, and who believes what he wants to believe. He would see the Queen's hiding the book and concealing its theft from him as a betrayal, almost certainly. And yet – he still loves her, has never wanted to lose her. He made Gardiner's people pay when they called her a heretic without the evidence for it.'

'None of this helps us with the question of who has the book, though,' Barak said.

'No,' I agreed. 'It doesn't.'

'What about my idea of a double agent?' Nicholas asked. 'Someone who told his masters about the book but then, before it could be taken, got it for himself, killing Greening in the process?'

'To what end?' Barak asked.

'Perhaps to smuggle it safely abroad.'

I said, 'If so, the only one who could have it now is Mc-Kendrick. Wherever he is.'

A sudden knock at the door made us all jump. The relief in the room was palpable when, in answer to my call to enter, Tamasin came in.

We all stood. After the business of bows and curtsies Tamasin smiled at us. 'So this is how you fathom out the secrets of the law.' Barak and I laughed, though Nicholas frowned a little at the latitude she allowed herself. But she and I were old friends, and Tamasin had never been a shrinking violet.

Barak said mock severely, 'We allow ourselves a little relaxation at the end of a hard day; a fine thing when women squirrel their way in to chide us for it.'

'Perhaps it is needed. Seriously, Jack, if you are finished I wondered if you would come with me to Eastcheap Market, to see if there are any apples in.'

''Tis late. And you know there are none ripe yet; only the dregs of last year's poor harvest, expensive for all they are shrunk and wrinkled.'

'I have such a craving for them.' She gave Nicholas an embarrassed glance. 'There may be some from France, now we are trading again.'

'God help my purse,' Barak said. But he put down his mug.

'I should leave too,' I said. 'There are some papers in my office I should take home. Wait while I get them, then I can lock up.'

'Thank you,' Tamasin said. She turned to my pupil. 'And how are you, Master Nicholas?'

'Well enough, Mistress Barak.'

'Jack tells me you do not lose papers and knock things over the way you used to,' she said mischievously.

'I never did,' Nicholas answered a little stiffly. 'Not much, at least.'

In the office I sorted out the papers I wanted. When I opened the door to the outer office again Nicholas had left, and Tamasin had seated herself on Barak's desk. He was gently winding a strand of blonde hair that had escaped from the side of her coif round his finger, saying quietly, 'We shall scour the market. But the craving will cease gnawing soon; it did last time.'

I coughed. We all went out. As I watched them set off into the late summer afternoon, bickering amiably as usual, that moment of intimacy between them, caught thus unexpectedly, clutched somehow at my heart. I felt sadly aware of the lack of anything like it in my own life. Except casting a fantasy at the Queen of England, like the most callow boy courtier at Whitehall.

✟

I HAD A QUIET dinner on my own, good food cooked by Agnes and Josephine and served by Martin with his usual quiet efficiency. I looked at his neat profile. What had he been doing that day Josephine saw him going through my desk? The uncomfortable thought came to me that Josephine was heavy-footed, and it would not be difficult for Martin to ensure she was not near before doing something illicit again. But I thought, more likely he had simply yielded to a momentary temptation, to see if he could find some money for his son. Temptation which, in any case, he had resisted, for I had carefully gone over my accounts and no money had ever gone missing.

Afterwards, it still being light, I took the papers I had brought home out to my little pavilion in the garden. They concerned a Court of Requests case for the autumn, a dispute between a cottager and his landowner over the cottager's right to take fruit from certain trees. As with all these cases the landlord was rich, the cottager penniless, the Court of Requests his only recourse. I looked up to see Martin approaching across the lawn, his footsteps soundless on the grass, a paper in his hand.

He bowed. 'This has just come for you, sir. Brought by a boy.'

He handed me a scrap of paper, folded but unsealed. 'Thank you, Martin,' I said. My name was drawn in capitals. I remembered uneasily the note telling me of Nicholas's kidnap.

'Can I fetch you some beer, sir?'

'Not now,' I answered shortly. I waited till he had turned his back before opening the paper. I was surprised but relieved to see that it was written in Guy's small spiky hand.

Matthew,

I write in haste from St Bartholomew's Hospital, where I do voluntary work. A man, a Scotchman, was brought in two days ago suffering from bad knife wounds, and is like to die. He is delirious, and has spoken all manner of strange things. Among them he has mentioned your name. Could you come, as soon as you get this note?

Guy

This had to be McKendrick, the only one of the Anabaptist group to escape the fight at the wharf. He must have been attacked after his flight, and very recently by the sound of it. I stood up at once, then as I walked to the stable, realized that Guy had simply signed his name, not prefixed it with the customary farewell of good fellowship, *Your loving friend*.

✝

I FETCHED GENESIS and rode up to Smithfield. I had not been there since Anne Askew's burning over three weeks before. I remembered noticing then how what was left of the old monastic precinct of St Bartholomew's was hidden by the new houses built by Rich.

It had been market day at Smithfield, and the cattle-pens were being taken away, boys with brooms clearing cow dung from the open space. Farmers and traders stood in the doorways of the taverns, enjoying the evening breeze. Ragged children milled around; they always gathered at the market to try and earn a penny here or there. The awful scene I had witnessed last month had taken place right here. One might have thought some echo would remain, a glimpse of flame in the air, the ghost of an agonized scream. But there was, of course, nothing.

I had never been to the hospital, which gave directly onto the open ground of Smithfield. I tied Genesis at the rail outside, paying one of the barefoot urchins a penny to watch him, and went inside. The large old building was in a dilapidated state, paint and plaster flaking – it was seven years now since the dissolution of the monastic hospital. I asked a fellow who had lost half a leg and was practising walking on crutches where Dr Malton might be. He directed me to the main ward, a large chamber with perhaps twenty beds in two long rows, all occupied by patients. I walked to the far end, where Guy in his physician's robe was attending to a patient. Beside him was his assistant, plump old Francis Sybrant.

They looked up as I approached. The patient in the bed was a girl in her teens, who whimpered as Guy wound a bandage round her calf, her leg held up carefully by Francis. Two wooden splints had already been bound to the leg.

'Thank you for coming, Matthew,' Guy said quietly. 'I will be with you in a moment.' I watched as he completed winding the bandage. Francis lowered the girl's leg slowly down onto the bed, and Guy said to her quietly, 'There, you must not move it now.'

'It pains me, sir.'

'I know, Susan, but for the bone to knit you must keep it still. I will call again tomorrow.'

'Thank you, sir. May I have my rosary, to pass the time — ?' She broke off, looking at me anxiously.

'Master Francis will give it to you,' Guy replied. He turned to his assistant. 'Give her some more of the drink I prescribed later. It will ease her pains.'

'I will, Dr Malton.'

Guy stepped away. 'I have put the man I wrote of in a private room.'

I followed him down the ward. 'What happened to the girl?'

'She assists at the cattle market for a few pennies. A frightened cow pressed her against the side of an enclosure. It broke her leg.'

'Will it mend?'

'It may, if she is careful. The bone did not come through the skin, so the leg will not go bad. I would be grateful if you would forget that she asked for a rosary. There are those who think this hospital still stinks of the old religion. Francis was once a monk here, by the way. He helps here still, through Christian charity.'

I looked at Guy in surprise. But there was no reason why his assistant should not be an ex-monk; there were thousands in England now. I replied, frowning, 'You know I would never do such a thing as mention that child's rosary to anyone.'

'It does no harm to put you in remembrance that it is not just radicals who have to be careful these days in what they do, and what they say.'

'I do *not* forget it.'

He gave me a hard look. 'And for myself, I take no note of words spoken by patients who sound impiously radical. As you will shortly see.' I took a deep breath. There was no give in my old friend nowadays.

✝

HE LED ME into a side ward. Like the main chamber it was but poorly equipped, a little room with a small window containing only a truckle bed with an old thin blanket and a stool. The window was open to let in air; the sound of voices drifted faintly in from Smithfield.

I recognized the man within at once: McKendrick, whom I had last seen running from the wharfside. He had been a physically powerful man, and had proved himself to be a fierce fighter. He looked utterly different now. His square face was covered with sweat, white as paper, and his cheeks were sunken. He tossed uneasily on the bed, making it creak, his lips moving in delirious muttering. Guy closed the door and spoke quietly. 'He was fetched in the day before yester-day. It is a strange story: a group of apprentices were hanging about outside one of the taverns near Cripplegate, around curfew, when all of a sudden a man rushed out of an alley into their midst. He was covered in blood and they caught a glimpse of two men pursuing him. Whoever they were, they turned tail when they saw the crowd of apprentices. They brought him here. It is a miracle he lived at all: he had been stabbed, thrice. He must have fought his pursuers and managed to run away. But the wounds have gone bad. He cannot live long; I think he will die tonight.' Guy gently lifted the blanket and under the man's shift I saw three wide wounds on his chest and abdomen. They had been stitched, but around two of the wounds the skin was swollen and red, and the third had a yellowish hue.

'Dear God,' I said.

Guy replaced the blanket gently, but the movement disturbed McKendrick, who began muttering aloud. 'Bertano . . . Antichrist . . . Pope's incubus . . .'

Guy looked at me sternly. 'When I heard some of the things he was saying, I put him in here. Safest for him, and perhaps for others.'

'And he has mentioned my name?'

'Yes. And others. Including, as you just heard, that name Bertano which you asked me about. Generally what he says in his delirium is nonsense, but I have heard him mention Queen Catherine herself. Disconnected talk, about spies and traitors at the English court. Mostly it makes no sense, and his Scotch accent is unfamiliar to me. But I have understood enough to realize he knows dangerous things, and is a religious radical. Once he cursed the Mass, saying it was no more than the bleating of a cow. Another time he spoke of overthrowing all princes.' Guy hesitated, then added, 'I see you know him.'

'I saw him only once, though I have been seeking him for weeks.'

'Who is he?'

I looked him in the eye. 'I cannot say, Guy, for your safety. I beg you, continue to keep him apart from the other patients; he knows dangerous things. Did he have anything on him when he was brought in?' I asked urgently. 'Perhaps – a book?'

'He had a copy of Tyndale's forbidden New Testament with his name inside, and a purse with a few coins.'

'Nothing else?'

'Nothing.'

I looked at McKendrick, quiet now, his breathing shallow. 'I would have prevented this, Guy, I hope you believe me.'

'Yes,' Guy answered, 'I believe that. But you are still involved in something deeply dangerous, are you not?'

'Yes.' I looked again at McKendrick. 'May I question him?'

'His mind is in a fever most of the time.'

'Would you leave me to try? The only reason I ask you not to stay is in case you hear something that might imperil your safety. I would not drag you into this bog as well.'

Guy hesitated, then nodded. 'I will leave you for a little. But do not tax him.' He went out, closing the door gently. There was a stool in the room, and I dragged it across to McKendrick's bed. It was getting dark, the sound of voices quieter as Smithfield emptied. I shook him gently. His eyes opened; they were unfocused, feverish.

'Master McKendrick?' I asked.

'Dominie McKendrick,' he whispered. 'I am Dominie. Teacher, preacher.'

'Dominie, who did this to you?'

I was not sure he had heard my question, but then he said wearily, closing his eyes tight, 'There were two o' them, two. They took me by surprise, though I'm careful. Jumped out of the doorway an' stabbed me. Two o' them. I got one o' them in the shoulder, managed to run.' He smiled sadly. 'Escaped in the alleys. Got to know the London alleys these last years. Same as the ones in Stirling, always running, running from the lackeys of popes and princes. But I weakened, loss o' blood.' He sighed. 'Running, always running.'

I bent my head close. 'Did you know your attackers, Dominie?'

He shook his head wearily.

'Were they two tall young men, one fair, with a wart on his face, the other almost bald?'

'Ay, that was them.' He looked at me, his eyes focusing properly for the first time. 'Who are you?'

'One who would punish those who attacked you.' Daniels and Cardmaker had underestimated the ex-soldier's strength and speed, and he had managed to run into the crowd of apprentices. But too late, it seemed, to save his life.

He reached a hand out from under the blankets, grasping mine. His was hard and callused, the hand of a man who had worked and soldiered, but hot and clammy. 'Did they kill Master Greening?' he asked.

'Yes, and his apprentice, Elias.'

His grip tightened and his eyes opened wider, blue and clear. He stared at me. 'Elias? We thought he was the traitor.'

'No, it was not him.' Nor you either, I thought.

McKendrick released my hand and leaned back on the bed with a groan. 'Then it can only have been Curdy, William Curdy we all thought such a true soul.' Yes, I thought, and Curdy is dead, unable to say who his master was. Killed by one of Richard Rich's men.

He looked at me. 'Are you one of us?' he asked.

'One of who?'

507

'The brethren. The believers in a new heaven and a new earth. Those our enemies call Anabaptists?'

'No. I am not.'

The dying man's shoulders slumped. Then he looked at me fiercely. 'I see it, among these dreams I have here. The greater vision, a future Commonwealth where all share equally in the bounty of nature, and worship the one Christ in peace. No princes, no warring countries, all men living in harmony. Is it a dream, do you think, or do I see Heaven?'

'I think it a dream, Dominie,' I answered sadly. 'But I do not know.'

A few moments later McKendrick slid back into unconsciousness, his breathing shallow. I stood, my knees creaking. I had learned what I needed to know and returned slowly to the main room, where Guy was writing notes at a desk at the back of the ward.

'He is unconscious again,' I sighed. 'Or perhaps in a sleep of wondrous dreams. There is nothing to be done for him?'

He shook his head. 'We doctors know the signs of coming death.'

'Yes.' I remembered Cecil telling me about the King's doctors saying he could not last long now. 'Thank you for summoning me, Guy. One thing more. When – when he dies, it would be safer for the hospital if he were buried under a different name. He is wanted in connection with possible treason.'

Guy looked at me, then spoke with quiet passion. 'I pray every night that whatever terrible thing you are involved in, it may end soon.'

'Thank you.'

I left the hospital. At home I sent a note to Lord Parr, telling him the Scotchman was found, and that he was not the spy. Very early next morning, Brocket woke me with two notes that had arrived with the dawn: one on expensive paper with the seal of the Queen in red wax, the other a second folded scrap from Guy. The first told me that I was required at Whitehall Palace again that morning, the second that McKendrick had died in the night. Again, Guy had signed his note only with his name.

Chapter Thirty-nine

AND SO I TOOK A BOAT to Whitehall Palace. I had no more information to bring Lord Parr about what might have happened to the Queen's book; and I realized that, with all Greening's group gone, its fate might remain unknown.

On the way to Temple Stairs I called in at chambers to tell Barak I would be away that day, I did not know for how long. He was alone – Nicholas and Skelly had not yet come in – and I summoned him to my room.

'Whitehall?' he asked.

'Yes. I found McKendrick last night.' I told him what had happened at the hospital.

'So the late Master Curdy was the spy.'

'So it seems.' I sighed. 'I have reached a dead end.'

'Then leave it to the politicians now,' he said roughly. 'You've done all you can.'

'I cannot but feel I have failed the Queen.'

'You've done all you can,' he repeated impatiently. 'Risked your life.'

'I know. And yours, and Nicholas's.'

'Then have done with it. If Queen Catherine falls, it will be through her own foolishness.'

✝

I ENTERED the palace by the Common Stairs again, the wherry jostling for space at the pier along with boats carrying newly slaughtered swans for the royal table and bolts of fine silk. The pier ran a long way out into the water, so that unloading could take place even at low tide. The tide was almost full now, though, just starting to ebb. Dirty grey water washed round the lowest of the stone steps. I thought for a moment of poor Peter Cotterstoke, tumbling into the river on a cold autumn day. As I left the boat, gathering my robe around me and straightening my cap, I looked upriver to the Royal Stairs. There, a narrow, brightly painted building two storeys high jutted out of the long redbrick facade of the palace. It ended at a magnificent stone boathouse, built over the water. A barge was heading towards it, oarsmen pulling hard against the tide. A man in a dark robe and cap sat in the stern. I recognized the slab face and forked beard: Secretary Paget, master of spies, and one of those who knew whether an emissary of the Pope called Bertano was truly in London.

I went into the maze of buildings, tight-packed around their little inner courts. Some of the guards recognized me by sight now, though as always at strategic points my name had to be checked against a list. All the magnificence within had become familiar, almost routine. I was accustomed now to avoid looking at all the great works of art and statuary as I passed along, lest they delay me. I saw two stonemasons creating a new and elaborate cornice in a corridor, and remembered Leeman saying how every stone in the palace was built on common people's sweat. I recalled that craftsmen were paid a lower rate for royal work, justified by the status that accrued from working for the King.

I was admitted again at the Queen's Presence Chamber. A young man, one of the endless petitioners, stood arguing with a bored-looking guard in his black-and-gold livery. 'But my father has sent to Lord Parr saying I was arriving from Cambridge today. I have a degree in canon law. I know there is a position on the Queen's Learned Council come vacant.'

'You are not on the list,' the guard answered stolidly. I thought, who was leaving? Was it me, now my work was done?

In the bay window overlooking the river some of the Queen's ladies sat as usual, needlework on their laps, watching a dance performed with surprising skill by Jane Fool. I saw Mary Odell sitting with the highborn ladies despite her lack of rank. The pretty young Duchess of Suffolk, her lapdog Gardiner on her knee, sat between her and the Queen's sister Lady Anne Herbert, whom I had seen at Baynard's Castle. A tall thin young man with a narrow, beaky face and wispy beard stood behind them, watching with a supercilious expression.

Jane came to a halt in front of the gentleman and bowed. 'There, my Lord of Surrey,' she said to the man. 'Am I not fit to be your partner at the dancing at Hampton Court for the admiral?' So this was Surrey, the Duke of Norfolk's oldest son, but reportedly a reformer, said to be a skilled poet, who last winter had been in trouble for leading a drunken spree in the city.

He answered curtly, 'I dance only with ladies of rank, Mistress Fool. And now you must excuse me. I have to meet my father.'

'Do not be harsh with Jane,' the Duchess of Suffolk said reprovingly; for the fool's moon face had reddened. But then Jane saw me standing a little way off, and pointed at me. 'There is the reason the Queen has gone to Lord Parr's chamber! The lawyer has come again to bother her with business! See, he has a back as hunched as Will Somers'!'

The company turned to look at me as she continued. 'He would have had Ducky taken from me. But the Lady Mary would not let him! She knows who her true friends are!' There was a glimmer in her eyes that told me Jane was indeed no halfwit; all this nonsense was deliberate, to humiliate me.

Mary Odell stood up hastily and came to my side. 'Her majesty and Lord Parr are waiting for you, Master Shardlake.'

I was glad to walk away with her to the Queen's inner sanctum.

✝

AGAIN THE QUEEN was seated on a high chair under her red cloth of estate; today she wore a bright green dress on which flowers, leaves, even peapods on a bush, were sewn to scale. Under her French hood I thought I caught the glint of grey strands in her auburn hair. Lord Parr stood to one side of her in his usual black robe and gold chain, and Archbishop Cranmer on the other, in his white cassock. As I bowed deeply I saw the Queen's chess set on a table nearby and thought: a black piece and a white.

All three had been studying a life-size portrait set before them on an easel, the newly painted colours so bright they drew the eye even amid the magnificence of Whitehall Palace. The background showed the dark red curtains of a four-poster bed, the foreground an open bible on a lectern and next to it the Lady Elizabeth, whom I recognized at once. She was wearing the same red dress as the day I saw her, when she had complained at having to stand so long, and being painted beside her bed.

Her trouble had been worthwhile, for the portrait was truly lifelike. Elizabeth's budding breasts contrasted with the vulnerability of her thin, childlike shoulders. She held a small book in her hands and her expression was composed, with a sense of watchful authority despite her youth. I read the meaning of the painting: here was a girl on the brink of womanhood, scholarly, serious, regal, and in the background the bed as a reminder of her coming marriageability.

The Queen, who had been looking at the portrait intently, sat back in her chair. 'It is excellent,' she said.

'It says everything that is needed,' Cranmer agreed. He turned to me. 'I have heard your latest news, Matthew,' he said quietly. 'That there *was* a spy in this group, and he is dead. His master is likely someone senior, a Privy Councillor, but we do not know who.'

'Yes, my Lord,' I added. 'I am sorry.'

'You did all you could,' he said, echoing Barak. I glanced at the Queen. She looked troubled now, her body held with that air of slight stiffness I had come to recognize as denoting strain. She did not speak.

'At least this group of Anabaptists is gone,' Lord Parr said. 'I'd have seen them burned!'

Cranmer said firmly, 'The guard who Leeman suborned at the palace, and the gaoler Myldmore, must be sent abroad. For all our safety.'

'You would have had them burned too, my Lord Archbishop,' Lord Parr growled, 'were moving them not necessary.'

'Only if earnest preaching could not bring them from their heresy,' Cranmer said, anger in his voice. 'I wish no man burned.'

'You have helped us greatly, Matthew,' the Queen said gently, 'with Leeman's information about Bertano.'

I asked, 'It is true, then, about him?'

Lord Parr glanced at Cranmer and then the Queen, who nodded. He spoke sternly. 'This is for your ears only, Shardlake, and we tell you only because you first brought us that name and would welcome your view. Only we four know about Bertano. We have not even told the Queen's brother or sister. And that man and boy who work for you must say nothing,' he added in a threatening tone.

'We know you have absolute trust in them,' Cranmer said mildly.

'Tell him, niece,' Lord Parr said.

The Queen spoke: heavily, reluctantly. 'A week ago, his majesty had a visitor brought to his privy quarters during the day. All the servants in the Privy Chamber were cleared out. Normally he tells me if a visitor from abroad is coming,' she added, 'but the night before this visit he said that it was for him alone to know about, and I was to stay on my side of the palace.' She lowered her eyes.

Her uncle prompted her gently, 'And then?'

'I know the meeting did not go well. His majesty sent for me to play music for him afterwards, as he does sometimes when he is sad and low in spirits. He was in an angry humour, he even hit his fool Will Somers on the pate and told him to get out; he had no patience for idle jest. I dared to look at him questioningly, for poor Somers had done nothing to warrant being struck. The King said, "Someone wants the powers granted me by God, Kate, and dares send to ask for them. I have sent back such answer as he deserves." Then he struck the arm of his chair so fiercely with his fist that it jarred his whole body and caused a fearful pain in his leg.' The Queen took a deep breath. 'He did not make me swear to keep his words confidential. So, though strictly it goes against the honour due my husband, because of the dire straits we have all found ourselves in, I confided in my uncle and the Archbishop.'

'And now we have told you,' Lord Parr said brusquely. 'What do you make of it?'

'It adds weight to the suspicion that what Vandersteyn learned on the Continent was true. Someone asking the King for the powers granted him by God. That can only mean the Supreme Headship, and only the Pope would demand that.'

He nodded agreement. 'That is what we think. If Bertano was an emissary from the Pope it sounds as though the price for a reconciliation was the King's renunciation of his Headship of the Church in England.'

'And from all the King said, a message was to be sent back to the Pope?'

Cranmer answered. 'I think it has already gone. And if it has, it would be through Paget.' He smiled humourlessly. 'And yesterday Paget told the Privy Council that after d'Annebault's visit, the King and Queen will be going on a short Progress – only as far as Guildford – and announced those of the council he has chosen to accompany him, all sympathizers with reform. Gardiner, Norfolk, Rich, all our enemies, remain in London, kicking their heels and keeping the wheels of government turning. Those who will be about the King's person, and have his ear, will be our allies.'

Lord Parr raised his hands. 'The pieces all fit.'

Cranmer smiled, more warmly this time. 'Those left behind did not look pleased to hear the news at the council table. I think Bertano's mission has failed at the start.' There was satisfaction in his voice, relief too.

I said, 'But there remains the *Lamentation*.'

'There is nothing more to be done about that,' Lord Parr said bluntly. 'Except hope that whoever stole it realizes they have squandered their chance, that the Catholic cause is lost, and – forgive me, Kate – that they dispose of it.' He added, 'The King will not turn his policy again.'

Cranmer shook his head emphatically. 'With the King, that can never be ruled out. But I agree, the trail on the book is quite cold.'

I looked at the Queen. 'Believe me, your majesty, I wish I had been able to recover it. I am sorry.'

'God's wounds,' Lord Parr said abruptly. 'You did your best, even if it wasn't good enough. And now, all that remains is for you to keep quiet.'

'I swear I will, my Lord.'

Cranmer said, 'Your efforts to serve her majesty will not be forgotten.'

It was a dismissal. I adjusted my posture a little, so I could bow to them without pain, for I was still suffering from when Nicholas had thrown me to the ground, to save me from the man with the gun. But the Queen rose from her chair. 'Matthew, before you go I would talk a little with you again. Come, you have seen my Privy Gallery, but not by daylight. Let us walk there. Mary Odell can accompany us.' She nodded to Cranmer and Lord Parr, who bowed low. I followed the Queen as she walked to the door, silk skirts rustling.

✞

WITH DAYLIGHT coming in through the high windows, showing the gorgeous colours to full effect, the Queen's Privy Gallery was magnificent. The little birds in their cages hopped and sang. The Queen walked slowly along; I kept a respectful pace or two away, while Mary Odell, summoned from the gallery, brought up the rear. The expression on her plump face was neutral, but her eyes were watchful, I saw, as I glanced back.

The Queen halted before an alcove in which a jewelled box was set atop a marble pillar. Within were coins of gold and silver, showing portraits of long-dead kings and emperors. Some were worn almost smooth, others bright as though new-minted. She stirred them with a long finger. 'Ancient coins have always interested me. They remind us we are but specks of dust amid the ages.' Carefully, she picked up a gold coin. 'The Emperor Constantine, who brought Christianity to the Roman Empire. It was found near Bristol some years ago.' She lifted her head and looked out of the window; it gave on to the Thames bank below the palace, exposed now as the tide ebbed. I followed her gaze, my eye drawn to a heap of rubbish from the palace that had been thrown onto the mud: discarded vegetable leaves, bones, a pig's head. Gulls swooped over it, pecking and screaming. The Queen turned away. 'Let us try the view on the other side,' she said.

We crossed the gallery. The opposite window looked down on another of the small lawned courtyards between the buildings. Two men I recognized were walking and talking there. One was Bishop Gardiner, solidly built, red-faced, dressed again in a white silk cassock. The other, younger man was sturdy, dark-bearded, saturnine: John Dudley, Lord Lisle, who had commanded the King's naval forces at Portsmouth last year. His defensive strategy had done much to ward off invasion. So the other senior councillor who favoured the radicals was back from his mission abroad. All the chess pieces were in place now. Gardiner, I saw, was talking animatedly, his heavy face for once wearing a civil expression. Something in their postures suggested Gardiner was on the defensive. Lord Lisle inclined his head. This, I thought, was how the real power-play went: conversations in corners and gardens, nods, shrugs, inclinations of the head. But nothing in writing.

The Queen joined me. An expression of distaste and fear, quickly suppressed, crossed her face at the sight of Gardiner.

'Lord Lisle is back,' I observed.

'Yes. Another ally. I wonder what they are discussing.' She sighed and stepped away from the window, then looked at me and spoke seriously. 'I wanted you to know, Matthew, the depth of my gratitude for the help you have given. I sense it has cost you much. And my uncle can be – less than appreciative. But all he does is for my interest.'

'I know.'

'It looks as though my book will never be found. It saddens me to think it may be on some rubbish tip, for all it may be safer there. It was my confession of faith, you see, my acknowledgement that I am a sinner, like everyone, but through prayer in the Bible I found my way to Christ.' She sighed. 'Though even my faith has not protected me from terrible fear these last months.' She bit her lip, hesitated, then said, 'Perhaps you thought me disloyal, earlier, for repeating words spoken to me by the King. But – we needed to know what this visit from abroad signifies.'

I ventured a smile. 'Mayhap a turn in fortune for you, your majesty, if the meeting went badly.'

'Perhaps.' She was silent again, then said with sudden intensity, 'The King – you do not know how he suffers. He is in constant pain, sometimes he near swoons with it, yet always, always, he must keep up the facade.'

I dared to say, 'As must you, your majesty.'

'Yes. Despite my fear.' She swallowed nervously.

I remembered what Lord Parr had said about how the King might react to disloyalty. For all that the Queen revered her husband, her fear of him over these last months must have been an unimaginable burden. I felt a clutch at my heart that she so valued me as to unburden herself thus. I said, 'I can only imagine how hard it must have been for you, your majesty.'

She frowned. 'And always, always there are people ready to whisper poison in the King's ear – '

Mary Odell, perhaps concerned the Queen was saying too much, approached us. 'Your majesty,' she said. 'You asked me to remind you to take these to the King when you see him. They were found down the side of a chair in his Privy Chamber.' She had produced a pair of wood-framed spectacles from the folds of her dress, and held them out to the Queen.

'Ah yes,' she said. 'Thank you, Mary.' The Queen turned to me. 'The King needs glasses now to read. He is always losing them.' She tucked the spectacles away, then began walking down the gallery again. 'The court will be moving from Whitehall next week,' she said, more brightly. 'The French admiral is to be received first at Greenwich and then at Hampton Court, so everything is to be moved.' She waved a hand. 'All this packed up, transported by boat, set out again in a new place. The Privy Council meeting in a new chamber. With Lisle and Hertford both present,' she added with a note of satisfaction.

I ventured, 'I saw Lord Hertford with his brother Sir Thomas Seymour at the palace last time I came.'

'Yes. Thomas is back, too.' She looked me in the eye. 'You do not like him, I know.'

'I fear his impulsiveness, your majesty.'

She waved a dismissive hand. 'He is not impulsive, just a man of strong feeling.'

I did not reply. There was a brief, awkward silence, then she changed the subject. 'You have knowledge of portraiture,

Matthew. What was your opinion of the picture of my step-daughter?'

'Very fine. It shows the coming substance of her character.'

She nodded. 'Yes. Prince Edward, too, is a child, well advanced for his years. There are those in my family who hope that one day I may be appointed Regent when he comes to the throne, as I was when the King went to France two years ago. If so, I would try to do well by all.'

'I am sure of it.' But the Seymours as well as the traditionalists would oppose her there, I knew.

She came to a halt. 'Soon the French admiral will come, and afterwards the King and I go on Progress, as you heard.' She looked at me seriously. 'You and I may not have another opportunity to talk.'

I answered quietly, 'A young courtier waiting outside said there is a vacancy on your Learned Council. Do you wish me to resign my position?'

'The vacant post is not yours but Master Cecil's. He asked to go. What he experienced at the docks was too much for him, not that he is a coward, but he fears if anything happened to him his wife and children would be left alone. And Lord Hertford has asked him to become one of his advisers. I consented; Cecil is a man of great loyalty and will say nothing of the *Lamentation*. As for you, Matthew, I wonder if it might be best for all if you were to leave as well.'

'Yes. After all, I was supposedly appointed only to find a missing jewel.' I smiled. 'And sadly, it indeed seems there is no chance of finding your book. Perhaps it would be – politic – for me to leave now.'

'So my uncle thinks, and I agree.' She smiled tiredly. 'Though I would still rather have your counsel.'

'If you need to call on me again – '

'Thank you.' She looked at me, hesitated, then spoke with quick intensity. 'One thing more, Matthew. Your lack of faith still troubles me. It will eat away at you from the inside, until only a shell is left.'

I thought sadly: was the real purpose of our talk for her to make another essay at bringing me to faith? I answered truthfully, 'I have wished for God, but I cannot find him in either Christian faction today.'

'I pray that may change. Think on what I said, I beg you.' She looked into my eyes.

'I always do, your majesty.'

A sad little smile, then she nodded and turned to Mary Odell. 'We should go back, sit with the ladies awhile. They will think we are neglecting them.'

We walked back up the gallery. Near the door she paused at a table on which stood a magnificent gold clock a foot high, ticking softly. 'Time,' the Queen said softly. 'Another reminder we are but grains of sand in eternity.'

Mary Odell went in front of us and knocked at the door. A guard opened it from the other side and we stepped through into the heavily guarded vestibule, with its doors leading to the Queen's rooms, the King's, and the Royal Stairs. At the same moment another guard opened the doors leading to the King's chambers, and two men stepped out. One was the red-bearded Lord Chancellor Wriothesley, the other Secretary Paget, a leather folder thick with papers under his arm. They had probably just come from seeing the King.

Seeing the Queen, they bowed deeply. I bowed to them in turn, and rose to see both staring at me, this hunchbacked lawyer wearing the Queen's badge, who had been walking with her in her gallery. Wriothesley stared with particular intensity, his gaze only relaxing a little when he saw Mary

Odell standing by the door: her presence showed the Queen had not been walking alone with a man who was not a relative.

The Queen's face immediately assumed an expression of regal composure; still, quiet, a little superior. She said, 'This is Serjeant Shardlake, of my Learned Council.'

Wriothesley's stare intensified again. Paget's large brown eyes held mine with a forceful, unblinking look. Then, turning to the Queen, he lowered his eyes and spoke smoothly. 'Ah yes, the man appointed to help you seek your stolen jewel.'

'You have heard of that incident, Master Secretary?'

'Indeed. I was grieved to hear of its loss. A present from your late stepdaughter Margaret Neville, I believe, God save her.'

'It was.'

'I see Serjeant Shardlake's name has been added to the list of those on your Learned Council. And I see young William Cecil has moved to Lord Hertford's service. He will be a loss, your majesty, he is marked down as a young man of ability.' I thought, yes, Paget would know of all the changes in the royal household; he would inspect all the lists and ensure nothing of interest passed him by. He would have learned that trick from Thomas Cromwell, his old master and mine.

The Queen said, 'Serjeant Shardlake is also leaving my council. My jewel has not been discovered, despite his best efforts. There seems little chance of finding it now.'

Paget looked at me again, that stony unblinking stare, and ran a hand down his long forked beard. 'A great pity the thief could not be caught, and hanged,' he said, a note of reproof in his voice. He patted his thick leather folder. 'If you would excuse us, your majesty, the King has just signed some important letters, and they should be immediately dispatched.'

'Of course.' She waved a hand in dismissal. Wriothesley and Paget bowed low, then passed through a small door leading into the labyrinthine depths of the palace. The Queen, Mary Odell and I were left standing with the impassive-faced guards. In their presence the Queen's face remained regally expressionless, giving away nothing of how she had felt at thus encountering Wriothesley and Paget. She knew that Wriothesley, at least, would have had her in the fire.

With a formal smile she said, 'Farewell, then, Matthew. I thank you again.'

I bowed low, touched her hand briefly with my lips; a scent of violets. In accordance with the rules of etiquette I remained bowed until she and Mary Odell had walked back into her quarters and the doors closed behind her. Then, painfully, I straightened up.

I left my robe bearing the Queen's badge with one of the guards before I quitted Whitehall, my relief tinged with sadness.

Chapter Forty

EARLY NEXT MORNING I sat at breakfast, morosely studying a printed circular from Paget's office, which had been sent to me by Rowland's clerk. It detailed the duties of those who were to wait in the streets to welcome Admiral d'Annebault's party when it paraded through London. Representatives of the Inns of Court were to take positions with the city dignitaries beside St Paul's Cathedral, and cheer as the French party passed. We would be present again at the reception of the admiral given by Prince Edward near Hampton Court Palace two days later, and at the great banquet fixed for the day after. I was not looking forward to any of it, and was still in a sad humour after leaving the Queen, my mission unfulfilled. I had been terse with Martin as he served me that morning, snapping because the butter was on the turn. As usual he reacted with a deferential lack of emotion, apologized, and went to fetch some more.

He returned, laying a fresh dish on the table. I said, 'I am sorry I spoke roughly just now, Martin.'

'You were right, sir,' he answered smoothly. 'I should have checked the butter. Although Josephine set it out.' I frowned; he could not resist the chance to criticize her. 'A visitor has called to see you,' he said then. 'Master Coleswyn, of Gray's Inn.'

'Philip? Ask him to wait. I will be with him in a moment.'

Martin bowed and left. I wondered if this meant Philip

had reconsidered investigating the story of Isabel and Edward's stepfather. I wiped my lips with my napkin and went through to the parlour. Philip, his handsome features thoughtful, was looking through the window at the garden, bright in the August sunshine. He turned and bowed.

'Matthew, forgive this early visit. God give you good morrow.'

'And you. I am glad to see you.'

'You have a beautiful garden.'

'Yes, my steward's wife has done much to improve it. How is your family?'

'They are well. Much relieved that matters of state have – settled down.'

I invited him to sit. He placed his palms together, then spoke seriously. 'Since our talk last week, I have struggled mightily with my conscience over what to do about Edward Cotterstoke. Considered my duty to God.'

'Yes?' I said encouragingly.

'I decided I could not let the matter rest. If there is any question of my client being involved with his stepfather's death, that would be a crime against God and man. Not only could I no longer represent him, I would be obliged at the very least to tell our vicar, who ministers to both our souls.' He took a deep breath. 'Last Sunday, after church, I spoke to Edward. I explained I had been told the story of his stepfather's death, and wondered whether that tragic event was in any way connected with his feelings towards Isabel.'

'How did he react?'

'Most angrily. He said the old barrister I spoke to had no right to divulge information about matters on which his mother had instructed him, however many decades ago, and that I should not be listening to such tattle.'

'Strictly he is right.'

Philip leaned forward, his expression urgent. 'Yes. But the fierce manner in which Edward reacted – you should have seen it. He was angry, but also perturbed. There is something hidden here, Matthew, something serious.'

'So I came to think when Isabel was my client.' I paused, then asked, 'Well, what next?'

'I believe now that I should talk to the old servant Vowell. Doing so without Edward's instruction is a breach of the rules, but nonetheless I believe it is my duty.' He set his lips tight. 'I will go to him today.'

'May I come also?'

He hesitated, then nodded agreement, giving a rare slant- wise smile. 'Yes. I would welcome your presence, and if I am to break the rules by taking my ex-opponent with me, I might as well be hung for a sheep as a lamb.' He took a deep breath. 'Let us go now. I came by horse. We can ride there.'

I got Timothy to saddle Genesis, then sent him to cham- bers with a note saying I would be in late.

✝

IT WAS STILL EARLY, the city just coming to life, as we rode to the Cotterstoke house at Dowgate. I glanced round periodically; it had become habit since the night of the fight on the wharf. But if I were still being followed, which I doubted, it was by someone very skilled. And perhaps now that all in Greening's group were dead, or in Vandersteyn's case fled, there was no longer a need for me to be watched.

We passed a thin, ragged old woman going from house to house calling out, 'Any kitchen stuff, maids?' She was one of those who collected kitchen rubbish to sell for a few pence, for use as compost in the vegetable gardens round London. She was old for such a heavy, dirty task. As I looked at her blackened face I remembered Barak talking of seeing his mother in the street. This old woman could even be her. Family quarrels, they were hard things.

We passed the Great Conduit in Eastcheap, maids and goodwives lined up with their pails to fetch water. Some of the beggars who always haunted the conduit left off troubling the women and ran to us, one coming almost under the nose of Philip's horse, making it shy. 'Take care, fellow!' Philip shouted, straining to bring his mount under control. 'He'll kick you if you're not careful!' As we rode on he said, 'By Heaven, that fellow stank. Could he not wash himself, seeing as he is lounging by the conduit?'

'Hard to keep yourself clean if you're begging in summer.'

He nodded slowly. 'You are right to reprove me. We must have charity for those who have suffered ill fortune. It is a Christian thing.'

'Of course. But perhaps we should not give them charge of the realm,' I added, half-mockingly. 'As the Anabaptists would wish?'

He looked annoyed. 'You know I do not approve those heresies.' He sighed. 'It is a common enough thing for papists to accuse reformers of being Anabaptists, but I am surprised you give credence to such nonsense.'

'I do not. I am sorry.'

'The Anabaptists are not of the Elect,' he continued severely.

'Do you believe people are divided between the Elect and the damned?' I asked seriously.

'Yes.' He spoke with certainty. 'Some are predestined by God for salvation, while those without faith burn forever. Read St Paul.'

'I have always thought that a harsh doctrine.'

'The justice of God may be beyond our comprehension,

but it is inviolable.' Philip looked at me seriously. 'Coming to faith, Matthew, may confirm one's place in Heaven.'

'And show one the way to right living; such as working to uncover whether one's client may be a murderer.'

He looked at me hard. 'That possibility is in both our minds.'

I nodded agreement. 'Yes. Let us find out.'

✠

THE COTTERSTOKE house was unchanged since the inspection, shuttered and silent, the stableyard to the rear again empty and bare in the sultry morning; it was hard to remember we were in the centre of the great city. Old Mrs Cotterstoke, I thought, lived here over fifty years. We tied up the horses. As we stepped into the sunshine, Philip, once more the practical lawyer, said, 'They should get the house sold. The value of money keeps falling. But neither of them will take a single step till this dispute is resolved.'

We walked back under the stableyard arch into the street, and knocked at the door. Shuffling footsteps sounded within and the old man Vowell opened the door. His watery blue eyes widened with surprise at the sight of us, standing there in our robes. He bowed quickly. 'Masters, I did not know you were coming, I have had no instructions. Is there to be another inspection?'

I realized from his words that he was unaware that I no longer represented Isabel. Philip replied amiably, 'No, good-man, but there are some questions you might help us with.'

Vowell shook his head, obviously reluctant. 'I do not know how I can help you. I was the late Mistress Cotter-stoke's servant all her life, but I knew nothing of her affairs. My only duty is to keep the house safe.'

I said, 'We have both been eager to see whether there

may be a way to resolve this dispute before it comes to court.'

'Little chance of that,' Vowell said sadly. 'But come in, sirs.'

He led us to the parlour. I noticed the old lady's half-finished embroidery still lay on its chair, facing the wall painting, and wondered if anything at all had been moved since she died. I looked at the picture. 'That is a very fine piece of work. Were you here when it was painted?'

'Yes, sir. I was little more than a boy then, but I remember thinking how lifelike it was. My late mistress, her first husband, and the two little children; all just as they were then. It saddens me to see it now, my mistress dead and the children at such odds.' He looked at us, something wary in his eyes now.

'I heard a story of the death of their stepfather,' Philip said. 'A sad tale.' Philip related the old barrister's story. As he spoke, the old servant's posture seemed to droop and tears came to his eyes. At the end he said, 'May I sit, sirs?'

'Of course,' Philip said.

Vowell took a stool. 'So you have learned that old story. I thought, with this new quarrel, it must come out sooner or later.' He clenched his fists, looking down at the matting on the floor, then seemed to come to a decision.

'Master Edward was eleven then, Mistress Isabel twelve. As children they were − not close. Both had proud natures, wanted their own way, and they often quarrelled. Their mother was often sharp with them too, I have to say. Though she was a good enough mistress, and she has provided for me in her Will −'

'Though the Will must be proved first,' I said. Vowell would not get his legacy till then.

The old servant nodded and continued, 'The children loved their father. When he died they were both so sad. I remember coming across them, crying in each other's arms.

It was the only time I saw that.' He looked up at us. 'Since my mistress died and this argument over the painting began, I have not known what to do or say. It has been a burden, sirs – '

'Then let us help you,' Philip said quietly.

Vowell sighed deeply. 'Mistress Johnson, as she was then, perhaps remarried too soon, only a year after Master Johnson died. But it was hard for her to keep the business going on her own, some people didn't like trading with a woman, and the children were too young to help. But her new husband, Master Cotterstoke, he was a good man. My mistress knew that. The children, though – '

I spoke quietly, remembering Barak and his mother. 'Perhaps they thought it a betrayal?'

He looked up. 'Yes. It was not – nice – to see them then. They would sit giggling and whispering together in corners, saying and doing – ' he hesitated – 'bad things.'

'What sort of things?' Philip asked.

'Master Cotterstoke had a fine book of Roman poems, beautifully written and decorated – it was all done by hand; most books then were not these blocky printed things we have nowadays – and it disappeared. All the servants were set to look for it, but no one found it. And I remember the children watching us as we searched, smiling at each other. Other things of the master's would go missing, too. I think the children were responsible. Yet Master Cotterstoke and especially the mistress thought it was us, careless servants. We always get the blame,' he added bitterly.

'The mistress and Master Cotterstoke were much preoccupied with each other then; the mistress had become pregnant. They barely noticed the children.' He shook his head. 'That angered them even more. I think Edward and Isabel had become much closer, united in their anger. Once

I overheard them talking together on the stairs. Master Edward was saying they would be disinherited, everything would go to the new baby, their mother scarcely looked at them any more . . . And then – '

'Go on,' I urged gently.

'Sometimes Master Cotterstoke worked at home in the afternoon, going over his accounts. 'He liked a bowl of pottage mid-afternoon. The cook would prepare it in the kitchen and take it up to him. One day after eating it he was violently sick, and very poorly for several days after. The physician thought he had eaten something bad. He recovered. But one of my jobs then was keeping down vermin, and there was a little bag of poison bought from a peddler that was good for killing mice. I remember just after Master Cotterstoke was ill, getting the bag from the outhouse to put a measure down in the stables and noticing that some had been taken – it had been almost full.'

'You mean the children tried to poison him?' Philip asked, horrified.

'I don't know that, I don't know. But when I spoke to the cook she said the children had been round the kitchen that day.'

Philip's voice was stern. 'You should have spoken up.'

Vowell was looking at us anxiously now. 'There was no evidence, sir. The children were often round the kitchen. Master Cotterstoke recovered. And I was just a poor servant; making an accusation like that could have cost me my post.'

'How did the children react to Master Cotterstoke's illness?' I asked.

'They went quiet. I remember after that, their mother looked at them in a new way, as though she, too, suspected something. And I thought, if she is suspicious of them, she will look out for her husband, there is little point in my saying anything. Yet it pricked my conscience, that I had not spoken.' He added sadly, 'Especially after — what happened next.' He hunched forward again, looking at his feet.

I said, 'The drowning?'

'The coroner found it was an accident.'

'But you doubted it?' Philip said sternly.

Vowell looked up at that. 'The coroner investigated everything, it is not for a servant to contradict him.' I heard a touch of anger in his voice now. 'There were enough unemployed servants trailing the road even back then.'

I spoke soothingly. 'We have not come to criticize you, only to try and discover what caused the quarrel. We understand Master Cotterstoke went down to the docks on business that day, and you and another servant accompanied him and the children. And then after a while the children came back, saying they had been told to wait with you beside the customs house till he returned.'

'Ay, that is what happened, as I told the coroner.'

'How did the children seem when they returned?'

'A little quiet. They said their stepfather wanted to look over some goods on a ship newly come in.'

I thought again, there was only the children's word for that. Anything could have happened when they and Cotterstoke were alone. The children could have pushed their stepfather into the water. They would have been fourteen and thirteen then.

I asked Vowell, 'Was Master Cotterstoke a big man?'

'No, he was short and slim. One of those fast-thinking, energetic little men. Not like my first master.' He stared up at the wall painting, where Edward and Isabel's father, in his smart robes and tall hat, looked out on us with patrician confidence.

'What were things like in the family after the drowning?' Philip asked.

'Things changed. They were told of their stepfather's dispositions, I imagine. That he had left his estate to his wife, and to all his children equally if she died first. In any event, Edward and Isabel seemed to alter. They had become close while Master Cotterstoke was in the house. They didn't go back to quarrelling like before, but they – avoided each other. And oh, the fierce looks they would give one another. Mistress Cotterstoke's attitude to them seemed to change as well, even before she lost the baby she was carrying. She had been sharp with them before, but now she almost ignored them. She sold the business, and arranged for Edward to start clerking at the Guildhall, which meant he had to live out. That was just a few months later.'

'So he did not inherit the business after all.'

'No. And though Isabel was only fifteen her mother seemed keen to marry her off; she was always inviting potential suitors to the house. But Mistress Isabel, as ever, would not be brought to do something against her will.' Vowell smiled sadly, then shook his grey head. 'There was a horrible atmosphere in this house, until at length Isabel agreed to marry Master Slanning and left. Afterwards Mistress Cotterstoke seemed to – I don't know – retreat inside herself. She didn't often go out.' He looked over at her empty chair. 'She spent much of her time sitting there, sewing, always sewing. Kept a strict house, though, kept us servants on our toes.' He sighed deeply, then looked up at us. 'Strange, is it not, with all the sad things that happened here, that she never moved, even when she was alone, the house far too big for her.'

I looked at the wall painting. 'Perhaps she remembered she had once been happy here. I notice her chair faces the picture.'

'Yes. She was sitting there when she had her seizure. Edward and Isabel seldom visited, you know, and never together. And the mistress didn't encourage them. It saddened me to see how they were with each other when they came here for the inspection. And that strange Will – ' He shook his head. 'Perhaps I should not have told you all this. What good can it do? It was so many years ago. Whatever happened, it cannot be mended.'

Philip stood pondering, fingering his bearded chin. Vowell gave a despairing little laugh. 'What will happen, sir? Shall I remain as caretaker of this empty house till I die? I don't like being here alone.' He added in a rush, 'At night sometimes, when the wood creaks – '

I felt sorry for the old man. I looked at Philip. 'I think we have learned all we need, Brother Coleswyn.'

'Yes, we have.' Philip looked at Vowell. 'You should have spoken before.'

I said, 'He is right that it can do no good to rake it all up now. Not a matter of a possible murder, so many decades ago, with no evidence to reopen the case.'

Philip stood silent, thinking.

'What will you do, sir?' Vowell asked him tremulously.

He shook his head. 'I do not know.'

✝

WE STOOD OUTSIDE in the stables, with the horses. I said, 'It may be that the children, or one of them, put Master Cotterstoke into the water. Clearly Goodman Vowell thinks so.'

'And their mother. It seems clear now: she made that Will to start a new quarrel. It was revenge.'

'But there is still no new evidence to overturn the coroner's verdict.'

'I think that is what happened, though.'

'So do I. Two children, grieving for the father, believing they might be disinherited by their mother's new husband – '

'Quite wrongly,' Philip said severely.

'They did not know that. Perhaps it started with little tricks, then they encouraged each other to go further, and as they spoke constantly of the rejection and betrayal each felt, maybe they drove each other to – a sort of madness.'

'Who put him in the water?'

I shook my head. 'I don't know.'

'Whoever did it was a murderer.'

'This all remains speculation,' I said emphatically. 'Likely, but not certain. Master Cotterstoke's drowning could still have been an accident. And the old man is right. Who could benefit from this being exposed, after forty years? And remember, you have a duty of confidentiality to your client. You can only break it if you think he is about to commit a crime, and that is hardly likely.'

Philip set his mouth hard. 'It is a matter of justice. I shall question Edward directly. And if he cannot satisfy my doubts, I shall cease acting for him and report the circumstances to our vicar. You are right about the lack of evidence, but if it is true he must still be brought to see the state of his soul. How could a man who had done such a thing ever be one of the Elect? Our vicar must know.'

'And Isabel? There is no point taking this tale to Dyrick. He wouldn't care. I know him.'

Philip looked at me. 'You would have me let sleeping dogs lie?'

I thought for a moment, then said, 'I think so. In this case.'

Philip shook his head decisively. 'No. Murder cannot go unpunished.'

Chapter Forty-one

NEXT DAY I WENT AGAIN to ask Treasurer Rowland for a copy of his letter to Isabel Slanning, and to see whether she had replied. I had done much thinking about what old Vowell had told Philip and me. It seemed all too possible that, forty years before, Isabel or Edward, or both, had killed their stepfather. Again I remembered Isabel's words to me, weeks ago, about her brother: *If you knew the terrible things my brother has done.* But what could be achieved by confronting them now, without new evidence? I knew Philip would be seeing Edward, perhaps had done so already. I had an uneasy feeling that the consequences of that old tragedy might ripple out anew.

My uneasiness was not assuaged when Rowland's clerk told me the Treasurer would not be available for appointments until Monday. It struck me that there was something a little furtive in the clerk's manner. I made an appointment for that day; it was three days hence, but it was at least a firm commitment.

✣

LATER THAT MORNING I was working in chambers, researching a precedent in a yearbook so that when the new term started next month I should have everything prepared. There was a knock at the door and John Skelly entered. His eyes behind his thick spectacles had a reproachful look, as often this last month. Not only had I frequently been out of the office, leaving the work to fall behind, but I knew he was conscious that Barak and Nicholas and I shared some secret he knew nothing about. It was better he did not, and safer for him, a married man with three children. But I knew he must feel excluded. I must talk to him, thank him for the extra work he had done for me, give him a bonus.

I smiled. 'What is it, John?'

'There is a visitor for you, sir. Master Okedene. The printer who came before.'

I laid down my book. 'What does he want?' I asked a little apprehensively, remembering how his last visit had led us to the tavern and the fight with Daniels and Cardmaker.

'He says he has come to say goodbye.'

I told him to show Okedene in. He looked older, thinner, as though his strong solid frame was being eaten away by worry. I invited him to sit.

'My clerk says you are come to bid me farewell.'

He looked at me sadly. 'Yes, sir. I have sold the business and we are moving in with my brother, at his farm in East Anglia.'

'That will be a great change in your life.'

'It will. But my family have never been at ease since Armistead Greening's murder and Elias's disappearance. I hear Elias has never been found, nor those others who used to meet with Master Greening.'

I hesitated before replying, 'No.'

He looked at me sharply, guessing I knew more than I was saying. I wondered what rumours were circulating among the radicals. Okedene sat, rubbing his brow with a strong square hand, before speaking again. 'I have not told my family of our encounter with Armistead's killers in that tavern, but knowing those people are still out there only makes me feel more strongly than ever that we are not safe. We must think of our children. Every time I see the ruin of Master Greening's workshop it reminds me, as it does my wife.'

'Ruin? What do you mean?' I sat up.

'You do not know, sir? The print-shop took fire, two weeks ago, in the night. A young couple, workless beggars, had got in there, and one of them knocked over a candle. You remember the building was all wooden; it burned quickly. Poor Armistead's press, the only thing of value he had, destroyed; his trays of type no more than lumps of useless lead. If we and the other neighbours had not rushed out with water to quench the flames, it could easily have spread to my house. And others.'

Okedene had spoken before of the printers' fear of fire. I knew how quickly it could spread in the city in summer. Londoners were careful of candles in a hot dry season such as this.

Okedene added, 'And those two killers are still in London. The fair one and the dark.'

I sat up. 'Daniels and Cardmaker? You have seen them?'

'Yes. I hoped they might have left the city, but I saw them both, in a tavern out near Cripplegate last week. I was passing; it was market day and very busy, they did not see me. But I would never forget those faces. I thought of coming to you then, but after what happened last time I felt myself best out of the business.'

'I understand. I have heard nothing more of them since the day of the fight.' I thought again of the feeling I had had of being followed at the wharf, the chink of a footstep on stone.

'All is settled,' Okedene said firmly. 'We go next week. We have sold the works to another printer. But I thought I would come to tell you I had seen those men. And to ask whether there has been any progress in finding who was responsible for killing Armistead Greening? Those two thugs were employed by someone else, were they not?' His eyes fixed on mine. 'Someone important? Someone who, perhaps, is still protecting them, for they still dare to show their faces in the taverns.'

I bit my lip. I had learned much since first meeting Okedene: who Bertano was, how the Queen's book had been stolen, what had happened to the others in Greening's group. But not the answer to the most important question, the one he had just asked. Who was behind it all?

'I think you are right,' I answered. 'I think Daniels and Cardmaker were employed by someone important, but whoever it was has covered his tracks utterly.'

His eyes fixed on mine. 'And that book? The one called *Lamentation of a Sinner*?'

'It has not been found, though – ' I hesitated – 'at least it has not been used to damage the Queen.'

Okedene shook his head. 'It is all terrible, terrible.' I felt a stab of guilt, for I had scarcely thought of him recently. An ordinary man whose life had been turned upside down by all this. 'I fear more troubled times may be coming,' he added, 'for all the heresy hunt has ended. People say the King may not last long, and who knows what will happen then?'

I smiled wryly. 'One must be careful what one says about that. Forecasting the King's death is treason.'

'What is not treason these days?' Okedene spoke with sudden fierce anger. 'No, my family is better out in the country. The profit we will make on our crops may be little, with the coinage worth less every month, but at least we can feed ourselves.'

'I am sorry my enquiries brought such trouble to you,' I said quietly.

Okedene shook his head. 'No, the fault lies with those who killed my poor friend.' He stood up and bowed. 'Thank you, sir, and goodbye.' He went to the doorway, then turned back and said, 'I thought I might have had some word, perhaps some thanks, from Lord Parr, for going to tell him privately what had happened that night.'

'He is not best known for gratitude,' I said sadly.

✝

LATER THAT morning my work was disturbed again, unexpectedly. From the outer office I heard Nicholas's voice call out, 'No!' followed by a tinkling sound.

I hurried out. I found Barak and Skelly staring in astonishment at him. He stood red-faced, his long body trembling, staring at a letter in his hand. On the floor at my feet I saw a golden coin, a half-sovereign: others were scattered around the room.

'What has happened?' I asked.

'He has just had a letter delivered,' Skelly said.

Nicholas stared at me then swallowed, crumpling the letter in his hand. Skelly stepped out from behind his desk and began going round the room, picking up the scattered coins.

Nicholas spoke coldly. 'Leave them, please, John. Or put them in the Inn chapel poor-box. I will not take them.'

'Nicholas,' I said, 'come into my office.'

He hesitated, but followed me in slowly, his movements strange and stiff. I gestured him to a chair and he sat down. I took my place on the other side of my desk. He looked at me with unseeing eyes. His face, which had been red, turned slowly white. The boy had suffered a shock. 'What has happened?'

He slowly focused on me, then said, 'It is over. They have

disinherited me.' He looked at the letter, which he still held. His face worked, and I thought he might break down, but he took a deep breath and set his features stiff, hard. I reached out a tentative hand to the letter, but he clutched it all the tighter. I said again, 'What has happened? Why did you throw those coins away?'

He answered coldly, 'I am sorry for my outburst. It will not happen again.'

'Nicholas,' I said, 'do not treat me like this. You know I will help you if I can.'

His face worked again for a moment. 'Yes. I am sorry.' He fell silent, staring out of the window at the quadrangle, then, his head still turned away, said, 'I told you my parents had threatened to disinherit me in favour of my cousin, because I would not marry a woman I did not love.'

'That is a hard thing to do.'

'My mother and father are hard people. They – they could not bend me to their will, so they found someone more amenable.' He gave a sad half-smile. 'The duel was the last straw; I did not tell you about that.' He turned and looked me in the face, his expression half-fierce, half-desperate.

'What duel?'

He gave a harsh little laugh. 'When my father was trying to get me to marry this poor girl against both our wishes, I made the mistake of confiding in a friend who lived nearby. Or friend I thought he was; certainly a gentleman.' He spoke the word, which signified so much to him, with sudden bitterness. 'But he had been overspending and his family had put him on short commons. He said if I did not give him two sovereigns he would tell my father that I did not intend to marry her.'

'What did you do?'

Nicholas spoke with a sort of bleak pride. 'Challenged the churl to a duel, of course. We fought with swords, and I cut him in the arm.' He clutched the letter again. 'Wish I'd taken half his ear off, like that rogue Stice. His parents saw he had been injured and came complaining to mine. When they confronted me I told them why we had fought, and that I would not marry.' He took a deep breath, and ran a hand down his face. 'It was then they decided to send me to law, and threatened to disinherit me. I did not think they would go through with it, but they have.'

'What does the letter say? May I see it?'

'No,' he answered quietly. 'I shall keep it, though, as a reminder of what parents can be. My father calls me undutiful, uncontrollable. The duel and my refusal to accept their choice of wife have undermined their position locally, my father says. Neither he nor my mother want to see me again. He sent this letter by special messenger, with five pounds. He says he will send me the same sum every year.' He fell silent again, then said, very definitely, 'I think it cruel, and wrong.' A fierce look came onto his face. 'Who do you think, sir, has done the greater wrong here?'

'They have.' I answered without hesitation. 'When you first told me about the girl I, too, thought that perhaps they would get over their anger. But it seems not.'

I knew that Nicholas would have liked to rage and shout, but he kept himself under control. He took more deep breaths, and I was glad to see colour returning to his face. 'I already have in my possession barely enough to pay for my pupillage with you, sir,' he said, his voice sad. 'I think I must leave.'

'No,' I said. 'You have learned almost enough now to earn your keep.' He looked at me and I could see he knew that was not true: he was still learning, and for a while at least I would spend as much time teaching and correcting him as benefiting from his labours. 'Or at least you will soon, if you continue to work hard, as you have during these last difficult weeks.' I smiled. 'And you have helped me in much more important ways.'

'I will not be a burden,' he burst out angrily. 'I will fend for myself from now on.'

I smiled sadly. 'The Bible tells us, Nicholas, that pride goes before a fall, and a haughty spirit before destruction. Do not leave me – us – because of pride, do not make that mistake.'

He looked down at the crumpled letter. I had an uneasy feeling that if he did follow his pride and anger he would end badly, for there was a self-destructive element to his nature. There was silence for several seconds. Then a knock, and the door opened. Barak entered, not with a flourish but quietly. He, too, held something in his hand. He came up to the desk and laid a neat little stack of half-sovereigns on it. Nicholas looked at him.

'Done it, then, have they?' Barak asked roughly. 'Your parents?'

Nicholas answered thickly, with a dark look, 'Yes.'

'I feared they might. They – can do bad things, parents.' Nicholas did not answer. Barak said, 'I know all about it. But I know another thing, too. Money is money, wherever it's from. There's as much here as five poor men would earn in a year. Take it, spend it, put two fingers up to them.'

Nicholas met his gaze. Then slowly he nodded and reached out his hand to the money.

I said, 'You will stay?'

'For now, sir, while I think.'

Barak clapped him on the shoulder. 'That's a good lad. Come on then, work to do.' He gave Nicholas a weary, worldly grin, which, after a moment, the boy returned.

☦

ON SATURDAY, I HAD the first good news in some time, though even that was not unmixed. I was sitting in the parlour, pondering whether to invite Guy for dinner the following week. I had been heartened by the small steps towards reconciliation we had taken at the hospital, but still worried that he might refuse. There was a knock at the door and Agnes Brocket entered. She seemed full of suppressed excitement. I wondered if there had been better news of her son. But she said, 'Sir, Goodman Brown, Josephine's young man, has called. He asked if he might talk to you.'

I laid down my pen. 'Do you know about what?'

She took a step closer, clasping her hands. 'Sir, perhaps I should not say, but I always think it well for people not to be taken by surprise in important things. So — in confidence — he wishes to ask your approval to marry Josephine.'

I stared at her. I liked Brown; I was glad Josephine had found a swain, it had made her happier and more confident. But this was unexpected. I said, 'This is sudden. Josephine is not—'

She flushed with embarrassment. 'Oh no, sir, no, it is nothing like that.'

'But they have not been seeing each other long, have they?'

'Nearly four months now, sir.'

'Is it so long? I had forgot.'

'They have no plans for a hasty marriage,' Agnes said, a trifle reproachfully. 'But I believe they are truly in love, and wish to be betrothed.'

I smiled. 'Then show Master Brown in.'

The young man was nervous, but reassured me that he intended a six months' engagement. He said that his master would be glad to take Josephine into his home; currently he had no female servant. But then he added, 'He is retiring at the end of the year, sir. Moving his household to his family property in Norwich. He would like us to go with them.'

'I see.' So after Christmas I would probably not see Josephine again. I would miss her. I took a deep breath, then said, 'You have always struck me, Brown, as a sober young man. I know Josephine is very fond of you.'

'As I am of her.'

I looked at him seriously. 'You know her history?'

He returned my look. 'Yes, when I asked if she would marry me she told me all. I knew her father was a bullying brute, but not that he had stolen her from her family during one of the King's invasions of France.'

'He was a hard, brutal man.'

'She is very grateful to you for ridding her of him, and giving her a home.'

'Josephine needs gentleness, Master Brown, above all. I think she always will.'

'That I know, sir. And as you have been a kind master to her this last year, so I shall be a kind husband.' His face was full of sincerity.

'Yes, I think you will.' I stood and extended my hand. 'I give my consent, Goodman Brown.' As he shook my hand I felt a mixture of pleasure that Josephine's future was thus assured, coupled with sadness at the thought that she would be leaving. I remembered how her clumsiness and nervousness had irritated me when first she had come to my household. But I had seen that she was troubled, recognized her essential good nature, and determined to be kind.

Young Brown's face flushed with pleasure. 'May I go and tell her, sir? She is waiting in the kitchen.'

'Yes, give her the good news now.'

✝

LATER I JOINED the two of them in the kitchen, together with the Brockets and Timothy, to drink their health. Timothy looked astonished, and also distressed. How that boy hated change. It worried me. Agnes acted as hostess, dispensing wine which I had asked her to bring up from the cellar for the occasion. Even Martin unbent so far as to kiss Josephine on the cheek, though I think he noticed, as I did, her tiny flinch, and while the rest of us made merry conversation he stood a little apart. Josephine wept, and young Brown drew her to him. She wiped her eyes and smiled. 'I will try not to be one of those wives who weep at every excitement.'

'I know you will be the best and most obedient of wives,' her fiancé said quietly. 'And I shall try to be the best of husbands.'

I smiled; I knew Josephine was no Tamasin, whose strong nature demanded a relationship of equality with her husband, sometimes to the disapproval of others. Josephine had been brought up only to obey, and I suspected sadly that she would find anything other than a subordinate role in life frightening. I had a sense, though, that she would be a good mother, and that that might give her strength. I raised my glass. 'May your union be happy, and blessed with children.'

As the others raised their glasses to toast the couple, Josephine gave me a look of happiness and gratitude. I decided that I would, after all, write to Guy.

✝

THEY CAME FOR ME at dawn, as they often do. I was still abed, but wakened by a mighty crashing at the door. I got up and, still in my nightshirt, went out. I was not frightened but angry: how dare anyone bang so loudly on the door at this hour? As I came out onto the landing I saw Martin was already at the door, like me still in his night-clothes, pulling back the bolts. 'I'm coming,' he shouted irritably. 'Stop that banging, you'll wake the house—'

He broke off as, opening the door, he saw Henry Leach, the local constable, a solidly built fellow in his forties. Two assistants with clubs stood at his side, silhouetted against the summer dawn. As I walked downstairs my anger turned to fear, and my legs began to tremble. The constable held a paper in his hand. Leach had always been properly deferential before, bowing when I passed him on the street, but now he frowned solemnly as he held the paper up for me to see. It bore a bright red seal, but not the Queen's. This time it was the King's.

'Master Matthew Shardlake,' Leach intoned gravely, as though I were a stranger.

'What is it?' I was vaguely aware of Agnes and Josephine behind me, likewise roused from bed, and then Timothy ran round the side of the house into view; he must have been up attending the horses. He skidded to a halt when one of the constable's men gave him a threatening look. I took a deep breath of air, the clean fresh air of a bright summer morning.

Leach said, 'I am ordered by the Privy Council to arrest you on a charge of heresy. You are to appear before them tomorrow, and until then to be lodged in the Tower.'

Chapter Forty-two

L EACH TOLD ME to go and dress. 'I have been asked to search your house for forbidden books. I have a warrant,' he added and held up a second document.

'I have none.'

'It has been ordered.'

His assistant had grasped Timothy by the collar and, quite unexpectedly, the boy slipped out of his grip and ran at the constable, grabbing at the warrant. 'No! No! It is false! My master is a good man!'

Leach held the paper above his head, easily beyond Timothy's reach, while his assistant took the boy by the collar again, lifting him up in the air. He made a choking sound. The man set him on the ground, keeping a firm hold on his arm. 'Don't try anything like that again, lad, or I'll throttle you!'

I glanced at my other servants. Agnes and Josephine stood wide-eyed, clutching each other. 'I thought this hunting people out of their homes was over,' Agnes whispered. Martin looked on impassively.

Leach said to me, 'I will conduct the search while you dress.' His tone remained level, official, disapproving, though I sensed he was enjoying the opportunity to humble someone of my status. He did not meet my eye.

I let him in. On that score at least I had nothing to fear; I had burned all my newly forbidden books and there was nothing concerning the hunt for the *Lamentation* in the house. He sent one of his men upstairs with me to watch me as I dressed; my fingers trembled as I secured buttons and aiglets. I tried to calm myself and think. Who had done this, and why? Was this part of some new plot against Queen Catherine? When I had been imprisoned in the Tower of London five years before, on treason charges manufactured by Richard Rich, Archbishop Cranmer had rescued me; could the Queen save me now? I put on my summer robe, laid out as usual last night by Martin, and stepped to the door.

My servants were still standing in the hall, Josephine with her arm round a weeping Timothy. It was to her, not my steward, that I instinctively turned. I grasped her hand and said urgently, 'Go at once to Jack Barak's house and tell him what has happened. You remember where it is? You have taken messages there.'

Though her own hands were shaking she composed herself. 'I will, sir, at once.'

'Thank you.' I turned to the constable, trying to muster a shred of dignity. 'Then let us start, fellow. I take it we are to walk.'

'Yes.' Leach spoke severely, as though I were already convicted.

Martin Brocket spoke up then, in reproving tones. 'Master Shardlake should be allowed to ride. A gentleman should not be led through the streets of London like a common fellow. It is not fitting.' He seemed far more concerned by the breach of etiquette than the arrest itself.

'Our instructions are to bring him on foot.'

'There is no help for it, Martin,' I said mildly. I turned to Leach. 'Let us go.'

We walked through the streets; thankfully few people were out and about yet, though a few stared fearfully at us as we passed, Leach in his constable's uniform in front, a bulky armed fellow each side of me. The arrest of a gentleman, a senior lawyer, was a rare thing; it did no harm for it to be seen in public, a reminder that everyone, regardless of rank and status, was subservient to the King.

✝

WE ENTERED the Tower by the main gate. The constable left me with a pair of red-uniformed Tower guards, the edges of their halberds honed to razor sharpness, the rising sun glinting on the polished steel of their helmets. I remembered the twist of fear I had felt when I entered here a few weeks ago with Lord Parr, to see Walsingham. Now the fate dreaded by all, being brought here a prisoner, had befallen me again. The ground seemed to sway under my feet as they led me across the manicured lawn of the inner courtyard towards the White Tower. Far off I heard a roaring and yelping from the Tower menagerie; the animals were being fed.

I pulled myself together and turned to the nearest guard, an enormously tall, well-built young fellow with fair hair under his steel helmet. 'What is to happen now?' I asked.

'Sir Edmund wishes to see you.'

I felt a little hope. Walsingham was a friend of Lord Parr; perhaps I could get a message to him.

I was marched through the Great Hall, then upstairs. Sir Edmund was engaged and I had to wait nearly an hour in a locked anteroom overlooking the summer lawn, sitting on a hard bench trying to gather my scattered wits. Then another guard appeared, saying brusquely that Sir Edmund was ready.

The elderly Constable of the Tower sat behind his desk. He looked at me sternly, fingering the ends of his white beard.

'I am sorry to see you again in such circumstances, Master Shardlake,' he said.

'Sir Edmund,' I answered, 'I am no heretic. I do not know what is happening, but I must inform Lord Parr that I am here.'

He spoke impatiently. 'Lord Parr cannot interfere in this, nor anyone else. You are brought by the authority of the King's Privy Council, to answer questions from them. Lord Parr is not a member of the council.'

I said desperately, 'The Queen's brother, the Earl of Essex, is. And I was with the Queen but four days ago. I am innocent of all wrongdoing.'

Sir Edmund sighed and shook his head. 'I had you brought here to me first as a matter of courtesy, to tell you where you will be spending today and tonight, not to listen to your pleas. Leave those for the council. My authority comes from them, under the seal of Secretary Paget.'

I shut my eyes for a second. Walsingham added, in gentler tones, 'Best to compose yourself, prepare for the council's questions tomorrow. As for tonight, you will be held in a comfortable cell, together with the others who will answer accusations with you.'

I looked at him blankly. 'What others? Who?'

He glanced at the paper on his desk. 'Philip Coleswyn, lawyer, and Edward Cotterstoke, merchant.'

So, I thought, this is Isabel's doing. But her harebrained ravings were surely not enough to have us brought before the council. Then I remembered Philip's fears that he was already under suspicion, and that Edward Cotterstoke was also a radical. Walsingham continued, 'You may have food and drink brought. Is there anyone you wish to send for?'

'I have already sent word to my assistant that I am – taken.'

'Very well,' he said neutrally. 'I hope for your sake that you acquit yourself satisfactorily tomorrow.' He nodded to the guard and made a note on his paper, and I was led away.

✝

THEY TOOK ME BACK through the Great Hall, then again downstairs, to those dank underground chambers. The same loud clink of heavy keys, the same heavily barred door creaking open, and I was led by the arm into the central vestibule, where Howitson, the big man with the untidy straggling beard, sat behind his overlarge desk. The guards gave him my name and left me in his care. He looked at me, raising his eyebrows in puzzlement for a moment at the sight of a recent visitor returned as a prisoner, before quickly adopting the blank mask of authority again. I thought of the guard Myldmore, who from what Lord Parr had said would soon be smuggled out of the country. I wondered what Howitson made of his employee's disappearance.

He called for a couple of guards and two more men appeared from the direction of the cells. 'Master Shardlake, to be kept till tomorrow, to go before the council. Put him with the others in the special cell for prisoners of rank.'

I knew who had occupied that cell recently; Myldmore had told me. Anne Askew.

✝

I WAS LED DOWN a short, stone-flagged corridor. One of the guards opened the barred door of the cell, the other led me inside. The cell was as Myldmore had described it, with a table and two chairs, but this time there were three decent beds with woollen coverlets, not one – they must have put in the other two when they heard three were to be brought in. The chamber, though, held the clammy, damp stink of the dungeons, and was lit only by a high barred window. I looked at the bare flagstones and thought how Mistress Askew had lain there in agony after her torture.

Two men lay silent on the beds. Philip Coleswyn got up at once. He was in his robe; the shirt collar above his doublet untied, his normally neat brown hair and beard untidy. Edward Cotterstoke turned to look at me but did not rise. At the inspection of the painting I had marked his resemblance to his sister, not only physically but in his haughty, angry manner. Today, though, he looked frightened, and more than that, haunted. He was dressed only in his shirt and hose. From those protuberant blue eyes, so like Isabel's, he regarded me with a lost, hopeless stare. Behind me the door slammed shut and a key turned.

Philip said, 'Dear Heaven, Matthew! I heard you were being brought in. Isabel Slanning must have done this – '

'What have they told you?'

'Only that we are to appear before the Privy Council tomorrow, on heresy charges. I was taken by the constable at dawn, as was Master Cotterstoke.'

'So was I. It makes no sense. I am no heretic.'

Philip sat on the bed, wiping his brow. 'I know. Yet I – ' he lowered his voice – 'I have had reason to fear. But I have been careful not to speak heresy in public. Edward, too.'

'And your vicar? Has he spoken carelessly?'

'Not to my knowledge. If he had, surely he would have been arrested, too.'

I nodded at the sense of this. 'The only thing that connects the three of us is that wretched case.'

Edward, from his bed, spoke softly. 'Isabel has undone us all.' Then to my surprise he curled up his legs and lay hunched on the bed, like a child. It was a strange thing to see in a grown man.

Philip shook his head. 'I fear you have been caught up in this because of suspicions against me and Edward.'

'But Isabel's conspiracy charge is ridiculous, easily disproved! Surely we would not be hauled before the council on Isabel's word alone. Unless,' I took a deep breath, 'unless her complaint is being used by someone else, someone who wishes to see me undone.'

Philip frowned. 'Who?'

'I do not know. But Philip, I have been involved, perhaps against my better judgement, in matters of state. I could have enemies on the Privy Council. But friends, too, powerful friends. Why would I be attacked now?' My mind was in a whirl. Could this be the moment after all when whoever was the holder of the *Lamentation* had decided to expose it? And question me about the hunt to find it? I had never spoken with the Queen or Lord Parr about what we would do with the *Lamentation* should we recover it; but I knew Lord Parr would almost certainly have the book destroyed. To ensure the King never saw it.

'Listen.' I grasped his arm. 'Have you ever specifically denied the Real Presence of Christ's body and blood in the Mass to someone who might have reported it?' I spoke quietly, lest a guard be listening at the door.

Philip spread his arms wide. 'Given what has happened this summer? Of course not.'

'And you, sir – ' I turned to Edward, still curled up on his bed – 'have you said anything that could be dangerous? Have you kept forbidden books?'

He looked at me. 'I have spoken no heresy, and I handed in my books last month.' He spoke wearily, as though it did not matter.

I turned to Philip. 'Then we must cleave to that, and tell the council the accusations against us are false. If someone is trying to use Isabel's accusations to get at me, we must show them up as nonsense.' I remembered, my heart sinking, how Treasurer Rowland had avoided making an early appointment with me to discuss Isabel's accusations further. Had someone got to him?

Edward sat up, and with great weariness, as though his body were made of lead, leaned back against the stone-flagged wall. He said, 'This is the vengeance of the Lord. Isabel is his instrument. It was all foreordained. Given what I have done, I cannot be saved. I am damned. All my life has been a fraud. I have lived in pride and ignorance – '

I looked at Philip. 'What does he mean?'

Philip spoke quietly, 'Two days ago I confronted him with what the servant Vowell told us. He thinks this is a judgement on him. He told me that he did indeed kill his father.'

'So it was true.'

Philip nodded despairingly.

Then we all jumped at the sound of keys in the door. The guard held it open. I was overjoyed to see Barak step inside. Beside him, carrying a large bundle, was Josephine. She looked terrified. With them came Coleswyn's wife, Ethelreda, with whom I had dined that fateful evening when Isabel surprised us. She, too, was clutching a bundle. Her face looked ghastly, her hood askew. 'Ten minutes,' the guard said, and slammed the door on us.

Barak spoke, his gruff tone belying the worry on his face. 'So, you've landed yourself here again. Josephine insisted on coming. Nicholas wanted to come too, but I wouldn't let him. State he's been in, he'd probably break down and start crying like a big girl.'

'He'd come at you with his sword if he heard that,' I said. In the midst of this horror, Barak had made me laugh for a second. I turned to Josephine. 'Thank you for coming, my dear.'

She gulped. 'I – I wanted to.'

'I am grateful.'

'She insisted,' Barak said. 'Brought a great pile of food for you.'

'Does Tamasin know what has happened?'

'In her condition? You must be fucking joking. Thank God when Josephine came to the house she had the sense to ask to speak to me on her own; Tammy thinks there's some crisis on at chambers. What the hell's happening?'

'I don't know. Isabel – '

I broke off at the sound of an angry voice. Ethelreda was leaning over Edward Cotterstoke, berating him angrily. 'Answer me, sir. Why did you tell the Tower authorities your wife and children were not to be admitted under any circumstances? I have had your good lady at my house; she weeps and weeps, it is cruel.'

Edward answered in a miserable voice. 'It is best my wife and the children never see me again. I am an unclean thing.'

Ethelreda stared at him, then at her husband. 'Has he gone mad?'

Philip looked at his client sorrowfully. 'Leave him, my love.' He sat on the bed and pulled her down to sit beside him. They clung together.

I spoke to Barak, urgently. 'Listen, I want you to go to Whitehall Palace, get a message to Lord Parr.'

He answered impatiently, 'I've just come from there. I got a wherry as soon as Josephine brought the news. I knew that was what you'd want. But they wouldn't let me in. It's chaos at the Common Stairs, stuff being moved out by the boat-load, to Greenwich for when the King meets the admiral, and to Hampton Court where they're all moving afterwards.

They wouldn't even tell me whether Lord Parr was there.'

'The Queen – '

'I tried that one, too. The guards didn't want to know. All I got was, "The Queen is not here. The Queen is going to Hampton Court."' He took a deep breath. 'It strikes me your friends in high places have abandoned you.'

'No!' I answered fiercely. 'Lord Parr perhaps, but never the Queen. Besides, this matter could have implications for them. There's no rumour of anything having happened to the Queen, is there?' I asked anxiously.

'No.'

'Listen, I will write a message. Get it to the Queen's servant, Mary Odell.' I spoke feverishly. 'Find out whether she is at Whitehall still or Hampton Court, and get it to her. Tell the guards they will be in trouble with the Queen if the message does not reach her.'

Barak had brought quill and ink, anticipating my request. I scribbled a note explaining what had happened and addressed it to Mary Odell. 'Seal it at chambers,' I told Barak. 'They like a seal. But for God's sake, hurry.'

'I'll try,' he said, but his tone was not hopeful.

The guard opened the door again. 'Time's up,' he said brusquely. Barak and Josephine went out with Ethelreda; she was weeping, and Josephine, though trembling herself, supported her. The door slammed shut again.

✝

I SAT BESIDE Philip on his bed and looked at Edward. I feared the state he was in, what he might blurt out when brought before the council. He was sitting up now, his head bowed. I whispered to Philip, 'He told you he killed his stepfather?'

Philip nodded sadly. Edward had heard me, despite my

lowered voice, and looked up, still with that expression of despair. 'Yes, I killed him, a man who was guilty of nothing, and I must answer to God for it. I have hidden the truth from myself and the world for forty years, blamed Isabel for everything, but now the secret is discovered I must answer for it along with her. Somewhere in my heart I always knew this time would come.'

'What happened, Master Cotterstoke, all those years ago?' I needed to try and reach this shocked and devastated man.

He was silent a moment, then said quietly, 'Our father was a good man. Isabel and I were always quarrelling, but though it merely annoyed our mother, our dear father would always settle things between us, bring us round. He was our rock. When he died, the sorrow, for Isabel and me – ' He shook his head, fell silent.

'And then your mother married again?' I prompted.

'When our father had not been in his grave a year.' I heard a touch of the old anger in his voice now. 'Another few months and her belly was swelling with a new child. She fawned on Peter Cotterstoke, ignoring Isabel and me. How we hated him.' He looked at me. 'Have you brothers or sisters, sir?'

'No, but I have seen families broken by hatreds before. Too many times.'

Edward shook his head sadly. 'Children – their minds can encompass such wickedness, such depravity. We were sure Peter Cotterstoke would give everything to his new child and disinherit us. Though we had no evidence.' He shook his head. 'We started by doing little things, stealing possessions of his and destroying them. Sometimes the idea was mine, more often Isabel's.' He shook his head. 'We got bolder; we burnt a book he valued – in a field, dancing round the little fire we made, tossing in the illuminated pages one by one. We were wicked, wicked.'

'You were but children,' I said.

He looked back at me bleakly. 'We tried to poison him. Not to kill him, not then; just to make him sick. But he was ill, very ill. We thought we would be discovered, but he never suspected us.' He shook his head sorrowfully. But your mother did, I thought, and watched for her husband. But not close enough.

Edward went on in that flat, toneless voice. 'Always Isabel and I kept a mask of loving childishness before him, and he did not see through it. We used to giggle at his innocence. And then Isabel had the idea of killing him. To secure that inheritance, and gain vengeance. For depriving us – as we had persuaded ourselves – of our inheritance.' He closed his eyes. 'And for not being our dear father, whose place no man could take.' A tear coursed down Edward's lined cheek. In that house, I thought, there was no reminder of their real father save that wall painting, no one left whom they trusted, whom they could talk to. Some children make friends among the servants, but I guessed neither Edward nor Isabel had been that sort of child. They had driven each other slowly but steadily into a kind of madness.

Edward continued, 'We talked of all sorts of plans to kill him secretly, but could not think of one that might work. I truly believe I never intended to match the word to the deed, though perhaps Isabel did. Then that day on the wharf – Peter Cotterstoke looking out over the river, right on the edge of the wharf; Isabel whispering in my ear that now was our chance. The tide was full and the water cold, he would not be able to climb out. It took only one push from behind, and I was a big boy, tall for my age.' He lowered his head. 'Strange, it was only afterwards that we realized what we had done. Murder. Isabel took charge, decided we must say we had left our stepfather at the wharf.'

Philip said, 'And no one could prove otherwise.'

'And then – then we learned he had not planned to disinherit us at all.' Edward hid his face in his hands, his voice scarcely audible. 'Mother suspected, somehow. Afterwards she could not stand the sight of us, got both of us out of the house as soon as she could. She had no interest in my family, her grandchildren. And that Will she made – ' He broke off.

I said, 'Her revenge.'

He shook his head. 'Yes. I see it now. I never thought Vowell had guessed, even on the day of the inspection when he was so upset. I have been blind, blind for so long.' He made a fist of his hand and banged it against his forehead.

I said quietly, 'All these years, you and Isabel have blamed each other, because it was easier than facing the truth.'

Edward nodded dumbly. 'A truth too terrible to bear.'

'In a way, all this time you have still been conspiring together, each determined to avoid your share of the blame.' It was a strange, turnabout thought.

'After it was done, I blamed her for pressing me to do it, while she said she never intended me to actually push him, it was just play-acting. We ceased speaking. But, in truth, it was both our sin. Though I hid it even from the sight of the Lord when I came to true faith. But He knew, and now He has His just vengeance.'

I did not reply. At law, both Edward and Isabel were guilty of murder. An open confession from either would see both hang, even now. I thought of their mother, suspecting all these years what her children had done, unable to prove anything but hating them. I took a deep breath. 'What will you do now, Master Cotterstoke?'

He shook his head. 'I will confess. That is what the Lord commands.'

I spoke carefully. 'You understand that your being brought before the Privy Council has nothing to do with your stepfather. It is about heresy. If you have not spoken heresy, it may be that you and Brother Coleswyn are being used to get at me.'

He stared at me with genuine puzzlement. 'I thought this arrest was concerned somehow with – with what we did. Though, yes, they did say heresy. But I could not understand why we were brought here, why the Privy Council should be involved.' He frowned. 'Why would the Privy Council have an interest in you, sir?' I noted with relief that he looked attentive as well as puzzled. I had brought him back to the real world, at least for now.

'Because I have been involved in – political matters,' I said carefully. 'I may have made enemies on the traditionalist side.'

'Those rogues! Lost and condemned by God I may be now, but I am not so far fallen that I do not still revile those enemies of faith.' A look of angry pride appeared on his face.

'Then for all our sakes, Master Cotterstoke, when they ask you at the council tomorrow whether you have ever pub/licly condemned the Mass, tell them the truth, that you have not.'

'In my heart, I have.'

'It is what you *say* that could burn you. Keep your beliefs locked in your heart, I beg you.'

Philip nodded. 'Yes, Edward, he is right.'

'But what we did, Isabel and I – '

'Leave that until after, Edward. After.'

Edward's face worked as he thought. But then he said, 'If

I am asked about my stepfather's murder, I must tell the truth. But if I am not, I will say nothing.' He looked hard at Philip. 'Afterwards, though, I must pay for my sins.' I thought, he is a strong man, hard and tough like his sister. And indeed it must have taken a strange, perverted strength of mind for him and Isabel to each blame everything on the other, for forty years.

✝

AFTER THAT the hours hung heavy. Philip persuaded Edward to pray with him, and they spent a long time murmuring in the corner, asking God for strength, and afterwards talking of the possibility of salvation in the next world for Edward if he publicly confessed his crime. At one point they discussed Isabel's cleaving to the old ways in religion, and I heard Edward's voice rise again, calling her an obstinate woman with a cankered heart, in those cadences of self-righteousness and self-pity so familiar to me from the time I had spent with his sister. I thought, if Edward confesses, Isabel, too, is undone.

The barred window above us allowed a square of sunlight into the room, and I watched it travel slowly across the walls, marking the passage of the afternoon. Edward and Philip ended their talk, and Philip insisted we eat some of the food that our visitors had brought.

Evening was come and the square of light fading fast when the guard returned with a note for me. I opened it eagerly, watched by Philip and Edward. It was from Barak.

I returned to Whitehall, and managed to persuade the guard to admit me to the Queen's Presence Chamber. The Queen has left for Hampton Court, with most of her servants, Mistress Odell, too, it seems. Workmen were removing the tapestries, watched by some sort of female fool or jester with a duck on a leash; when the guard asked if she knew where Mistress Odell was she said Hampton Court, and when he said I brought a message from you she turned and made childish faces at me. I got the guard to ensure the note is forwarded. I am sorry, I could do no more.

Jane Fool, I thought, who had taken against me so fiercely. I put down the note. 'No news. But my message has been forwarded to – an important person.'

Edward looked at me with incomprehension, as though this were all happening to someone else; he had retreated inside himself again. Philip said nothing and lowered his head.

✝

IT WAS A LONG, long night. I slept fitfully, waking several times, tormented by fleas and lice that had been drawn from the bedding. I think Philip slept badly too; once I woke to hear him praying softly, too quietly for me to make out the words. As for Edward, the first time I woke he was snoring, but the next time I saw the glint of his open eyes, staring despairingly into the dark.

Chapter Forty-three

THEY SAT IN A LONG ROW behind a table covered with green velvet, six members of the King's Privy Council, the supreme body answerable to him for the administration of the realm. All wore the finest robes, gold chains and jewelled caps. Philip Coleswyn and Edward Cotterstoke and I were given seats facing them, the three Tower guards who had brought us in taking places behind us. My heart pounded as I thought, this was where Anne Askew had sat, and many others as well these last few months, to answer the same charge of heresy.

Sir Thomas Wriothesley, Lord Chancellor of England, waved a beringed hand in front of his face. 'God's death, they stink of the Tower gaol. I've said before, can people not be washed before they are brought here?' I looked at him, remembering his fear at Anne Askew's burning that the gunpowder round the necks of the condemned might hurt the great men of the realm when it exploded. Nor did I forget that he had tortured Anne Askew together with Rich. He caught me looking at him and glared at my presumption, fixing me with cold green little pebble eyes.

All the councillors had documents before them, but Sir William Paget, sitting at the centre of the table in his usual dark silken robe, had a veritable mound of paperwork. The square pale face above the long dark beard was cold, the thin-lipped mouth severe.

On Paget's left sat Wriothesley, then Richard Rich. Rich's face was expressionless. He had made a steeple of his slim white fingers and looked down, his grey eyes hooded. Next to him Bishop Stephen Gardiner, in cassock and stole, made a complete contrast. With his heavy build and powerful features, he was all force and aggression. He laid broad, hairy hands on the table and leaned forward, inspecting us with fierce, deepset eyes. The council's leading traditionalist, with his supporters Wriothesley and Rich beside him. I wondered if he had known of Anne Askew's torture.

Two other councillors sat to Paget's right. One I hoped was a friend: Edward Seymour, Lord Hertford, tall and slim, his face and body all sharp angles. He was sitting upright. I sensed a watchful anger in him and I hoped that if it emerged it would be to our advantage. Beside him sat a slim man, lightly bearded, with auburn hair and a prominent nose. I recognized the Queen's brother, William Parr, Earl of Essex, from my visit to Baynard's Castle. My heart rose a little on seeing him: he owed his place at the council table to his sister. Surely if she were in trouble today he would not be here. His presence made up a little for the absence of the figure I had hoped most of all to see – Archbishop Cranmer, counterweight to Gardiner. But Cranmer, whose attendance at the council was said always to be motivated by strategy, had stayed away.

Paget picked up the first paper on his pile. He ran his hard eyes over us, the slab face still expressionless, then intoned, 'Let us begin.'

✟

WE HAD BEEN brought to Whitehall Palace by boat. The Privy Council followed the King as he moved between his palaces, and I had thought we might be taken on to

Hampton Court, but apparently the council was still meeting at Whitehall. First thing that morning the three of us, red-eyed, tousled and, as Wriothesley noted, smelly, were led to a boat and rowed upriver.

At the Common Stairs there had been a great bustle, as Barak had described; servants were moving everything out. A little procession of laden boats was already sculling upriver to Hampton Court. I saw huge pots and vats from the royal kitchen being carried to one boat and thrown in with a clanging that reverberated across the water. Meanwhile a long tapestry wound in cloth was being lifted carefully into another waiting boat by half a dozen servants. A black-robed clerk stood at the end of the pier, ticking everything off on papers fixed to a little portable desk hung round his neck.

One of our guards said to the boatman, 'Go in by the Royal Stairs. It's too busy here.'

I looked at my companions. Philip sat composed, hands on his lap. He caught my eye. 'Courage, Brother,' he said with a quick smile. It was what I had said to him when he grew faint at Anne Askew's burning. I nodded in acknowledgement. Edward Cotterstoke stared vacantly at the great facade of polished windows, his face like chalk. It was as though the full seriousness of his position had only just sunk in.

The boat halted at the long pavilion at the end of the Royal Stairs, green-and-white Tudor flags fluttering on the roof. We climbed stone steps thick with the dirty green moss of the river, then a door in the pavilion was opened by a guard and we were led into the long gallery connecting the boathouse to the palace, fitted out with tapestries of river scenes. We were hustled along the full length of the pavilion, past more servants carrying household goods, then into the palace itself. We found ourselves in a place I recognized, the vestibule which formed the juncture of the Royal Stairs with three other sets of double doors, all guarded. I remembered that one led to the Queen's Gallery, the second to the Queen's privy lodgings and the third to the King's. It was the third door which was now opened to us by the guards. A servant carrying a decorated vase almost as large as himself nearly collided with me as he emerged, and one of our guards cursed him. We were marched quickly to a small door, the lintel decorated with elaborate scrollwork, and told we would wait inside until the council was ready. It was a bare little chamber stripped of furniture, but with a magnificent view of the gardens. A few minutes later an inner door opened and we were called into the council chamber itself.

✠

PAGET BEGAN BY getting each of us to confirm our names and swear on a Testament to tell the truth before God, as though we were in court. They had that power. Then he said, with a note of heavy reproval which, I suspected from long dealings with judges, was intended to intimidate us, 'You are all charged with heresy, denial of the Real Presence of the body and blood of Christ in the Mass, under the Act of 1539. What do you say?'

'Sirs,' I said, surprised by the strength in my own voice, 'I am no heretic.'

Philip answered with a lawyer's care, 'I have never breached the Act.'

Edward Cotterstoke closed his eyes and I wondered if he might collapse. But he opened them again, looked straight at Paget, and said quietly, 'Nor I.'

Bishop Gardiner leaned across the table, pointing a stubby finger at me. 'Master Shardlake uses words similar to those his former master Cromwell employed when he was arrested at this very table. I remember.' He gave a contemptuous laugh. 'Parliament found differently. And so may the City of London court, if we decide to send them there!'

Paget glanced at Gardiner, raising a hand. The Bishop sat back, scowling, and Paget said, more mildly, 'We have a couple of questions which apply only to you, Master Shardlake.'

He nodded to Wriothesley, who leaned forward, his little red beard jutting forward aggressively. 'I understand you were recently sworn to the Queen's Learned Council.'

'Yes, Lord Chancellor. Temporarily.'

'Why?'

I took a deep breath. 'To investigate the theft of a most precious ring from the Queen's chambers. Bequeathed to her majesty by her late stepdaughter, Margaret Neville.' I was horribly aware that I was lying through my teeth. But to do otherwise meant revealing what I had actually been looking for and causing grave danger to others. I glanced at Lord Hertford and William Parr. Neither returned my look. I swallowed and my heart quickened. I had feared the floor might seem to tremble and shake beneath me but it had not, yet.

'A rare and precious object,' Wriothesley said, a note of mockery in his voice. 'But you have not found it?'

'No, my lord. And so I have resigned my position.'

Wriothesley nodded, the little red beard bobbing up and down. 'I understand there have been several sudden vacancies in the Queen's household. Two senior guards, a carpenter, Master Cecil who now serves the Earl of Hertford. Most mysterious.' He shrugged. 'I wondered whether he was fishing or had just noted these changes and wondered if they were more than coincidence.

Then Richard Rich spoke, looking not at me but down at his clasped hands. 'Lord Chancellor, these domestic matters are not part of the accusations. Master Shardlake has advised the Queen on legal matters for several years.' Rich turned to look at Wriothesley. I realized with relief that his own involvement in my investigations meant it was in his interests to help me. Wriothesley looked puzzled by his intervention.

Gardiner knitted his thick black brows further, glowering at Rich. 'If this man – ' he waved at me – 'and his confederates are under a charge of heresy, any links to her majesty must surely concern this council.'

Lord Hertford spoke up suddenly, sharply. 'Should we not first find whether they are guilty of anything? Before turning to subjects the King wishes closed.' He emphasized his words by leaning over and returning Gardiner's fierce stare.

The Bishop looked set to argue, but Paget raised a hand. 'Lord Hertford is right. In the discussions over whether this matter should be included in today's agenda, we agreed only to ask these men whether they had breached the Act. The evidence before us relates solely to that question.'

'Flimsy as it is,' William Parr said. 'I do not understand why this case has been brought before us at all.'

I looked between them. Someone had wanted the charge of heresy against us to be put on the council agenda. But who? And why? To frighten me, assess me, to see me condemned? To try and get at the Queen through me? Which of them was accusing me of heresy? Gardiner was the most obvious candidate, but I knew how complicated the web of enmities and alliances around this table had become. I glanced quickly at my companions. Philip remained composed, though pale. Edward sat upright and attentive now, some colour back in his cheeks. Mention of the Queen had probably brought back to him what I had told him in the Tower, that this interrogation might concern the religious factions on the council. In this regard at least, whatever his dreadful turmoil of mind, Edward would try to serve the radical cause.

'Then let us get straight to the point,' Gardiner said reluctantly. 'First, have any of you possessed books forbidden under the King's proclamation? Philip Coleswyn?'

Philip returned his gaze. 'Yes, my Lord, but all were handed in under the terms of his majesty's gracious amnesty.'

'You, Edward Cotterstoke?'

He answered quietly, 'The same.'

Gardiner turned to me. 'But you, Master Shardlake, I believe you did not hand in any books.' So I had been right: they kept a list.

I said evenly, 'I had none. A search was made of my house when I was arrested yesterday morning, and nothing can have been found, because I had nothing.'

Gardiner gave a nasty little half-smile, and I wondered for a dreadful moment whether a forbidden book had been planted in the house; such things were not unknown. But he said only, 'Did you ever possess books forbidden under the Proclamation?'

'Yes, my Lord Bishop. I destroyed them before the amnesty expired.'

'So,' Gardiner said triumphantly, 'he admits he had heretical books that were not handed in. I know, Master Shardlake, that you were seen burning books in your garden.'

I stared at him. That was a shock. Only Timothy had been at the house that day, and he had been in the stables. Moreover he would never have reported it. I remembered his frantic anger when they had come to arrest me the day before. I answered quietly, 'I preferred to destroy them. The proclamation declared only that it was illegal to keep books from the list after the amnesty expired. And I have had none since before that date.'

Wriothesley looked at me. 'Burning books rather than handing them in surely indicates reluctance to draw your opinions to the attention of the authorities.'

'That is pure supposition. It was never said that a list would be kept.'

Paget gave a tight smile; he was a lawyer too, and appreciated this point, though Gardiner said scoffingly, 'Lawyer's quibble,' and glowered at me. I wondered, why this ferocious aggression? Did it betray his desperation to find a heretic linked to the Queen?

Lord Hertford leaned forward again. 'No, my Lord, it is not a quibble. It is the law.'

William Parr nodded agreement vigorously. 'The law.'

I looked along the row: enemies to the left of Paget; friends, I hoped, to the right. Paget himself remained inscrutable as he said, 'Master Shardlake has the right of it, I think. It is time we turned to the main matter.' He reached into his pile and pulled out some more papers, handing three sheets to each of us in turn across the table, his hard unblinking eyes briefly meeting mine. 'Members of the council have copies of these letters. They concern a complaint by a former client of Master Shardlake, Mistress Isabel Slanning, sister of Master Cotterstoke here. We have called her as a witness today.' He turned to one of the guards. 'Bring her in.'

One of the guards left. Edward's face twisted briefly; a horrible, tortured look. Gardiner, taking it for guilt, exchanged a wolfish smile with Wriothesley.

I looked at the papers. Copies of three letters. Isabel's original complaint to Rowland, accusing me of conspiring with Edward and Philip to defeat her case. A reply from

Rowland, short and sharp as I had expected, saying there was no evidence whatever of collusion, and pointing out that unsupported accusations of heresy were seriously defamatory.

It was the third letter, Isabel's reply, that was dangerous. It was dated a week before and was, by her standards, short.

Master Treasurer,

I have received your letter saying that my allegations of collusion between Master Shardlake, Master Coleswyn, and my brother, to defeat my just claims, are unsubstantiated. On the contrary, they are just, and the heresy of these men clear and patent. Master Shardlake, taking farewell of Master Coleswyn after going to his house for dinner, said in my hearing that the way to salvation is through prayer and the Bible, not the Mass. I am sending a copy of this letter to his majesty's Privy Council, so the heresy of these men may be investigated.

So that was why Rowland had been avoiding me: he wanted no association with matters of heresy if they became official. I had been concerned that Isabel had overheard Coleswyn's words on the night of the dinner. Yet she had misremembered or falsified what happened: that evening Philip had adjured me to pray and study the Bible, as the only sure path to salvation. I had made no reply. And neither of us had mentioned the Mass. What Philip had said marked him as a radical reformer but not a heretic; just as, from what I had been told was contained in the *Lamentation*, the Queen's views marked her. They were risky views to express, but not illegal. I frowned. Paget's office must receive a dozen such letters a week, written from malice by quarrelling family members, former lovers, business enemies. At most, the accuser would be questioned by an official from the council. Why indeed had such nonsense been brought here?

Another door opened and Isabel, dressed in her finery as usual, entered. Behind her came the tall, black-robed figure of Vincent Dyrick. He looked uneasy.

Edward stared at his sister, a long, unfathomable look. Isabel, whose expression a moment before had been haughty as always, seemed to quail a little at the sight of these great men. She glanced quickly at her brother, who only stared back at her stonily. Then she curtsied. Dyrick bowed, rising to look at the men behind the table, his eyes scared, calculating slits.

Hertford said bluntly, 'It is not customary for those brought before the Privy Council to be allowed lawyers.'

Paget answered firmly, 'Two of the accused are lawyers themselves. In the circumstances it is reasonable to allow the witness her legal representative.'

I looked at the Secretary, the King's Master of Practices; it was still impossible to discern whose side he was on. But someone had made a miscalculation if he thought Vincent Dyrick would help Isabel. He was obviously here under pressure; he was not a man who would willingly appear before such a powerful group to plead a pack of nonsense.

Paget addressed Dyrick. 'We have been discussing the correspondence. You have copies?'

'We do. And Mistress Slanning knows them by heart.' That I could imagine.

Paget grunted, and looked at Isabel. 'You say there was a conspiracy between these three men to cheat you, motivated by their being heretics?'

Isabel turned to Dyrick. 'You must answer yourself, mistress,' he said quietly.

She swallowed, then replied, hesitantly at first but with growing confidence. 'Master Coleswyn and my brother attend the same church, where the preacher is known to be radical. Coleswyn and Master Shardlake dine together, and once I heard them speaking heresy afterwards. And Master Shardlake knowingly chose an expert who would look at my painting and undermine my case.' She was speaking rapidly now. I wondered, could she actually believe what she was saying? I knew from experience how people could twist facts to suit what they wanted to believe, but this was a very dangerous forum for such self-delusion. She continued, 'Edward will do anything to thwart my case, he is wicked, wicked — '

Edward answered, quietly, 'No more than you.'

Paget glanced at him sharply. 'What is that supposed to mean?'

Philip spoke up. 'Only that the conflict between my client and his sister goes back to events when they were children.' Isabel's face took on an expression of fear as she realized that Philip had just referred obliquely to what she and Edward had done near half a century before — and that he might refer to it openly now. Her face paled, the wrinkled flesh seeming to sink. She looked terrified.

'And this expert?' Paget looked at Dyrick.

'His name is Master Simon Adam, an expert on house construction. My client says there are — rumours — that he may have radical sympathies.'

'More than rumours,' Isabel said boldly. 'A friend told me her servant knew the family — '

'That is third-hand hearsay,' I said flatly.

Isabel turned to Dyrick for support. He was silent. Edward Seymour said, 'Master Shardlake advised you to pick this Master Adam?'

Isabel hesitated, then said, with obvious reluctance, 'No. But I asked him for a list of experts. This man's name was first on the list. He put it first so I should pick it, I am sure.'

'Mistress Slanning insisted on my providing a list of

experts, and chose Master Adam against my advice.' Could she really be misremembering what had happened to this extent? Looking at her, I realized she could.

And then William Parr, Earl of Essex, did something which shifted the whole balance of the interrogation. He laughed. 'Sound choice,' he said. 'Nobody comes before Adam, not since the world began.'

Hertford and Rich laughed too, and a wintry smile lifted the corner of Paget's mouth. Isabel's face was like chalk. Gardiner, however, banged his fist on the table. 'This is no matter for levity. What of the heresy spoken among these men?'

Philip said, clear and steady, 'My Lords, there was no heresy. And it was not Master Shardlake who spoke the words referred to in Mistress Slanning's letter. It was I, as I took farewell of him at my door.' I gave him a glance of gratitude. 'And I did not mention, let alone argue against, the Real Presence.'

'Well, madam? Is that right?' Edward Seymour asked sharply.

Isabel looked genuinely confused. 'I thought – I thought it was Master Shardlake who spoke about the Bible, but it may have been Master Coleswyn. Yes, yes, I think it was.' For a second she looked embarrassed, but rallied. 'Either way, those were the words.'

'And the Mass?' Paget asked.

'I – I thought they said that. I am sure – I thought – ' Flustered, she turned to Dyrick, but he said flatly, 'You were there, madam, not me.' Isabel looked at him, helpless for once in her life. She began to tremble. It was known that Dyrick would take on anyone as a client, the more blindly aggressive the better. But Isabel Slanning had proved too wild a card even for him.

Then Rich said, his voice contemptuous, 'This woman is wasting our time.'

Gardiner glared at him again, then said to Philip, 'But you did speak those words about faith coming through study of the Bible, and prayer?'

'Yes. But that is no heresy.'

Blustering now, Gardiner went on, 'All know the King mislikes this endless talking over religion. As he said in his speech to Parliament last Christmas, though the Word of God in English is allowed, it is only to be used for men to inform their consciences.'

'And that is what Master Shardlake and I were doing, informing our consciences.' Philip looked at Isabel. 'Rather it is Mistress Slanning who makes light use of God's Word, to further her personal quarrels.'

He had spoken well, and left a silence behind him. After a moment Wriothesley said to him, 'You swear neither of you denied the Real Presence when you met?'

'I did not,' I answered.

'Nor I,' Philip said.

Paget looked at Isabel. 'What were you doing at Master Coleswyn's house that evening, Mistress Slanning? You were not at the dinner?'

She swallowed. 'I see it as my duty, when I suspect heresy, to watch and wait for it. That I may inform the authorities.'

'You spied on them,' Lord Hertford said flatly.

Paget leaned forward, his voice hard. 'Yet you did not see fit to inform the authorities of this alleged collaboration between heretics until the Lincoln's Inn Treasurer rejected your accusations.'

'I – I did not think at first. I was so angry at my brother's lawyer conspiring with mine – ' She looked at Edward, who stared at her strangely, his expression blank yet intense.

William Parr said, 'Is it not manifestly clear to all that this woman's claims are those of an ill-natured litigant – unfounded, motivated by mere spite – and that these men are guilty of nothing?'

Lord Paget looked between us, then inclined his head. 'Yes. I think it is. Mistress Slanning, you are a vicious and vexatious creature. You have wasted our time.' Isabel gasped, fighting now to control her emotions. Paget turned to us. 'Gentlemen, we will discuss this a little further between ourselves. All of you wait outside until council business is finished.' He made a signal to the guards and we were led away.

✝

WE WERE RETURNED to the room where we had waited before. As soon as the door was closed I spoke to Philip in heartfelt tones. 'Well done, and thank you. You answered well.'

He replied sorrowfully, 'One must speak more with the wisdom of the serpent than the innocence of the dove, where matters of faith are concerned. Jesus Christ said so.' He looked at me. 'Do you think we will be released now?'

'I have every hope. Isabel made a fool of herself. We are lucky I have friends on the council, and Rich has his own reasons not to see me brought down. Paget, too, seemed won over to our side.'

'Yes.' He frowned. 'Gardiner and Wriothesley would have taken the chance to examine us further about our beliefs, which for me at least would have been – a concern.'

Edward had sat down on the windowsill, his back to the magnificent view of the river, and put his head in his hands. I said to him, 'You did well too, sir.'

He looked up. It was as though all the energy had drained

from him once more; he seemed again the exhausted, tormented figure of the day before. He spoke quietly, 'You told me I must stand firm, lest they use these allegations to build a case against the Queen's friends. But now it is over – the other matter remains: what Isabel and I did.' He looked at Philip. 'And I know I must pay.'

Before Philip could answer, the door opened. Richard Rich entered. He looked at Philip and Edward, who stood hastily. 'You two,' he snapped, 'outside. Wait in the corridor with the guards. I want to talk to Shardlake.'

Philip and Edward did as he ordered. Rich pushed the door shut and turned to me. His face wore a strange expression, half-admiring, half-angry. 'Well, Master Shardlake, you got out of that one. With my help. It was a strange thing to give it, sitting between Wriothesley and Gardiner, who, knowing our history, thought I would be glad to see you burned.' He laughed mirthlessly. 'A strange feeling.'

I looked back at him. He deserved no thanks, for like Dyrick he had sought only to protect his own skin. I kept my voice low. 'Who wanted that matter brought before the Council, Sir Richard? Normally such a silly accusation would surely not have gone there? And why? Was it to do with the Queen? Gardiner said—'

Rich waved a hand dismissively. 'Gardiner seizes every chance that comes his way to take a tilt at the Queen. He's wasting his time; he should realize by now that ship has sailed.' Rich took off his cap, revealing his thick grey hair. 'But you are right about it being silly, and I have been trying to find out who pressed for it to be included on the council agenda. I was not consulted. Paget decides, on the basis of advice from many quarters. I dare not press the matter too closely.' His thin face was momentarily pinched with worry, reminding me how he had looked at Anne Askew's burning. How he must dread her book appearing on the streets.

'So it could have been anybody?'

'Gardiner, Wriothesley, the Duke of Norfolk, though he was not present today – anyone – ' His voice rose angrily. 'Lord Hertford, for all I know. He and his brother Thomas were with Paget yesterday, and shouting was heard, I know that.'

'But Hertford is on the reformist side. He helped me.'

'He seemed to, I grant you. But on the council people may take one line in public and another in private.' Rich's voice lowered to an angry whisper. 'The Parrs and Seymours would both like the Regency of little Edward when the King dies, and Seymour and his brother quarrel constantly. Sir Thomas Seymour thinks he should have a place on the Privy Council, but the King knows he has not the ability. More knives are sharpened every week.' He gave me a look of hatred. 'And as for my private feelings, do not think I will help you again, crookback. Unless it is in my own interest. I *would* gladly see you burned. And watch with pleasure.'

I smiled wryly. 'I have never doubted that, Sir Richard.'

'Then we understand each other.' He bit off the words. 'Now, the council says you can go, the guards will take you out.' Then, with those grey eyes burning, he said, 'You have been lucky. If you have any sense left you will keep well away from here. Do not think the time of crisis is over.' Then, in an undertone – more to himself than me – he added, 'Of late sometimes I have wished I, too, could run like a rabbit.'

Chapter Forty-four

W E WERE LED to the Common Stairs. The guards got into their boat, leaving us in the midst of all the removals. As a large, ornate cabinet was heaved out of the door by four men a drawer fell open and a little mouse jumped out onto the landing stage. It stood for a moment in the forest of legs, not knowing where to run, till someone saw it and kicked it into the river.

I managed to hail a passing wherry. We sculled down-river, away from Whitehall; I hoped for ever. The three of us sat in silence, still recovering from our ordeal. I noticed a tear on Edward's cheeks: he was weeping, silently. The boatman looked between us curiously.

I spoke quietly to Philip. 'Can you look after him?'

'I will take him to my home, do what I can.' He looked sadly at his client. 'Will you come with me, Edward?'

Edward looked at him. 'Yes,' he whispered. 'I know what must be done now.' He shook his head in anguish. 'The disgrace, the disgrace to my wife and children.'

'We can talk about that later. When you are rested. About what God requires of you.'

He shook his head violently. 'I shall never rest again. I do not deserve it.'

I said to Philip, 'I must go to my house.' I needed to speak to Timothy; I could not imagine that he had betrayed me, but I must know.

We rounded the bend in the river. In the distance, past the riverside houses and the docks, the square solid shape of the Tower was visible. I turned away.

✝

I FOUND TIMOTHY at his accustomed place in the stables, sitting on an upturned pail eating bread and cheese. He jumped up as I entered, astonishment and relief on his face. 'Sir! Thank the Lord you are back! We thought you—' He broke off.

I stood, weary and dishevelled, looking down at him. 'I am released,' I said quietly.

'We none of us knew why – '

'I have been questioned by the King's Privy Council. Do you know how serious that is?'

'All know that,' he answered quietly.

'It was, among other things, about an allegation that I owned forbidden books.'

Timothy stepped backwards, his eyes widening, and my heart sank as I began to believe that, after all, he had given me up. But I kept my voice low. 'Do you remember an afternoon, about three weeks ago, when Martin and Agnes and Josephine were out? I told you to turn visitors away, as there was something I needed to do.'

He backed away another step, up against the wall. He looked frail and thin, his arms and legs like twigs. Genesis looked round, sensing something strange between us. I asked, 'Did you watch me that afternoon, Timothy? Did you see what I did in the garden?'

The boy nodded, misery on his face. 'You burned some books, sir. I came into the house and watched you, from a window. I know I shouldn't have, but I – I wondered what was so secret, sir.'

'There is a surfeit of secrets in this world,' I said, angrily now. 'And stable-boys spying on their masters can cause grave trouble. Had you heard of the King's proclamation?'

He looked frightened. 'What proclamation, sir? I know only that all must obey his commands.'

'He recently made a proclamation forbidding ownership of certain books. I had some, and that was what I burned. In the garden, that day.'

'I – I didn't know they were forbidden, sir.'

Standing there, the boy looked pathetic. And the thought came to me, he is but thirteen, and thirteen-year-olds are nosy. I asked, very quietly, 'Who did you tell, Timothy?'

He hung his head. 'Nobody, sir, nobody. Only when Master and Mistress Brocket came back, Mistress Brocket said something had been burned in her vegetable garden, it looked like papers. Master Brocket went and stirred them round, brought back a few unburned pieces. I was in the kitchen. I saw him. He knew I had been alone here that afternoon, sir, and he asked who had been burning papers. He said he would strike me if I lied, so I told him it was you.'

'Martin,' I said heavily. So, Josephine had been right about him all along. And he was not just a thief, he meant to do me harm. 'You let me down, Timothy,' I said sternly. 'I shall talk with you again. But first,' I added grimly, 'I must speak to Martin.'

He called after me, 'I didn't mean for anything to happen to you, sir, I swear. If I had known you might be arrested –' His voice rose to a howl behind me as I walked away to the house.

✞

MARTIN BROCKET was in the dining room, polishing the silver, running a cloth round a large dish which had belonged to my father. He regarded me, as usual, with cold eyes and a humble smile. 'God give you good afternoon, sir.' Evidently he had decided, with deferential tact, not to refer to my arrest at all.

'Put that down, Martin,' I said coldly. The shadow of an emotion, perhaps fear, crossed his face as he laid the silver dish back on the table. 'I have been talking to Timothy. Apparently the boy told you he saw me burning books in the garden.'

I discerned only the slightest hesitation, then Martin answered smoothly, 'Yes, sir. Agnes saw the burned papers and I asked Timothy about it. I thought he might have been up to mischief.'

'Somebody has,' I answered flatly. 'I was questioned about those burned books at the Privy Council this morning.'

He stood stock-still, the cloth still in his hands. I continued, 'Nobody knew what I had done, save the friend who was questioned with me.' Still Martin stood like a statue. He had no answer. 'Who did you tell?' I asked sharply. 'Who did you betray me to? And why?'

He laid the cloth on the buffet with a hand that had suddenly begun to tremble. His face had paled. He asked, 'May I sit down?'

'Yes,' I answered curtly.

'I have always been a faithful servant to my employers,' he said quietly. 'Stewardship is an honourable calling. But my son – ' his face worked for a moment – 'he is in gaol.'

'I know that. I found Agnes crying one day.' He frowned at that, but I pressed him. 'What has that to do with what you did?'

He took a deep breath. 'Rogue though I know my son John is, I feared he might die for lack of food and care in that

584

gaol if I did not send him money, and I could only get him out of it by paying off his debtors.' His eyes were suddenly bright with anguish and fear.

'Go on.'

'It was in early April, not very long after Agnes and I came to work for you. John had had a fever of the lungs in that vile place last winter, and nearly died. We were at our wits' end.'

'You could have come to me.'

'It is for me to care for Agnes and John – me!' Martin's voice rose unexpectedly, on a note of angry pride. 'I would not go running to you, my master, soft though I saw you were with Josephine and the boy.' There was a note of contempt in his voice now. There, I thought, that was why he disliked me. He had an iron view of the place and responsibilities of servants and masters. It had led him to betray me rather than ask for help.

He pulled himself together, lowering his voice again. 'I had arranged to have what money I could scrape together delivered to John in prison by a merchant of Leicester who travels between there and London, and who knew my story.' He took a long breath. 'One day, as I was leaving his London office, a man accosted me. A gentleman, a fair-haired young fellow wearing expensive clothes.'

I stared at him. 'Was he missing half an ear by chance?'

Martin looked startled. 'You know him?'

'Unfortunately I do. What name did he give?'

'Crabtree.'

'That is not his real name. What did he say?'

'That he was an acquaintance of the merchant, had heard of my son's trouble and might be in a position to help. I was puzzled. I know there are many tricksters in the city, but he was well-dressed and well-spoken, a gentleman. He took me to a tavern. Then he said he represented someone who would pay well for information about you.'

'Go on.' Martin closed his eyes, and I shouted, 'Tell me!'

'He wanted me to report your movements generally, but especially if you had any contact with the Queen's household. Or any radical reformers.' He bowed his head.

I persisted. 'And this was in April?'

'Yes. I remember the day well,' he added bitterly. For the first time he looked ashamed.

I ran my hands through my hair. Stice, the servant of Richard Rich who I had reluctantly worked with, had been spying on me since the spring. But as I thought it through, it began to make sense. April was when the hunt for heretics linked to the Queen was getting going. Rich knew I had worked for her; if he was able to link me to religious radicals, he might be able to incriminate her by association. This could have been a small part of his and Gardiner's campaign to destroy her. But of course he would have found nothing. Then, after the campaign against the Queen failed in July, and Rich found me hunting for Greening's murderers – and, as he thought, Anne Askew's book – he could easily have switched from spying on me to using me.

Yet it did not add up: I had not burned my books till the end of July, when Stice and I were already working together, and if it was actually Rich who brought that matter to the Privy Council, then why had he helped me today, when it was likely to bring him into bad odour with Gardiner? But the paths Rich followed were so sinuous, it could all still be part of some larger plan. I had thought him sincere this morning, but Rich could never, ever be trusted. I had to talk this through with Barak.

Martin was looking at me now, a twitch at the corner of his mouth. 'Crabtree gave me the money I needed to start to pay down the debts. But only little by little, and all the while the interest was mounting. Agnes, she was at the end of her tether.'

'I know.'

'And Crabtree kept demanding information.' Brocket looked at me in a sort of desperate appeal. 'I was bound to him, he could expose what I had done, if he chose.'

'That is the problem with being a spy. Where did you meet?'

'In a house, a poor place, barely furnished. I think it was used for business.'

'In Needlepin Lane?'

He shook his head. 'No, sir, it was at Smithfield, hard by St Bartholomew's Hospital.'

'Exactly where?'

'In a little lane off Griffin Street. Third house down, with a blue door and a Tudor rose above the porch.'

It did not surprise me that Rich kept more than one place for secret meetings. He owned half the houses round St Bartholomew's.

'I suppose Agnes and I must go now, sir,' Martin said quietly.

'I take it she knows nothing of this.'

'No, sir. She would not have let me do it. She would have argued, it would have upset her mightily – women, they do not understand the hard necessities men can be driven to.' He attempted a quick half-smile, man to man, as though we could at least agree on the vagaries of women. I stared back at him coldly. Though he recognized how dishonourably he had behaved, he had still not apologized. And he had disliked me from the beginning, as I disliked him. That made the next thing I said easier.

'You will not leave yet, Martin. The game is not quite played out. A game involving the highest in the realm, which your betrayal has involved you in. When did you last meet Crabtree?'

He began to look worried. 'Last Wednesday. I meet him once a week at the house near St Bartholomew's, to give him what information I have. If there is urgent intelligence I am to leave a message that I wish to see him at a tavern nearby. I did that when I learned you had been burning books.' He had the grace to lower his head as he said that.

'For now you will say and do nothing. We shall go on apparently as before. I may need you to go to the tavern with a message, I do not know yet.'

He looked seriously worried now. 'Could Agnes and I not just leave now?'

'No. And if you go before I say you can, I will ensure you never work again. Now, I have to send a message to Hampton Court.'

Martin looked frightened. He must have realized Stice was connected to the heresy hunt, that politics was involved, but he had doubtless preferred not to think about it. 'Is that understood?' I asked sternly.

'Yes, sir. I will do as you command.' He took a deep breath, and before my eyes his face composed itself into its normal expressionless mask. He rose from his chair, a little shakily, and took up the silver bowl.

✞

MY APPOINTMENT with Rowland was for two o'clock, and it was almost that now. My stomach rumbling with hunger, I left the house and walked down to Lincoln's Inn. When I was shown into his chamber the Treasurer was sitting behind his desk as usual. He smiled at me, quite unashamed. 'So the Privy Council let you go, Brother Shardlake?'

'Yes. They recognized Mistress Slanning's accusations for the rubbish they were.'

He inclined his beaky head, stroking the ends of his long beard. 'Good. Then the matter is over, with no disgrace to Lincoln's Inn. Secretary Paget sent a message asking me not to see you before today.' He smiled. 'They like to do that, ensure that the people to be brought before them have no advance warning.' My anger must have shown in my face, for he added, 'Take care what you say next, Brother Shard/lake. Do not abuse me as you did once before: remember who I am.'

I replied quietly, 'I know exactly who you are, Master Treasurer.' He glared at me with his flinty eyes. 'As the Slan/ning matter is over,' I continued, 'I take it there is nothing more to discuss. Except that, in light of my arrest, I presume someone else will attend the ceremonies to welcome the admiral later this week.'

Rowland shook his head. 'You do presume, Brother Shardlake. The message from Secretary Paget was that if your appearance before the council led to your arrest for heresy I should find a substitute, but if you were released you should still attend. They want someone of serjeant rank and you are the only one in town, except old Serjeant Wells, who is entering his dotage and would probably turn up on the wrong day. So you will attend as planned, starting with the parade through the city on Friday. I take it you have the requisite robes and chain.'

'The robes, no chain. Who can afford a gold chain these days?'

He frowned. 'Then get one, Serjeant, in the name of Lincoln's Inn, which you will be representing.'

I could not resist one piece of insolence. 'Perhaps the Inn could provide me with one. After all, it has recently acquired the late Brother Bealknap's estate. You will have his chain, surely.'

'Gone to the Tower mint to be melted down like the rest of his gold,' Rowland snapped. He waved a hand. 'Now, that is enough, Brother.' He pointed a skinny, inky finger at me. 'Get a chain. And a shave as well. You look a mess.'

✝

I NEEDED TO GET the news about Brocket to Lord Parr as fast as possible, but I was hungry, and exhausted already. As I crossed the square to the refectory I realized both my hands were clenched tight into fists. Timothy's stupidity, Brocket's betrayal and Rowland's insouciant rudeness had left me in a state of fury.

Feeling a little better for my meal, I went into chambers and asked Barak and Nicholas to come to my room. From the expression on Nicholas's face Barak had told him about my arrest. When the door was closed behind us Barak said, 'Thank God you're out.'

'No reply to the message you took?'

'Nothing.'

I sat looking at him. It hurt that those I had served seemed to have abandoned me. The Queen most of all. I said, 'Well, I must get another message to Hampton Court now. Something else has happened. It had best go direct to Lord Parr.'

'Perhaps it might be better for me to take this one,' Nicholas said. 'The guards there may have instructions to hold Jack off; another messenger may get through more easily.'

I looked at him; the boy seemed himself again, after the

dreadful hurt his father's letter had caused. Yet I sensed a new sadness and seriousness in him.

Barak nodded agreement. 'God's blood, Nick boy, you're learning the ways of politics fast.' He gave him a mocking look. 'So long as it's not just a chance to see all the ladies inside Hampton Court.'

He answered quietly. 'On my oath, after what has just happened to Master Shardlake, I have no wish to step into a royal palace.'

'Thank you, Nicholas,' I said. There was still loyalty in chambers at least, and my spirits rose a little.

'But what happened at the council?' Barak asked.

I told them about my appearance there, Rich's unexpected help, and Martin's disloyalty, concluding with my encounter with Rowland. I asked ruefully, 'Has either of you a spare gold chain you don't need?'

'Rowland's an arsehole,' Barak said. 'The way he cheated Bealknap, it almost makes me feel sorry for the old rogue.' He looked at Nicholas. 'If you make a career in the law, be sure you don't turn out like either of them.'

Nicholas did not reply. I studied him. What would he do when his period with me came to an end in a few months? Run for the hills, if he was wise. But I hoped he would not.

'So you still have to go to the ceremonials?' Barak said. 'I'm going with Tamasin to see the admiral arriving at Greenwich on Friday. She insisted.'

'I should like to see that,' Nicholas said.

'I wish it were all over, these ceremonies that I must attend.' I looked at him. 'Try all you can to get the message through that I am about to write. It may be possible, now, to set up a meeting between Brocket and Stice at the house and then grab Stice. We may be able to find out exactly what Rich has been doing.'

Barak raised his eyebrows. 'How? He won't willingly betray his master. He's not some youngster who got himself involved with crazy Anabaptists, like Myldmore and Leeman.'

'I'll leave that to Lord Parr,' I answered grimly.

He looked at me askance. 'I quite agree; but that's a bit ruthless for you, isn't it?'

'I have had enough.'

'What is Rich up to? We all thought he'd changed tack after the heresy hunt ended and Anne Askew's book was taken. That he was helping you. But it was him, through Stice and Brocket, who reported your burning those books.'

'Rich can never be trusted. And yet I can't see either why he would report my burning the books to the council now. It was risky, I could have spilled the truth about Anne Askew.'

'Rich always turns with the political wind, doesn't he?'

'Yes. He started as Cromwell's man.'

'What if this was a double-bluff? Rich gets the matter onto the council agenda along with the Slanning complaints because he knew that your burning the books wasn't illegal, and that the Slanning charges were all shit?'

'Why would he do that?' Nicholas asked.

'Because he is turning with the tide towards the reformers,' Barak answered excitedly. 'The whole performance could have been intended to show a shift of loyalty on his part, by siding with Lord Hertford and the Queen's brother.'

'That sounds too devious to be credible,' Nicholas said doubtfully.

'Nothing is too devious for those courtiers,' I replied vigorously. 'But the problem with that idea is that Rich knew nothing of the Slanning case. He didn't know Isabel would have no evidence and make a fool of herself as she did. And he seemed genuinely worried afterwards.' I sighed. 'Only

Lord Parr can help to sort this out. And he ought to be told about it.'

Barak said, 'The Queen's brother will have told him.'

'Not the whole story.'

'What role is Secretary Paget playing in all this?' Nicholas asked. 'They say he is the King's closest adviser.'

'No: his closest *servant*. There is a difference. He is the King's eyes and ears, the ringmaster, if you like. From all I understand, he never challenges the King over policy. He remembers Wolsey and Cromwell too well.' I smiled wryly. 'He is the Master of Practices, not Policy.'

'He must have an eye to the future; when the King is no longer here.'

'Well said,' Barak agreed. 'He'll be looking out for his own interest; he'll no doubt jump to whichever faction is most likely to win.'

'He is like all of them,' I said angrily. 'He will do anything to anybody. And people like me are the pawns, useful in the game but dispensable. And now, Nick, smarten yourself up a little, while I write this letter.'

✝

I DID NO WORK FOR the remainder of that afternoon. After sending Nicholas with the message, I went out and sat in the shade on a bench under an old beech tree, occasionally nodding to colleagues who passed by. Nobody, thank God, knew I had been in the Tower a second time, though doubtless the news would get out, as it always did. Exhausted, I closed my eyes and dozed. After a time I heard something fall onto the bench beside me and, opening my eyes, saw it was a leaf, dry and yellow-tinged. Autumn would soon be here.

I turned at the sound of someone calling my name. John

Skelly was running towards me. I stood. It was too early for a reply from Hampton Court. 'Master Coleswyn has called to see you, sir,' he said as he came up. 'He seems agitated.'

I sighed. 'I will come.'

'I thought you no longer represented Mistress Slanning, sir. I thought your involvement in that case was over.'

I said with feeling, 'I wonder, John, if that case will ever end.'

But it was about to, and for ever.

Chapter Forty-five

P HILIP WAS WAITING in my office. He looked haggard. 'What has happened?' I asked breathlessly. 'Not more accusations?'

It was more a tremor than a shake of the head. 'No, not that.' He swallowed. 'Edward Cotterstoke is dead.'

I thought of the desperate figure in the boat that morning. Edward was not young, and the last few days had turned his world upside down. 'How?'

Philip took a deep breath, then started to sob. He put a clenched fist to his mouth, fought to bring himself under control. 'By his own hand. I took him home, fed him and put him to bed, for he seemed at his last gasp. He must have taken the knife from the kitchen. A sharp one.' He shuddered, his whole solid frame trembling. 'I went to see how he was, two hours ago, and he had slit his throat, from ear to ear. It must have taken great force.' He shook his head. 'There is blood everywhere, but that is the least of it. His soul, his soul. He was in great torment, but such a sin . . .' He shook his head in despair.

I remembered Cotterstoke's words on the boat, talking of the disgrace that confessing to his stepfather's murder would bring his family. He had said he knew what had to be done. I said, 'He felt he deserved death for what he did, and believed he was damned anyway; he did not want his family to suffer.'

Philip laughed savagely. 'They will suffer now.'

I answered quietly, 'Suicide is a terrible disgrace, but less than murder. His family will not see him hang, nor will his goods be distrained to the King.'

'There could have been some other way; we could have talked about it, talked with our vicar. This is – is not – sane.'

'After what had just happened to him, anyone might lose their reason. Perhaps God will take account of that.'

✝

A REPLY FROM Hampton Court arrived just as I was going to bed. Martin brought it up, his expression a deferential mask as usual. I examined the Queen's seal carefully in the privacy of my room, to ensure it was unbroken, before opening it. The letter was from Lord Parr:

Matthew,

Forgive my not replying to your earlier messages: there has been much to do, with the move to Hampton Court and the arrangements for the admiral's coming, and also I have been ill. Furthermore, Jane Fool told the guard your first message was not urgent; out of spite against you, I think. I have seen that she is well punished for it, despite the Queen and the Lady Mary's softness towards her.

Neither I nor the Queen knew you were to appear before the Privy Council; Paget kept that to himself, though the Queen's brother told me afterwards. We do not know who pressed to have the matter brought there; thank heaven the Slanning woman made a fool of herself, and Rich had motive to speak on your behalf.

Regarding your faithless steward, yes, keep him on for now. But other than that, do nothing. I will have the house you mentioned watched.

I will write further, and we may see each other at the ceremonies.

By the way, your boy, the messenger, did well. He was gentlemanly and polite, which is not always true of your other man.

I felt relieved as I laid down the letter. Lord Parr's tone was friendly; the observation about Barak made me smile. The Queen and her uncle had not, after all, abandoned me. The story about Jane Fool rang true. I wondered, not for the first time, whether she was a fool of any sort at all, or merely a woman who had found a profitable role in pretending it.

✝

NEXT DAY WAS the 17th, only three days before the admiral's arrival at Greenwich, and I still needed a gold chain. I went to a shop in the goldsmith's quarter, one of the smaller ones, guarded outside by a large man ostentatiously bearing a club. Barak accompanied me. Asking around on my behalf, he had discovered the service this shop provided.

Inside, another man was posted beside an inner door. The owner, a stout elderly fellow, came over and gave me a deep bow. 'God give you good morrow, sir.'

'And to you. I require a gold chain; I have to be at the ceremony welcoming the French admiral on Saturday.'

'Ah yes, his progress through the city. It has brought some good business.' He looked me over professionally. 'A lawyer, sir? Is that a serjeant's coif you wear?'

'Well observed.'

'It is the nature of my business, to judge who people are. You should buy a good long chain, with thick links.' He smiled unctuously.

'I look only to rent one, for a week.'

The man stared. 'Rent?' He shook his head. 'People are expected to wear their own chains on such an occasion, of a size in accordance with their status. To rent one — ' he shook his head sadly — 'that might be thought shameful among your colleagues, if it got out.'

'So it would,' I agreed. 'That is why I asked my clerk here to find a goldsmith who rented chains discreetly.'

'Best look one out and save time,' Barak told the gold smith cheerfully. 'I know you rent them for a good price.'

That got the goldsmith moving: he went into the back room and returned with a heavy chain with large, solid links. It was a little dirty, but gold is easily cleaned. I wrote a note confirming receipt, paid over a half sovereign as deposit, and asked Barak to put the chain in his knapsack.

'Don't you want to wear it?' he asked mockingly.

'Not till I have to.'

☦

I HAD AGREED to go down to Greenwich with Barak, Tamasin and Nicholas on Friday, to watch Admiral d'Anne bault's arrival. He would be welcomed by the King and stay the night at Greenwich Palace before his procession through London on Saturday. Going to see this would help me get used to it all, before playing my, mercifully small, part later.

The four of us met at Temple Stairs. There were many people waiting for wherries and tilt boats to take them down river; mostly family groups in their best clothes, for the day had been declared a public holiday. One young man stood alone, his expression grave; he had only one leg and stood on crutches. I wondered if he had been a soldier in the war.

Our turn came and a tilt boat, with a white canopy to shield us from the sun, took us down the busy river. Even the boatman was dressed cheerfully, a garland of flowers in his cap. Tamasin sat under the canopy with Barak, Nicholas and me on the bench opposite, Nicholas wearing a broad hat against the sun. I had on my robe, but no chain.

Tamasin looked cheerfully out over the brown water. 'I wonder if we shall get close enough to see the King. They distributed a leaflet giving the details. He will be on the royal barge just below Greenwich, and the admiral's barge will pull up beside it for the King to welcome him aboard.'

I looked at her. Her time of sickness was over and she was blooming. She wore the dress she had worn at George's birthday, yellow, with a bonnet, a little ruby brooch at her breast. She met my gaze and leaned over, putting her hand on mine. 'I know this will be hard for you, sir, after last year. Forgive my enthusiasm, but I do not see much spectacle.'

'While I see too much. But no, Tamasin, enjoy the day.'

The river turned south, past the Isle of Dogs. The path winding around it was filled with people of the poorer classes, walking down to watch the admiral's arrival. Beyond the muddy path was marshy woodland dotted with vegetable gardens that cottagers had set up, their shacks in the middle. Guard dogs tied to posts barked furiously at all the passers-by.

Greenwich Palace, built by the King's father as a symbol of the new Tudor dynasty, came into view, with its splendid facade and pointed towers. Boats were pulling into the bank on both sides of the river, passengers disembarking and walking on to get as close as possible to the palace. Our boat pulled in to the left-hand bank. Beside the palace I saw a great barge at anchor, brightly painted in Tudor green and white, an enormous English flag flying from the prow. A dozen liveried oarsmen sat on each side, now and then sculling with their oars to keep the craft steady. The barge had a long cabin gilded with gold and silver. Purple curtains had been pulled back to show those within, but they were too far away to make out. Tamasin leaned over the edge of the crowded path to see better, risking a fall into the mud below, and Barak pulled her back. 'Control yourself, woman.'

For a while nothing happened. We stood amid the watching, murmuring crowd. Beyond the barge a long row of mighty warships was moored along the south shore. The King's great ships, which I had seen last year at Portsmouth. Streamers in many colours, some a hundred feet long, were hung from the masts and swung gently in the light river breeze. The ships themselves I remembered: enormous, magnificent, their upper decks brightly painted. One, though, was absent: the King's favourite warship, the *Mary Rose*, now sunk at the bottom of the Solent.

There was a crash as gunports opened along the sides of the ships. Cannon appeared and fired volleys; no actual cannonballs, of course, but emitting thick clouds of smoke and making enough noise to shake the pathway. People shouted and cheered. Nicholas joined in enthusiastically, waving his hat in the air. Some women whooped at the noise, though Tamasin glanced at me with a sombre face.

Then they appeared, coming fast upriver; first a French warship, guns firing on both sides, then over a dozen French galleys, long and narrow: sleek, fast vessels of war. They were brightly painted, each in a different colour, and their cannon, set in the prows, fired off blasts in reply to ours. The largest galley, covered from prow to stern in a white canopy decorated in gold fleur-de-lys, pulled alongside the King's barge.

It was too much for me. The sight of those galleys, which I had last seen firing at the *Mary Rose*; the smoke; the gunfire that shook the ground. I touched Barak on the shoulder. 'I have to go.'

He looked at me with concern. 'God's blood, you look

sick. You shouldn't go alone. Nick, get a boat.'

'No!' I answered stubbornly. 'I'll be all right, you stay here.'

Nicholas and Tamasin were also staring. Tamasin took my hand. 'Are you sure? I could see you were troubled earlier.'

'I will be all right.' I felt ashamed of my weakness.

'Nick,' Barak said peremptorily, 'go back with him.'

The boy stepped forward. I opened my mouth to protest, then shrugged.

'Call on us later,' Tamasin said.

I nodded. 'I will.'

I walked away, fast as I could through the crowds, Nicholas for once having to lengthen his long stride to keep up with me. The endless crash of cannon suddenly ceased; the admiral must have boarded the King's barge at last.

'Watch out there!' a man called out as I nearly fell into him. Nicholas grasped my arm.

'He's drunk, sodden old hunchback,' another man observed. And in truth it was as though I were drunk, the ground like a ship's deck, seeming to shift and slide beneath my feet.

✝

WE GOT A BOAT TO the Steelyard stairs. When we stepped off I felt strange, light-headed. Nicholas said, 'Shall I walk you home?' He was embarrassed, and had hardly spoken during the journey.

'No. We'll walk to chambers.'

Today being a holiday and so many people down at Greenwich, the city was quiet, as though it were a Sunday. I was walking steadily again now, but thought with renewed grief of my friends who had died on the *Mary Rose*. Their faces came before me. And then I found myself saying an inward goodbye to them all, and something lifted in my heart.

'Did you say something, sir?' Nicholas asked.

I must have murmured aloud. 'No. No, nothing.' Looking round, I realized we were at Lothbury. 'We are close to the Cotterstoke house,' I said. 'Where that painting is.'

'What will happen to it now?'

'Edward's half of his mother's estate will go to his family. In these circumstances I imagine his wife will want to get rid of the house as soon as possible, painting or no painting.'

'Then Mistress Slanning may get her way.'

'Yes. I suppose she may.'

He hesitated, then asked, 'Will Master Coleswyn tell Edward Cotterstoke's wife why her husband took his life? That old murder?'

'No. I am sure not.'

I realized the old servant, Vowell, would know nothing of Edward's death. Perhaps I should tell him, and make sure he kept his mouth shut.

☦

THE OLD HOUSE was quiet as ever. Nearby a barber had opened his shop, but there was little custom and he stood leaning disconsolately against a wall under his striped pole. I remembered Rowland saying I needed to shave before taking my place for d'Annebault's progress through London tomorrow; I would do so after visiting Vowell. I knocked at the door.

He opened it at once. He looked agitated, his eyes wide. He stared at us in surprise, then leaned forward and spoke quietly, his voice shaking. 'Oh, sir, it is you. I sent for Master

Dyrick.' He frowned. 'I didn't think he would send you in his place. Sir, it may not be safe for you.'

I lowered my voice in turn. 'What do you mean, fellow? I have not come from Dyrick.' I took a deep breath. 'I came to tell you poor Edward Cotterstoke is dead.'

Vowell wrung his hands. 'I know, and by his own hand. One of his servants told someone who knows me. Wretched gossiping women, everybody knows already. Mistress Slanning—'

'Isabel knows?'

'Knows, sir, and is here.' He cast a backward glance at the gloomy hall. 'In such a state as I have never seen anyone. She insisted I let her in. She has a knife, sir, a big knife she took from the kitchen. I fear she may do as her brother did—'

I raised a hand; the frightened old man's voice was rising. 'Where is she?'

'In the parlour, sir. She just stands looking at the painting – she will not move, nor answer me – holding that knife.'

I looked at Nicholas. 'Will you come with me?' I whispered.

'Yes.'

We stepped inside, past Vowell. The door to the parlour was open. I walked in quietly, Nicholas just behind. There, with her back to me, stood Isabel. She wore one of her fine satin dresses, light brown today, but had cast her hood on the floor. It left her head bare, long silvery-grey tresses cascading down her shoulders. She was staring at the wall painting, quite motionless, and as Vowell had said, a broad, long-bladed knife was clutched in her right hand, so tightly that each bony white knuckle stood out. The image of her mother and father, of little Edward and her own young self, stared back at her, appearing more real than ever to me at that terrifying moment.

She did not even seem to be aware that we had come in. Vowell stayed outside; I heard him breathing hard in the corridor.

Nicholas stepped quietly forward, but I put up a hand to restrain him. I said softly, 'Mistress Slanning.' Strange, even in that extremity, I could not allow myself the presumption of calling her by her first name.

I would not have thought her body could have tensed any further but it did, becoming quite rigid. Then, slowly, she turned her head to look at me. Those blue eyes, so like her brother's, were wild and staring. Her brows drew together in a frown.

'Master Shardlake?' she said in a quiet, puzzled voice. 'Why are you here?'

'I came to speak to Vowell. To tell him your brother is dead.' I moved my right hand a little. 'Mistress Slanning, please let me have that knife.' She did not reply; her breath came in short pants, as though she were trying to hold it in, to stop breathing. 'Please,' I implored. 'I wish only to help you.'

'Why would you help me? I tried to destroy you, and Edward and that lawyer Coleswyn. I called you heretics. As you are.' Her grip on the knife tightened, and she lifted the blade slightly.

'I think you were not yourself. Please, mistress, give me the knife.' I took half a step forward, stretching out my hand.

She slowly lifted the knife towards her throat.

'No!' Nicholas cried out, with such force and passion that Isabel paused, the blade almost at her neck, where the arteries pulsed under the wrinkled white skin.

'It's not worth it!' he said passionately. 'Whatever you did, madam, whatever your family did, it's not worth that!'

She stared at him for a moment. Then she lowered the knife, but held it pointing outwards. I raised my arm to protect myself, fearing she would attack: Isabel was a thin, ageing woman, but desperation gives strength to the weakest. But it was not us she attacked; instead she turned round again and thrust the knife into her beloved picture, stabbing at it with long, powerful slashes, so hard that a piece of plaster broke off beside the crack in the wall that the experts had noticed. She went on and on, making desperate grunting sounds, as more of the paint and plaster crumbled. Then her hand slipped and the knife gashed her other arm, blood spurting through the fabric of her dress. She winced at the unexpected pain and dropped the knife. Clutching her arm, Isabel crumpled in a heap on the floor, and began to cry. She lay there, sobbing desperately with the grief and guilt of a lifetime.

Nicholas stepped forward quickly, picked up the knife and took it outside to Vowell. The old servant stared at Isabel in horror through the doorway. The painting was now scored with innumerable slashes, spaces where pieces of plaster had fallen revealing the lath behind. A tiny stream of plaster dust trickled down. I saw that the section of the painting she had attacked most fiercely, now almost entirely obliterated, was her mother's face.

I looked at Nicholas, who was pale and breathing hard. Then I knelt beside Isabel. 'Mistress Slanning?' I touched her shoulder lightly. She flinched, huddling further away from me, as though she would squeeze herself into the floor, clutching at her injured arm.

'Mistress Slanning,' I said gently. 'You have cut yourself, your arm needs binding.'

The sobbing ceased and she turned her head to look at her arm. Her expression was bereft, her hair wild. She looked utterly pitiful. Lifting her eyes, she met mine briefly before shuddering and turning her face away. 'Do not look at me, please.' She spoke in an imploring whisper. 'No one should look at me now.' She took a deep, sobbing breath. 'He was innocent, our stepfather, a good man. But we did not see it, Edward and I, till it was too late. Our mother was cruel, she left that Will so we would quarrel, I understand it now. It was because both Edward and I loved the painting so. Mother never wanted us to visit her, but I would come sometimes, to see the painting. To see our father again.'

I looked at their mother's empty chair, facing what was left of the painting, the embroidery still lying on the seat.

'He died so suddenly, our father. Why did he leave us? Why?' She wept again, the tears of a lost child. 'Oh, Edward! I drove him to that unclean act. All these years I could have confessed; the old faith allows that if you repent and confess your sins it is enough, you are forgiven. His faith did not allow even that. But I — ' her voice fell to a whisper — 'my hardened heart would not allow me to confess. But it was both of us together did that thing, both of us!'

I jumped at the sound of a sharp knock at the door. I heard Vowell and another voice, and then Vincent Dyrick strode into the room, gown billowing theatrically behind him, his lean hawk face furious. He looked at Nicholas and me, at Isabel weeping on the floor, then gaped at the wrecked painting.

'Shardlake! What have you done? Why is my client in this state?'

I rose slowly to my feet, my knees cracking and my back protesting in pain. Isabel was looking at Dyrick; it was the same puzzled, otherworldly look Edward had worn in the Tower, as though she barely understood who he was.

'Ask her,' I answered heavily.

Dyrick was staring again at the painting. Perhaps he saw the prospect of endless fees from this case trickling away like the plaster dust still falling from the ruined wall. 'Who did this?'

'Isabel, I fear.'

'Christ's wounds!' Dyrick looked down at his client. Isabel was still hunched over, so ashamed she could not meet our eyes. 'See her condition – ' He pointed at me. 'I cannot be held responsible for anything she has done! It was she who insisted on sending a copy of that complaint to the Privy Council. I tried to dissuade her!'

'I know. And I may tell you, since Isabel is your client and you must keep it confidential, that Edward and Isabel conspired to murder their stepfather the best part of half a century ago. Edward has killed himself, and Isabel might have done the same had we not come in time.' I looked again at the painting. 'This is a tragedy, Dyrick. One made worse by the tangles of litigation, as their mother intended. My efforts with Brother Coleswyn to find a settlement only uncovered a horror,' I added sadly.

I stepped wearily to the door. Dyrick looked down at Isabel.

'Wait!' he said, turning. 'You cannot leave me alone with her, in this state – '

'Vowell will help you bind her wound. Then, if you will take my honest advice, you should send for her priest. Make sure it is him, she is of the old religion and it matters to her. He may be able to help her, I do not know.' I turned to Nicholas. He was looking at the face of Isabel's father, still staring out from the wreckage with his benevolent, confident, patrician air. 'Come, lad,' I said. We walked past Dyrick, past old Vowell, out into the street.

There, in the August sunshine, I turned to Nicholas. 'You saved her.'

'She came to this, even with a good and loving father,' he said quietly. And I realized with a chill that his parents' letter had brought thoughts of suicide to Nicholas as well. But he had rejected them, and that was why he had been so passionate with Isabel. 'What will happen to her?' he asked.

'I do not know.'

'Perhaps it is too late for that poor woman now.' Nicholas took a deep breath and stared at me, his green eyes hard and serious. 'But not for me.'

✠

EARLY THE FOLLOWING afternoon I stood at the front of a great concourse outside the church of St Michael le Querne, which gave onto the open space at the west end of Cheapside. More crowds lined the length of Cheapside, along which Admiral d'Annebault would shortly progress. Mayor Bowes, whom I had last seen at Anne Askew's burning, stood alone on a little platform. I waited in a line with the aldermen and other leading citizens of London, all wearing our gold chains. As at the burnings, a white-robed cleric stood at a makeshift lectern, but on this occasion he was to deliver an oration in French, welcoming the admiral to the city. There was a steady murmur of voices, while water tinkled in the conduit by the church.

The admiral had come by boat from Greenwich to the Tower that morning, all his galleys following. The previous evening I had taken Nicholas with me to visit Barak and Tamasin, and had spent a quiet night playing cards. I had not told them what had happened to Isabel – it was no thing for Tamasin to hear in her condition. Then I had gone home and slept late, to be woken by the crash of guns from the Tower welcoming the admiral. Even out at Chancery Lane the noise rattled the windows. From the Tower d'Annebault would progress through the city, finishing at St Michael's Church, accompanied by the Queen's brother, William Parr, the other great men of the realm following.

Martin helped dress me in my very best. I put on the gold chain which I had set him to cleaning last night. Neither of us said a word. Then I walked down to the church. As I left I saw Timothy peering through the half-open door of the stable, looking disconsolate. I knew I must speak to him about Martin's betrayal; but for now Lord Parr had sworn me to secrecy and I gave the boy only a severe look. Too severe, perhaps, but I was still sore troubled by what he had done, and by my experiences of recent days.

A royal official lined us up, peremptorily ordering the mayor and aldermen into position like children. The sun beat down, making our heads hot under our caps and coifs. The golden links of our chains sparkled. Streamers and poles bearing the English flag beside the fleur-de-lys of France fluttered in the breeze, and bright cloths, too, had been hung from the upper windows of houses and shops. I remembered how only a year before I had seen dummies wearing the fleur-de-lys used in target practice by new recruits to the army – hundreds of men who had marched to Portsmouth from London to resist the threatened invasion.

Next to me Serjeant Blower of the Inner Temple stood proudly, his fat belly sucked in and his chest thrust out. He was in his fifties, with a short, neatly trimmed beard. I knew him slightly; he was too full of himself for my taste. It was said that Wriothesley was considering appointing him a judge. 'We have a fine day to greet the admiral,' he said.

'I cannot remember such ceremonial since Anne Boleyn's coronation.'

I raised my eyebrows, remembering how that much-acclaimed marriage had ended.

'Are you going to be present when Prince Edward meets the admiral tomorrow?' Blower asked. 'And at the Hampton Court celebrations?'

'Yes, representing Lincoln's Inn.'

'I too,' he said proudly. He looked askance at my chain. 'Have you had that long? By the smell of vinegar you have just had it cleaned.'

'I only wear it on the most special occasions.'

'Really? It looks somewhat scratched.' Blower glanced proudly down at the broad, bright links of his own chain. Then he leaned closer and said quietly, 'Could you not find time to shave, brother? We were instructed to. It is a pity your hair is dark, your stubble shows.'

'No, Brother Blower. I fear I have been very busy.'

'In the vacation?'

'I have had some hard cases.'

'Ah.' He nodded, then quoted the old legal saying, 'Hard cases make bad law.'

'They do indeed.'

He gave me a sidelong look. I wondered if news of my appearance before the council had filtered out. Servants would speak to servants at Whitehall, the city and the Inns of Court. A rousing cheer sounded from Cheapside. People had been told to cry a welcome as d'Annebault passed. Blower pulled his fat stomach in further. 'Here he comes,' he said eagerly, and shouted a loud 'Hurrah!'

Chapter Forty-six

AFTER THE CEREMONY I went home. I was exhausted, and with another one to face on Monday, and a third the day after. For all his poor conduct at the Battle of the Solent last year, Admiral Claude d'Annebault had cut an impressive figure riding up to St Michael's: a large, handsome man of fifty, on a magnificent charger, the Earl of Essex riding beside him. I was glad to see the Queen's brother so prominent; another sign the Parr family was secure.

After the welcoming address the mayor had presented the admiral with great silver flagons of hippocras, and marchpane and wafers to refresh him after his journey. My back hurt from standing so long, and I slipped away as soon as possible, wanting only to spend the remainder of the day quietly by myself. I walked home. As I entered the house I heard Josephine and Agnes talking cheerfully in the kitchen about the wedding, fixed now for January. I thought, poor Agnes, she knows nothing of what her husband has done. Soon she will be leaving with him.

Martin came out of the dining room, a letter in his hand, his manner deferential as usual. 'This came while you were out, sir.'

'Thank you.' I recognized Hugh Curteys's handwriting. Martin said quietly, 'Sir, is there any more news concerning

– that matter? About my going to that house?' Though his face remained expressionless, I saw the signs of strain about his narrowed mouth and eyes.

'No, Martin,' I replied coldly. 'I will let you know as soon as I have instructions.'

'Will it be soon?'

'I hope so. I do not know. I will tell you as soon as I do. You brought this on yourself,' I added.

✝

IN MY ROOM I read Hugh's letter. Apparently Emperor Charles had decided to curb the independence of the Flanders cities: *'There have been arrests of many reformist citizens here, and in other places in Flanders, and there are like to be imprisonments and burnings. Certain English and other foreigners have crossed into Germany.'* I wondered if Bale was among them, Anne Askew's book hidden in his luggage. Probably; he must have become used to moving quickly since he fled England after the fall of his patron Cromwell. This would surely delay the publication of Anne Askew's writings now.

The letter continued: *'Many in the English merchant community are worried, and I fear if the atmosphere in the city changes for the worse I, too, may consider going to Germany.'*

I sighed; I thought my ward had found a safe haven, but it seemed not. I remembered that it was over Hugh's wardship case that I had first crossed swords with Vincent Dyrick. Thoughts of Dyrick led me to Isabel; what would happen to her, now that the whole weight of what she had done – and Edward's death – lay upon her? I remembered her frantic, deranged slashing at the painting she had fought for so single-mindedly. On an impulse, I sat down, took up quill and ink, and wrote a note to Guy:

I have not seen you since I visited that poor man at
St Bartholomew's, but you have been in my thoughts. There
is a woman I represented in a case – a sad family matter –
who is now in great travail of soul. She is of the old faith,
and I asked her lawyer to arrange for her priest to see her,
but I am anxious how she fares. If you have time, perhaps
you might visit her. I think perhaps you could comfort her.

I added Isabel's name and address, signed the note 'your loving friend', and sanded and sealed it. There, I thought, he will see I do not cavil at religious counselling being offered to one of the old beliefs, and he might even be able to do something for Isabel, though I feared her mind was broken now.

✞

ON THE MORNING of Monday 23rd I dressed in my finery again and went down to the stables. Today's ceremony was to welcome d'Annebault to Hampton Court. It was to take place three miles from the palace, beside the river, and the admiral was to be greeted by little Prince Edward. It was the boy's first public occasion. Those of us coming from the city had to ride out there, but it was some consolation to me that during the occasion we would remain on horseback. I had gone to be shaved yesterday and my cheeks were smooth: Blower would not be able to make remarks at my stubble today.

I had asked Martin to tell Timothy to ensure Genesis was well rubbed down, and his mane tied in plaits. When I entered the stable I was pleased to see the boy had done a good job. He did not look me in the eye as he placed the mounting block beside the horse. As I slid my feet into the stirrups, though, he looked up and smiled nervously, showing the gap where his two front teeth had been punched out when he was still an orphaned urchin, before I took him in.

'Master,' he said nervously. 'You said you would talk to me again about – about the burned books.'

'Yes, Timothy. But not now. I am due at an important occasion.'

He grasped the reins. 'Only – sir, it must have been Martin who told people about the books; I wouldn't have, yet Martin is still in his place, and he was sharp as ever with me last night.' He reddened and his voice rose a little. 'Sir, it isn't fair, I meant no harm.'

I took a deep breath, then said, 'I have kept Martin on for my own private reasons.' Then I burst out, 'And what he did pains me less than your spying. I trusted you, Timothy, and you let me down.' Tears filled the boy's eyes and I spoke more calmly. 'I will speak to you tomorrow, Timothy. Tomorrow.'

✝

A BROAD HEATH by the river had been chosen as the site for the ceremony. When I arrived almost everyone was there. Near a thousand yeomen had been commandeered for the day, dressed in brand new livery with the King's colours. City officials and we representatives from the Inns were again shepherded to places in the front rank, facing the roadway. A little way off, with a guard of soldiers, the great men of the realm waited on their horses. All those I had seen at the Privy Council were present: Gardiner, his solid frame settled on a broad-backed horse; Rich and Wriothesley side by side; Paget stroking his long forked beard, a little colour in those flat cheeks today, surveying those around him with his usual cool eye. The Earl of Hertford looked stern and solemn, while beside him Thomas Seymour, with his coppery beard combed and no doubt perfumed, wore a happy smile on his handsome face. Others too: Lord Lisle, who had proved a better commander than d'Annebault at Portsmouth last year, and other lords in their finery, the feathers in their caps stirring in the river breeze. The water was blue and sparkling, reflecting the bright sky.

And at their head, on a smaller horse, sat the boy, not yet nine, who was King Henry's heir, the control of whom after the King died was the focus of all the plotting by the men behind him. In a broad-shouldered crimson doublet with slashed sleeves, a black cap set with diamonds on his head, Prince Edward was a tiny figure beside the adults. He sat firmly upright on his horse, though. He was tall for his age, his thin little face stiffly composed. His serious expression and small chin reminded me of his long-dead mother, Jane Seymour, whose likeness I had seen in the great wall painting at Whitehall. I pitied him for the weight that must soon fall on him. Then I thought of Timothy: I had been too hard with him; one should not hold a grudge against children. I would speak to him when I returned.

Once again my allotted place was next to Blower. The big Serjeant nodded to me but said little; he kept leaning forward, looking towards the party behind Prince Edward, trying to catch the eye of Lord Chancellor Wriothesley, who might give him his coveted judgeship. Wriothesley did see him, but in answer to his nod and smile gave only a little frown as though to say, 'Not here.' I remembered the old saying, big fleas have little fleas to bite them.

At length we saw d'Annebault's party approach slowly along the riverbank. There must have been three hundred of them; I knew d'Annebault had brought two hundred men over from France. From the English party heralds stepped forward, blowing trumpets. The admiral, accompanied again by the Earl of Essex, rode up to Prince Edward and bowed to the little boy from the saddle. The Prince began delivering, in a high childish voice, an address of welcome; he spoke without pause, in perfect French. At the end the admiral's horse was led forward and he and Prince Edward embraced.

✝

THE ADDRESS OVER, the French party and the bulk of the English lords rode away to Hampton Court, the Prince and the admiral leading the way, a tall soldier holding the reins of Prince Edward's horse. Those of us left behind, as usual on such occasions, relaxed immediately, everyone swinging their shoulders and drawing deep breaths, pausing to talk with friends before riding back to London. I supposed that for civility's sake I would have to ride back with the disgruntled-looking Blower, but as I was about to speak to him I felt a touch at my arm. I turned to see Lord Parr standing at my elbow, accompanied by two serving men, one holding his horse.

'My Lord,' I said. 'I did not see you with the Prince's party.'

'No, the Queen's household is not involved in this. But I came, and would speak with you.'

'Of course.' I looked at the old man; in his note he had said he had been ill, and indeed he looked frail, leaning hard on his stick. He nodded to his men and one helped me dismount while the other took Genesis's reins. Blower looked at Lord Parr with surprise, not knowing that I had acquaintance with such a senior figure. He bowed to Lord Parr and rode off, looking more put out than ever.

Lord Parr led me away a little, to stand beside the river. 'You had my letter?'

'I did. I have spoken to my steward Brocket and he stands ready, though very reluctantly.'

'I am still trying to discover who put that item on the council agenda. But I make no progress, and Paget is as close-mouthed as any man can be.'

'He was fair at the council,' I observed. 'He seemed genuinely concerned to find the truth or otherwise of the allegations.'

'Ay, perhaps.' Lord Parr sighed deeply. 'I am getting too tired for all this. After the admiral leaves next week the King and Queen are going on a short Progress to Guildford, so I must move these old bones yet again.' He looked out over the river for a moment, then spoke quietly. 'The King is taking none of the traditionalist councillors with him, not Gardiner, nor Wriothesley, nor Norfolk. Lord Hertford and Lord Lisle, though, will be accompanying him.' He looked at me, a keenness now in his bloodshot eyes. 'The tide is shifting fast in our favour. The King has not seen Bertano again; he is cooling his heels somewhere in London. Rumours are beginning to spread of a papal emissary here. And if I can prove that Rich has been playing some double game, perhaps seeking to damage the Queen through you, it will anger the King, and help the Queen. And the Parr family,' he added. 'But before I do anything with that man Stice, I must know more. No sign of those others, I take it, the men who killed Greening?'

'Daniels and Cardmaker? No, the printer Okedene saw them about the town, but I have not.'

'Who did they take the Queen's book for? Not Rich, I am sure, he would have used the *Lamentation* at once.'

'Could its release still harm the Queen?'

'I think so.' He paused, then made a fist with his bony hand. He shook his head. 'It is her hiding the book from him that would anger him most, I know.'

'The disloyalty, rather than the *Lamentation*'s theology?'

'Exactly. Though her stress on salvation by faith alone would hardly help. And the King's illness makes him all the more unpredictable. One never knows how he may turn, or in what direction.' For a second Lord Parr seemed to sway, and I put out a hand. But he righted himself, taking a deep breath. 'Give me a few days, Master Shardlake, to try and worm out some more information. And I will have a watch set on that house where Stice meets your steward.' He turned, and we walked back to our horses.

'I will contact you soon,' Lord Parr said after we had mounted. 'Keep that steward safe. Is he well frightened?'

'I think so.'

'Good.' As I turned away he said, 'I almost forgot. The Queen sends you her best wishes.'

✠

I RODE SLOWLY back to the city. I had not gone far, though, when another horseman pulled up beside me. To my surprise I saw it was young William Cecil, his face serious as usual.

'Brother Cecil. I had not thought to see you again so soon.' I allowed a note of reproach to enter my voice. He had been of great help earlier, but now Lord Parr must feel his absence greatly.

'Brother Shardlake.' His thin lips set slightly at my tone.

'How goes your service with Lord Hertford?'

'Well, thank you.' He hesitated. 'His secretary retires soon, it is possible I will take his place.'

I inclined my head. 'You made a good move, then.'

He pulled his horse to a halt, and I, too, stopped. The young lawyer looked at me squarely, fixing me with those large, keen blue eyes. 'Brother Shardlake, I was sorry to leave the Queen's service. But an offer of serious advancement came and I had to take it.'

'As men do.'

'Also, I confess, after that turmoil on the wharf, I did some serious thinking. About what I am – and am not – capable of. I am not a fighting man, and I have a young family to consider. My talents, such as they are, are best put to use behind a desk. Where,' he added, 'I can serve the cause of reform. Believe me, I am sincere in that, as in my continued love and respect for the Queen.'

I dared to say, 'But your first loyalty now is to the Seymours, not the Parrs.'

'Both families serve reform. And I followed you today, Brother Shardlake, to tell you something I thought you should know. Lord Parr's health is failing. I did not know how ill he was when I left, but my purpose now is to tell you that if your involvement in the Queen's matters continues – and I know you have appeared before the Privy Council – you must rely on your own judgement as well as his.' He looked at me earnestly.

'I saw just now that he was not well,' I said quietly.

'And under pressure, with all this – ' Cecil cast an arm behind him at the disappearing cavalcade. 'He has much to do at Hampton Court, the Queen is to play a prominent role at the ceremonies there.'

'I know. I will be attending tomorrow.'

There was no need for him to have ridden up to me to tell me this. 'Thank you, Brother Cecil,' I said.

'If I hear anything that may be of use to you or the Queen, I will tell you.'

'What do you think has happened to the Queen's book?'

'Lord Parr thinks it destroyed,' Cecil said.

'Do you?'

'I do not know. Only that the moment for the conservatives to use it to maximum advantage has passed. The wind is blowing fast in the other direction now. Perhaps whoever took it realized that and destroyed it.' He shook his head. 'But likely we shall never know.'

We rode on, talking of the ceremonies and the autumn Progress that was to begin afterwards, apparently going only to Guildford for a couple of weeks because of the King's health. We parted at the foot of Chancery Lane. 'This mystery is not yet unravelled,' I said. 'If you do hear anything, please inform me.'

'I will, I swear.'

As I rode down Chancery Lane I thought, yes, you will, but only so long as it serves the Seymours as well as the Parrs.

Chapter Forty-seven

I TURNED INTO MY HOUSE, aware of the sweat stiffening on my forehead under my coif, and rode round to the stable. Now I would speak to Timothy. But the boy was not there; Martin or Agnes must have set him some task around the house. I dismounted wearily, removed my cap and coif, and went indoors.

Immediately I heard the sound of a woman crying in the kitchen; desperate, racked sobbing. I realized it was Agnes Brocket. Josephine murmured something and I heard Martin say in loud, angry tones, 'God's bones, girl, will you leave us alone! Don't stare at me with those cow eyes, you stupid creature! Get out!'

Josephine stepped into the hall, her cheeks burning. I said quietly, 'What is happening?'

'Oh, sir, Master and Mistress Brocket –' She broke off as Martin stepped out, having heard my voice. His square face was angry. But he pulled himself together and asked quietly, 'May I speak with you, sir?'

I nodded. 'Come to the parlour.'

When the door was closed I said, 'What is it, Martin? You have not told Agnes about your spying?'

'No! No!' He shook his head impatiently, then said more quietly, 'It is our son.'

'John?'

'We have had a letter from the gaoler at Leicester. John

621

has another sickness of the lungs, a congestion. They called a doctor and he said he is like to die. Sir, we must go to him. Agnes insists we leave today.'

I looked at him. I realized from the desperation in his eyes that, whatever the consequences, Agnes would go to her son. And Martin, who for all his faults loved his wife, would go, too. 'When was the letter sent?' I asked.

'Three days ago.' Brocket shook his head despairingly. 'It may be too late already. That would kill Agnes.' When I did not reply he said, suddenly defiant, 'You cannot stop us. You may do what you like. Give me bad references, spread the word round London about what I did. Tell the Queen's people. It makes no difference, we are going today.'

I said, 'I am sorry this has happened to you.'

He did not reply, just continued staring at me with that desperate look. I considered, then said quietly, 'I will make a bargain with you, Martin Brocket. Take one more message to that tavern, now, saying you have important news and will be at the house in Smithfield at nine tomorrow night.'

He took a deep breath. 'We go today,' he repeated, an edge to his voice now.

'I do not expect you to keep the appointment. Others will do that. But to set the wheels in motion you must deliver the message, in your writing, in person.'

'And in return?' he asked, suddenly bold.

'In return, I will give you a reference praising your household skills and diligence. But I will not say you are a trustworthy man, for you are not.'

'I was honest all my life,' Martin replied, a tremble in his voice, 'until John's actions brought me to this.' Then he added spitefully, 'I might not even have agreed to play the spy but for the fact I never respected you, Master Hunch – ' He broke off, realizing he was about to go too far.

I answered quietly, 'Nor did I respect you, Martin, proud, narrow man that you are. With a wife too good for him.'

He clenched his fists. 'At least I have one.'

In the silence that followed I heard Agnes sobbing uncontrollably again. Martin winced. I spoke quietly. 'Come to my study. Write me that note and deliver it. While you are gone I will compose a reference. I will give it to you when you return. Then you can get out.'

✝

IN THE STUDY I thought, what is sure to bring Stice, and perhaps Rich, to that house? I told Martin to write '*I have urgent news concerning the visit of an Italian gentleman*'. There, that would do: Lord Parr had told me that rumours of Bertano's presence were starting to leak out. Rich would be keenly interested. I had Martin add: '*Please make sure we are alone. It is all most confidential.*'

When the note was written and I had gone over it, Martin left for the tavern; I wrote out a reference for him in ill conscience. I wondered whether he might throw the note away and not deliver it, but before he left I warned him again that very senior people were involved in this, and oddly I also felt that his pride would ensure that he honoured this last promise. Josephine took Agnes upstairs to pack. I stood at my parlour window, looking out on the sunny lawn, full of sad thoughts. A wife. I would have wished the Queen for a wife. I wondered whether perhaps I was a little mad, like poor Isabel.

There was a knock at the door. Agnes Brocket entered, her face weary and tear-stained. 'Martin has told you our news, sir?'

'About John? Yes. I am sorry.'

'Thank you for letting us go, sir. We will return as soon

as we can. Martin has gone out on a last piece of business.' She smiled wanly.

So Martin had not told his wife they would not be return-ing. No doubt he would make up some story later. Poor Agnes, so honest and hard-working, so full of goodwill. Her son in prison, her husband's deceits kept from her. I said gently, 'I have been looking out at my garden. You have done much good work there, and in the house.'

'Thank you, sir.' She took a deep breath, then said, 'My husband, I know he is not always easy, but it is I who insisted we must go to John today – the fault is all mine.'

'No fault to want to see your son.' I reached for my purse which I had put on the desk. 'Here, take some money, you will need it on the journey.' I gave her a half-sovereign. She clutched it tightly and lowered her head. Then, with a des-perate effort at her old cheerfulness, she said, 'Make sure Timothy and Josephine stay out of mischief, sir.'

I waited till Martin returned and confirmed he had deliv-ered the message. I gave him the reference. I did not want to watch them leave, so I left the house again and walked to Lincoln's Inn. I needed to speak to Barak and Nicholas and take their counsel.

✝

I TOOK THEM BOTH into my office and told them what had just happened. I said, 'This means Stice must be dealt with tomorrow.'

'What grounds are there to lift him?' Barak asked. 'He hasn't done anything illegal, and Rich won't be pleased.'

'That's a matter for Lord Parr. I will look for him at this great banquet at Hampton Court tomorrow afternoon. My last assignment for Treasurer Rowland. From what I gleaned from the instructions, it will be just a matter of standing round with hundreds of others,' I said bitterly, 'showing d'Annebault how many prosperous Englishmen with gold chains there are. Though most are struggling with the taxes to pay for the war, while many thousands more that he will not see struggle simply to exist.'

Barak raised his eyebrows. 'You sound like one of the extreme radicals.'

I shrugged. 'Anyway, I should be able to find Lord Parr then.'

'What if you don't? Among all that throng?'

'I will.' Then all the anger that had been building in me in these last few days burst out and I banged a fist on my desk, making the glass inkpot jump and spill ink. 'I'll find what Rich and Stice have been up to. Damn them, spying on me for months, kidnapping Nicholas, cozening me into working for them. I'll have no more of it! I'm tired to death of being used, used, used!'

It was seldom I lost my temper, and Barak and Nicholas looked at each other. Nicholas said tentatively, 'Might it not be better to leave the matter where it is, sir? Your faithless steward is gone. Anne Askew's book is taken abroad, the Queen's book vanished. And it was taken by different men, not Stice. There is now no trace of the men who killed Greening and those others in his group.'

'And no evidence at all they are connected to Rich,' Barak agreed. 'Quite the opposite.'

'There has always been some – some third force out there, someone who employed those two murderers,' I said. 'But we have never been able to find out who. Whatever Rich and Stice's reason for spying on me – as they have been since well before the book was stolen – it may be nothing to do with the *Lamentation*; but it *is* to do with the Queen. Brocket said he was told particularly to watch for any contact between us. For her sake I have to resolve this. And, yes, for mine!'

Nicholas looked at me seriously. 'Do you want me to come to the house tomorrow?'

Barak nodded at him. 'There is no guarantee Stice will be alone tomorrow.'

'Lord Parr has sent a man to watch the house, he'll know who's coming and going.'

'You should still have somebody with you, sir,' Nicholas persisted. I looked at him; the expression on his freckled face was sincere, though I did not doubt that his youthful taste for adventure had been stirred again.

Barak said, 'Well, if he goes, I'd better go too, to keep an eye on you both.'

I hesitated. 'No, you have both done enough. I'm sure I can persuade Lord Parr to send some men.'

'But if you can't — ' Barak raised his eyebrows.

I looked at them. I realized that from the moment I had sent Brocket with the message I had wanted them to offer to come. And both of them had made their offer mainly from loyalty to me. My throat felt suddenly tight. 'We will see,' I said.

Nicholas shook his head. 'I wish we could have discovered who was behind those men who stole the Queen's book.'

Barak laughed. 'You're doing a lot of wishing, long lad. It doesn't look like Rich but it's not impossible. Or it could be Wriothesley, or either of them acting on Bishop Gardiner's orders.'

'Yes,' I agreed. 'But I don't know. The Lady Mary could even be involved, with that so-called fool Jane; though I doubt that now. Or even the Seymours, working against the Parrs.'

Barak raised an imaginary glass. 'Here's to the King and all his family, and all his grand councillors, and the great Admiral d'Annebault. To the whole bloody lot of them.'

✝

I RETURNED HOME TIRED, and with a guilty conscience. It was my feeling of being used that had caused me to lose my temper, but what was I myself doing if not using Barak and Nicholas?

The house was quiet, the late afternoon sun glinting on the window panes. A rich man's house; in many ways I was lucky. I thought of Martin Brocket and poor Agnes, now no doubt riding hard northwards, kerchiefs round their mouths against the dust. At least the money I had given Agnes should ensure them decent mounts. I would have to rely on Josephine and Timothy until I could find a new steward.

Josephine was in the kitchen, preparing the evening meal. 'They are gone?' I asked.

'Yes, sir.' I could see she had been crying. She added, a little hesitantly, 'Sir, before he left, Master Brocket went to the stable, to take leave of Timothy.' I frowned. Martin had never had any time for the boy before, thinking I spoiled him. 'I don't know what he said, but I saw Timothy afterwards and he was upset, he was crying and wouldn't say what about. Then he ran back to the stable. He will be sad that Agnes is gone. He has – not been himself of late.'

'I have had – well – cause to be displeased with Timothy. I meant to speak to him today. I will do it now.'

She looked relieved. 'I think that a good idea, sir – if I may say,' she added hastily.

I smiled at her. 'You may, Josephine. You are in charge of the household now.' Her eyes widened with a mixture of pleasure and apprehension.

C. J. SANSOM

I went to the stable. I could hear Genesis moving inside. I took a deep breath as I opened the door. 'Timothy,' I said quietly, 'I think we should have that talk — '

But there was nobody there, only my horse in its stall. Then I saw, on the upturned bucket where the boy habitually sat, a scrawled note addressed to *Master Shardlake*. I picked it up. I unfolded the note apprehensively.

I am sorry for what I did, my spying on you that day. I was bad. I never meant harm to you, sir. I swear to Lord Jesus. Master Brocket says he and Mistress Agnes are leaving and it is all my fault, it is because of what I did. I do not deserve to stay in your house so I go on the road, a sinner in lammentation.

A sinner in lamentation. The misspelt word jolted me. But its use was common now, in a land where more and more believed they had great sins to lament before God. I put the note down, realizing that my terseness with the boy had done more damage than I could have imagined. Martin had delivered the note to the tavern for me, I was sure, but then he had taken his anger and bitterness out on a child. The foul churl.

I crumpled the note in my fist. Then I ran back to the house, calling to Josephine. 'He is gone! Timothy. We must find him!'

Chapter Forty-eight

JOSEPHINE WENT TO FETCH her fiancé, young Brown. He was happy to help look for Timothy and he and Josephine went one way, I another, to search all the surrounding streets, up beyond Newgate. But although Timothy could not have been gone more than an hour, we found no trace of him. Only when it grew dark did I abandon the search, returning to a deserted house where I lit a candle and sat staring dismally at the kitchen table. I cursed Brocket, who had deliberately humiliated the boy. I realized that I had come to think of Timothy almost as my own son, just as I had come to see Josephine, in a way, as a daughter. Perhaps that was why I had been so hurt by what Timothy did, and had in turn hurt him, by letting my anger fester. Foolish, foolish, I. It would have been better for us all had I looked on them only as servants.

As I sat there, hoping Josephine and Brown would return with Timothy, Bealknap's words as he lay dying came back to me: *What will happen to you?* Almost as though he had foreseen the disasters that would come.

Then I drew a deep breath. I remembered again how, last autumn, Bealknap had made those uncharacteristic overtures of friendship; for a while seeming to be always hovering nearby, as if wishing to engage me. And then he had fallen badly ill – in the first months of the year, that would have been; at just about the time I took Martin on. I had thought

C. J. SANSOM

Martin's spying was connected with the heresy hunt. But what if Bealknap, too, had been trying to spy on me? Perhaps Stice had first recruited him and then, when Bealknap's efforts to worm his way into my confidence failed, and he fell ill, Stice had gone looking for another spy and found that my new steward had money worries.

I ran a shaking hand through my hair. If Bealknap had been spying on me, that would explain his deathbed words. But who could have had an interest in me as long ago as last autumn? The heresy hunt had not yet begun and I was not even working for the Queen then.

My reverie was interrupted by the sound of a key turning in the kitchen door. Josephine and Brown entered, looking exhausted. Brown shook his head as Josephine slumped at the table opposite me. 'We can't find him, sir,' he said. 'We asked people, went into all the shops before they closed.'

Josephine looked at me. 'Timothy – he has good clothes, and surely anybody who saw that gap in his teeth would remember it.'

Young Brown put a hand on her shoulder. 'There are many toothless children on the streets.'

'Not with Timothy's smile.' Josephine burst into tears.

I stood up. 'Thank you for your help, both of you. I am going to Jack Barak's house now. He may have some ideas.' He would, I was sure; he had been a child on the streets himself once. 'With your employer's permission, Goodman Brown, we shall resume the search at first light tomorrow.'

✝

'OFFER A REWARD.' That was Barak's first suggestion. I sat with him and Tamasin in their parlour, nursing a jug of beer. As always, it was a cosy domestic scene: baby George abed upstairs; Barak mending a wooden doll the child had broken; Tamasin sewing quietly by candle-light, her belly just beginning to swell with the coming child.

'I'll do that. When we go out tomorrow. Offer five pounds.'

Barak raised his eyebrows. 'Five pounds! You'll have every lost urchin in London brought to your door.'

'I don't care.'

He shook his head. Tamasin said, 'What is Josephine's fiancé's first name? You always speak of him just as Brown.'

'Edward, it's Edward. Though I seem to think of him as just young Brown.'

She smiled. 'Perhaps because he is taking Josephine away from you.'

'No, no, he is a fine lad.' I thought of his uncomplaining willingness to help tonight, his obvious love for Josephine. She could not have done better. Yet perhaps there was some truth in what Tamasin said.

She said, 'I will go out tomorrow with Goodwife Marris. I'll come to your house in the morning and we can divide the city into sections.'

'No, you won't,' Barak interjected. 'Going up and down the streets and stinking lanes. No.' He put down the doll. 'I'll talk to some people; plenty of the small solicitors and their servants would be happy to look for the boy for five pounds.' There was still amazement in his voice at the size of the sum I was prepared to lay out. 'Have you paid the latest instalment of your taxes?' he asked me.

'Not yet. But remember I got four pounds from Stephen Bealknap.' I frowned slightly, thinking again of his deathbed words.

'Make sure you find him,' Tamasin told her husband. 'Or I will be out looking the next day.' She asked me, 'Is tomorrow not the day you go to Hampton Court?'

'Yes. But I do not have to be there till five in the afternoon. I'll search for Timothy till I have to leave.'

✝

NEXT MORNING, while Barak was busy rousing people to join the hunt, Josephine and Goodman Brown and I went out again. They took the road eastward, to see if the boy had left London; if he had, he would be impossible to find. But he had spent all his life in the city, he must surely be here somewhere.

There was a little crowd in Fleet Street, for today was hanging day and people always gathered to watch the cart that carried the condemned to the great gibbet at Tyburn, its occupants standing with nooses round their necks. Some of the crowd shouted insults, others encouraged the condemned to die bravely. Though I shuddered as always at this spectacle, I stopped and asked people if they had seen Timothy. But none had.

I went along Cheapside, calling in all the shops. I had dressed in my robe and coif, to impress the shopkeepers, but perhaps some thought I was mad as I asked each a set of questions which soon became a chant: 'I am looking for a lost stable-boy . . . ran away yesterday afternoon . . . thirteen, medium height, untidy brown hair, his two front teeth missing . . . Yes, five pounds . . . no, he hasn't stolen anything . . . yes, I know I could get another . . .'

I asked among the beggars at the great Cheapside conduit. At the sight of a rich gentleman they crowded round me, their stink overpowering. There were children among them, filthy, some covered in sores, eyes feral as cats'. Women as well, too broken or mad even to be whores, in no more than rags, and men missing limbs who had been in accidents, or the wars. They were all blistered by the sun, with cracked lips and dry, matted hair.

More than one said they had seen Timothy, holding out a hand for a reward. I gave each a farthing to whet their appetites and told them the extraordinary sum of five pounds awaited if they produced the boy – the *right* boy, I added emphatically. One lad of about twelve offered himself in Timothy's stead, and bared a skinny arse to show what he meant. One of the women waiting for water at the conduit called out 'Shame!' But I did not care what they thought, so long as Timothy was found.

✝

THERE WAS ONE further resource I had not tapped. Guy had met Timothy several times at my house, and the boy liked him. What was more, if something happened to him, he might turn up at St Bartholomew's. Despite the distance that had come between us, I needed Guy's help.

His assistant Francis Sybrant opened the door and told me his master was at home. He looked at me curiously, for I was dusty from the streets. I waited in Guy's consulting room, with its pleasant perfume of sandalwood and lavender, and its strange charts of the human body marked with the names of its parts. He came in; I noticed he was starting to walk with an old man's shuffle, but the expression on his scholarly brown face under the thinning grey curls was welcoming.

'Matthew. I was going to write you today, about Mistress Slanning. I am glad you told me about her.'

'How does she fare?'

'Not well. Her priest has spoken with her, but she told him what she and her brother did, and allowed him to tell me, but then broke down again badly. I have prescribed her a sleeping draught; she has a good household steward, he will keep her from doing what her brother did, so far as anyone can. Perhaps in a little while she may confess fully, and receive absolution.'

'Do you think confession would rest her mind?'

He shook his head sadly. 'I think it will never rest again. But it would ease her.'

'Guy, I need your advice on another matter – nothing to do with the great ones of the realm,' I added as his expression became wary. I told him Timothy was missing, and he readily offered to look out for him at the hospital. But he added sadly, 'There are thousands of homeless children in London, more every week, orphans and those cast out from their homes, or coming in from the countryside. Many do not live long.'

'I know. And Timothy – it is partly my fault.'

'Do not think of that. I am sure you are right, he is still in the city, and your offer of a reward may find him.' He put a comforting hand on my arm.

†

I RETURNED TO the house shortly before lunchtime. Barak was there, and said he had half a dozen people out looking. He had told those who had joined the hunt to recruit others, on the promise that each would get a portion of the reward if they found the boy. 'Contracting the job out,' he said with a grin. 'I've got Nick out looking too, we've more than caught up with the work at chambers.'

'Thank you,' I said, grateful as ever for his practicality.

'I think you should stay here now, to hand over the reward if someone finds him. What time must you be at the banquet?'

'Five. I must leave by three.'

'I'll take over here then.' He stroked his beard. It was tidy as usual, Tamasin kept it well trimmed. 'You'll look for Lord Parr?'

'I'll make sure I find him,' I answered grimly.

'Remember, Nick and I are available tonight, if we're needed.'

'Tamasin — '

'Will be all right. You'd be mad to go there alone.'

'Yes. I hope Lord Parr will supply some men, but bring Nicholas back here after the search for Timothy, and wait for me. Just in case. Thank you,' I added, inadequately.

Chapter Forty-nine

B Y THREE O'CLOCK, several ragged boys had come or been brought to my door, but none was Timothy. I left Barak and took a wherry upriver to Hampton Court. I had done my best to clean the London dust from my robe before I left. I carried the rented gold chain in a bag; wearing it in the city would be a sore temptation to street robbers. I was tired, my back hurt, and I would have liked to lie down rather than be forced to sit on the hard bench of the boat.

'Going to the celebrations to welcome the French admiral, sir?' the boatman asked.

'That's right.'

'They enlisted me last year, sent me to Hampshire. Our company didn't go on the King's ships, though. We came home after the French fleet sailed away. I lost a lot of money through being taken from my trade.'

'At least you came back with your life.'

'Ay. Not all did. And now we've to welcome that Frenchie like a hero.' He turned and spat in the river as the high brick chimneys of Hampton Court came into view in the distance.

✝

ONE OF THE many guards posted at the landing stage led me into the Great Court fronting the palace. The wide lawned court backed on to high walls, and in the centre was the Great Gate leading to the inner court and the main buildings, whose red-brick facade looked mellow in the sunlight. Hampton Court was a complex of wide interlocking spaces, a complete contrast to the cramped turrets and tiny courts of Whitehall – less colourful, but more splendid.

In the Great Court I saw two large temporary banqueting houses, skilfully painted to look like brickwork, with the flags of England and France flying from pennants above. Even the smaller of the two structures looked as though it could seat a hundred people. Some of the royal tents had also been put up, their bright varied colours making a vivid picture. Hundreds of people, mostly men, but a goodly number of women too, stood conversing in the wide courtyard, all in their finest clothes. Servants bustled to and fro, handing out silver mugs of wine and offering sweetmeats from trays. There was a steady hum of conversation.

An usher marked my name on a list – there was a list, of course, and anyone who did not turn up would hear about it – and told me that at six o'clock the King and Queen would walk with Admiral d'Annebault and their households from the Great Gate, cross the Great Court and enter the banqueting halls. Later there would be music and dancing. All of us were to cheer loudly when the trumpets sounded. Until then I was told I should mingle, just mingle.

I took a mug of wine from a servant and made my way through the throng, looking for Lord Parr. I could not see him, though there were many other faces I recognized. The old Duke of Norfolk, in a scarlet robe with white fur trim despite the heat, stood with his son the Earl of Surrey, whom I had seen with the ladies in the Queen's Presence Chamber at Whitehall. Both looked over the crowd with aristocratic disdain. In one corner Bishop Gardiner in his white surplice was talking earnestly to Lord Chancellor Wriothesley.

Both looked angry. Edward Seymour, Lord Hertford, peregrinated across the court, looking over the crowd of city dignitaries and gentry courtiers with confident, calculating eyes. On his arm was a thin woman in a green farthingale and feathered hat. I recognized her from my first visit to Whitehall Palace to see the Queen; she had asked if I was another hunchback fool. It had annoyed the Queen. Only five weeks ago; it seemed like an age. Many said that Hertford's wife, Anne, was a shrew who ruled him in private, for all his success as soldier and politician. She certainly had a sour, vinegary face.

The wine was very strong. That and the hubbub made me feel a little light-headed. I saw Sir William Paget in his usual dark robe, walking with a woman who despite her finery had a pleasant, homely countenance. He turned to her as she said something, his hard face softening unexpectedly.

I recalled the boatman spitting in the river. All this splendour for d'Annebault, ambassador of France. I wondered where Bertano, the Pope's emissary, was. Not here, for sure: his mission was still a secret. Perhaps he had already left England. As I walked slowly around, trying to spot Lord Parr, I began to find the gold chain heavy and the sun hot. I halted for a moment under the shade of one of the broad oak trees beside the outer wall.

I felt a tap on my shoulder and I turned: Sir Thomas Seymour, in a silver doublet, with a short yellow cloak over his shoulder and a matching cap worn at a jaunty angle. 'Master Shardlake again,' he said mockingly. 'Are you here as a member of the Queen's Learned Council?'

'No, Sir Thomas. As a serjeant of Lincoln's Inn. I no longer serve the Queen.'

He raised his eyebrows. 'Indeed? Not out of favour with her majesty, I hope?'

'No, Sir Thomas. The task she set me came to an end.'

'Ah, that missing jewel. Wicked, that some servant should steal an object of such great value to the Queen and get away with it. He should have been found and hanged.' His brown eyes narrowed. 'It *was* a jewel, wasn't it?'

'It was.'

Seymour nodded slowly, fingering that long, shiny, coppery beard. 'Strange, strange. Well, I must find my brother. We shall be sitting at the King's table at the banquet.' He smiled again, with preening self-satisfaction. You vain, stupid man, I thought. No wonder not even your brother wants you on the Privy Council.

My feelings must have shown on my face, for Seymour frowned. 'A pity you will not be dining. Only the highest in the land will be seated at the banquet. It must be uncomfortable for you, standing about here. See, even now you shift from foot to foot.'

I knew Thomas Seymour would never part without an insult. I did not reply as he leaned close. 'Watch your step, Master Shardlake. Things are changing, things are changing.' He nodded, smiled maliciously, and walked away.

I looked at his back, and that ridiculous cloak, wondering what he meant. Then, a little way off, I spied Mary Odell, in a dress of deep blue, the Queen's badge on her cap, talking to a young man in an orange doublet. She looked bored. I crossed to her, removed my cap and bowed. The gold links of my chain tinkled.

'Master Shardlake,' she said, relief in her voice.

The young man, handsome but with calculating eyes, looked slightly offended. He twirled the stem of his silver goblet. I said, 'Forgive me, sir, but I must speak with Mistress Odell on a matter of business.'

He bowed stiffly and walked away. 'Thank you, Master

Shardlake.' Mistress Odell spoke with that agreeable touch of humour I remembered. 'That young fellow is another would-be courtier, keen to talk with someone close to the Queen.' She grimaced.

'I am glad to have served,' I answered with a smile. Then, more earnestly, 'I need to speak with Lord Parr urgently. I hoped to see him here.'

She glanced back at the Great Gate behind us. 'He is in the Palace Court, with the Queen and her ladies, waiting for the King to come out with the admiral.'

'Could you fetch him? I am sorry to ask, but it is very urgent. He is expecting to talk to me today.'

Her face grew serious. 'I know you would not ask on a trivial matter. Wait, I will try to find him.'

She walked away, her dress swishing on the cobbles, and was allowed by the guards to pass through the Great Gate. I took some more wine and a comfit from a waiter. Looking over the crowd, I saw Serjeant Blower with a couple of aldermen, laughing heartily at some joke. William Cecil passed with an attractive young woman who must be his wife. He nodded to me but did not come over. Then, a little way off, I saw that Wriothesley was now talking to Sir Richard Rich, their heads together. I looked back at the gate. The feather plumes on the guards' steel helmets stirred in a cooling breeze from the river. The sun was low now.

Lord Parr appeared at the Great Gate, looking out at the throng. He craned his neck, trying to find me in the crowd. He looked tired. I walked over to him.

'Master Shardlake,' he said, irritation in his voice. 'I am needed inside. The King and Queen and the admiral will be out in ten minutes.'

'I am sorry, my Lord. I would not interrupt, but we must act against Stice tonight. He will be at the house near

St Bartholomew's at nine. Have you heard any more? Has anyone been to the house?'

The old man shifted his weight a little uneasily. 'My man says Stice came briefly yesterday, but soon left again.'

'Alone?'

'Yes.'

I spoke urgently, 'Then if you could spare a couple of men to go tonight, I will go too. Stice must be questioned. Even if we have no cause – '

Then Lord Parr said firmly, 'No.'

'My Lord?'

'Things have changed, Master Shardlake. Charles Stice must be left alone.'

'But – why?'

He leaned in. 'This is confidential, Shardlake. I have had a direct approach from Richard Rich. He is in bad odour with Gardiner, for several reasons; his speaking up for you at the Privy Council did not help. He has offered to aid the Seymours and Parrs against Norfolk and Gardiner. He has changed sides, following the wind again.'

I looked at him in amazement. 'The Queen will work with Rich now? But she loathes him.'

'She will,' Lord Parr answered firmly. 'For the sake of the Parr family, and the cause of reform. Rich is on the council, he is important, the King respects his skills, if not the man. As do I.'

'But – why has he been spying on me? And may he not have information about the *Lamentation*?'

Lord Parr shook his head firmly. 'Rich will do nothing to harm the reformers now. Even if he had the book, which I do not believe he ever did.'

'If he is your ally now should you not ask him?'

Irritation entered the old man's voice. 'Our agreement

involves my drawing a veil over all his activities this spring and summer. Those are not to be discussed. That includes what he did to Anne Askew, and everything else. As for his spying on you,' he added more civilly, 'in due course, when the time is right, I will ask him.'

Stunned, I continued to stare at Lord Parr. He flushed, then burst out with sudden impatience, 'God's death, man, do not stand there with your mouth open like a fish. These are the necessities of politics. Rich and his people are to be left alone.'

And with that, the Queen's Chamberlain turned away, back to the Great Gate.

✝

I STEPPED BACK, feeling as though I had been punched in the stomach. So Rich was finally turning his coat. And, I thought wearily, Lord Parr was right; these were the necessities of politics. Why should it matter to any of them what Rich had done to me? I looked across to where he stood talking to Wriothesley; Wriothesley's face was red, they were arguing. The alliance between them, which had led to the torture of Anne Askew, was over now.

A trumpet blew, then another. The guards at the Great Gate stood to attention and everyone ceased talking and looked towards it in silence. Then the King appeared in the gateway, Admiral d'Annebault at his side. The King was dressed more magnificently than I had ever seen before, in a yellow coat with padded shoulders and fur collar, a cream-coloured doublet set with jewels, and a broad white feathered cap on his head. He was smiling widely. One arm rested on his jewelled stick, the other round the shoulder of Archbishop Cranmer. No doubt he needed Cranmer to hold him up. Fortunately it was but a short walk to the banqueting houses. On d'Annebault's other side, her arm through the admiral's, was the Queen. She wore a dress in Tudor green and white, her auburn hair bright under a green cap, a light smile on her face. She looked radiant: knowing her inner turmoil, I marvelled again at her composure.

The royal party was followed by the men from the King's household, and women from the Queen's ladies in their bright new livery, led by Lord Parr. The crowd in the Great Court parted to let them walk through to the larger of the two banqueting houses. I joined the others in raising my cup. There were claps and shouts of 'God save the King!'

Now the junior members of the households halted and turned towards the second, smaller banqueting house. Guards opened the doors of both and I glimpsed cloth-covered tables on which candles in gold sconces were already lit against the coming dusk. The leading men of the realm — Norfolk and Gardiner and Paget, the Seymour brothers and others — left the crowd and followed the King, Queen and d'Annebault into the larger banqueting house. From within I heard lutes starting to play.

The Lady Mary had now appeared through the gateway, followed by her own retinue. Jane Fool was there, and began dancing and frolicking round Mary, who laughed and bade her cease. They, too, passed into the royal banqueting house.

The crowd outside relaxed, as a fresh column of servants came through the Great Gate carrying large trays of food from the Hampton Court kitchens. They were followed by a group of guards bearing torches, which they slotted into brackets set into the walls of the Great Court and on the trunks of trees. As the servants handed round cold meats and more wine, I saw some people were getting drunk; in Serjeant Blower's party, one or two were swaying slightly. Son of a drunkard myself, the sight revolted me.

I looked over all these rich men and women and thought of Timothy, somewhere alone out on the streets. The notion came to me that perhaps the Anabaptists had something after all: a world where the gulf between the few rich and the many poor did not exist, a world where preening peacocks like Thomas Seymour and Serjeant Blower wore wadmol and cheap leather, might not be so bad a place after all.

I waved away a waiter carrying plates in one hand and a silver dish of swan's meat in the other. I was shocked by what Lord Parr had said. It was dusk and the breeze felt suddenly cold. My back hurt. My mission was over. I should go and tell Barak and Nicolas they would not be needed.

I saw that Rich and Wriothesley were still engrossed in their argument, whatever it was. They would be in trouble if they did not soon make their way to their appointed places in the royal banqueting hall. Then I saw somebody else I recognized. Stice. I stepped back into the deepening shadows of the tree. He wore an expensive grey doublet, with 'RR' embossed on the chest, and as he passed at a little distance a torch picked out the shiny scar tissue of his damaged ear. The way he was moving puzzled me; he walked stealthily as he moved towards the royal banqueting house, constantly seeking cover, slipping behind those who stood between him and his master. There could be no doubt, I realized suddenly: Stice was avoiding Rich, not seeking him. Rich and Wriothesley were still arguing fiercely; Rich waved a waiter aside so violently that the man dropped a tray filled with goblets of wine. People laughed as the waiter bent to pick them up, Rich berating him angrily as though it were the waiter's fault. Stice took the opportunity to move swiftly to the guards at the doors of the banqueting house. A steel-helmeted soldier put out a hand to stop him.

Stice pulled something from the purse at his belt and

showed it to the guard. I could not make it out but it looked like a seal, that of one of the great men of the realm, no doubt. Not Rich, who still stood with Wriothesley, glowering at the unfortunate waiter, for Stice would have pointed to him. As the guard examined the seal, Stice cast a quick glance over his shoulder at Rich. Then the soldier nodded to him, and Stice entered the tent.

I stood there, my heart thudding. For I realized now that Stice, like Curdy the spy, had more than one loyalty. A man in Richard Rich's employment had outmanoeuvred his master. Stice had used that seal to get himself into the royal banquet, and his purpose in hurrying there now must be to tell his other master, whoever that was, about the note retrieved from the tavern where Brocket had left it, the note mentioning the 'Italian gentleman'. But who, among those leading men, was Stice's other master? Whoever it was, he had ordered Stice to spy on me, for many months. Rich had been telling the truth, after all. I stared intently at the open doors, but I could only vaguely make out the bright-clad courtiers moving to take their seats.

Rich and Wriothesley realized they were late. They began walking towards the banqueting house with long strides, not speaking. The guards let them through. Would Rich see Stice now?

No. For a moment later Stice walked briskly along the outside wall of the banqueting house, ducking as he passed a window; he must have left through a rear entrance. Keeping close to the tree, I watched as he stepped rapidly away to the river steps, and disappeared.

A group of minstrels walked into the centre of the Great Court, strumming their instruments for the crowd. People cheered, and as I watched a space was cleared. Men and women began dancing, robes and skirts whirling. I thought

C. J. SANSOM

for a moment, Lord Parr should be told about Stice, especially if Rich was on his side now. But he was inside the main banqueting house. I had seen how difficult it had been for Stice to gain entrance; and I no longer had the Queen's seal to show anyone, for I had returned it along with the robe with her badge on it.

Stice must already be on his way back to London by boat, to go to what he thought was a rendezvous with Brocket. I clenched my fists. Obstinacy and anger rose in me. Well, it would be me and Barak and Nicholas whom Stice would be meeting. Three of us against one, we would take him easily, and we would finally have some answers.

Chapter Fifty

BARAK AND NICHOLAS were waiting for me at home, drinking beer in the kitchen. I had hailed a boat quickly at the Hampton Court stairs; a long line of wherrymen was waiting to bring people back to London once the festivities ended, and I was leaving early. I asked the boatman whether I was the first to depart; he replied that one of his fellows had picked up another customer a few minutes before. As we pulled downriver I saw another boat a little ahead of us, a man in grey doublet and cap sitting in the stern. I told the boatman to slow a little so I might enjoy the cool airs of evening; in fact it was to let Stice get out of view. It was peaceful out there on the river, the boatman's oars making ripples that glinted in the setting sun, insects buzzing over the water. I asked myself: is this right, what I am doing? And I answered yes, for surely Stice's true master was the one who had ordered the murder of the Anabaptists and taken the *Lamentation*. There might be a chance of recovering the Queen's book after all.

✝

BACK HOME, there was no news of Timothy. Barak, who had remained at the house all afternoon, had had several visitors who said they knew where the boy was but wanted the reward first. Barak had dealt with them bluntly. Nicholas had also returned. I thanked them for their efforts, telling myself that for the next few hours I must put Timothy's fate from my mind.

Looking at Barak and Nicholas, I considered again whether what I was doing was right. This was for the Queen and the murdered men, but I knew also for myself, because I wanted answers. Barak and Nicholas had come equipped for danger; Nicholas's sword was at his belt and Barak had one, too. Both knew well how to use them.

I told them about seeing Stice at Hampton Court, and what Lord Parr had said. When I had finished I asked them once more, 'Are you sure you wish to do this?'

'All the more, now,' Barak said. 'With Brocket gone it's our last chance.'

'What did you tell Tamasin?'

He looked uncomfortable. 'That we were going to continue searching for Timothy this evening.'

'I'm glad of the chance to get back at that churl who kidnapped me,' Nicholas said. 'But sir, if we catch him, what do we do with him? We can't take him back to my lodgings as we did with Leeman, my fellow students are there.'

'I've thought of that. We'll keep him in that house until morning; question him ourselves, then take him to Lord Parr.'

'I'll get answers out of him.' Barak spoke coldly. 'He wouldn't be the first.' I thought, no, there are things you did when you worked for Cromwell that we have always drawn a veil over. I did not dissent.

'Can we be sure Stice will be alone?' Nicholas asked.

'I got Brocket to ask him to come alone as always. And Lord Parr's man who is watching the house says Stice only came there once, and by himself.'

Barak said, 'I got one of the men helping me on the

search for Timothy to walk up and down that street this afternoon and report back to me. I didn't want to go myself as Stice knows me. It's a lane of small, newly built houses, much better places than on Needlepin Lane. Most of the houses have porches, quite deep. We could hide in one and watch until just before nine. We might even see Stice arrive.'

'Very well.' I looked out of the window. It was quite dark now. I thought, at Hampton Court they would be dancing by torchlight in the courtyard, sounds of loud revelry coming from the King's banqueting house. Several more banquets, as well as hunts, were planned for the next few days. The Queen would be at all of them. Then I thought of Timothy, alone on the dangerous streets for a second night. I collected myself. 'Let us go now,' I said. 'But remember, Stice is a man who will stop at nothing.'

'Fortune favours those with justice and honour on their side,' Nicholas said.

Barak responded, 'If only.'

☩

THE STREETS WERE QUIET as we walked up to Smithfield. Fortunately it was not a market day and the big open space was silent and deserted. We went down Little Britain Street, following the wall of St Bartholomew's Hospital, then turned into a broad lane, a reputable row of newly built two-storey houses, most with glass windows rather than shutters, and little porches, too. Candles flickered behind most of the windows but at a house that was in darkness Barak waved us into the porch. I hoped the owner would not return expectedly; he would think himself about to be robbed.

Barak pointed to a house on the opposite side of the lane, a little further down. 'That's the one. There's a big Tudor rose on the arch above the porch, as Brocket mentioned. You can just see it.'

I followed his gaze. The house's shutters were drawn and all was silent.

We stood, waiting and watching. A serving woman came out of a nearby house with a bucket of dirty water and poured it into the channel in the centre of the road. We tensed as the light of a torch appeared at the top of the lane, and voices sounded. It was, however, only a link-boy, leading the way for a small family party who were chattering happily, returning from some visit. They disappeared into one of the houses further down the lane.

'What time is it?' Nicholas asked quietly. 'It must be near nine.'

'I think it is,' Barak said. 'But it doesn't look like Stice is here yet.'

'He could already be inside,' I whispered. 'At the rear of the house, perhaps.'

Barak's eyes narrowed. 'All right, let's wait till the clocks chime. Stice wouldn't be late for this one, not if he's been all the way to Hampton Court and back to consult his master.'

We waited. When the bells rang out the hour, Barak took a deep breath. 'Let's go,' he breathed. 'Rush him as soon as the door opens.'

⟨✠⟩

WE HALF-RAN ACROSS the street. I glanced up at the Tudor rose on the lintel of the porch, as Barak hammered on the door. He and Nicholas both had their hands on their sword hilts, and I grasped my knife.

I heard quick footsteps, sounding indeed as though they were coming from the rear of the house. There was the glimmer of a candle between the shutters. As soon as we heard the handle turn on the inner side of the door Barak put his shoulder to it, and crashed inside. The interior was dim, just a couple of candles in a holder on the table. By their light I saw Charles Stice stagger back, hand reaching to the sword at his waist. But Barak and Nicholas already had their blades pointed at his body.

'Got you,' Nicholas said triumphantly.

Then, at the edge of my vision, I saw rapid movement as the men who had been waiting on either side of the door stepped quickly out. Two more swords flashed. Barak and Nicholas turned rapidly as two well-built young men ran at them from behind. I recognized them by the candlelight: one fair with a wart on his brow, the other almost bald. Greening's killers, Daniels and Cardmaker.

Barak and Nicholas were both quick, managing to parry the blows. Meanwhile, drawing my knife, I lunged forward, ready to plunge it into the neck of the bald man, but he was faster than me. Though still fighting against Nicholas, he managed to half-turn and elbow me in the face with his free arm. I staggered back against the wall. The distraction, however, was enough to allow Nicholas to gain the advantage, and begin to force him back.

Barak, meanwhile, was facing not only the other man in front but Stice behind. And before he could turn, step aside and face both of them, Stice raised his newly drawn sword and slashed at Barak's sword-arm. To my horror the razor-sharp weapon, with the full force of Stice's arm behind it, slashed down into Barak's wrist just above his sword. Into it and through it, and I cried out at a sight I shall never forget: Barak's severed hand, still holding his sword, flying through the air and hitting the ground.

He screamed, turned and grasped his arm, which was spraying blood. Then Stice stabbed him in the back with his sword. Barak looked at me. His face was a mask of astonish-ment, his eyes somehow questioning, as though he wanted me to explain what had just happened. Then his legs gave way and he crashed to the floor. He lay on his face, unmov-ing, blood pumping from the stump of his wrist.

In a fury, I flew at Stice, knife raised. My move was unex-pected and he did not have time to block my path with his sword. I aimed for his throat but he ducked and the knife slashed his face instead, from mouth to ear. He cried out but did not drop his sword, instead raising it to my throat and forcing me backwards, pinning me against the wall.

'Stop now!' he shouted. 'You can't win!'

Glancing to the side, I saw the other two had Nicholas. The bald man shouted, 'Drop the sword, boy!' Nicholas gritted his teeth, but obeyed. His weapon clattered to the floor. He looked in horror at Barak, face down on the floor. Stice withdrew his sword from my throat. He reached into his pocket and pulled out a handkerchief to staunch the blood welling from his cheek. I caught a glimpse of white bone.

Barak made a sound, a little moan. He was still alive, just. He tried to raise his head but it dropped back to the floor with a crack and he lay unmoving again. Blood still poured from his wrist, and more from the wound in his back, making a dark patch on his shirt.

'He's still alive,' the bald man said with professional inter-est.

'Not for long,' Stice replied. 'He'll bleed out soon if nothing else.' Blood dripped down the hand holding the kerchief to his face. 'He was once known as a fighter,' he added, with sudden pride.

I looked at Stice, and spoke savagely, through bruised lips. 'At least you'll have a scar on your face to match that ear.'

He looked at me coldly, then laughed. 'So, you caught Brocket out, did you?'

'It was me who sent the message.'

Stice smiled. 'Brocket seemed to have found out something big. I thought it time to bring him in person to my master, so I arranged help to secure him.'

'So all of you were working together, all the time?'

'That's right. All part of the same merry band, working for the same master.'

The fair-haired man, his sword still pointed at Nicholas's throat, said, 'He'll be pleased then? We've caught a big fish, as well as this long minnow?'

Stice sat on the edge of the table. 'Yes. He'll be keen to find out why he mentioned an Italian.' He winced at the pain from his face. 'God's wounds, I'll have to get this stitched. But we must take Shardlake to him first. The boy as well. Bind their hands; we'll ride. I'll get treatment at Whitehall. He's waiting there.'

Whitehall? I thought. But the royal family and high councillors had all moved to Hampton Court.

'It's past curfew,' the fair-haired man said. 'What if the constables see us?'

'With my seal, they won't challenge us. Not when they see who we are taking them to.'

There was a sudden bang on the wall separating the house from its neighbour. A man's voice shouted, 'What's going on?' The voice was cultured and angry, but frightened too. 'What's all this noise?'

Stice called out, 'We're having a party! Fuck off!' His confederates laughed. There was silence from the next house. I looked down at Barak, quite still now, blood still flowing from his severed wrist, though less freely. I glanced at his severed hand, lying a foot away on the floor, still holding his sword. 'Right,' Stice said decisively. 'Time to go.'

I said, 'Who is your master? It's not Richard Rich, is it? I was at Hampton Court, and saw how you avoided him. Who are you really working for?'

Stice frowned. 'You'll find out soon, Master Hunchback.'

The bald man nodded at the prone Barak. 'What about him?'

'Leave him to bleed out,' Stice replied.

I said desperately, 'Leave him to die here? Leave a body in this house to be found? That neighbour is already worried. He'll be looking in the windows tomorrow. Then there'll be a coroner's enquiry – in public – and they'll do a search to find out who owns the house.' I continued rapidly, for I knew this was my last dim hope of saving Barak's life, if indeed he was not already dead. 'It's known that Jack Barak works with me. Whatever you have planned for me, this is murder and it won't be allowed to rest. Not when the Queen hears – she won't let it.'

'Our master could soon stop a coroner's enquiry,' the bald man said scoffingly. Stice frowned, though. He looked down at Barak; his face, from what I could see, was still and ashen against his brown beard. He could be dead already. I thought of Tamasin, pregnant. I had brought him here.

'The hunchback could be right,' Daniels said uneasily.

'All right,' Stice agreed. 'Our master would wish us to be careful. Here, one of you make a tourniquet with your hand-kerchiefs, or he'll bleed all over us as well as the floor.'

'I know where we can put him.' The bald man gave a little giggle. 'I came here round the back ways. There's an empty building lot the people round here have turned into a rubbish heap. Two streets away.'

'All right,' Stice agreed. 'Bind those two now.'

Cardmaker produced a length of rope from the bag at his belt, which he must have brought for Brocket. He cut it in two with his knife, then approached us. 'Hands behind your backs.'

We could do nothing else. I looked desperately at Barak's prone form as they bound our hands behind us. Meanwhile Stice bound Barak's arm tightly with a handkerchief, making a tourniquet to lessen the flow of blood, and tied another securely round the stump. Bright red blood immediately began to seep through. Then Stice said, 'Daniels, throw him across your horse. We'll put these two on the horse we brought for Brocket, tie their legs together under the horse's belly. If we're stopped on the way to Whitehall, say they're traitors and we've arrested them.' He looked at Barak's severed hand lying on the floor in a pool of blood, still gripping his sword. 'God's teeth, what a mess. We'll have to come back and clean this up after. Our master often uses this house.'

They took us out to the back, where there was a stable, three horses waiting. It was horrible to see Barak unconscious, being lifted up under the arms by Cardmaker and dumped over the back of one of the horses as though he were a sack of cabbages. From what I could see, the bleeding was much less, though a few drips still fell to the ground. But I knew enough to understand that even if Barak still lived, he did not have long, perhaps fifteen minutes, before he bled out.

Stice looked at me over his handkerchief, his eyes bright with savage pleasure. 'It'll be up to my master whether the two of you live. He'll get a surprise; he was only expecting one frightened steward.'

Chapter Fifty-one

W E RODE DOWN THE LANE behind the stables. Nicholas and I had been placed, hands bound, on one of the horses, Nicholas in front. It was a moonlit night, though the narrow track between the garden fences of the new houses was hard to see. Then we turned into a second lane, running down the back of another row of houses. Halfway down the lane there was a square plot where for some reason no building had been put up. As Cardmaker had said, it was a rubbish heap. I saw an old bed frame, broken stools, household refuse and a huge heap of grass clippings where servants had been scything the gardens. It had mulched down into a soft green compost. The rubbish heap stank.

We halted. Stice's men dismounted and Barak was lifted from his horse and tipped, head first, into the compost. I seldom prayed nowadays — even if God existed, I was sure that he was deaf. Now, though, I prayed hopelessly that somehow my friend might live.

We rode back to the main road. It was hard merely to keep my balance. My face throbbed from where I had been elbowed. Stice's confederates walked one on either side of us; Stice, leading the horse which had carried Barak, rode in front, still dabbing at his face with his handkerchief. We came out onto Smithfield and passed the front door of the hospital. I wondered if Guy was working within.

We were stopped at Newgate by a constable. Lifting his lamp and seeing our bound hands and Stice's bloody face, he asked Stice sharply what was happening. But Stice took out a seal, thrusting it into the man's face. 'Official business,' he snapped. 'Two traitors to go to Whitehall for questioning. As you'll see from my face, they made a fight of it.'

The London constables knew the different seals of all the great men, it was part of their training. The man not only withdrew, but bowed to Stice as he did so.

✝

WE RODE ON through the quiet streets, past Charing Cross and down to Whitehall. I wondered why we were being taken there rather than to Hampton Court. Surely, apart from the guards, there would be only a few servants left to maintain the place? Yet such considerations hardly mattered in comparison to what had happened to Barak. I was sitting tied up on the horse, my back was excruciatingly painful and my face throbbed. A wave of exhaustion washed over me, and my head slumped forward onto Nicholas's back. He took the weight, saying over his shoulder, 'Stay awake, sir, or you will fall.'

'Just let me rest against you a little.' Then I said, 'I am sorry, sorry.' He did not reply. Whatever happened now, I must try to save Nicholas at least.

✝

AS EXPECTED, Whitehall Palace was dark and deserted, only a few dim lights visible within. But the guard at the gatehouse had obviously been told to expect Stice, for as we rode up he stepped forward. Stice bent to speak to him; there were some murmured words and then I heard the guard say, 'He's waiting in the Privy Council Chamber. Rode here from the Hampton Court celebrations half an hour ago.'

Two more guards came out of the gatehouse. Stice dismounted and quickly scribbled a note, and the first guard ran into the building with it. No doubt it was to inform Stice's master that he had come back not with Brocket, but with me.

The two guards accompanied us across the courtyard, the horses' hooves clattering loudly on the cobbles. We came up to the wide doors of the King's Guard Chamber. Stice dismounted and cut the ropes binding us. Nicholas helped me to dismount, and I stood a little shakily at the bottom of the steps. Stice, bloodied handkerchief still held to his face, turned to Daniels and Cardmaker. 'Thank you, goodmen, for your work these last two months. Your money is in the gatehouse. Leave London for a while, find some alehouses and brothels in another town to spend your wages. But keep in contact, in case you are needed again.'

The two murderers bowed, then turned away without another glance at us. I watched them go, the men who had killed Greening and Elias and those others. Hired murderers, strolling cheerfully to collect their reward. I looked at Stice, who glared back at me. 'I will leave you as well now, Master Shardlake. I need to get your handiwork on my face seen to. I doubt you will leave here alive, which is a comfort. If you do, watch out for me.' Then he followed his henchmen back to the palace gatehouse. Nicholas and I were left with the two guards. One inclined his halberd towards the doorway of the Guard Chamber. 'In,' he said brusquely.

I looked at Nicholas, who swallowed hard. Then we mounted the steps, one guard ahead of us, one behind.

✝

THE MAGNIFICENT STAIRCASE leading up to the King's Guard Chamber was quiet and barely lit, only two men posted at the top; the torches in their niches showing empty spaces on the wall where paintings had been removed to Hampton Court. One of the guards at the top said we were to be taken to the Privy Council Chamber, where I had stood and sweated the week before. 'He's not ready yet, you can wait in the Privy Chamber. It's empty as the King's not in residence here.'

We were led through a series of dim rooms until we reached a large chamber. The walls were almost bare here too, everything no doubt removed to the Privy Chamber at Hampton Court. We were ordered to stand and wait, a guard staying with us. I looked at the opposite wall, and saw that it was covered from floor to ceiling by a magnificent wall painting, irremovable, for it was painted directly onto the plaster just like the Cotterstoke family portrait. I had heard of Holbein's great mural, and now, in the dim flickering candlelight, I looked at it. The other large wall painting I had seen at Whitehall had shown the present King and his family; this one, however, was a magnificent display of dynastic power. The centrepiece was a square stone monu-ment, covered in Latin words which I could not make out from where I stood. The old King, Henry VII, stood on a pedestal with one lean arm resting on the monument, his sharp foxy face staring out. Opposite him was a plump woman with arms folded, no doubt the King's mother. Below her, on a lower step, stood Queen Jane Seymour. I thought again how Prince Edward resembled his mother. But it was the present King, standing below his father, who dominated the mural: the King as he had been perhaps half a dozen years ago: broad-shouldered, burly but not fat, his hand on his hip and his bull-like legs planted firmly apart, with an exaggerated codpiece jutting from the skirts of his doublet.

This image of the King had been reproduced many times and hung in countless official buildings and private halls, but the original had a life and power no copyist could imitate. It was the hard, staring, angry little blue eyes which dominated the painting, whose background was in sombre colours. Perhaps that was the whole point of the mural, to make those who were waiting to see the King feel as if he were already watching and judging them.

Nicholas stared open-mouthed at the mural and then whispered, 'It is like looking at living people.'

Another guard came in then and spoke to the first. We were taken roughly by the arm, and led out, through a second and then a third magnificent chamber, before we reached a corridor I recognized; the Privy Council Chamber. We came up to the door. The guard standing before it said, 'Not the boy. He says to put him somewhere till he knows whether he needs to question him.'

'Come on, you.' The first guard pulled Nicholas's arm, leading him away. 'Courage, Master Shardlake,' Nicholas called back to me. Then the remaining guard knocked at the door, and a sharp voice I recognized called, 'Enter.'

I was pulled inside. The guard left, shutting the door behind me. There was only one man in the long chamber, sitting on a chair at the centre of the table, a sconce of candles beside him. He looked at me with hard eyes set in a slab face above a forked beard. Master Secretary Paget.

'Master Shardlake.' He sighed wearily. 'How much work and effort you have made for me.' He shook his head. 'When there is so much else to do.'

I looked at him. 'So you were behind it all,' I said quietly.

My voice sounded thick and muffled, my face swelling now where I had been struck.

His expression did not change. 'All what?'

Recklessly, far beyond deference now, I answered, 'The murder of those Anabaptists. The theft of the – the manuscript. Spying on me for the last year, I know not why. Nor care.' I gulped a breath, my voice breaking as a picture came into my head once more of Barak dumped on that rubbish heap.

Paget stared back at me. He had the gift of sitting still, focused, like a cat watching its prey. '*Murder?*' His tone was admonitory, accusing. 'Those men were heretics, and traitors too, who would gladly have killed me, or the King, or you for that matter, to advance their perverted notions. They had easier deaths than they deserved, they should have been burned. They were stupid, though. When my spies among the radicals warned me of a nest of Anabaptists in London, my man Curdy infiltrated it with ease. Now *there* was a loyal servant, and he *was* murdered.' Paget drew his heavy eyebrows together in a frown.

'He was killed in a fight.'

'Yes. By one of Richard Rich's men.' He waved a hand contemptuously. 'Rich was after what Anne Askew wrote before she was burned, I know that. I believe John Bale has it now.' For the first time Paget laughed, a flash of surprisingly white teeth amid the coarse brown of his beard. 'That may come back to haunt Sir Richard yet.'

'You suborned Rich's servant,' I said.

Paget shifted a little, settling more comfortably in his chair. 'I keep my eye on those who work for the great men of the realm, and sometimes I find men among them of such ambition they can be persuaded to work for me and earn two incomes. Though organizing a watch to be kept on you, Shardlake, that was a nuisance, a waste of Stice's talents, I thought. And there was nothing to find. Until – ' he leaned forward, frowning now, his voice threatening – 'until last month.' He paused, then spoke slowly and deliberately. 'A moment ago you mentioned a manuscript.'

I did not reply. I should not have spoken of it. I must keep my control. I waited for Paget to question me further, but he only smiled cynically. 'The *Lamentation of a Sinner*,' he said, 'by her majesty, the Queen Catherine.'

My mouth fell open. 'Yes, Master Shardlake,' he went on, 'it was me who arranged for that book to be taken from the heretic printer Greening, as soon as Curdy told me it had been brought to his group by that wretched guard.'

I closed my eyes for a moment. Then, having nothing left to lose, I said, 'No doubt you took it to further your own ends in the power struggle. Have you been waiting, like Rich, to see which way the wind will blow, whether the Queen would fall and Bertano's mission succeed, keeping the *Lamentation* in reserve? Be careful, Master Secretary, that the King does not find you have kept it from him.'

I was speaking recklessly, dangerously. 'Mind your words with me, master lawyer,' Paget snapped. 'Remember who I am and where you are.' I stared back at him, breathing heavily. He inclined his head. 'You are right that the King was gracious enough to receive an emissary from the Bishop of Rome, but it seems that as a condition of peace His Holiness, as he styles himself, demands that the King surrender the Headship of the Church in England – the Headship to which God has appointed him. Bertano is still here, but I think it is time now he took himself back to his master. How did you know of his presence?' he asked sharply.

'The Anabaptists were overheard,' I said quietly. 'You

rogue, that cut such a swathe of murder through ordinary folk to serve your ambition.'

'My ambition, eh?' Paget asked coldly.

'Yes.'

And then, to my surprise, he laughed grimly, and stood up. 'I think it is time for you to see what you never guessed, master clever lawyer. Even Stice did not know anything of this.' He picked up the sconce of candles and walked past me to the door. 'Follow me,' he said with an imperious sweep of the arm, throwing the door open wide.

I got up slowly. He said to the guard outside, 'Accompany us.'

The guard took a position beside me as Paget opened a door opposite. I found myself in a darkened gallery filled with beautiful scents, like the Queen's gallery, though wider and twice the length. As we walked along, our footsteps silent on the rush matting, the sconce of candles in Paget's hand showed glimpses of tapestries and paintings more magnificent than any I had seen elsewhere in the palace, before we passed marble columns and platforms on which rested gigantic vases, beautiful models of ships, jewelled chests with who knew what within. I realized this must be the King's Privy Gallery, and wondered why the contents had not been taken to Hampton Court. We passed an enormous military standard, the flag decorated with fleur-de-lys; no doubt a French standard seized when Henry took Boulogne. It was covered in dark spots. Blood, I realized, and remembered again Barak's severed hand flying through the air. I jumped at something small running along the wainscoting. A rat. Paget frowned and barked at the guard. 'Get that seen to! Bring one of the ratcatchers back from Hampton Court!'

At length we reached the end of the gallery, where two further guards stood beside a large double door. Glancing through a nearby window I saw we were directly above the palace wall, on the other side of which I could see the broad way of King Street. A group of young gentlemen were walking past, link-boys with torches lighting their way.

'Master Secretary.' One of the guards at the door bowed to Paget, and opened it. I blinked at the brightness of the light on the other side, then followed Paget in.

It was a wide chamber, beautifully furnished, and brightly lit by a host of fat buttermilk candles in silver sconces. The walls were lined with shelves of beautiful and ancient books. In the spaces between the shelves, splendid paintings hung, mostly depicting classical scenes. A window looked out directly over the street. I realized we must be inside the Holbein Gate. Under the window was a wide desk littered with papers and a dish of comfits beside a golden flagon of wine. A pair of spectacles lay atop the papers, glinting in the candlelight.

The King's fool, little hunchbacked Will Somers, stood beside the desk, his monkey perched on the shoulder of his particoloured doublet. And sitting beside him, in an enormous chair, staring at me with blue eyes as hard and savage as those in Holbein's portrait, for all that they were now tiny slits in a pale face thick with fat, was the King.

Chapter Fifty-two

INSTANTLY, I BOWED as low as I could. After what I had happened to Barak I had given Paget none of the deference due to him, but faced with the King I abased myself instinctively. I had time to take in only that he wore a long caftan, as on the day Lord Parr showed him to me from the window, and that his head with its grey wispy hair was bare.

There was a moment's silence. The blood rushed to my head and I thought I might faint. But no one was permitted to rise and look the King in the face until he addressed them. I heard him laugh. It was a laboured, creaking sound, oddly reminiscent of Treasurer Rowland. Then he spoke, in that same unexpectedly high voice I remembered from my brief encounter with him at York, though underlain with a new, throaty creakiness. 'So, Paget, my Master of Practices, he found you out. Someone has punched him in the face.' That creaky laugh again.

'There was a fight, I believe, your majesty, before Stice took him,' Paget said.

'Have you told him anything?'

'Nothing, your majesty. You said you wished to do that.'

The King continued in the same quiet voice, though I discerned a threatening edge to it now. 'Very well, Serjeant Matthew Shardlake, stand.'

I did so, my bruised face throbbing, and looked slowly up

at the King. The pale bloated face was lined, full of pain and weariness. His grey beard, like his hair, was thin and wispy. His huge bulk strained against the satin arms of his chair, and his legs stuck out, swathed in thick bandages. But grotesque and even pitiable as he now was, Henry's gaze remained terrifying. In the portrait outside it was the eyes which seemed most chilling, but in the living man it was the tight little mouth, straight and hard as a blade between the great jowls; angry, merciless. Looking at him my head swam for a second; it was as though none of this were real, and I was in some nightmare. I felt oddly disconnected, dizzy, and again I thought I might faint. Then in my mind's eye I saw Barak's hand fly through the air in a spray of blood, and I jerked convulsively.

The King held my gaze another moment, then turned and waved at Somers and the guard. 'Will, top up my goblet, then take the guard and begone. One crookback at a time is enough.'

Somers poured wine from the flagon, the monkey clinging to his shoulder with practised ease. The King lifted the goblet to his mouth and I caught a glimpse of grey teeth. 'God's death,' he murmured, 'this endless thirst.'

Somers and the guard went out, closing the door quietly behind them. I gave Paget a quick glance; he looked back with that flat, empty gaze of his. The King, his eyes locking on mine again, spoke in a voice full of quiet menace. 'So, Master Shardlake, I hear you have been spending time with my wife.'

'No, your majesty, no!' I heard the edge of panic in my own voice as I answered. 'I have merely been helping her to search for, for – '

'For this?' With difficulty the King reached behind him to the desk, his surprisingly delicate fingers clutching at a sheaf of papers. He heaved himself round again, holding it up. I saw the Queen's writing, the first page torn in half where Greening had grasped it as he died. The *Lamentation of a Sinner*.

I felt the ground shift beneath me; again I almost fainted. I took deep breaths. The King stared at me, waiting for an answer, the little mouth tightening. Then, from beside me, Paget said, 'Naturally, Master Shardlake, when I learned from my spy in that Anabaptist group that they had stolen a book written by the Queen, I told his majesty at once. He ordered the book brought to him, and the sect extirpated. It has been in his possession all this time.'

I stared foolishly at the manuscript. All this – all the weeks of anxiety and fear, the terrible thing that had happened to Barak tonight – and the *Lamentation* had been in the King's possession all along. I should have been furious, but in the King's presence there was no room for any emotion but fear. He pointed a finger at me, his voice rasping with anger. 'Last year, Master Shardlake, when the Queen and I were at Portsmouth, I saw you at the front of the crowd as I entered the city.' I looked up in surprise. 'Yes, and I remembered you, as I do all those I have had cause to look on unfavourably. You failed once before to discover a stolen manuscript. At York, five years ago. Did you not?'

I swallowed hard. The King had insulted me in public, then. Yet he would have done far worse had he known that I had succeeded in discovering that particular cache of papers and had destroyed them on account of their incendiary contents. I looked back at him, fearing irrationally that those probing eyes could see into my very mind, that they could see what I had truly done at York, and even my treacherous thoughts this very afternoon about the Anabaptists' creed.

The angry edge in the King's voice deepened. 'God's blood, churl, answer your King!'

'I – I was sorry to have displeased you, your majesty.' It sounded craven, pathetic.

'So you should have been. And when I saw you last year at Portsmouth, when you had no reason to be there, I had Paget make enquiry, and learned you had visited my wife at Portchester Castle. And that you did lawyer's work for her. I allowed that, Master Shardlake, for I know that once, before our marriage, you saved her life.' He nodded slowly. 'Oh yes, Cranmer told me about that, later.' His voice had softened momentarily, and I saw that, indeed, he still loved Catherine Parr. And yet he had used her as a tool in his political machinations all these months, had allowed her to go in fear of her life.

His voice hardened again. 'I do not like my wife receiving visitors unsanctioned by me, so when I returned from Portsmouth I arranged to have you watched.' He laughed wheezily. 'Not that I would suspect my Kate of dalliance with an ugly brokebacked thing like you, but these days I watch all those who might take too great an interest in those I love. I have been betrayed by women before,' he added bitterly. 'My wife does not know that I watch certain of her male associates. Paget is good at employing discreet men to observe and spy. Eh, Sir William?' The King half-turned and gave Paget a blow on the arm which made him stagger slightly; he blinked but did not flinch. The movement meanwhile set the King's whole vast body, uncorseted under the caftan, wobbling and juddering.

I swallowed hard. 'Your majesty, I hold the Queen in great esteem, but only as her employee, and as a subject admiring of her kindness, her learning—'

'Her religion?' the King asked, suddenly and sharply.

I took a deep breath. 'It is not a matter her majesty and I have discussed at length.' But I remembered those conversations in the gallery. I was lying, plain and simple, because terrifying as the King was, to reveal the truth might still endanger the Queen. My heart thumped in my chest, and it was hard to keep my voice from shaking as I continued. 'And when I spoke with her, in London and at Portsmouth – someone was always present, one of the ladies, Mary Odell or another – ' I was almost stammering, my words tumbling over each other.

Paget looked at me contemptuously and said, 'Stice's spies, the lawyer Bealknap and afterwards the steward Brocket, reported no dealings between you and the Queen or her court for a year. But then last month, out of the blue, you were sworn to the Queen's Learned Council. With the mission, people were told, of finding a missing jewel. But as the steward Brocket overheard you saying to Lord Parr's man Cecil, it was actually the *Lamentation of a Sinner* you sought. A search that led you to join Richard Rich in his hunt for Anne Askew's ravings.'

I remembered when Cecil had visited me after Elias was murdered. The *Lamentation* had been mentioned then. That rogue Brocket must have been listening at the door. If they know all this, I thought, there is no point telling lies about a stolen jewel. With horror, I realized the depth of the trouble I was in, and felt my bruised face twitch.

The King spoke again, in a strangely quiet voice. 'Anne Askew. I did not mean her to be tortured. I only gave Wriothesley permission to use strong measures.' He wriggled slightly in his chair, but then added sternly, 'That is his fault, and Rich's. Let them suffer if her writings are published.' Then the King looked at me again, and spoke with biting coldness. 'But the Queen should have told *me* this manuscript existed, and that it was stolen, not set forth a search under cover of lies about a missing jewel. What say you to that, lawyer?'

I swallowed hard. And I decided that whatever I said must be calculated to protect the Queen, to deflect any possible charge of disloyalty from her. Otherwise, truly, it would all have been for nothing. I took a deep breath. 'When Lord Parr consulted me, just after the book was stolen, the Queen was quite distracted, frightened, too, after – recent events.' I knew that with what I planned to say next I could be signing my own death warrant: 'It was I who asked her to let me try and find the book secretly, using the story of the stolen jewel.'

'I will be questioning Lord Parr tomorrow,' Paget said quietly.

I felt relief at that. I knew the Queen's uncle, whatever his faults, would also do his best to deflect responsibility from the Queen to himself. And to make sure our stories tallied I said, 'Lord Parr did agree that we should try to find the book secretly.'

'Who else knew?' the King asked sharply.

'Only Archbishop Cranmer. The Queen knew the book might be considered too radical, after she wrote it. She sought his opinion, and he said the manuscript should not be published. But before it could be destroyed, it disappeared. Stolen by that guard,' I dared to say. 'So she did not deceive you, your majesty, she intended to destroy the book at once lest it anger you.'

The King was silent, his brow puckered. He shifted his legs, wincing. When he looked at me again the expression in his eyes had changed. 'The Queen was afraid?' he asked quietly.

'Yes, your majesty. When she discovered its disappearance she was astonished, confused – '

'She would have been. Coming after all these months of Gardiner and his minions trying to turn me against her.' His voice rose angrily, but I was – for the moment – no longer the object of his fury. 'Gardiner told me she was a heretic that denied the Mass; they would have broken my heart again!' He leaned back in his chair. 'But I knew their ways, I knew my Kate was faithful and true, the only one since Jane. So I told them I would do nothing without strict proof. And they brought none, none!' His face was red now, sweating. 'Those rogues, that would have had me turn against Kate, and take me back to Rome! I have seen through them, they will pay—'

The diatribe ended in a bout of painful coughing which turned the King's face puce. The *Lamentation*, which he had been holding on his lap, began to slide to the floor. I leaned forward instinctively, but Paget, with a quick frown at me, returned it to the King before taking his goblet, hastily refilling it, and handing it back to him. Henry drank deeply, then sat back in his chair, gasping. Paget murmured, 'Your majesty, perhaps too much should not be said in front of this man—'

'No,' the King said. 'This he should know.' He looked at me. 'When the manuscript was brought to me, I feared what it might hold. But I have studied it.' Then, quite unexpectedly, he gave a prim little smile. 'Its sentiments are a little thoughtless, but – ' he waved a hand dismissively – 'the Queen is but a woman, and emotional. Nothing is said here against the Mass. The book is not heretical.' His tone now was pompous, judgemental, as befitted one authorized by God Himself to decide such matters, as Henry truly believed he was. 'Kate fears too much,' he concluded. I thought, how fast his emotions change, and how he wears them on his sleeve. At least when he chooses to. For the last few months had shown, too, how coldly secretive he could be. Yet his last words gave me hope for the Queen.

'May now be the time to tell her you have it?' Paget asked him, hesitantly.

'No,' the King answered sharply, the edge back in his voice. 'In these days the more things I keep safe in my own hands the better.' I realized he had kept the manuscript to himself because, until Bertano's mission failed, there remained at least the possibility that he might still decide against the reformist faction. Then a Protestant Queen would be a liability, and the *Lamentation* could still be a weapon. He loved the Queen, yes, but ultimately, like everyone in the realm, she was only a pawn on his chessboard. He would have killed her if he thought he had to, little as he wished it. And it would, of course, all have been someone else's fault.

He studied me again. 'So, it was you that inclined the Queen to keep its loss a secret?' A query in his voice now. I remembered Lord Parr telling me how suggestible the King was, how he believed what he wanted to believe, and also that to him disloyalty was the greatest of sins. Now, I was sure, he wanted to believe Queen Catherine had not taken the initiative in hiding the theft of the *Lamentation* from him. He would rather the blame fell on me, whom he despised and who, politically, counted for nothing at all. Perhaps he had already chosen me as a scapegoat, perhaps that was why he had told me so much. But after what had happened tonight, I no longer cared. 'Yes, your majesty,' I answered, perhaps signing my death warrant a second time.

He considered a moment, then he said petulantly, 'But Kate still deceived me —'

I took a deep breath. Somehow I was fluent again, fluent as at the climax of a court hearing. 'No, your majesty. It was I who hunted for the *Lamentation* behind your back.'

With a struggle, the King managed to sit more upright in his chair. He was silent a moment, trying to decide just what the role of his wife had been in all this. Then he seemed to reach a conclusion. He leaned forward, eyes and mouth set mercilessly now. 'You are an insolent, base-born, bent-backed common churl.' He spoke the words quietly, but I could feel his rage. 'Men like you are the curse of this land, daring to say they answer only to themselves on religion and the safety of the realm, when their loyalties are to *me*!' His voice rose again. 'Me, their King! I call it treason, treason!' He looked at me in such a vengeful way that, involuntarily, I took half a step back.

'Do not dare move unless I give you liberty!' he snapped.

'I am sorry, your majesty.'

Seeing my abject fear seemed to change his mood again. He turned to Paget and spoke scornfully. 'How could I ever think such a poor reed of a creature could be any sort of threat to me, hey?'

'I do not think he is,' the Secretary answered quietly.

The King considered a moment. 'You say one of the two men working for Shardlake is dead.'

'By now, yes.' Paget's tone was completely indifferent.

'And the other, that was brought here with him?'

'Little more than a boy.' Paget ventured a smile. 'A tall young fellow, with red hair, as your majesty was in his youth, though I believe this churl is nothing like so well-looking.'

The King smiled at the flattery. And I realized that Paget was trying to soften the King's anger, and I wondered why. There was a moment of silence as the King considered further, but then shook his head. 'This man suborned the Queen to keep secrets from me. That is treason.' He looked at me again, those little blue eyes buried in their wrinkles still hard and merciless. 'And I would be rid of him, he is a pestilential nuisance.'

I bowed my head. I felt cold, my racing heart had slowed. Treason, I thought. I would be dragged to Tyburn at the tail of a horse, hanged until almost dead, cut down, and then the executioner would cut out my innards. And naked, I thought strangely, quite naked. Then finally I would be beheaded. I thought, can I face that, can I act with courage as some have? I doubted it. And when I was dead, would I go then to hell? Would I burn for lack of faith, as Philip Coleswyn would believe? I stood there, in the King's study, quite still. The image of Barak, thrown on that rubbish heap, came to me again.

Beside me, Paget drew a deep breath. He spoke slowly. 'Your majesty, a trial for treason before a jury would make the recent problems concerning the Queen public. And also the deaths of those Anabaptists. We do not want that getting out. Not at this time.'

'He can be condemned by Parliament, through an Act of Attainder.'

'That would make it all the more public.'

Henry waved a hand, as though this were a trifle, but I could see from his expression that he realized it was not. Paget took another deep breath, before pressing home his point. 'Even if Shardlake were put quietly out of the way, it would become known, and some might see it as a move against the Protestant side. The new political balance is still very delicate. We do not want to upset it unnecessarily.'

He fell silent; Henry was glowering at him now. It was a scene I imagined Henry playing out with anxious chief advisers repeatedly over these last thirty-seven years; the King angry, demanding ferocious measures, his councillors trying to warn him of the possible damaging consequences.

The King sat, considering. At length he grunted, a strange sound like a pig's squeal, full of frustration. He gave me a savage look. 'But surely we could do him quietly to death.'

'I have no affection for this man, your majesty, believe me. But still I do not think that a wise move. The Parrs, in particular, would be concerned if he disappeared.'

The King sighed. 'You give me straight advice, Paget, you always have. Even though I may dislike to hear it.'

'Thank you, your majesty.'

Henry gave him a sharp look. 'And you know on which side your bread is buttered, eh? Always you act to further my will, never go down your own road, like Wolsey and Cromwell?'

Paget bowed deeply. 'I serve only to implement your majesty's chosen policies.'

'Yet I would be rid of this man,' the King repeated. He gave me a long stare, unblinking as a snake's. I knew my life, and Nicholas's, hung in the balance. An eternity seemed to pass before he spoke again. 'Paget is right. You are a serjeant and it is known that you have been working for the Queen. Your disappearance would make a stir.' He took a deep breath. 'I will let you go, Master Shardlake, you and your boy. For policy reasons alone. But take note of this.' He leaned forward, his voice rising again. 'You will never, ever, again come anywhere near the Queen, or any royal palace, or do anything that might, even possibly, bring you to my notice. Do you understand? I do not wish to hear of you, still less see you, ever again. And if I do see you, it will not be your bent back I see, but only – your – head!' The last words were accompanied by the King banging on the arms of his chair. He leaned back, breathing hard. 'Now, Paget, get him out of here. And send in Will Somers, I need distraction.'

Master Secretary bowed and then, beckoning me, walked backwards to the door; it was forbidden to turn one's back on the King. I followed, dreading to hear the King summon me again. Paget knocked on the door, it was opened from outside by a guard, and we backed through safely. Will Somers, the monkey still perched on his shoulder, stood outside with the guards. Paget inclined his head sharply to the door. Somers and the guard who had been with the King slipped back in. The sound of the door closing brought me an overwhelming rush of relief.

Paget led me back up the corridor. Then I felt the floor sway and slide under me again and had to lean against the wall, breathing hard. Paget looked at me, his face expressionless. 'A narrow escape, I think,' he said, his voice hard. 'You were lucky, Master Shardlake.'

I felt steadier now. 'Will he – could he – call me back?'

'No. He has made up his mind now. You spoke very well, all things considered,' he added reluctantly. He inclined his head. 'Was it truly you that persuaded the Queen to let you search for the book?'

I did not answer. Paget gave a little smile. 'Well,' he said. 'It does not matter now.'

I looked at him gratefully, despite myself. Given all that had happened, it was a strange paradox that it was Paget who had saved me at the end, for without his intervention I knew I would already be on my way to the Tower, Nicholas as well: he would not be the first innocent caught in the King's net. I took a deep breath. 'Did the King come all the way from Hampton Court for this?'

Paget gave a quiet, mocking laugh. 'You flatter yourself, lawyer. No, he and Admiral d'Annebault are going hunting in St James's Park tomorrow. He came here unofficially to spend the evening in peace. He is tired, he had to do much

standing today, he wanted a little time away from them all.'
Paget looked out of the window, down at King Street,
deserted at this hour. 'His study is always kept ready for him.
Here he can rest, work, watch the doings of his realm from
the window.' He added quietly, 'It is not easy, being a King.'

I dared not answer, and Paget continued in a strangely
dispassionate tone. 'I think, you know, your search for the
Lamentation these last few weeks may have saved the Queen.'

I stared at him. 'Do you?'

He stroked his long forked beard. 'Yes. When I first
brought him that book, Bertano had not yet arrived. The
King indeed found no evidence of heresy in the *Lamentation*
– it sails close to the wind in places, but as he said, it does not
deny the Mass. But the Queen had hidden its existence from
him and that rankled seriously.'

'Disloyalty,' I murmured.

'Quite so. The Queen could have been in trouble there
and then. For several days he considered arresting her. But
then your hunt for the book, and Rich's for Anne Askew's
writings, caught his attention and he ordered me to let the
matter play itself out, although of course those Anabaptists
had to die.'

'Curdy was your spy.'

'Yes. And when the allegations from that Slanning
woman came before me, I decided you should be brought
before the Privy Council, so I could see for myself whether
there might indeed be a chance you were a heretic.'

'So we were all moved like puppets,' I said bitterly.

'Be grateful that you were. That allowed time for
Bertano's mission to fail, and the King's mind to turn finally
and decisively against the conservatives.'

I looked at his slab of a face and thought, you enjoy all
this; you would side with radicals or conservatives alike to

keep your position. Another of those great men in the middle, bending with the wind.

Paget spoke again, his voice stern now. 'Of course, you will forget everything that was said in there, not least what the King let slip about authorizing strong measures against Anne Askew.'

I took a deep breath. 'Of course, Master Secretary.'

His eyes narrowed. 'And you heard what the King said. Make sure he has no more trouble from you. Do not cross me again, either. And now, fetch your boy; then get out of here. And, as the King said, never, ever, return.'

Chapter Fifty-three

PAGET BECKONED a guard, then without further word led the way back through the King's Gallery, then to the Presence Chamber. He crossed the room to speak briefly with one of the guards standing there. I looked again at the Holbein mural, the King in his prime; the swagger, the square hard face, the ferocious little eyes and mouth. The candlelight caught Jane Seymour's face, too: demure, placid. Paget returned with the guard. 'Take him to the boy, then get them both out of the palace. Quickly.' And then Master Secretary turned and walked away, without so much as a nod or a backward glance, his long black robe swishing round his legs. He was done with me. The mind of the King's Master of Practices had probably already returned to its coils of conspiracy.

Nicholas was crouched in the corner of a small, bare receiving room, his long arms folded round his bent knees. When he stood I saw spots of blood on his doublet. Barak's blood. 'Come, Nicholas,' I said quietly. 'We are free, but we must go quickly.'

The guard led us along the dark corridors to the Guard Chamber, then down the stairs again, across the cobbled court, and through the gates. As soon as we were out in the street Nicholas said, 'I thought we were undone.'

'I, too. But I think we are safe, so long as we never come here again.' I looked upwards at the Holbein Gate and its windows, wondering if the King were watching. I turned away hastily; it was dangerous now even to glance in that direction.

'Stice and his men, are they – ?'

'Free as air,' I answered bitterly, looking at him. His face looked haunted. 'But do not ask me to tell you more, ever.'

He ran a hand through his red hair, then gave a little choking laugh. 'I was told before I came to London how magnificent the royal palaces were. And I have seen for myself, it is true. And yet – fear and death stalk there, even more than in the rest of the world.'

I smiled with desperate sadness. 'I see you are beginning to learn.'

'In there – I felt it.' He gulped. 'What now? What of – Jack?'

'We must go back to get him at once,' I said, though I was terrified of what we would find there.

✞

WE REACHED the lane near an hour later, the clocks striking one shortly before we arrived. It was easy to find the place. I half-ran to the rubbish heap, full of dread at what I might see, then drew up abruptly. Barak's body was gone.

'Where is he?' Nicholas asked in astonishment. 'He couldn't have – got up?'

'That would have been impossible. Someone has taken him.' I looked frantically round the darkness of the lane, but there was nothing to be seen.

'But where?'

I thought hard. 'If someone found him, they might have taken him to St Bartholomew's. It is hard by. Come, we will go there first.'

We arrived at the hospital ten minutes later: Nicholas had

had not only to accommodate his long stride to my own, but almost to run. The doors were closed, but a porter answered our knock, holding up a lamp. I spoke urgently. 'We wish to ask whether a man was brought here tonight. He had a sword wound to the body and – he had lost his hand.'

The man's eyes narrowed. 'Was it you that left him there? A man so wounded, left on a dungheap?'

'No, it was not us, we are his friends.'

'Old Francis Sybrant found him, and brought him in.'

The porter still looked at us dubiously. 'Please,' Nicholas asked. 'Does he live?'

'Just, but he's as near death as a man can be. He has been unconscious since he came.'

'Has the doctor been sent for? Dr Malton?'

The man shook his head. 'A doctor only comes once a day.'

'Well, send for Dr Malton now,' Nicholas said. 'He is a friend of my master here, and also of the man brought in by Francis Sybrant.'

I looked at Nicholas's face in the lamplight. I would swear new lines had appeared on it since this afternoon. I reached for my purse and thrust two shillings at the porter. 'Here. Get someone to fetch Dr Malton, then take us to Barak.'

The porter stared at the coins in his palm, then back at me. 'Who's Barak?'

'The man who was brought in. Please, hurry.'

He scurried away, leaving us in the vestibule. Nicholas smiled wryly. 'With all the money you're giving away, sir, you'll have none left.'

I thought, insolence, the boy becomes more confident. Then I thought of Timothy, and wondered whether he was lost to me as well. Between the fight at the house, and my ordeal at Whitehall, I had forgotten him.

The porter returned, his manner obsequious now. 'I will take you to your friend. Sybrant is with him. He is in a chamber we keep for those who may need the last rites.'

✝

BARAK LAY IN the same room where the Anabaptist McKendrick had died, in the same bed, a cheap candle on a chair beside it. His clothing had been removed and the blankets covered only his lower body; his strong scarred torso was as pale as though he were dead already. He lay on his side, a bloodstained bandage covering the place on his back where he had received the sword-thrust. His right arm, the stump of the wrist thickly bandaged, lay on a pillow. I put a hand to my mouth.

The door of the little room opened and a man with a lamp entered. I recognized Guy's assistant, Francis Sybrant. His brow furrowed when he saw me.

'You, sir? You were here before – to see that other man who was attacked – '

'The porter said you brought Barak in. How – ?'

'I was coming on duty earlier this evening. I come by the back ways, always. Often one finds sick beggars, sometimes people who have been injured and abandoned, though never like this.' He looked at us accusingly. 'You left him there?'

'No! We were prisoners, we could do nothing. Dear God, you must have come on him just in time.' I thought, perhaps my prayers had been answered after all. 'Please, this man is a good friend, can you tell us – ' my voice faltered – 'will he live?'

Sybrant looked at us dubiously. 'That wound in his back – it was made by a sword?'

'Yes.'

'It has damaged no vital organs that I can see, but between that and what was done to his hand – he has lost much blood. Too much for him to survive, I fear.'

'He is a strong man.'

Sybrant shook his head. 'He would need to be exceptionally so to survive this. Has he family?'

I exchanged an anguished look with Nicholas. I had put thoughts of Tamasin from my mind. 'Yes,' I answered haltingly. 'And a child. His wife is expecting another.'

Nicholas said, 'Perhaps it may be better if she is not told till the doctor comes.'

Sybrant said, 'Dr Malton has been sent for.'

'You are right, Nicholas,' I said. 'I will wait for Guy.'

Nicholas turned to Sybrant. 'Is there anything we can do?'

The old man looked at the ashen figure on the bed. 'Only pray, sirs, pray.'

✞

GUY ARRIVED soon after, a heavy bag over his shoulder. He appeared shocked, haggard, for he had known Barak and Tamasin almost as long as I. He looked at us, then at Barak lying on the bed. He drew in his breath sharply. 'What happened to him?'

'There was a sword fight; he was stabbed in the back and his hand sliced off.'

'Dear Jesus!' Guy looked angry. 'Was this sword fight part of this mission of yours?'

I lowered my eyes. 'Yes.'

'Were you there?'

'Yes. But we were taken prisoner. We have only just been released.'

Guy moved across to the bed. 'Does Tamasin know?'

'I thought it better to wait for you.'

He did not reply, but knelt over Barak, gently removing the bandages from the wound on his back and examining it closely, then uncovering that dreadful stump, still oozing blood, white bones visible against the torn flesh. I closed my eyes. Gently, Guy replaced the bandages. He looked at me again, his face as sombre as I had ever seen it. 'The wounds show no sign of infection — yet. They must be cleaned, properly. But he has lost enough blood to kill most men.' He stood up briskly. 'I must get fluid into him.'

'Will he live?'

'He is far more like to die,' Guy answered starkly. I realized how hard it must be for him, having to treat a critically injured patient who was also a friend. 'I knew something like this would happen, I knew it! Are there going to be any more men brought to me dead and crippled through whatever it is you are doing?' His voice was full of rage.

'No,' I answered quietly. 'It is over. It ended tonight.'

He looked at me, his face hard as stone. 'Was it worth it, Matthew?' There was an angry tremor in his voice. 'Was it?'

'I think one person was saved — a woman.'

'Who? No, I think I can guess.' He raised a hand. 'Tell me nothing more.'

'My master did not wish it to end like this,' Nicholas said.

'I do not doubt that,' Guy answered in gentler tones. 'Now, Master Nicholas, would you ride to Mistress Barak's house, and fetch her here?'

I protested, 'But in her condition — '

'Jack will probably die tonight,' Guy said quietly. 'What do you think Tamasin would say if she were denied the chance to be with him at the end?'

'Then let me be the one to tell her.'

'The boy will be quicker. I would rather have you here. And I may need your help if Francis is called away to other patients.' He turned to Nicholas. 'Tell Mistress Barak only that there has been an accident. Say I am in attendance.'

He nodded sombrely. 'I will.'

'Hurry now. Use my horse, it is outside. And tell Francis to come in and assist me.'

Nicholas looked at me. I nodded, and he hurried from the room. When he was gone Guy said quietly, 'Can you face her?'

'I must.'

He bent and opened his bag. Barak lay unmoving.

✝

IT WAS NEAR AN HOUR before Nicholas returned with Tamasin. Guy had been working to clean Barak's wounds the whole time, moving deftly and quietly. I sat in the chair next to the bed, so exhausted that, despite the appalling circumstances, I had dozed off, waking with a start when I almost tumbled from the chair. By the light of a lamp which Sybrant held up I saw Guy re-bandaging Barak's wrist, a concentrated expression on his dark face, suppressing God knew what emotions. He paused to glance across at me. 'You slept near half an hour.'

I looked at Barak. His breathing was ragged, irregular. Guy said, 'I tried to make him drink something, poured some apple juice into his mouth. It made him gag, and waken for just a second.'

'Is that a hopeful sign?'

'He did not swallow. I have to get some nourishment into him, so his body can make more blood to replace all he has lost.'

Then I heard footsteps outside. Nicholas's fast, heavy

tread, lighter steps behind. The door opened; Nicholas held it as Tamasin came in, her eyes wide, breathing hard and fast. When she saw the state of her husband I thought she might scream or faint but she only looked at Guy. 'Is he dead?' she asked in a trembling voice.

'No, Tamasin, but he is very badly hurt.'

I stood up and indicated the chair. 'Tamasin, please sit down.'

She did so, but without looking at me, brushing aside some strands of blonde hair which had escaped from her coif. She held her stomach with her free hand, as though to protect the baby within from the sight on the bed. She spoke to Guy again. 'Nicholas said Jack was badly injured. He would not say why, but I pressed him and he said there was a sword fight. He said Jack had lost a hand. Dear God, I see now that it is true.' Her voice still trembled but she made a fist of her hand, willing herself not to break down.

Nicholas said, 'She insisted I tell her, Dr Malton — '

Guy nodded. 'Yes, there was a fight.'

Tamasin turned her face to me, full of fury. 'Why? Why was there? Why did you get Jack to lie to me about where he was tonight?'

I said, 'I needed help. He gave it, as he always does.'

She shook her head angrily. 'I thought he was past all that now, I've suspected there was something going on for weeks but I told myself he would never endanger himself again, nor you lead him into trouble.' She cried, 'Well, it is for the last time. He cannot do your dirty work any more now, can he? Even if he lives? And if he does, he will not work for you again, not ever. I shall see to that!'

'Tamasin, I am sorry, more than I can say. You are right. It was my fault. But if — when he recovers — he can come back to work for me, in the office — '

Tamasin answered savagely, 'How? What can he do? When he will no longer even be able to write?'

'I will arrange something – I will make sure you do not lose – where money is concerned – I will take care of you –'

She stood up, fists bunched at her side. 'I see how you have taken care of my husband! You will leave us alone, never come near us again!' Nicholas reached out a hand to steady her, but she slapped it aside. 'Get off me, you!' She turned back to me. 'Now, get out! Get out!' She put her face in her hands and sat down, sobbing.

Guy said, 'You should go, Matthew. And you, boy. Please, go.'

I hesitated, then walked to the door. Nicholas joined me. Just as we reached it we heard a sound like a groan from the bed. Whether from all the commotion or from hearing his wife's voice, Barak appeared to be waking. I glanced back at Tamasin; she reached out to her husband. I took a step back into the room but she cast me such a look that without further ado I let Nicholas lead me out.

✝

HE TOOK ME HOME, carrying a lamp the porter gave him. He could see I was nearly spent. He had the sense not to speak, only to take my arm when I stumbled a couple of times. I asked him once, 'Do you think, now he is awake, Jack may live?'

'Yes, I'm sure.' He spoke with a confidence which, I could tell from his voice, he did not feel.

He walked me up the path to my door. As we approached, it opened and Josephine stood in the doorway. The only one of my household left now. As I came up to her I saw she was smiling. She said, 'We found him. Edward and I. At that pond on Coney Garth where he goes to fish sometimes. He was there, trying to catch something to eat.' Then she saw my face and her eyes widened. 'Sir, what has happened?'

I walked past her into the kitchen. Timothy, filthy dirty, sat at the table with Edward Brown. As I came in the boy essayed a nervous smile, showing the wide gap in his teeth. He said tremulously, 'Josephine said you were not angry any more, sir.'

I said, my voice breaking, 'No, Timothy, I was wrong to hold a grudge so long. And what Martin Brocket told you was untrue. His leaving was not your fault. Are you safe?'

'Yes, sir.' He looked at me, then at Nicholas standing in the doorway behind. 'But sir, has something happened to you?'

'It is nothing.' I laid my hand on Timothy's, small and thin and dirty. I thought, at least I did not lose him. Of all those whose lives had been uprooted by the trap the King and Paget had set, he was the least important – to them, though not to me, not to me.

Epilogue

T HE CROWDS STOOD SIX DEEP outside Whitehall Palace. They lined both sides of the roadway, up past Charing Cross and along Cockspur Street. Some said people were standing all the way to Windsor. Everyone was huddled in their warmest clothes; the sky was blue but there was an iron-hard frost in the air, the puddles grey and frozen, a bitter wind from the east. Some from the poorer classes, in leather jerkins or threadbare coats, were shivering and hunched in the cold. But they stayed, determined to see the spectacle.

I wore my heavily furred winter robe, but no gold chain. That had been returned to the goldsmith back at the end of August. For on this royal occasion there was no great central figure to impress. King Henry VIII was dead, and his funeral procession about to begin.

✝

THE KING, it was known, had fallen gravely ill again during the short royal Progress to Guildford in September,

689

and never fully recovered. He worsened again in December and at the end of January he had died. The gossips at the Inns of Court had had much to chew over in recent months. It was, as ever, hard to distinguish truth from rumour, but most agreed that during the autumn the religious radicals had utterly triumphed; Bishop Gardiner had been publicly struck in the face by Lord Lisle in the Privy Council, and the King had refused to see him in the weeks before he died. It made sense to me: the conservative faction had bet every-thing on the Queen being found guilty of heresy, and on the success of Bertano's mission. Both gambits had failed and the King, knowing he was dying, had turned to those who would ensure that the Royal Supremacy over the Church was preserved for his son.

In December the Duke of Norfolk and his son the Earl of Surrey had been suddenly arrested, the Earl accused of illegally quartering the royal arms with his own. Parliament had passed an Act of Attainder convicting both of treason; the young Earl had been executed in January, and Norfolk, the arch-conservative, would have followed him to the block had not the King died the night before the execution. It sounded to me like a put-up job – the King had used such methods before, to rid himself of Anne Boleyn and Thomas Cromwell. For now the old Duke remained alive, in the Tower.

It was said that as he lay dying at Whitehall the King had called for Archbishop Cranmer, but by the time he arrived Henry was past speech. And when the prelate asked him to give a sign that he died in the faith of Christ, he had been able only to clutch Cranmer's hand. No confession then for Henry, no last rites. His death – perhaps by accident – had been one which Protestants could approve. And yet, extraordinarily, the King in his Will had ordered traditional requiem Masses to be said over his body. Henry, in death, was as inconstant as he had been in life.

✝

'VIVE LE ROI Edward the Sixth!' So the heralds proclaimed the new King, that thin, straight-backed little boy. The new Council which the old King had appointed by his Will made shortly before his death, to govern England during Edward's minority, was dominated by those identified with the Protestant cause. Lord Lisle and the Earl of Essex, Catherine Parr's brother, had places. So, too, did those in the middle, who would bend with the wind: Paget remained Master Secretary, Wriothesley was still in place on the Council, and Rich. All had bent to the King's final change of path. But not Bishop Gardiner; he was left seething impotently on the sidelines. It was said that radical religious reform would soon be coming.

Within the reforming camp, the Seymours had won out over the Parrs. There was to be no Regency for Catherine Parr, despite her hopes. She was now merely Queen Dowager, while the council had immediately appointed Edward Seymour, Lord Hertford, as Protector of the young King. He it was who sat now at the head of the Council table, to which he had also appointed his brother Thomas.

All sorts of stories were flying around that the King's Will had been doctored after his death, Hertford conspiring with the careerists to insert a clause concerning 'unfulfilled gifts' from the King which allowed the new council to award them titles, setting their loyalty in stone. Certainly there was a great crop of new peers: Richard Rich, for instance, was now Lord Rich of Lees in Essex. But exactly what had happened in the days just after the King died, nobody knew for sure; perhaps no one ever would.

☩

ATTENDANCE AT the funeral procession was officially encouraged, but not compulsory. Most of the great crowd, like me, had come, I think, to witness the passing of an epoch. The younger people present would have known no other ruler, and I could only dimly recall, when I was seven, my dear mother telling me that King Henry VII was dead and a second Tudor had ascended the throne.

I shook myself and rubbed my gloved hands together. Opposite, Whitehall Palace was silent and empty; the procession was to begin at the chapel of Westminster Palace, further south. Next to me, a voice proclaimed, 'Ay, a chill day, but perhaps there now begin the days of true religion.'

Nicholas, on my other side, murmured, 'Days of snow, from the feel of that wind.' His Lincolnshire accent lengthened the vowels of his words.

'Ay,' I agreed, 'I think you are right.'

The boy had been a rock to me these last months. In chambers he had worked with a new energy and intelligence, taking over much that Barak had formerly done. Though he needed supervising, and could be too haughty in manner for some of Barak's more lowly friends among the clerks and solicitors, he was learning fast. He still made mistakes and, as those promoted rapidly often will, had taken on a certain insolence that needed gentle correction. But I had come to see that under his bravado and flippancy there was a core of steel in Nicholas Overton. I did not know how long he would stay with me, or even why he was so loyal: perhaps he needed to root himself somewhere after the quarrel with his family. Whatever the reason, I was grateful, and had invited him to accompany me to the funeral procession today.

When the two of us reached Whitehall I saw a large crowd of lawyers, their status ensuring them places at the front of the crowd, just north of the great Holbein Gate. They were all in their black robes and most had their hoods up against the cold; for a moment they reminded me of a crowd of monks. Heads turned as we approached; as I had anticipated, news of my arrest and appearance before the council had got out and was soon an item of gossip, as was the fact that Barak, known round Lincoln's Inn for his wit and disrespectfulness, was gone. I nodded to people I knew with formal politeness. Treasurer Rowland, his long nose red with cold, looked at me disapprovingly. Vincent Dyrick, a woman and three children at his side, gave me a quick glance before turning away. And right at the front, William Cecil raised a hand in greeting, and gave me a nod. I returned it, thinking how well Cecil had done; Secretary now to the Earl of Hertford, already this young man was becoming a power in the land.

A familiar figure shouldered his way through the lawyers and called a greeting. I had not seen Philip Coleswyn since the summer, but took his hand gladly as he led Nicholas and me to stand beside him in the front row. I asked after his family and he said all were well. He looked relaxed and content, his terrible anxieties over the summer long gone. When he asked after my health I said merely that I was well. Even though I wore my coif, and had the hood of my robe up against the cold like everyone else, Philip glanced at my head. Perhaps someone had told him that after that night in

August my hair had turned completely white; first just at the roots, giving me the aspect of a badger, but growing out until only white was left. I had got used to it.

†

'THEY'RE LATE,' Nicholas observed, stamping his feet.

'There is much to organize at Westminster,' Philip said. 'There are near two thousand men going to Windsor, on horse and foot. Everyone will have to be in their correct place.'

'And it is nothing to them if common folk are kept waiting,' I snapped. Philip looked at me, struck by my bitter tone. I thought, I must be careful, people will be taking me for an Anabaptist soon, and that creed of equality would have no more of a place under the new regime than it had under the old, however radical the religious changes which might come. I looked up at the windows above the wide arches of the Holbein Gate. There was the King's study, to which he had called me on that dreadful night. He would never watch his people from his window again. All at once, I felt free.

Philip asked, 'I do not suppose you have heard how Mistress Slanning fares?'

'I have, in fact.' Guy had kept me informed. He had been furious with me that night in August, and rightly so, but in the weeks that followed, when I was subject to blacker moods than ever in my life, he helped take care of me, counselled me. His compassion won out over his anger, for which I was eternally grateful. I looked at Philip, wondering how he would take what I had to say: 'She is gone to France, as people may since the peace. She has returned to the Catholic faith and entered a nunnery, somewhere out in the French countryside.'

'A nunnery?' He sounded shocked.

'I do not know if she has taken any vows yet. There is a long preparation.' I wondered if Isabel had, at last, made her confession. 'I think it is best for her, she would find it hard now to face the world. She has given her worldly goods to the nuns. Edward's share of that house will pass to his family, for she had none left living.'

Philip inclined his head disapprovingly. 'However comfortable a refuge the papists may provide, she has lost any chance of salvation.'

Nicholas looked at him narrowly. 'Then you believe that when she dies she will burn, sir, as Mistress Anne Askew did, but in her case for all eternity?'

'God's laws are beyond human understanding, boy,' Philip answered firmly.

I spoke quietly, 'If such are his laws, then indeed they are.' I thought of Hugh Curteys, my ward. As the persecution of Protestants had intensified in Antwerp the previous autumn, Hugh had moved to Hamburg, and worked now with the German Hanse merchants. This great struggle between Protestants and Catholics all across Europe could now make anyone a refugee, a prisoner, or worse.

✝

STILL THE PROCESSION did not come, though officials had begun scurrying to and fro around the Holbein Gate, under which the procession would pass, one of them shivering in a clerical cassock. I remembered how the vicar had been late at the infinitely smaller ceremony a month before, when Josephine married Edward Brown. The wedding had been celebrated in the little parish church Edward attended; his family and friends from the Inn had come, together with Edward's master. Josephine had no family and I had given her away; I had been proud to do so, though I would miss her greatly. They had moved to Norwich last week. I had hired an old fellow called Blaby, a grumbling creature, to look after my house until I found a new steward; apart from him, the household now consisted only of Timothy and myself. Gently, very gently, I was nudging the boy towards an apprenticeship with the Lincoln's Inn farrier when he turned fourteen, which I would finance to give him a chance in life.

Then I saw them, for the first time in six months, near the front of the crowd a little way off. Barak and Tamasin. Tamasin wore a thick coat with a hood, but looked pale; I knew from Guy that, a fortnight before, on the night the King died, she had given birth to a healthy daughter. She should not be out in this cold so soon, but I imagined she had insisted.

Barak, beside her, still looked sick. There was a heavy puffiness to his features now, and he had put on weight. I saw, with a clutch of sorrow at my heart, how the right sleeve of his coat trailed empty. He glanced up and his eyes met mine. Tamasin looked up too; when she saw me her face stiffened.

'They're coming!' Murmurs and an excited shuffling in the crowd, heads craning to look towards the Holbein Gate. From beyond, the sound of sung prayers in the clear cold air. But then, for another minute, nothing happened. People shuffled and stamped their feet, some beginning to mutter and grumble a little in the bitter cold.

A movement nearby. I turned to see Barak sidling through the crowd towards us. Tamasin stayed behind, glaring at me, fierce as ever.

Barak took Nicholas by the arm with his remaining hand. 'How are you, Nick boy? I haven't seen you since that night. Are you all right?'

'Yes – yes. And you?' Nicholas sounded surprised, as

indeed he might, for when he had gone to visit Barak one night in October, Tamasin had slammed the door in his face. Money which I had sent to her via Guy had been returned without a word.

'How's he treating you?' Barak asked, inclining his head towards me. 'Keeping you busy?'

'Yes – yes. We miss you at chambers.'

Barak turned to me. 'How goes it with you?' His eyes, like his puffy face, were still full of pain and shock.

'Well enough. But I have wished for news of you – '

'Listen,' he said quietly. 'I'll have to be quick. Tammy doesn't want me talking to you. I just wanted to say, I'm all right. When I'm a bit better I've an offer from a group of solicitors to work with them; interviewing clients, finding witnesses, that sort of thing. Work where you don't need two hands. So don't worry.'

'I am desperately sorry, Jack, desperately,' I said. 'Tamasin is right to think it was all my fault.'

'Balls!' Barak answered with something of his old vigour. 'It was me decided to get involved with all that, me that told her lies about what I was doing. Am I not still a man with responsibility for my own decisions?' A spasm of anger crossed his face and I realized that, in his own eyes, he was not fully a man any more. I did not reply.

'How does the new baby fare?' Nicholas asked. 'We heard you have a daughter.'

Barak spoke with a touch of his old humour. 'Can't keep anything quiet within a mile of Lincoln's Inn, can you? Yes, she's lusty and healthy, lungs on her like her mother. We're going to call her Matilda.'

'Congratulations, Jack,' I said quietly.

He glanced over his shoulder at Tamasin. 'I'd better get back. Listen, I'll be in touch when I'm working again. And this – ' he gestured to his empty sleeve – 'Guy's making me some sort of attachment now the stump's healed. It won't be anything like a hand but I suppose it'll be better than nothing. As for Tammy, give her time. I'm working on her. Easier for her to blame you than me, I suppose.'

There was some truth in that. Yet she had every reason to blame me for Barak's maiming, as I blamed myself. He gave me a nod, then walked back to his wife. Tamasin had seen him speaking to me; the look she gave me now had in it something despairing, defeated, that cut me to the heart. I turned away.

The murmuring had ceased, the crowd fallen silent again. Beyond the Holbein Gate the singing of prayers was growing louder as it approached. People bared their heads. I lowered my own hood, feeling the icy air against my coif. Two officials on horseback rode under the main arch, looking up the roadway to ensure the way was clear. Then beneath the wide arches walked the choir and priests of the Chapel Royal, still singing. There followed perhaps three hundred men in new black coats, carrying torches. The poor men who, by tradition, headed the funeral processions of the great. Well, there were plenty of poor men in England now, more than ever there had been.

The men who came next, on horseback, dozens of them bearing standards and banners, were certainly not poor: the great ones of the realm, flanked by Yeomen of the Guard. I glimpsed faces I recognized – Cranmer, Wriothesley, Paget. I lowered my head in a pretence of mourning.

Eventually they all passed, and the great hearse approached. A lawyer behind me leaned round Nicholas, saying impatiently, 'Aside, beanpole, let me see!'

The hearse was drawn by eight great horses draped in black, each ridden by a little boy, the children of honour, carrying banners. It was richly gilded, with a cloth-of-gold canopy covering the huge coffin, on top of which lay a wax effigy of King Henry, startlingly lifelike, though looking not as I had seen him last summer but as he was in the Holbein mural: in his prime, hair and beard red, body solidly power-ful. The effigy was fully dressed in jewelled velvet, a black nightcap on its head. The face wore an expression of peace and repose such as I doubted Henry had ever worn in life.

Bells began to toll. People lowered their heads, and I even heard a few groans. I looked at the effigy as it passed and thought, what did he really achieve, what did his extraordin-ary reign really bring? I remembered all that I had seen these last ten years: ancient monasteries destroyed, monks pen-sioned off and servants put out on the road; persecutions and burnings — I shuddered at the memory of Anne Askew's head exploding; a great war that had achieved nothing and impoverished the country — and if that impoverishment con-tinued to deepen, there would be trouble: the common people could only stand so much. And always, always under Henry, the shadow of the axe. I thought of those who had perished by it, and in particular of one I had long ago known well, and still remembered: Thomas Cromwell.

Beside me Philip said softly, 'And so it ends.'

✝

IT WAS A FORTNIGHT later that the horseman brought the note to chambers, riding from Chelsea through the heavy snow that had lain for days. Henry was buried now, and little King Edward crowned. There was a tale that while lying overnight on the way to Windsor, Henry's body had exploded, that stinking matter had dripped out and attracted the attention of a dog, fulfilling an old friar's prophecy that the dogs should lick Henry's blood as they had Ahab's in the Bible. But that sounded too neat, and I doubted it had happened.

I was working in my room when the messenger arrived, while outside Skelly prepared a case for court and Nicholas laboured, inky-fingered, over a deposition. I recognized the seal at once. That of the Queen; the Queen Dowager, as she was now. I opened the letter, bright light from the snow-covered square outside making the copperplate lettering stand out on the white paper. It was brief, from a secretary, asking me to attend her the following afternoon at Chelsea Palace.

I laid it down. I had not expected to hear from Catherine Parr again; after that confrontation with the King, I had tried, so far as I could, to put her from my mind. But the King's edict against my coming near had died with him. I had been sorry that Catherine Parr had not, as she had hoped, been appointed Regent, though glad when people said the King had been generous in his Will to her, as well as to the Ladies Mary and Elizabeth; each now had great wealth and status of their own. People said Catherine Parr might marry again, in time, and the name Thomas Seymour was mentioned.

✝

I RODE TO Chelsea alone. Genesis plodded his way out of London slowly, for the roadway was covered with compacted snow and ice. Chelsea Palace, on the riverbank, was a fine new mansion of red brick, set in wide gardens which would be beautiful when spring came; I estimated it could easily house a staff of two hundred. The guards at the gate still wore the Queen's livery. I was admitted, a steward taking me to the house. Inside, servants passed quietly to and fro, but there were no guards on the doors as at Whitehall, no sidling politicians. He led me to a door at the rear of the mansion, and knocked. A familiar voice bade him enter.

I followed the steward into a large room. I recognized some of the items displayed there from the Queen's Gallery: an ornate clock, her box of coins which lay on the table beside a chess set. The Queen Dowager herself stood with her back to a large bay window, her black mourning clothes and gable hood contrasting with the snow-covered lawns outside. I bowed low. She dismissed the steward.

'Matthew,' she said. 'It has been many months.'

'Yes, your majesty.'

Her pale face was as attractive and composed as ever. In her stance I discerned a new relaxation, a new authority. Gently, she said, 'I am sorry that your efforts to help me ended – badly. I know now who had the *Lamentation*. And what happened to you – and your poor servant.'

I wondered, did she know that I had lied to the King for her? I could not tell from looking at her, and I must not ask. 'The book has been returned to you?'

'Yes. By the Protector.' I discerned a little bite in her voice at mention of the man who had taken the position she had hoped for. She added, 'I plan to publish it later this year.'

I looked at her, surprised. 'Is that – safe, your majesty?'

'Quite safe, now. Master Cecil has offered to write a preface. He thinks, like me, that the *Lamentation of a Sinner* may help some suffering souls to salvation. He remains a good friend.'

'I am glad. He is a young man of great talent.'

'And you shall have a copy, signed by me.'

'I – thank you.'

She came a step closer. 'But I say again, I know what the search for it cost you.' Her hazel eyes looked into mine and I thought suddenly, yes, she knows I told the King a lie: that I had been responsible for the decision to search for the book rather than telling him it was missing. Along with her uncle, whom I remembered Paget was to question the next day, and who must also have taken a share of the responsibility.

She said, 'I will be grateful to you, unto death.'

'Thank you, your majesty.' There was an awkward pause, then I asked, 'How fares Lord Parr?'

'He has gone back to the country,' she answered sadly. 'To die, I fear. His great service to me last year was too much for him, ill as he is.'

'I am sorry to hear it.'

She looked at me earnestly. 'If he was ever rough with you, it was only through love for me.'

I smiled. 'I always understood that.'

She moved over to the chess set. The pieces were laid out for a new game, and I wondered for a moment whether she might ask me to play. But she only picked up a pawn and set it down again. 'It is because I owe you so much that I have sent for you.' She smiled. 'To offer you some employment, if you wish to take it.'

I did not reply. Not politics – I would say no to that, even to her.

The Queen Dowager pressed her palms together. 'My circumstances are much changed now. I am a widow, free to remarry. In a little time, I may.' She coloured then, and looked quickly down, as though knowing that I and many others would disapprove. I thought, so the rumours are true, it is Thomas Seymour. My heart sank and I thought: what a waste.

I think the expression on my face gave me away, for she took a deep breath, and said, 'If and when that time comes, I am afraid I should not be able to employ you, or see you again.' Yes, I thought, it is Seymour, who detests me as I do him. But then, what had she meant by employment?

She continued, 'You will know about the – promotions – that have taken place since the late King's death.'

'Only the gossip,' I answered cautiously.

She smiled sadly. 'Do not worry, Matthew. I am going to tell you something which should be kept confidential for now, but only because it is in your interest to know.'

I spoke quietly, 'Forgive me, your majesty, but I wish to know no more secrets. Ever.'

'It concerns Richard Rich,' she said, her eyes on mine. 'Baron Rich, as we must now call him.'

I bit my lip, did not answer. The Queen Dowager looked down at the chessboard. 'Rich shifted his allegiances just in time. He has been promoted, and I fear he is about to be promoted further.' She looked at me intently. 'Thomas Wriothesley is a peer now, too, but strangely he of all people has had an attack of conscience, and is raising difficulties regarding some of the powers Lord Hertford is taking to himself. Wriothesley will not long remain Lord Chancellor. That is the word I have, and I trust my source.' Thomas Seymour, I thought, the Protector's brother. 'His successor will be Rich.'

I took a deep breath. 'It is what he has lusted after for years.'

'Anne Askew's book has already been smuggled in from the Continent. Its revelations regarding Rich will soon be public. The Protector already knows them.' She frowned, then bent to the chessboard and moved a knight forward. 'But he wants Rich for Lord Chancellor – he is a clever and experienced lawyer, he knows the ways of politics intimately, and –' she sighed – 'people fear him.'

'Rich, Chancellor, head of the legal profession. He will be able to destroy my career.' I shook my head. Well,

I thought, perhaps now was the time to retire. I had been thinking of it last summer, before the trouble began. But then I thought, stubbornly, I do not want to be forced out. I like my work, and I have responsibilities: Timothy, Nicholas and, yes, Barak. And I thought, too, where would I go? What would I do?

'I am sorry, Matthew.' The Queen Dowager raised an arm as though to take mine, then dropped it. 'I fear your position as serjeant at the Court of Requests may soon be given to another.'

'Yes. Rich would do that to me, and worse. Perhaps another accusation of misconduct; which this time will not be dropped. I am sure Treasurer Rowland would not be sorry to cooperate with him.'

She nodded sadly. 'That is possible.' Then she continued, her voice serious. 'But not if you also have a secure position with someone of high enough status.'

I looked at her, puzzled. 'But your majesty, you just said that you – '

'I do not mean me.'

'Then who?'

She smiled. 'You will not know yet, but I have been given the guardianship of the Lady Elizabeth. She is to reside with me here, along with her tutor and her staff. She has been left numerous properties by her father. She is a young lady of great wealth now. As is the Lady Mary, who if she accommodates herself to the religious changes that are coming, may marry. As for our young King – ' her smile widened – 'he is a fine boy, healthy and clever. If he lives even so long as his father he could reign near half a century.' I saw her happiness that her side had won, even if her own family had not reached the pinnacle.

'The Lady Elizabeth is far from the throne. In due time

no doubt she will marry into the senior nobility. For now, she is but thirteen, and under my guidance. A council must be appointed to deal with her estates, and in the nature of things there will be much legal business to be done. To begin with, her new properties must be conveyed into her name.' She took a deep breath, smiled again. 'I would like you to take on all the legal work connected with her properties. It will be regular employment. You would report not to me but to her Treasurer, Sir Thomas Parry. He will instruct you when legal advice is needed. He will be based near the law courts rather than here.' She added, 'I have spoken to the Lady Elizabeth. She remembers her meetings with you, and readily agreed to my suggestion.'

I stood, thinking hard. Elizabeth might be the least important of the King's children, but an assured place working for her household would provide ample protection against unwarranted persecution by Rich. And my official appointment to the Court of Requests was indeed all too likely to go. This new appointment would bring a steady flow of legal work, in the field of property law too, my specialist area.

The Queen Dowager said, 'A new start, Matthew, for us both.' She gave a hesitant smile, with something of apology in it.

I looked at her and thought again, how could this sophisticated, beautiful and profoundly moral woman marry a creature like Thomas Seymour? But perhaps Catherine Parr, after so many years of duty, felt the right to her own choice. And Seymour had good looks, if nothing else.

'You will take the post?' she asked.

I looked at her, and nodded. 'I will.'

'The Lady Elizabeth is not here at present, she is down at Richmond Palace. I would like you to go there now, take your oath to her. I sent a message you might come today. My barge is ready.'

I said, smiling, 'You knew I would accept.'

'I knew you would let me do this for you.'

I nodded, slowly, in acknowledgement. 'Thank you.'

She regarded me seriously. 'Elizabeth is not yet fourteen, yet already she has the will and intelligence of an adult. There is one thing she asked me to say to all those appointed to work for her. From another girl her age it might be child-ish boasting, but not Elizabeth.'

'What is that?'

The Queen Dowager smiled ruefully. 'My dogs will wear my collars.'

'Yes,' I answered quietly. 'I can imagine her saying that, and meaning it.'

She stepped forward, and now she did take my hand and pressed it tightly. 'Goodbye, Matthew. I shall never forget all you have done. Or the true regard in which you hold me. Believe me, I understand that, and value it.'

She looked me in the eyes, then stepped away. I was too choked with emotion to reply, as I think she saw, for she rang a bell for the steward to come and take me down to her barge. There were tears in my eyes, which I tried to hide with the depth of my bow.

Outside the steward said, respectfully, that he would ensure Genesis was taken safely back to Chancery Lane for me. He led me outdoors, and I huddled into my coat as we walked down the path between the snow-covered lawns to the river. He helped me into the barge waiting at the landing stage, where two liveried oarsmen sat. They pulled slowly out into the slate-grey Thames. I glanced back once at Chel-sea Palace, then turned to face the oarsmen. They carried me downriver, to Elizabeth.

ACKNOWLEDGEMENTS

As well as my friends in the writing group, many thanks to Maria Rejt, Liz Cowen, Sophie Orme, Antony Topping, Chris Wellbelove and Wes Miller. Thanks once again to Graham Brown of Fullerton's for meeting my ceaseless stationery demands.

I would also like to thank Dr Stephen Parish for advice on Henry VIII's medical symptoms. My interpretation of what happened to Henry during the last months of his life is of course entirely my own.

My last Shardlake novel, *Heartstone*, centred on the sinking of the King's warship *Mary Rose* during the battle of the Solent in July 1545. Since its publication the new Mary Rose Museum has opened in Portsmouth, showing the surviving half of the ship with, as a mirror image, the widest ranging and most beautifully presented collection of Tudor artefacts anywhere in the world. It is truly an extraordinary place, which I have been privileged to be associated with, and I am again grateful to the museum, the staff and especially Rear-Admiral John Lippiett, for continued insights into the vanished world of the 1540s.

Many works were invaluable for my research. Catherine Parr has received some deserved attention in recent years. Janel Mueller's (ed.) *Katherine Parr: Complete Works and Correspondence* (Chicago, 2011) is a work of fine scholarship, as well as an exhaustive compendium, which includes the text of *Lamentation of a Sinner*. Anthony Martinssen trod the biographical ground a generation ago with *Queen Katherine Parr* (New York, 1971). Two excellent recent biographies are those by Susan James, *Catherine Parr* (Stroud, 2008) and Linda Porter, *Katherine the Queen* (London, 2010). For other characters, Dairmaid MacCulloch's biography, *Cranmer* (London, 1996), was yet again an invaluable resource. Samuel Rhea Gammon's *Statesman and Schemer: William, First Lord Paget – Tudor Minister* (Devon, 1973) is an excellent biography of this unshowy, and therefore perhaps neglected, Tudor politician. Along with McCulloch, he gives the remarkable Bertano affair the attention it deserves. Glyn Redworth's *In Defence of the Church Catholic: The Life of Stephen Gardiner* (Oxford, 1990) was very helpful, though it failed to convince me that Gardiner did not play a leading role in the events of 1546. Stephen Alford's *Burghley: William Cecil at the Court of Elizabeth I* (Yale, 2008) was helpful on Cecil's early career and first steps on the political ladder.

Dakota L. Hamilton's *The Household of Queen Katherine Parr* (unpublished PhD thesis, Oxford, 1992) was a treasure trove on the structure of the Queen's Court. Simon Thurley's *Whitehall Palace, The Official Illustrated History* (London, 2008), *Whitehall Palace, An Architectural History of the Royal Apartments 1240–1690* (London, 1999) and his *The Royal Palaces of Tudor England* (Yale, 1993) brought the vanished palace back to life, although a good deal of my reconstruction had of course to be imaginative. David Loades's *The Tudor Court* (London, 1996) and Maria Hayward's *Dress at the Court of King Henry VIII* (London, 2007) were also of great help.

For the wider London world, Liza Picard's *Elizabeth's London* (London, 2005) was once again invaluable and, as with MacCulloch's *Cranmer*, never far from my side. James

Raven, *The Business of Books* (Yale, 2007) was especially helpful on the early printing trade. Susan Brigden's *London and the Reformation* was another book which, again, was always near to hand. Irvin Buckwalter Horst's *The Radical Brethren: Anabaptism and the English Reformation to 1548* (Holland, 1972) was a mine of information on the early Anabaptists.

My description of Henry's funeral is based on the account in Robert Hutchinson, *The Last Days of Henry VIII* (London, 2005).

Thanks also to Amanda Epstein for discussing the legal aspects of the Cotterstoke Will case with me, and to Jeanette Howlett for taking me to Sudeley Castle, where Catherine Parr lived during her sad fourth marriage, and where some beautiful examples of her clothing and possessions survive, as does her tomb, where I left some flowers in memory of Henry's last, and to me most sympathetic, Queen.

HISTORICAL NOTE

THE LAST YEAR OF Henry VIII's life saw some of the most tumultuous political events of his entire reign: a major heresy hunt, an attack on the Queen, radical changes in foreign policy, an attempt at reconciliation with the Pope and, at the end of 1546, a switch in control of the Privy Council from religious traditionalists to radicals, who were left in charge of England upon Henry's death. Unfortunately the sources are very thin, which leaves events open to a wide variety of interpretations. The historian Glyn Redworth has said, rightly, that 'all accounts are obliged to be in the nature of interpretative essays'.*

My own attempt at interpreting the events of 1546 forms the background to the story of *Lamentation* (except of course for the fact that Catherine Parr's *Lamentation of a Sinner* was not, in the real world, stolen). So I will start with those elements of the story where the facts are clearer, before moving on, for those who may be interested, to my own venture at an 'interpretative essay' on what happened in the tumultuous last months of Henry's life.

✝

IN 1546, ENGLAND'S ruling elite, as well as the common people in London especially, were split between those

* Redworth, G. In Defence of the Church Catholic: The Life of Stephen Gardiner (1990)

sympathetic and those hostile to religious reform. It was a matter of degree, and many people either kept their heads down to avoid trouble, or, among the ruling classes, bent with the wind for political advantage. And the wind blew very fiercely in the mid-Tudor period, as Henry VIII, following the split with Rome in 1532–3, lurched between traditional and radical religious policies for a decade and a half.

Most of those in the reforming camp were not social radicals, except for one group, which became a bogey for the traditionalists: the Anabaptists. In Holland and Germany various sects had grown out of Luther's Reformation, and the Anabaptists (or adult Baptists) believed in returning to the practices of early Christianity. These beliefs included holding goods in common, which meant overthrowing the feudal ruling classes – although they seem to have been more ambivalent about the rising merchant classes. When they took over the German city of Münster in 1534, the local Protestant rulers joined with Catholics to exterminate them, but the Anabaptists continued as a persecuted minority in north-western Europe. A very small number fled to England, where they may have made contact with the survivors of the fifteenth-century Lollards, but were quickly caught and burned. In England they were very few; but a Dutch Anabaptist coming to London in 1546 and forming a small group there would have been possible.

Of course, like the group in *Lamentation*, these men would have been vulnerable to infiltration by official spies, of which there were plenty. The slowly emerging world of London printing (at this period most books were imported from the Continent) was watched by the authorities, with printers often being reformers, and some having contacts with exiled English polemicists in Germany and the Netherlands, of whom John Bale (a religious, though not a social, radical) was the most feared. And Anne Askew, hiding in London in 1546, was captured by informers – and later tortured in the Tower by Wriothesley and Rich. She was one of many brought before the Privy Council for questioning during the 1546 heresy hunt; although, as Shardlake observes in my novel, it would have been very unusual for an accusation as weak as Isabel Slanning's in the story to go that high.

✠

LONDON IN 1546 was a tumultuous, violent, sectarian and impoverished place. It was only a year since the country had faced a serious threat of invasion. The King's French war had, literally, bankrupted England – Continental bankers were refusing to lend Henry any more money – and the debasement of the coinage continued apace, to the impoverishment of the lower classes especially. The harvest of 1546 seems to have been a good one, which was probably just as well for the elite; bad harvests later in the decade contributed to large-scale rebellions.

✠

WHITEHALL PALACE, located on the fringes of the city, was an utterly different world. The palace, seized by Henry VIII from Cardinal Wolsey, was extensively expanded and enriched by the King, although its development was restricted as it was bounded on the east by the Thames, and on the west by the great thoroughfares of Whitehall and King Street, leading from London to Westminster. The problem was solved by building the recreational side of the palace on the western side of the roadway, and bridging the road with the magnificent Holbein Gate, where Henry had his private study. The two great paintings mentioned in the book – one showing Henry and Jane Seymour with the

King's father Henry VII and his Queen, and the other showing Henry and Jane Seymour (by that time long dead) with Henry's three children, and two figures in the back-ground who are believed to have been the royal fools Will Somers and Jane – were highlights of the magnificent decor-ation of the palace. Scrots's portrait of the young Princess Elizabeth was painted at this time, and can be seen in the National Portrait Gallery in London. Baynard's Castle, which like Whitehall Palace no longer exists, was home in 1546 to the Queen's wardrobe as well as to her sister Anne and brother-in-law William Herbert.

✝

THE ELITE governing England at the end of Henry VIII's reign was divided by religion, but it was also divided into family blocs. Catherine Parr, like all Henry's queens, placed family members in positions of importance within her household, such as Lord Parr and Mary Odell, while her brother-in-law William Herbert was an important member of the King's private chamber, and her brother William Parr took a place on the Privy Council, the King's executive council, as well as the earldom of Essex.

This would now be called nepotism, but the Tudor view was entirely different – people were expected to advance mem-bers of their own family networks. So far as the royal court was concerned, this led inevitably to distant relatives and family hangers-on making their way to court in the hope of a place in royal service, as described in the book.

The Parrs were all on the reformist side, and their family loyalties seem to have been exceptionally tight; more so than their reformist allies and potential political rivals, the Sey-mours, the family of Prince Edward's mother Jane Seymour. Thomas Seymour was a drag on his brother Edward, now

Lord Hertford. Nonetheless Lord Hertford was close to Henry and had considerable political ability, although when he actually rose to the top after Henry's death he proved inadequate for the job. Meanwhile, during 1546 William Paget, the King's Secretary, appears to have moved from being a protégé of Bishop Gardiner's to an ally of Lord Hertford.

✠

AT THE SAME TIME a young man named William Cecil was beginning to make his career on the fringes of politics. I have invented his position on Queen Catherine's Learned Council, although he was certainly a friend of the Queen, and moreover wrote the preface to *Lamentation of a Sinner* when it was published in 1547. During that year he first appears on the record as Edward Seymour's secretary, beginning the meteoric rise which was to culminate, in 1558, when he became chief adviser to Elizabeth I. Edmund Walsingham, meanwhile, was the uncle of Elizabeth's famous future spymaster, Thomas Walsingham.

✠

THE FACT THAT all these people knew each other is indicative of just how tiny the Tudor elite was – essentially a group of titled country landowners, though increasingly open to men from the gentry and merchant classes, who sought positions at court to amass wealth and, like Rich and Paget, went on to create their own great estates. Paget and Rich were both lawyers of undistinguished lineage but great ability, who were first chosen for service by Thomas Cromwell – as Shardlake observes, six years after his death much of the political elite still consisted of men whom Cromwell had advanced. 'Gentleman' status, meanwhile, was everything for young men like Nicholas Overton, who guarded it jealously;

allowed to wear swords and colourful clothes of rich material forbidden to the common populace, they were brought up to see themselves as quite different from the common run.

✝

FOR THE VISIT of Admiral d'Annebault in August 1546 I have followed closely the short account in Charles Wriothesley's *Chronicle*. As one traces the ceremonies, one realizes their huge scale. Henry played a prominent role, but this was to be his last hurrah. Five months later he was dead. Greeting the admiral near Hampton Court was also Prince Edward's first public appearance.

✝

Catherine Parr and the Politics of Henry VIII's Last Months
– An Interpretative Essay

Historians have long puzzled over the huge upheavals in English politics during the last months of Henry VIII's life. The source material is fragmentary, mainly scattered correspondence and ambassadors' reports, and the reliability of one major source regarding Catherine Parr, John Foxe's *Book of Martyrs*, has been called into question. Historians are divided over Foxe; he was a radical Protestant who wrote, highly polemically, about the sufferings of Protestant martyrs in the years before Elizabeth I ascended the throne. Some have said that Foxe is too biased to be credible, adding that where Catherine Parr is concerned he was writing seventeen years after the event he described. Others respond that Foxe was meticulous about trying to get his facts right, whatever gloss he put on them. I tend to agree with those who say that Foxe was an honest and assiduous gatherer of witness testimony, while also agreeing with pretty much everyone that his chronology was notoriously unreliable – of which more below.

If one looks at a timeline of political events in 1546, two things stand out. The first is that during the spring a major heresy hunt was ordered from within the court, targeting people who had denied the truth of transubstantiation. Transubstantiation is the doctrine which claims that during the ceremony of the Mass, the bread and wine are physically transformed into the actual blood and body of Christ; many Protestants, however, disagreed. It was over this point that, in 1539, Henry VIII drew a firm line. Under the 'Act of Six Articles' of that year, denial of transubstantiation, or 'sacramentarianism', was defined as heresy. One recantation was allowed; a refusal to recant, or a second offence, was punishable by burning alive.

In the 1546 heresy hunt the net spread widely, and those questioned by the council included the younger son of the Duke of Norfolk – who was interrogated about his presence at potentially subversive 'preachings in the Queen's chamber' in Lent – and Henry's courtier and friend George Blagge. The Queen was clearly under threat herself, as we shall see. The heresy hunt climaxed with the burning of Anne Askew and three others at Smithfield on the 16th of July. (The description of this in this book is based on the account by Foxe.) Meanwhile, though few even in Henry's circle knew this, plans were being made for a papal emissary, Gurone Bertano, to be received by the King in London in August, to explore whether a rapprochement with Rome, after thirteen years of separation, was a possibility.

One gets the impression from this timeline that the ship of state which, steered by Henry, had for years veered wildly between support of traditional Catholic practice – but without the Pope – and a more thoroughgoing reform, set a firm course during the early months of 1546. With increasing speed it sailed towards the extirpation of Protestant heresy and the victory of those who favoured a traditionalist position – and possibly some agreement with the Pope.

Then suddenly, around the end of July, the ship of state turns round and steers, even faster, in exactly the opposite direction. The heresy hunt stopped dead in July, and some who had been convicted were quietly released, George Blagge being pardoned personally by the King.

In early August, Bertano arrived. He had his first and only meeting with the King on the 3rd. We do not know what was said, but the meeting was clearly unsuccessful. Afterwards, Henry wrote a letter to the Pope to which the Pontiff never replied. Bertano remained in a 'safe house' until late September, not seeing the King again, until word of his presence began to get out and he was ordered to go home.

✝

DURING THE AUTUMN months Henry steered the metaphorical ship of state ever faster in a Protestant direction. He went on a Progress to Guildford, which was intended to be brief but was lengthened, probably because he fell seriously ill, and for over a month he stayed at Windsor on the way back. During this period, as was normal during Progresses, the Privy Council was split into two: those attending the King and those left in charge of business in London. Access to the King, as ever, was all-important, and the councillors Henry chose to be with him until he returned to London at the end of October were all either radical sympathizers or those who would bend to the wind, whichever way it blew.

✝

IN NOVEMBER, Bishop Gardiner, the leading conservative, found himself marginalized and denied access to the King. Then, in December, the other leading traditionalist, the Duke of Norfolk, and his son, the Earl of Surrey, were suddenly arrested and charged with treason. By now Henry's health was deteriorating fast. He shut himself up at Whitehall Palace with his closest advisers, and in late December wrote a last Will, which appointed a council of sixteen to govern England until his nine-year-old son reached his majority. All the council members were either Protestants or centrists.

✝

SPRING 1546 SAW, as well as the start of the heresy hunt, a complete about-turn in foreign policy. The two-year war against France had been a disastrous and costly failure. The English occupied Boulogne, but were besieged there, supplied by boat across the Channel, strongly opposed by French ships, at enormous cost. Despite his advisers' entreaties during the winter of 1545–6, Henry refused to end the war.

Meantime, relations were uncertain with the Holy Roman Empire, which was at odds with its own Protestant subjects. England remained formally at war with Scotland, and the Pope continued to be an implacable foe. In March 1546 the ever warlike Henry finally accepted that this dreadful mess would have to be sorted out. Peace negotiations began with France, and a settlement was reached in June. Admiral d'Annebault, who had led the French fleet against England the year before, was invited to come to England as ambassador in August, and enormous celebrations were planned. This was surely a signal of Henry's intent to make a lasting peace.

At the same time Henry negotiated a new treaty of peace with the other major Catholic power in Europe, the Holy Roman Empire. Peace with Scotland, too, was encompassed in the French treaty.

✝

MOST ASTONISHING of all was the arrival, via France, of the papal emissary Bertano. The previous year Pope Paul III had convened the Council of Trent, part of whose purpose was to see whether the Protestant powers could somehow be reconciled with the Holy See. This, I think, is the context for Bertano's visit – to establish whether some arrangement could be made between England and the Pope, some formula to allow Henry to keep his Supreme Headship of the Church, which he genuinely believed had been awarded him by God, while making some friendly arrangement with the Pope. Theologically, however, the Royal Supremacy and the papal function were irreconcilable, and on this diplomatic front at least, Henry failed.

✝

IF, AS THE TIMELINE suggests, March 1546 was the crucial date for changes in both domestic and foreign policy, what happened during that month? I think the answer lies in a development often overlooked – the collapse of Henry's health.

It is impossible at this distance to be clear what was wrong exactly with Henry by the 1540s, but some things can be said confidently. The old idea that the King suffered from syphilis is long discredited – there is no evidence for this, and much against. At the core of Henry's problems seems to have been lack of mobility. David Starkey has suggested in his *Six Wives: The Queens of Henry VIII* (2004) that in Henry's jousting accident in 1528 he broke his left leg; it healed but left a piece of detached bone in his calf, which decayed and formed a large and painful ulcer. In any event, Henry gradually had to give up his former regime of very active exercise and, as the years passed, he became increasingly immobile. His portraits show growing obesity, especially in the period 1537 to 1540, during his late forties, between his marriages to Jane Seymour and Anne of Cleves.

By 1544, measurements for his armour showed a waistline of 54 inches; even a modest further weight gain might give a waistline of around 58 inches by 1546; even for a man of 6'2", this puts Henry at the outside edge of gross, morbid obesity. Why did a man who had so prided himself on his appearance allow this to happen? The most likely explanation is that his initial weight gain and immobility, especially given the Tudor elite's diet of meat and sweetstuffs, would have made likely the development of type 2 diabetes, a disease not understood at the time. If this happened it would have added another element to the vicious cycle of immobility and weight gain, for Henry would have been constantly hungry and thirsty.

By 1546 it seems that walking any distance was difficult and painful for the King. He already sometimes used a 'tram' (a type of wheelchair) to get around the palaces, and had a 'device' to get him up and down stairs. And his gross obesity and immobility would have made him prone to yet another problem, deep-vein thrombosis in his legs, both of which were now described as ulcerated (a condition consistent with diabetes). Blood clots would form in the legs, then could become detached and travel to the lungs (to trigger a pulmonary embolism). If the clot can dissolve, a patient can survive, but otherwise dies. The descriptions of Henry's medical crises from 1541 seem consistent with a series of pulmonary embolisms, the last of which killed him in January 1547, although he would also be liable to strokes or heart attacks — all his organs would have been under tremendous strain.

If Henry did become diabetic as well as morbidly obese around 1540, he could also have become impotent. He had no problems in making his first three wives pregnant, but none of his last three conceived. Catherine Parr was in some ways an odd choice for a sixth wife; she was past thirty and had already had two childless marriages (neither, as in popular myth, to men too old to sire a child). Henry badly needed a second male heir. Prince Edward (again contrary to popular myth) was not a sickly child, but child mortality in Tudor England was high and, if he died, Henry would be back where he had started, without a male heir. Yet in 1543 he married a woman who was a most unlikely candidate to bear a child. Catherine Parr did not fall pregnant during her three-and-a-half-year marriage to Henry, but she conceived during her subsequent marriage to Thomas Seymour. So Catherine was not incapable of bearing children; but Henry by now may well have been.

None of this, of course, was the King's fault. If what I suggest is right, Henry was trapped in a dreadful cycle of pain, immobility and consuming hunger. He seems to have suffered no major health crises in 1544 or 1545, but in March 1546 he did fall very ill, perhaps with an embolism, and his life was feared for, although he recovered after some weeks of convalescence. His next health crisis did not come until September, although it was then followed by a whole series of illnesses which culminated in his death in January 1547. I suggest, though, that the March 1546 crisis was bad enough for Henry's doctors (who, while they may not have been very good at preserving life, would have known well the signs of impending death), his councillors, and Henry himself to realize that he probably did not have long to live, and preparations needed to be made for Prince Edward's succession. Some final choice between the radical and conservative factions on the council now had to be made, and the crises in foreign policy had to be resolved. The frantic round of diplomatic and political activity that began then and continued for the rest of the year stemmed, I think, from Henry's March illness.

✝

AND SO TO my attempt at an interpretation of the plot against Catherine Parr (I think there was only one, not two as has sometimes been suggested, and it spanned several months). Recent historical work – by Susan James, Linda Porter and Janel Mueller – has given us a much clearer picture of Catherine. She was an attractive, sophisticated woman who had spent her life on the fringes of the court (the Parr family were minor players in the royal household during her childhood) and would have known the King for years. After the death of her second husband, Lord Latimer, she herself later wrote to Thomas Seymour that she had wished to marry him, but the King had set his sights on her. Thus, she believed, she was called by God to marry Henry, and she meant to, surely, in order to influence his religious policy so far as she could. Her letter indicates she was already a reformist sympathizer when she married Henry.

Catherine, who had great style, was an extremely successful and sophisticated performer of the visible and ceremonial aspects of Queen Consort, including the entertainment of foreign ambassadors. She was also, it seems, a very sympathetic personality; loyal and trustworthy and, one detects, with a sense of humour.

Unlike most Tudor women, Catherine had received a good education from her mother, Lady Maud Parr. She learned Latin as a girl; it became rusty, but she picked it up again when she became Queen. She also studied other languages – in the last months of Henry's reign she was learning Spanish, a useful language then for diplomacy. She had a wide range of interests, collecting clocks and coins, and was clearly drawn to scholarship. Her intelligence, while very considerable, seems to have been broad rather than of great depth and focus – in that, she resembled Henry.

Religious influences on Catherine before her marriage to the King in 1543 were contradictory; her brother, Sir William Parr, her uncle Lord William Parr (following the early death of her father, the principal male influence on the family), and her sister and brother-in-law Anne and Sir William Herbert, were all reformist sympathizers. Her mother Lady Maud Parr, however, had been a lady-in-waiting and friend to Catherine of Aragon, but she died in 1529 before Henry expelled his first wife from the royal household. The Boroughs, the family of Catherine's first husband, were reformist sympathizers, but her second husband, Lord Latimer (her marriage to whom appears to have been happy), was a traditionalist. However, her later letter to Thomas Seymour seems to me to indicate she was already travelling a reformist path by 1543. She was to journey further.

✝

CATHERINE PARR was not, nor would she have claimed to be, a serious theologian. Her little book *Prayers and Meditations*, published in 1545, is quite orthodox. The *Lamentation of a Sinner*, however, probably written over the winter of 1545–6, shows a writer passionate about salvation, which could only be found through reading the Bible and ultimately through faith in Christ. Confessional writings in this vein were common at the time, though not from an English Queen.

Catherine tells of how her own love of the world's pleasures blinded her for a long time to God's grace, before she succumbed to Him. She writes with the fiercely self-critical religiosity of similar contemporary 'confessions' and 'lamentations'. There is enough in the *Lamentation* to ground suspicion of her among traditionalists, because of her belief in salvation coming through a personal relationship with Christ, and study of the Bible, rather than through the practices of the official church. However – and this is vital – the *Lamentation* says nothing at all about, or against, the Mass.

Writing it at all was risky, although in the winter of 1545–6 Henry had taken a new and radical step against the old religion in appropriating the chantries, where Masses were said for the dead, although this move was probably motivated primarily by his desire to get hold of some much-needed money – their endowments were large. But in the early months of 1546 Catherine's caution seems to have quite deserted her in her public association with reformers and, according to Foxe, in openly arguing religion with the King.

☩

ACCORDING TO Foxe, '*In the time of his sickness, he (Henry) had left his accustomed manner of coming, and visiting his Queen: and therefore she would come to visit him, either after dinner or after supper.*' This surely dates this part of the story to March–April 1546 (though most authorities put it months later); as this was the only period before the autumn when Henry was so seriously indisposed. Foxe tells us that Catherine took to lecturing the King on religion, and one night was careless enough to do so in the presence of Bishop Stephen Gardiner, the leading conservative, who, again in that crucial month of March, had returned from a long foreign embassy and quickly gained the King's ear. Gardiner, according to Foxe, subsequently told the King:

. . . how dangerous and perilous a matter it is, and ever hath been, for a Prince to suffer such insolent words at his subjects' hands: the religion by the Queen, so stiffly maintained, did not only disallow and dissolve the policy and politic government of Princes, but also taught the people that all things ought to be in common; so that what colour soever they pretended, their opinions were indeed so odious, and to the Princes estates so perilous . . . (that they) *by law deserved death.*

Then, according to Foxe, Gardiner persuaded the King to begin an investigation into radical religion, in the Queen's household as well as elsewhere – having frightened Henry, among other things, with the mention of people who wished to hold all goods in common, in other words the Anabaptist creed, although Catherine's (and indeed Foxe's) beliefs were very far from Anabaptism.

If I am right and this happened in March–April when the King was convalescing, that fits with the records of arrests and enquiries which began in April and went on till July. But why, some have asked, should the religious conservatives focus on Queen Catherine Parr? It seems to me that she was the obvious target – she was the centre of a group of highborn ladies who, certainly during Lent in 1546, met together to hear sermons and discuss religion. They included her sister Anne (wife of Sir William Herbert), Lady Denny (wife of the chief gentleman of Henry's household, Sir Anthony Denny) and potentially most important of all, Anne Stanhope, wife of Lord Hertford. If heresy was proved against Catherine, not only would Henry's sense of betrayal by a woman he still loved be terrible (there is no evidence at all that he *wanted* rid of Catherine Parr in 1546, rather the reverse), but likely all the women in her circle would fall too, and with them, crucially, their husbands. Catherine Parr, therefore, was the keystone in the arch; knock her out and the whole reformist edifice faced total collapse.

The heresy hunt went on for three months. The spring and early summer of 1546 must have been a desperate time for Catherine, but she seems to have maintained her composure and behaved calmly throughout. Everyone in her circle seems to have stuck loyally together; though this is hardly surprising – if one fell, all fell. It is possible that searches took place within the Queen's household, and certainly she gave some books (which may have included *Lamentation of a Sinner*) to her uncle Lord Parr for safekeeping in April.

By July nothing had been found against her. By then the questioning of suspects seems to have been largely over. No evidence had been discovered against anyone within the circle of the court except for Henry's courtier and friend George Blagge, and nobody from within the Queen's circle. If Thomas Wriothesley and Richard Rich were actively seeking out heretics on behalf of Bishop Gardiner (and possibly, behind the scenes, the Duke of Norfolk), by July they must have been getting desperate.

✝

THEN, IN LATE June and early July came the extraordinary and gruesome story of Anne Askew, whose memoir, the *Examinations of Anne Askew*, was smuggled out to Flanders, and published the next year by John Bale. Anne Askew, or to use her married name, Anne Kyme, was the wife of a Lincolnshire gentleman. She was aged around 25. By the standards of the time, her behaviour was extraordinary. A radical Protestant who had openly denied the Real Presence in the Mass, she left her husband, a religious conservative, and their two children to come to London and preach in 1545. She had relatives there, certainly a cousin, and distant connections to low-ranking courtiers. Soon she was brought before the Common Council of London, where she denied she was a heretic. Nonetheless, a year later she was back, and this time, although her initial technique in argument was to hedge, she eventually admitted enough to be found guilty of heresy. She refused to recant, and having been brought before the Privy Council and questioned by Gardiner, among others, she was convicted at the end of June and sentenced to be publicly burned, along with three men, on the 16th of July.

There is no evidence that Catherine Parr and Anne Askew ever met or corresponded. They may have had acquaintances in common, but again that is not surprising given the small size of the Tudor elite. Once condemned, according to law, Anne should have been held in prison until her execution. However, at the beginning of July she was sent to the Tower, where, according to her memoir, she was questioned again by Rich and Wriothesley; this time specifically about her links to women in Catherine Parr's household. Not only was she questioned, she was tortured by Rich and Wriothesley personally, to the horror of the Lieutenant of the Tower, who was present. Asked specifically about her links to ladies in Queen Catherine's circle, Anne admitted she had had gifts of money from men who claimed to be servants of the Duchess of Suffolk and Lady Hertford, but denied any direct links to them or the Queen. It was not illegal to bring prisoners money to buy food; in fact these donations were necessary to keep them alive.

There seems no reason to doubt Anne Askew's story; Rich and Wriothesley's behaviour has all the hallmarks of a last, desperate effort by the religious conservatives to find some evidence damaging to the Queen. Desperate indeed, for torture of a person already convicted – and a woman from the gentlemanly classes – was not only illegal but scandalous; even more so when Wriothesley – as Lord Chancellor, the most senior law officer in England – had himself turned the rack. It was too extreme for the Tower Lieutenant, who promptly went off and told the King, who was horrified. It has been suggested the King himself may have secretly ordered the torture, but there is no evidence to support this accusation one way or the other. It seems more likely to me that Henry was genuinely angered at this attempt to torture someone into providing accusations against the Queen when months of enquiry had failed to find anything credible.

Henry was, by now, already angry with the conservatives. He said that in arresting the courtier George Blagge they had come 'too close to his person' and Blagge was pardoned. Given this move, the scale of the King's anger at those who had tried to torture Anne Askew into providing something harmful to the Queen can only be imagined.

✟

IN FOXE'S ACCOUNT, there was a second plot against Catherine, involving a warrant being issued for the Queen's arrest, a copy of which, however, was conveniently dropped where it would fall into her hands. This event has been convincingly dated by Dakota Hamilton and others to July 1546. According to Foxe, Catherine's response was to rush to the King and persuade him that she had never intended to lecture him on religion, only to engage his mind to distract him from the pain in his legs. Again according to Foxe, the gambit succeeded. Henry accepted Catherine's submission, and Lord Chancellor Wriothesley, when he arrived with the warrant to arrest the Queen the next day, was insulted and beaten about the head by Henry and ordered from his presence – in other words, completely and publicly humiliated.

This has, to me, the flavour of a deliberate ruse by the King, rather than a spontaneous sequence of events as reported to Foxe by two survivors from Catherine's ladies (though it may have looked genuine to them). To begin with, it is hard to guess the legal grounds on which Catherine could have been arrested in July, since extensive enquiries about her and her ladies had revealed nothing at all. If Henry had actually wanted to dispose of her, he could easily have manufactured something, as he did when he wanted to rid himself of Anne Boleyn and Thomas Cromwell, and was soon to do again with the Duke of Norfolk.

It is worth noting in this context that three years before, when Archbishop Cranmer had been the subject of accusations of heresy by Gardiner, the King had turned the tables on the conservatives in a very similar manner, agreeing that Cranmer should be called before the Privy Council, but giving him his ring beforehand to show to the council as proof he still had the King's support. The outcome was that a commission to investigate Cranmer was appointed, but headed by Cranmer himself! This tactic had the benefit of humiliating one party (in both cases the religious conservatives) while reminding the other (first Cranmer, then Catherine) very firmly who was in charge. Given the failure of the heresy hunt, it would have been quite characteristic of Henry to humiliate Wriothesley in this way, while forcing

Catherine, like Cranmer earlier, to play a part in the deception – and in Catherine's case, publicly to admit that as a woman it was her place to learn from, and not lecture, her husband.

I think, therefore, that the arrest warrant was nothing more or less than a put-up job, designed to humiliate Wriothesley and also to signal that the heresy hunt was over and the Queen still in Henry's favour. Catherine herself was likely ordered to be involved, and the whole thing stage-managed by Henry himself.

By the end of July, when new jewellery was ordered for her for the forthcoming visit of Admiral d'Annebault, Catherine Parr was clearly and visibly once more high in the King's favour. Her brother, as Earl of Essex, rode at the admiral's side on his procession through London in August. And in October, crucially, Catherine's brother-in-law Lord Herbert was promoted to Deputy Chamberlain, a position which was to be of critical influence in the King's last days. The Parrs had successfully weathered the storm.

☧

THERE REMAINED Bertano's visit, but as noted previously, it was a failure. When the papal emissary arrived early in August, hopes of some sort of accommodation with the Pope seem to have been immediately dashed. And from now on the King began to move, steadily, back towards the reformers. He may well have feared that if Gardiner and Norfolk were left in charge of the realm during his son's minority, they would take England back to Rome. And Henry's first priority was always to ensure that the Royal Supremacy passed to his son. Such a fear on the King's part was not unrealistic; a decade later Gardiner was to be key lieutenant to Henry's daughter, Mary I, when she returned England, briefly, to papal allegiance.

☩

AFTER THE FAILURE of Bertano's mission, the focus turned back to relations with France, and much attention was devoted to the preparations to welcome Admiral d'Annebault to London at the end of the month. The sheer scale of the celebrations, in a country financially ruined by Henry's war, has, I think, been rather ignored. There had been no such celebrations to welcome a foreigner, at least not since the arrival of the ill-fated Anne of Cleves in 1539. Archbishop Cranmer's secretary, Ralph Morice, later recounted how Henry stood at one of the Hampton Court banquets for d'Annebault, with one arm round the ad-miral's shoulder and the other round Cranmer's (a sign of favour to both, although Henry by now may have found it difficult to stand unsupported) and, according to Morice, made the astounding statement that he and the French king would soon abolish the Mass and establish a common Communion. This was never remotely possible, of course (Francis I of France remained firmly Catholic), but for the King to say such a thing even in jest could only be a sign of radical intention, quite unthinkable even a few weeks before.

☩

THE BALANCE OF POWER on the Privy Council had shifted back towards the reformers with the return from abroad of the Earl of Hertford and Lord Lisle, and it was mainly reformers who accompanied Henry on his Progress at the beginning of September. This Progress was intended to be unusually brief, lasting only a couple of weeks and going only so far as Guildford, but Henry fell ill again during this time and moved from Guildford only to Windsor, where, halfway back, he stayed until the end of October. During most of that time the conservatives on the Privy Council remained in London dealing with routine business, while the radicals were with Henry. As was Catherine Parr.

Henry may well have spent these autumn months plotting his final decisive moves; perhaps his latest bout of severe illness gave him further intimations of mortality. In November and December Gardiner was sidelined, at one point struck in the face at a council meeting by Lord Lisle — without consequences for Lisle, though it was a serious offence — and repeatedly denied an audience with the King. Then, in December, Norfolk and Surrey were arrested, found guilty of treason and sentenced to death. The ostensible cause was Surrey's quartering of the royal arms with his own, but the whole affair smacks of a manufactured attempt to get rid of Norfolk. As the senior peer in England, he thought he should have control of Henry's successor, the young Edward; as noted already, Henry had used far-fetched accusations of treason before to dispose of Anne Boleyn and Thomas Cromwell. Surrey was executed in January 1547; Norfolk himself was due to follow his son to the block on the 28th, but the King's death in the early hours of that morning saved him; he languished instead in the Tower of London for the next six and a half years.

In early December, Henry was seriously ill again and seems never to have recovered fully. The last two months of his life appear to have been passed entirely at Whitehall. Some historians have seen the fact that Henry was apart from the Queen during the last month of his life as politically significant. Certainly Catherine did not get the Regency she had hoped for. However, though she spent Christmas at Richmond Palace, away from the King, her chambers were prepared for her at Whitehall in mid-January, although it is not known whether she actually took up residence, before Henry fell ill for the final time, just afterwards. But the point is not that Henry did not see the Queen during these last weeks of his life, but that he saw hardly *anyone* except Secretary Paget, and – significantly – the two chief gentlemen of his bedchamber.

Always in Henry's reign, the gentlemen of the bedchamber, chosen by him and with the closest access to his person, wielded serious political power. His two chief gentlemen during most of 1546 were Anthony Denny, a radical sympathizer, and his deputy William Browne, a conservative. In October, Browne was moved and his replacement was none other than William Herbert, the Queen's brother-in-law and a reformer. This surely puts paid to any idea that the Parrs were out of favour following the heresy hunt.

Henry also, inevitably, saw much of his doctors. His long-standing chief physician, the reformer William Butts, had died in 1545 and was succeeded by his deputy, Thomas Wendy, another radical who also served as chief physician to the Queen. Indeed, it has been suggested that he was the man who got a copy of her arrest warrant to the Queen in July, either secretly or, as I think more likely, acting as go-between in Henry's scheme to humiliate Wriothesley.

✝

WITH THESE MEN in close attendance, the King wrote his last Will at the end of December. The Will has caused much controversy. For the last few years of Henry's life, with so many documents to be signed and the King in poor health, use had been made of a 'dry stamp', a stamp with a facsimile of the King's signature. When Henry approved a document, it was stamped and the King's signature inked in, most often by Paget. One would have expected the King to sign his own Will, but the dry stamp was used. The Will, too, was not entered on the register of court documents until a month after its signature, by which time Henry was dead.

Without venturing too far into this area of controversy, the provision that during Edward VI's minority the realm was to be governed by a council of sixteen persons, with a strongly radical balance, almost certainly reflects Henry's intention in December. However, it is quite possible that the clause giving Secretary Paget the power to make 'unfulfilled gifts', the details of which Paget said the King had confided to him personally, was a forgery. After the King's death on the 28th of January 1547, Paget and Edward Seymour quickly seized the initiative; peerages and gifts of money were handed out liberally to members of the council as 'unfulfilled gifts', and the council made Lord Hertford Protector.

✝

HERTFORD BECAME, for a while, something like a dictator. A new religious policy of Protestant radicalism began. The Mass was abolished, church interiors whitewashed, a new Prayer Book installed. Whether Henry VIII wished for any of this is very doubtful, but he had secured his main aim – the preservation of the Royal Supremacy for the young Edward VI. By the time Edward reached fifteen, in late 1552, his own personality as a radical and rather severe reformer was emerging. Had he lived as long as his father, which no one saw any reason to doubt, a Protestant revolution, as thoroughgoing as that which took place in 1560s Scotland, would probably have become firmly established. But by one of history's ironies, Edward died from tuberculosis in 1553, a few months short of his sixteenth birthday.

The throne then passed to the King's elder daughter

Mary, who reversed course all the way back to papal allegiance, renounced the Royal Supremacy, re-established monasticism and married the Catholic Prince (later King) Philip of Spain. But in 1558, after only five years' rule, Mary too died, probably of cancer, and the throne passed to Elizabeth, who re-established Protestantism, albeit of a distinctly moderate kind.

It has often been suggested that the 'Protestant' and 'Catholic' factions at Henry's court were motivated more by desire for power than any religious conviction, and indeed many councillors – Paget, Rich, Cecil and others – managed to survive and hold office under both Edward and Mary, the younger councillors continuing to serve Elizabeth. But Edward's senior councillors, who implemented radical Protestantism, were mainly former Henrician radicals, while Mary's were mainly former Henrician conservatives. This reminds us that while many clerics and councillors were motivated by the desire for power and wealth, it is a mistake to think the Tudor ruling classes took religion lightly.

✝

THE STORY OF the last two years of Catherine Parr's life is tragic. To her disappointment, she did not become Regent. Then this most capable and usually astute woman decided to follow her heart rather than her head, and quickly married her old love, the Protector's brother Thomas Seymour. The result was disastrous. She moved with him (and the teenage Elizabeth) to Seymour's castle at Sudeley. There, at thirty-five, Catherine fell pregnant for the first time. Thomas Seymour, who had probably married Catherine because of her status as Queen Dowager, diverted himself during his wife's pregnancy with sexual abuse of the fourteen-year-old Elizabeth. When Catherine found out, Elizabeth was sent away from the household of the stepmother she had been close to for four years.

In September 1548 Catherine gave birth to a daughter, but like so many Tudor women, she died shortly afterwards from an infection of the womb. In the delirium of her last days she accused her husband of mocking and betraying her.

Seymour, who seems by now to have been hardly sane, then launched a crack-brained plot, in February 1549, to seize his young nephew Edward VI, and perhaps make himself Protector in his brother's place. He had no support whatever, was immediately arrested and executed for treason in March 1549. Elizabeth, hearing of his execution, is said to have remarked, 'Today died a man of much wit and little judgement.' As so often, she summed things up exactly.

Catherine's baby, the now orphaned Mary Seymour, passed into the care of Catherine's friend the Dowager Duchess of Suffolk, but disappears from the records after 1550, and must have died in infancy like so many Tudor children. It was the saddest of endings to the story of Catherine Parr.